BLACKMARK

THE KINGSMEN CHRONICLES
BOOK ONE

JEAN LOWE CARLSON

DRAGONLIGHT PUBLISHING, LLC

First Print Edition: 2016, updated 2022

ISBN 978-1-943199-12-9

CONTENTS

AUTHOR'S NOTE

Welcome to the Kingsmen Chronicles, and thanks so much for your interest in this series!

This world has been brewing in my brain a long time, and since Blackmark was first released in 2016, I've made some over-arching decisions for the series that created a few discrepancies in the text of this first book.

Those discrepancies have been corrected, and a major overhaul of the language in this first book has been undertaken to bring the writing in-line with the rest of the series.

I hope you enjoy the epic, adventurous world of the Kingsmen – here's to many more books to come!

Onward to glory,
Jean Lowe Carlson
August 27th, 2019

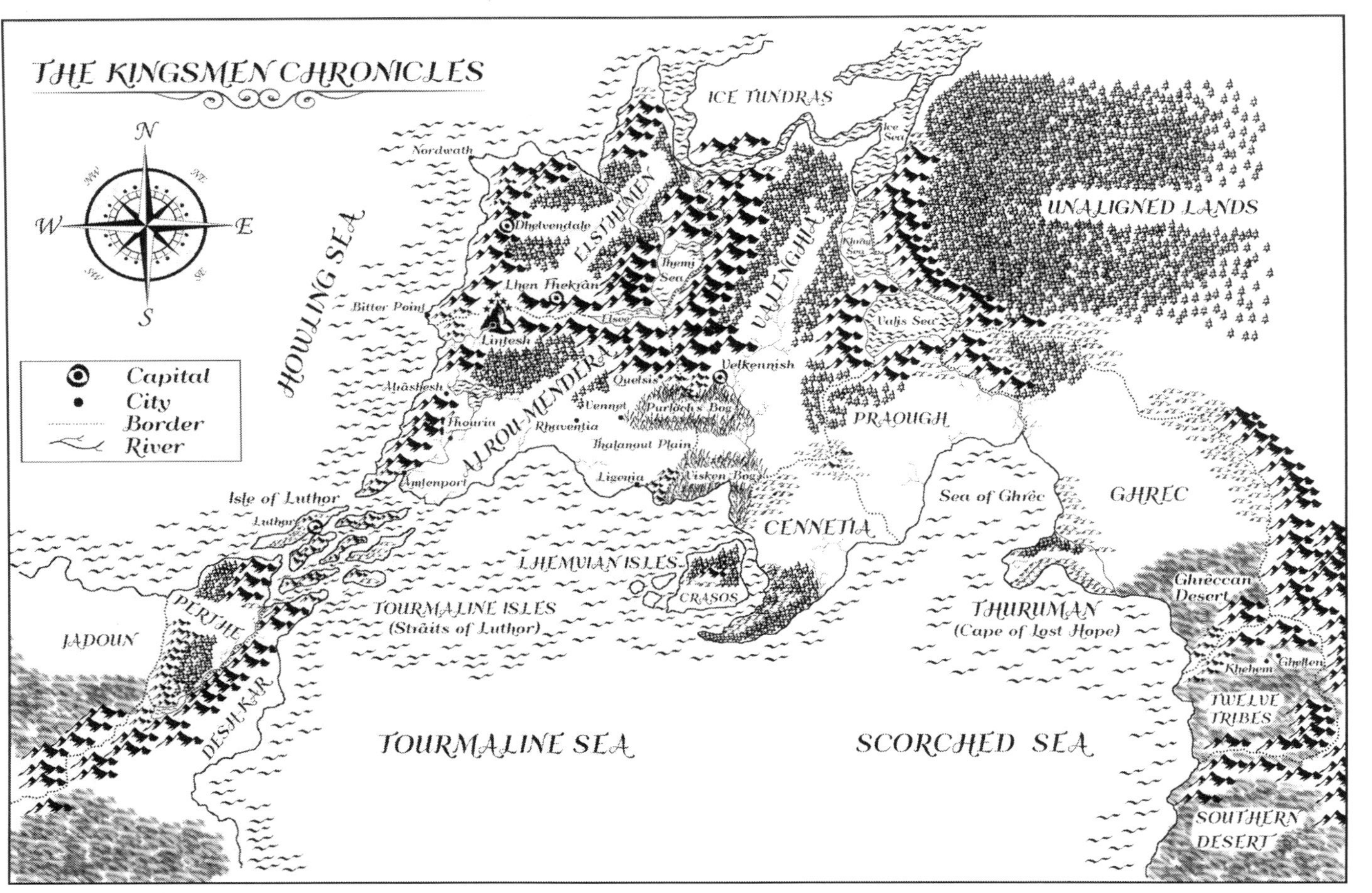

THE KINGSMEN CHRONICLES
N
E
S
W
Capital
City
Border
River
HOWLING SEA
ICE TUNDRAS
Ice Sea
UNALIGNED LANDS
Nordwath
Dhelvendale
ELSTHUMEN
Themi Sea
Lhen Thekrân
Bitter Point
Lintesh
VALENGHIA
Valis Sea
Velkennish
ALROU-MENDERA
Quelsis
Vennyt
Purloch's Bog
Rhaventia
Thourin
PRAOUGH
Thalanout Plain
Amtenport
Ligenia
Visken Bog
Isle of Luthor
Luthor
CENNETIA
Sea of Ghrēc
GHREC
LHEMUIAN ISLES
CRASOS
TOURMALINE ISLES
(Strâits of Luthor)
THURUMAN
(Cape of Lost Hope)
Ghrēccan Desert
JADOUN
PERTHE
DESJLKAR
Khehem
Ghelten
TWELVE TRIBES
TOURMALINE SEA
SCORCHED SEA
SOUTHERN DESERT

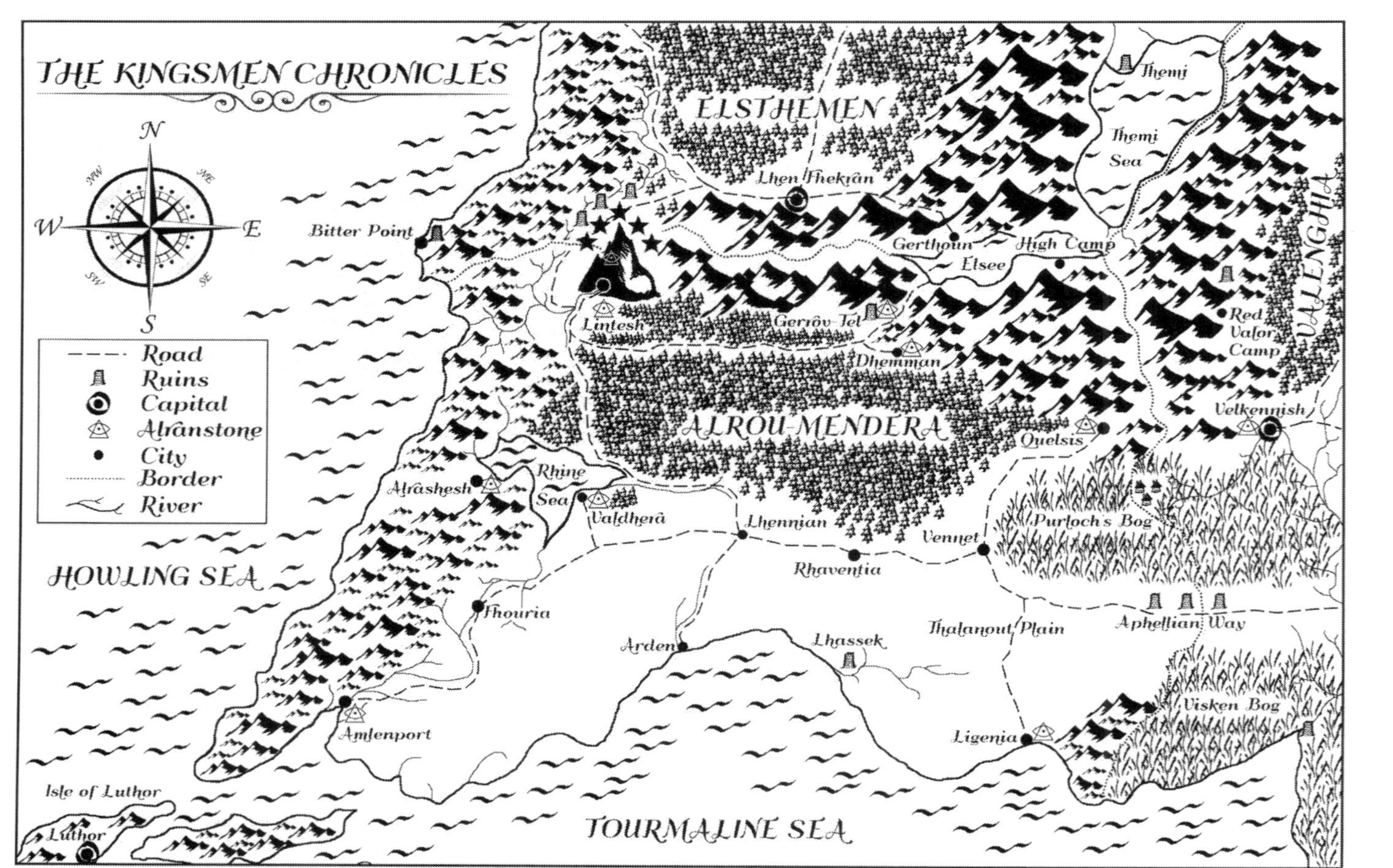

THE KINGSMEN CHRONICLES
N
E
S
W
NW
NE
SW
SE
Road
Ruins
Capital
Alrânstone
City
Border
River
ELSTHEMEN
Lhen Fhekrân
Themi
Themi Sea
Bitter Point
Gerthoun
High Camp
Elsee
Lintesh
Gerrôv-Tel
Dhemman
Red Valor Camp
VALENGHIA
Velkennish
ALROU-MENDERA
Quelsis
Alrashesh
Rhine Sea
Valdherâ
Lhennian
Vennet
Purloch's Bog
Rhaventia
HOWLING SEA
Fhouria
Thalanout Plain
Aphellian Way
Arden
Lhassek
Visken Bog
Amlenport
Ligenia
Isle of Luthor
Luthor
TOURMALINE SEA

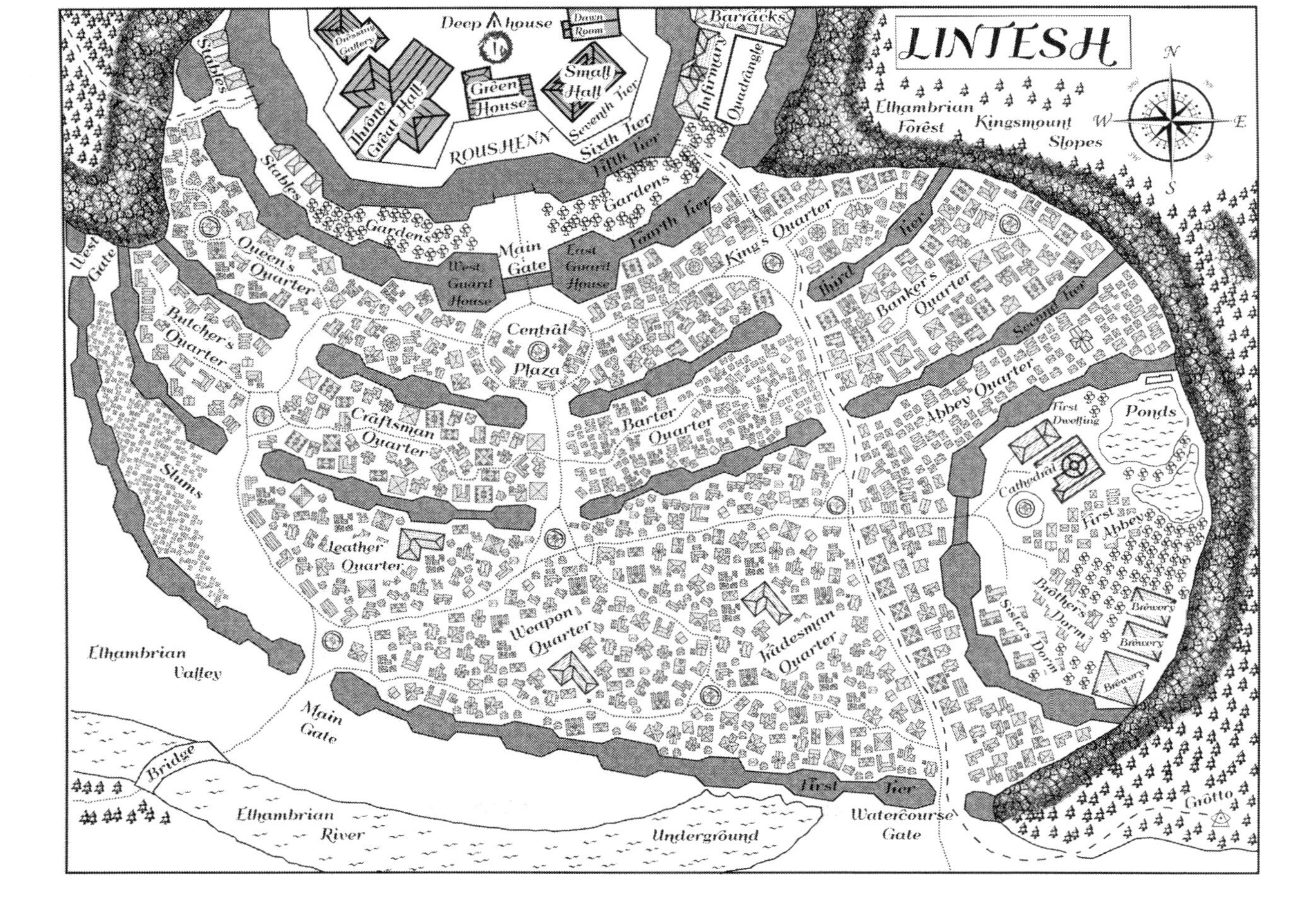

LINTESH
N
E
S
W
Elhambrian
Forest
Kingsmount
Slopes
Deep house
Dawn Room
Dressing Gallery
Throne
Great Hall
Green House
Small Hall
Seventh Tier
ROUSHENN
Sixth Tier
Fifth Tier
Barracks
Infirmary
Quadrangle
Stables
Stables
Gardens
Gardens
Fourth Tier
West Gate
Main Gate
West Guard House
East Guard House
King's Quarter
Queen's Quarter
Butcher's Quarter
Central Plaza
Third Tier
Banker's Quarter
Second Tier
Abbey Quarter
First Dwelling
Ponds
Cathedral
First Abbey
Brother's Dorm
Sisters Dorm
Brewery
Brewery
Brewery
Craftsman Quarter
Barter Quarter
Slums
Leather Quarter
Weapon Quarter
Tradesman Quarter
Elhambrian Valley
Main Gate
Bridge
Elhambrian River
Underground
First Tier
Watercourse Gate
Grotto

PROLOGUE

ELOHL

Elohl den'Alrahel darted through the night, his black cowl raised against the windswept silence of the city. Doubling his pace as he slipped through the darkness, his doeskin boots whispered over the cobblestones as choked alleys loomed around him; hushed streets in the King's City of Lintesh. The plaque of an alehouse creaked in a snowmelt wind, the rim of the sky lightening against the glacier-shrouded mountains. Dawn was coming, and Elohl's stomach clenched in a bilious knot as his tense heartbeat filled his ears.

He was running out of time.

His people were running out of time.

Elohl moved on faster, blending into the shadows as he absorbed the night. With the *wyrric* senses that were his birthright, a spectral imprint of the city formed in a vast sphere around him as he moved. Scents of piss-pot and jasoune marked a whorehouse; the banging of a shutter spoke of an abandoned home. Dodging a barrel by a tingle to his feet, he avoided a low roofline by pressure near his face. A void at the end of the alley loomed ahead and Elohl had a sensate picture of towering stone – his destination. Approaching, his heart raced as the outer wall of Roushenn Palace coalesced before him.

The palace of the King of Alrou-Mendera.

Elohl's fingertips touched the wall's darkness, hacked out of the southern face of the Kingsmount. Coarse, Roushenn's blue byrunstone granite had been carved by wind and rain, snow and ice over eons, leaving plenty of holds. Climbing by the same instinct that allowed him grace in the darkness, Elohl's fingers and resinous tips of his boots found purchase. His fingers tingled as he ascended; an image of cracked bones lanced his consciousness and Elohl passed that hold by. His foot throbbed as he stepped to a lip – urging him toward a ledge strong enough to support his weight.

The byrunstone wall yielded its secrets until Elohl was soon up and over. Sensing no sentries inside its reaches, Elohl dropped the last length, landing in thick vegetation. The nighttime gardens were drowned in the whisper of ferns, and Elohl soon found the palace gardener's entrance, just as his sister Olea had prepared him. Sidling into the shadows of the stone arch, Elohl removed Elsthemi-steel picks from a pouch in his leathers. His touch was softer than featherwisp as he eased his tension tool and pick into the door's iron lock. He was nearly done when a pair of Palace Guardsmen crunched by upon the gravel walk. Their eyes swept the darkness and Elohl froze in the shadows, fear lancing his gut.

Discovery would mean a stint in the dungeons for invading the King's fortress tonight.

But Elohl's charcoal garb was meant for the night, and the guards passed on. The lock clicked and Elohl sighed in through the door like a shroud, his insides tight as tripwire. Torches guttered in iron sconces, licked by ghastly currents in the hall. His breath echoed in the vaulted gables, his hands trembling as if the nightwind blew through him rather than through the vaulted hall.

Inhaling, Elohl took a measured breath to control his emotions. Only his success could halt the march that his people, the Alrashemni Kingsmen, had begun this day. For centuries, the Kingsmen had sworn loyalty to Alrou-Mendera. Elite warriors and peacekeepers for the King, they were the strength and heart of the nation. But in a few hours they would arrive here at the palace, clad for battle to show their outrage at an unfounded accusation. A King's Summons that demanded each and every one of them re-swear fealty at Roushenn Palace.

Or get charged with High Treason and be put to death.

Received three days ago, the Summons accused the Kingsmen of unspecified crimes. It was an unprecedented edict from an untrusting King – though King Uhlas den'Ildrian had previously trusted the Kingsmen his entire reign. Charging the Kingsmen with treason was insanity, and Elohl tried not to think about what would happen if his people arrived here in a few hours, clad for war as they demanded explanation. Or if the King ordered his Palace Guard to arrest his nation's peacekeepers.

Bloodshed could be the only result – bloodshed Elohl hoped to prevent by his actions tonight.

As he moved down the byrunstone hall, he steadied his purpose. Down a corkscrewing stair, he twisted through the labyrinthine bowels of the palace, orchestrated to hopelessly confuse invaders. It was this part of his task Olea had quizzed him on ruthlessly in the past three days, and Elohl moved swiftly through the torch-lit shadows, every turn committed to memory.

At last, he arrived at a pair of massive ironwood doors deep inside the mountain. Taking in their imposing height, he absorbed their carved tableau illuminated by a nearby torch. A stylized wolf and dragon curled around each other, locked in battle and ringed in fire. Snarling with hackles raised, the wolf's fangs were sunk into the dragon's neck, while the serpentine dragon pierced the wolf's belly with its talons. Though both tore at each other, the tableau's circle was perfectly balanced – as if neither were winning. Awed, Elohl stood a moment, his skin tingling strangely. No one knew what the wolf and dragon signified, nor why certain places in Alrou-Mendera were inscribed with the image.

An ancient sigil from a people long lost.

With a shiver, Elohl roused himself. Setting his attention to the iron lock, it clicked open to his picks, revealing a looming black maw. The Deephouse was a taproom for servants and guards, and Elohl's nostrils caught the acrid spice of hopt-ale and the syrupy scent of mellon-blume wine as he stepped inside. But the darkness of the stone cavern wasn't absolute. Elohl froze in the shadows, and setting his back against a stand of kegs, he peered toward the byrunstone bar. The glow of a lantern confirmed his suspicions.

Someone else was here tonight – and they shouldn't have been.

Four figures stood around the lantern upon the polished bar, their leathers roughshod in the way of mercenaries. Cowled with their heads down, they conversed in murmurs, the edge of a knife catching the light as one gestured at a vellum spread upon the bar. Elohl cursed internally. His destination, the highwall in the furthest depths of the cavern, could only be accessed by the natural stone arch behind the bar. To get to the stair-access, he had to maneuver past the night-time agitators. Determination snarled through him and Elohl edged along the kegs, his senses tingling. Moving out of the deepest shadows, he kept low – creeping towards the stone stairs.

"Ho, there! Halt!"

A war-roughened voice ripped the darkness and Elohl froze, his pulse thundering in his ears as heads turned. A burly man cursed and pulled a knife as a slender weasel of a fellow hurried to roll up the vellum. But the laughter of a woman came then, blonde hair shining from beneath her thieves' hood as her leather-buckled figure rounded the bar. The dry-sour scent of cider reeked from her as she sidled close, along with a cloying jasoune perfume as she reached up and uncowled Elohl – her smile lecherous.

"Yurgas! You've scared the poor Penitent half to death!" Her blue eyes glimmered as she put a black glove to Elohl's face, then slid her hand down his neck, stroking his jerkin's high collar. "You're built like a heron, lad! So slender and tall. And with such lovely storm-grey eyes. What a waste in a Jenner!"

Elohl blinked, realizing she thought he was of the priesthood, the Jenner Penitents that brewed the concoctions which filled the alehouse. He adopted the ruse, placing one foot behind the other and dropping into a bow, two fingers to his lips in the manner of a Jenner. "My Lords. My Lady. Blessings upon you in this late hour."

He felt the agitators ease. But if they had ever truly looked at a Penitent, they would have known the young man before them wore no Jenner garb. Elohl's long charcoal leather jerkin was quadrant-split for fighting, with blackened steel buckles etched with the Kingsmount and Stars. His hood was oiled leather rather than cloth, flowing seamlessly into his jerkin to keep off rain. Even though he'd not worn his sword across his back tonight, only dual longknives on his harness, to politicos his Alrashemni Kingsman garb would have been unmistakable. But Kingsmen were a rare enough sight across the nation that meeting one never happened for some folk. So these brigands believed as they wanted to believe, and saw a Jenner Penitent walking his Mercy in the early hours.

"Here lad." The swarthy man behind the bar growled. "Have a pull and go. Bar's closed."

A thick glass tumbler slid across the polished stone of the bar, straight to Elohl's fingertips. His nostrils caught the tang of distilled cider and he knew his best option was to play the ruse. With a nervous chuckle, Elohl picked up the tumbler just like a Penitent might if discovered coming down for a drink in the dead of night. "Just a taste, I suppose."

"Not so pure after all!" The woman laughed, urging the tumbler to his lips. "Have a sip, lad."

Elohl gazed at the amber liquid, wondering if it would be his last drink this side of Aeon's Oblivion; or if it would be a mourning for his kin who might see oblivion today. Either way, a drink would ease his nerves. Tossing it back, Elohl clapped the tumbler to the bar with a grimace. Jeers greeted his buzzing ears as he fought to not cough from fumes screaming up his throat.

"Three whole pulls! He drinks like the High Brigade!" The man behind the bar laughed. "Jenner sure can keep his liquor."

"Ain't no Jenner."

A battle-rough voice spoke again from the darkness, and the place in Elohl's gullet where the cider had passed cooled in terror as he realized his ruse was forfeit. His gaze flicked to the shadows; to the man who had marked him. Elohl's skin tingled, feeling the man's predatory gaze like a war commander, and he forced himself to pin the mercenary-commander with a gaze as stern as his father's. It was a Kingsman's stare, and the man hesitated in the darkness. But though Elohl had his father's strong, sinewed build, at twenty years old he was only a Seventh Seal – unfinished. He hadn't the experience of commanding men to war; he hadn't matched his skills against a hundred enemies yet.

The mercenary-commander saw it. Stalking into the light, the man's bear-thick bulk tensed, roped scars upon his left cheek twisting up into a malicious snarl. "If he's a Jenner, he won't fight me. If he's a Kingsman, he will."

"Now, Yurgas! The lad couldn't be a Kingsman!" The blonde spoke as her gaze flicked uncertainly between them.

"Oh, he's a Kingsman." The brute's blue eyes were cold as iron upon Elohl. "See that pride in his gaze, that ramrod spine? Pride and training. And Kingsman Greys, even tooled with the right sigils."

"They's on to us?" The skinny fellow rasped urgently. "You said they got no clue what's in for 'em tomorrow night—!"

"Still your tongue or lose it!" The commander barked.

"I only thought—"

"You didn't think, so shut your hole. This one's barely of age, ain't you boy? Just shy of your Blackmark, scared and pissing yourself." A cruel smile twisted the commander's lip as his iron-blue gaze perused Elohl. "Your kin would be here carving out our hearts right now if they knew you were caught in a devil's lair listening to *privileged* information. But you're alone, aren't you? The Kingsmen don't know what's in store for them tomorrow. And so they'll come to the palace in a few hours, just as you've come tonight, without backup. Meaning that your presence here is happenstance. And no one will ever know what happened to you."

Suddenly, the mercenary-commander lunged – a dagger in his meaty hand. A ripping sensation seared Elohl's neck and he twisted, the slash cutting only air where his neck had been. Launching to the wall behind the bar, Elohl scurried up as the marauders cursed. A tingle of instinct rippled Elohl and he dropped his right hand just before a knife hit the stone where his hand had been. Regaining his grip, he climbed like the *eloi* lizards for which he was named – as more knives went whirring upwards.

"Skewer him, dammit!" The commander rasped. "The Lothren will send us to Halsos if tomorrow's events play wrong because of a single lad!"

Below, two mercenaries began climbing, their scrabbling peppered with grunts and oaths. Though the commander's words chilled Elohl's veins with ice, he missed no holds as he angled up the highwall. Cursing himself for missing critical information about the Kingsmen's fate this day, sparks caught his attention far below and Elohl scrabbled faster, realizing what was about to happen.

"Heave! Hit him, dammit!"

With roars of glee, the mercenaries sent liquor-bottles with flaming spouts whizzing through the air. Smashing upon the highwall, blazing spirits doused the stone to Elohl's right. Gouts of fire surged as another bottle smashed to his left. Elohl's only option was up as a third bottle smashed below his foot. His lungs pumped air as smoke choked him, but he was above their throws now. Opening his sensate sphere, Elohl felt for the high corner where the item he'd come for was supposed to be, the item Ghrenna had seen in her vision.

A talisman that had the power to save the Kingsmen from whatever was coming.

Moving with his senses, Elohl found the gap in the wall Ghrenna had described, just below a rift that led out to the night. Anchoring with fingers and toes, Elohl tucked his nose to his shoulder so he could breathe as he reached a hand into the gap. Touching a wooden box, he fished it to the edge. Coughing as smoke burned his eyes, Elohl snugged a finger under the metal clasp and flicked the lid open. His fingers touched a moth-eaten velvet lining, then a filigreed object. Retrieving the item, he squinted at it in the cavern's red light. An ornate metal clockwork the size of a medallion gleamed in his palm – layered with precious metals like a puzzle, with thirteen spokes like the Jenner Sun.

Elohl's gut dropped as his chest compressed. The box was just as Ghrenna had described it, but the object was all wrong. *Look for a ring of star-metal, of a dragon fighting a wolf around a drop of blood,* Ghrenna had told him three days ago, her voice hollow from her trance. But this wasn't a star-metal ring at all. And as Elohl held it, a sensation suddenly speared him like the clockwork was burning. Lancing up his arm like fire ants, it drove through his body, knifing his heart. Elohl gave a violent tremor, nearly losing his grip upon the wall as his heart clenched. His hand spasmed into a fist around the clockwork as a blistering rage surged through him. But as quickly as the feeling overpowered him, it fled.

And then, the clockwork broke.

A cry escaped Elohl, the despair of a man with all the gods against him. Quickly, he opened his hand but the damage was done; the item was in pieces. Smoke was thick and Elohl choked, his throat burning, his limbs weak from whatever the clockwork had done to him. A mercenary scrabbled for purchase beyond the flames and stuffing the clockwork into his belt pouch, Elohl lifted his chin, smelling the sweet night breeze beyond the smoke. Muscles of his torso and thighs bunching, Elohl hurried up through the rift in the top of the cavern, and emerged upon the roof of the palace.

Doubling over in the grey-opal dawn, Elohl coughed hard, eyes watering from burning vapors as his limbs trembled. Curses pursued him and Elohl hurried across the palace roof, vaulting boulders tumbled from the mountainside. Suppressing his anguish, he coughed hard as he ran. He had to return the item he'd found to Ghrenna; perhaps her vision had changed in the hours he'd been away.

Perhaps a new one had come to explain this unexpected turn.

That thought was all he had to spur him as he ran. Next to a grand dome, Elohl backed over toes first, finding rough handholds where the carving-out of the palace met the Kingsmount. It was hundreds of lengths to the ground from the Upper Tiers, but he made his way steadily down as he managed his breath and fatigue. A tingle in his foot led him left, a pulse in his other foot led him right, until he found a crevasse that got him down to the paving stones behind a weaver's shop. Dawn blushed the eastern peaks of the Kingsmountains rose and gold.

But the lightening sky could not brighten Elohl's despairing heart.

Picking up his feet, Elohl ran. A dark shadow melted to his side as he streaked through the dawn city, his twin sister Olea keeping easy pace. His twin was a soothing balm to his torpid emotions, entering his *wyrric* sphere like sunlight upon a frozen lake. Darting through alleys, Olea's shadowy form leaped benches and ducked awnings with serenity, longknives flashing in her hands as she ran.

Elohl's twin was as fine as her blades, her slender height honed into effortless grace as she spoke with unruffled breath, "Did you get it, Elohl? Was it there?"

"No." Elohl didn't break stride though his breath was ragged. "The box was there, but not the star-metal ring. This was there instead."

Ducking into an alley that seeped with the acrid tang of a tannery, Elohl halted, unbuckling his leather pouch. Opening it quickly, Olea's pale opal eyes narrowed upon the item, her straight dark brows forming a line. Setting her jaw, she looked up, then buckled the pouch to her own belt with fast fingers.

"We'll discuss this later. I can hear five men following. And – something else."

"Five? There were only two following me out the top of the cavern—" Elohl glanced back down the alley. But Olea's *wyrric* hearing was keener than a wolfhound and Elohl knew better than to gainsay her. They ducked down the alley, back the way they had come tonight as rough stone workshops and taverns now abandoned their spectral nighttime forms. Elohl's heart sank as he skimmed over the paving stones. Unbuckling his jerkin, he tugged his shirt lacings open as he ran, baring the Inking upon his chest, the black Kingsmount crowned with five stars. He rubbed the still-tender marking, illegally Inked by Ghrenna just three days ago.

Elohl didn't deserve it; he hadn't earned it yet.

But they might be the last marks Inked upon any Kingsman now that their task had failed.

Racing under the Watercourse Gate, Elohl found the guards still sleeping from the pith-crest Olea had slipped into their ale earlier. Speeding out into the chatter of the Elhambrian Forest, they streaked to the mossy grotto from whence they'd come. In a group of boulders burbling with a natural spring, a man-sized Alranstone stood, covered in arcane glyphs with three eyes carven into it – the

Stone they had come through hours ago. The eye at the top began to open as they approached, some ancient *wyrria* transforming the gray-blue byrunstone to a gleaming inset of lapis. Splaying his hand towards its blue iris, Elohl called out his name and lineage as he ran.

"Elohl den'Alrahel, den'Urloel, den'Alrashesh! Blessings to the Kingsmen! Blessings to the *Alrashemni—*"

But before he could finish the words that would activate the Stone, Elohl felt something slide into his mind. Not the rush and tingle of the Stone, this was a smooth current of *wyrria*, arresting his mind like a tide's flow takes a ship. Causing the incantation to fall from his lips as it caught him, he stumbled to a halt beside the Stone. Pulling at him, it made him turn like a nightmare; gazing toward the edge of the clearing.

There, in the grey hues of dawn, a behemoth stalked them down. Beside Elohl, Olea was captive also – held by the approaching presence. The black monstrosity chittered as it came, its massive claws clacking like language, segmented legs punching the moss. In the growing light, the scorpion's chitinous plates glittered like stars, black with a horrible allure. Arching over its broad back, the behemoth's tail was ready to strike, its high barb shining with a drop of poison in the sun's first rays.

A man rode upon its back. Dressed in a herringbone-weave leather jerkin so black it ate the sun's rays except for shining silver studs, the man's face was hidden inside his deep hood. Maneuvering with only a touch of his hand, he rode the scorpion without a saddle, an enormous longsword with a black-wrapped handle strapped to his back. The man's dark eyes stared Elohl down from the shadows of his hood – and a quicksilver sensation swept Elohl, rolling him. He collapsed, one knee driving into the earth, his hand upon the Alranstone the only thing keeping him upright as Olea gave a sharp cry and fell to her knees also. Horror swept Elohl as the man smiled deep within his hood – and the quicksilver sensation inside Elohl's mind formed speech.

I can't let you leave, boy. Not with what you have witnessed tonight. Open for me. Open your mind. Spill for me what you saw, what you heard...

Vast weaves of silver light slammed into Elohl like a tidal wave hitting a jetty. Terror gripped him as he felt his mind break, shredded open for the scorpion-rider. But suddenly, from his hand upon the Alranstone, a presence went humming through him like a thousand bees. A warming glow filled Elohl as the

Stone's massive eye came fully open, flooding the glade with blue light – and the final words of the Stone's incantation were thrust into Elohl's mind.

Trapping Olea's hand beneath his, Elohl screamed out, "*Open Stone of Alran, pass me free!*"

Blue light dimming, the Alranstone acquiesced to his command. The black rider's face contorted in fury as he vaulted from his scorpion, drawing his massive sword with a roar, swiping down to sever Elohl from the Stone.

But he was too late. In a flash and a clap of thunder, Elohl and Olea were threaded into the Alranstone's core. Elohl screamed in agony as his innards contorted with a searing wrench, his body twisted into a mobius. Sunbursts flared before his eyes as emptiness filled his lungs like being rolled beneath ocean waves. But before he could focus upon any of these things, he and Olea were spat out upon the other side.

Stumbling to their knees in a clearing far from the grotto, breathless and retching.

1

ELOHL

Throwing his hand of battered playing cards to the rough wooden table, a vague smile lifted one corner of Elohl den'Alrahel's wind-chapped lips. With drunken curses and incredulous grins, his High Brigade climbing team groaned, tossing their hands facedown with little grace as Elohl revealed his cards – a trump of Kingsmount and Plinth over a straight flush of black stars. Rubbing his short beard, Elohl curried a hand through his cropped black hair, then leaned back in his chair – giving his weather-hardened frame a good stretch as he laced his hands behind his head.

"Kingsmount high. Pay up, louts."

His men chuckled with good humor as they swigged their ale, before reaching for their purses. Cracking bitel nuts, they flicked the shells to the straw-strewn boards of the muddy alehouse, causing a stray shell to launch into the barmaid's cleavage. She scowled at the rough Brigadiers, picking it out as she huffed past with trenchers of stew, an old man in homespun tuning the strings of his gourd-shaped oube by the quarried stone fireplace. There would be music beneath the alehouse's blackened rafters this evening – a rarity in the King's Army, especially at the remote High Brigade basecamp near the war-torn Valenghian border.

But Elohl was going to miss it.

"Aeon's prick, Lead Hand!" Russet-haired Ihbram den'Sennia, Elohl's Second Hand, threw down his cards with an affable smile – showing impeccable white teeth in his tanned olive skin. "Couldn't you let us win this once? You are leaving today. Could at least give us a chance to win back all the coin you've fleeced from us these past ten years."

"You want your coin back?" Elohl's lips twitched in a smile as he fastened the buckles of his worn military jerkin and adjusted his bracers. "Play me again, Ihbram."

"And give you one final chance to cock my ass?" Ihbram's lance-sharp green eyes glimmered with humor. "I don't think so."

"Actually, getting your ass cocked might be a better way to make some money, rather than playing me at Alrouhelia." Elohl smiled slyly.

"Take your coin and get the fuck out of here. Asshole." His Second Hand grinned back.

With a laugh, Ihbram slid his leather purse across the bitterpine table, and the rest of Elohl's climbing team did the same. Most accepted the farewell whupping from their commander with grins and swigs of ale. But there was one who was not pleased, and had never been pleased with his First-Lieutenant and Lead Hand. Wereth den'B-hariye, a wiry man with a face of steel surged to his feet unsteadily across from Elohl, a hateful scowl turning his graying mustachios down even more than usual.

"Den'Alrahel!" He slurred. "You can't just take our coin and sail! You owe us!"

"Do I?" Elohl's grey eyes were suddenly stone-hard as he raked his winnings into his leather belt purse, his gaze chilling the table to silence.

"Yeah, you damn well do." Wereth snarled as he leaned in across the table, challenging – his wiry hand straying to the rope-knife at his hip. "Go drown yourself in the Elsee; but not with my coin in your purse. I'll have it back. Now."

"Whoa there, Wereth..." Ihbram's clear voice was reasonable as he held out a hand, moving into a cautionary position between Wereth and Elohl. But Elohl moved around Ihbram, motioning his Second Hand out of the way with a nod.

"I've put up with you," Elohl's steely gaze pinned Wereth, "for nearly two years. Ever since you were ousted from den'Mhessua's team for falling asleep drunk on watch. Den'Mhessua wanted your dumb ass up in a noose for your negligence in protecting your brothers, and I counseled him to let you live. I don't owe you; you owe me, Wereth. I'd say a bit of your coin for saving your neck is a fair trade, wouldn't you?"

"Fuck you." Wereth sneered, his fingers on the hilt of his knife. "You don't give a shit about my life, let alone your own. You drink yourself into oblivion just like the rest of us, *Lead Hand*. Everyone knows you're a suicidal cunt! You don't even try to hide those wrist scars of yours."

"Hey now!" Ihbram surged forward but Elohl held his hand out over his Second Hand's chest.

"You want a chance at me, Wereth?" Elohl dropped his voice, emptying himself of care for the man in front of him. "Today's your day. By tonight I'll be gone, and you'll never have another chance. So what are you waiting for?"

"Fucking *Blackmark!*"

Wereth's face was purple as he lunged with his rope-knife, fast as a keshar's raking claw. But Elohl moved with the speed of *wyrric* instinct – whipping one longknife to den'Bhariye's throat before his team could so much as startle. His surge made low whistles sound around the table. Elohl's team had seen how fast he could move and the precision his *wyrria* lent him – the reason he set true climbing routes up passes and kept men around him alive, both in battle and out of it. Elohl had earned his authority time and time again in blizzards, navigating around crevasses, and saving men from falling to their deaths by a fast anchor to the line. They had been saved by his longknives or his sword – thrust suddenly between them and an enemy.

But rarely did they see that instinct used on a fellow Brigadier. Elohl's team had little understanding of what seethed beneath his crust of glacial calm. As Elohl's uncompromising gaze held den'Bhariye's, daring him to even flinch, the moment stretched – Elohl's authority bristling through the hushed tavern with his storm-grey gaze every bit his father's now but harder; older. Ten years in the High Brigade did that to a man.

Ten years in an unforgiving war that might have been stopped had the Kingsmen had any say in it.

"Put it away, Elohl." Ihbram den'Sennia spoke from his right. "He's not worth a hanging. You've only got two hours of service left."

Elohl took a deep breath, the single breath of his Kingsmen training. Glacial ice slipped into place inside him once more, sluicing his rage. Sliding his knife back into its sheath, Elohl watched Wereth simmer before him, hateful like so many were now against a Kingsman because of an accusation of treason none could conjure evidence for. Hateful simply because common men needed someone to hate when their families starved from rations shunted to armies for ten years.

"I'm no traitor to the Crown," Elohl spoke, cold. "And killing a soldier of the Crown would be treason; even a shit excuse for one such as you. *Kingsmen* do not commit treason."

Den'Bhariye snarled. His knife snaked up, fast. But Elohl was faster, surging forward in a heron-smooth strike with the heel of his open palm slamming den'Bhariye square in the chest. It was a blow to shame, learned long ago at the capable hands of Elohl's father. Toppling backwards over his chair, Wereth sprawled out over the sodden floorboards – as Elohl's team erupted into laughter.

"Cunt." Den'Bhariye's scowling mustachios scowled harder as he slunk away to the bar. Though he spit as he went, the man was broken. Satisfaction spread through Elohl as he turned to make his farewells, clasping hands with the veteran climbers of his primary team.

"Nice strike, Lieutenant. I daresay, we'll miss you. And those instincts of yours." A grinning Jovial den'Fourth put away his short knife now that the fight was over, though he'd been ready to dive in to protect his commander just like Ihbram. Proffering his arm, Jovial's mouth quirked in his aquiline face. He was a good climber and a friend, eight years on Elohl's team, and as they clasped wrists Elohl felt a sudden pang, realizing he was leaving everything of his life behind yet again.

Just like ten years ago.

"Jovial. Nice climbing with you." Elohl spoke, masking all emotion.

"Don't be so sullen, Lieutenant!" Jovial slapped him on the shoulder. "Maybe we'll see each other again someday. Until then, watch your back on the road. I can't be ready to knife everyone who insults you in a tavern."

"I'll keep that in mind." A small smile lifted Elohl's lips as a somber-eyed Harlis den'Sellen turned to him next, saying his goodbyes with respect for his First-Lieutenant. The other men on Elohl's team followed suit in the lazy, frozen way of the High Brigade, saluting with two fingers and a nod. Elohl clasped Ihbram's climb-corded forearm last as the other men moved off, giving their commander and his closest friend space to converse in the thin daylight near one grimy window. Elohl eyed his Second Hand as they faced each other, taking in the weatherworn creases at Ihbram's eyes and mouth. Grey streaked Ihbram's roguish copper waves, braided back from his face in the Elsthemi

Highlands fashion – Highlands blood somewhere down his mostly Cennetian family line.

"Travel safe, friend," Ihbram spoke quietly, a kind glimmer in his bright green eyes.

"Ten years of war in the highpasses might be enough for a man," Elohl murmured back. "Your serve is up, same as mine. You don't have to jump right back into the fray, Ihbram."

"Fifteen years for me, you forget." Ihbram den'Sennia grinned as he lifted his pewter tankard and swigged off the last of his ale, amused.

"You sure you want to join the lowlands campaign against Valenghia?"

"Nah." Ihbram chuckled. "But where is an old soldier like me supposed to go? Anyway, just 'cause I'm going to the lowlands doesn't mean I'm joining the war-front. I might just sneak over the border, find a little silver-haired Valenghian gal with high bosoms and a good, roaring fire, know what I mean? A man can't climb until his fingers bleed all the time."

"Deserter." Elohl snorted, though he smiled.

"Go where the gold is, Elohl." Ihbram grinned, baring very white teeth in the midst of his trimmed red beard. "Get a little of what I want for a change. Fuck these mountains."

"Fuck these mountains," Elohl agreed. "Walk me to the pier?"

Ihbram nodded and they fell into a military stride, at once possessing the clip of a soldier and the exhausted amble of a veteran Brigadier. Exiting the alehouse, they stepped off its waterlogged boards into the three-inch mud that was ever-present in the Eleskis, except when it snowed. Now it was raining, and when it rained in the heights of the Kingsmountains, it rained and rained, depressing.

Thick mud squelched up around the stout leather of their knee-high Brigadier boots as they slogged on in their oilcloaks. Stopping by the log bunkhouse, Elohl fetched his rucksack with his belongings, which weren't much. It struck him suddenly that his life had come to so little. A single rucksack filled with rope, ice axes and claw-feet for climbing, and longknives to engage Valenghia's Red Valor once a skirmish began. His military-issue longsword he now strapped to his back, heaving the rucksack over it but leaving the sword's handle free just in case.

And his Kingsmen Greys – stuffed into the bottom of his pack.

Surveying his empty bunk, Elohl realized how far he'd strayed from his youth. Though a talented fighter, the lad he'd been when he'd come here had been used to comfort. But that lad had become numb to hardship quickly, mired in the routines of war, and now there was nothing else. The High Brigade of Alrou-Mendera suffered skirmishes every summer as the Valenghian Red Valor tried to find a way through the passes to weaken the border.

And they froze every winter, in snows thirty feet deep.

It was tiring, and Elohl was more tired than he'd ever been. But he'd learned practicality in the highmountains, how to be emotionless in bad times – and he pushed his emotions away now, drowning them beneath the glacial calm he'd perfected. They were always bad times these past ten years, more or less, and Elohl's tread was heavy as he stepped from the bunkhouse boards. Huddling in his oilcloak, he and Ihbram slogged through the sleeting rain to the lakeshore. At the pier on the Elsee, a twin-masted sailing craft waited to take those whose service was ended on their long trek home.

But home was a place Elohl no longer had, all the Kingsmen now gone. Faces surfaced in Elohl's mind; the laughing gaze of Olea. His father's stern jaw; his mother's sweet smile. The hot rage of Dherran; Suchinne's perfect calm.

Ghrenna.

Cerulean washed over Elohl's vision, sweeping him away for a moment. The dark blue of her eyes always came to him in times like these – as if Ghrenna watched him from afar. He could almost smell her pine-clean tundra fragrance; almost see her pale throat and the way her white hair curled around her ears. But Elohl set his jaw and drowned that thought also, surveying the dock. There weren't many waiting for the boat from the High Brigade. Most of the climbing team Elohl commanded still had a few years of service left, and no one from his original team had made it ten years except Ihbram.

Not many made it home from the High Brigade.

"Where will you go?" Ihbram spoke at Elohl's side. It was a trick he had, picking up on people's thoughts. Elohl and others had accused the man of reading minds, but Ihbram always laughed it off with a flash of his impeccable white teeth.

"Olea was in Lintesh last I heard. So I go to Lintesh."

"That was eight years ago, Elohl; your last letter from Olea." Ihbram eyed him warily. "That's a big risk going right back into the keshar's maw after everything that happened."

"It doesn't matter," Elohl murmured, submerging sensations of failure so acute still that his throat gripped, as rain pattered off his nose. "I'm going to

Lintesh. If Olea's not there anymore, I'll follow her trail until I find where she went."

"Your twin hasn't written in all this time. You think—"

"Don't say it." Elohl shot his friend a hard look. "Don't even think it. Olea's alive. Just like... all the rest."

Ihbram nodded, wrapping his oilcloak tighter as he watched crates being loaded and boatmen lashing down cargo. Ihbram knew when to let something go. After ten years fighting together in the High Brigade, living to keep each other alive, the two men knew each other better than Elohl knew his own twin at this point.

"I got a cousin in Quelsis," Ihbram murmured at last. "Ihlen den'Almen. Friend of mine is a friend of his. He'd get you on your feet. Get you hooked up with a trade."

"I have a trade."

Ihbram stopped Elohl with a hand to the arm, his bright emerald gaze deadly serious beneath the hood of his cloak. "Being a Kingsman isn't a trade, Elohl. Not anymore. Your people are gone, disappeared and probably dead. Nothing you can do will bring them back. Whomever penned that Summons and captured you Kingskinder sent you out here to die, all to keep the worst secret our nation has ever known. If you go back to Lintesh, they'll be that much closer to ending you."

"I have to go back, Ihbram." Restlessness stirred in Elohl, of business unfinished. "You don't know what it's like, knowing I failed the Kingsmen, my people."

"You did what you could."

"I didn't. I failed at Roushenn Palace and my kin disappeared and then I got caught. Olea got caught. Ghrenna. Dherran. Suchinne. All the Kingskinder."

"They didn't get caught because of you, jackass. Sheathe those words. You've survived out here ten years – that's an Aeon-fucked miracle, Elohl! Don't be suicidal again, not like when you first arrived here. Go get yourself a girl and a nice little farm and leave the whole Kingsmen thing be."

Elohl regarded Ihbram, knowing his friend's words for truth yet unable to heed them. "I'll be in Lintesh, looking for Olea."

Ihbram narrowed his eyes. "You can't stay put near people for longer than a fortnight and we both know it. You're a ronin keshar if ever there was one, Elohl. I give you two weeks before you leave the city and isolate yourself."

"I'm a man of solitude."

"You're a man punishing himself for the past, Elohl. There's a difference. Do you even know what you want out of life?"

Elohl was silent, feeling emotions try to melt through his glacial calm like a volcanic vent beneath a snowfield. Guilt, fatigue, rage, responsibility – he could name them all, but didn't allow himself to feel them. "I just want peace, Ihbram, is that so much to ask? This turmoil I feel – I just need some peace."

"Peace comes at a price, Elohl." Ihbram held his gaze with level concern. "All men pay that price in war. The only way to find true peace is to allow yourself to live again. To move on."

The bronze steerage-bell was rung from the ship and Elohl glanced over. Boatmen scurried up the masts, unfurling sails and loosing lines from the dock. He was going to miss his ship if he didn't move, and there wasn't another one for two more months. Turing to Ihbram, Elohl proffered one climb-weathered hand. "Keep yourself well, Ihbram."

"Keep yourself *alive*, Elohl." Ihbram grasped his arm solemnly. "Because I won't be around to do it anymore."

"I'll keep that in mind."

It was a brutal truth, and they shared a moment of silent understanding – of climbs weathered and battles waged, of nights huddling close for warmth with death always a thin breath away. But at last, it was time. Elohl turned, striding down the rain-slicked pier, leaving his truest friend behind in the mud. Mounting the chipped gangplank, Elohl settled his pack at the railing for one last view of the storm-shrouded peaks of the Eleskis.

There was no belowdecks for soldiers, but Elohl was used to weather in the Kingsmountains. Wrapping his oilcloak tighter around himself, Elohl snugged the hood and hunkered upon his pack, not letting himself think any further than Lintesh. It was death in the highmountains to think too far ahead. Two coarse-bearded veterans from the High Brigade saluted their First-Lieutenant as they settled their packs at the rail also – veterans with scars like Elohl's and the same empty-hard visage.

Nodding, Elohl turned away. He wasn't their First-Lieutenant anymore; he wasn't Brigadier-Captain Arlus den'Pell's steadiest ice-ax anymore.

He wasn't anything anymore.

The rain deepened as the marine crew lofted the sails and swung them about, wind driving the wet against Elohl's bearded cheeks. If anyone had been looking, they might have thought some of those raindrops were tears. But no one was looking at a man with hard grey eyes who was no longer young, whose chiseled face could have been menacing or sorrowful. No one was looking at a man whose hands were weathered like the ice they'd climbed for ten years, but were steady when he killed. No one was looking at a Kingsman who bore the mountain-and-stars Inkings, but who had never really been one.

Because Kingsman wasn't a trade.

Not anymore.

2

OLEA

Eyes closed in the new day, Olea den'Alrahel took a deep breath, embracing the peace of the Roushenn Palace fight-yards. Morning sunshine streamed down through the cedars, warming her skin. Gravel crunched at the edge of the yard as someone passed; a bumblebee rumbled near her ear. Mellow scents of lavender and lemon-balm came from gardens that ringed the grounds, while camphor breathed out from the Palace Infirmary adjacent. No voices disturbed her this early, no one here to bother their Captain-General before the palace needed her to be on point for yet another day.

But today wasn't just another day. Today was the day Elohl was supposed to be discharged from service. High Brigade, a post men didn't come home from – where soldiers froze to death, or fell upon a climb, or got skewered by Valenghians in battle. It had been ten years since they had last seen each other.

Ten years; eight without letters, not knowing if he still lived.

Erupting into motion, Olea banished all thought. Moving like a summer breeze through the quadrangle, her longknives flowed through her fighting forms like they'd been born in her hands. Strong yet yielding, her slices were made to separate limb from joint. Dancing in the sunlight, Olea never needed to open her eyes. Life was in the roll, the pivot, and the lunge. Death was in the cut, the jab, and the parry with her unseen foe – all of it done to a slow rhythm of breath learned long ago.

A sound alerted her; the careful slide of a boot scraping dirt. It would have been missed by anyone else, but Olea honed in upon her sudden opponent, knowing where he was without needing to see. Fenton den'Kharel had stepped into the ring with her this morning. Her First-Lieutenant in the Roushenn Palace Guard always smelled of peat and honey, a light musk that spoke of living rough, fighting hard, and eating clean off the land – the life of a soldier in the highpasses of Alrou-Mendera. Sometimes Fenton didn't bother being quiet when he approached, but sometimes he tested her, seeing how well she could track him with her *wyrric* hearing. Stepping in with the barest crunch of dirt, his breath was smooth. Drawing his longknives, Fenton let only the lightest whisper of steel over leather attune Olea to his readiness.

"I can hear you, you know." Olea spoke, a smile lifting her lips. "Don't even try to be stealthy, Fenton. Even your scent gives you away."

"Curses. Foiled again." Fenton spoke, his smooth baritone betraying a chuckle. "A man can but try. Ready?"

Fenton closed the distance, and with a slicing of dual longknives they engaged, Olea with her eyes closed. A fighting-style of ripple and flow, their sparring had no hit, no clash, no muscle. Flowing around each other like water, they tore into each other with subtle grace without contesting strength. Curling around Fenton's blades as they sought her body, Olea rolled around for strikes as fast as a whirlpool. But Fenton den'Kharel was just as deft, Olea's blades never once finding a home in his flesh.

Fenton had learned the movements of the Kingsmen sometime during his long years as a soldier, even though he wasn't one.

After a while, Olea heard Fenton step back. The crunch of his boots in the dirt was obvious as he signaled a halt with a soft chuckle. His breath was easy, though they had dueled for nearly a half-hour; the sunlight changed behind Olea's closed eyelids. The forest around the fight-yards had erupted into birdsong, a whole cadre of bumblebees in the lavender now. And the new recruits in the trainees' hall were awake, with a cacophony of young men's noise and jeering.

Olea opened her eyes at last.

"Good morning, Captain-General."

Fenton had gathered both his longknife hilts into one hand and was wiping a light sweat from his brow with his forearm. His gold-brown eyes were placid as he smiled at her, as if they had seen the future and the past and neither was anything to fear. Bared to the waist, his whip-lean stature was average, his well-made body all sinew without any meat to spare. The morning sun picked out golden highlights in his dark auburn hair, kept military short. And though he seemed unnotable at first glance, something about Fenton was intensely striking, something that simmered inside him despite his genial nature. The fighter in Fenton was unquestioned – and the serenity of spirit he possessed was never to be taken for granted.

"I thought you'd be up on the ramparts already for First Survey, Captain." Fenton's gaze glinted with subtle mischief. "Aren't you late?"

"Going to report me tardy, Lieutenant?" Olea gathered her longknives in one hand, wiping sweat from her own brow. Fenton pushed her when they fought, eyes closed or no. Besides Olea, he was the Guard's most talented fighter, and had been ever since he'd arrived at the palace ten years ago.

Fenton laughed. It was a good laugh, the laugh of a man who kept a level head and lived for the best things in life. As Fenton lifted his eyebrows and cocked his head toward the infirmary, Olea nodded, and together they strode from the dirt ring toward the wash-trough by the infirmary doors. Wetting a clean cloth from the pile under the eaves, Olea did one for Fenton also. He nodded his thanks and they both sluiced off.

The summer day was balmy, the wash-water refreshing as it cascaded down Olea's skin. The quadrangle was beginning to fill up with new recruits from the trainees' hall now, sauntering out from their gabled stone dormitory. Shucking white shirts and cobalt jerkins, they took to the field as young men do, pushing each other and jesting. Recognizing their Captain-General, they became flustered at seeing her washing in her short training breeches and halter. Every pair of eyes alighted on her chest, at her Kingsmount and Stars inked in black. As many times as the recruits had seen it these past weeks, they still stared. Eight years into Olea's tenure as Captain-General of the Palace Guard, even Guardsmen who had known her from the first still stared.

It was unheard-of to meet a Kingsman these days, much less one who bared her Blackmark openly.

"Captain!" Many of the new recruits spoke hastily, saluting.

"As you were, gentlemen." Olea gave a curt command while donning her gear. Her trainees had been warned what her Inking meant – that she would have their asses on the ground before they could blink if they challenged her. Nearly dressed already, Fenton's calloused swordsman's hands were just finishing his jerkin's last buckle as a smile of amusement lifted his face. A fire lived inside Fenton, giving him a deceptively languid briskness. Wearing Guardsmen cobalt, his jerkin's cross-over flap was buckled so the high collar was tight, a clean white shirt beneath. His black breeches were spotless, as were his black kneeboots, his sword and longknives hanging from his baldric as they should.

Olea was supposed to keep her cobalt jerkin done up in proper military fashion like Fenton's, but she preferred to leave it open so she could breathe. Buckles gaping to mid-chest as she finished dressing, and leaving her upper shirt-laces lax also, Olea displayed a decent swath of cleavage in the hot summer morning. But her silver pin of office as Captain-General of the Palace Guard glinted untarnished upon her collar on the left – something she never let slide.

"Don't they have any standards for Guardsmen these days?" Fenton grinned as Olea finished up – his way of teasing; light and subtle.

"I have standards for *them*, Fenton." Olea smiled, unwinding her long blue-black curls from their braid and currying her fingers through them, which produced even more stares from her recruits. "If I don't shine my boots, my trainees just look the other way."

"I think your boots attract the least attention, really."

Fenton's lips lifted in amusement as his eyes flicked purposefully to Olea's cleavage, then to the recruits, and Olea looked up from sliding her longknives home on her baldric. A number of trainees looked away fast, blushes coloring more than a few cheeks as boots scuffed the dust. They all looked so young, Olea thought suddenly, like she and Elohl when they'd been caught after the Summons and pressed into military service ten years ago. But these lads were here because they wanted to be. Every face was smiling, eager to begin a new adventure in one of the most lauded positions the nation of Alrou-Mendera had to offer.

And serving under one of the most renowned women in the nation.

"All right you lot!!" Olea's Second-Lieutenant Aldris den'Farahan suddenly strode out from the infirmary and into the yard. Tow-haired and chisel-cheeked, he wrapped his hands in linen as he came, already bare-chested for a day of training. A ladykiller and ruffian who reveled in it, Aldris gave Olea a ribald wink as he whisked a quarterstaff from the rack, striding to the nearest lime-marked sand ring.

"Staves!" Aldris bellowed at the recruits. "Quit staring at your Captain-

General like puppies that pissed on her boots, I don't care how fetching she is!! You think you're the first to throw yourself upon your sword for her love? Think again! Hup!!"

Fenton laughed at Olea's side; a good laugh that was serene and true to his nature. "You're going to set a bad example for the new men, leaving your buckles undone, Olea."

"I'll show you an example," Olea shot him a look, unusually moody today, "about fighting and loyalty. And using what you have to your advantage. *Fight well today, gentlemen!*"

Olea roared it suddenly, a snarl of combat in her voice with the gravel of a seasoned commander. Her roar arrested every ear in the yard and satisfaction filled her, that they were all looking at a Kingswoman who still commanded for the royal house. "Fight well and the best man at his task, as judged by your Second-Lieutenant, gets the honor of having a drink with their Captain-General in the Deephouse tonight! My treat!"

Laughs went up in the yard, with a few whistles and catcalls. Olea winked at Fenton, mimicking her normally far more lighthearted self.

"You heard her, gentlemen!" Grinning, Aldris gave Olea a salute from the sand ring with his quarterstaff. And then whipped out keshar-fast at the closest recruit, dropping the man to his ass with the end of the staff behind his knees. "Get to weapons! And quit thinking about fucking our Captain!"

"I get plenty of fucking, boys," Olea called from the sidelines, "but not by you! Move it!" She turned as more laughs went up, feeling the surge of loyalty from her recruits rise along with their humor. Men needed thoughts of sex and drinking to keep them motivated while they got bludgeoned all day.

As they turned to walk inside, Fenton sidled close. "Kingsmen. Trouble, aren't you?"

Olea smiled wistfully as they moved into the high-gabled gloom of the infirmary. It was a joke between them, though a sobering one. Trouble was something she and Fenton shared, something that had brought them together as friends ten years ago when Olea had first come to the Roushenn Palace Guard. On the surface Fenton was easy as a spring breeze and calm as a draft horse, but he was troubled down deep somewhere, just like Olea. But Fenton den'Kharel didn't talk about his past and Olea never pried – and he never pried into hers.

"Tell you what, Fenton." Turning, Olea set a hand to Fenton's jerkin, needing something to banish her brooding about Elohl. "Play Ghenje with me tonight, after my rounds."

Fenton's gold-brown eyes lit with a sudden fire, positively twinkling with dark mischief and making his handsomeness utterly delightful. His lips were made for smiling, and they curled up at the corners, teasing. "You know you'll lose. Playing Ghenje with me is a proud man's curse."

"I know." Olea raked her fingers through her long blue-black curls as she grinned at her First-Lieutenant, playing lighthearted. "But somebody's got to cheer you up."

"I'm not the one who showed up at dawn on the practice grounds to work off steam." Fenton narrowed his eyes, terribly shrewd in his quiet composure. It was one of the reasons Olea had promoted him years ago. He saw through her bravado, down to the bitter dungeon her thoughts paced. "You only lose at Ghenje with me when you need some serious distraction, and you rarely come out to the practice grounds at dawn these days. I know because I'm here every morning. Out with it. What's up?"

Olea sighed. Her mood dropped like a stone, unable to be propped up anymore despite the blithe day and banter. Leaning against a stone column in the quiet infirmary, Olea resisted the urge to rub her Inking. Pulling one longknife from its sheath on her baldric, she tested her knife's edge with the back of her thumbnail, curling off a small shaving. Her appearance might have been shit, but her weapons were always impeccably cared-for, just like her mother had once shown her.

"Elohl's supposed to have been discharged today."

"Your twin?" Fenton straightened, watchful, coming over to stand beside her at the column.

"I haven't seen Elohl in ten years, Fenton. He stopped writing eight years ago. I don't really even know if he's alive."

Fenton went silent a long moment. In a rare breach of decorum, he slid a hand out, gripping Olea's fingers in the quiet of the infirmary. He stood gazing at their hands, their breach of military propriety something to be sacrificed in lieu of long friendship. When he finally spoke, his voice was gentle. "High Brigade's a tough company. If Elohl made it two years, he made it ten. I should know. That was my company before I came here."

"Thanks." Olea looked up, comforted. "I just – I don't even know if he'll come looking for me."

"He'll come." Fenton spoke as he squeezed her hand and released it. "He knows where you were last, and from what I've heard, Kingsmen don't break their promises."

"Don't let anyone hear you talking like that." Olea's glance was sharp.

"What are they going to do, kill me?" Fenton chuckled, an old sadness haunting his smile. "Then who's going to run half the Palace Guard? Do you have any idea what you'll do?"

"You mean if Elohl doesn't come?"

"Or if he does?" Fenton's murmur was gentle. "What if he needs you? Would you abandon the palace, and your Dhenra?"

Olea paused, her breath stolen. "Don't ask me to make that choice, Fenton. I serve the royal family and the Dhenra Elyasin. This is where I'm needed."

"But if Elohl lives, he might ask you to go off looking for—"

"Cease! That is *enough*, Guardsman." Olea hissed. She hadn't heard any footsteps nearby, but Roushenn Palace had a way of learning people's secrets.

"Captain." Fenton's demeanor cooled, though the change was subtle, only around his eyes.

Olea's breath rushed out, realizing the wound she had dealt her friend. Reaching out, she squeezed his hand. "Forgive me, Fenton. I'm just – tight as tripwire today."

"Understandable." Fenton murmured kindly, in his miraculous way of suddenly banishing anger. "I can't imagine what you've endured. That you've become the Crown's most formidable ally these past years says something about your character, Olea. Your determination to truly be what you are – a Kingsman through and through. I respect that."

Olea smiled, her mood easing at last as she released Fenton's hand. "I have to go. I should polish my boots before my shift."

Fenton laughed as he glanced at all the scratches and worn places on Olea's boots and leather jerkin. "Fat chance. You need three days to clean all that up. Why don't you make Aldris do it?"

"He's going to school you at Stones and take your pay again, Fenton, if I make him fix my gear and tell him you suggested it." Olea grinned.

"Yeah, but I whip his ass at Ghenje – I win it all back." Fenton chuckled, a dark competitiveness in his gold-brown eyes. "And if you play me, I'll win double. All because you won't polish your boots."

"That's why I have you." Olea clapped him on the shoulder with a smile. "You're utterly efficient and you set a great example for the men."

"I just have good habits."

"I know your habits, Lieutenant. They're far better than good. Who knows where you studied, but you didn't learn how to fight like you do in the High Brigade."

Fenton sobered at Olea's statement. In that moment, the fine lines at his eyes made him seem ageless – and Olea wondered not for the first time how old he was, and about his history. But his age was a secret Fenton never divulged, along with much of his past. Fenton had come to the Roushenn Palace Guard already ruthlessly efficient, a veteran soldier. He'd been in the High Brigade before joining the Guard, and it was rumored he'd served in the Fleetrunners before that. The Guard-Captain before Olea had seen Fenton's promise and set him to training the advanced guard right from the moment he'd started. Fenton had been offered the position of Guard-Captain when the old Captain had retired. But for some strange reason, he'd turned it down.

And ceded the post to Olea, becoming her First-Lieutenant instead.

"Keep well, Olea." Fenton spoke, gripping Olea's shoulder and letting her go. "Bring your brother to meet me when he gets in."

"I will. Keep well, Fenton."

Olea clapped Fenton upon the shoulder, then turned, putting a hand to her sword to keep the scabbard from banging against the byrunstone column as she moved away. As she whisked through the massive chamber, sidling around woven dividers towards the door, people tracked her from occupied beds. One man in tan Palace Huntsman's leathers, idling at the palace apothecary station and drinking a medicinal tea, gazed at her appreciatively. But as she approached, his gaze flicked to the center of her chest, noting the black Inking there – and abruptly flicked away.

Olea gave him a hard look as she passed, the stare she gave her Guardsmen when they were severely out of line.

The huntsman lifted his mug to his lips, trying to hide from her entirely.

3

GHRENNA

From atop the byrunstone guard-wall, Ghrenna den'Tanuk studied the ornate manse in the balmy summer night. Hunkered beneath a cover of eldunne trees in her Kingsmen Greys, Ghrenna conducted an unconscious inventory for the evening ahead; checking her lock picks, fighting and throwing knives, and sleeping darts on her leather harness. Touching her wavy white-blonde hair in its bun, she checked the comb at her crown to make certain her dark hood remained in place tonight. Taking a long draw from her threllis-pipe, she locked it between her teeth where it would stay all evening.

Visions came when they came, and threllis was imperative – its numbing sedation just enough to keep her in control of her faculties while she was at work.

Tonight's destination was the manse of the wealthy Couthis Emry den'Thorel, their score the family's heirloom jewelry. Ghrenna didn't relish thieving; it was a poor profession for her Kingsman training, but she couldn't hold a regular trade, thanks to her visions and their resulting seizures. Tonight, Ghrenna's muscles were loose, her mind calm except for a dull headache. Headaches plagued her also, and this one was nothing notable as she gazed at the hulking byrunstone manse in the darkness, quiet as a fennewith-haze. Only three guards maintained a perimeter, pivoting at predictable intervals, their movements lax as a lazy wolfhound gnawed a carcass on the steps. Four lights burned in the upper halls and in the basement kitchens, to be expected – and avoided.

Ghrenna made the *proceed* hand signal to her Guild-mate Shara den'Lhoruhan beside her, dressed in regular thieves' gear, and Shara nodded, lifting her dart tube to blow a white flag to the foot of the wall behind them. The two grapples Ghrenna had set suddenly had tension, and presently Luc den'Orissian and Gherris den'Mal, also part of Ghrenna's Guild, mounted the wall next to her and Shara. Waiting for them to get settled, Ghrenna's dark blue eyes flickered over the guards and the dog. They hadn't changed their patterns, and they weren't watching the wall.

She made a hand signal to the group. *Proceed.*

No alarm was raised as they slipped over the wall and through the dappled shadows. A row of cypress trees had been foolishly planted all the way to the house, providing excellent cover, and halting her company at the end of the cypress row, Ghrenna signaled for sleeping-darts. Three properly blown darts and the guards collapsed upon the manse's front steps, dreaming until tomorrow. The dog, however, had Gherris' knife buried in its throat, which he strode forward to retrieve. Five years younger than Ghrenna, Gherris was Alrashemni Kingsman also, a Second Seal when the Summons came. Excellent with knives, he was an asset, but Ghrenna had never seen him smile.

Though his eyes flashed with pleasure at the kill.

Key rings were removed, the guards looted and hauled into the bushes. Ghrenna made the *proceed* signal again and Luc stepped to the door, finding it unlocked. He squirted oil on the hinges anyway, obsessive, and with her back to the door as she scanned the night, Ghrenna could see his merry green eyes lit with mischief beneath his dark hood as he worked. He saw her watching; winked and grinned. A born rogue, golden-handsome Luc was a creature of the gutter. Street performing in his youth had graduated to hustles in his adulthood, relying upon his wit and tall good looks, which had eventually matured into professional thieving. It was rumored there was no lock Luc couldn't pick, no man he couldn't swindle, and no woman he couldn't seduce.

At last, Luc hauled on the iron handle of the door, which opened without a sound. The company stepped inside, melting into the darkened hall like graveyard mist. Luc stepped to the left wall with Ghrenna, while Gherris and Shara took the right. Shara pointed the way she had scouted at the masked ball the night prior, signaling *third floor, second door on right, lockbox.*

Ghrenna nodded and took point, trusting Shara implicitly, her constant ally since they'd abandoned the Fleetrunners eight years ago. Memorizing buildings and personnel rotations was Shara's specialty, and their journey to the third floor of Couthis Emry den'Thorel's manse was uneventful. The rumors Shara had elicited at the party were proving true. A wealthy addict, the young Couthis was careless, throwing lavish parties to smoke *fennewith*, which sent even the hardiest addicts into languid largesse. Most of the manor's retainers had quit recently, not wanting to be associated with Emry's antics. It was largely rumored young Emry was going to get his throat slit some deep night when he was high.

Maybe tonight.

Gherris toyed with his knife as they paused outside the appointed door, practically itching for a kill as the company tucked into the shadows next to a pair of ancient armor-suits. Looking down, Ghrenna watched light play beneath the ironbound door as Luc oiled the hinges. The flickers were strong, the blaze of a fire, and after a minute of listening and hearing nothing, Ghrenna decided to risk it.

Pick it, she signed to Luc.

He set to, his skills needed this time.

Five minutes, Ghrenna signed to Shara. *Fighting, leave. Yells, leave. Silence, send Luc.* Shara nodded and so did Luc, finished with his lock picking. Gherris merely watched, brooding. He wanted a real kill tonight – Ghrenna could practically smell it.

With one last glance at Gherris, Ghrenna slipped inside. The door was silent thanks to Luc's obsessiveness, shutting behind her with barely a click as Ghrenna's dark blue eyes roved the bedroom. She was a shadow in the wan firelight, pristinely still against the dark wood of the door. Invading rooms was her specialty, and sometimes her Guild-mates even forgot she was there, only a curl of smoke from her pipe or a flash of her hair giving her away. No matter how long Ghrenna needed to wait for the perfect score, she could, patient and practical. *Courhe den'Byrune*, she had been nicknamed by her team, the Heart of Byrunstone. In a trade ruled by hotheaded men, Ghrenna was a valuable irregularity, her levelheadedness a boon. Her efficient scores kept her in good with her threllis supplier, and better yet, thieving was generally a profession without brutality if one was fast, quiet, and effective.

Unlike war.

Ghrenna would never go back to the war-front. Never again would she wear the uniform of Alrou-Mendera, conscripted ten years ago against her will. She would wear her Kingsmen Greys, recovered from Alrashesh after her desertion from the army, until her death – come Halsos' Burnwater. The Kingsmen had taken Ghrenna in when she had been abandoned by her real parents from the tundra. And though she was not born Alrashemni, she would honor the Kingsmen until the end of her days.

But tonight could be navigated without death if Ghrenna was careful – no matter what Gherris craved. From across the room, Ghrenna saw a whip-lean man lay sprawled upon the canopied bed, shirtless. His breeches were undone, baring an emaciated abdomen, and a naked woman sprawled next to him, her limbs pale by fire's light. Ghrenna's gaze flicked around the room, noting servant's doors, empty sitting-chairs, and a lounging-couch by the fire.

And the iron lockbox etched with filigree, just behind the bed.

Taking a breath, Ghrenna eased over the ornate Praoughian carpets – when one of the side-doors opened. Blending into a pillar of the canopied bed with their dark velvet curtains, Ghrenna went immaculately still. As always, when she willed herself to be unseen, a *wyrric* coolness rose in her mind. It came now, licking out like a gossamer breath as a maid entered, stoking the fire noisily, though the couple on the bed lay drug-deep and dead to the world. The maid sniffed as she glared at the couple, fists on her hips as Ghrenna's heart pounded in the maid's line of sight. But as if Ghrenna's mind eased into the maid's, whispering and causing her gaze to slip past, she missed Ghrenna entirely. Returning to the door, the maid slammed a tray of food upon the desk with a pitcher of water, then spun on her heel and left, closing the door.

Ghrenna breathed out in relief. She'd not been seen, and the couple on the bed hadn't stirred. She gave it another moment then silently approached the desk, examining the lockbox. The thirty-bennel hasps were solid, but the locks were nothing Luc couldn't handle. A rhennel-bolt, an uringle-puzzle, and a fhass-key, the three old-fashioned locks wouldn't stall him.

But the uringle-puzzle would be noisy, no matter how much oil Luc gave it. Sidling over to the bed, Ghrenna observed the couple, removing her pipe from her mouth so they wouldn't smell it. As Ghrenna bent close, watching the slow rise and fall of the man's chest – Couthis Emry, clearly heavily sedated – she realized the noise of the lock-picking probably wouldn't matter. Emry had the look of the addicted bourgeois, gaunt with a smudge of shadows beneath his closed eyes, sprawled out like he just might sleep through anything. But as Ghrenna bent closer, watching the woman's ribs not move in the fire's light, she reached out, gently touching the woman's wrist. She was cold – cold and very dead. Ghrenna backed off just as the door she had come through opened, the quick pace of Luc's footsteps entering.

Ghrenna threw Luc a quick flurry of signing as he rounded the edge of the bed. *Woman dead. Man drugged. Puzzle, key, and bolt. Proceed.*

Luc's blonde eyebrows lifted inside the shadows of his hood as he approached the lockbox. *You killed her? Byrune.* He signed back, his wicked white grin flashing in the fire's light.

Ghrenna shook her head. *Drug-death.*

Luc looked slightly crestfallen, then grinned again as he set to work. Luc loved a scandal, but not as much as he loved lock picking. The fhass-key he oiled and picked first, smooth as silk. The rhennel-bolt he picked second, the bolt snapping back with a report that would have wakened any normal person, though Emry merely snorted, one hand sliding down to fondle himself in his drugged haze. But the puzzle-lock was as noisy as Ghrenna had predicted; each time Luc turned the dial it made a groaning creak, which caused him and Ghrenna both to wince and the drugged man to shift uneasily.

He'll wake. Abort? Luc signed, pausing with eyebrows lifted.

Ghrenna shook her head. *Proceed.*

Luc turned the dial again, and it gave a hideous shriek. The man on the bed came awake with a deep gasp as if rising from the grave. Ghrenna had a moment to decide. If she hit him with a sleeping dart, the sedative could overdose him with so much fennewith already in his system. But then she saw his eyelids fluttering – that he still languished deep in drug-addled dreams.

Cool with calculation, Ghrenna was on the bed in a flash.

"Shh, Emry..." Ghrenna laid a hand on the Couthis' chest, playing the part of his dead woman. Pushing him back down to the mattress with a gentle touch, she willed him to see her as his lover. Tendrils of her mind reached out, smoothing into him, whispering, and Emry went without a fuss, though his rapid blinking indicated fennewith hallucinations. Ghrenna had no idea what his mind was conjuring, whether he would scream and wake the manse, or spin on in blissful abandonment. Either way, threllis would calm him, so she leaned in, exhaling smoke into the man's mouth and nose. At the same time, she willed him to be calm, the tendrils of her mind pouring out towards him like the tide of her smoke.

His eyelids fluttered slower as he took a deep inhalation.

"Anjelica..." he breathed, running his hands up over Ghrenna's buttocks. A stifled guffaw came from Luc, still clicking through the puzzle.

"I'm here, my love." Ghrenna ignored Luc as she leaned in, wafting more smoke into Emry's mouth and nose, then gave him a long, slow kiss as her *wyrric* tendrils plucked at his mind. Reaching down, she massaged his crotch, willing him to focus on the eroticism of the touch. Anything to keep him from noting the noise of the puzzle-lock – and seeing that Ghrenna was not the woman who lay next to him, dead.

"Mmm, threllis." The Couthis pawed at Ghrenna's throat. "Give me a draw, love. Make me spin..."

Ghrenna held her pipe to his lips, and he sucked greedily like a babe at teat, inhaling and holding it for a ten-count – a practiced addict.

"Mmm, Cheridwen Hills... where did you get Cheridwen?" The Couthis' eyelids slipped closed as smoke sighed from between his flushed lips.

"I keep a little just for us, love." The clicking from the puzzle-lock stopped. Ghrenna heard a *chunk* as Luc pulled the lockbox open, and then the sweet slither of velvet pouches as he began to raid it.

Emry's eyebrows knit at the sound, and he struggled to pull his eyes open. "Is that Julinne? Aeon, tell her to keep it down! Give us another draw, love..."

Ghrenna gave him her pipe again, letting him take deep inhalations as she willed him to relax. She massaged his crotch and Emry moaned, low and obliterated. When she reached to reclaim her pipe, he did not fight her, his arm falling limply to the coverlet. But as his arm fell, it brushed the dead woman, and he shied away. "Ugh, who put a fish in my bed...?"

"That's just the tray, love." Ghrenna hastily pushed the dead woman over, willing Emry calm. "Julinne brought us some cold khremm. Here, let me move it off the bed." Ghrenna shot a look at Luc and he played his part right on cue – lifting the tray upon the desk and setting it back loud enough for it to clink. "There, love. It's on the table now."

"Mmm, kiss me, sweetling..." Couthis Emry slurred as his needy hands began pawing at Ghrenna's harness and jerkin. "Kiss me again. You were so ripe at the ball... kiss me like that. Are you dressed? Leather? I like leather. Yes, let's have sex again, let's undo all this..."

Luc was finished, now waiting by the door as Ghrenna gave the drug-addled Emry another deep kiss then stood, extracting herself. "Just a moment, love. I need to use the chamber-pot."

"Go fast, love." Couthis Emry settled into the lavender sachet-pillows, his words hardly a whisper as his ardor flagged. "Go fast..."

Ghrenna paced quickly to the door where Luc waited – grinning. He flicked her nose with his long fingers and she narrowed her eyes, and then they were out the door. Gherris and Shara were vague shadows in the hall, falling into step as the quartet retreated. Watching for movement, they made their way back out the front door of the manse, paced the garden, and slipped up and over the wall. Only once they were a league away, moving through a forested swath north of the manor, did Luc start braying laughter.

"Ghrenna, you ice-hearted bint! Seducing a man buried in fennewith, and next to a dead woman, no less! And right in front of me? *Byrune*!"

"We're not exclusive, Luc. I'm not beholden to you or anybody." It was Ghrenna's regular answer. Luc wasn't the only man who warmed her bed, though she knew he wanted to be. He laughed it off, his pride too great to show hurt that Ghrenna wouldn't settle for anyone these past eight years.

"You killed someone tonight?" Pacing in the darkness beneath the trees, Gherris shot Ghrenna a sour look. Ghrenna took a deep inhalation, not wanting to address Gherris' bloodthirsty nature tonight, though Luc conveniently answered for her.

"The woman was already dead, Gherris. Fennewith overdose. There wasn't any need for your *talents.*"

Gherris grunted, turning to stare out at the night as they walked.

"Well, despite the excitement, or Gherris' lack thereof," Luc continued, "we managed to acquire a good haul, ladies and gents. Back to our digs to divvy it? You girls can take our tithe to the Consortium. I have an appointment I'd rather not miss later tonight."

"Appointment?" Shara glanced over, her bubbling laugh bright in the darkness. "Are you losing all your share dicing again, Luc?"

"Losing?" He tweaked her nose and Shara batted him, but Luc paced on blithely. "I never lose, ladies. And after what I saw this evening? Lord Luc feels lucky tonight!"

"You're no lord." Shara grinned as she gave him a false punch to the gut.

But Ghrenna was a thousand leagues away from her comrades' banter, thinking about the dead woman's cold skin. Suddenly, her headache lanced as a vision surfaced with a feeling of chill ice and glacial water inside her body. Her stride paused as she blinked, drawing deep on the threllis-pipe between her teeth. A ship on a long lake rose in her mind, mountains rearing up into a cloud-heavy sky. A man hunkered by the rails as wind lashed rain against his beard-roughened cheeks. His lost grey eyes were as beautiful as the sea under storm-clouds, and the vision stopped her breath.

Stopped her heart for just a moment.

Elohl.

As if Ghrenna's body had been pulled straight to him, she could feel Elohl; the set of his jaw, the emptiness of his beautiful, commanding stare. And in that moment, a feeling of hopelessness rose in her; a deep sensation of need. Elohl's need – and Ghrenna's own. Taking a tremendous pull from her threllis-pipe, Ghrenna pushed back the headache that now rose like a demon in the wake of her vision.

Though she could never push back her love.

4

ELOHL

Contemplating the sharp crags of the Eleski mountain range, Elohl took in the view one last time as his ship pulled up alongside the dock on the southwestern shore of the Elsee. Snowcapped peaks faced him this morning, their shining tips uncaring of the hardships of men. The day had dawned glorious, but it had been a miserable night aboard the boat, sluicing rain. Elohl had huddled between the ships' railing and his pack, trying to stay warm and unable to. Freezing, he'd slept fitfully between rings of the ships' bell and shouts of sailors, until the sun finally rose at dawn.

Muddled dreams had plagued him, half-remembered things now as the day shone in strange contrast to his nightmares. In his dreams, a door had loomed above him, snarling with a fighting wolf and dragon. The box and puzzle from his youth surfaced; his throat had choked with smoke. The steel-eyed man in herring-bone leathers had been there, a snarl of contempt upon his face as he broke into Elohl's mind.

And lake-blue eyes had watched it all – wrapping him in their chill tundra silence.

Elohl could still feel those dreams. As if Ghrenna stood just behind his shoulder reliving his nightmares with him, Elohl could almost feel her inside his body as he rubbed a hand behind his neck, working out the kinks that stitched him. Stepping down the gangplank, he felt the sun warm on his skin, his breath misting as vegetation by the lakeshore curled with steam where the sunbeams struck. Hefting his pack upon his shoulders, Elohl reached up, adjusting his sword for trekking. The touch of cool steel eased him, something about it like the memory of Ghrenna.

Practical. Implacable.

Surveying the shore, Elohl noted there were no wagons to cart him to Lintesh. The handful of Brigadiers had left the boat at the first inlet early this morning, a cart-track through the mountains to Quelsis. Wagons waited at this stop for the Longvalley Brigade; lord's sons who only served two years in a valley surrounded by impenetrable mountains patrolled by the High Brigade. A cushy post, the Longvalley boys saw little of the Valenghian Red Valor, and were soft. Young faces with hardly a beard to them, they clambered up on the wains as if every bone ached, moaning about the rain.

But Elohl was a veteran Brigadier, and hardship was familiar. He'd never had a wagon to cart his gear in the highpasses and he didn't need one now. Shaking out his oilcloak, he slung it across his pack to dry, re-shouldered his burden, and took to his feet upon the byway. Behind him, he heard the crack of a whip and a lowing of oxen as the Longvalley wains rolled out. One splashed through the cart-track as it passed, spattering Elohl's cloak with mud.

No one offered the Brigadier a ride as the carts rolled by, and the teamsters didn't slow.

At last, they were out of sight and Elohl was alone walking the ruts as sun flooded down through the scattering clouds. Signs of late spring were here in the lowmountains; daffodils and red harlen-bush in bloom, leaves of leatheroak and shudder-maple beginning to darken as the warm days rose. It would be full summer down in the King's City, and something about that thought made heat sear up Elohl's throat suddenly, clenching his chest. Unbuckling his jerkin, he unlaced his shirt, craving fresh air. It left his Inkings bared in the sunlight that cascaded over the road, but there was no one to see it out here, no one to challenge him or call him Blackmark.

Still, unrest itched over Elohl like stinging ants this morning. Halting, he scanned every shadow along the byway, but there was no one. When suddenly, he could see it just as it had been ten years ago – when he'd first come to the High Brigade. Late summer, the leaves of the trees curling and browned; cicadas thrumming in his ears. The creaking of the cart's wheels as it bumped over ruts, causing a chafing pain where iron manacles bit his wrists and ankles. Elohl had watched this same scenery then, his heart full of anguish and his mind broken with a young man's fear. His world had crumbled; his people were gone. He was a captive and soon had a choice to make – to serve the King as a Brigadier or be put to the sword.

He'd almost chosen the sword.

Elohl's throat tightened. He pulled his shirt open more, closing his eyes and fighting for calm. Woods were just woods. A cart-track was just a cart-track. He'd breathed summer air for ten years after that day and he lived to breathe it still. At last, the burning in his chest subsided and Elohl opened his eyes, drawing a deep inhalation. Reaching up, he touched the leather-wrapped pommel of his sword, finding the steel cross-guard smooth and cool beneath his fingers.

Elohl took a step forward – and walked on.

The morning passed, uneventful after that except for the sighting of a magnificent eight-point buck browsing by the roadside. Just as Elohl was considering stopping for a noon meal of elk jerky from his pack, he spied a sprawling cottage near the road. A cheery affair with a byrunstone foundation, a pine-board porch, and wicker-woven furniture, smoke drifted from the chimney, a sigil of Innship carved on a signboard out front. Halting in the road, Elohl regarded the inn. If he continued on, there was no guarantee of lodging further down the road. And though he could sleep rough by the roadside, the promise of a real bed rather than a soldier's cot or pine boughs was alluring.

Tromping up the porch, Elohl announced his presence by knocking mud off his boots on the porch boards as he drew his shirt lacings closed to hide his Inkings. A pretty young woman with a long honey-blonde braid over one shoulder peered through the summer screen, paused, then opened it. Good smells of bread and stew drifted out as she looked him up and down, taking in his worn military gear with an arched blonde eyebrow. "High Brigade?"

"Yes, milady." Elohl nodded, suddenly conscious of how he must look to her. For the first time in years, he found himself wishing he had stopped to shave and wash.

"Milady! Goodness, do I look that old? Just Eleshen! Eleshen den'Fhenrir." She laughed, her pretty heart-shaped face instantly more friendly. Elohl saw the cordage on her wrist relax and heard the hollow thump of a cast-iron pan being set down just inside the doorframe. Her work-roughened hand came into sight as she opened the screen with a beaming smile. "Well? Come in! Eleshen's Boarding Rooms, right here. I've got *mitlass* on the stove, though we don't get many visitors. Those Longvalley lord's boys never stop, you see, and all I really get are Elsee fisherfolk and High Brigade fellows like yourself. Though not many of those, either. What's your name?"

"Elohl. Elohl den'Alrahel." Slinging his pack to the porch, Elohl left it in the sunshine to dry, bending to unbuckle his sodden boots and leave them out also.

"Den'Alrahel. The name's familiar, but I can't say why for the life of me just now!" Clucking her tongue, the innkeeper henned over him as she held out her hand impudently, though she wasn't any older than Elohl. "I'll set your cloak on the line to dry, Brigadier. I can take your jerkin and shirt, too. Just give them here, now!"

"It's fine, really. I'll just let them dry as I eat." Elohl spoke, moving her hands away as she reached out, trying to open his unbuckled jerkin and strip it from his shoulders.

"No, they need drying, you are just soaked through!" The innkeeper wouldn't have it as her fingers fussed, and Elohl finally relented, letting her help him out of his jerkin. But when her feisty hands tried to pull his damp shirt from his trousers, he flinched back, not wanting her to see his Inkings.

"No, really, I'll just leave it on."

"You're going to take sick in a wet shirt like that, sunshine or no." She eyeballed him, her green eyes critical. "Spring isn't over yet up here. Or have you got the belly-blisters? Let me see now, I have a salve for that."

"No, it's not that, just—"

"Just what? Shuck it, or you don't eat!"

A flash of irritation lanced Elohl and he blinked. He'd forgotten what it was like to have women in your life, how charming and demanding they could be. This one didn't care how often he'd starved in a blizzard, rubbing his chest with blue hands to keep warm. She didn't care that he could walk a hundred leagues in three days and still climb to a lookout. She didn't care how many men had tried to knife him or cut his line on a climb, or had stolen in to slit his throat in his bunk.

She won't care about my Inkings.

Elohl paused, then pulled his wet shirt off over his head. He heard the innkeeper's sharp intake of breath and when their eyes met, hers were full of pity. She held out her hand for the shirt and he gave it up. But instead of taking the clothes away, she piled the wet laundry on a side table and grasped his hand, pulling him through the main lodge-hall and towards the kitchen fire. "Sit, please! My hearth is yours. Please, you must not pay for your meal, it wouldn't be right. You must eat and rest the night. No charge."

"I'm more than happy to pay. I can afford it." Elohl spoke, embarrassed and thinking he must look penniless with his worn gear and scruff of beard.

"No! No charge. I insist!"

"No, really, a Brigadier's stipend is more—"

"I don't get many Kingsmen here." She interrupted, then blushed furiously and looked down before looking back up, bold. "Please. It's the least I can do for your service. For your *real* service, I mean."

Elohl blinked, undone by surprise. It had been a long time since someone had said such a thing to him, and it stung to hear it now after wanting it for so long. Wordlessly, he sat upon the long bench at the rough kitchen table by the fire, succumbing to a riot of emotions too thick to tease apart. When the innkeeper Eleshen placed a bowl of mutton *mitlass* in his hands, he found his hands trembling. She pressed his hands between hers and Elohl's gaze flicked up, meeting hers – seeing his own raw pain reflected in her eyes.

She flushed crimson and looked down, releasing his hands. Then bustled away, whisking up his laundry and marching out the back door of the guesthouse. Elohl heard her singing a lilting march as she pinned his clothes to the line; an Alrashemni war-song. It dove into him like a striking of swords on the practice grounds at Alrashesh and his chest burned, his throat tight as he watched the innkeeper through the open window. He saw her rub her eyes before stomping back up the porch. Inside she was all business, offering him fresh-baked bread with rosemary salt, winter pepperberry jam, and sheepsbutter flavored with thyme. Pouring a tot of ale for Elohl and leaving a flagon of well-water, she hustled off to the back rooms, leaving him to eat.

Elohl lifted the ale, swigging it back to drown a myriad of emotions before digging in to his stew and bread. But where once drinking had drowned his memories, now it simply made him brood. As Elohl finished his meal, the innkeeper Eleshen returned. Whisking to the table, she swept up the dishes with a quick smile, then shucked them into the kitchen washbasin with a deafening clatter. Washing with gusto, her movements were sloppy and imprecise. Elohl found he couldn't remain seated. It was habit from the highmountains to take care of his own messes, and it felt strange to have someone do it for him. Rising he approached, taking up a dish and scouring with a woven rag alongside her.

"Now, see here! You don't have to...! I mean, that's not for you to—"

As Elohl scrubbed, Eleshen's gaze flicked to his upturned wrists. Seeing the ragged scars there, one at each wrist, she made a dismayed sound – and Elohl quickly turned his hands over, the tanned skin at the backs of his forearms showing only rope-burns and fighting slashes he'd taken over the years.

"Aeon!" Eleshen's cheeks went crimson as she shifted her stance in a hasty, uncoordinated way. "I'm so sorry! I didn't mean to – I mean they were just there...!"

Seeing his self-inflicted scars had upset her; Elohl could feel it like a wave pulsing through her body. The flustered innkeeper stepped backwards suddenly and stumbled over a wooden stool behind her – falling sideways and upsetting the washbasin. Elohl's reflexes were quick as a darting heron. With the *wyrric* instinct that had kept him alive far too long, he stabilized the washbasin with one hand and caught her around the waist with the other, pulling her close.

The pretty innkeeper's breath was high above her woven corset and white blouse. Her weight felt good to Elohl; her slender waist fit in the crook of his arm. A need stirred, something denied most of his years in the High Brigade, as cerulean eyes surfaced in his vision. But suddenly, the truth was plain to Elohl. If Ghrenna was alive, she hadn't come to him. She hadn't seen his whereabouts in any vision, or she didn't care to search. He was alone in the wilderness and her twin lakes in his mind were just that; lakes to drown himself in.

Memories that he had drowned himself in for years – of a woman long gone.

But this woman here and now, sweet and kind. Elohl's nose was in her hair, his lips breathing in her good scents of rosemary soap and lavender honey. She made a low, obliterated sound, molding to him like a cloak in the rain, as if she could feel his vast need. His breath was fast; hers was faster. But Elohl wasn't a rogue. He inhaled deep to control his emotions, just as he had been taught long ago.

Setting the innkeeper Eleshen on her feet carefully, he stepped back. "Forgive me, I didn't mean to – you could have been hurt..."

But the words had hardly left his mouth when she moved, her lips rising to his. His careful calm shattered with that kiss. How sweet she tasted; how warm she was. Suddenly, Elohl's arms were around the pretty innkeeper, drawing her close, his heart full of need just as her lips were. And then they were sinking to the kitchen floor, finding a sudden and unexpected sweetness to round out the mitlass and the bright spring sunshine.

* * *

THE INNKEEPER ELESHEN lay in the crook of Elohl's arm as sunlight filtered to the kitchen floor, her blonde braid woefully disheveled from their lovemaking. Splaying her fingers across Elohl's bare chest, she traced his Inkings as Elohl pulled her closer, smelling her hair with a contented sigh. Closing his eyes, he relaxed upon the pine boards, cold mountain nights melting away like a soothing balm. As sunlight filtered through his eyelids, deep blue drifted across his vision; serenity infinite as a mountain lake. Elohl found himself gazing into those crystalline depths as the still water watched him – as if eyes drifted up out of its fathomless blue. High tundra scents came to him; pine boughs and air so cold it tasted of wintermint.

A whiff of char drifted through his vision, acrid like pine resins aflame.

"Oh, no! My bread!" Eleshen suddenly sat up. Launching to her feet, her half-bound corset spilling open, she flew to the byrunstone oven. Hauling the metal door open, she coughed at the scorch within. Elohl wrinkled his nose as smoke poured forth, Eleshen hauling four blackened rosemary loaves from the oven and unceremoniously tossing them into the fire.

"Well, that's that." Eleshen huffed, watching them burn. Looking back, her pretty face was full of humor. "I guess I had better things to do this afternoon than tend bread."

Returning, she straddled Elohl with devious intent and he gave a satisfied sigh. Reaching up to stroke her messy braid where it fell over her breasts, he slid his other hand up her bare thigh, gripping the crease where thigh met hip, enjoying her weight upon him. "Bread is the least of our concerns..."

"Are you really one of them, Elohl? A Kingsman?" With a sweet but wistful smile, Eleshen's fingers traced his Inkings, the mountain in the center of his chest with the topmost star at its peak. Her touch stirred Elohl, where he had been nothing but cold and hard for years. Like little runnels of sunlight, Eleshen found his deepest ice, making things melt deep within.

"It's nice to not be called Blackmark for once." Elohl found himself smiling as she touched him.

"Blackmark." Eleshen snorted. "What a horrible slur for such a beautiful promise. A promise of everything you are, to your King and country."

"Not just to our King, but to our kin." Elohl corrected gently. "Before we promised service to Alrou-Mendera, we promised it to ourselves. Before we were Kingsmen, we were Alrashemni – and still are."

"But your oath goes hundreds of years back, doesn't it?" Eleshen countered. "To be the right-hand spear of the King, his to call for justice on any matter be it through might of arms or intelligence of negotiation. Did you learn the Kingsmen arts of peacemaking?"

"Some," Elohl stroked her fingers, his smile soft. "I am Alrashemni, but I'm not a Kingsman, not quite. At age twenty, I only reached my Seventh Seal by the time my people disappeared, a year shy of my full training. I don't actually deserve to wear these marks. They're worn after your Eighth Seal at age twenty-one. When you become fully Inked and take the Oath of Allegiance to the King of Alrou-Mendera. Only then can you be truly called a Kingsman, rather than simply born Alrashemni."

"What do they mean, the marks?" Eleshen spoke as she traced the rightmost star, near an old blade-slash Elohl had gotten his first year in the Brigade.

"Our Inking is called the *Chirus Alrashemni*." Elohl spoke, indulging her. "It means *Dedicated of the Land*, a title we receive when we pass our Eighth Seal. The mountain is a double-reference to the Kingsmount – representing the nation – and also our enduring vow to the King's house. The five stars are for the five tenets of Alrashemni life: strength, flexibility, wisdom, knowledge, and patience."

"The central star is larger than the others. Why?" Eleshen queried.

"The central star represents wisdom," Elohl murmured. "In all things, we are guided by our deepest intuition, the inner heart which knows before the mind. Intuition drives who we are and allows us to achieve wisdom in mediation. Being a Kingsman is not about killing. It's about negotiation and peacemaking. Violence is and has always been considered a last option."

"But you are trained killers. You learn killing arts nearly from birth." Eleshen lifted an eyebrow.

"When a rabid boar attacks, the sword that is honed the sharpest pierces best."

Elohl countered, wondering where all this was going, and why she was so interested in the Kingsmen.

"Poetic."

"Practical."

"Had you killed anyone before you went to war, Elohl?" Eleshen reached up, stroking Elohl's short beard. "Did you kill the men who came to take you after the Summons?"

Eleshen's questions dipped too far, upsetting his newfound sunshine, and Elohl sobered suddenly. Diving inside him like knives, her questions opened wounds of failure best forgotten. Pulling her hand gently from his face, Elohl cradled it to his chest instead – what had once been lithe and young now lean and hard from rough living.

And scarred. Too many scars.

"It doesn't matter now." Elohl tried to keep his voice calm, though it came out hard-edged.

"But your entire clan just disappeared after that Summons, an accusation of treason from your very own King!" Eleshen's lips pursed, fierce. "They must have killed everyone; your parents, your teachers! And then they banished the Alrashemni children to the furthest war-campaigns like criminals—"

"I said it doesn't matter!" Elohl sat up, unseating Eleshen with a growl and lacing his trousers. The glacier that protected his heart had shifted from their sun-drenched afternoon, and it shouldn't have. Emotions were too close, fished up by the innkeeper's prodding. As Elohl strode from the kitchen, his heart gripped him. Pushing out the back door, he ripped his cloak and belongings down from the wash line, even as Eleshen flashed out the door after him, one hand clutching her barely-laced shirt closed, the other hand on his forearm.

"Please, forgive me! I didn't mean to upset you! Please, I just—"

"Leave it alone!" Elohl growled in a raw passion. Cerulean swallowed his vision for a moment, and Elohl felt suffocated. Taking the long, slow breath of his training, he yanked his shirt on over his head. "The Kingsmen are dead. The Alrashemni courts are empty. Leave it alone, Eleshen."

"I know, I just – Kingsmen saved my family!" Eleshen clutched her arms now, miserable. "I wouldn't be here but for them. In the raid, they were just suddenly there, protecting us! My father was Dhepan of Quelsis. Valenghian raiders had crossed the border in the night. But somehow, the Kingsmen knew. They sent fifty – just fifty. And fifty Kingsmen kept our city safe from hundreds of raiders."

"The Raid of Quelsis." Slowly, Elohl turned. And suddenly he could see Eleshen's pain, just as fresh and raw as his – all from seeing a Kingsman walk through her door this day. "Fifteen years ago. Valenghians snuck through the Borderlands and burned Quelsis in the middle of the night. My father was among the fifty Kingsmen protecting the city."

"Your father?" Eleshen stepped back, her gaze flicking over Elohl's iron-wrought frame and tall stature, his black hair that shone with blue highlights in the sun, and his opal-grey eyes. "Den'Alrahel. That's where I know that name! Urloel den'Alrahel – you look like Urloel!"

"My father was Rakhan of the Court of Alrashesh." Elohl's throat burned as he spoke. "He led the defense at Quelsis."

"He did. He worked with my father, during the siege."

A long pause stretched then, as something knit between them – a cord of pain, or maybe promise. A feeling of destinies thickened the air, and Elohl's hand twitched. If his sword had been in his fingers, he'd have cut that cord. But though there was pain here, there was also peace. Hadn't he found it already, in an afternoon of warmth and good sweat, and sunlight filtering through his closed eyelids?

"Come back inside." Eleshen pleaded, earnest. "I could... use some help with the pots."

Glancing at the road, Elohl noted the angle of the sun. It was long past mid-afternoon, the sun already on its way down the mountains, the shadows growing long. A part of him howled, not wanting to go back out into the cold, hard night. Cerulean plucked at his vision, and with a sigh, Elohl scrubbed a hand over his short beard, pushing the vision away.

Reaching out, Eleshen took him gently by the fingers.

And with a subtle tug, led him back inside to the warmth.

5

DHERRAN

Pain exploded across Dherran den'Lhust's face as he slipped a punch and was anticipated by his hulking opponent. Blood spattered the yellow earth of the summer-ring as Dherran's lip split – the only blow that had landed upon him this fight. Cheers rang from the crowd, fists pumped for some violence in the match at last. Eyeing the big man from between his raised hands, Dherran flowed out of the way of the next five swings, moving with ease in the scalding summer heat by a twist of his hips here, a shift of his feet there.

Making his opponent's massive fists pummel only air.

In the center of the dirt ring surrounded by spears, time paused, an eternity of noise flooding Dherran's ears as he focused on his breath. Rhaventia's main square was packed for its annual summer celebrations, the prize fights the top attraction. Pennants flew from every gable, awnings hot with reds and yellows reflecting the noon sunshine. Coarse farmers and laborers crowded the ring of tall spears, pressing in and swigging bottles of ale. Their eyes shone rabid as they watched Dherran and his hulking opponent, both shirtless as they fought for the final title today.

But just as Dherran was taking the measure of the big man with the shockingly red hair opposite him, his measure was being equally taken. Though glistening with sweat and breathing hard with all his seeking punches, there was little to no weight behind the big man's swings. In the sweat-drunk heat of the day,

Dherran stayed relaxed in his quick, small movements, his lean bulk slipping effortlessly away from each punch as he counted on exhausting his adversary. He could hit the man and hit him hard, but it was far more satisfying to watch the lout's fury mount, watch the veins in his temples bulge, and see his face become blister-red with embarrassment.

A trickle of perspiration beaded down Dherran's eyelashes and he blinked it away.

"Come on, Rorouk! Hit the Blackmark again!"

"Knock the treasonous whoresson on his ass, Rorouk!"

Shirtless in the summer-ring, Dherran's black Alrashemni Kingsman Inkings were plain upon his broad chest. Though his Inkings incensed the crowd, a snarl of pleasure lifted Dherran's lips at the jeers. As Big Red threw a stretch of punches that hit nothing but the breeze, Dherran let himself enjoy the moment, knowing he was superior to his massive opponent. Knowing he was a better man than these louts who leered and jeered, spit and drank. Dherran lived for the pleasure of a fight, for sweating out his rage beneath the high summer sun. Once upon a time, those sour jeers towards Kingsmen would have been enough to make him a raging boar in the ring, forgetting his training and giving his opponent opportunity.

But time had taught him lessons. That rage got you hit, and hit hard. And so Dherran enjoyed the slurs and curses, knowing he was better than they – and he would show them all, right here, right now and in every summer-ring all season.

But suddenly, his opponent backed off a pace in frustration. His wrapped fists still up, Big Red's seething blue gaze fixed upon Dherran as he bellowed, "Come at me, cocksucking Blackmark! Come at me or I'll tie you to a post and fuck your dead mother in front of you! Royal Kingswhore!"

The man made a gesture that was hard to misinterpret.

And just like that, Dherran's easy flow was gone. He felt his rage rise until his ears rang with it. He felt it flash, seething and hot, just as it had when he was young among his comrades Elohl and Olea, Suchinne and Ghrenna on the training field. Back then, he would have been taken by his rage. But now, even in the grips of red that washed his vision, he was able to find peace in the burning. Rather than let it sweep him like he once had, Dherran held his anger, cherished it.

Nourished it.

Now, the swing Dherran had been waiting for came. Frustrated, Big Red threw his weight behind a right hook and Dherran gave a quick twist of his hips, allowing the punch to flow past his chin. And then he put power behind his tight thrust to the man's neck. True power; rageful power. The power of the charging boar that knows no right or wrong.

Big Red crumpled from Dherran's punch, his blue eyes rolling up in his head. Falling to the yellow dirt in a heap of thick flesh, he was out cold. Roars of disappointment filled the square from the quick, uneventful match, men shaking fists as bottles of ale were tossed in anger, shattering on the black-tipped spears behind Dherran in showers of glass.

"You Blackmark shit!"

"Bloody Kingsman!"

Dherran spat blood to the dirt, signifying his disdain for the callous, lowborn men around him as battle filled him. Spreading his arms, Dherran let himself be taken by the red rage, buzzing filling his ears as red shrouded his vision.

"Have you gotten no *pleasure* from this fight today?!" He roared above the clamor of the crowd. "Then I am pleased! You should have no pleasure for your bigotry!! Fuck you and fuck this whole fucking town!! May it *burn!!*"

Dherran turned with a florid growl, his blood boiling. His opponent still hadn't moved, and was being slapped to no avail by his support-team. The large bronze gong reverberated through the dirty heat of Rhaventia's main square as Dherran strode from the ring. Red fury took him as he paced along the spear-lined passage to his ready-tent. With a roar, Dherran batted aside the heavy canvas flap, tearing at his handwraps as he strode into the stifling gloom. He heard a whisk of canvas behind him and the flitting steps of Grump, who raced forward to finish unwinding Dherran's wraps with nimble fingers.

"Dherran, my lad, they're piss-mad! Your first punch! You could have at least given Rorouk a chance. Fastest Final Match in Rhaventia's history! And unfortunately, the most uneventful." The lithe little old man chuckled, his rapid speech unconcerned as his clever fingers unwound the cloth strips.

"Fucking cunt had it coming! Did you hear what he *said?!* Did you?!"

Loosing his rage at last, Dherran swung a fist, which Grump ducked nimbly like the little grey forest-mouse of a man that he was. The punch connected with a stout beam of the ready-tent and the whole pavilion trembled. When Dherran pulled his fist away, it came bloody, a great dent left in the solid barreloak beam. Grump clucked his tongue in reproach, then fetched the water bucket, rinsing

Dherran's damaged knuckles and giving him the dipper. Dherran drank deeply, then dunked his head, simmering under the cool trickles of water.

"I heard, I saw," Grump quipped, his breezy manner a contrast to the shouting beyond the pavilion. "He called you a royal Kingswhore, then mimed fucking your face. What more do you want, Dherran? You're talented, but no one likes you for it. Notorious." Grump winked, then thumped him on the shoulder, a butterfly's brush upon Dherran's solid bulk.

But suddenly, Grump's manner changed. Alert like a sharper-hawk, he cocked his head. In his ebbing rage, Dherran heard the rising roar beyond the tent. A whiff of pitch and lamp-oil touched his nostrils and Dherran paused as a cold fear hit him. "We have to get out of here, don't we?"

"Well, my boy, you don't exactly play the crowd." Grump grinned with hard amusement, scenting the air. "It's time for our little trio to move on, I think. Shall we make an unforgettable exit?"

With that, Grump was in action, flitting to Dherran's gear upon the wooden benches. Sinewed hands fast, Grump stuffed gear into saddlebags as Dherran erupted into motion also. Rage fed him like a swift stream as he quickly gathered his shirt, jerkin, sword harness, and gauntlets, cinching everything on with a speed that didn't match his bulk. Alert to the mob, Dherran heard spears clack as they were pulled from the summer-ring, men banging them together in violence. Voices boiled in drunken recklessness, though their words were indistinct.

Dherran smelled the acrid scent of burning pitch.

The mob was coming.

"Horses? Khenria?" Dherran's gaze flicked to Grump.

"Through that panel." Grump gave a flourishing bow, their saddlebags slung over his wiry frame.

"Let's go." Dherran ducked out the rear tent flap, his rage deepened into wrathful lava towards the populace of Rhaventia. Their horses were tied to the stout pilings of the pavilion's rear entry and skinny Khenria den'Bhaelen was there, dressed in her usual men's leather jerkin and trousers, her homespun cowl up despite the heat. Fingers flying, she pulled the lead-lines as Grump lashed saddlebags in place. Their escape was hidden, but just as Dherran was about to take his bay gelding from Khenria's nervous fingers, the mob broke around the side of the tent.

"There's the Blackmark!"

"Grab him!"

Dherran turned to face the mob. Grump was mounted on his grey gelding, and Khenria was up on Dherran's bay, the horses snorting and pacing as the crowd closed in. Hatred burned in the mob, torches hefted in a number of hands, and spears. Without pause, Dherran advanced. Dodging a wild spear-thrust from one untrained drunkard, he hit the fellow just below the ribs with his elbow, huffing him over in the dirt and taking his spear.

"You've seen me in the ring with fists!" Dherran bellowed, letting the rage in his hot green eyes be felt by the mob as he brandished the black-tipped spear. "Who will be the first to see what I can do with a weapon?!"

Fear took the faces of those at the front as they drew up short. Townsfolk, farmers, none actually wanted to face the death they saw in Dherran's eyes. They saw how he held the spear, a weapon known practically since birth for a Kingsman. But those behind were pressing forward as frightened men backed up, colliding with drunken fellows in the back. A punch was thrown.

And that was all it took.

Brother turned on brother like a forest fire jumping a dug trench. But the melee gave Dherran his moment. With a running leap, he launched from a step-stump by the picket line, up over the rump of his stout bay. The horse whinnied at the perverse treatment, but it was used to Dherran's getaways. With his spear in hand, Dherran reached around Khenria to grab the saddle-horn as he kicked the bay into motion. Grump wheeled also, kicking his stout grey into a gallop and taking the lead out of town.

As they galloped across the broad flagstone square, Dherran roared like a lion. Beneath the fluttering pennants by the trader's stalls, townsfolk shied back from the horses' hooves and Dherran's roar. Twisting in the saddle, Dherran hurled the black-tipped spear, skewering the ground in front of the pursuing mob. Men flooded to the sides of it, pulled up short in surprise.

And like some great beast, they halted – roaring behind Dherran and his comrades, furious at their escape.

Gaining the dusty tracks of Harrow's Road, Dherran and his companions raced out of Rhaventia just as the late afternoon sun dipped below the mountains. They ran the horses hard before Dherran felt the lather on his bay's withers far too slick beneath his hand. Reining to a walk, he let both horses and riders catch their breath. His stout bay Muk was tired, but Muk and

Merrow were not daunted by a quick getaway, and neither were Dherran's companions.

Angling Muk into the forest and feeling Merrow follow, Dherran heard heavy hoof-falls turn into dull thumps as they reached a thick carpet of forest loam. Grump took the lead then, walking them away from the road a league, his sense of direction unerring. Stopping their trio at a ring of balewick trees with high, thick foliage to keep off summer thunderstorms, Grump slipped out of the saddle. Khenria dismounted with Dherran after her, tying his horse to a tree with enough lead for grazing. Turning, Dherran listened for sounds of pursuit. But the forest held only the usual – the chirp of hedge-sparrows, scathing chatter from a grey squirrel, and whispers of wind through the leathery balewick leaves.

"Doubt they have six horses between the lot of them," Grump chattered, starting to gather fallen branches from beneath the trees to start an evening fire. "We'll be all right here, Khenria, mark my words! Uncle Grump has got us a fine fat purse, and we'll be in the money for months yet! You want kipper-flisk, child? Uncle Grump will get it for you, next town we come to!"

"Assuming there *are* any towns left open to us. Bigoted assholes." Dherran spoke hotly, hauling saddlebags off the exhausted mounts and setting them at the edge of the mossy camp.

"Now, now." Grump spoke as he piled his sticks by a balewick tree. "We've got the entire swath of eastern provinces to visit yet. Vennet, Quelsis, Arodantia, Pleinne. Plenty of places left to incite riots, my boy. The summer is still young!"

"They'll remember me from last year," Dherran countered, bitter. "They'll keep us out, because of the riots that followed my wins last summer."

"Maybe, maybe not." Grump dismissed. "You'd be surprised how people forget certain things and the faces that accomplished them. Memory is a fleeting thing, Dherran."

"You didn't cause a riot in Nevarre." Khenria's grey eyes were earnest as she bent to help Grump. Her short blue-black curls were whipped into a crest from riding, her men's jerkin and breeches allowing movement of her skinny frame as she gathered. "Your fighting doesn't cause riots in every town."

"Just most of them," Dherran sighed, irate. "That's three riots already this summer. And it was only my fifth series of fights!"

"Last year was worse," Khenria countered with a sly grin. "You had five riots by midsummer. Maybe you're losing your edge."

"My *edge?*" It took Dherran a moment to realize her comment had been a joke. And suddenly, it broke him. Like water pouring over hot stones, his rage fizzled and Dherran's exhalation became a chuckle. Humor had always dissipated his heat, but it had to be the right kind; a subtle, caring humor.

And Khenria had it, just like Suchinne once had.

But Dherran's demeanor cooled, remembering Suchinne – remembering how she'd died. Dherran's regiment, the Stone Valley Guard, had been summoned to the Valenghian front, engaging a vicious battle in the foothills near Quelsis. He'd found Suchinne in the Quelsis Foreguard, only hours too late as he picked through the dead. Speared, raped – it was obvious in what order things had been done. The spear through her middle had been Valenghian, but when Dherran found a Menderian Lieutenant's pin on the ground beside her, he'd snatched it up in a blinding, terrible wrath.

And found the Menderian soldiers who'd done it.

"Dherran? Where did you go?" Khenria's voice was small at his side, as her slight hand settled to his forearm. Blinking, Dherran surfaced from red memories.

"Nowhere." With a wry twist of lips, he pulled away. "I'll get some more sticks for the fire. Be back soon."

Khenria blinked at his rebuff, but something in her understood and she didn't pursue him. Striding from the ring of trees, Dherran made for a massive boulder nearby, a great swath of stone bigger than ten barns. Approaching the behemoth covered in moss and last years' leaf litter, Dherran took deep breaths to cool his memories. His inner turmoil eased as he considered the stone; its groundedness, its cool solidity. Shadows smoothed across its blue-grey surface, the sun's rays picking out emerald highlights in the moss. As Dherran stared at those green glimmers, his vision began to expand from its hot, narrow spear – until it opened up all together.

Inhaling fully, Dherran took a breath without his rage at last.

It had been Suchinne who had shown him how to study objects to cool his temper. But this object was actually something of interest. Walking the near side, Dherran found the enormous swath of rock had a peculiar shape, like a hand palm-down in the earth with five elongated fingers. Laying with its massive fingers splayed into the ground, the vegetation suggested it had had been there for centuries, even a few trees now brazenly growing out of the top of the thing.

"Grump!" Dherran called. "Come look at this!"

Grump flitted over with a bundle of sticks under his skinny arm, his head cocked and his grey brows knit. "Well, you've found something, boyo! Yes, indeed!"

"It looks like a hand!" Khenria exclaimed as she came up behind Grump. "A hand extended in warding!"

"Looks like a piece of one of those monoliths we saw last year when we tracked along the Aphellian Way." Dherran murmured, intrigued.

"Not from the Aphellian Way," Grump spoke, reaching out to smooth one gnarled hand over the rough stone. "Those are all protected by a magic long lost. Some have been toppled by time but not broken. No, this probably came from far up in the mountains. Stones like these are found stranded, left down in this valley from glaciers long receded. The mountains further up are riddled with broken pieces of ancient lore. Someone was here upon this continent, long before us. And they weren't shy about leaving their mark on this land."

"Fantastic." Dherran murmured, smoothing his hand over the mossy stone. Feeling the immensity of it, he imagined how tall the original monolith would have been, suddenly feeling small next to something wrought by such an ancient people.

"Look here, boyo!" Grump suddenly turned upon him. "You don't get out of making camp just because you fought today. *Idle hands make an idle future!* That's what—"

"Gramma den'Aldriye always used to say. Yeah, yeah." Dherran murmured, stepping away from the enormous stone and brushing moss off his hands.

"Get to work, Dherran! Hup, hup! *The faster you gather, the faster you sup!*" Khenria bent to pluck a stick from a clump of telmenberry vines as she quoted one of Grump's platitudes. She threw the stick at Dherran, and he let it hit his chest. He saw how it pleased her even though they both knew how fast he could have dodged it. Grinning, Dherran ambled back to camp with them to unpack saddlebags and untie bedrolls from the horses. Laying out their cooking utensils, he suddenly remembered something.

"Grump. How much did we win today?"

Making a fire in the center of camp, Grump piled medium sticks into a cone with small tinder. "Guess."

"Ten and thirty!" Khenria spoke as she lined a space for the fire with stones.

"Not even close! Up near twenty." Grump chortled, obviously proud of his betting skills.

"Gods above, Grump!" Dherran glanced over. "What were the odds against me? I already won five bouts in that town over the past week."

"The odds were eleven to one, boyo, despite your winning. There are plenty who dislike a Kingsman and bet with their hatred rather than their brains. *Blind men run into deep wells.* I put in everything we had and took a cut for the trades I arranged besides. But your opponent was a champion in three regions of Alrou-Mendera this year! Had a nasty right hook and sixty pounds on you. He was anticipated to knock you flat. Though I daresay I knew better."

"He was fat and slow," Dherran dismissed, embarrassed that the odds against him had been so bad.

"He was thick and fast," Grump challenged. "You were faster. And because of it, I got us nineteen and eighty-two Rou. Best *that,* kiddos." Grump was smug, striking flint and steel into his bundle of tinder and blowing on the flame.

"Do I get a horse now?" Khenria laughed, jostling Grump.

"Anything you want, dear heart." Grump waved her off, away from his smoking bundle. He came to all fours as he tucked his small flame into the tinder of the cone, blowing gently to get the fire licking upwards. "We have plenty now for a third horse, and a number of months room and board to boot. We won't have to live out in the woods over the winter."

"Good thing everyone hates a Kingsman." Dherran growled, pouring water from one of their bladders into a pot to make their evening tea.

"Not everyone hates a Kingsman. Don't you ever say that." Khenria's voice cracked and Dherran looked up, seeing her dark, intense stillness. Khenria had an anger of her own, a match to Dherran's. Ferocity was there in her set lips, in the defiant angle of her chin; a hawk-eyed woman beneath her lanky youth. More and more, Dherran saw the steely strength of the Alrashemni in her, beautiful in a vicious way like Suchinne had once had. Khenria's dark grey eyes held fury in the fading day. Her brush-cut black curls caught the fire's glow, blazing with blue highlights.

"I know," Dherran murmured, his heart softening to her ferocity. "But I still owe you a nice feather mattress, don't I? Always getting us kicked out of decent lodgings."

Khenria's lips quirked. And though an ache flushed Dherran's chest, it was a calm sadness of delicate things lost and a safe life forgotten. Dherran's joke was more than half-true. He owed Khenria a lot more than he could ever repay. With his mother's coloring – the straw-blonde hair and green eyes that were gradually drowning out the elegant darkness of the Alrashemni – Dherran didn't look like a Kingsman. But he had the Inkings, and Khenria had recognized them when she and Dherran had met at the stream two years ago. He'd been naked, soaking in the river. She'd been hiding in the forest's fringe, watching him. She'd approached him because of those marks, because of the trust she put in them and the life she remembered. And from a solo journey of misery since he'd defected from the Stone Valley Guard after Suchinne's death, Dherran had suddenly acquired a family.

He owed Khenria everything because of it.

But Khenria took on a thoughtful cast now, silent, and suddenly Dherran thought he had said something wrong. Unlike Suchinne, Khenria was moody, sometimes ferocious as a keshar, sometimes playful, sometimes distant. She'd had a hard life after the Summons, a childhood of abuse and desperate living, and Dherran felt distinctly uncomfortable now as if he'd triggered something.

His gaze broke from her hawkish steel, flicking to find Grump. But as usual, Grump had melted away once the fire had started, to fetch the bounty of the forest. Dherran made himself busy by pouring herbs for tea and setting the pot to boil. Still silent, Khenria organized their bedrolls, erecting a lean-to of oiled canvas between the trees in case of rain.

At last, Dherran heard light feet returning, Grump only making his presence known for their sake. Dherran turned, noting Grump's gather-pouches were full to bursting as he stepped into the fire's light, two fat rabbits slung over his shoulder.

"Summer bunnies are out!" Grump chortled as he shed the rabbits to the moss.

Finished with the lean-to, Khenria snatched the rabbits up, using her belt-knife to skin and eviscerate them with stunning alacrity. Dherran forgot sometimes that she'd been starving and wild when Grump had found her at age ten, adopting her to his nomadic ways. She'd escaped an abusive foster-family and managed to stay alive a number of months on her own, but had been close to death as autumn had turned to winter. Grump had taught her woodscraft and kindness, and his sweet chatter had re-socialized her.

Somewhat.

"Soon it will all be bunny-stew," Grump spoke as he picked through a pouch full of yellow chandria mushrooms, "bunny-jerky, bunny-pies, and now that we have money for flour, salted bunny-crunch wraps! Though we've got to wait for the dragon-snaps at the end of summer for that."

Dherran smiled as he stepped in, helping Grump slice up the mushrooms he had foraged, as Khenria tore up some bitter greens. They hardly ever needed supplies from town when they lived rough, Dherran an adept hunter with his bow, and Khenria learned in Grump's foraging skills. In a little while, a fragrant stew was bubbling heartily in the pot, and as Khenria began honing her knife, Dherran motioned her up. She sprang to her feet, Dherran tossing her an extra practice sword from his bedroll, which she snatched from the air like a cat.

And their regular evening sword-bout began.

Even in his youth, Dherran had been an expert swordsman, a capable teacher when he wasn't busy getting pissed off. He took Khenria through combinations to get her heated, until she was breathing hard and damp with sweat. At last, she gave him a wide opening, and Dherran moved in. One fist to her chest, he knocked out her wind, his blade sliding to her throat. But the little hawk was handy with steel, and even as she doubled over coughing, Dherran felt her boot-knife prick his ribs. He laughed, stepping back as Khenria glowered, rage in her fine-boned features. Womanly and hot with wrath, her glower made Dherran's chuckle falter as he inclined his head.

"Fair enough. It was a dirty blow. But you have to expect your opponent to fight filthy sometimes. You did just right, Khenria. When someone fights like a caged keshar, you do the same. And if you really feel your life is in danger—" his hand whipped to a fly-blade in his jerkin, throwing it faster than a viper. Khenria slipped to one side as the knife brushed past her cheek, burying in the tree behind her.

"You could have killed me!" Her lips dropped open, realizing what he'd just done.

"But you felt it. Good job." Dherran inclined his head. "We're done."

He turned, making for the fire. But a breath of wind raised his hackles and Dherran spun, catching Khenria's sneak attack upon his blade, sliding past her in a two-handed upward parry that left her spinning to an uneven seat upon the moss. As Dherran whipped the tip of his blade to her throat, Khenria's eyes glittered coal-dark in the firelight.

"I almost got you, Dherran."

Dherran's sword-tip didn't waver. "Test me, Khenria, and find out what I'm really made of."

"I'll test you. Just you wait." Her eyes had changed to a dark smolder that left Dherran rattled as he pulled his sword up and thrust it back in its scabbard. He didn't offer Khenria a hand up, merely gazed at her a long moment.

"Stew's ready! Come and eat." Grump suddenly chimed in.

Moving away, Dherran sat upon a spread hide before the fire. Khenria sat beside him, fetching her bowl and portioning her fill. She stared at him as they ate, and Dherran felt like a skinned rabbit beneath her gaze. Suchinne's gaze had pierced him like that, like talons. And now there was another hawk in Dherran's life, a tempestuous one that was far less predictable. Dherran hunched his shoulders in the deepening night, draining the dregs of his bowl.

Grump prattled on, oblivious to the tension in their camp.

6

OLEA

Striding from the infirmary to the West Guardhouse for her rounds, Olea jogged down grandiose byrunstone staircases to the deepest halls of Roushenn. Few folk were about in the bowels of the palace, the corridors echoing and silent. Turning right, she entered the vaulted reaches of the West Armory, a hall of antiquities from the martial history of Alrou-Mendera that had a passage up to the guardhouse. Full of iron displays of armor, glass cases full of weapons and medallions, plus tapestries of lord's crests adorning the walls, Olea's soft footsteps echoed in the hall's cavernous silence.

Though it was intriguing, Olea felt a pang as she always did when traversing this hall. All evidence of Alrashemni Kingsmen antiquities had been removed from the space, and their absence was notable. Gazing at armor upon iron displays, she saw countless niches barren, entire suits removed. Sword-displays hung empty for ten paces, glass cases pocked with dented blue velvet where medallions of bravery had once lain.

Even in her first year at the palace, Olea had never seen evidence of Alrashemni honor here. All of it had been removed after the Kingsmen's disappearance – and gazing around now, a feeling of barrenness rose in Olea, an aching sensation of loss. Here had been evidence of how her people had served their kings, and now only their absence remained like a hole in the heart of Roushenn.

Kingsmen had been all but erased from Alrou-Mendera's history, as if a hand of destiny had swept them from the continent.

Olea's chest clenched as she moved swiftly through the hall. This was no place to linger, not with everything else she was thinking about with Elohl's discharge. If he lived, he'd not be honored any more for his service than Olea was for being a Kingsman at her post.

That was all too plain here – staring at her from every empty display.

Olea was about to exit when a hot curse suddenly issued from behind a suit of gold-plated armor nearby. As she moved toward the sound, glancing behind the iron stand, Olea saw a young woman with long gold-blonde hair dressed in a jade silk gown sitting on the floor of the niche. Looking up, startled and fierce, the woman's regal features and piercing green eyes relaxed as she noted who had found her. Her tear-stained cheeks flushed, her eyes all the more brilliantly green for the red that rimmed them.

"Dhenra Elyasin." Olea dropped to one knee, bowing with her hand to her sword – halting her other hand and moving it back to her side rather than press it to her Inkings. Even after ten years, bowing like a Kingsman was a hard habit to break.

"Captain-General. As you were." Dhenra Elyasin den'Ildrian smiled ruefully, scrubbing tears from her high cheekbones with determined hands.

"Are you all right, Dhenra?" Olea asked, her straight brows furrowing to see her liege in such a state.

"Oh, fine! Just fine." The young Dhenra laughed harshly as she leaned her head back upon the armor she rested against. "Let's see. Why am I fine? Well, there's fourteen suitors vying to become King when I rise into my throne at Highsummer, all of them trying to manipulate me with trade agreements. My dead father's Chancellate, always in my ear, bullying me because I'm a woman and they don't think I can rule. And Castellan Lhaurent – why must I supervise the palace household when I have a kingdom to run and an ongoing border-war with Valenghia to manage?" Elyasin closed her eyes with a tired sigh. "Leave me, Captain. I wish to be alone."

"You are unguarded, Dhenra." Olea observed gently.

"And who is going to accost me here?" Dhenra Elyasin's eyes snapped open, with the same rash temper her brother Alden had once possessed. "The Ghost of Roushenn? No one uses these halls, it's why I come down here." Scrubbing her fingers through her lush golden hair, she combed her bright waves over one shoulder angrily. "What am I going to do, Olea? A marriage? Aeon's tits! This is harder than managing the war in Valenghia!"

Another tear leaked down the Dhenra's face and she scrubbed it away angrily – angry with herself. Elyasin had never enjoyed weakness, not as the high-spirited girl who'd used to gape at Olea upon the practice grounds, and certainly not now as a woman. With a furiously strong demeanor and a keen mind, at twenty-two Elyasin was still the same person who, at twelve years old and fascinated by Olea's Inkings, had demanded to learn the sword and other arts of the Kingsmen. Olea had relented and taught her Dhenra in secret, a secret kept even from her father King Uhlas den'Ildrian.

A secret they still shared twice weekly.

"You have time, Dhenra." Olea spoke, her heart stirred by the fury of the young woman before her. "Take any advice you require to gauge trade agreements. Walk among the people in Lintesh and ask what they need. Your coronation is still a month away at Highsummer. Even so, weddings and treaties can wait. Alrou-Mendera has had unwed queens before. Foster goodwill in the wake of your father's passing, and your people will stand by you no matter how you choose to rule."

"You give me the best advice yet again, Olea. Unsought-for." Elyasin's golden brows eased, now gazing at Olea in a thoughtful manner. "Why is that?"

"Kingsmen always speak truth to our liege, Dhenra."

"Everyone wants *something* from me." Elyasin lifted one golden eyebrow, shrewd. "All my suitors, the Castellan, the Chancellate. They all look at me as if I'm supposed to do what they say, offering counsel and expecting me to be their puppet because I'm young, and a woman. No one offers advice freely, not without expectation of return. So what do *you* want from me, Captain?"

The question took Olea aback and her face opened in honesty, even the suggestion that she might be manipulating her Dhenra abhorrent. "I want nothing from you, Dhenra. All I've ever wanted is to see you succeed. You have strength and a keen mind. And I would like to see a powerful, outspoken Queen ascend the throne."

"Won't that be the day?" The Dhenra smiled wryly. "The taciturn suspicion of my father King Uhlas, followed by the reign of an outspoken Queen."

"Your father was a man of deep and unfathomable plans, Dhenra."

"Yet for all his planning, I am surrounded by wolves and not allies!" Elyasin snapped, rising in a lithe movement from the floor. Her silk gown poured down her fit, curvaceous body like water as one hand settled to the jeweled dagger that always rode her waist, her jade eyes flashing fire.

"I don't even know who my true allies are, Olea! My father kept his own counsel and his secrets were known to none. And now I know nothing! These past nine months since his death, I've not known where to turn. Once the Kingsmen were allies that could always be depended on. My father spoke so highly of them when I was a child, calling them his *truest vanguard!* And then he reaped them down with accusations of treason and no one knows why! Do you?"

Olea went very still, her heart racing as her soon-to-be-Queen raged upon this line of inquiry. Her hackles rose as she pondered how much to say to her Dhenra – how much was safe. It was one thing for common folk to speculate on what had happened to the Kingsmen, but for the Dhenra to know so little of such a definitive event in her own nation was dangerous. Olea had always assumed King Uhlas would have told his daughter what had really happened when it was time for her to become Queen. But Uhlas had never told his son Dhenir Alden about the Kingsmen disappearance. Olea knew that much, as many nights as she had spent in Alden's confidence. But Uhlas had never told Elyasin, either.

And now he was dead and couldn't tell anybody.

Horrors were surfacing, burned into Olea from that awful time ten years ago. Like a nightmare, she could still feel a cavernous dread from the day she and Elohl had taken that Alranstone to Lintesh, and had nearly been killed by that scorpion-rider. When they'd returned to Alrashesh, the rest of the Alrashemni Kingskinder had been gone, left for their safehouse in the fortified ruins of Kepsburg-on-the-Rhine. Olea could still smell the dry peat of the yards and hear the empty silence of the stone battlements in Alrashesh, as they'd run to the training amphitheater to pack supplies and follow.

When that Aeon-awful creak of a hundred bows drawn at once had lanced Olea's ears.

Archers had ringed the ramparts of the practice yard's amphitheater. Hidden, and somehow also concealed from Olea's hearing, they'd been waiting for someone to make the vast mistake of coming back to Alrashesh – someone who could tell them the location of the Kingskinder. Olea, Elohl, and their companions had formed a bitter ring in the dusty amphitheater with weapons drawn. And then, the same tall man in black herringbone armor that had accosted them in the Alranstone grotto had stepped from the archers and swordsmen.

And Olea's world had been torn apart.

"Olea? Are you all right?" The Dhenra's murmur broke into Olea's memories, Elyasin watching her with a gaze every bit as shrewd as her deceased father.

"Forgive me, Dhenra." Olea spoke, taking a long breath. "Today is the tenth anniversary of when us Kingskinder were arrested and conscripted into service. It weighs on me."

"I didn't realize, Captain..." Elyasin blinked, her brows lifting. "But all the more that this issue be discussed. For ten years, our realm has been in the dark about what happened. Tell me, what do you know of the Kingsman Summons? Do you know why my father charged them with High Treason?"

"What do you know about it?" Olea countered. "Let's start there."

"Little, unfortunately." The Dhenra tapped her fingers on her gown, thinking. "My father Uhlas was always tight-lipped about it, even when my brother Alden confronted him years ago. I was so young when it happened, and Alden and I were away at the Summer Palace on the Elsee. No one I ask knows what actually occurred here at Roushenn; not the Chancellate, not Castellan Lhaurent, not the Guardsmen or even the maids and cooks. The annals say the Kingsmen are dead, but there was no trial, no public execution. No one actually *saw* them die. Nearly two thousand Kingsmen were shown courtesy, taken to rooms throughout the bowels of the palace, and then – nothing. In the morning, all the rooms were empty. The Kingsmen simply showed up here at Roushenn and were never seen again. Some chronicles say they abandoned their King, used magic to disappear into the mountain like wraiths."

"If that was the case, they would have come for us Kingskinder." Olea scowled. "But none of our elders ever came for us, Dhenra. The few younger Kingskinder I've been able to trace went to foster-families, while those past their Fifth Seal were split up into military service."

"Were *pressed* into service, like slaves." Elyasin's face twisted in disgust. "Slaves in my own country, serving their lifeblood up to my father against Valenghia!"

"It is my *honor* to serve the Crown, Dhenra." Olea held her gaze, honest.

"Even after what my father did to your people?"

"You are not your father."

"No, I am not. And I will find out what happened, and why. I dislike secrets in my realm."

"Everyone in Roushenn keeps secrets," Olea murmured. It was a common adage about the palace, labyrinthine fortress that it was.

But the phrase struck a violent chord with the Dhenra, who clenched one fist, a livid scowl upon her face. "Not from me, they don't—"

"Your highness!" A smooth voice suddenly cut the air like an oiled whip. Startled, Olea looked around, seeing the King's Castellan Lhaurent den'Karthus moving down the hall with imperious efficiency in his tall, gaunt frame. Dark brows level, his pearl-grey eyes pierced Olea above his high cheekbones, his cropped black beard and hair immaculately groomed though streaked with grey. The Castellan's dove-grey silk doublet, robes, and breeches were pristine, his silver chains of office hanging from his doublet's high collar. Rings of gold graced every finger, an ornate ring of dusk-grey metal with a ruby upon his left index finger. Everything about the man was polished and well-oiled – right down to his scented breath and buffed nails.

"Captain den'Alrahel." Castellan Lhaurent gave Olea a cold look as he neared. "Why did you not alert someone of the Dhenra's whereabouts? She is needed in the Small Rotunda to meet Prince Ilkresh of Crasos."

Olea set her jaw, instantly irritated at the Castellan. Whenever he approached, his soft-booted silence made Olea think of rainbarrel eels. She didn't trust Lhaurent, though he'd never given anyone a reason to think he was disloyal. All the same, Olea had her suspicions about what he was up to. Thievery, perhaps. Embezzlement. Maybe plotting to murder someone to better his own station.

"Castellan Lhaurent," Olea growled. "I'm sure the Dhenra can manage her schedule to her liking."

Lhaurent's eyes narrowed upon Olea's wild blue-black curls, her undone buckles and laces, and the Inked star on her chest, his tone dripping scorn. "You are a *mess*, Captain. It is a wonder anyone lets you remain in service, sloppy as you are."

Olea was about to retort when the Dhenra stepped from behind her suit of armor. Elyasin's back was straight, her posture imperious. "Leave us, Lhaurent. I was in need of a report from my Captain-General before her rounds. You may tell Prince Ilkresh that I will be along presently. Invite him to music, wine, and delicacies in the Viewing Gallery. I will be no more than fifteen minutes."

The Castellan betrayed a small surprise at the Dhenra's fierce demeanor, though he gave a languid bow. "As my Dhenra wishes, so shall it be done."

Turning on his heels, he glided from the hall, as if his ego had never been bruised by his Dhenra's sharp dismissal. Elyasin watched her Castellan go, her posture still impeccable. But once he turned the corner, she suddenly fiddled with her knuckles, a nervous tic. "Aeon, I never hear him coming! If I did, I'd be able to prepare myself better for his dour critiques."

"He's like an eel, Dhenra." Olea commented darkly. "All that oil in his hair greases his passage."

"Olea!" The Dhenra snorted, her lips quirked in laughter as she turned. "For shame. Lhaurent is a loyal subject, both for my father and his father before him. He is a fixture of this palace these past thirty years, and no one runs Roushenn with such grace as he."

"Are you certain he's loyal?" It was out before Olea could take it back. She never heard Lhaurent approaching either – and with her *wyrric* hearing, it was one of the things that made her intensely suspicious about the man.

The Dhenra's smile changed suddenly, into something deeply thoughtful and calculating – a look like her father Uhlas once had. "Are you certain he is not, Captain?"

"My suspicions have no proof, Dhenra." Olea spoke, setting her jaw. "Alden and I never had any proof of anything."

"Suspicions and proof of *what?*" Elyasin stepped closer, intent.

"Treachery against the Crown."

"Castellan Lhaurent?!" Elyasin looked shocked.

"Not necessarily." Olea shook her head. "But someone who knows these halls."

"Explain." Elyasin raised one regal eyebrow, cool as stone.

Olea took a deep breath. In Elyasin's sharp gaze, she read the steady depth of Uhlas, and Olea could not lie to Uhlas' daughter. Elyasin had been denied the truth from so many sides, it was against Olea's oaths as a Kingswoman to withhold any more. Even if it placed her liege in a precarious situation, Elyasin had a right to know. She would be Queen in four weeks' time, and Olea clenched a fist, feeling pain but knowing she had to speak at last.

"Two years ago, just before he died," Olea began, steadying her voice against a flood of awful memories, "your brother Dhenir Alden and I were looking into the

Kingsmen disappearance. It was one of the reasons we were spending so much time together, openly. Looking into why your father was acting so paranoid and secretive. We had just started to dig into some dire leads when Castellan Lhaurent exposed our... *intimate* affair. *For the good of the realm*, he said, to bring Alden and I's improper relationship before the Chancellate rather than speak with your father the King about it privately. It put your father in a terrible position, Dhenra, having such a shameful family matter be made public. But what Lhaurent's exposure of our affair truly did... was stop Alden and I's investigation into the Kingsmen disappearance."

"Two years ago." Elyasin's eyes had gone wide. "That was when the Chancellate voted for you to be beheaded because of the scandal. I remember that day."

"Your father was merciful." Olea nodded soberly. "He sent me to the cells instead, and put Alden on a trading ship to Ghrec with the merchant fleet."

"The ship that crashed..." Elyasin's face fell, infinitely sad.

Olea nodded, trying not to think about that horrible time. "That lighthouse should have been lit, Dhenra. That ship never should have crashed coming back into port."

"You think someone orchestrated Alden's death?" Elyasin's green gaze flicked to Olea, sharp. "Darkened the lighthouse on purpose to crash the flagship that night? Because of what you two were investigating?"

"Because we were investigating the Chancellate in regards to the Kingsmen Summons." Olea nodded. "And the palace household. And the Generals. There were whispers of rumor leading into all those arenas, Dhenra, rumors we were about to follow. But we were stopped before we could find anything conclusive. And then Dhenir Alden was killed on that ship. Only someone very powerful could have bribed the lighthouse-master of Amlenport to darken his charge for a night when the ship of the King's son was coming into harbor."

Elyasin was very pale, and very silent as she rubbed her knuckles violently. "Walk with me, Captain-General. I have a request to make of you."

Olea nodded and offered her arm. The Dhenra took it regally, resting her fingers upon Olea's sleeve. It was unusual to have a woman so high-ranking in the military these days. But there had been a time when it had not been, and Olea knew the rituals of respect that bound a Kingswoman to her liege as she escorted her Dhenra from the hall, and down Roushenn's labyrinthine corridors.

"Captain, I want you to re-open your investigation into the Kingsmen disappearance."

"Yes, Dhenra." Olea startled, but did not lose her step.

"Use what resources you must. I will give you a writ for the treasury and to excuse you from your regular duties, but keep your activities *very* discreet. You are trained in espionage?"

"Yes, Dhenra."

"No one must know, unless you can recruit someone to aid you that you absolutely trust. I *must* know why the Kingsmen Summons was dispatched, what led to it, and what happened afterwards, in detail. Before my coronation in four weeks at Highsummer."

"Yes, Dhenra. May I speak freely?"

"Always." Elyasin glanced over.

"Why are you looking into this? If it got Dhenir Alden killed, why take it up now?"

The Dhenra paused and Olea halted, Elyasin's golden brows furrowed. "Because I think the Summons of the Kingsmen was wrong. Everything I have read in the ancient histories speak of the Alrashemni Kingsmen with high honor, citing them as the Crown's most trusted alliance and most reliable weapon. But all the events of the past thirty years concerning the Kingsmen have been scrubbed clean. I am in the dark, Captain, and I don't like being in the dark. My father left me a vast kingdom, but he also left me vast worries. You have always been forthright with me, and my brother Alden loved and trusted you like none other. You have given me wise council, and you have kept every secret I have ever told you. If all the Kingsmen were like you, then I think my father's Summons was amiss. And perhaps precipitated by... something else. Something that may still trouble our nation. And that, I will not abide under my rule."

Olea's throat tightened. Sinking to one knee in the hallway, she bowed her head in respect. Elyasin was proving wise beyond her years, but Olea couldn't help but wonder if the Dhenra subjected herself to the same unknown tides that had ripped the heart out of the Kingsmen, and of her beloved Dhenir Alden.

"You place yourself in danger if you pursue this, Dhenra. Like Alden did." Olea spoke softly. "Whomever is behind this... if they hear of it, they may try to strike you down before your coronation. Before you truly have the power to move against them, independent of the Chancellate."

"Yes. I know." Elyasin murmured. "And if we find that my father actually was the source of the Summons, and did something so horrible with the Kingsmen he could never tell me, then that is that. I will hate him for his decision, but it was his to make as King. But if not..."

"The Summons didn't come from Uhlas." Olea breathed, knowing she had to tell her Dhenra everything.

"*What*?" Elyasin went utterly still.

"Alden and I found one thing out for certain with our inquiries two years ago." Olea's murmur was softer than specters in the looming hall. "That King Uhlas wasn't at Roushenn when the Summons went out, nor when the Kingsmen arrived. He was in Valenghia, making a secret last-hour effort to stop oncoming war with the Valenghian Vhinesse. His signature on the Summons document was a very precise forgery. *Your father never gave that Summons.* Someone else did. Someone, or someones, very close to him. And you have inherited all your father's Chancellate, Dhenra, and his staff, and all his Generals..."

"All those who were close to my father are now close to me." Elyasin's words were hushed as she realized the terrible truth. Fingertips brushed her shoulder and Olea knew her cue to rise. She came to her feet, gazing at the fierce, calm Dhenra as Elyasin reached out, trailing her fingers over Olea's Inkings.

"Find out what happened, Olea. I trust you, just as Alden trusted you. Find out what happened to the Kingsmen, and who was behind my father's reign. And once we know..." Elyasin's eyes went flinty. "I will clean out my rule. And start fresh."

"Be careful, Dhenra. I admonished Alden to be careful—"

"But my brother was not careful enough, was he?"

"Alden was never one to take care." Olea blinked back a prickling of tears as her heart twisted. She could still feel the closeness of him even now. His soft breath at her ear in sleep, the way his lion-rich laugh used to ring through the practice yard when she bested him. The warmth of him, so smooth and hard, in bed.

Elyasin reached up, stroking Olea's wild hair away from her cheeks. The Dhenra's face was sad, but the set of her jaw was uncompromising, just like her father's. "Do this for me, Olea. I know I put you at risk, but I have no one else I trust..."

Corralling back her grief with a single, slow breath, Olea offered her arm once more. "I will not fail you, Dhenra. Ever."

7

JHERRICK

Staring down into the glassy eyes of the dead boy, Jherrick den'Tharn watched the fey blue light of Roushenn Palace's Hinterhaft flicker over the boy's pale features. Hunkering by the body, Jherrick's cobalt Guardsman jerkin creaked in the cavernous silence, a catacomb-thick darkness filling the corridor behind the walls of Roushenn. Wisping globes of blue light traversed the catacomb's vaulted ceilings, swirling like sand in a glass. Curious about death, the fae-wisps floated down toward the floor, inquisitive like fireflies around the corpse. One wisped close to the boy's face, lighting his smooth features with their sallow emptiness. Purple bruises stood out on the boy's neck, four strong fingermarks on each side.

Jherrick hadn't killed the boy. Those weren't his orders. Waving one hand at the blue globe, Jherrick made it waft back to the upper reaches of the hall. With the same straw-gold hair, fair skin, and sea-grey eyes, the lad could have been Jherrick's brother in another life. Twelve or thirteen, the boy had been on the cusp of manhood, that transition where a kitchen page starts waiting at table to move up and become a proper servingman. Jherrick had started that way, before he'd been moved into the Palace Guard.

Deal with that. Castellan Lhaurent had said.

Deal with that. Like the dead boy was just some rotten cord of wood to be heaped upon the slag-pile.

Resolute, Jherrick grasped the lad's arm, hauling the weight up over his strong shoulders. Though lean for his twenty-three years, Jherrick was all muscle, honed to perfection upon the dry side of a sword. Most of his official time was spent reading through lists and ledgers with Guard-Captain Olea den'Alrahel in the West Guardhouse, but his unofficial time was spent doing odious chores such as this for the Khehemni Lothren, many of which required a fit frame.

And a hardened mind.

As Jherrick moved at a brisk walk through the Hinterhaft behind Roushenn's walls, the arched catacomb soon opened into a massive space whose heights were lost but for the blue globes. Traversing it to a particular section of wall, Jherrick pushed on the stone, hearing some mechanism click. The wall pivoted to reveal a little-used servant's corridor in the palace, torch-brackets far apart this deep inside the mountain. It had been the lad's bad luck to have taken this shortcut with the spice delivery he'd been making from one larder to another.

And his further bad luck to lean against this particular section of wall.

Few people stumbled upon the five sections of wall in all of Roushenn that could access the Hinterhaft. Four of them had been partially blocked by armoires and bookcases, so one had to sidle into a shadowy niche to give the wall a push. But this one was left unblocked for deliveries, and so it was that Jherrick now delivered the dead lad back out like a sack of grain, stealing along the quiet corridor.

Arriving at the palace's east garden door, Jherrick stepped out to the soft, warm night. Summer was here, and a peeping of frogs followed his quiet movements, the only mourning the dead boy would ever get. Unease gnawed Jherrick's gut as he pushed through a little-known door in the rear of the guard-wall that led directly to the Kingswood. Patrolled by Guardsmen of Jherrick's own allegiance, he received shadowy nods. Nodding back, he moved off down the path with his burden, his boot-falls thumping dully on the thick loam.

Shadows filled the Kingswood from a slivered summer moon, the double hoot of a bridge-owl reaching Jherrick's ears. Water spilled over rocks as he stepped over a stream, the night silent but for this music around him. The night was Jherrick's protection in his duty, and his solace. Sometimes he thought he heard the night speaking to him, as if spirits lingered in the rustling leaves, whispering of absolution for his young life gone so utterly wrong. It made him come to peace to believe it, ignoring the heavy burden across his shoulders.

But his midnight sojourn ended as the cedar and barreloak hollow where the wolves knew to expect their meat loomed suddenly. A sallow slope of last-year's leaves showing deep rents and claw marks from constant scuffle over gristle and sinew, it was a dark place, riven with desperate energy. The smell of death lingered here, the cloying stench of entrails ripped and bones cracked, a latrine acridity no midnight wind could ever scour clean.

Surveying the scene, calm now in shifting shadows, Jherrick's stomach churned, knowing how much torn flesh the boy's body was about to become. Knowing how the wolves would prowl in, wary at first. And when the meat was found unable to fight back, they would surge in with yips and growls, teeth flashing, worrying the boy's body until cold blood coated their muzzles black in the night.

A howl sounded; a little too near. Jherrick's sword was in his hand, fast. Suddenly, he knew he couldn't leave the boy there, not to be ripped apart like all the others. His flesh was too young, too pure.

Too *good* to make a meal for wolves.

Backing out of the hollow, Jherrick moved away from the slope, his sword still out. Eyes watched him, glinting in the moonlight. He could almost hear the pack's tension in the dark, like bowstring pulled taut for a long shot. And they could feel his own readiness, his sword glinting as much as their eyes in the darkness – that he was a predator in the night as much as they.

"Come try me," Jherrick murmured. "Come for your meat if you dare. But this one's not coming to you. Not this time."

His legs were strong beneath his load, his posture fierce. He'd drop the body to fight if he needed to, but it wasn't going to come to that. Jherrick could feel the pack drifting away like smoke, back through the silver-dark cedars.

A ready enemy was no enemy to fight.

"Smart choice." Jherrick murmured as he slid his sword away. Now that the possibility of a fight had passed, he let his body shudder out its tension, relieved. Hefting the body more securely atop his shoulders, he thought of where to take it. And suddenly, he knew. The boy's mother was a mushroom-hunter for the palace. Jherrick knew she went out every dawn from her modest cottage in the Second Tier, taking the same path through the Kingswood to her favorite spots. Jherrick angled for that path, picking his way off-trail through fern and snake-vine.

Dawn kissed the pale sky as he found the right trail. Gently, he settled the boy's body in the cedar-strewn path, and unsheathing one longknife, he sliced the boy's purse strings, taking his leather pouch. Raiding the boy of a lapis pendant that wasn't worth much and a stout ring of silver with a decent sapphire, he knew the mother would find the lad, think he'd come to visit her, and that highwaymen had gotten him.

Jherrick's gaze roved the scene, making sure it looked right. The boy looked almost peaceful curled on his side. Like a fire-yarn where a boy stumbles into a ring of fae-caps and emerges on the cusp of manhood, it seemed like he merely slept from his time in fae lands. Jherrick was about to leave, when he paused. Something pulled at him; the memory of a family lost. Kneeling, he set the ring upon a flat white stone in the path, as if it had been carelessly dropped.

Slipping back into the vegetation, a sense of rightness filled him at what he had done. Early-summer henianthus was in bloom, and the bush he hid behind was fragrant with purple bells, their scent easing through his tired body. A chorus of titwidget erupted around him as the sunlight from the eastern side of the Kingsmountains dappled the forest.

At last, the mother came into view. Young with long blonde hair bound over her shoulder, she was a true woodswoman of Alrou-Mendera, strong like Jherrick's own mother had been. Wearing breeches, a fitted hunting-jacket, and boots for foraging, her gaze swept the verge, a basket upon her arm.

And then her gaze swept the path ahead. She stopped. Gasped. Ran. Fell to her knees screaming. Weeping. Jherrick saw her glance at the flat white stone in the path, then pick up the sapphire ring, glinting in the sunlight. A long wail ripped through her, and she flung herself over her dead son.

It was somehow worse than the howl of wolves.

Bitterness twisted Jherrick's gut, and he melted back into the vegetation, a shadow in the underbrush.

"Has the lad been dealt with?"

Lhaurent den'Karthus's voice was smooth with a lack of care as Jherrick stood at attention in the yellow lantern light of the octagonal hall. Accessed through the Hinterhaft, this room had been made long ago for war-council during times of siege, occupied by a massive octagonal table and throne-carven chairs going to dust. Iron chandeliers hung from the highest gables, with candles unlit for eons. Poring over a red-inked map spread upon the table, Lhaurent sat in the largest of the thrones in his impeccable grey velvet doublet and robe, sipping a cup of tea.

"Well, den'Tharn?"

"He's been dealt with." Jherrick's voice was colder than the iron in the chandeliers as he responded, and Castellan Lhaurent glanced up, his attention piercing Jherrick to the quick.

"Do you have something you'd like to say, Khehemnas?"

"I serve the Khehemni Lothren. Whatever their bidding." Jherrick stilled his emotions, blank.

Lhaurent kept him pinned for a moment more. "Good. Then I have another task for you."

"May the Lothren guide me." Jherrick knew the words. Although he wasn't so certain about this particular member of the Lothren. The dead boy had not been Alrashemni Kingsman. That hadn't been for the Khehemni Lothren's cause, killing that boy. That had just been murder, ordered by Castellan Lhaurent to keep the Hinterhaft of Roushenn Palace a secret.

"Careful, young friend," Lhaurent murmured, his steel-grey eyes still watching Jherrick. "Remember the Kingsmen who slew your family and the reason your vows to the Khehemni Lothren were made. Understand that sometimes the blood of innocents must spill to serve a larger function. When you are tempted to be merciful, you must hone yourself. You have sworn to be the weapon of the Broken Circle, the spear for the Khehemni Lothren's purpose."

"Yes, my Lothren."

Lhaurent eyed him a moment further, then settled his teacup upon its gilt-edged saucer with a soft clink. "I believe you have rounds this evening in the West Guardhouse? With Captain Olea den'Alrahel?"

"Yes, my Lothren."

"Then I have a new assignment for you. Keep a close watch upon your Captain-General. She is serving a purpose currently for the Dhenra Elyasin, something outside her usual duties, and the Khehemni Lothren want to know what it is. You are dismissed from your regular tasks in the Hinterhaft until we know what Olea den'Alrahel is up to. If it's something decidedly intrusive to our purposes... we will have to arrange a way to dispose of her. She has become less than cooperative lately with me."

"May the Lothren guide me."

Though Jherrick eased, knowing he was dismissed from corpse clean-up for a while, something inside him clenched at Lhaurent leveling a threat against the Guard's Captain-General. But making his body serene and his face empty, as he had trained for so many years, Jherrick made certain Lhaurent would never know about that thought.

Nor would he ever know about Jherrick's mercy with the dead boy.

Lhaurent gazed at him for a long moment. At last, he waved one regal hand, his ruby ring flashing in the light. "Dismissed."

* * *

BEYOND THE GRIMY West Guardhouse window, Jherrick saw the sun was on its way down behind the Kingsmount at last. The late-afternoon gloom of the Guardhouse was stifling, and cataloguing the day's reports at his stout desk, Jherrick was looking forward to a dip out at Elhambria Falls in the Kingswood at the end of his shift. Carrying a dead lad nearly three leagues this morning had only worsened the knots in his shoulders, and he was craving the pummeling of the waterfalls. Near Jherrick's desk, the barreloak door of the Guardhouse had been propped open to get what little breeze there was today.

The view to the plaza suddenly affording him a glimpse of his quarry – Olea den'Alrahel.

Striding across the flagstones before the main palace gates, the market in the plaza nearly packed up for the day, his Captain-General moved with elegant purpose. Jherrick sat up, tracking her, watching Olea's long, wild curls catch the wind as she moved. Her hair was a shade of black so pure it gleamed blue in the late afternoon light, her grey-opal eyes gathering the sun as if she shone from within. Her hand upon her sword with her cobalt jerkin unbuckled, Jherrick caught a glimpse of the star upon her chest as she neared.

On her way to the West Guardhouse, Jherrick knew the Captain-General would spend her evening inspecting the lists, approving the payroll before it was brought to Chancellor Evshein den'Lhamann. She had a few hours of reading ahead of her tonight; reports of behavior from her Guardsmen, considering promotions and demotions. Jherrick knew her schedule by heart, even though he couldn't follow her by day. But the Khehemni Lothren kept Jherrick close to her here in the West Guardhouse, perfectly poised to gather everything the Guard-Captain knew – and whatever she let slip.

Jherrick watched her slender swordswoman's hips as she rounded the broad fountain in the center of the plaza. Picking up her stride, she was about to make her usual leaping run up the steps of the guardhouse, when a brawny young man sauntered by. Jherrick saw the man's gaze flick over Olea's Inkings, then narrow.

He spit.

Olea rounded on him. Jherrick saw her blithe mood sour as she took the insult with her straight dark eyebrows pinched in a scowl. Sidling from his desk with a grace he never exhibited in the guardhouse, Jherrick eased to the open door, watching their interaction from the shadows.

"Do you have something you'd like to say, fellow?"

Olea's bell-clear voice rang out like a duelist's challenge in the dusty heat and the man turned, facing her. Dressed in stonemason's roughspun with his sleeves rolled up from a hard day's labor, blue byrunstone chalk covered his hands, smudging his clothes and face. He spit again near the Captain-General's boots and drawing up before her like a bear, the mason growled, "Blackmark bitch."

Jherrick saw his Captain-General go deadly still. A smile stole over Jherrick's lips, watching the show – knowing what was coming.

"That's *Guard-Captain-General Kingswoman Blackmark bitch* to you, mason. Do we have a problem here?" Olea's voice was saccharine, her smile so sweet it burned.

The stonemason's thick lips screwed up as if he might spit again, and on her this time. Olea's sword flashed out faster than Jherrick could blink, the tip nicking the mason's stout neck. "Give me a reason, fool."

"You can't threaten a citizen!" The mason flinched back from her blade, incredulous.

"An insult to me is an insult upon your *Crown,* fellow." Olea's dark eyebrows arched, her sweet berry-ripe lips set in a flat line. "Do you want to take that risk? I don't have to kill you, you know. Only hamstring you and slice your wrist tendons and drag you down to the cells. You'll never stand again, never work again. Never walk again."

And though his beady eyes were furious, they also flinched. Olea was a ruthless bitch when she wanted to be, and Jherrick's lips curled into a dark-edged smile his Captain-General had never seen.

And never would see.

"You got any family who call you son?" Olea's words wafted through the muggy thickness of the late afternoon, up the steps of the Guardhouse. The mason took a deep breath, but Jherrick and anyone else watching could see he was bested. Such a big, thunderous man and Olea den'Alrahel had broken him, just like that.

"Yes, milady." He spoke sullenly, though with respect now.

"Then go home." Olea lowered her blade.

Jherrick's gaze flicked around, but few people were in the plaza now to see the stonemason's immense embarrassment. Without a word, the man growled and turned, hulking back to whatever hovel he called home in the King's City. Olea was putting up her sword when a man loitering at the far edge of the byrunstone fountain caught her attention.

Olea halted, watching him.

Jherrick stilled, eyeing the man also.

Sitting upon the lip of the wide fountain, the brawny fellow had a casual appearance. Broad arms were crossed over a muscular chest in a homespun flax shirt. Like a blacksmith, thick with muscle and iron-hard hands, he looked like he had spent a lifetime hammering steel or wielding it. With his military-cropped dark curls and a ragged scar down his face, he'd probably been discharged from service in Valenghia, shoeing horses on the battlefield and wielding a war-axe on the side. The rugged fellow stared out towards a weaver's shop, but neither Olea nor Jherrick were fooled.

Jherrick was certain the big blacksmith had been staring at Olea not a moment before – watching her encounter with the stonemason.

Jherrick saw his Captain-General frown, narrowing her eyes upon the fellow at the fountain. As Jherrick watched, the man's dark gaze flicked to Olea. Putting his palm to his chest, his other hand dropped to his side where a sword should have hung, and he nodded again. It was a small series of movements, but they filled Jherrick with electricity, a thrill passing through him. He saw Olea go very still, as the man settled back into his casual pose at the fountain.

Jherrick knew the man was waiting for Olea. He'd performed the Kingsmen salute, plain as porridge. But a chill passed through Jherrick, thinking about reporting this to Castellan Lhaurent. The dead boy's face rose in Jherrick's mind, and countless innocent faces replaced it, shuffling like a deck of cards – bodies he had disposed of for Lhaurent. The Castellan was Jherrick's only touchstone within the Khehemni Lothren, as per the rules of secrecy within the organization, though Jherrick was aware of one other Lothren member in the palace. Olea was Alrashemni Kingsman, the enemy, a member of the clan who'd killed Jherrick's family.

But how many bodies had she asked Jherrick to dispose of? Not a single one.

Jherrick slipped back into the gloom of the Guardhouse before Olea could march up the steps. His mind churning, his muscles clenched as her bootfalls slapped stone. When she finally shucked her baldric with a clatter at her scroll-strewn desk next to his, he'd gotten composure of himself enough to look around. His captain flopped into her chair, boots up on her desk atop a pile of papers. With an exasperated grumble, she curried her hands through her long tumble of blue-black curls, mussing them in frustration.

"Aeon-damned bigots."

"I'm sorry?" Jherrick played his affable, mousey alter ego as he turned from the stacks of tomes that chronicled supplies and inventory costs. It was a ruse he was comfortable with, this bumbling, shy personality. But Jherrick's mind was sharp enough to work at ledgers and lists, and that was no ruse. It was one of the reasons he was fit to maintain this post, both for the Khehemni Lothren and for the Crown. Jherrick paused with an open tome near his nose, blinking owlishly as if he couldn't read the text because he'd neglected to grab his sham spectacles from his desk. Olea grinned at him. Swinging her boots off her desk, she rose, fetching Jherrick's wire-framed spectacles from his desktop.

"Here. Don't ruin your bloody eyes. They're bad enough."

She tossed the spectacles to him in a nice, slow arc, the kind of thing any lad of seven could catch. Jherrick fumbled them, dropping his tome with a thick slap of leather hitting stone, and bobbling the spectacles too, which fell to the stone with a clatter.

"Sorry..." He mumbled, allowing a blush to flame his cheeks as he hastily bent to retrieve both spectacles and tome, awkward.

"My fault." Olea moved to him with a laugh, clapping him on the shoulder. "I should know better than to throw things at you. What have we got to do this evening, Jherrick?"

"The next batch of volunteers from all over Alrou-Mendera have come in." Jherrick spoke, stepping into his usual ruse with fluid ease. Years of practice had given him an easy familiarity with Olea, one that he realized suddenly, was no longer feigned. "Plenty of families want to send starving children into the Palace Guard this year, Captain."

"How many?" Olea's smile became a grimace.

"So far? One thousand and sixteen. And the consideration deadline is still two weeks away."

"Aeon!" Olea's lovely face saddened, her lips wry. "I could use the men on the walls, but we can't take even a hundred of those. Not with the rations we've got. This war... everything's going to the Valenghian front. Every bushel of wheat. Every barrel of pears."

"No one wants to send their sons to war, but all of them need the coin, Captain. The Palace Guard are the only faction not slated for border-holding against Valenghia or anywhere else. And we get three squares, plus extra coin to send home."

Olea nodded, her bright demeanor covered in a thoughtful shroud. She heaved a sigh, then settled to her desk, boots up again. Crossing her slender arms beneath her breasts, a soft scowl took her features. "Read us the lists, Jherrick. We'll sort through those thousand and see if we can't find any with promise before they make a long trip here for the physical trials. I'll not have starving families spend more coin to get their sons to the capitol if we can't take them. Even if it takes all night, we'll make a decision on them before morning and start drafting the proper refusal documents."

"Yes, Captain." Jherrick moved to his desk, fetching the vellum sheaves with the names he'd tabulated. He remembered to put on the spectacles he didn't need, then glanced at Olea. Gazing out the door into the wilting light of early dusk, her curls were haloed in a stray beam of sunlight. She mussed them absently, and Jherrick's body tightened for her. He had the thought that if she ever pulled a blade on him, he might just take a sword in the gut to hold her.

He pushed it away. He would report her movements; it was his duty. A duty he'd taken an oath to uphold. An oath inked in blood to the Khehemni Lothren.

"First candidate," he read from the vellum, peering through his spectacles. "Otis Altshi of North Cathrae. Aged seventeen. Ploughman, leather-binder, woodsman..."

8

ELOHL

As Elohl and Eleshen sat once more at the rough wooden table in the kitchen, Eleshen serving him winterberry tea with honey, Elohl realized he hadn't meant to be so harsh with her. It was habit from captaining men upon the glaciers, but battle was now far behind. When she slipped her fingers out to touch his in apology, Elohl stood and moved around the table, watching her rise also. They met, her fingers tentative as she reached up to touch his jaw. Questions still occupied her lovely eyes, but became drowned in ardor as Elohl corralled her close around the waist. Her cheeks flushed as he slid a hand beneath her hair, gripping her nape – feeling an animal tension rise.

An agony of heat and need surfaced between them, and Elohl's lips fell open, feeling it. Holding back, Eleshen watched him; daring him with her lovely green eyes. With a growl of frustration, Elohl pressed her to his lips, heat rioting through him with that kiss. Boiling heat flamed every nerve, hard and good – and in a rush, Elohl scooped Eleshen up, carrying her to the back bedroom.

Their second tryst was fast, a deed of forge-hot fury. But when it was done, they took comfort in each other with languid kisses and slow delight as the darkness deepened, chill with a night breeze off the glaciers. With only a single candle lighting the room, Elohl glanced down now, seeing Eleshen snuggled into his warm protection, curled up against his right side. Cinching her closer around her shoulders, Elohl kissed her temple, then allowed himself to fall toward sleep.

Dozing in the night's hush, Elohl languished, a deep blue lake behind his eyes. On his back with his left arm up beneath his pillow, the tips of his fingers touched his longknife hidden there. Cold steel filled his dream like lake-water; a numbing depth as he was submerged, every nerve deadened and chilled. But as he languished, something began to wake him, to heat – his senses suddenly boiling like the lake had become a cauldron.

Elohl's body twitched, his hand clamping down on the hilt of his knife. With his eyelids closed, he came fully awake – aware of something else in the room. Someone else. No board had creaked beneath an ill-placed footstep; no breath had disturbed the shadows of the room.

And yet as he cradled Eleshen, he felt someone watching.

Feigning sleep, Elohl allowed his body to relax. His breath was deep, his muscles calm as if he were still dead to the world. And yet, every nerve was on fire, his sensate sphere tingling wide. He didn't need to open his eyes; he could feel the fellow to his left in the shadows near the open door. Candlelight flickered across his lids as a breath of air disturbed it. Peeper frogs chorused in the snowmelt darkness. The intruder's presence intensified with coiled readiness.

Elohl's fingers tightened around his knife.

Suddenly, his neck tingled. A vision lit his mind, of Eleshen slashed and bleeding, Elohl with a knife piercing through his neck. The man came at him from the shadows then, a stab at his neck meant to take his spine by the full width of the blade. Faster than thought, Elohl rolled over Eleshen. Protecting her, he thrust back with his longknife as the intruder's stab missed him. Elohl met resistance, his longknife driven deep into the fellow's stomach. The man grunted. Elohl's right hand tingled, and flashing out, was just in time to seize the man's wrist as a second slash came. Slamming the fellow's wrist against the stout bedpost, he hauled his blade up with his triceps, gutting the intruder. Hot blood poured over Elohl's hand, wrist, and back. It was a mortal wound and the man spasmed as Elohl smashed the man's hand against the bedpost again. That hand sprung open, the knife clattering away. Whipping his head back hard, Elohl broke the intruder's nose with a sharp crack.

The man fell back with a grunting wheeze, hitting the wall and sliding to the floor.

Launching from the bed naked, an animal violence took Elohl, his senses on fire, his body taking over as his mind went to a primal place. Blood and filth slicked him as he pinned the intruder's knife-hand beneath his knee, then gripped the man by the face and slammed his head into the floor again and again. The man released his second knife and Elohl kicked it away, pinning his own longknife to the fellow's throat. Kneeling in blood and waste, Elohl had him. Filth leaked thick through the fellow's fingers as he clutched his abdomen, gasping.

"Move and you die!" Elohl growled, his blade poised to skewer the man through the throat. Some part of him registered Eleshen was awake, shouting in alarm and taking up the candle from the bedside – bristling with a knife of her own.

"I'm dead anyway." The intruder rasped, blood trickling from his mouth as it gushed from his middle, his breath heavy with pain. Elohl's strike had gone up under his ribs, deep. Not close enough to pierce his heart, but slicing enough of his lungs and the large artery near his spine that he wasn't long for this world.

"Tell me who sent you." Elohl growled, his longknife poised as he kneeled naked on the slick boards.

The man's coughing chuckle was full of froth, his blue eyes piercing Elohl with fervor even as they faded. "Abandon your protector, Kingsman, and this is what you get – more of us..."

"What do you mean, my protector?! And more of whom?! Tell me who you are!" Elohl snarled, a bestial rage roaring through him.

Limbs lax, his head fallen back, the assassin smiled a grave-ready grin as the blood-pool upon the floor formed a lake of black rouge beneath him."Too late, Kingsman. Too thorough. Torture us next time, but the outcome will be the same. We'll tell you nothing. And still, the Lothren will come for you..."

With a last bloody gurgle, the man's eyes dimmed. Elohl released him with a growl, slamming the assassin's head into the floor once more in fury. But the man had no complaints now, and nothing more to tell him.

Just like all the others.

The quiet roared in Elohl's ears like thunder in the silent room. Sitting back upon his heels, Elohl could feel nothing but the buzzing of his senses and the grip that tightened his muscles, ready for more fighting. His chin lifted, his entire body listening for movement in the night. They'd always sent two before, whoever these Lothren were. One to slash and sacrifice; one to try for Elohl's back. But this time, the dark hall and the vegetation outside were empty, not even a doe's heartbeat pulsing in the night.

Peeper frogs chorused again outside. Chill air freshened the room from the open window. A shiver took Elohl from head to heels, sloughing away his readiness. Taking a deep breath, the single breath of his training, he let his body shiver the rest off to the night. Reaching out, Elohl hauled the dead man away from the wall, then began to strip the intruder of his soft leather boots, his hooded assassin's jerkin, then the rest. He was liberating the man of his trousers when Eleshen finally spoke, her voice only minimally breathy.

"What are you doing?" Eleshen asked, the candle in her hand throwing shivering shadows over the scarlet-black blood.

"Looking for a mark." Elohl shimmied the man's pants off under his hips and shucked them, laying the assassin out bare upon the bloody boards.

"A mark? An assassin's mark? Has this happened before?" Eleshen breathed.

"Enough times." Elohl gestured for her to step forward with the candle so he could see better. She did, claiming more bravery than he expected, kneeling just outside of the black pool. Elohl saw nothing upon the man's flesh, no mark nor scar other than the regular ones born of battle. Reaching out, he let his fingertips peruse the man's skin instead, sliding his fingers over the man's shoulder, bicep, and arm, searching for a mark only his fingers could feel.

"Have they ever had a mark before?"

"No." Finished with the man's front, Elohl tunneled an arm through the sticky blood and hauled the fellow over on his face. Just an anonymous corpse now with his face down in the blood, it was easier for Elohl to see only dead flesh before him rather than a man. Starting all over, he scoured the fellow's back with his gaze, then his fingertips. Eleshen breathed softly at his side, her composure fierce and interested.

"How many assassins have been sent after you, Kingsman?"

Elohl looked around, to see a bitter humor upon her face in the candlelight. "I've had eight attempts on my life since I entered the High Brigade. Though they weren't all assassins."

"What?" Eleshen blinked. "Well, what were the other attacks?"

Feeling nothing but the usual scars upon the man's broad back, Elohl closed his eyes now, searching the entire body with his *wyrric* senses to see if he could feel anything else. "The rest were High Brigade fellows, whipped to anger over a perceived slight. Six came at me once. Four jumped me in a bar another time. But whether they were roused to violence by their own means or by someone else..."

"You didn't kill those Brigadiers who attacked you, I hope." Eleshen blinked, frowning.

"Killing a soldier of the Crown is treason." Elohl opened his eyes, holding her gaze with a glacial intensity. "Even if they do jump you six-to-one while your trousers are down in the privy. I've had my climbing-rope cut by men I thought I could trust, and found myself at the end of a blade in my bunk by fellows like this one here. I've been spat on and called *Blackmark* and *traitor* more times than I can count, and been lunged at by stupid fools in a drunken rage. I'm anathema in my own nation, and praise falls not at all for the marks I bear. I'm a honed sword pressed into service for a King that betrayed me. Is that what you want to hear? The romantic story of the Kingsmen, Eleshen?"

"I'm sorry! I just—"

"Being a Kingsman isn't glorious, not like the old songs. There are no heroes anymore, and no one ever called me noble. Let us be plain, for you've seen now what I am. I'm a killer, Eleshen. And I'm tired. Marked, and tired."

Eleshen fell quiet a long moment, watching him. Elohl rose to his feet, finished with the corpse. There was no mark upon the man. He knew that when he searched the clothes and weapons, there would be nothing there, either – just like all the others.

Beside him, Eleshen clutched her nakedness with a somber silence, though she'd not gone for a robe. Elohl sighed, compassion flooding him. Wiping his hands upon the dead man, he stepped to the bed where a blue night-gown hung upon the bedpost. Lifting it, he draped it gently around her shoulders. "Here. You'll get a chill."

"What about you?" She asked as she shrugged it on.

"I'm used to the cold."

"I'm sorry, Elohl." Her jade eyes softened, the tension in her brows easing. "For what you've been through."

Stepping close, Elohl gazed down at her, the ice around his heart slipping. Reaching out, he cupped her jaw, smoothing a climb-roughened thumb over her chin and leaving a small smear of blood in its wake. "Don't be sorry for dead men, Eleshen."

"You're not dead, dammit."

Elohl swallowed hard, his truth too plain in her words. "I may not be dead. But I can't live."

"Why not?" Eleshen's body was warm as she slid closer, her fingers stealing up and touching his where they rested upon her face.

"Because the justice that I want, I can never have. The King is dead. And the secret of my people's demise has gone with him to his grave. In all these years, I've discovered nothing. Not a breath of what happened. Not a word..."

Eleshen's fingertips slipped down, touching Elohl's Inking despite the blood on his chest. "Come to the kitchen. We'll wash and stoke the fire, then figure out what to do with – that." Her gaze flicked to the body, then back to the hardened plains of Elohl's chest. Her fingers stopped, touching a blistered scar just to the left of his Inking, over his heart. Flicking to his scarred wrists, her gaze returned to his chest as comprehension engulfed her. "This scar – you tried to burn it off. Your Inking."

"A year into my service." Elohl's gaze slipped to the cold hearth, to the stand of iron pokers there. "But I spasm when I try to inflict self-harm. It never takes. Just like my body never lets me lie still beneath an assassin's blade." Elohl couldn't look at Eleshen as a soft silence filled the room.

"Do you still want it gone? Your Inking?" She murmured at last.

Elohl took a deep breath, knowing what she was really asking as a stubborn heat flared deep inside his body. "No. I would like to earn it first."

Stepping back, Eleshen's fingers slipped down to Elohl's hand. "Come to the kitchen."

Elohl heaved a sigh. Trailing at the ends of the innkeeper's fingers, he came to her call.

CRADLING a bluestone mug across the kitchen table from Elohl, Eleshen's robe was tightly cinched as dawn sweetened outside, the light violet beyond the kitchen windows. The hearth-fire stoked, the kitchen was cozy once more, and dressed in his shirt and breeches, Elohl watched her also, his bare foot resting up on his wooden bench. After the violence earlier, they'd wrapped the assassin's body in a sheet, and still naked, Elohl had hauled the corpse out into the forest. Half the night had been spent scouring the bedroom, and only afterwards had Elohl washed, though it felt good to be clean and clothed now.

"So tell me why you never defected from the High Brigade." Eleshen began, re-opening their conversation. "Never sought out any Kingsmen over the years to find out the truth of what happened."

"To desert the King's army without proper dismissal is treason." Elohl's fingers traced the rim of his bluestone mug upon the table as he responded. "As a Kingsman, I respect the promise I made when these Inkings were confirmed upon me, though the King did not respect his promise to me."

"Even now, you have honor toward a man who wronged you." Eleshen murmured, shaking her head with a wry wonder in her gaze.

"My honor is superficial," Elohl murmured, his fingers tracing his mug. "I never deserted the King's army, but my Alrashemni Inking is technically unlawful. If any true Kingsman saw me and knew me for one Seal short of my full eight, my life would be forfeit. But my comrades and I made a choice ten years ago, to Ink ourselves though we were too young, because we feared the worst. We were desperate youths, and it was a desperate act we committed in the eleventh hour."

Blessedly, Eleshen didn't push deeper, though Elohl could see questions burning in her eyes as he sipped his winterberry tea. Inside, heat in his throat warred with a chill in his heart. One sought to flood out, following an inevitable river that led straight into dark memories. One was still, urging him to take his hard-won calm and leave all else alone. Elohl could feel the innkeeper simmering in her own righteousness, not comprehending his inner war of whether to pick up a life long dead. A life Ihbram had wisely warned him against resuming.

Especially considering tonight's events.

Eleshen simmered a moment longer, but at last sighed. "I am a stalwart supporter of the Kingsmen, I just want you to know that. When they were accused of High Treason, my family did what we could to rally in their defense. We sent a delegation to the King's City, but there was never any trial. The Kingsmen had just... disappeared. I just want to know the truth of what happened."

"I never found out the truth, either." Elohl scrubbed a hand through his hair, then over his short beard. Visions surfaced; a black door in the night, a snarling wolf and dragon rising before him. The glint of metals in the darkness, a puzzle now broken. Cerulean eyes like a deep blue lake as they gazed up at him. Hair so white it shone like pearls spread over the emerald moss of the forest floor as he moved with Ghrenna, breathing scents of pine tundra from her neck as she cried out his name...

Elohl pushed that thought away. "I should say no more. If anyone finds out you've been speaking with a Kingsman about the Kingsman Treason, you'll be a target."

"Still. I would like to know what happened to you. Besides, who is around to hear us?" Eleshen whispered, her pretty face lit by the hearth fire, her cheeks rosy and lips sadly secretive.

"I was followed here, Eleshen." Elohl spoke quietly, setting his tea aside. "Someone might come for you. Torture you for information. I don't want to place you in harm's way. Not after... your kindness."

"Well." Eleshen huffed, then sipped her own tea, taking a decisive swig. "I'm already *in* harm's way. After my family showed support for the Kingsmen, the Palace Guard came after us. We had to go underground; separate from each other. I came here with my father, rest his soul. My mother and two younger sisters went elsewhere. That's why I've been here these past seven years. Keeping an inn like a common barmaid when I should be stepping into my station as Dhepan of Quelsis in the wake of my father's passing."

Elohl couldn't help but soften, pulled out of his sorrows as he contemplated Eleshen's situation as the eldest daughter of a powerful Dhepan who'd been hunted for the very same reasons Elohl had been. He reached out, grasping her hand across the rough table, and watched Eleshen gaze at their clasped fingers. It was comfortable, holding hands with her. The ferocious Dhepan-heir-in-exile reminded him of Alrashemni women; unafraid, cocky. Eleshen didn't have battle-training, but she had spitfire.

And Elohl was fairly sure she had used that iron frying-pan at the door on more than one occasion.

He smiled, a true smile. Chuckled.

"What?"

"I was just thinking of your fry-pan at the door." Elohl smiled softly.

"Oh." Eleshen flushed to her roots. "Well. Not all men as are honorable as you."

"You just watched me kill a man tonight. How can you possibly say I'm honorable?"

"Why do you think you're not?"

The question took him aback. "Because I'm a killer, Eleshen."

"*When a rabid boar attacks, the sword that is honed the sharpest pierces best.*

That was a fairly rabid boar that invaded my rooms just now, wouldn't you say?" Her pretty mouth lifted at the corner as a beat passed between them, a moment of understanding.

"You should have been one of us, Alrashemni Kingsman." Elohl murmured with a slight smile. "You've the wit for it."

"Maybe I should have. But I was born into a different life." Leaning forward on her elbows, Eleshen was raptor-keen suddenly. "Tell me of the Alrashemni, Elohl, of your people's history. I've finally got one captive in my inn, and I want to know."

"I'm hardly your captive, woman." Elohl's mouth quirked.

"So you say. But tell me something you can speak of. Your people aren't native here, are they?"

"No." Elohl shook his head. "But we've been in Alrou-Mendera for a thousand years. We came from somewhere far to the southeast where sands cover the land, bleak and barren, ringed in mountains."

"Why did your ancestors leave their home?"

Sipping his tea, Elohl stretched his legs out along the bench towards the fire. Gazing into the flames, he thought about stories his mother had told him on cold winter nights, sitting around the fire in a kitchen much like this.

"There was a terrible war." Elohl murmured at last. "We had to leave. Even with the battle-skills my people had, coming from such a harsh place, it's said our abilities weren't strong enough to combat whatever occurred. The Alrashemni go far back, even further than that desert land. It's said we're originally descended from a people that lived to the east, beyond Ghrec and the Unaligned Lands. When our forebears arrived in the desert, we were literate, and gifted, arriving among nomadic desert tribes who knew nothing of mathematics and letters and such. We rose to leadership because of our learning and inborn talents, and for our clever negotiation and adjudication."

"So how did your people become associated with the King here?" Eleshen asked.

"It's said that the King of Alrou-Mendera once made a pact with my people, that they would use their skills on his behalf in exchange for us being left alone to govern ourselves. In the King's hour of need he could call upon us, the most capable warriors and mediators available to him, and we would honor our oath. Loyalty means much to Alrashemni. Though some groups of Alrashemni settled in other nations also, swearing oaths to lieges there. It was once said there were Alrashemni in Valenghia, and that Elsthemen was founded by Alrashemni."

"And your skills?" Eleshen asked again. "Are they magic like the stories say? Are your people imbued with fae talents given to them by demons, making them expert spies and assassins?"

"There's no magic precisely, not like the tales." Elohl chuckled wryly. "But we're taught certain skills with such precision for them to seem magical. Though some Alrashemni are born with... *oddities* that give them unique abilities."

"And did your unique abilities warn you of the Summons?" Eleshen queried, rapt with attention.

Elohl stopped, his eyes flicking from the fire to meet Eleshen's. In her deep interest, Elohl felt a promise of solace, encouraging him to unburden himself. Gazing back to the flames, Elohl could feel his story ready to slip out – like he'd only done once before when he'd told it to Ihbram den'Sennia.

"I saw the emissary who came from Roushenn Palace," Elohl murmured to the fire. "One of the King's Chancellate, den'Khenner. He came with a small guard but he bore the King's banner. They rode in at noon through the gates of Alrashesh, and my sister and I were in the yard, training at quarterstaves. My father Urloel stepped aside when the delegation arrived, and spoke with the Chancellor. We thought it was a request for men to go to the Valenghian front, as tension was high from constant raids over the border. But my father's face spoke otherwise. I'd never seen him so angry. He kept his voice low, but his face was a thundercloud. He kept flexing his hands as if he was going to draw his sword right then and there. He showed the King's emissary to the Receiving Rotunda, and my sister and I spied on the proceedings from the gallery."

"What happened?" Eleshen's voice was rapt as she leaned in.

"My father started shouting the moment the doors were closed. He erupted into a tirade of cursing, livid. I had never heard him curse except when having stitches sewn. The Chancellor was just standing there smirking, as if my father was proving his point. When my father finally calmed down, the Chancellor handed him a writ with the King's seal and signature, and said, *Three days, at dawn*. Then turned on his heel and left."

"The Summons?"

"Yes." Elohl sighed. "The Alrashemni Kingsmen had been accused of High Treason for unspecified crimes. To prove our loyalty, we were to march to the palace in three days, to re-swear our Oath of Fealty before the King. It was a sham, but my father knew we had to go. If we didn't, disobeying the King's Summons, it *would* have been High Treason. All those past their Eighth Seal were Summoned. Us Kingskinder between our Fifth and Eighth Seal were instructed to take the little ones to a safe place in the mountains until the Inked returned."

"But they never came back."

"It was worse than that. They *knew*, Eleshen." Elohl spoke quietly. "My father didn't trust the Chancellor or the Summons, and knew they were walking into something bad. They went heavily armed and dressed in the Greys, as if for war. Us older Kingskinder took the children out of Alrashesh to a secret lake fortress nearby. But five of us went on an errand, something that might have been able to stop the Summons and save our people. It failed. When we came back we were captured, and they forced the location of the other Kingskinder out of us. They captured all the children, split us up. I was sent under guard to the High Brigade that same afternoon, forced to swear military oaths or be put to the sword. I chose the oaths. Ten years of service, to the day. Yesterday."

"And your twin?" Eleshen's murmur was soft.

"She was made a Lieutenant in the Palace Guard a number of years back, which is how she found me. I used to have letters from her, and I wrote her every month. I've been writing this whole time, but I haven't gotten anything back for eight years now." Elohl settled at the end of his story. Eleshen was silent, then put her hand to his inner wrist. Her fingers perused his jagged scar there, and Elohl felt suddenly that he had to unburden himself of those events, too.

"I first tried to kill myself only a year into my High Brigade service," he murmured. "It seemed easier than to face everything I had lost, all the ways I'd failed. But all the times I tried, my fingers simply slipped upon the knife, spasmed. I could never quite seem to do myself in, no matter how many times I attempted it. And Ihbram... was always there to pull me back up from my fall."

Elohl stared at his wrist in the firelight another long moment. At last, he looked up, settling his tea mug to the table. Eleshen squeezed his hand. "More tea?"

"Please." He nudged his cup forward with climb-hardened fingertips.

"You know what happened in Lintesh, don't you, after the Kingsmen marched?" She poured them each another round of tea, then set the kettle back on its iron trivet.

Elohl took a deep breath. "I've heard the rumors. Were you there?"

"Yes," she nodded. "I was seventeen. Old enough to come learn statesship at court, so my father brought me to Lintesh. The Kingsmen marched into the city in flawless formation that day, clad for battle. It was frightening to see so many of them all together like that, like a sea of ravens. Rumor had already passed through the city of their treason, and most feared they were going to make war upon the palace. But they didn't. The Kingsmen didn't make a sound as they marched. You could hear a dove's wings in the Central Plaza, it was so quiet, like watching ghosts. They flowed up the palace steps, flanked by Guardsmen. When they shut the doors, that was the last anyone ever saw of the Kingsmen. My father and I waited in Lintesh seven days. But they had simply disappeared. My father was livid and sought a direct audience with the King, demanding to know what had happened. He never got his audience. Palace Guard came after us in the night at our lodgings. We had to flee."

"My sister heard as much, also," Elohl sighed. "Her letters stopped shortly after that. She hadn't found any trace of the Kingsmen within the palace; not a blade, not a buckle. She'd walked those labyrinthine halls from dusk to sunup every night, and in two years, found nothing."

"Vanished." Eleshen murmured. "Roushenn keeps its secrets. Cursed stones."

"Cursed." Elohl mused, rubbing a hand over his beard as images surfaced in his mind – a snarling wolf with its fangs deep in a roaring dragon, clawing the wolf in turn.

His fingertips settled to his mug, tracing the rim.

Fixing him with a piercing gaze, Eleshen stared at his Inkings, just visible over the edge of his shirt. "How did you know to Ink yourself, Elohl? What was this errand you went on in the three days before your parents arrived at the palace? What was it that could have saved your people, but failed?"

Elohl met her gaze, his eyes hard. "Too much, and not nearly enough."

9

OLEA

The sun was high, the morning sweltering as the weather had been for the past week. Hundreds of lengths above the ground, Olea made her rounds upon the Seventh Tier battlements of the palace, the bustling market far below minuscule, wagons of firewood looking like matchsticks at the fountain before Roushenn's gates. Her eyes raw from too little sleep, Olea blinked, pushing back exhaustion. It had been a week since her charge from the Dhenra to investigate the Kingsmen disappearance. An entire week of good dreams and nightmares as old wounds surfaced – sweet dreams of her and Dhenir Alden together and devastating ones of them exposed.

The wind shifted, the shrill cry of a ferrow-hawk coming to Olea's ears from far up the crags of the Kingsmount. Up ahead, her Second-Lieutenant Aldris den'Farahan waited for her on the battlements. She could already see mirth all over his chisel-cheeked face as he slouched against the stones in a way that showed off his honed body, one hand upon his sword with the wind rifling his short gold-blond hair. Olea glanced over as she came abreast of him, and he fell into step beside her with a winsome smile.

"Report," Olea spoke briskly.

"All quiet on Tiers Five, Six, and Seven, Captain. We had a thief climb as high as Tier Five last night, but three of my men took him down. He's been transferred to Undercell Four, if you'd like to question him."

"Damage?"

"None. We did a sweep of the Royal Galleries, the Dawn Room, the Throne Hall, and the Receiving Hall, but everything seemed in order. He had no valuables on him. Just a few weapons, a grappling hook, and a lock picking kit."

"Why was I not summoned?" Olea scowled, wondering why the regular protocol had been ignored.

"Pardons, Captain." Aldris rubbed his short blond beard, his green eyes relentlessly teasing. "When my men went to get you, they heard... *sounds*... in your quarters. I made the call to not interrupt you if everything was in order."

Olea gave her Second-Lieutenant her sternest eyeball. "In the future, Aldris, you summon me for a disturbance inside the Fourth Tier, no matter what. Are we clear?"

"Perfectly, Captain." Her Second-Lieutenant was attempting to be chagrined, but couldn't quite manage it – Aldris never could. Five years older than Olea, Aldris had served in the Palace Guard since before her time. Still in his prime, he was a handsome man, of quick temper but quicker with charm, indulging in his blond good looks. His wit was like a tiger's claws, but he was as competent as they came.

Though today, his rare lapse of judgment had saved Olea from explaining things better left alone.

"Just come get me next time." Olea sighed, mussing her curls with one hand.

"Yes, Captain." Aldris gazed at her sidelong with a grin. Olea could tell he was barely holding his tongue, and only because there were men of his garrison within earshot.

"Walk with me, Aldris." Olea gestured along the battlements and Aldris fell into step beside her. The Seventh Tier of Roushenn commanded a view of the entire valley, but Olea noted that Aldris' gaze was all for her today; furtive glances with a grin that said he didn't know whether to tease her more about the sounds his men had heard last night in her rooms, or behave himself right now. The heat was searing, and Olea tugged her shirt open above her half-buckled jerkin to catch the breeze, her Inkings bared above her halter's cleavage. Even though she was in a mood this morning, she was pleased to see Aldris grin more.

It was always thus between them, innuendo without substance.

"Tell me, Aldris," Olea gazed out over the byrunstone rooftops of Lintesh as she walked the edge of the tier, "what do you know of the Kingsmen?"

"I know there's a really hot one standing in front of me right now. Great ass. Nice tits. Black Inkings she likes to show off to get a rise out of people."

"Don't you have any respect, Lieutenant?" Olea eyeballed him, though her lips curled into a smile.

"Not so much, Captain." Aldris rubbed his short blond beard and grinned wider. "I was a pain in the ass long before you came along to flog me with your good looks and charm. Besides, I was never much interested in politics. Women, sure. Drink, definitely. Doing my job when I was on watch and getting into brawls when I wasn't? Absolutely."

"I know your sordid history, Aldris." Olea's mouth quirked.

"I was a hothead in my youth, Olea. What can I say?" He grinned wider.

"You're still a hothead."

"Touché."

"So what do you know of the Kingsmen?" Olea pressed again.

Suddenly, Aldris stopped her with a hand to her arm as he turned to face her, his expression shrewd and deadly serious. There was a good mind inside Aldris when he wasn't testing Olea's patience – and an even better swordsman. "What's this all about? Why are you asking me this now after all these years we've been friends? I thought you didn't like to talk about what happened to you..."

"I asked you a question, Lieutenant. Answer it." Olea's eyes hardened.

"You only take that tone with me when something serious is up." Aldris scoffed, not intimidated by her demeanor. "What's going on? Olea. I'm your Third-in-Command. Just what are you looking into?"

Olea took a long breath, wondering how to phrase things without dragging Aldris into her charge. Aldris was like Fenton, sharp as tacks and hard to fool. "I just need to hear what you know. What you saw the day of the Kingsmen Summons."

Aldris gave her a wary eyeball, and Olea knew she wasn't fooling him. But with a short sigh, he finally began to talk. "It was surreal, you know? I saw them march into Lintesh, from way up here. All the men who were Seventh Tier with me at the time are retired or transferred on now. I was the youngest of the lot, but we started wagering: on whether the Summons was true, what kind of treason the Kingsmen had committed, what was going to happen."

"What do you recall of the Kingsmen?"

"They were a hard lot." Aldris' gaze flicked to her chest, to the Inked star there. "Hard, but calm, you know? When I was a boy, I remember a bunch of Kingsmen settled a dispute among the grain merchants. We couldn't get bread here in Lintesh, not for a week or more because the merchant bank were gouging prices and the farmers wouldn't sell their grain so low. But the Kingsmen came, and damn if that dispute wasn't settled that very afternoon."

"And the day they marched on the palace?"

"I don't know much, sad to say." Aldris spoke levelly, holding Olea eyes with a serious gaze. "I remember going down to the barracks after my shift. I thought I would see a few Kingsmen wandering the palace like a lot of folk do at night. But I never saw a one of them. Maybe they were just a private lot, sticking to their rooms, but I didn't even see them in the kitchens for a late-nighter. And the next day, the maids said they'd all gone. Left in the night. Gone more surely than the Ghost of Roushenn does when the torches flicker. But how do so many people leave so suddenly? Strange, you know? It was too bad. I was hoping to see a few of them up close."

Aldris held Olea's gaze, and there was something angry in his eyes before the teasing glint returned. "But now I get to see a Kingswoman up close everyday. And someone else did last night, apparently. Up close and *personal* from the sound of it."

"Is there something you'd like to ask, den'Farahan?" Olea growled, not wanting to discuss her nightmares with Aldris and explain that she hadn't had a man in her rooms last night. No man had graced her quarters for nearly two years, not since Dhenir Alden's death.

But Aldris didn't know about any of that.

"There are many things I'd like to ask you, Captain, if they weren't likely to get my head on a platter." His lips curled up wryly as her noted her mood sour. "Such as why you're looking into the Kingsmen disappearance. But I know when to keep my mouth shut. So I'll ask something safer." Aldris' voice was husky as he stepped close. "Do you have magic thighs that men get lost in? Is that what happened to the poor fellow last night that the lads heard you sighing for in your rooms?"

"Yes." Olea glared at him, setting her hands to her hips now. "Happy?"

Aldris exploded with laughter, like he often did while drinking and dicing or walking the ramparts with Olea. He was a friend and he knew it, pushing the limits constantly. Sidling close, he teased her more, merciless. "Magic thighs, Aeon be damned! Who was the lucky fellow that got trapped in there last night? Den'Rhashak? Den'Sulith? I hear he has a monstrous cock, nearly as long as all six feet of him. Or are you fucking the Black Ghost of Roushenn? Is that why no one ever sees these men entering or leaving your quarters? He just slips through the walls into your bedchamber at night, sliding right in to his pleasure..."

"Stow it, den'Farahan." But Olea felt herself truly smiling now. Aldris was always teasing her out of her brooding, and her mood lifted until she could feel the bright promise of the day at last. Fenton was her safety, keeping her calm. But Aldris was her partner in crime, quick with a laugh and an ale.

"What other magic do you have besides your hot gates?" Aldris chuckled as he stepped away.

"The kind of magic that can pick out a conversation all the way down there." Olea nodded over the ramparts, down at the throng in the market far below. "If the wind blows just right."

"That old tale again?" Aldris' handsomely chiseled face made a tutting pout. "Would you swear it on your sword? Or better yet... on mine?"

"No *swearing* with your sword up here while you're on duty, den'Farahan. I'll hear it."

"I may just have to swear some very *specific* oaths, Captain," he grinned, "while I'm up here with my sword. To see if you can hear any of it."

"Make all the noise you like, Lieutenant, just be sure the wind is blowing in the opposite direction." Olea turned to go, walking along the ramparts towards the stairs down to Tier Six. But she had not gone fifty paces before a whisper upon the wind caught her ears.

"Wish I was the Ghost of Roushenn..."

She turned, giving Aldris a raised eyebrow. Stunned, he stared at her a moment, then burst into laughter so loud that Guardsmen all along the tier turned to look.

* * *

Down in the West Guardhouse at the end of her day, Olea was unable to concentrate upon the week's supply lists. As Captain-General of Lintesh and Roushenn Palace, it was her job to review lists not just for the Guard, but also for the companies at the Valenghian border as they came into the capitol. The tedious list of grain and fruit blurred before her, until at last Olea gave up, signing the whole damn thing. The guardhouse had emptied and she was alone now with Corporal Jherrick den'Tharn, her secretary. But just as Olea was about to dump all the week's lists upon young Jherrick's desk so he could do one last review before they went to Chancellor Rudaric den'Ghen, her attention suddenly alighted upon a curious discrepancy.

Olea hesitated at the edge of Jherrick's desk, the list still to hand.

"Something off, Captain?" Jherrick looked up with a frown, scrubbing a hand through his wheat-blond hair. He blinked blond-lashed grey eyes behind his spectacles, then took them off and cast them thoughtlessly to the desk. Jherrick hated wearing his spectacles and was forever fussing with them. Olea supposed it was considered weak for a Guardsman to need spectacles, and he didn't wish to appear more physically inept than he already was.

Jherrick had only four years in the Guard. And though he was wire-honed and strong, in the practice yards he was atrocious, with wild blade swings and balance so awful it was like both his legs had been put on backwards. The palace serving-lad with no family had almost been cut from the recruits until Olea had found out he was learned with numbers and languages. She'd needed someone with brains to work with her in the Guardhouse, and thankfully, Jherrick was exceptionally brainy.

And thus had secured his position at her side day in and day out, other than his occasional guard-duties in the Upper Cells.

"Jherrick..." Olea set the ledger down in front of him, her finger marking one spot. "Why is Lintesh sending two hundred barrels of prunes to the Valenghian border every month when we're only sending a hundred new recruits? The recruits only need a barrel apiece to keep their bowels regular when they get on front-rations."

Jherrick blinked at the ledger, but didn't don his spectacles. "Unusual constipation, Captain?"

"That would be some constipation, to need that many prunes." Olea chuckled.

Jherrick sat back in his chair, putting one boot up against the desk, thinking – the two of them often casual in the Guardhouse when no one else was about. "Maybe they're feeding the new recruits too much wheat-mush when they get to the border. Stopping them up so they don't shit themselves when they catch their first skirmish. Then they need more prunes to get everything out afterwards." Jherrick grinned like a younger version of Aldris, though something somber in his nature could never match Aldris' levity.

"Could be." Chuckling, Olea scuffed her boot on the floor as she put her hands on her hips. "But check into it, will you? It could be a calculation error, but that many prunes would imply we're sending far more recruits to the eastern border than we are. Unless there are magical troops appearing from nowhere to go fight for us against Valenghia... then we've got some prune thievery going on."

"The prune thief." Jherrick chuckled, his eyes glinting with mischief. "Let's see... whom do we know that is chronically constipated and would want to steal all the realm's prunes?"

"Lhaurent den'Karthus." Olea made a sour face. "Clean all his bullshit right out of that ass of his."

"You really don't like the Castellan, do you?" Jherrick leaned his chair back on two legs, lacing his fingers behind his head and giving Olea a considering glance.

"Does it show that much?" Olea lifted an eyebrow, though she smiled.

"As much as your Inkings do, Captain." Jherrick chuckled, though it seemed something dark shone in his grey eyes now.

Olea had to chuckle. But then she yawned. It was far too late.

"Tired, Captain?"

"This week has been a special kind of hell." Olea nodded. "Double-check those numbers, make sure they're correct before you run it up to Chancellor den'Ghen's quarters."

"Yes, Captain. And may I suggest? Chamomile, hops-bud, and fheldarin-seed. Boil the seed and buds first, then add the flowers. The tea will take you right to sleep."

Olea smiled and it was natural. She was fond of the whip-smart young man, even though he was terrible with a sword. "Have a thing for herbs, Jherrick?"

"My mother was a master herbalist, Captain." He gazed at her, thoughtful, though something in his eyes was still somber. "I learned a thing or two. Before she died. That tea puts me to sleep every time."

"Have trouble sleeping, do you?"

"I mean no insult, Captain. But how I sleep is none of your concern." Jherrick's blond brows knit as he sat back, evaluating his captain with his arms crossed over his slender-muscled chest and cobalt jerkin. Olea was mildly surprised at his frank rebuke, as he was usually quite amiable. But looking closer tonight, she saw he had shadows around his eyes and tight lines at the corners, as if he hadn't slept well, just like her. But as it was with Fenton, Jherrick was closemouthed about his life, and Olea respected privacy. She clapped him on the shoulder in conciliation.

"I did not mean to pry. Have a good night, Jherrick. And I will try that tea."

"Goodnight, Captain." He nodded, breaking into a smile. "Rest up. More missing prunes to hunt down tomorrow."

Olea laughed and Jherrick chuckled, then pulled the list in front of his nose and bent to, sans spectacles. Striding out the guardhouse door and into the cool twilight, Olea saw that traffic around the fountain had dwindled, the markets packed up for the day, awnings of shops around the plaza down and windows shuttered.

She was about to turn toward the palace gates, when suddenly a thrill passed through her. And turning, she saw him. The massive bear of a man with short black curls who had saluted her a week ago was leaning against the lip of the fountain yet again. Olea saw him note her watching; a subtle change in his posture, though he did not look directly at her. With grace uncommon for a man with such a blacksmith's solid bulk, he rose – striding off into the evening shadows.

Her heart thundering, Olea followed, knowing he wanted her to track him. Keeping to the deepest darkness like he'd been born to it, he strode a winding course through the evening city, down to the lower Tiers, Olea using her *wyrric* hearing to pick his footsteps out across portals and down byrunstone alleys. At last, he turned into a tight alley in the Tradesman Quarter, and Olea sidled around a shadowed corner, peering down the cobbles. Ducking through the double-door of a workshop with a silversmith's sigil upon the signboard, the man left the door cracked, spilling warm lantern-light into the alley's end.

Easing behind a stack of crates, Olea blended into the evening's shadows. Watching the doorway for a space of heartbeats, she scanned the hushed alley and darkened rooftops. Closing her eyes, she honed her hearing, waiting for the surreptitious footstep of anyone who might have followed her. But every clink of cutlery and howl of hungry babes was to be expected in the city's poorer quarter at suppertime.

Her heart in her throat, Olea strode forward with one hand upon her sword – heading toward the light.

10

GHRENNA

In the dream, the sun bore down, dust blowing around Ghrenna's boots as she, Elohl, and the three other Seventh Seals held their weapons bared in a prickly ring of death. The only sound upon the wind was their breathing at the center of the training-amphitheater in Alrashesh; so scared and young, untested in war as archers held steely attention all around then in the amphitheater's upper gallery. In their tight standoff, Ghrenna's dark blue eyes met Suchinne's steady brown ones, then moved back to the cobalt-jerkined Palace Guardsmen before her. The creak of leather and the crunch of boots in dirt came as swordsmen held blades bared around the five Kingskinder, also.

A pair of ravens winged above, calling out their displeasure as sweat trickled beneath Ghrenna's arms. Holding her yew-bow ready but not yet drawn, her attention was trained upon the palace swordsmen directly in front of her. Stillness filled her; tension for a fast draw. Slung across her back, her quiver chafed from running, and counting each breath, Ghrenna tried to keep her pain at bay. But already her neck ached, the sun too bright. One of her worst spells was coming because of their failure at Roushenn Palace today – and from the trap they'd stumbled into returning to Alrashesh.

Though pain was coming like a landslide, Ghrenna forced herself into further stillness, willing her body to hold firm. She was a faster draw than the palace archers around her – though if it came to that, she and Elohl and the rest would probably all die together.

"As I said," the stocky Roushenn Palace Guardsman in his cobalt jerkin before Elohl rumbled again. "There's no need to die today. Put down your weapons. We only have a few questions for you."

"Bullshit!" Dherran snarled from Ghrenna's left, incensed.

"We already told you." Olea's voice was reasonable next to Elohl. "Our families marched three days ago for Lintesh, as they were supposed to for the King's Summons. The younger Kingskinder have been sent to the Court of Dhemman while our families are away. Only us five Seventh Seals were left behind, to caretake Alrashesh. We were just out hunting this morning."

It was a weak ruse; Olea had always been a terrible liar. The Guardsman before them chuckled. "Can't negotiate your way out of this mess, girl. We're here for all you Kingsmen children. To keep you... safe. Trust in the King now and come with us."

"You're here to slaughter us!" Dherran answered with a hot-tempered growl. "Our parents were summoned as *traitors* by King Uhlas den'Ildrian! How can you say we should trust him? The Kingskinder are safe, as planned by *our people*, and we'll die before we give them up. So go fuck yourself. And your King."

Dherran spat at the man, florid. He was working himself into a rage, and once he did, even Elohl couldn't stop him. He was going to lash out soon, breaking their tight circle of protection. But from the corner of her eye, Ghrenna saw petite Suchinne step close to Dherran in her forest leathers, her fingers falling upon his fist where he gripped the handle of his sword, white-knuckled. The raging boar shivered beneath Suchinne's steady dark gaze – and though he growled at her intervention, he stepped back, their ring unbroken.

Though Ghrenna watched their interaction, something told her to run rather than stand here. Something rippled inside her, her headache drumming hard in her temples. Something was coming, far worse than the trap of Guardsmen they had stumbled into. Something she could feel inside her mind, crackling with the energy of an oncoming storm as the stocky Guardsman answered Dherran with a chuckle, resting his hands atop the pommel of his sheathed sword.

"Where is the famous Kingsman patience I have heard of?"

"It's being tested." Elohl stepped forward then, standing between the Guardsman and Dherran, whom Suchinne was still pacifying. Elohl was slender, but had an advantage of height on the blue-jerkined guard, and Ghrenna knew those grey eyes of his were unnerving when he used them right. As he did now, the Guardsman shifting, uncomfortable.

"Please." Olea spoke again, her pacifying gestures well-practiced. "We've told you everything. If your men are weary, you are of course welcome to rest…"

Lies.

A single word came from beyond the amphitheater, a strong baritone pummeling the air like summer thunder. The voice seemed outside Ghrenna's ears yet inside also; a rolling sensation within her mind that tilted her equilibrium and made her stomach clench in a violent knot. Summoned to that voice, Ghrenna felt a vision surfacing as lancing erupted inside her head. A firebrand thrust through her mind, splitting it as her legs turned to water. Her eyelids fluttering, she collapsed, spilling to her hands and knees in the dirt, her bow dropped to the dust.

Images ripped through Ghrenna's head as vomit rose. She clenched her teeth, keening, spasming, her entire body jerking like a spider in death-throes as the vision rolled through her. Vaguely, she was aware of Elohl pulling her into his arms in the dirt, urging her to breathe. His gentle hand cupped her brow until at last her spasms ceased and the images began to roll back, though her head still beat like an Elsthemi war-drum. The vision flooded her; every terrible promise of it, unescapable. A promise that brutal voice had made inside her mind – that everything she'd seen was about to become reality.

Right now.

"They're going to capture us, Elohl…!" Ghrenna gasped through gritted teeth. "The Kingskinder. I saw it. He's coming…"

"Who's coming?" Elohl murmured by her ear, cradling her close. "What do you mean, Ghren? What did you see just now?"

"*Witch!*" The big Guardsman growled, his face ashen as unease spread through the archers and swordsmen. That word speared Ghrenna; that taunt from her childhood in the frozen wastes of the tundra. So many people had spat that word at her, at a little girl who could only absorb the terror of their hate. And it had only continued as she'd grown. Never from the Alrashemni, but from villagers, simple people who knew only to hate someone different, someone *outlandish.*

Cradling her in the dirt, Elohl had gone very still, with a deep fury that Ghrenna could feel. He knew what that word meant to her.

"Leave her be." Elohl's soft murmur carried to each and every ear in the yard. Though his words were barely audible, his cold fury pressed through the amphitheater, carrying unmistakable authority just like his father. As he helped Ghrenna to her feet, she felt Elohl's chill tension. Everything had gone terribly wrong at Roushenn Palace this day, and though he was furious right now, he was also drowning. Elohl was a chasm of stillness to most people, but Ghrenna could feel his turbulent currents. In his depths, Elohl was despairing. Despairing that they would survive this. Despairing that he'd not found the ring from her vision in Roushenn's cavern.

Despairing – that he'd failed to keep their people safe.

But more than torture, Ghrenna saw in Elohl's storm-grey eyes the magnetism that drew them together time and time again. For a moment, neither could look away from each other, though the world crumbled around them. It gave Ghrenna strength as she at last pulled away, able to stand on her own as she found that place of deep stillness she needed to keep her pains at bay. Leaving her bow in the dirt, Ghrenna unsheathed her longknives, ready. Elohl turned to the Guardsman, leveling his sword as waves of rage rippled from him, glacier-cold.

"We have no quarrel with you, Guardsman, just as we have no quarrel with our liege King Uhlas den'Ildrian, to whom we Alrashemni Kingsmen are consummately faithful." Elohl's grey eyes bored into the guard, flat and merciless like chips of the Kingsmount. "But it's up to us to protect the Kingskinder until our families return. Not our King. So if you wish to die today, step forward to take us, or threaten the Kingskinder again. And know that any who slaughter a Kingsman or Kingskinder unjustly will pay the Fifth Price. This is the vow of our people."

Uncertain glances were shared among the swordsmen. The big Guardsman chuckled, but beneath his bravado, fear showed. "An oath of vengeance? That you'll come and kill five out of every six people we know if we cross you? Isn't that a bit extreme, lad?"

"Come for us, and see what Kingsmen truly are." Elohl's voice was cold, fury burning within him.

But the ranks of blades parted then, as an approaching figure crunched to the front, his face hidden in the deep shadows of his hood. A sliding sensation moved through Ghrenna, churning her stomach. Suddenly, she knew from whence that voice in her mind had come. The Guardsmen in cobalt stepped aside to admit the unhurried man – his jerkin of a foreign make, a herringbone weave of blackened leather set with silver studs, his gauntlets and greaves the same. A two-handed broadsword rode his back, his stature enormous, his torso and limbs mercilessly thick and strong in the way of the Unaligned Lands to the far north-east.

"What have the Kingsmen gotten themselves into this time?" The man's speech held a lilting accent as his chuckle grated like fists over gravel. Drawing his sword from his back in a long, slow arc, he leaned upon the pommel with the tip planted in the dust. "Oh, my thousand pardons. Kings*kinder*. These ones are Inked, but they've not earned it yet, have they?"

Ghrenna felt something slide into her mind upon the tide of that voice, like a silver-black coil slithering into her thoughts. Stiffening, she pulled back, deeper into stillness as her headache flared – though a keening cry spilled from her lips.

"Whatever you're doing to her, stop it." Elohl growled.

"See my face, boy." The man grated. "Know the one who will break your northern friend. And you." The towering black-armored swordsman lifted one hand, casting back his hood to reveal a strong-boned face of Unaligned descent. Deeply tanned, he was in his prime, with thick lips, high cheekbones, and grey streaks in his dark brown hair. As the swordsman eyed Elohl from his massive height, Ghrenna heard Elohl hiss in surprised recognition.

And the man's thick lips twisted up in subtle humor.

"I nearly had you at the Alranstone this morning, boy. But there's no Stone here to wrest you from my clutches now. Let us continue what was so rudely interrupted. Show me now. Let me feel what you witnessed last night that you shouldn't have. Open for me..."

And then, with a dire cry, Elohl fell to his knees in the dust, trembling violently. His gaze pinned to the man in herringbone leathers, sinew stood out in Elohl's neck as he strained against whatever was happening, his breath fast. His pulse pounded at his neck and he cried out again, shivering. He narrowed his eyes as if to close them, but they stopped, arrested, his dark eyelashes trembling from strain as his jaw clenched. The man in herringbone leathers cocked his head for a long moment, a strange smile suddenly lifting his lips. At last he moved his chin, and Elohl was released.

Panting hard, Elohl's head fell, a cry of pain issuing upon his breath.

"Nothing," the black-clad man murmured, bemused. "You overheard nothing of import in the palace. It is just as well. I do not welcome spilling the blood of Leith's line from your throat today. But you." The man's hard gaze came to rest upon Ghrenna. "You are another matter, girl."

Our kind get more than name-calling of witchery, you know. The man's dagger-keen thoughts pierced Ghrenna's mind suddenly, slicing through her carefully-woven protection. *We get burned as children. Set to the torch. You should see my scars, northern girl, when my village tried to burn me for what we can do. Count yourself lucky that your family simply gave you away. Ah... but you don't know what you can do yet, do you? If you did know, you could stop me. Open for me now. Open, northern girl... spill to me the secrets I want to know.*

With an awful sneer of dominance upon his thick lips, the man's consciousness slammed through Ghrenna like a fist. Her mind broke. Her barriers crumbled. She screamed as she fell to the dust, as his touch pummeled into her, uncovering her thoughts. Ghrenna couldn't stop him as she writhed in the dust of the amphitheater, her mind revealing her vision – showing him how he would find the location of the Kingskinder, how he would find the trail to the ruined fort by the old beech grove.

How he would find them all, catching every last child of the Kingsmen and clapping them in irons.

Vaguely, Ghrenna was aware that her wrists and ankles were being shackled as she writhed in the dust. Elohl and the others were shackled also, though they only screamed in pain as they twisted and writhed. The man in black armor had broken them all with a thought, rendering all their battle training useless as they curled into helpless balls from unceasing pain. He laughed as he had them hoisted like sacks of twitching grain over the shoulders of the swordsmen.

Ghrenna faded to darkness as she passed out, the man's baritone laugh still in her ears.

STARTLING AWAKE, Ghrenna's limbs flailed, knocking a wine bottle and her threllis-pipe from her bedstand in the semi-dark of the cavernous underground grotto. The bottle smashed upon the stone floor, wine and pottery scattering with a tinkle in the lamplit gloom. The glass pipe only rolled beneath her four-post bed, deep under the tattered laces and mildewed sheers of the canopy's drapes.

Her mouth full of cotton as her head pounded with a five-day ache, Ghrenna leaned over the bed to find her pipe, though doing so raised her pain to a cascading fury. Keening, she eased back to the tattered pillows, breathing raggedly in her sweaty silk undershirt.

"Hmm?"

Beside Ghrenna in the bed, honey-blonde Shara stirred, blinking blearily. Turning over, she nestled back down into the tattered covers, pulling them up over her mussed golden locks. Shara was still good and drunk from a scouting party they'd done only hours prior, but Ghrenna's inebriation had worn off during her nightmares. Pulling away the sweat-soaked covers, she brushed back her damp white-blonde waves. Tottering to her feet, she avoided shards of broken bottle as she stepped over arcane white sigils set into the stone floor, lurching to the tarnished silver washbasin at one edge of the vast byrunstone grotto. She made it just in time. Like clockwork, all the delicacies she had eaten the night before came up in a ragged rush as she vomited into the basin.

Ghrenna coughed, spat, and blew her nose. Lifting the basin, she tossed the contents down the cave-abyss to her left, hearing it splatter on its way down to Aeon-knew-where – far enough that she and Shara wouldn't smell it later. Rinsing her mouth with a cup of water from the pool of underground seepage near the basin, she spat over the abyss. Drinking water slowly, she at last felt her headache roll back.

Her senses clearing, Ghrenna monitored the underground cavern for intruders. Silence echoed to a ceiling of unseeable heights, despite oil-lamps that burned near the bed. Lace-filigreed stone extended upwards into the darkness, curling room dividers like unrolled scrolls. Sigils tattooed the ancient space; glyphs set in luminous white metal covered every inch of stone, interspaced by tarnished silver mirrors. Here and there, the writing gathered in inset cupolas of doors. And though Ghrenna and her guild-mates had thoroughly explored the cavern beneath Fhouria that they called home these past six years, they'd never been able to disturb those sigil-laden doors, nor pry the precious metals from the walls.

Something protected this place, indestructible to the ravages of time. And except for tarnish and dust it held firm like a fortress. All except the entry they'd found in Fhouria's sewers, a blue byrunstone door smashed into massive blocks as if it had burst outward from within, long ago. Each block had been covered with whorls of white metal, a monstrous sigil written *through* the sundered stone. Adopting the place, they'd set the broken entrance with traps.

And never once had there been any unwelcome intruder.

Ghrenna breathed a sigh as the cavern echoed around her, Shara falling back into soft snores in bed. As she stood at the basin, thinking back over her dream, she suddenly realized she'd had a vision after it – of a cottage with an Innship sign in the mountains. She'd seen Elohl, harder-worn than she had ever seen him before; the storm-grey of his eyes grim, a short black beard upon his jaw. His chiseled face had been hard, closed – in pain.

Ghrenna's heart flooded out, feeling his agony. The spreading ache in her chest swamped her and she hitched a breath. Elohl's despair was just as strong now as it had been ten years ago. Even though she could still feel his arms around her, she also felt that they were both alone in the wilds. Something held them apart – after ten years of dreaming about him Ghrenna had never seen any clue in her visions as to where exactly he was.

She had no destination, no place she knew to go find him.

But he'd been at ease in the last part of her vision, a woman in his arms. His heart was still aching, though soothed a little by kindness. Ghrenna flushed, seeing her vision again, watching them make love upon pine planks drenched in sunshine. Heating, she brushed a hand over her sweat-soaked silk, watching Elohl's ironspar frame, intense as he had ever been. Afterwards, Ghrenna had seen him standing bare-chested in morning's light, next to an Alranstone. Beautiful gold Inkings were writ upon his skin, and the woman was touching them – admiring him with her fingertips as if Elohl were hers.

Ghrenna watched this future or perhaps this past and found herself jealous. Dashing a hand over her eyes, she doused her face with water from the seepage basin, rubbing away sweat.

"Ghren?" Shara's sleepy murmur startled Ghrenna. She turned toward the grand bed, seeing Shara sit up, lit by the oil-lanterns.

"It was just a dream, Shara. Go back to sleep." Ghrenna murmured, currying water through her long white-blonde waves.

"Want to talk about it?" Shara yawned as she gave a languid stretch, her beautiful curves the envy of all women.

"No." Returning to the bed, Ghrenna sat, rolling out the screaming tension in her neck. Reaching out, Shara brushed a hand down Ghrenna's hair, and

Ghrenna stilled beneath that touch, soaking it in. Soothing like a sister, touch was a mutual comfort ever since they had defected from the Fleetrunners together eight years ago.

"You know you can tell me," Shara murmured. "Dreams are important, Ghren. Sometimes they give us insight." Ghrenna had still never told Shara she had true visions, but Shara knew Ghrenna had vivid dreams, strange and often accurate. Though they'd never precisely discussed it, Ghrenna was fairly certain Shara knew she was a Seer, after such a long friendship. Though Shara had never told Luc and Gherris.

"I saw Elohl." Ghrenna relented at last. Collapsing sideways upon the pillows, she drew her feet up onto the bed as Shara scooted close, cuddling Ghrenna's back and stroking her hair.

"Again?" Shara murmured, her breath soft by Ghrenna's ear. "How was he?"

"Alive. Barely."

"How many dreams of him does that make now?"

"Too many." Ghrenna absorbed Shara's petting, her eyelids settling closed.

"You've not had as many dreams of your other Kingsmen comrades, Olea and Dherran. And still just the one of your little friend, right? What was her name?"

"Suchinne." Ghrenna's throat closed. She saw it again, as she did whenever she was disturbed. Suchinne on the battlefield, run through by a spear but not dead. Pinned to the bloodsoaked ground and raped by five of their own Menderian soldiers before the light left her dark eyes. Suchinne, kicked like trash by the last man, furious that the Blackmark bitch had died before he was finished.

Dherran, finding his beloved hours later – becoming consumed by an unstoppable rage.

"Suchinne." Shara wound her arms tighter around Ghrenna. "*May the All-Mother protect our sisters, who fall in battle.*"

They shared a soft silence in the lantern-lit darkness before Ghrenna spoke again. "I dreamed of Elohl, in the mountains somewhere. He was with a woman, in a cheery inn. It smelled like pine and rosemary bread..."

"He's still out there somewhere, Ghren. Waiting for you." Shara spoke as she smoothed Ghrenna's white locks.

"He's not waiting for me." Ghrenna choked, swallowed back tears. Crying would only make her head pound, which would make her smoke more threllis, which would cost more, which meant she had to thieve more. Which meant more lives got risked, which was something Ghrenna wouldn't tolerate.

It wasn't practical to let her emotions run away with her.

Ghrenna's gaze alighted on her fat thieving-purse from Couthis Emry's mansion a week ago, tossed upon her gilded bureau by the cavern wall. Slipping from Shara's arms, she rose, padding to the bureau, her fingers taking up the soft deer-leather purse. She dumped it out, her cut of the spoils clattering upon the bureau's top – a number of pieces of jewelry plus a hefty sum of gold and bank notes. Running her fingers over a gilded amulet with a snarling wolf, she picked it up, examining it. The wolf wasn't the same as her vision; the one on the ruby ring Elohl should have found in that cavern ten years ago. Her Seeing back then had been wrong. The only vision that had ever been wrong. Elohl's face filled her thoughts and Ghrenna's throat closed.

"What is it?" Shara murmured from the bed.

"Nothing. Just an oddity for my collection." Turning towards a teak table at the far end of the grotto, Ghrenna added the amulet to her collection in a wide basket there. Her fingers roved the eighty-odd pieces in the basket – jewelry depicting a dragon or a wolf, none were the same as that ruby ring she'd Seen ten years ago. Fine-wrought sundials in layered metals cluttered the basket also, with wound gears, pieces of Glockenzart from Praough worked by specialty jewelers.

And yet, none of these pieces looked even remotely similar to the intricate clockwork Elohl had found all those years ago. That piece had been like this cavern, its true nature filled with a magic lost to time. Ghrenna had felt it when she'd touched the scattered gears in Elohl's belt-purse after he and Olea had stumbled through the Alranstone. A tingle in her mind, of *wyrria* and secrets. Secrets they might never know.

Secrets that were too late to uncover.

Tracing the wolf medallion in the basket, Ghrenna turned from the table, padding back to bed.

11

ELOHL

Elohl had stayed for over a week at the inn. Eleshen had put him to work, and the days had passed in a small, comfortable life of scrubbing laundry, chopping firewood, and thatching the roof of the barn out back. She'd charmed him with her feisty ways and humor, the first sweetness he'd truly enjoyed for ten years. With the routine had come a kind of contentment, though restlessness had grown in Elohl during his stay; of things left unfinished. As the days passed, it finally became overwhelming, until this morning Elohl had blinked wide awake knowing his peace could not be found here – no matter how serene this simple life could be.

Now, Eleshen and Elohl faced each other in the main room of the guesthouse, Eleshen tossing her blonde braid defiantly as she planted herself right in the middle of the doorway. The frustrating little woman had packed some clothes and an overabundance of food the moment she saw Elohl making preparations to leave. And now she stood in front of the door wearing men's breeches and a laced leather bodice, her arms crossed and scowling, her petite, curvaceous form barring his way to the road.

"You can't come with me to the King's City," Elohl growled for what felt like the hundredth time. "It's dangerous in Lintesh, and I'm a marked man."

"Like Halsos I can't," Eleshen spoke back, raising a golden eyebrow at him defiantly. "It's dangerous *here*, Elohl. Your enemies, whoever they are, followed you. So like it or not, I'm already a target. And I'm safer with you."

Elohl wouldn't lift a hand to forcibly move her from the doorway, even though irritation rose hot within him. With a low growl, he turned, marching for the door to the back porch instead. Like a barbed dart, Eleshen scurried around him, chucking her pack in his way and thrusting her arms out so he nearly bowled her over – as she managed to trip over her boots and fall into his arms.

Which he was starting to believe wasn't entirely a lack of coordination.

But once Eleshen was near, Elohl caught her spice and lavender scent, and his frustration made it even more alluring. He meant to tell her to move – but found himself shucking his pack to the floor as he drew her close, kissing her hard. She was on her tiptoes, kissing him back as Elohl wrapped his arms around her waist. Fire twisted in Elohl's gut as he drew back from their kiss at last.

"You'll be killed if you come to Lintesh. Move aside and let me go alone."

"Make me." Eleshen spoke fiercely, her cheeks hot and her jade green eyes hotter as she held him close. "I'm not letting you go off by yourself, as frustrating as that may be for you. I'm a frustrating woman. But you need a frustrating woman in your life to *keep* you alive."

Elohl's hands dropped from her like he'd been burned by firebrands – her words far too much like Ihbram den'Sennia's. Elohl had been living like a dead man for years, his glacial calm a replacement for true feeling. And now that he'd begun to thaw, emotions roiled, unpredictable and wild. Eleshen baited that raw part of him, sinking her spice and temper into his ice and cracking it wide.

But she couldn't follow him to Lintesh. Elohl knew danger would dog him all the way because of his Inkings. He had to do something that would make sense to her stubborn temper, that would convince her of the danger he drew like a lodestone.

So Elohl did something he'd never done. Like a calloused cur, he set one hand to a longknife on his harness, drawing cold steel. He only bared his blade halfway, but the warning was enough. As Eleshen moved back with a squeak of astonishment, Elohl sheathed his knife, swiped up his back, and walked out of the guesthouse, banging out the back door and tromping down the porch. Rounding the side of the inn from the backyard, he marched on without looking back, his weatherworn boots sending up puffs of dust on the sun-dry road – though his heart clawed at him for the vicious move he'd just pulled.

But he'd not gone fifty paces before his *wyrric* senses felt someone following. A scuff of dainty boots came to his ears; a faint scent of spice breathed on the wind. He walked on, seeing if she would stop, but it was a vain hope. Eleshen wouldn't be deterred, whisking solidly along in his wake. At last, Elohl closed his eyes, taking the single breath of his training. He stopped and turned, eyeing Eleshen in his best commander's manner, staring her down. Seeming almost tiny beneath her massive pack, she fiddled with her braid but didn't look away, her chin elevating like a defiant horse.

"What?" She quipped peevishly, pursing her lips and setting her hands on her hips. "You need me. Even an idiot can see you're going the wrong way."

"I came that way ten years ago, and I remember it like a nightmare." Elohl pointed down the road to the south. "I'm not going the wrong way. Go back to the inn, Eleshen. This isn't a game." Turning, Elohl hefted his pack higher on his shoulders and marched on.

"I'm not playing, you great idiot!" She shouted as she struggled to run beneath the weight of her pack, huffing to catch up with him.

Slowing as if she pulled strings that went directly to his heart, Elohl sighed and turned. "There's no shortcut to Lintesh through the mountains."

"Not for *regular* people. Only for Kingsmen." Eleshen's eyes glittered as she smirked like she had all the apples in the world stuffed in her blouse, pointing some distance up the mountain to his right. "The way to Lintesh for a Kingsman is *that* direction."

"An Alranstone?" Elohl nodded up the mountainside, understanding at last. "There's one up there?"

"Perhaps." Her smirk grew wider. "But you'll have to let me come with you. Besides, traveling by Alranstone would save you the week you lost dallying with me."

Elohl stilled, remembering the last time he had journeyed by Alranstone. A wrenching sensation filled him, a twisting grip in his guts as if some great beast had seized him, trying to rip him apart. A grotesque rush and pressure like being drowned and threaded through a needle all at once surged through him as he felt a thunderclap in his ears. All of it came rushing back, as he remembered his failure all those years ago. Of returning empty-handed, to an empty Alrashesh.

"No." Elohl murmured to the breeze.

"Why not?" Eleshen's brows lifted, her pretty heart-shaped face surprised.

"Tales say Kingsmen can travel by Alranstone any time they please!"

"The old tales are misleading."

"Well," Eleshen scuffed the heel of one boot through the dirt. "You could at least *try* it. It's a half-day's hike, up in a valley just over that rise. There's a bunch of tumbled ruins, a settlement with a Stone in the middle of it all. We won't be set back but a day if it doesn't work."

"Unmarked can't travel by Alranstone. It will leave you behind if I go that way." Elohl gazed up the ridge, searching for a spot level enough to indicate a road.

"That's crap." Eleshen pursed her lips like she'd eaten a sour grape. "I've heard Alranstones work for Kingskinder. They're Unmarked."

"Fine." Elohl sighed, then gestured towards the ridge. "But if you get left behind by the Stone, leave it be. Don't come following me all the way to Lintesh. It wouldn't be safe for you to travel alone."

"Any safer than it is for me to keep an inn alone?" Her eyebrows quirked as she smirked, then pushed past him, marching down the road to the south.

With a torpid sigh, Elohl hitched his pack higher upon his shoulders then picked up his feet, trailing in her dust. Not half an hour later of mutual stubborn silence, they spied a deer-track sprouting off to the west through the ditch. But the levelness of the ground where the track went suggested ancient stones beneath the verge, and as Elohl stepped off the road to scuff his boot down through a hummock of moss, he found flat flagstone beneath the tilth. Squatting, he brushed moss from the stone's surface, noting how level it was.

"This was a road, once." Elohl spoke, intrigued as he gazed up the ridge, the track switching back at long intervals like a well-planned road would have. "A well-traveled one. Men don't put this much effort into just any thoroughfare."

"My father and I used to take this track up to the ruins." Eleshen responded as she squatted next to him. "Most of the local hunters and trappers know it, though no one comes here on purpose. Legend says the ruins were once a keep, a fortress stronghold. When we get there, you'll see, the foundation-stones are massive. But most of it is fallen except one main quadrangle that's all blocked with tumbled stones; everything looks like it was badly sieged. Father and I found stone blocks we think came from the towers nearly a league down the ridge."

"Probably just ripped downstream by snowmelt," Elohl commented. "I've seen boulders taken some distance in the mountains by spring floods."

Straightening, Eleshen gazed along the main road, back the way they'd come.

Shading her eyes, she squinted and Elohl rose from his crouch, glancing also. A lone man walked the road in the midday sunshine, his bearing erect and his stature fit. As Elohl squinted, he could make out a pack upon the man's shoulders, and the cut of his jerkin and trousers were military. High Brigade, in fact. As the man drew nearer, Elohl made out the lively features and pale blond hair that was Jovial den'Fourth, one of his own climbing team.

"Trouble?" Eleshen whispered at his side.

"No." Elohl shook his head, puzzled. "One of my former men. But what he's doing coming this way I can't rightly fathom. He's not due to be discharged for two more years yet."

"Maybe he's come to find you? Maybe your discharge was a mistake?"

Elohl cocked his head, his dark brows furrowing. Her words seemed logical, yet something within him stirred like a mongrel dog prowling around an uncommon scent. "Arlus den'Pell gave me a formal dismissal himself. There was no mistake. Unless there's been a tremendous attack over the passes from Valenghia and they need me – but then they would have sent a rider. Stay behind me. I don't expect trouble from Jovial, but he's... lecherous."

"Would you be jealous if he tried to kiss me?" Eleshen batted her eyelashes.

"Just stay behind me." Elohl sighed. She did.

Jovial was another minute approaching, hailing Elohl with a relieved smile upon his face, his blue eyes bright over his high cheekbones. "Lieutenant den'Alrahel! Thank Aeon! You've no idea what an ordeal it's been, getting even one man through to you!"

"Jovial!" Elohl took a step forward, closing the gap as his man drew close. "What's the matter? Trouble in the passes?"

"Trouble for sure, that needs addressing, sir."

Slinging his pack to the dust, Jovial moved forward with his arm proffered in greeting. Elohl stepped in, reaching to clasp Jovial's arm. When suddenly, his muscles twisted so badly that Elohl stumbled, his hand spasming past his subordinate's grip. Shock flooded Jovial's face, as Elohl's own surprise rushed through him at his body's reaction.

But then he saw the short knife hidden in Jovial's other hand, poised to thrust in and gouge his kidneys the moment they clasped in greeting. Eleshen's shriek confirmed what Elohl's body had already known – as Jovial recovered, a snarl twisting his handsome features as he spun in, jabbing and swiping. A trained fighter, the man was a surge of mad intent as Elohl stumbled back, blocking like wildfire as shocked flooded him. Slipping Jovial's thrusts, he managed to get both hands to the longknives on his weapons harness, protecting Eleshen as he corralled her behind him.

"Assassin!" Elohl snarled, fury seething through him as he brandished his weapons. "Tell me who you are!"

"Don't you know me, Elohl?" Jovial's eyes were chips of ice as he threw down the short assassin's blade and pulled his own longknives now for a fight. "I'm Jovial den'Fourth. Just one loyal Brigadier, come to collect his commander. Or rather, your body."

Elohl roared, blistering with anger – but in that moment, his adversary snarled and lunged. They clashed, muscles straining in a clinch, their breath hot face to face as they struggled. Suddenly, Jovial slipped out, taking a nasty cut on his shoulder as they began to truly fight, slipping and swiping. Close and fast, a knife-fight was deadly. And though Elohl's *wyrric* senses spared him anything deep, he had a number of slashes in the first moments of the fight, shallow cuts above his thick leather bracers, his shirtsleeves shredded and nicks on his neck.

Jovial was the same, his knives flashing as Elohl went silent, entering a space of utter precision. A cut swiped at his windpipe and Elohl blocked with a forearm. Lancing in, his knife dove for Jovial's jugular and the man slipped sideways though Elohl's blade left a gash. Compacting, Jovial drove a set of fast swipes at Elohl's groin, and twisting, the swipes hit Elohl's hips, scoring his belt and leathers instead. Elohl lunged, swiping to scissor-gut Jovial, and pivoting, Jovial kept his belly whole as his blade dove at Elohl's flank. Slippery with non-lethal cuts, both men breathed hard, a musk-thick sweat evaporating to the morning as the iron tang of blood filled the air.

But Jovial had been on Elohl's climbing team eight years. And there had been that time on a climb over Selten Pass when an icicle had taken Jovial in the side of his left eye, leaving that eye half-blind. Elohl seized that advantage now with cold precision, driving deep into Jovial's blind left side and taking a nasty swipe across his chest to get in – slicing Jovial's forehead. Blood poured into Jovial's eyes and he roared blind, blocking too low as Elohl dug at his ribs, thinking Elohl meant to shiv him. Unseen, Elohl angled his longknife in and up, burying the slender blade deep between Jovial's ribs.

Right into his heart.

The man gasped. His knees buckled at the killing blow, but rushing energy made him keep fighting. He swiped again and Elohl took it across his back, feeling it score through his leather jerkin as he shoved his blade deeper, slashing with his other longknife across Jovial's throat. Jovial crashed to the ground and Elohl let him fall with the first blade still buried in him to the hilt.

Only one sentence escaped his ruined throat as he died. "Den'Sennia can't save you now..."

Breathing hard, Elohl stood over the body as emptiness blew through his heart like a chill wind. Still vibrating from the fight, he barely felt his wounds. Jovial had asked for no mercy and Elohl had shown none. And now, gazing down at a face he knew like a brother, Elohl felt his throat grip at last. A man he'd once called friend lay dead before him, his bright blue eyes glassy and dull. A man he'd once trusted, commanded, trained, stood side-by-side with upon the battlefield with snow up to his knees and blood up to his elbows.

Elohl crouched, his gaze lingering upon Jovial's once-laughing face. "Just another assassin... just like all the rest."

His own pronouncement knifed Elohl to his core as he wondered how many more were out there – men he had once called friend now tracking him. Emotions warred within him; disgust, rage, sadness. With a sigh, Elohl retrieved his knife and wiped it on the body. He couldn't bring himself to shuck Jovial's clothes to look for marks. Elohl had seen him naked at the bathing-houses of High Camp enough times to know he bore nothing but the ordinary scars of battle.

Gazing at Jovial a moment more, Elohl drew his glacial calm back into place. Standing, he winced as he felt the nasty slash across his back at last, seeping with blood beneath his jerkin. The chest was bad too, runnels of blood making Elohl's bracer slippery and coating his hand. His gaze flicked to Eleshen, seeing her frightened nearby, breathing fast. But she'd stood her ground just like last time, her own boot-knife in her hand, her pack shucked to the dust.

"You would have fought for me." Elohl murmured, something about her defiant manner touching him.

"Glad I didn't have to." She breathed back.

Turning to the trail by the roadside, Elohl nodded up the mountain. "Up off the main road?"

Eleshen nodded, wordless for once. Elohl grasped the wrists of the dead man, hauling him off the road and under a spreading cendarie that would hide the body from any passersby. Returning, he scuffed dirt with his boots, covering the blood that had soaked into the road until it looked like a pack of wolves had simply brought down a deer. The silence persisted as Eleshen and Elohl took the mossy track beneath ancient cendarie and pine, boxwood and birch.

But Elohl's wounds called. At a stream up the ridge, he shucked his pack and pulled off his sliced-up shirt and jerkin, washing blood off in the water. Breathing deeply to manage the pain, he let Eleshen tend the deepest wounds on his back and chest, then fished out his jerkin and shirt of his Kingsman Greys from the bottom of his pack and donned them. Climbing again in silence, they listened to the chirr of tit-widgets as they switched back again and again, the trail ascending thousands of feet up along the ridge. And though it was grueling, Elohl managing his wounds and Eleshen managing her enormous pack, they said not a word as they tromped determinedly on, each buried in thought.

It was late afternoon by the time they gained the valley beyond the ridge. In the sun's slanting rays, they found the secluded valley true to Eleshen's word; a sprawling ruin nestled in the side of the mountains. The foundation-stones of a massive keep still rose from the ground, though the turrets were mostly decimated and the forest had all but taken it back. A number of smaller foundations, houses and outbuildings, stood in precise semi-circles along more byrunstone roads out from the keep at the valley's southern end. But enormous trees had worked their roots deep into the sprawling ruin, some nearly three hundred years old, and all was quiet as specters beneath the spreading canopy.

Eleshen led the way, and at last they came to a clearing of tall grasses and dirt over flagstones. Angling up the mountainside and dug down into the ground, the ruin arced upwards in a series of tiers, forming an amphitheater, at the bottom of which was a massive Alranstone. Larger than any Elohl had yet seen, this Stone towered four man-heights, and had not two or three eyes amidst the whorls and carven sigils, but seven. One above the next, climbing to its pinnacle, all of the eyes were lichen-covered and closed, serene in their everlasting sleep.

Dropping his pack, Elohl approached, marveling at the Alranstone. He'd never really sensed them beyond the usual pressure he felt from stone, but this one felt different, compelling. Elohl felt the rush of the Stone's awareness as he approached within its Sight, prickling his wounds. As if it pulled at him, Elohl stepped up, extending one hand to touch the rough-chipped surface. A tingle crawled across his palm and wrist, like a wind blowing through his body and up into his mind. Disorientation swept him as if he looked out over the entire amphitheater, and Elohl had the sudden urge to climb the thing – a need to sit at the very top of the Stone and stare out over the valley and the highmountains beyond.

"So what do we do to make this thing work?" Eleshen spoke at his side.

Elohl blinked, pulled from his trance. With a blowing whisper, the sensation of vertigo was gone, and he glanced over to see Eleshen gazing up at the Alranstone's towering height. "Put your hand to the Stone with mine," Elohl murmured. "I'll say a few words, then it should take us in. It will hurt badly, but don't fight it."

"Hurt?" Surprise flitted over her features.

"Badly." Elohl repeated, preparing himself as much as her. Rolling out his shoulders, he readied himself for the pain. Memories rose of the last time he'd done this, and Elohl drowned them deep. Concentrating on the sensation of the rock beneath his palm, Elohl murmured, "Elohl den'Alrahel, den'Urloel, den'Alrashesh. Blessings to the Kingsmen. Blessings to the *Alrashemni*. Open, Stone of Alran, pass me free."

A shivering tingle lanced through his skin, a moment of recognition from the Stone; that someone stood penitent before it and words of passage had been spoken. But then it was gone. Looking up, Elohl saw all of the eyes upon the towering column were still closed. Disappointment clenched his gut, though relief eased his shoulders. He sighed and stepped away, walking to his pack and rummaging through it for something to eat. Finding some mutton jerky and a roundel of cheese, he sat upon his pack just like he once had when stymied upon a climb – taking the time to rest and feed his belly, and to think.

Though his fingers still tingled with an urge to climb.

"That's it?! Are you jesting with me?" Eleshen strode up beside him with a huff, dumping her pack next to his. "I don't get it. You're a Kingsman! Why didn't it work for you?"

"Alranstones are unpredictable, Eleshen." Elohl chewed his jerky as he stared up at the towering byrunstone column, his wounds throbbing as if they'd been reopened by the Stone's strange reaction to him. "Alranstones are a cautionary tale among the Alrashemni. Three hundred years ago, there was a war in one of the Valenghian border passes, and Rakhan Tourliat den'Tharn led a great host to a Stone rather than towards the battle, because he thought they could make better time. But it wouldn't open for him. Every man and woman in his host tried their hand, and failed. They lost two days, then had to turn around and trek into the mountains. The battle was over when they arrived. The pass was lost, and they had to fight in the Longvalley. It was a bloody skirmish, lasting a full summer, when it could have been solved in days. Rakhan Tourliat lost his life that summer, as did most of the five hundred he led to war. All because of the Alranstone."

"Aeon be merciful!" Eleshen spoke, her golden brows arching. "But you said you've traveled by one before."

"It's said that great need allows Alranstones to see you." Elohl gazed up at the seven closed eyes as emotions roiled inside him, his fingers still itching to climb the column. "But not always. Sometimes they're asleep, buried so deep in dreams they don't recognize you. Sometimes they're awake, but deem you unfit to travel. Tourliat needed to protect the border pass for his King, but even the need of five hundred Alrashemni was not enough to grant him passage. And my need? To find a sister who might be dead and look for a people ten years gone? Apparently, my need isn't enough."

"I'm sorry, Elohl." Eleshen's hand settled upon his arm. "But did you feel anything from the Stone? Anything at all?"

"I felt its awareness. But it passed on."

But even as Elohl spoke, tingling speared his hand and wrist again, his fingers cramping as if they were already climbing. Ghrenna's face surfaced in Elohl's vision, her lake-hued eyes with her long dark eyelashes drowning him. Her white-blonde hair was gathered in a loose bun, a few wisps loose by her high cheekbones. Her head turned suddenly as if she was attentive to him, baring her slender throat and fine jaw. The movement was elegant and alert, with the precise stillness that had drawn Elohl to her all those years ago. Her hair was done in an ornate weave; thick braids twisting through each other like she belonged among the wild kings of the north.

But Ghrenna had never worn her hair in braids, and Elohl blinked, confused. A wind blew through him like a northwesterly over icecaps and the image of Ghrenna passed. Elohl shivered, unnerved by the sensations he was having near this Stone. Glancing over, he saw Eleshen staring up to the Stone's heights, shading her eyes with one hand from the late-afternoon sun.

"So what do all the eyes of an Alranstone do?"

"Truly?" Elohl gazed upwards also. "I have no clue."

12

THEROUN

Chancellor Theroun den'Vekir rubbed a battle-hardened hand over his temples and down his grey-blond beard as he gazed down at the map, its markings blurred by the steady illumination of the iron-wrought lamp upon his broad cendarie desk. His jaw was tight, his green eyes strained from too many late nights studying trade routes these past weeks. Poring over reports during war was a familiar routine. But these lists in his sparse quarters in Roushenn Palace weren't war reports, but details of trade from Alrou-Mendera's neighbors. Cross-checking each with the Houses who had come to court Dhenra Elyasin, Theroun searched for the Dhenra's best advantage for an upcoming marriage and alliance.

Which was a battle all its own.

Sitting at the far side of the desk, Thaddeus den'Lhor, Theroun's secretary-lad, shuffled through a stack of papers. Standing rather than sitting like his secretary, the right side of Theroun's body twinged as he leaned over the desk in his millitary-esque leather jerkin and breeches. Shifting, Theroun breathed into the pain. He still had most of his health despite his old wound, his body lean, his diet rigorous. But that knife through his ribs had ended his career commanding armies at the Valenghian border. Walking was painful; mounting a horse almost impossible. Standing made his side ache where his lung had collapsed, but he wouldn't sit. Battle-hardened with discipline, Theroun still moved through his sword forms daily, breathing into this wretched pain just as he was doing now.

One old General put to pasture.

"Tell me about the Tourmalines, Thad." Theroun barked casually as his gaze raked the map, his manner brisk despite the late hour. "The Islemen control the Straits of Luthor. How much of our spices come through them?"

Thaddeus, still keenly attentive, snatched up a document, his wire-framed spectacles reflecting the lamplight as he scrubbed a bony hand through his wild blond hair. At twenty-two, Thad had never been a fighter and his lanky frame showed it in his fawn-colored breeches and silk palace jerkin. But his green eyes were cunning, his wit something Theroun had wanted to see in his own sons, once upon a time.

"The Islemen send us thirty thousand bales of hopt-blume and fifteen thousand barrels of fennewith annually," Thad spoke, unperturbed by Theroun's warlike demeanor. "Not to mention a decent amount of wesl-root, bitterbark, and threllis. Plus, Jadoun controls all the seeproot, vheldan, and morris-blossom. Most of your average battlefield apothecary gone, if we can't get healing-herbs through the Isles, sir."

Theroun ground his jaw, despising fennewith. Chewing enough for severe wounds made soldiers useless in battle, not to mention hallucinating out of their gourds. Crossing his arms over his chest, Theroun pinned his secretary with his gaze, ready to impart a lesson of trade and nations to the young man. "So if the Dhenra turns down the suit of King Arthe den'Tourmalin of the Isles, you're supposing our regiments will take a hit. Soldiers unable to be healed because our herbs are controlled by the Isles. And how likely do you think it is that the Dhenra will take King Arthe for her husband?"

"I don't think it likely at all, sir," Thaddeus blinked from behind his spectacles as he realized Theroun was testing him. "Which is why I'm worried about our apothecaries. King Arthe is too much like Uhlas once was. He's old and he's been married once already. Marrying him would be like Elyasin marrying her own father. Sir."

"You're all too right, Thad." Theroun chuckled, scanning the trade routes through the Isles and knowing Thad's logic was sound even though he was missing a big consideration. "But the Islemen control trade from Luthor, Jadoun, and Perthe, to the whole Eastern Bloc. If they halted trade to us... well, let's just say cutting us off would mean cutting off trade between all the western and eastern nations. And what happens when official trade is halted through such a crucial and prosperous choke-point?"

"Trade goes underground." Thaddeus blinked. "Smuggling."

"Yes." Theroun agreed with a curl of smile. "The ships that come through from Perthe and Jadoun are old smuggler's vessels from the Perthian Rebellion. The men who captain them are practiced smugglers. The Isles would rather reap taxes by proper shipping through their straits, rather than force it underground because of a slight from Alrou-Mendera."

"So we can do without the Islemen, if Elyasin chooses someone else to marry?" Thad ventured.

"Just because the Islemen prefer harmony doesn't mean we can do without them, Thad." Theroun shook his head. "They are powerful allies, and make our lives easier in every way, from the wool carpets beneath our boots to the porcelain basins we shit in. Careful alliances have been curried with the Isles for generations. They are perhaps the strongest nation in our part of the world, despite having so few people and such little land."

"They rely upon us for millet, silth, and wheat." Thaddeus spoke as he shuffled to another paper in the stack, scanning it. "And cendarie for ships."

"The grains they might get elsewhere," Theroun folded his arms over his chest as if studying for a battle, "but not cendarie. Does any other nation supply them with cendarie?"

Thad shuffled through a number of papers, then looked up. "No."

"No." A smile lifted one corner of Theroun's mouth. "King Thronos den'Ildrian secured that trade, Uhlas's grandfather. The Islemen can make ships out of leavonswood, bairn, and ironwood, but they prefer cendarie. The Elsthemi have plenty, but they have few accessible harbors, ice-bound half the year. Valenghia and Praough have inferior milling techniques for shipbuilding. Control the wood for ships, control the Isles, Thad. The Islemen will not abandon us if we turn down their King's marriage proposal. We already have a true alliance, stout as my desk and made from the very same wood."

Theroun slapped one strong palm upon the stout red wood of his desk, making Thaddeus jump. But the lad recovered well. After three years as Theroun's secretary, timid Thaddeus was getting used to the martial manner of his superior. Sitting back, Thad took his spectacles off, dangling them from one hand as he lipped the metal that wrapped around his ears. Theroun liked that look. Thaddeus was being shrewd when he did that, and surprising things often emerged from his mouth.

"Speak." Theroun barked casually, knowing the lad had something to say.

"Sir," Thad began. "Why are we still in a war with Valenghia? We've had them stymied at the border for years, neither army really able to invade the other. Your lance along the Aphellian Way was the greatest push into Valenghian territory in all ten years of the war. We're exhausting men and resources on both sides, preventing mutually-beneficial trade. What for?"

Theroun stared the lad down, ready to test Thad's wits again. "If we cease our attentions at the border, the Vhinesse will invade us. She wants the borderlands."

"No." Thad shook his head. "The border is poor farming. Just one bitter valley right between two impassable bogs that stretch for hundreds of leagues. And the Longvalley and Highmountains? Rocky soil, glacial moraine. The Vhinesse has plenty of ripe tilth, especially now that she's annexed Cennetia and Praough. The city-states of both southern nations were weak. We're not. She's wasting her resources attacking us. I think it's something else."

"Like?" Theroun pressed. He knew the answer to this riddle, though Thaddeus didn't.

"Like..." Thaddeus chewed his spectacles like a horse nibbling the bit as his gaze took a faraway cast. "Maybe there's something behind the war? I don't know. Say, a secret cabal? Ever read the history of Cennetia? They had a secret order called the Illianti that manipulated the Centos of each city-state for hundreds of years, pitting them against each other to benefit the order. They were finally routed in 1120 by Centos Lugro Apante, who made an alliance with Centos Revio Duonti. Duonti provided the key, discovering the Illianti mark, a brand upon the inner ankle. Through Apante's military might, they put the Illianti to the torch."

"I've read Qentus Atolychi's *Inner Sanctum*." Theroun chastised mildly, though he still wanted to see how far the lad would take it. "But continue."

"Oh. Sorry." Thaddeus looked chagrined, though he pressed on. "Could there be something like that happening here, sir? On both sides, manipulating the thrones to keep the war going?"

"Could be. What makes you think I know anything about it?"

"You knew King Uhlas." Thaddeus shrugged. "Some speak of you as close as brothers. And you were on the Valenghian front for a long while at his orders."

"I was also *removed* from the Valenghian front at his orders, Thad." Theroun corrected mildly. "Dishonorably discharged for my actions at the Aphellian Way ten years ago, just after the Kingsmen Summons."

"Sorry." Thaddeus knew Theroun's martial history and blushed in the fire's light, chewing his spectacles. A long silence passed between them, which at last Thad broke, his green eyes curious yet bold. "Were there Alrashemni Kingsmen in your army, sir? When you went mad along the Aphellian Way ten years ago? Did you have them crucified along with the Valenghian Alrashemni you caught when you went on your... rampage... after the Kingsmen Summons?"

"Strung up mostly, but yes." Theroun corrected levelly. "Most of our own Blackmarked Kingsmen deserted in the night when they realized what I was doing after the Summons. Predominantly, the Alrashemni I caught at that time were Valenghian, as my army drove up the Thalanout Plain and deep into the Vhinesse's tilthland. The stories are wrong about my crucifixions. I only crucified some of the Blackmarks I caught. Mostly I strung them up along the Aphellian Way, three to four on every Monolith. Lynching a man is far easier than building a cruciform."

Thaddeus hesitated at the grisly description, but the lad had gumption tonight. "You desecrated the Monoliths of the Way. Bronze that never tarnishes, copper that never turns green. Limestone that never erodes, and obsidian that never flakes. Ancient effigies of worship for peoples of three lands, made by gods long forgotten. You defaced them with corpses – for leagues."

"Most of the Blackmarked Alrashemni were still alive when I strung them up, Thad. Get your history straight." But Theroun was impressed with the lad's courage tonight. Thaddeus had never had the guts to ask Theroun about the details of the Aphellian Way before. The young man was growing bolder in his statecraft.

Thaddeus was silent a long moment as he weighed Theroun's forthrightness about his past. "But you did kill some of your own men. Soldiers of Alrou-Mendera. King Uhlas' soldiers. That was treason."

"There's a reason I got the nickname Black Viper of the Aphellian Way, Thaddeus, and that King Uhlas removed me from service for my actions," Theroun murmured. "A viper will strike anyone when enraged. Friend and foe are not viewed separately to the viper."

"Do you regret it?" Thaddeus met Theroun's gaze by the fire's light. "What you did?"

Theroun had asked himself that question a thousand times. There was really only one answer. "No. I do not regret lynching and crucifying Alrashemni, even the ones in my own regiment, after the bastards killed my family. But I regret how it pained King Uhlas. My heart was mad with rage. I thought it justified, that those who had been so treasonous to their King and escaped his Summons be punished for it. And in my grief… well. Grief plus fever-wounds makes rage run hot like tundra-wolves."

"Do you still hate the Kingsmen?"

"The Kingsmen are gone, Thad."

"Not entirely. Guard-Captain Olea den'Alrahel wears the Inkings. If she's alive, there are probably others out there. Somewhere."

Theroun's lips quirked, proud of his apprentice's reasoning skills. His back facing the wall, his face hidden in the shadows so only Thad could see, he gave a very small nod. He knew Lhaurent kept an extensive network of spies in the palace, and was nearly certain there were hide-holes for watching and listening in the walls, though he'd never had his suspicions confirmed.

"Holy *Aeon!*" Thaddeus cursed softly as he sat forward, intrigued. "There are Kingsmen still out there! Living ordinary lives? Where?"

"Where would you hide if you were one of the most elite warriors ever to walk this land?"

"The army." Thad blinked. "They're still hiding in the army. Specialty units that see a lot of action. High Brigade. Fleetrunners. Maybe the Stone Valley Guard…"

"Smart, Thaddeus. A very smart *theory*." Reaching for a wine goblet upon the table, Theroun had a long draught. He was about to invite the lad out for a walk to discuss the topic further, when a knock came at the door.

"Come!" Theroun barked. A lanky page peeked around the doorframe, terrified of the once-General within. "Yes? Out with it, lad!"

The boy made a hasty, inelegant bow, trembling. "You're needed by the Dhenra, sir. She wishes to run over the trade details of the Isles once more."

"At this hour?" Theroun scowled. Elyasin needed sleep, not to be pouring over trade routes in the wee hours of the night yet again. But she was being careful, taking each suitor into deep consideration, and he respected her care despite her whip-quick temper. She was Uhlas' daughter, after all.

"Scurry off and tell the Dhenra I will attend her immediately." Theroun barked at the trembling page. The terrified lad was only too eager to oblige. Turning to Thaddeus, Theroun gestured at the papers upon the table. "Lock these up in my desk. Attend me at seventh bell tomorrow, so we may prepare for the Dhenra's suitor negotiations."

"Yes, sir." Thaddeus knew the routine, beginning to sort and stack the trade documents. But before Theroun could leave, Thad piped up. "Sir? Before you go. I was doing an inventory of the gemstones we trade to other nations, in case any of the suitors inquire, and I came across an abnormality."

"Continue." Theroun set one hand quietly to the desk, frowning.

"The emeralds from the Hallow Mines," Thad went on. "The mines report almost thirty *hecante* of emeralds mined every month, but only fifteen *hecante* are reported shipping out from Amlenport to our trade partners."

Theroun's eyebrows rose. This was news. "That's a *lot* of emeralds missing, Thaddeus. How long has this been going on?"

"I looked back through the lists." Thad shuffled, though his green eyes were sharp. "The issue has been overlooked for almost seven years. Though it was only two *hecante* of emeralds missing at first. Chancellor Evshein oversees the nation's gemstone lists. Doddering old fool to have overlooked so many missing emeralds, sir?" Thaddeus ventured.

Theroun scowled as his gaze flicked to the lad, seeing that Thad didn't believe his own question. "You've met Evshein. Do you think there's any infirmity in that withered old mind, Thad?"

"Not at all, sir." Thad's answer was decisive. "What's Chancellor Evshein up to then?"

"Nothing promising." Theroun growled. "I'll look into it. Dig no deeper, and do not approach Evshein about it."

"Sir."

Theroun turned to go, his hand upon the latch. It was a stunning amount of gemstones missing, and Thad was astute to have caught it. Theroun was going to have to ask his superiors in the Chancellate about it, or Castellan Lhaurent, and that wouldn't be a cozy conversation. They probably wouldn't tell him what it was for.

Theroun wasn't high enough up in the Khehemni Lothren to know most details.

* * *

SWIRLING a dark red vellas-wine in a silver goblet, Theroun enjoyed the way the wine caught the firelight. He'd returned from the Dhenra's suites an hour ago, as Elyasin had finally become fatigued. She'd dismissed six suitors already, Menderian lords of middling means. The real negotiations would begin tomorrow, with two suitors of significant wealth who could be of benefit to a nation at war. As Theroun's gaze drifted over trade routes for the thousandth time, he took a sip of wine, enjoying its deep plum notes. His habits of war drove him to pour over the document obsessively, as he'd once done with battle-plans. There had been nights upon campaign when he'd gotten only three hours' rest, yet been the first to march from his tent in the morning to set a good example for his men.

Theroun's gaze drifted to the Valenghian border, memories of ten years ago pressing in like ghosts at the edges of his vision. It had only been three days after word had reached him of the Kingsmen Treason and disappearance that he'd staggered back to his command tent, knifed in the ribs by an Alrashemni assassin while taking a piss out in the darkness. Holding his bloody ribs, his agony had been exquisite as he realized his command-tent was far too quiet. Seeing his guards murdered, their throats slit in the moonlight, he'd thrown back the canvas flap to find his wife, daughter, and two sons with their throats slit also – their pools of blood wine-red by the light of the braziers.

Theroun stroked the rim of his wine goblet with his finger, staring at the Thalanout Plain between its two flanking bogs. That fucking Alrashemni Kingsman with his black Inkings so brazenly displayed had gotten a knife in Theroun's ribs, and he hadn't even heard the man coming, just like he hadn't heard the rest of them slaughtering his family. But Theroun had gotten a blade in the assassin's neck before he could strike again. General Theroun den'Vekir had always been fast with a blade; fast like a viper. But all the same, his family had died that night.

At traitorous Blackmarked hands.

Theroun felt the cramp of his old wound and took a long, slow breath. Valenghia enjoyed unceasing war with Alrou-Mendera now as skirmishes fluttered at their borders and raids dipped into the highpasses and valleys. The Vhinesse's army had driven a neat wedge through the Lheshen Valley near Quelsis for a time, though they'd been beaten back by the Fifth, Eighth, and Ninth Cavalry, attended by the Fleetrunners and Stone Valley Guard. But it was all a sham. All the battles, skirmishes, drives and counter-drives. Theroun knew the truth behind the war now, unlike when he was simply a General out marshaling armies on the field.

Not even Theroun's thoughtful, stolid King Uhlas had known the truth – duped like all the rest of the nation.

Sipping his wine, Theroun gazed at the fire's embers. Nothing was simple anymore, and Theroun no longer served just House den'Ildrian. Now he had other masters, and it was his sworn duty to let the war rage as long as it took to kill all the treasonous Alrashemni Kingsmen still hiding in the military. A part of him felt bad for the surviving Alrashemni, the ones still serving their nation in secret. They were a doggedly righteous lot, and their own dedication to their damn Kingsmen oaths was going to get them picked off, battle by battle. But they would have that glory, unlike him. Theroun's only regret was that he couldn't be out there.

That he was here, dishonorably discharged and rotting away inside this palace.

A knock sounded upon Chancellor Theroun's ironbound door and his grip tightened on his silver chalice. Only one man came to his quarters so very late, and it was never good news.

"Come!" Theroun barked, stilling his irritation beneath the implacable iron of a professional war-maker. Flowing around the door, Castellan Lhaurent den'Karthus hardly pushed the door open and thus hardly needed to close it. Theroun gave the tall Castellan his customary glower as he rose from his chair by the fire and set his wine goblet aside. It wouldn't do to glower any less or more than he usually did, as he didn't want Castellan Lhaurent or Chancellor Evshein – his superiors in the Khehemni Lothren – *ever* knowing just exactly what he thought of them.

"What is it, Lhaurent? It's past late, and the Dhenra has preparatory talks tomorrow with the Isles and Ghrec."

Castellan Lhaurent cleared his throat, his hands clasped. Oiled back from his high forehead, his black hair shone in the fire's light, his grey eyes calm. Impeccably groomed in his grey silks, his silver chains of office hung neat and straight from his doublet's high collar. "Apologies, Chancellor. I have come with a change of petition from our mutual beneficiaries for your activities tomorrow. You are to focus your attentions on the suit of the Elsthemi Highlanders. Convince the Dhenra that her other suitors are less attractive than King Therel Alramir of Elsthemen."

"Explain." Theroun drew a breath, scowling at this news.

"The First Sword of Elsthemen," Lhaurent gave a slippery smile, "is prepared to act for our cause if Elyasin chooses King Therel Alramir as her intended. So we are going to make *sure* she chooses the renegade Highlander wolf-King for her husband, and no other."

"What do you mean?" Theroun ground his jaw. "What is the First Sword of Elsthemen prepared to do if Elyasin weds King Therel?"

"Don't be obtuse, Theroun, it doesn't suit you." Lhaurent's smirk became subtler, his eyes grey velvet, smooth and deceptive. "Elsthemen's First Sword has finally agreed to attack the Dhenra at her coronation. For the cause."

"He's going to assassinate her." Theroun's stomach dropped as his scar-ruined side twisted. The Khehemni Lothren had demanded much of him over the years, influencing the Dhenra, using his Chancellate position to push Uhlas into endless counter-strikes against Valenghia. But this was madness. Theroun had had nothing to do with either King Uhlas' nor Dhenir Alden's deaths at the Khehemni Lothren's hands.

But now, a familiar rotten flavor filled his mouth like seven-day carrion.

"You fucking bastard." Theroun seethed, his jaw clenched. "You planned this, didn't you? The Khehemni Lothren maneuver far, but you... this brazen play has your stink all over it, eel. Just like Uhlas and Alden's deaths did. Wiping out the King's line. Ending the den'Ildrian reign."

"War necessitates sacrifices, Theroun." Lhaurent murmured mildly. "I thought you discovered that upon the Aphellian Way?"

"That was different." Theroun's side twisted as he thought about being adjunct to slaughtering Uhlas' daughter.

"Was it?" Lhaurent's smile was smooth. "Because I do believe the objectives of those acts and this one are the same. Provoke war, to kill as many Alrashemni hiding in the ranks as possible."

"You want a war with the Highlands." Theroun could see it now, despicable as the filth he wiped from his own ass. "King Therel of Elsthemen will retaliate if he's blamed for his First Sword's assassination of the Dhenra. He'll fight like a junkyard dog. And our Lothren representatives in the Chancellate will push our nation to war, killing off yet more Alrashemni in the ranks."

"Elsthemen is teeming with blackmarked mongrels." Lhaurent picked a piece of lint from his silk robes. "We simply aim to cull the pack, just as we did in Valenghia."

"Will Alrou-Mendera cease war with Valenghia to engage one with the Highlands?"

"I think not. The Khehemni Lothren command us to engage both fronts at once." Lhaurent's answer was practiced, soft with false demureness.

"But Alrou-Mendera can't sustain a two-front war, especially against Elsthemen!" Theroun erupted, slamming his fist into the stout table beside him. "The Highlanders have keshar they fucking *ride* to battle! Those tawny cats can leap fifteen feet and bring down a horse at full gallop! Ever seen a man get his head crunched in a keshar's maw? There's little left but brain spatter, and those fangs can reach a heart through the shoulder. We'll lose too many men. We risk losing the entire fucking country if the Khehemni Lothren push this forward!"

"Nevertheless," Lhaurent continued, his hands clasped calmly before him. "Our ancient enemies, the Alrashemni, are strong in Elsthemen. They are aware of the Khehemni, and pick us off like hawks do rats. The Lothren have declared that the hiding Alrashemni Kingsmen must be *pinned* in the ranks. We will never get it done with Elyasin upon the throne. She's far too sympathetic to their plight."

"That's a lot of good netting put to waste, to catch a few minnows." Theroun stared Lhaurent down, furious at what the secret ruling body of the Khehemni was going to cost the nation. "The Lothren will be condemning thousands of Menderian men to death; *loyal* soldiers. You'll thin our ranks until the Valenghian Vhinesse gets the idea to *really* test Alrou-Mendera's mettle, seizing her opportunity to smash through and drive straight to the capitol. She's a bitch, and knows her warfare."

"The Valenghian Vhinesse is well in hand." Lhaurent did not flinch. "She will not challenge the Lothren, nor push our agreed upon border-war further than we wish her to."

"Are you sure of that?" Theroun growled.

"I am." Lhaurent's small smirk was eerie, his grey eyes shining with the pleasure of secrets. "She is ours to command. It is enough."

"She is the Lothren's to command? Or yours, personally?" Theroun ground his teeth, resisting the urge to shove a blade right through Lhaurent's greasy throat.

"She serves the Khehemni Lothren." Lhaurent's small twitch of lips showed his vast pleasure as he smoothly evaded Theroun's question. "And she keeps up a *very* expensive war because we wish it. Not to mention the... benefits she receives from the arrangement, which I assure you are ample."

"What are you doing for her that convinces her to keep such a war going, Lhaurent?"

"*I* am not doing anything, Theroun." Lhaurent lifted a well-calculated eyebrow. "I am merely following the Lothren's command. When the Khehemni Lothren need information, or persuasion, or need someone dead, I simply supply. Right now, they need a *lot* of someones dead – in Elsthemen and Alrou-Mendera. Which is *your* job. Push the Dhenra to yield to the suit of King Therel Alramir of Elsthemen. Tout their wealth, their bloodlines. There is much that is attractive about the Elsthemi, and Therel. He is young and good-looking. And fairly well-behaved."

"Except that time he cut a maid up and stuffed her into a trunk in his rooms." Theroun growled, citing a popular rumor about the renegade young King of the Highlands.

"*That* cannot be proven." Lhaurent coughed smoothly.

"But isn't King Therel aligned with the Khehemni, if his First Sword is?"

"Therel is not aware of our agents." Lhaurent shook his head. "The man is a rogue like Dhenir Alden once was, not to be trusted. But some of his men are *very* loyal to the cause. Three of whom are in his entourage right now, including his First Sword."

Theroun went silent. Lhaurent did not blink nor did he fidget, his hands still gracefully clasped. He appeared benign and servile, but Theroun knew he was far from either. Theroun wondered again just how high up Lhaurent was in the Khehemni Lothren. Far enough to know exactly what was going on, which Theroun didn't. Yet Lhaurent had surprising information sometimes, that Theroun wondered if he shared with the Lothren. Lhaurent's broad-ranging network of spies were intensely loyal to him, for what reason Theroun couldn't fathom – though he wondered sometimes if those spies were even loyal to the Lothren at all.

"Tell me about the emeralds, Lhaurent." Theroun confronted him bluntly. "And don't bullshit me. You know where they're going, and why Chancellor Evshein's been signing off on the documents."

"Wars are expensive, Theroun." Lhaurent lifted an eyebrow with a chuckle. "Evshein is merely providing... a bit of pay. To recruit the men we need when war breaks out on the Elsthemi border."

"Recruiting men from where?" Theroun's fingers lingered near the knife at his belt.

"Abroad. And that is all I will say on the matter."

Theroun ground his jaw, his fingers spasming at the hilt of his knife as pain ripped through his side. "You're an eel, Lhaurent. Someone's going to put a sword through you someday and roast you for supper."

"Is that a threat, *Chancellor?*" The Castellan smirked darkly, just the hint at one corner of his lips as rage flashed in his calm grey eyes now. "Or have you forgotten why you swore allegiance to the Khehemni Lothren just after your madness on the Aphellian Way? So many Alrashemni Kingsmen to kill, so little time before a man dies to see revenge done for his family and his own crippled worthlessness. I'm watching, Theroun. Step wrong, tell the Dhenra, or do any little thing that compromises Elyasin's demise and you *will* be pinned again, but not by a Kingsman. And that's not a threat, my friend. That's a promise. But play our little game, and see all your desires to annihilate Alrashemni Kingsmen bear blood-ripened fruit."

"*You're* watching?" Theroun growled. "Don't you mean the *Lothren* are watching?"

"Take my words as you like them."

With that, the Castellan turned smoothly, clasping the iron handle of the door and flowing around the frame. Theroun scowled, watching the Castellan go. He hadn't raided the banks of the Trius with only fifty men, slitting throats in the dead of night for this. To be disrespected by this silken cur and treated like a lackey. Those cream-smooth hands of Lhaurent's hadn't done a lick of work in his entire life. Theroun thought he could *smell* eels in the man's wake. Or perhaps it was just jasoune-bloom, reeking like a west wind through Lintesh. Perfume for a woman's bedchamber, not the smell of a man.

Theroun found he was gripping the hilt of the knife at his belt, hard.

He should have thrown it. Right into the Castellan's back.

13

DHERRAN

Dherran gripped the woman's hips, driving himself up into her as she straddled him. But the buxom brunette was a professional, and ground down upon him as she gripped him with her strong thighs, her green eyes flashing by the candle light in the inn's small room. Dherran gave her everything, and she absorbed it as she raked her long nails down his chest, making Dherran hiss through gritted teeth, so very close. Reading his body like Dherran read others in the ring, she reached out, slapping him hard across the face. Dherran gasped at the sting of it, then came with a roar, spasming hard beneath her – reaching up to seize her neck and haul her down into his kiss as he shuddered.

Breathing hard, he released her, the hot forge inside him cooled at last. She ran a thumb over his lips, but Dherran was finished, and turned his head away. "Your coins are on the bureau."

"You're not one for lingering." Arching an eyebrow at his tone, she rose, wiping between her legs with a washcloth from the porcelain basin by the bed. Her chuckle was scathing as she bent, lifting her red silk gown from where it had puddled upon the floor and hooking the bodice closed. Raking her coins from the bureau, she eyed him as Dherran rose from the bed, going to the basin to splash water on his face and curry it through his blond hair. "You're beautiful to look at Kingsman, and a pleasure to fuck. But you're a bastard, aren't you?"

"You're not my lover. You're not my friend. So get lost."

"Prizefighters." She combed her tousled mane with her fingers, brushing it out over one shoulder as she went to the door. Pausing with her fingers on the handle, she looked back. "My name's Cecilia. If you want me again during your stay, just talk to the landlady downstairs."

Dherran wanted to tell her no. He wanted to tell her he didn't need it. But he knew the truth. He would need her again tomorrow, and the next day. And she had been good, letting him rage inside her the way he needed to. "Tomorrow. This time again."

A small smirk lifted her lips as she nodded and stepped out – victory.

Dherran settled back to the bed, not bothering to draw the covers up after she'd gone. Summer in Vennet was balmy, and the past two nights had proved stifling at the inn. Their trio had money, but it wouldn't do to waste it, so their lodgings were modest. But it was clean, and Dherran rolled to his back on the firm bed, turning his head to stare into the collection of candles that burned in the unlit fireplace for the hot night.

The flames licked low, the window open to the night breeze outside. Soothed, Dherran's eyelids began to droop as memories rose, of a fine-boned woman in his hands. Delicate, her skin was supple, her muscles hard as she rode him, bliss upon her lovely face. Her dark brown eyes half-closed, her sighs eased into Dherran's ears, the only sound Suchinne had ever made as she'd climaxed for him. Suchinne, whom he could wrap entire in his arms, who could still his rage with a touch, who could control this beast inside him with a glance. Dherran drifted, feeling her, hearing the croaking of frogs outside and watching the flicker of the candles. Time stretched – but suddenly he snapped awake, roused by a touch of cold steel at his throat.

"Got you, Dherran."

Dherran's breath hissed, in relief and exasperation to discover who had gotten the drop on him. "It's the middle of the fucking night, Khenria. We're not bouting. Go back to bed."

The candles had dwindled to stubs and gave little illumination to Khenria's stealthy movements in the shadows. But Dherran felt her slide onto the bed, her knife blade not moving from his throat as she settled upon his naked body. Dherran's breath caught to feel her, so firm and lithe with only her thin cotton undergarments between them. Khenria's lips were close to his, her breath hot upon his face.

"I don't want to go back to bed." She murmured, her voice low in the half-dark.

"I'm not playing." Dherran growled, though he was betrayed by his rising intrigue, trapped against her where he knew she could feel it. "Get off me or get your wrist broken."

"I'm not playing either, Dherran." Khenria continued, brushing her full lips across his. "Do you know where I go when we're in the cities, where I was last night? To whorehouses. I'm not innocent, Dherran, not like you and Grump think I am."

"Maybe you want to fuck, Khenria, but not with me." Khenria had always been her own creature, and Dherran knew she slipped away from their group when they were in cities. He'd never questioned her business, but now that he knew the truth, need boiled in his veins – the same surging tirade he had always felt with Suchinne.

"I've tried to tell myself I didn't want you," Khenria's dark gaze glittered in the low light, dangerous and sexy. "But when I watch you fight, I feel this... vast animal inside you. This terrible, amazing passion. I've watched through cracks in the door; you let out your magnificent rage with the whores. I want to feel it. I want you to unleash that animal passion upon me. I want to fight like you do. I want to fuck like you do..."

The knife slipped away; Dherran felt it plunk to the covers beside his head. Khenria's fingertips stroked his neck as her lips brushed his, so full and soft – bold with desire.

Dherran pulled back, though his loins screamed at him for a fool. "I can't do this, Khenria." He spoke, breathing hard now. "You're beautiful, but—"

"But you're what I want." Khenria's slender fingers eased over Dherran's chest, tracing his Inkings. "You're a Kingsman, like I should have been. I knew when I saw you that day in the river. I knew you'd come to make it right, everything that happened after the Summons."

"I'm *still* trying to make it right." Dherran murmured, his lips brushing hers as his body roared with need, though he tried to hold back. "I'm trying to teach you the Kingsmen arts as they were taught to me. But I can't if we do this. It's too... complicated. Grump trusts us. I can't—"

"Touch me, Dherran." Khenria breathed as she slid her hips over his. "Take me. Train me, right now. Tonight, you're mine – either with my knife buried in your throat or your cock buried between my legs."

"Khenria..." But Dherran's resolve was feeble as his body betrayed him – his lust nearly as strong as his rage. Sliding his hands around her slender waist, he felt her warm flesh beneath her thin undershirt, so good in his hands. But Suchinne's memory was still too near, and she would have asked him to do better. Pulling back with a frustrated growl, Dherran rolled Khenria to the bed in one quick motion, pinning her. She hissed, a dark pleasure flashing in her eyes at his sudden dominance, and it nearly made Dherran break. But he held her pinned at her wrists. Khenria was his student and he was her teacher – and engaging this passion would only make things maddening.

"I'm not taking you, Khenria. You're my student, not my lover. Get out of my bed." Dherran pushed off her to standing, though he was still breathing hard, fighting a dark need that blossomed between them. With a scathing growl, Khenria rolled off the bed, her ardor evaporating like a hot wind as she stared him down in a fury now.

"Fine! If that's the way you want it, Dherran... fine!"

Stalking to the door, she opened it, slamming it hard behind her as she left. Dherran tried not to give a damn. But his heart twisted as he lay back down, remembering a beautiful dark-eyed little hawk.

And a new little hawk that he wanted to pin him with her talons. Badly.

* * *

KHENRIA'S MOVEMENTS around Dherran were obvious this morning, pissed. Banging her cup on the rough table of the inn's main room, she kicked out the bench to take a seat by Dherran for breakfast. Flipping her knife restlessly in one hand, her grey eyes pinned him, ignoring the bustle of the inn as their trenchers of eggs and ham in gravy arrived. She didn't eat as Dherran set to, the inn a drone of sound around them as people talked and laughed, every table in the dining room full though Grump had yet to come down for breakfast. Suddenly, Khenria's fingers twitched, flicking her knife to thunk point-down into the table a hair's width from Dherran's hand.

"Oops." She spoke, simmering with fury as he blinked at her in astonishment.

"*Oops*?" Dherran hissed, trying to keep it quiet in the busy inn. "What the fuck, Khen!?"

Khenria turned a gaze upon him that could have ripped rabbits limb from limb, her full lips tight. Suddenly, she reached out, sliding her hand over Dherran's thigh to stroke his crotch under the table.

"Stop that." Dherran growled as he pressed down upon her hand. He said stop, but he also hoped she wouldn't stop. Dherran had lain awake for an hour after he'd dismissed her last night, trying to remember Suchinne but finding his memories had been replaced by Khenria. And now she stroked him, cruel and challenging, and he rose for her just as hard as any man who wanted a woman.

"I said stop." Dherran repeated, his mutter breathier than it should have been.

"Make me," Khenria growled back, sidling close upon the bench as she slid her hand down behind his belt now – into his pants. "I want you to take me, like a Kingsman. And I'm not going to stop until I have what I want."

It was all Dherran could do to not moan in the bustle of the inn around them, as he breathed a single slow breath, fighting for control. "Being a Kingsman isn't all about fucking and fighting, Khenria. It's about negotiation, and balance."

"The only negotiation you ever do is with your fists. And your cock." Her chuckle was ruthless as she stroked him. "So let's negotiate."

"Negotiation was never my strong suit. That was Olea."

Her hand stilled. "Who is Olea? Someone you knew from before?"

Dherran cursed internally. After Suchinne had died, he'd sworn he would never mention the five Kingskinder and their failure. With every punch and every drunken sousing, he tried to forget that time. A time when he'd been nothing but a young man with a quick sword, a foul temper, and a fierce bird-boned woman who had always been there to keep him in check.

"Stop touching my cock. And my past." Dherran gave a sour growl, and Khenria scowled ferociously. Removing her hand from his breeches, she surged to her feet. Ripping her dagger from the table, she hurled it point-first into the floorboards, turning a number of heads.

"Best two out of three, Dherran." She spoke coldly.

"No. I won't fight you when you're mad." Dherran growled low, a few men nearby sniggering to hear their fight. "And I won't disabuse Grump's trust."

"Fuck you!" Khenria gestured angrily across to room towards the hearth, where Grump had appeared, leaning against the cold stones of the fireplace and watching Dherran and Khenria's interaction with steady eyes. "I'm not a child, and he's not my keeper! He's just a lonely old man who found me out in the woods!"

"Khenria!" Dherran surged to his feet also, intimidating. "Apologize! Grump saved your hide—"

"It's all right, Dherran." Grump's voice was sad as he moved over from across the room. "The girl's got to grow up sometime. I'm just glad she chose you, after all that gallivanting she's prone to."

"What?!" Khenria was agog at Grump, her mouth fallen open as her gaze flicked around the dining room, her face crimson. "How – you followed me?"

"You're not so sneaky, girl. Uncle Grump has ears like a fox and footsteps thrice as quiet." Grump had that look he got sometimes, like the world had failed him sometime long ago as he spoke. A hard glint was in his normally merry eyes with a tightness to his shoulders as he settled to the bench opposite. "I followed you enough to know what you were up to. And you and Dherran weren't particularly quiet when you crawled into his bed last night, sweet child."

"I'm not a child!"

"So you said." Grump sighed, careworn as he laced his fingers on the table. The look he gave Khenria, of such fatherly kindness and heartache, almost ripped Dherran apart. "A lonely old fool needs company, and I was tired of being alone when I found you. I will understand if you choose to leave me and go with Dherran. I got along in the world before the both of you, and I will do so again."

"No." Dherran's voice was firm. "We're a team, and there's a prize-fighting purse to be had here in Vennet, not to mention the wagers. We need you, Grump."

"Two is pleasure, three is a pain," Grump murmured, staring past their trio, out the open door of the inn to the bright morning sunshine.

"You've got us in a damn fine pickle, sweetheart." Dherran growled to Khenria. "Happy?"

"Me?" Khenria's snarl was brutal. "You're the one who can't keep your prick in your trousers, in *every* town we stay at."

"For fuck's sake!" Dherran's temper surged. And with it came lust, thundering down upon him like boulders crashing down a mountain. Khenria glanced down, noting his rising ardor as her lips curled into a sneer. Dherran scrubbed his fingers through his blond hair with a growl, defeated by his temper, his desire – and the sultry, bitchy little hawk before him.

Turning, he took his temper and his forge-fire outside, knowing that if he stayed around people, someone was going to get hit. People stared at him, whispering all around and Dherran roared, "*What?!*" as he strode to the door. They shrank back, a number of folk scuttling away as he jogged down the steps, making straight for a rain barrel at the side of the inn. There, in the shade beneath a boxelder, he dunked his head in the cold water. Currying water from his hair with both hands, he braced his fists on the barrel, trying to focus on the water's ripples to calm himself.

He tried to think of Suchinne, but in the water's eddies, he only saw Khenria's face, beautiful and haughty, sexy and stormy. Suddenly, Dherran saw his own face in the water, and the vision was like a slap in the face, realizing how similar he and Khenria were. Feeling a presence nearby, he looked up to see the her staring at him from the corner of the inn. He couldn't look away, his breath stolen as she gripped him with a surging intensity, her short ruff of curls blue in the sunlight like a bird's wing, her grey eyes piercing him.

Her posture was defiant – the strength of the Kingsmen in her very soul.

Dherran choked. Without a word, he pushed off the rain barrel and strode away, unable to face it. Walking from the inn, he wandered the town's market. In dusty avenues between shops, he moved in and out of the shadows of bright awnings and rickety stalls, trying to manage the tension that filled his chest and cramped his muscles. Turning to a saddle-maker's stall, he looked over a pair of leather stirrup-straps, needing some to replace his hard-worn ones. Suddenly, he felt Khenria at his elbow. A boot-knife pierced his ribs, and hidden by her body, no passersby saw it. Brushing her fingers over a saddlebag with vines tooled upon it, Khenria stepped casually to his side as Dherran collected his things.

But as she smirked from getting the drop on him yet again, rage suddenly filled Dherran. Reaching out quickly, he snagged her wrist, forcing her knife-hand up behind her back and pulling her close to his chest. To anyone else, it would have looked like an embrace, but Dherran knew how much it hurt. Khenria hissed as he forced her wrist higher, straining her shoulder. She gave a squeak, struggling, but his grip was iron, and at last, her hand spasmed, dropping her knife to the dust. Anger blazing, Dherran crushed her close as she was disarmed – giving her a long, deep kiss.

A punishing kiss for what she was doing to him.

She struggled in his arms, caught between arousal and panic at being trapped, and Dherran let her go. She stepped back – and the hot slap she dealt him could have nailed him to the ground if he hadn't been ready for it. People were watching now, smirking at their lover's quarrel. As Dherran massaged his jaw, he tasted blood at his lip.

"There's more where that came from." Khenria spat, though her body was hot for him in her every movement as she heaved hard breaths, blushing. Dherran decided to let her stay that way. If she wanted to punish him then he would damn well punish her. But nearby, he suddenly noticed Grump lingering at a tinker's stand, looking over a one-person teakettle. Dherran sighed, an empty feeling replacing the rage in his gut as he watched Grump. Khenria looked over also, sobering as she saw Grump at the tinker's booth.

"He's buying his own supplies." She spoke quietly. "Do you really think he'll leave us?"

"You said some pretty hurtful things at breakfast, Khen." Dherran admonished. "He saved you; you owe him. And you're acting like a spoiled princess, without a care to his feelings."

"I didn't mean to." She sighed, looking more womanly than ever as her straight black brows knit in a tired frown. "I just get this heated feeling sometimes. And then I can't control it. What I do or what I say."

A laugh escaped Dherran, bitter. He'd said damn near the same words to Suchinne once, when they had been barely teens. And now he could see so clearly that Khenria was just like him. Rash, impulsive, rageful. Sexual. Dherran and Khenria were two fucked-up peas in the same goddamn pod, but something deep inside him loved her for it.

Khenria glanced over, scowling.

"I'm not laughing at you," Dherran murmured. "I'm laughing because you're far more like me than you'll ever know. You want to know how I fight so well? Because I can control that heat. I learned the hard way. But sometimes it gets the best of you. Sometimes you need someone else to help you control it."

Feeling clearheaded from the revelation at last, Dherran started to walk back to the inn's stable, and Khenria fell into step. "But I have you to help me control it."

Dherran shook his head, knowing a part of the answer to the riddle that lay between them. "You and I lose our control around each other, Khen. Sure, it's like a pressure valve, letting off the steam, but..." Dherran nodded back over his shoulder in the direction of the tinker's wares. "Grump is the kind of man who can help you control your rage. Not me."

Back near the inn, they had reached the stable, and Dherran stepped down the rows of stalls to his horse Muk. Ducking through the boards, he set about unbuckling his stirrups and threading the new leather straps on.

"You had someone teach you how to control your rage, didn't you?"

Dherran looked up, to see Khenria cool now, leaning against the wall of the stable with her arms crossed. "I did. A long time ago. Her name was Suchinne den'Thaon."

"How did she die?"

Dherran's hands paused at the stirrups, having not expected Khenria to be so perceptive. "She died in battle, on the Valenghian border. Suchinne was sweet by nature, but that calm allowed her to be ruthless in war. In all the years we trained together, I never bested her."

"You?" Khenria's eyebrows shot up. "She bested you?"

"Constantly. And she was smaller than you." Dherran smiled, thinking of how many times tiny Suchinne had thrown him ass-over-ears in the practice yards at Alrashesh. Cinching the new stirrup-strap tight, he made a flat knot with the extra leather, letting the leg-flap fall back into place. "She bested me the same way I best you. You get angry when you fight. The only times you surprise me are when you're cool and collected, like at the saddle-shop just now. But once you're hot, you're beaten."

"Why don't you like me, Dherran? Why don't you want me? Why do you only see me as... someone you have to train?" Dherran glanced up, hearing something new in her voice, something fragile as Khenria leaned into Muk, her cheek to his muscled neck. She wouldn't make eye contact with Dherran as the great bay horse turned his head and snuffled her short hair, lipping it. Throwing the second stirrup-leather up over the saddle, Dherran reached out, drawing Khenria close. She didn't resist as he lifted her chin and found her grey eyes red-rimmed, full of tears she was trying not to shed.

"Hey..." Dherran spoke, alarmed to see her like this – as if he'd broken something inside her, something that looked strong but was fragile as glass. Lowering his chin, he gave her a soft kiss, just a chaste touch of lips. "It's not like that, Khenria. I do like you, Aeon and all the gods, I do. But... I have to be your mentor, not just think about fucking when we're around each other. Someday you're gonna face a real enemy. And if I haven't taught you enough, you're gonna get killed. And then that death is on me." Dherran kissed her again, softer, sweeter this time. He didn't want to pull away, his own eyes stinging as Suchinne's memory crowded close. "I can't lose you like I lost her..."

Khenria snuggled close, burying her face in his chest. Breathing in hitches that weren't quite sobs, she kissed his shirt over his Inkings. "I'm sorry, Dherran. I've been awful to you lately."

"It's not me you need to apologize to," he murmured as he stroked her hair, kissing her temple.

She nodded into his shirt, then sighed. And with that sigh, all the tension went out of her. They held each other a long moment, listening to the snuffle of horses and smelling sweet clover upon the dust in the barn. It was sweet and tender, and it made Dherran's heart ache in a way he hadn't felt for years, until at last, Khenria pulled away.

"Did you make it into the fights this week, Dherran?"

"I saw the festival lists last night." Dherran nodded. "I've got the fourth slot in the last men's bare-knuckle round five days from now."

"Do you think you'll win?"

Dherran paused, searching for words. "I always enter the ring like it's my last moment to live. That's how you stay alive to enjoy another day. That's why I fuck like I do afterwards. My people may have died, the woman I used to love may have died... but I have people to live for."

Khenria's eyes brightened, realizing what he meant. The moment expanded around them, and Dherran saw her fierce beauty then, ready to be what she was born to be. He had a sense of rightness that they had met, even though it was tempestuous like summer storms. Ever since the river, he had known what she was, and she him. Something fierce pulled them together, just as it had when she'd approached him that day, and Dherran was a fool to pretend it was just mentorship in the Kingsman arts that connected them. He felt the heat and passion that bound them together – even stronger than it had been with Suchinne, because Khenria and Dherran both had it.

Desire. Passion. Love.

And suddenly, Dherran knew it was time.

"Khenria den'Bhaelen." Dherran spoke softly. "Are you ready to take your First Alrashemni Seal, your first step towards becoming a true Kingsman at last?"

Gazing up at him in surprise, Khenria's breath caught in her throat. As a fire Dherran knew all too well lit in her fierce grey eyes. "Really?"

"There's a women's amateur free-hand competition in five days, before my fights." Dherran continued soberly. "No weapons. No dirty play. Honest fighting, but any style goes. The purse is a straight hundred if you make it through the fourth and final round. As your mentor, I have but one condition for you to pass your First Seal, win or lose."

"What?" Khenria spoke breathlessly, eager.

"You must control your temper. If I see you break a heat, you fail."

And at his pronouncement, the fierce little hawk placed her open palm to the center of her chest – ready to begin her Kingsmen Seals at last.

14

ELOHL

Elohl and Eleshen laid out their bedrolls where they'd dropped their packs, just outside the ring of the Alranstone's Sight in the grassy amphitheater. The itching sensation that had taken Elohl gradually subsided, and ignoring his wounds, Elohl gathered wood then made a fire. Returning from being gone twenty minutes, Eleshen stepped towards their camp with a brace of rabbits. As Elohl lifted his eyebrows at her, noting she wore no bow nor arrows, she pulled a small sling out of a pocket of her breeches and grinned at him.

The rabbits made an adequate dinner, and Eleshen pulled a small flask from her pack to augment their meal, passing a few pulls of home-distilled hopt-ale Elohl's way. She'd been remarkably quiet all day after the attack on the road, but as peeper frogs began their evensong beyond the ruined glen, her insatiable curiosity at last got the better of her.

Rolling onto her front upon her bedroll, she gazed at Elohl intently by the fire's light. "You said the Alrashemni have peculiar abilities," she began, "and you are a *very* fast mover, Elohl. Normal men don't move the way you did when you fought those assassins. How *do* you move so quickly?"

Elohl's mouth quirked, feeling inclined to story-tell tonight as a fresh wind in the pines licked smoke from their camp up through a break in the trees. The evening was soft and violet around them, and Elohl took a long draw from the flask, feeling the liquor dulling the pain of his knife-slashes. "I suppose it's a little bit talent, a little bit training, and a little bit—"

"Magic?" Eleshen smiled slyly.

"*Intuition.*" Elohl countered. "Among the Alrashemni, such peculiar or intuitive gifts are known as *wyrria*, but it's not really magic, it's more like keen inborn skills. When I move, I feel a... sphere of sensation around me in the air, and it tells me things that are about to happen. When I climb or fight, I can feel when something will threaten me. Something presses me, and I flow around it – moving *with* it so it can't harm me, rather than against it. Because of my inborn gift, I carried a record for safest lead-climber in the High Brigade."

"Safest in how many years?"

"Ever. Three hundred and seventy years." Elohl spoke plainly. "I never set a bad route. It's part of why I became a Lead Hand right after I got to the mountains and was raised to First-Lieutenant within two years. My instincts didn't just keep me safe, it kept my men safe out on the glaciers, and during skirmishes with the Red Valor. I held point, because of my talent. I was always first up the ice, first over a chasm, and first into the fray. Always."

"And still, men tried to kill you." Eleshen whistled softly.

"My Inkings carry stigma." Elohl murmured as he glanced up over the tops of the trees, watching the last glow of white glaciers in the fading light. "I was marked as a traitor, no matter how many men I saved out there. People see my black hair and grey eyes, they see the Kingsmount and Stars, and they spit, they call me Blackmark to my face. They don't even know why they hate. They've just been told to." Elohl's fingers found a stick near his boots and tossed it into the fire.

"What about your sister?" Eleshen asked, rapt with curiosity. "Is she gifted also?"

"My twin sister Olea has incredible hearing." Elohl smiled, thinking of Olea. "She can hear footsteps a league off if the wind blows just right."

"And your other comrades from your youth? What gifts did they have?" Eleshen queried.

Glancing over, Elohl was unable to resist comparing Eleshen to Ghrenna as he thought about his old comrades back in Alrashesh. Eleshen was as bright a woman as Ghrenna had been a mystery, even after all the years Elohl had spent loving her. He felt he knew everything there was to know about the feisty, rebellious innkeeper the moment they met, seeing into Eleshen's heart as easily as his fingers read a route. But despite his love for Ghrenna, the deep pull that had caught them together again and again, Elohl felt he'd never really known her.

Lake-blue eyes rose in his vision; the flash of ornate Elsthemi-style white braids by a soft throat. Elohl's brows furrowed, once again finding it strange that he remembered Ghrenna with her hair in Highlander fashion – a way she'd never actually worn it.

"One of my closest friends was named Ghrenna den'Tanuk," Elohl murmured at last. "She was gifted with a rare talent others really did think was magic. Known as True Seeing, she was able to see paths into the future. She was adopted into the Alrashemni, but was originally of the tundra people far north of Elsthemen. She had a portent of someone's death at age three, and her mother traveled all the way to our Court and dumped her, terrified that the child had caused it. Ghrenna's visions when she was young were random flashes, but under tutelage she learned to wield them until she was able to see a proper sequence of events. She would have terrible headaches whenever a vision came, though, that would leave her debilitated for days. Legends tell of True Seers being able to hone their skills using Alranstones. But Ghrenna used to sit for hours before the one near Alrashesh, and she said that sitting near it helped control the headaches, but that was all."

"That's awful. What happened to her?" Eleshen spoke sympathetically.

"I don't know." Elohl spoke quietly. "My sister found her name in a military roster of the Fleetrunners eight years ago, but there was a report she'd vanished." A silence stretched, the hiss and crackle of green wood the only punctuation to Elohl's dark thoughts.

"What other gifts were there among your people?" Eleshen spoke up at last, beginning to unwind her hair from its braid over her shoulder with deft fingers as she listened.

With a sigh, Elohl settled back upon his elbows, stretching his boots to the fire but careful to not pull his wounds. "My father Urloel had a way of convincing people to do anything he said when his tone was just right, but he had to control his anger in order to use it. Our fletcher Fherrow could call birds by imitating their song. A bird would come right to him, let him pluck as many feathers as he liked, and he would snap his fingers and it would fly off. Then there was an old woman, Shelhaina. She could control the flow of water. With just a finger in the stream, she could make it flow *backwards*."

"Sounds like magic to me." Eleshen was rapt with her chin in her hands now, her long honey-blonde locks tumbling free. Elohl found himself admiring those golden tresses, wanting to run his fingers through them as he smiled. Despite having to fight a friend to the death today and his wounds, there was something about this place that soothed him. It felt safe, as if the fortress still stood, holding back the violence of the night and protecting them with its vigilance.

Eleshen saw him smile, and smiled back brightly. Scooching her bedroll closer, she wormed it across the grass until she was close enough to rest her head on Elohl's thigh. He reached out, his climb-calloused fingers brushing her hair, combing it back from her slender neck so he could see her jaw.

"Shelhaina said it wasn't magic," Elohl murmured, continuing his tale as he listened to the night. "She said she could *feel* the currents of water. And when she could feel it, she could change it."

"Strange talents, and a strange folk." Eleshen sighed under the care of his fingers, gazing at the fire. "What about your own gift? Has it ever betrayed you?"

A deep worry moved in Elohl at her question, a fear that always lurked at the edge of his consciousness. "I have to train hard, Eleshen. Like you saw today, just because my body warns me of danger doesn't mean I can't be damaged. If my opponent's fast, or when I'm exhausted... sometimes I can't get out of the way quick enough. And if I don't practice, all the time—"

"You might miss."

"I do miss." Elohl spoke quietly. "You've seen the scars I carry from blades. You've seen my new wounds today. I'm not untouchable, Eleshen. I'm fast and my instinct gives me an edge, but sometimes my body fails even if my instincts never do."

"Have you ever met anyone faster than you?"

"Not so far." Elohl shook his head. "But that doesn't mean it won't happen someday."

There was a long pause as Eleshen absorbed this information, motionless beneath his fingers. "What other strange things have you seen, Kingsman? What other magnificent wonders are out there?"

Elohl went quiet, thinking about the things he'd seen in the highmountains. "The passes are riddled with ancient secrets, and ruins like these. Old fortresses so destroyed they're little but foundations. But there are also monoliths. I saw a giant man sitting in a carven throne once, facing east. He took up the entirety of the cliff face we were climbing. We climbed right up over his lips to his cheek and over his left ear. And then there are the palaces of ice."

"Are you toying with me?" Eleshen glanced up, raising an eyebrow.

"No." Elohl smiled as his fingertips skated over her jaw and neck, admiring how her skin looked like burnished gold in the fire's light, enjoying the simple touch. "There are palaces of ice in the glaciers. Right on the border of Valenghia, someone once tunneled magnificent citadels into the ice, forming vast columned halls. Most are broken now, treacherous with mazes of cracks, their halls riven with the flow of the ice over time. Sometimes we used them as stop-overs, to weather bad storms. But the most incredible thing I saw..."

"What was it?"

"A white spire." Elohl smiled, remembering. "If I died tomorrow, I would go knowing I've seen perhaps the most beautiful thing in the world. The clouds cleared suddenly, when we were halfway up a hard climb near Bhorlen Pass. Across a valley of snow we saw it, like a needle piercing the heavens, with a pinnacle so sheer I didn't even know if I could climb it. Reflecting the sun like mirror-glass, it was blinding, so white it seemed to glow in the thin air. I forgot I was climbing, forgot my own body, forgot everything but that radiance just for a moment. And then the clouds closed in..."

"Did you ever see it again?"

"No." Elohl shook his head, stroking her lovely hair. "Such a sight is blessed to a man only once in his lifetime."

"Who do you think built such a structure?"

"Ancient gods." Elohl mused, surprisingly whimsical tonight. "There was a fable in the highpasses, that once a godlike people occupied these lands, with luminous wings and haunting black eyes like starlit obsidian. That they built such monoliths, indestructible to the ravages of time. But so many of the ruins I saw were ravaged. Only this remained supreme – as if placed there to stand defiant in the face of time."

"Maybe it was a marker," Eleshen mused. "A reminder to all those who would come after, to never forget them."

"But they were forgotten. Just like the Kingsmen will be, one day." Elohl's peace fled, thinking about the Kingsmen disappearance and his capture in Alrashesh, twitching in pain and bound in manacles. His new wounds seared and the solace of the night left him, leaving him feeling sore and tired from a day best forgotten.

"I think I'll turn in, Eleshen."

Elohl shifted his legs, forcing Eleshen to sit up. Kicking his boots off, he rolled over on his bedroll. He heard Eleshen pause, but at last Elohl felt her scooch her own bedroll up next to his. And then she was worming into his blankets, throwing hers atop them both as she snuggled in, smelling of spice and sweet lavender. Careful to not pull his wounds, Elohl lifted his arm, allowing her to curl around him as he cinched her close. She felt good, clean and soft, and the way she wrapped her legs around him and nuzzled her face into his chest made his peace slowly return.

"Elohl?" She murmured sleepily.

"Hmm?"

"What are you going to do when you get to Lintesh?"

He gazed up at the overhanging foliage, lit by the dying fire. "Try to find Olea. Last I knew, she was in the Palace Guard."

"Can I help?" Eleshen yawned sleepily, her words barely audible now as she drifted towards sleep, snuggling closer. "I owe the Kingsmen... your father. He saved... burning ... the timbers were falling... saved me..."

Elohl tugged the blankets about them as his heart swelled, feeling her simple goodness crack his cold glacier yet again. Finally, he understood why she was so determined to help him. Elohl's father Urloel had saved Eleshen during the Raid of Quelsis, and she felt she owed him a debt.

He saved her, so she's trying to save me.

"I don't think I can stop you coming with me." Elohl spoke quietly as he pressed his lips to her forehead. "I don't think anything could stop you from doing exactly what you want."

Eleshen sighed something unintelligible as a smile curled her lips. Elohl kissed her forehead again, stroking her hair as he stared up at the dark canopy, listening to the sounds of the night.

IT WAS LONG past midnight when Elohl startled awake. The fire was nearly out, only wisps of smoke now in the chill darkness. Spreading his sensate sphere wide,

Elohl canvassed for intruders. But the sprawling amphitheater was quiet, feeling only of trees and small, flitting creatures.

An owl hooted up in the pines, a rush of wings buffeting Elohl's senses as it dove – followed by the swift shriek of a mouse. Elohl was about to roll over again when he suddenly felt a thrumming vibration ripple through the ground – and he knew what had woken him. Reaching a hand out, he pressed it to the grit-covered stones beside his bedroll, and the thrumming came again. But this time, it shivered up through the bones of his hand, lancing his wrist all the way to his shoulder and searing into his back and chest. With a hiss, Elohl snapped his hand back, then gently unwound himself from Eleshen. Slipping from between the covers, he came to a ready crouch beside his bedroll, a longknife to hand.

The pulse came again. This time, it thrummed through the hand Elohl held pressed to the earth as he crouched, and up through both legs where his feet contacted the ground. But now it was like a rush of blood through his limbs after a good climb, or like sinking into a hot bath, almost pleasant. Setting his blade down, confused, Elohl pulled off his wool socks, balancing upon the balls of his bare feet upon the grassy stones.

The thrum came again and Elohl's head snapped up, fixing upon the towering Alranstone, the sensation's origin. Moonlight illuminated its high peak, bared through the encircling canopy. Gazing upwards, Elohl saw the topmost eye of the hulking column was slit open now – a glassy red half-orb reflecting the light of the moon.

Spreading his sensate sphere to its fullest, Elohl kept low, scanning the surrounding foliage as he approached the column with his hands ready. But nothing accosted him, and the area around the Stone seemed empty even of wildlife as he gained the column. Pressing one palm to its rough-hewn surface, he felt the tingling of its Sight pass over him. Closing his eyes, the tingling rushed through his body like fire-ants as the thrum came again. More powerful now, it was like a roll of thunder in the night – and in its shivering pulse Elohl thought he heard a word.

Climb.

His limbs moving like a string-puppet in a mummer's show, Elohl set his fingers to niches in the stone. Ignoring his wounds, his feet and fingers found purchase as he had done a thousand times, his body pushing upwards in a smooth, powerful flow. Well-worn, the Stone had chinks and niches aplenty, and in no time, he was facing the great half-lidded eye at the very top. Fire opal glittered through its iris, riven with cracks of crimson and orange as if made of living flame. As Elohl watched, it seemed the lid retracted more, gazing at him. And as the eye opened, he saw it was set with not just fire opal, but also deep onyx for the pupil.

Like a man watching him – like an ancient King, judging him.

Climb.

The shivering pulse came again, rippling through his hands and feet, and shuddering from the command of that word, Elohl flowed upwards again. Reaching the moonlight-drenched pinnacle, he folded his legs, taking a seat upon the massive column. The campsite spread below, grasses silver in the moonlight where they punched up through the amphitheater's well-fitted stones. Still asleep, there was nothing to disturb Eleshen at the fire's embers, and Elohl lifted his gaze to the highmountain valley visible through a gap in the trees. Austere glaciers lifted up behind him, along an impassable ridge. Moonsilver lit their white expanse, making them glow with a holy radiance, though Elohl knew the truth of those life-taking crevasses and sundering springmelt flows.

But though his wounds throbbed from climbing, the world seemed peaceful from his high perch as a breeze caught the pines, rustling them in a spreading ring around the Stone. Like he'd felt all night, something here was protective, fierce and loving in its vigilance. Nothing would accost him here, Elohl somehow knew – not tonight. It loosened his muscles, easing his throat, and he gave a deep sigh. Heights had always felt safe to him, being able to see far. But this perch was particularly satisfying, alone but not lonely, released and expansive – as if it was the only place in the world he was supposed to be.

You see far, Rennkavi, but not far enough.

Startled, alertness rushed through Elohl, his heart pounding. No one was near, nothing imprinting his sensate sphere, and yet a feeling of awareness pressed him. Someone was watching him – and the words he'd heard rippled through his mind, churning over and over like waves breaking against a rocky headland. An image flashed through Elohl's thoughts, of pressing his fingers to the stone, with a command that he should do it. Slowly, he set his fingertips down to either side upon the uneven stone, and as he did, a shock pulsed through him, rocking him. Searing with heat-lightning, a sensation like summer forest fires filled Elohl – crackling with energy and blistering through his sinews.

The Alranstone began to pulse, moving waves of heat through Elohl like a steadily-beating heart. Elohl moved in an ocean of fire, pulled by its ebb and flow, and when he thought he could take no more, it suddenly synched to his own heartbeat. A blaze of heat flooded Elohl, obliterating – and as it did, he saw in his thoughts a man standing before him upon the Stone, strong and tall with corded sinew, his eyes like umber flames. Golden-tanned and bare-chested, he wore leather breeches and boots, his lion-red mane braided back from his face in Highlander fashion. A keshar-claw pendant inset with gold sigils dangled on a fine golden chain about his neck, fur-lined bracers gracing his forearms, a ruby set in gold pierced into his right ear. A complex pattern of sigils tattooed in red and white spread over his chest and shoulders, a mountain and five stars inked in black at their center.

But the form of the mountain was different, not the Kingsmount Inked upon this man's chest, and as Elohl stared, the man in his mind grinned, a feral glint to his hard umber eyes like a wildcat. His searing gaze was steady upon Elohl, holding the command of a battle-lord, his face chiseled and ancient though still in his prime. White streaked the bright russet at his temples, white dappling his short stubble also. His presence pressed into Elohl, blistering as he spoke again.

You have a lot to learn about the world, Rennkavi.

Who are you? Elohl furrowed his brow, fighting to reply through their mind-connection. *And what is Rennkavi?*

Tossing back his head in a roaring laugh at once cultured and rogue, the man crouched before Elohl, reaching out battle-scarred fingers. *Your community has not confirmed you. But I confirm you now. My name is Hahled Ferrian, Brother King of the Highlands. And you are Rennkavi of the Tribes.*

Rennkavi? What do you mean? Tribes?

But the man did not reply, only pressed his palm hard against Elohl's chest, right at his Inking. Fingers of blazing light suddenly pressed *through* Elohl's body, directly into his heart – the light flooding him, searing him with a heat that glowed rather than burned. Diving into the glaciers that filled Elohl, the glow consumed them, evaporating them in a rush of wind that left nothing in its wake but illumination. Like he'd been filled by the beauty of the white spire he'd seen long ago, bliss filled Elohl – causing his heart to crack wide open.

His palms fell open in ecstasy; Elohl's fingertips grazed the Stone as his chin lifted to the night. All he could feel was expansion as he took a long, shuddering breath. Through closed lids, he could see the world beyond himself – *feel* it for the very first time. All the pain, all the pleasure. All the hope, all the disillusion. All the love and the hate. The beauty of the moon above pierced his heart and tears pricked beneath his eyelids. The wind that rustled the pines breathed through his pores, calling him. The sweetness of Eleshen was a spear in his heart as he felt her far below.

And then blue eyes surfaced, far away. Calling him. Oh, how she called him. Rivers of light poured through Elohl, flooding from his very soul, reaching for her. Calling back to her as if he stood upon the tallest peak of the most austere mountain range, flooded by all the colors of the dawn and by the illumination of his own beating heart. Just as he nearly had her, nearly touched that deep stillness of cerulean, his light was suddenly lanced by fire – his consciousness snapped back to the column beneath him and the stern barbarian King standing tall in his mind.

Focus! We have little time. I have been waiting for you, Rennkavi, searching for you throughout my long life. You didn't come when we thought you would, when our hopes were high and the time was ripe. But you are here now, so now is where we must begin. The other has failed his Naming, though he had all the right bloodlines, sundering the Tribes when he should be uniting them. I thought he was the one, long ago, but now I know my grievous mistake. This must be repaired. You must correct my mistake, Rennkavi. I have been waiting here, holding the Lineage for you, Unifier of the Tribes. You must take it now! You must take the Lineage... take up your duty and the Goldenmarks!

Elohl eyes blinked open. He shivered in the wind atop the column, the man's presence pressing in upon his heart until Elohl's blood thundered in his ears. Compelled by a force beyond his understanding, those wild eyes scorched him, urgent. Demanding he take what was offered, the man's touch pressed deeper, reaching for something. As it did, something began to rise inside Elohl. Shuddering, he seized with a monstrous bliss as a raw power, wild and tremendous, rose up within Elohl's own soul. Rising to the touch that commanded it to awaken, a leviathan of light surfaced with the power of a hundred burning suns, flooding Elohl with agony and ecstasy.

Accept it. The man pressed his hand deeper, his russet eyes searing. *You must accept it. Allow it to take you. For all our sakes...*

Elohl took the long, slow breath of his training as obliteration beckoned. Tipping into it, he could see nothing but light, filling him and expanding to every horizon. Suddenly, Elohl felt how beautiful it would be to give himself to it. To let it take him, completely – let it take all his pain, his despair, everything that had chilled his heart for ten ravaging years. Gazing into that light, he felt himself begin to slide into it, wanting it.

Wanting such peace and obliteration.

With that thought, Elohl let go. The leviathan rushed up, engulfing him. And plunged into an ocean of molten light, the illumination took Elohl – completely.

15

OLEA

Entering the silversmith's workshop, Olea found herself in a well-lit space, the mountainous man she had trailed from the fountain standing at his ease beside a long wooden workbench. An acrid tang of smelted metals reached her as a fire crackled in a hearth equipped with bellows for forging. But rather than the coarse tools of a smithy, this workshop had careful racks of well-polished small instruments, and progressive magnifying apparatus upon the workbench. A display of silver and goldworks stood to one side, the bracelets, ear-cuffs, and amulets pieces to show an artisan's careful craft, delicate with filigree.

Which was all at odds with the enormous man who now faced her, waiting a few paces inside the door, but not so close that Olea felt threatened. Dark-haired and grey-eyed in the classic Alrashemni way, he watched her as she surveyed the workshop then gazed upon his massive physique. A long rent of old scars tore down the left side of his face, trailing down his neck and over his collarbone – leading to a patch of vicious scars upon his broad chest, just visible where his homespun shirt laced.

His gaze traced her also, landing upon her Inkings.

"You are careful, Kingswoman," he spoke at last, in a rumbling basso like boulders colliding. "For a moment there, I thought you weren't following me."

"I was trained to be careful." Olea returned, watching him for any sudden moves. "As were you."

"Show me." He nodded his chin at her Inkings.

"You first." Olea narrowed her eyes upon him.

With a sigh like trees falling down a ravine, he stripped off his brown leather jerkin. Pulling his white lambswool shirt off over his head, he relaxed his shoulders, careful to not rip the fine weave. His shirt he folded neatly upon the bench as Olea perused his brutishly alluring bulk. Though rippling muscle moved in his arms, chest, and stomach like he'd trained all his life for battle, he had no Inking, no trace of the Kingsmount and Stars. And though the man was built like a bull, intimidating, Olea felt a strange gentleness in his nature.

But the scarring in the center of his chest was what truly caught her attention. Ruinous, his scars were where an Inking should have been, whitened with time and puckered. If he had taken a sword through the chest as the scars suggested, it would have killed him. But no wound of battle had made those, nor the strange scars that tore down the left side of his square-jawed face to his brawny chest.

"I burned it off." The Kingsman rumbled, watching Olea. "It took seven applications of searing iron to get the whole Inking. It hurt too much to wear it any longer, knowing I had failed our kin."

Olea's throat tightened; tears pricked as his statement touched her in a place so deep it had no name. And then her fingers were shucking her baldric from her shoulder, unbuckling her Guardsman jerkin, unlacing her shirt. And then it was all off, her trappings of palace life cast to the floor like so much rubbish. Bare-chested like he, she stood with her woe and pride bared before this Kingsman – the only one she had ever met since the horror of the Summons.

As Olea breathed the metallic air of the workshop with her torso bared to the cold night air, his gaze softened. At last, he gave a rumbling sigh, smiling sadly at her Inking. "You're too young. You would have been a child when that was done."

"I was twenty. I had my Seventh Seal."

"And so you gave yourself your Eighth. Without the community's approval."

"I *had* my community's approval." Olea growled, dipping to retrieve her shirt and pull it back on. "Five of us Seventh Seals were marked by one of us who knew the Way of Ink. We had the khemri venom; we had our Eighth Seal dreams. We survived them. And we did it because the rest of our community was about to die, Summoned by a traitorous King."

They faced each other, Olea bristling and angry, him gauging her words with a careful calm. Olea had trained herself to be thick-skinned over the years, but feeling a Kingsman's disapproval was something else. But the stern, gentle mountain suddenly crumbled before her. Slowly, the big man came to one knee, the palm of his right hand settling to the scars in the center of his chest. His other hand dropped to his side where a sword should have been as he bowed his head.

And in the light of the workshop lamps, Olea saw tears.

"Eighth Seal," the Kingsman rumbled in his deep basso voice. "Your community welcomes you. The Alrashemni Kingsmen welcome you. Awaken to your new life, *Chirus Alrashemni*, and to your purpose."

Olea stood tall, her anger whisked away in a wash of ferocious pride. If he could have shattered any further, the Kingsman did, tears cascading down his square-jawed face as Olea strode forward, kneeling before the massive man and gripping his face in both hands.

"You welcome me... without knowing anything about me?"

"You are one of us. One of the last of us. How could I not welcome you?" The silversmith's dark grey eyes were red-rimmed with pain, and driven by some unknown instinct, Olea pulled him close. It startled him, and she felt him almost pull away. But then the Kingsman gave a great shuddering sigh. Their lips met, just a touch. A long moment passed, a touching of hearts as they kissed – and then the moment broke as they both pulled back.

It wasn't love, and it wasn't lust. But it was like coming home.

Olea wound her arms up around his neck, and with great tenderness, the mountain of a Kingsman brushed a hand over her hair. His muscles were solid beneath Olea's hands, his half-bound black curls shining in the lamplight just like hers. Olea hadn't expected him to soothe her long years of loneliness and woe simply by holding her as they knelt upon the workshop floor. But when he finally helped her to her feet, he looked down at her with fierce pride, brightening her life. For his part, he couldn't cease stroking her curls as Olea's sword-calloused fingers reached up, tracing his scars.

"I don't even know your name, Kingsman," Olea murmured at last.

"Vargen." He chuckled, relief flickering over his scarred visage. "Vargen den'Khalderian. Silversmith."

"My name is Olea den'Alrahel."

"Alrahel?" His dark eyebrows lifted in surprise. "You must be Rakhan Urloel's daughter, from Alrashesh."

"I don't remember any Vargen in Alrashesh." Olea pulled back slightly, surprised. "I would have remembered you."

"I'm not from Alrashesh. I'm from the Third Court, from Dhemman up in the eastern mountains." The Kingsman was thoughtful, his face the chiseled wisdom of ancient gods. But his demeanor was kind as he touched her center-most Inked star reverently. "All the Courts were Summoned, and we met upon the Kingsroad and marched upon Lintesh as one. Afterwards, I returned to Dhemman, only to find it had been emptied. Our children were gone. I traveled all that winter, to the First Court of Alrashesh, then to the Second Court of Valdhera, looking for the Kingskinder, for anyone. They were the same. Abandoned. Looted. Empty but for crows and wolves and pikefish in the streams."

"We were captured after the Summons," Olea murmured. "Split up, the younger Kingskinder sent to foster homes and the older ones pressed into military service."

"There are more out there?" The Kingsman's breath caught in his throat. "Safe? Alive?"

"A few. Did you have a child?"

"I did. A son." Vargen sighed. "His name was Khergen. He was eleven when his mother and I had to leave him for the Summons. I've looked everywhere for him. Every year, I pick up my shop and move to a new city. But Khergen was blond like his mother, with green eyes – a common coloring in Alrou-Mendera. And now I don't know what he might look like. I may never find him."

"I'm sure he would remember his father. He will find you."

"It is kind of you to say, but I don't hold much hope." Vargen spoke as he brushed back her riotous tumble of blue-black curls again. "Not after so long. Even though I swore on my sword that I would find him."

"Do you even have a sword still?"

"I do. My own sword is in a trunk in the back. Along with everything else." He smiled sadly.

"So you burned your dedication away, but kept the trappings?" Olea's fingers trailed over his scars, visible above the edge of his shirt lacings.

"Men do things they don't understand when they grieve."

"And the rest of your family?" Olea hated to ask.

The Kingsman's deep breath told her everything she needed to know. That single breath of their training. That single moment to feel everything of one's emotions before stilling them beneath the calm for which Kingsmen were famed.

A single breath, in which to feel all the heartbreak of the world.

"My wife died. Elsiria died the night we came to Roushenn Palace. Along with all the rest."

And suddenly, Olea knew what story he would tell. A story of heartache and pain, misery and death. In Vargen's sorrowful grey gaze, she read that none of the Kingsmen had survived the Summons. That each and every one of them that had traveled to the palace had met a horrible end. In his single breath, he had stilled a mountain of emotions for which there were no words.

A woe that was beyond weeping.

"Tell me," Olea whispered at last. "Tell me everything."

VARGEN CRADLED a tiny tea mug in his massive bear paws as they sat across from each other now, fully dressed and perched upon the high stools of his long wooden workbench. Sipping the mellow tea he'd prepared, Olea tasted winter-mint and elderbloom, an Alrashemni recipe to calm and enliven the mind while they talked through what she expected to be the long hours of the night.

"It's hard to say exactly *what* I saw the night of the Summons," Vargen spoke at last, opening their conversation after ten minutes of silence while he'd prepared tea at the hearth.

"Why is that?" Olea asked, sipping and listening intently.

"Because everything... moved." Vargen responded as he cradled his cup in his big hands, as if its warmth could soothe him. "The walls, the furniture, the mirrors – even the chandeliers! I've tried to recall it in detail, but specific memory still eludes me. The awful disorientation of that poison, those walls—"

"Steady." Olea reached out, settling her hand over his. "Start at the beginning."

With a deep, shuddering breath, Vargen nodded, then began again. "We arrived at the palace in full strength. Over two thousand Alrashemni came to the Summons, even elders who could no longer walk were carted through the city and carried up the steps of Roushenn. The King's Summons had been explicit. *All* those past their Eighth Seal were to journey forth, or else there would be war against us. We were labeled traitors to the crown if we did not come, accused of High Treason but without any specifics as to why the charge was being leveled. For what, I never did find out. But that was not my duty. I wasn't Rakhan. My wife Elsiria and I marched at the front of the column. We were expecting conflict, but though King Uhlas den'Ildrian had amassed a presence of Palace Guard throughout the city, it seemed they were merely escort."

"As if he was not expecting trouble."

"And truly, I don't think he did." Vargen nodded as he sipped his tea. "Some were soothed, marching through quiet streets. Some, like myself and Elsiria, found ourselves suspicious. Why threaten us with High Treason, punishable by death? If the King had summoned us simply to renew our vows *en masse*, that's all he needed to say. We would have come peaceably, without weapons."

"But he didn't. The Summons was a threat."

"And so we came armed, in our Greys." Vargen nodded again. "But the streets were quiet. And when the column arrived at Roushenn Palace, a delegation came to greet us in the Great Courtyard. A few of the King's Chancellors bowed and greeted us politely, but the King and his family were strangely absent. The Castellan invited us to overnight in the palace; rooms had been made ready, for *all* of us. We were told we would see the King and renew our vows in the Throne Hall come dawn, as all of us had done when we were newly made Eighth Seals. We were invited into the palace, and a veritable army of servants escorted us to overnight quarters. I had not thought Roushenn could hold such a mass of folk, but as we turned down this winding hallway or climbed that innumerable staircase, burrowing deep into the mountain, I realized that warren for what it truly was. A trap. You are Palace Guard, are you not?"

Olea nodded. "I am Captain-General of the Palace Guard and Fourth Captain of the Realm, behind the captains of the Fleetrunners, High Brigade, and the Whitecaps, our naval regiment. I report directly to the King. Or at least, I did. Now I report to his daughter, the Dhenra."

Vargen's brows rose, impressed. "You've done well, considering the charge of treason leveled against those who bear the Inkings."

"I was given a chance by the late Dhenir, Alden den'Ildrian."

"I suppose you were. In any case, you must know that palace was built to forestall a veritable army of invaders. I had not believed the tales to look at it from the outside, but once we were within, I realized how far back into the mountain it truly goes. And how much of a labyrinth it was."

"There are whole wings that are entirely closed off," Olea agreed, "places no one goes because the tunnels are too labyrinthine, and even servants invariably get lost. I heard an estimate from Castellan Lhaurent once that the palace could hold an army of ten thousand in its bowels. It doesn't just carve into the mountain, it's beneath the foundations of this city – beneath our very feet. All the sewers of Lintesh run through shafts that sink deep beneath the extensions of Roushenn. The Unterhaft is a maddening labyrinth, almost all of it closed off. But it means that Roushenn has rooms and kitchens and storerooms aplenty when there is a host to house."

"I had no idea it was so extensive." Vargen grunted, his dark eyebrows rising. "And did you know that the walls move? That there is a hidden palace *behind* the palace proper?"

Surprise lanced through Olea in a vicious strike, as a cold fury bubbled up in her gut. "*That* I did not know."

"When I saw it, I thought I had gone mad," Vargen murmured, gazing down into the dregs of his tea. "There were four of us in my room, including myself and my wife, but the quarters were spacious. Mirrored chandeliers, furniture good enough for any lord, with two bedrooms, each with a four-post bed. Mirrors were everywhere, set into the walls between stone columns, even some of the furniture was set with an inlay of tiny mirrors like dragon-hide. It was opulent; far too much for hosting us. Myself and my wife, and Khennir and his wife Rhenna were on our guard. But as the night wore on everything seemed quite regular. We were provided food and wine, and a servant to taste everything. The fireplaces were lit; our beds were turned down. Until finally, there was nothing to do but go to sleep. Khennir and I agreed to keep a vigil and leave our wives to rest. But that's when everything became madness."

"How?" Olea sat on the edge of her stool, her hands clasped tight around her mug as a twisting dread filled her.

"I smelled something." Vargen continued, fiddling with his mug. "Sweet but putrid, like oranges or lemons gone to rot. My world began to tilt and reel. I tried to stand, draw my sword, but it was like the room tipped on its edge. A deafening ringing began in my ears, and my stomach roiled. I'd been through the trials of poison, but this was like nothing I'd trained for. The walls began to *move*, involuting towards each other, sliding, rotating. Mirrors shifted, reflecting everything in a mass confusion. Furniture moved, *doorways* moved! I tried to lurch to the bedroom to find Elsiria, but in my fugue I realized I didn't even know where the bedroom was! I supported myself upon a drapery, but the wall started folding towards the one next to it. I tipped and got crushed between the two walls as they came nearly together."

Vargen lifted a hand to the scar that ran down the side of his face and over his collarbones. "This was from getting crushed between the walls. Found out later I had three broken ribs. But once the walls spat me out, I realized I was in a vast vaulted cavern, tinged with wan blue light and littered with free-standing walls and furniture. I turned back to where I thought my wife's room was, and realized I was looking *through* a mirror. Elsiria was on the other side, her room still changing, shifting. She had her blade out and was trying valiantly to stand and fight, but she was as poisoned and disoriented as I. And then I saw a flash of ... something. My mind thought it was a knife, but that wasn't right. It was like five knives, like a hand of knives ripped across her throat. And I thought I saw..." Vargen shuddered and closed his eyes. Olea's heart keened for him, for them all, nightmares still potent even after so long.

"Saw what?" She had to ask.

Eyes still closed, he took a long draught of tea, then swallowed. "I thought I saw a demon."

"A demon?"

Vargen's eyes opened. "I can't really say. I must have been hallucinating from the poison in the air. But I thought I saw... some massive creature. Lanky, it was tall as two men and stood upright just like a man does, but hunched over. Leathery black skin, barely visible in the darkness, with knives for claws. An abomination. Fear engulfed me to see it. But such a thing is fable; no worldly creature looks thusly. It must have been a man in costume, with knives. And in my fugue I hallucinated... something else."

"A demon." Olea went very still, recalling a similar demonic creature she'd seen that same night, the giant scorpion ridden by the man in herringbone leathers. But this creature Vargen described sounded different. And Olea thought suddenly that Vargen's tale could be absolutely true. She had seen something, experienced something that night beyond her capacity to reason.

And so had he.

"I had seen my share of battle, and so had my wife." Vargen heaved a deep sigh, continuing on. "I had made peace with the fact that the sword might someday take her. But this was madness. I think my mind broke from it, from my terror. Everything ceased moving after she died. I hacked at that mirror with my sword and pummeled it with my bare fists until they bled, my ribs screaming agony. But nothing moved. Not for me."

"How did you get out?" Olea murmured.

"I must have gone unconscious. I woke some time later, half-buried in a black curtain. I looked through the mirror, but her body was gone. There was nothing for me to do but find my way out. I can't tell you how long I wandered that fey blue darkness. I passed mirror after mirror, rooms empty of people but full of furniture, jumbled like it had all been forgotten. It was like I was trapped in a dream world, behind the real one. At last, I passed halls where there were people beyond the mirrors, servants and Guardsmen all going about their business. Palace folk, but no Alrashemni. They were oblivious to my presence behind the walls. No one could hear me or see me. Finally, I found myself heading down a plain tunnel cut into the byrunstone. It was utterly dark and I followed it by touch until I waded through sewage, finally touching a ladder. I followed that up through a storm grate at the edge of the city. I had the presence of mind to shuck my jerkin and stow it, at least. Steal some clothes from a wash line. It wasn't safe to be a Kingsman, not anymore. Somehow I knew the rest of us were dead. That what had happened in my quarters had happened to us all. Demon or man, we had been played false, right from the King's own hands. And it was all done very quietly, arousing not a single voice of protest in the night."

Olea sat silent a long time, both hands gripped around her cup, her heart cold like byrunstone. At last, she looked up. "Do you remember which storm grate you came up through?"

"Yes." Vargen gave a tired sigh. "But you have to understand, I was severely drugged. I didn't count my steps in the darkness. I don't know which turns I chose in the twisting sewers. I got out by luck. I've tried to get back in a few times, but I end up just slogging through shit and piss all day."

Olea rolled her shoulders, trying to work out her tension. At last she sighed, her scowl bitter. "Lhaurent. I'm *sure* he knows about some of this."

"The Castellan?" Vargen murmured. "I've wondered so, in dark nights where sleep eluded me. His smile when he greeted us at the palace gates had the feel of eels that night. All the Chancellors seemed that way. Composed. Calm. Welcoming. Do you think they knew about the back passages of Roushenn? About what was going to happen?"

Olea chewed her lower lip, considering it. "Those back-palace places you described aren't on any map of Roushenn I've seen, and I've never observed a single wall move. But there are times... when I'm *sure* a different piece of furniture sat in a particular hallway the day before. Or when I walk a passage I've walked a hundred times, only to find it takes a strange turn I didn't remember. I always come out where I'm supposed to be, but... sometimes the journey getting there is different. I mentioned it to Castellan Lhaurent once and he sneered at me, said I had been drinking too much, believing tales of Roushenn being haunted with the Black Ghost and all. But after tonight – I have to find out. Maybe the Castellan and the Chancellate know about the walls and maybe they don't, but the Dhenra's safety is in my hands. And if what you say is true, then Roushenn is far from safe."

Vargen drained the last of his tea. "Now that I've told you, what are you going to do?"

Olea set her cup carefully aside. "I've been charged by Dhenra Elyasin to find out what happened to the Kingsmen and why. And I intend to do just that. If you'll help me."

"I pledge myself to you as best I can, Kingswoman." Vargen nodded soberly as he set a massive palm to his chest. "Know that my hands are yours. My sword is yours, as I should have protected all our kin the first time. I will do whatever needs doing. But this task... I want to do."

Olea nodded, then rose. "I need a few days to think. Give me three days and I will return at nightfall. Thank you for the tea, Vargen. And thank you... for the truth."

Olea didn't mention their kiss and neither did Vargen. It had been right at the time, two lost hearts finding out they were no longer alone. Olea stepped towards the door, her stride purposeful. But a smattering of small metal pieces caught her eye upon a workbench and she stopped. Changing course, she walked over to a repair in progress, her long fingers trailing over a number of minuscule gears from a Praoughian wind-watch.

"You repair Praoughian clockworks?"

"I don't get many, but yes. Why?" Vargen nodded, his brows furrowed in confusion.

"Can you look at something for me?" Unbuckling a leather pouch at her belt, Olea slid out a small white silk bag, dumping out a number of tiny gears in brass and silver, gold and copper. Motioning her over to a focus-lamp to get a better look, Vargen trained a series of lenses upon her palm.

"What is it? Those gears look like nothing I'm familiar with."

"I don't know." Olea spoke as she left her palm out for his inspection. "It's a puzzle of some kind. My brother Elohl found it in the palace the night before our kin died. He said it was one piece initially, but when he touched it they fell apart. Can you put it back together? Can you tell me what it is?"

"I can try. But what do you think they're for?" Vargen's glance was curious.

"It may be a key to why our kin were killed," Olea murmured as she carefully returned the pieces to the bag and pressed it into Vargen's palm.

"Then I will do everything I can to solve this puzzle."

Vargen closed his fist protectively around the silk bag, and something about it touched Olea's heart. Stepping forward, she reached up, giving the Kingsman a quick kiss. Before he could say anything, she opened the workshop doors, stepping out into the chilly night. Taking a single breath, she moved off through the dark-choked alley, one hand resting upon her sword as she paced the silent street.

The fingertips of the other played across the topmost star of her Inkings, as a seething rage burned in her gut.

16

GHRENNA

The iron tang of blood filled Ghrenna's mouth, but she couldn't swallow it. She tried to open her eyes, but they stuck as if sealed shut with horse glue. Her hearing pulsed like a slow tide though memory was coming back now through her fog. She recalled crouching upon the estate wall, her jaw locking tight with a spasm, not even able to shriek as a vision hit. Her limbs splayed out from beneath her and she remembered falling, with the vague impression of being caught in strong arms. A flurry of motion and sound had happened then, which must have been her guild-mates rushing her away from the manor they'd been about to rob. Ghrenna recalled watching silveroaks sway in the moonlit dark as her body finally gave up, everything lax as she was carried in someone's strong arms.

"Ghren? Ghrenna? Can you hear me?"

Ghrenna tried to form words to respond to Luc's question, but all movement failed her.

"What the *fuck* was that back there!?" Gherris' voice was a raw snarl, sandblasting her ears.

"Shut up Gherris!" Luc's voice rose again with a fierce bite. "She's had a Thren-Maule seizure. We need to get her to a physician."

"At this time of night? Dressed like we are?" Gherris growled.

Ghrenna struggled to open her eyes, but only managed a flutter. Their voices were too loud, too harsh for her pounding head. Someone unbound her hair and it fell over her ears, curtaining her –probably Shara. Shara knew that when her headaches hit, every sensation was misery.

“Shut up, both of you,” Shara interjected. “She’s coming around. Ghrenna? Can you hear me?”

“I told you all that shit she smokes will be the death of her.” Gherris spoke sullenly.

“It’s the only thing that keeps her headaches at bay!” Shara snapped back.

“A little threllis never hurt anyone,” Luc’s warm hand traced Ghrenna’s brow. “I’ve never seen it do anything like that. I don’t think it’s the smoke.”

“You’ve never seen anyone smoke as much as she does.”

“True,” Luc’s voice was considering. “But I’ve spoken with an apothecary who smoked *nearly* as much. They use it for chronic fugue-headaches and to forestall seizures. She vomits in the morning, doesn’t she? And her appetite is weak until midday? If she’s seizure-afflicted, I bet she’s never even without her pipe when it’s just the two of you girls around the cavern, is she?”

“How did you know all that?” Shara murmured with astonishment.

“I know a lot more than you give me credit for. Come on, Ghren, whiff this.” Something that reeked like a cross between a sewage canal and a dead porcuphensis wafted past Ghrenna’s nose. But she found herself gagging, her eyelids finally popping open to see Luc above her. “There you are,” he breathed, his fingertips stroking her face as he smiled grimly, a worried tightness to his green eyes. “You gave us a turn, woman. Don’t you *ever* fall off an estate wall like that again!”

Ghrenna struggled to sit up and Luc and Shara helped, propping her up on pillows as she realized she was back in the grotto in her own bed. Relief filled her, knowing no enemy could accost her here while she was weak. Now that she was conscious, her vision rippled through her. Hundreds of men in dark grey had stood defiant in a blue-cobbled plaza. Pennants had fluttered in the breeze from five different nations. So many different peoples had been in the vision, from redheads of the far north to bronze Cennetians of the south. And beyond that, massing at the city’s walls, an army the likes of which she’d never seen, filling the plain. Ghrenna took a deep breath, trying to return to her pain-riven body, though a part of her wanted to stay in this astonishingly strange future she had seen.

"How did you get me home?" Ghrenna grated, her voice raw.

"Luc carried you," Shara spoke as she stroked Ghrenna's hair. "He caught you, too."

"Fifteen-foot fall, little *Byrune.*" Luc grumped affectionately. "Nearly wrenched my shoulder off keeping you from splatting like a ripe fig-melon on the paving-stones."

Pacing near the armoire, Gherris rounded on them, furious. "You're a liability, Ghrenna! Always smoking! These headaches... and now this!"

"Like you should speak!" Luc rounded on the younger man with a snarl, his patience evaporated. "You just can't wait to slit a throat for your sick pleasure every damn night! You want to go be bloodthirsty, you sick fuck? It's called the King's army. Go sign the fuck up!"

"Everyone calm down," Ghrenna struggled up from the pillows to show she was hale. But sitting up made her head a cascade of misery, and she clutched her temples as stars burst across her vision.

"Here, sweetie." Shara had her glass-blown pipe packed from the copper threllis canister by the bed and lit. Ghrenna took it, brushing her white-blonde waves back, then had a long pull, the thunderous roil of her pain dulling some.

"You can barely move!" Gherris gestured at her angrily. "And right to the smoke!"

Ghrenna pinned Gherris with her eyes – pinning him to the wall with her gaze. She put everything into that stare, letting him feel how out of line he was, and that just because he was a Kingskinder didn't mean he'd earned her respect. Filling herself with stillness, Ghrenna murmured. "*Alrashemnesh aere phelo Areseitya rhavesin.*"

"*Areseitya?*" Gherris blanched as he stared at her. "Are you fucking with me?"

Luc cleared his throat, glancing from one to the other. "Um... what did I miss?"

Gherris spared him a glance. "She's says she's a Seer. *Areseitya* means True Seer in Alrashemni. It's used for people who have visions."

Luc was staring at her now, his lips fallen open in astonishment. "Um, like... the Three Seers of Wyr? Like that old fae-yarn?"

"No." Gherris shook his head. "Fucking childish drivel. True Seers don't have visions about lost chickens, Luc. True Seers have visions like, when the fuck we are going to die. Visions like, who killed the little girl found strangled in the street."

"Did you see something, Ghrenna?" Luc was appraising her now. "Is that why you seized?"

"What was it, Ghren?" Shara was calm, the only person in Ghrenna's guild that knew she was finally admitting the truth of who she was.

"I saw Kingsmen." Ghrenna's gaze was still on Gherris. "Hundreds of Kingsmen with pennants from a number of nations. Dressed in the Greys at Roushenn Palace and arrayed for battle."

"*What?*" Gherris startled, though he was attentive as he came over to the bedpost, a flicker of hope in his young, cruel face. "But I thought all the Kingsmen were dead! Are you saying there are *hundreds* alive out there somewhere?"

"My vision could be wrong." Ghrenna took a long pull from her pipe, eyeing him. "They generally aren't wrong, save for one ten years ago. But it was something so important—"

"That now you don't trust them." Luc's voice was somber beside her, taking everything in stride.

"Was that vision about the Alrashemni also?" Gherris watched her carefully, something knowing in his dark gaze.

"Yes." Ghrenna nodded. "Myself and four other Seventh Seals I knew acted on that vision, but it was wrong. We were arrested after the Summons, split up. One is in Lintesh now, she's Captain-General of the Palace Guard. One is a prize-fighter. One died in battle. The last was discharged from service in the High Brigade recently, I think." Ghrenna's mind strayed as the threllis kicked in. She saw Elohl's sinuous limbs again, saw him fucking that woman with the honey-blonde braid. It sparked a bitter possessiveness and Ghrenna pushed it away.

Getting angry would only heighten her current pain.

"Lintesh. That's only a week's ride," Gherris mused, wheels turning in his mind. "We could go to Lintesh, find your friend. See if she knows anything about these Kingsmen you saw..."

"We go to Lintesh, and what? Your parents are suddenly alive again Gherris?"

Ghrenna's words were bitter, a shocked silence filling the grotto as her guild-mates stared at her. Gherris' words had voiced a temptation Ghrenna had often had. But it was safer to stay here in this beautiful tomb than to go back and face how she had sent her friends off on a fool's quest from her false vision. How she had spilled the Kingskinder's whereabouts to the brute in herringbone leathers who had broken her mind. It was safer to stay here thieving like a rat then to face the judgment in Olea's eyes.

Or Elohl's.

"This future..." Ghrenna sighed more gently as she settled to the pillows, staring at the rotted lace of the canopy, "it was just a flash, Gherris. A future I have no idea how or when it will come. Futures are tricky, with numerous branchings. Most of the visions I see are common-thread events, which means they happen right as I see them. I've only seen a few true futures, and one was wrong. Deadly, horribly wrong. And everything went wrong because of it."

Ghrenna's gaze flicked to her clockwork collection – feeling all her shame just as fresh as the day she'd been carted to the Fleetrunners.

CONVERSATION ABOUT GHRENNA'S vision had turned to argument, had yielded to a break for food, which had morphed back into argument. Tempers were frayed, everyone worn from a long night as Ghrenna paced the grotto now, stretching out her limbs. Lounging on her bed with his boots up on her blankets, Luc stared up at Ghrenna's frayed canopy with his hands laced behind his head, as Shara picked through a cheese plate on the bureau and Gherris slouched against the bedpost, fiddling with one of his knives.

"We can't go to Lintesh. What would we tell the Consortium?" Ghrenna mused, taking up their argument again as she pulled on her threllis pipe.

"Fuck the Fhouria Thieves' Consortium." Gherris growled. "We're paid up. They get more from us in one night then they do from other guilds in a month. I say we go to Lintesh and find out about the Kingsmen. We can do some thieving while we're there for easy cash."

"If there's cash, I'm in." Shara quipped reasonably, munching some cheese. "Thieving comes easy in any city as long as we stay together."

"Lintesh is not just *any* city." Luc eyed Shara, a glimmer of anger in his eyes. "You wanna tangle with Palace Guard? Be my guest. Only the best thieves work Lintesh, and their Consortium is a tight-knit bitchfest."

"You grew up in Lintesh, didn't you Luc?" Ghrenna paused to lean against one stout post of her bed.

"I left when I was twelve." He nodded, staring up at the frayed lace. "I'm not going back."

"Well, we go together or we don't go at all." Shara sighed with irritation. "Split up, we're useless to work the jobs we work. Luc can't climb for shit, I can't hardly lockpick, Ghrenna can't work a party, and Gherris has no restraint. Unanimous vote, or we don't go."

"I'm in." Gherris threw his knife to the stone without a moment's hesitation.

"I'm in, too." Shara threw her knife in also. "The gentry are beginning to recognize me here in Fhouria. I gotta move on."

Ghrenna took a long draw on her pipe as her head lanced. Going to Lintesh would mean facing her past, but if there was one person who was in a position to understand the political machinations of the Crown, it would be Olea. Drawing a knife from her harness, Ghrenna flipped it, then put it away. "I have to think on it. Give me the night."

"Luc?" Gherris was all tension as he glanced at their most senior member.

Luc hadn't moved on the bed, his long hands still laced behind his head. "Nope. I told you, I'm not going back to Lintesh."

"Fucking *ghennie!*" Gherris snarled. "Throw your knife in, or so help me, I'll gut you!"

"Nope. And your threats aren't helping me change my mind."

"Come on, Luc," Shara wheedled. "We're getting played out here in Fhouria, and you know it."

"Nope."

Ghrenna sighed, exhausted, her mind constantly drifting to Elohl. Threllis helped her focus, but sometimes that focus turned to obsessiveness. And Elohl was *not* what she needed to be obsessing over right now. "Let's discuss it again tomorrow. We all need sleep."

"Fuck that." Gherris' eyes were wrathful ink. "I'm going out."

"Going to go kill somebody to feel better?" Luc was still staring up at the canopy.

The simmering tension between the two men snapped like bowstring. Gherris was a flash of motion as he surged from the bedpost, but Luc was faster. Luc's knifepoint pricked the hollow of Gherris' throat mid-lunge, before the younger man could raise his blade. Livid with rage, Gherris was frozen, not even a hair of his short-cropped black curls moving as he breathed hard, trapped.

While Luc had only risen halfway from his reclining leisure.

"Back off, boy," Luc growled, showing the killer that lived beneath his merriment. Ghrenna had seen it before, and each time it was like Luc had ripped a mask from his face to reveal a demon beneath. He was a man who rarely angered, but Gherris had just pushed his limit. Gherris slowly lowered his knife, sliding it back in his harness. Stretching out a hand, Ghrenna placed it on Luc's, slowly pushing his knife away from Gherris' throat.

"Let's just get some sleep." She murmured. "We can talk it over again in the morning."

"Fuck that." Gherris snarled, using Ghrenna's intervention to hulk off towards the entrance of the grotto as Luc slid his knife away.

"Do you need anything, Ghren?" Shara turned towards Ghrenna with a wry smile. "Would you like me to sleep in here with you tonight?"

"No. I'll be fine." Ghrenna shook her head, her headache dull now and the after-flashes of her vision fading. "Go get some sleep in your own chambers tonight."

"There's cheese and fruit over here on the bureau, if you need anything. I'll see if I can go talk some sense into Gherris." Shara gave a kind smile, then slipped from the cavern the way Gherris had gone. Turning to Luc, Ghrenna found he'd settled back to the bed, his boots up on her covers once more.

"Are you going to be my keeper tonight?" Ghrenna murmured around her pipe, lifting an eyebrow.

"Your bed is a haven of comfort, milady." Luc glanced over with a teasing grin, though it was tight. "There is no place I would rather be."

"You can go back to your chamber, Luc. Really. I'll be fine."

"Not with a problem like yours. Sometimes people who have seizures stop breathing after an episode. So I'm sleeping here tonight."

"How do you know so much about seizures?" Ghrenna frowned. "Were you apprenticed to a physician once?"

"Trying to pick into my past isn't getting you any sleep, Ghren."

Luc patted the coverlet next to him and Ghrenna realized he was right. Moving towards the bed, she shucked her gear to her silk undergarments as she crawled under, exhausted. Reaching down to unbuckle his boots, Luc kicked them off as Ghrenna scooted backwards and he reached out, pulling her close and spooning her. They didn't often sleep together just for comfort, but it happened every now and again. Ghrenna was grateful tonight as she pushed away images of Elohl, burrowing into her pillows and breathing in Luc's warm sandalwood musk.

Setting her pipe upon the bedstand, Ghrenna left it lit so she could breathe the last of the smoke as she fell asleep. She was just drifting off when Luc shifted with a sigh and sat up. Ghrenna heard the clatter of his leather harness hit the grotto floor, then his jerkin, and his shirt. He flopped back to the pillows, winding his arms about her middle, his bare chest pressed against her back.

"Ghren? You awake?" He murmured as one hand caressed her ribs. "I can't go back to Lintesh, Ghrenna."

Blinking open bleary eyes, Ghrenna rolled over to see Luc's green gaze by the lantern-light. Frowning with an unusual moroseness, all his regular merriment had fled. As she watched him, he sighed and rolled to his back, staring up at the canopy.

"Why? What is it about Lintesh? You're never this stubborn about anything, Luc." Ghrenna spoke, worried.

"My family will find me if I go back there."

"I thought you grew up on the streets." Ghrenna blinked. "That you didn't have any family."

"Partly." He gave a sour grimace. "My family didn't have a lot of time for me, we'll put it that way. I escaped to the streets whenever I could, to get away from them. Ever heard of the Lhorissians?"

"King's Physicians." With an astonished blink, Ghrenna rose up to one elbow, ignoring the vicious throb in her head. "Are you saying you're of the line of the King's personal doctor? That you grew up in Roushenn Palace?"

"Yeah, don't remind me." Luc's smile was pained. "But I'm not the firstborn son. Firstborn sons become King's Physician. Second sons don't get much. An apothecary post in some obscure township, sometimes a post in one of the bigger cities. I wasn't the favored child."

Ghrenna blinked at him, finally understanding the man lounging upon her bed. It made sense now, Luc's haughty manners, his teasing demeanor that wouldn't have been out of place in a King's court. His gambling and the strange idleness that ran undercurrent to everything he did, his more than competent ability with weapons – all habits he would have picked up living in a palace. "But the King's Physician is knighted. And so are his sons, even if they don't ascend the post. You *are* a lord!"

"Yeah, Lord Luc after all..." His chuckle was sad. "But I can't go back there."

"So your family will find you. So what? You don't have to become King's Physician."

"Oh, but you're wrong." Luc rolled towards her, gazing at her with a bitter humor. "My older brother Arlas died four years ago. A messenger came to find me recently from Lintesh. He was nosy, asking around, and someone sent the fellow to a tavern I gamble at. The messenger found me, told me my father died a number of months back, just a few weeks before the King himself. I had to take him to a quiet alley and kill him, so he wouldn't send word back about me."

"So your father and older brother are dead. What about your other brothers?"

"There are no more sons." Luc murmured. "I'm supposed to ascend the position. And they'll keep sending fellows after me until they haul me back to Roushenn. When this messenger doesn't return, the Chancellors will send someone more capable..."

"Could you do it?" Ghrenna frowned in thought. "Do you know what you need to, to ascend the post of King's Physician?"

"Oh I know it, all right." Luc chuckled roughly. "A thousand and one remedies for all the worst maladies. Drummed into me since I was three years old, usually at the end of a switch. But that's not the reason I'm slated to follow my father's line."

"What is?"

"This." Reaching out, Luc splayed his fingers over Ghrenna's face with a light touch. And where they went, her headache rolled back to nearly nothing. She closed her eyes, drinking in ease as Luc's fingers roved her scalp, stroking her hair and playing along her jaw. Smoothing tension from her brow, he traced gently over her closed eyelids, removing pain from her eye sockets like drawing blood with leeches. Ghrenna couldn't open her eyes. It was bliss to be this relaxed, to have her head humming with peace. There was still a trace of pain, but it was far away as she breathed softly in rapture.

"Better?" He spoke, ceasing.

"Gods, Luc... what did you do?" Ghrenna sighed, floating in bliss.

"What I was born to do." His chuckle was wry. "Only one person in three generations of Lhorissians has the healing hands. But the King keeps us, just in case one of us develops the gift. My gift rose when I was eleven. I escaped Lintesh shortly thereafter, but every now and again, I'll get a messenger like the one who found me. They're good with weapons Ghren, and they don't take no for an answer. What I did for you tonight will wear off, but every healing will make your headaches better. I'll do it for you, but *swear* to me you won't tell anyone. I'm not the King's pet. And I never will be."

Ghrenna's eyes blinked open, no pain behind them for the first time in ages. "I swear, Luc. But the King's dead. The Dhenra is supposed to ascend the throne in a few weeks."

"I'm not her pet, either." Luc's green gaze was fierce in the lamplight.

Ghrenna was silent a long moment, processing this revelation. She reached out, touching Luc's bright golden hair and feeling herself smile for the first time in ages. "You're a lord. I always thought there was something peculiar about you."

"Yeah, yeah. Don't rub it in, alright? And besides, I'm not peculiar. I'm handsome." His lips smiled now, but as his hand settled at her waist, his face went from teasing to stern suddenly. "You scared me tonight, Ghren. I thought I was going to lose you. There are few things that could make me betray my gift... but seeing you fall off that wall tonight was one of them."

"I'm not yours, Luc." Ghrenna murmured, though after what he'd done for her, Ghrenna felt her usual reticence recede. Luc was a good man, and in his fierce gaze she saw what he'd never say. That he adored her. That he would do anything, including throwing himself into danger, just to keep her safe.

"Would you come to Lintesh? If I went?" Ghrenna murmured at last.

Luc's body tensed. But then he gave a sigh as he rolled to his back, staring up at the mildewing canopy. "I have to. I can already tell you're going; I can see it in your eyes. You won't be able to let this go, not after tonight. I had my suspicions about your health for years, but visions?" He lifted his hands in a helpless gesture. "I have to go. I have to keep you safe."

"You don't have to do anything for me, Luc."

"That's where you're wrong." Luc rolled to face her again. Reaching out, he trailed his fingers down her neck, sliding them behind to her nape. Bliss seeped from him, deep into Ghrenna's muscles and up into her skull. She found herself melting into his touch, arching back as he held her by the neck, her lips falling open as she breathed softly with ease – and need. Luc stared at her with an answering need, and soothed by his gift tonight, her heart opened to it. Ghrenna reached out, stroking his jaw, watching his lips part to her touch. His green eyes burned as he pulled her close, cinching her tight against his body, his hand where it touched the small of her back radiating bliss. Turning his head, he lipped her thumb; sucked it deep into his mouth. Pleasure rippled through Ghrenna from his gift and his natural seduction, making her need more.

She came to him, desiring something solid, needing someone here and now. Melting into Luc, Ghrenna let him draw her into a deep kiss as he licked pleasure into her mouth, as he bit it gently into her lips. He kissed her hard, and Ghrenna arched for him – pushing Elohl's face and visions from her mind until the dawn.

17

OLEA

In her dream, Olea sat at an enormous banquet table, the Throne Hall nearly silent now as she languished in her cups near one roaring hearth. Everything was bedecked with yhulen for the Soldier's Ball at midwinter, their glossy spiked leaves and red berries catching the light of flames. The cavernous hall was clearing, the revelry nearly dead so close to midnight solstice. Roaring fires still filled every massive bluestone hearth, the long trestle tables filthy with spilled food and wine. The ball had been a merry event for most of Olea's new comrades in the Palace Guard, most bringing wives and fiancées to dance and drink in the King's own hall. A number of Olea's comrades had asked her to dance, but all had given up as the night burned low. Two foolish women giggled past upon the arm of the handsome ruffian Aldris den'Farahan. He glanced Olea's way and winked.

Olea snorted into her goblet, regretting it as wine lanced up her nose.

Pulling a piece of parchment from her jerkin, Olea fiddled with it, a charcoal nib to hand. Fuzzy and spinning, she set the charcoal to paper and a rough scrawl appeared, then another. Hashed shading created texture, trees and hills. Strong marks created walls and turrets, a practice yard and an amphitheater. Absorbed, Olea's hearing numbed to a buzz, blocking out the hall around her as she returned to a better time, a better place, with every inelegant mark. Dulled by drink, she heard the scrape of a boot behind her – too late. A hand fell upon her shoulder and she startled, her charcoal scrawling over the page as she sprang unsteadily to her feet – knocking the bench over as she whipped one longknife from its sheath with a hiss.

To find herself leveling it at her King.

A quick in-breath came from the only servant left in the hall. The fires were glowing embers now in every hearth, the tables cleared. Olea was alone in the hall but for King Uhlas den'Ildrian standing before her, tall and stern at the end of her blade. Clad in a black jerkin and breeches, a white ermine pinned about his shoulders, he looked almost plain. But his bearing was regal, his grey-shot dark hair cut military short, his deep grey eyes steady. His body was lean, sword-honed as he stood before Olea, her knife still brandished. She hated him. She hated the way he stared her down, unmoved by the steel in her hand. She hated the way he didn't react, like his heart was nothing but ashes. She hated the way he stood there as if he cared nothing for the Kingswoman before him and feared her skill not at all.

Like she was beneath him.

Like the Kingsmen had only been good enough to purge from the nation like rats.

"A cup of Arinul wine for my Guardsman, then leave us." King Uhlas' voice was as hard as his eyes, and the servant scurried to comply. Soon Olea's knife-hand was filled with a cup and no longer with a weapon, though she didn't remember her King disarming her. But her knife sat there upon the table, glinting in the low firelight as King Uhlas beckoned for her to sit. Olea sank unsteadily to the bench as he righted it, then sat next to her. He gazed at her drawing, pulling the parchment close.

"Impressive. Is this someplace you know?"

"Alrashesh." The word ground out like broken glass from Olea's wine-ruined throat.

"I see." King Uhlas sat back, regarding her. His gaze flicked to the parchment, studying it, then back to her. "I shall have to annex it, won't I?"

Seething anger flowed through Olea's veins, a hot temper she'd cultivated since being carted to the palace in manacles six months ago after her arrest in Alrashesh. "By the Serthas Code three-six-oh-three, you can do no such thing. The Court of Alrashesh is *private* property, belonging to the yet-living descendants of the Alrashemni."

"You know your law." The King's face betrayed nothing.

"You've watched me in the Library Annals often enough. Stalking me, really." Olea took a disrespectful mouthful of wine without asking her liege's permission. But King Uhlas did not react, his iron gaze steady.

"You have poured through more tomes of law and languages in the past six months than I think my Chancellate have ever seen. You dislike my Summons. You think it unlawful?"

Fighting the spin of the room, Olea indulged in the looseness of her tongue, not caring if it put her in the stocks. "Your Summons was shit, you bastard! And someday I'll prove it."

King Uhlas's iron-hard eyes pierced her. At last, a smile lifted the corners of his lips. "Yes. I'm sure you will."

The dream shifted then, the fire-lit gables of the hall diminishing until they were Olea's own chamber. A single candle burned to push back the night, the air through the open window clear with the sweet cool of morning. Olea twisted in her sheets, not alone in her narrow bed. Dhenir Alden den'Ildrian was there, holding her, her head cradled on his well-muscled chest as the fingers of his hand traced her breast. He glanced at the window, his glorious dark hair and alabaster skin haloed by the candle's light.

"Sun's almost up, Olea. I should go." He murmured gently, though he didn't move.

"Stay." Olea sighed, sweaty and spent.

"Father knows I'm not getting much sleep these days." Alden chuckled mischievously, making Olea want to ride him all over again.

"The rumors you've planted say you're out whoring in the Queen's Quarter. Uhlas doesn't know you're here, and no one else does either." Olea retorted as she snuggled in, not about to let him go.

"Dhenirs can go out whoring," Alden chuckled as he cinched her close. "What they can't do, is fuck Lieutenants in their Guard."

"So make me Captain-General of the Guard then." Olea grinned into his chest. "You gave me my original promotion six years ago, after all."

"*Father* gave you your original promotion."

"What?" Olea raised up to one elbow, confused. Alden looked like King Uhlas, dark haired, slender-muscled and tall. He was a near-perfect copy of his father except for the storms that roiled him, where Uhlas was nothing but calm precision. "I thought *you* promoted me, after I bested you just after midwinter my first year in the Guard!"

"Whoops." Alden gave his seductive chuckle as he reached out to stroke Olea's cheek. "I actually wasn't supposed to tell you that. But since it's been six years, I suppose it doesn't hurt for you to know the truth. You remember that morning you and I fought after the Soldier's Ball, and you bested me?"

"I do." Olea lifted an eyebrow at him. "You gave me my first promotion that same night."

"Well, that afternoon after you schooled my ass, my father and I were on a hunt in the Kingswood. I told him that the Kingswoman trainee had bested me, and he reined his horse, looked me in the eye, and said, *promote her*. Just like that. And then he made me promise not to speak a word of it. Ever."

"Why?" Olea spoke, frowning.

"Who knows?" Alden shrugged in that careless, handsome way of his. "Father has schemes within schemes and secrets within secrets. He's always been that way. But he's been different lately. I catch him pacing sometimes, gazing at the walls and mirrors as if he expects brigands to jump out of them. He's taken to riding out to the First Abbey on a weekly basis, even if it's just for an hour, and he never takes the same men. I think he's becoming paranoid."

"What does he do at the Jenner Abbey?"

Alden shrugged again. "Fenton has been with him a few times. He says they go to the compound. But father never lets any of the guards come in with him past the Abbey gates. He's always met by the Abbess, Lenuria den'Brae."

"Strange." Olea settled back into the crook of Alden's arm. "But he's always been secretive. Did I tell you he used to watch me in the Library Annals? All that autumn just after I got here, before you and I met. I used to go read to calm my mind."

"You do need a lot of calming, Kingswoman." Dhenir Alden mussed her black curls affectionately.

"I'll show you how much calming I need...!" Olea bit him on his shoulder and Alden laughed, full-throated and amused in that joyous, daring way Olea so loved.

"I surrender! No, but tell me, what did my father say to you in the Annals?"

"He didn't say anything. Just watched me – probably more than twenty times." Olea mused, thinking about it. "He did approach me at the Soldier's Ball that year though, the night before you and I bouted. I was drunk and pulled a knife on him. But he offered me wine instead of having me arrested. I got loose-tongued and told him I thought his Summons was unlawful, and that I was going to prove it. I actually called him a bastard right to his face. I thought he would have hauled me off to the dungeons. But he just... smiled. And then I met you on the practice grounds the very next morning."

"Strange. I've seen what father does to men who pull a weapon on him. Death is the least of their worries." Alden shifted next to her, then sat up. Settling back against the headboard, he rifled a hand through his sweat-slicked hair, then draped one arm across the headboard – an incredulous smile playing along his lips. "Sweet Aeon. Father set us up."

"What?" Olea blinked.

"Father set us up!" A low chuckle rumbled in his chest as Alden shook his head, his storm-grey eyes incredulous. "He told me to go observe the first-year Guards that day on the practice fields! He didn't say that the most beautiful, dangerous woman I would ever meet was going to be there, half-clad out in the snow and burning with passion." His gaze flicked to her, seductive. "Which he knows I can't resist."

"Why would your father set us up to meet the same morning I pulled a knife on him?" Olea's brows knit. "And why tempt you into someone's bed who's not a royal?"

"Maybe I need watching." Alden chuckled as he stroked Olea's jaw with his fingers. "Maybe he wanted someone close to me... to protect me. Personally."

Alden was joking, but Olea sobered as she sat up also, the sheets draping around her naked hips. "Maybe he did. You spent that whole first year trying to woo me. And when that didn't work, you set me in your personal guard these past five years. For five years I've been your shadow, always at your side."

"Four of which I've had you all to myself, in my bed." Alden chuckled, stroking Olea's Inkings and the tops of her breasts. "What can I say? I can't resist having the most beautiful Guardsman in the whole company near me. One who doesn't give fuck-all, and displays her Kingsman heritage proudly for everyone to see..."

"I'm the only Kingsman in the Guard." Olea's thoughts spiraled as she considered it.

"You're the most beautiful Kingsman in the Guard." Wrapping his arms around her, Alden pulled Olea in, kissing her collarbones.

"No. I'm the *only* Kingsman in the Guard, Alden." Olea moved back, gripping his chin and forcing the headstrong Dhenir to look at her. "Your father knows it. If what you say is right, he set you up to see my Inkings when I was fighting that day on the practice grounds in just my halter. I bested you that day, and your father knew you couldn't resist that. He set you up to take the *only* Kingsman in the guard into your bed. Don't you see? To bind us close – far closer than any of your other protectors. And Uhlas turns a blind eye to the things I'm teaching Elyasin. Fenton has told me Uhlas lingers in the shadows sometimes, watching Elyasin spar with me. He *wants* his daughter to learn Kingsman arts..."

"He wants us both to be close to the Kingsmen." Alden had turned thoughtful now. "To the only one we know. You."

"But it doesn't make sense. Why Summon the Kingsmen and accuse them of treason, then cause them all to disappear if he wants his children to be close to a Kingsman now?"

"Unless my father didn't give the Summons. Aeon's holy fuck!" Alden scrubbed a hand through his short black hair as his storm-ridden eyes churned. "Den'Selthir spoke the truth...!"

"Who? What?"

"You know how I went last month to the Valenghian front?" Alden spoke as his gaze snapped to Olea. "To do inspections for father? Well, one of the local lords in Vennet put our company up for the night. A Vicoute – Arlen den'Selthir. He was a genteel fellow, but he had the way of the sword about him. Indeed, we dueled at swords that evening for exercise, and he was probably the best swordsman I've ever come across. But as we sat in his steam-rooms that night, he told me something curious. I was asking about the war and how it had impacted his lands, and he told me my father had come through just before the war broke out. That Uhlas had stayed with den'Selthir in secret, on his way to Valenghia to treat at the eleventh hour with the Valenghian Vhinesse. But Arlen told me something else. That Uhlas had stayed with him the *very night* the Kingsmen Summons went out. And that Uhlas had ridden on to Valenghia the next day. I didn't believe the man at the time, but now..."

Olea let her breath out as her gut cramped, sick. "If that's true, it would have taken Uhlas two weeks of hard riding to make it back to Lintesh. He wouldn't have been at Roushenn Palace when the Summons went out, nor when the Kingsmen arrived! When they disappeared – he wasn't here!"

"My father didn't give the Summons." Alden looked green. "Sweet Aeon. He didn't want the Kingsmen dead! Someone else did. Someone else Summoned them, welcomed them here – and disposed of them. All before my father could do anything about it!"

"Someone with access to his seals, and close enough to copy his handwriting. That's what Uhlas meant when I told him his Summons was shit and someday I'd prove it, Alden! He told me, *I'm sure you will!*" Olea gripped Alden's wrist, hard. "He was haunting me in the libraries watching me hunt for the truth. And he put us together... so we'd find it!"

"Aeon's mercy!" Alden's head fell back against the bed frame. "He can't tell the nation. He can't tell anyone. My father can't risk speaking about this, Olea, he doesn't know whom to trust! No wonder he's been acting like a paranoid fuck for so many years. It must be one of the Chancellors..."

"Or a few of them." Olea's voice was soft. "Alden. We're talking about the disappearance of *two thousand* fighters. All in one night, quietly. That's not the kind of event a single person orchestrates."

"There must be a secret group opposing my father." Alden's gaze was sharp upon her. "The Kingsmen were *his* army, Olea. I remember him always telling me that when I was a boy. *In dire times, summon the Alrashemni Kingsmen. They will always do right by their King and country, and are the only ones you can trust to be your peacekeepers and personal guard.* So my father made sure the only Kingsman he knew would be by my side night and day. And Elyasin's." Alden reached out, stroking Olea's Inkings.

"I'm not the only one," Olea breathed. "I'm not the only Kingsman left alive. There are a number of the children scattered throughout the military. Though not any full-trained Kingsmen that I know of."

"Just children... like you were." Alden's fingers stole over Olea's chin, his thumb brushing her lips as he stared at Olea a long moment, his storm-grey eyes so very sad. And then, something in his gaze hardened. "I'm going to start asking around about the Summons. About what really happened. We need answers, and if my father's afraid to go after them... then we'll have to."

"I don't think that's wise, Alden." Olea gripped his wrist. "Uhlas has been cagey for a reason. He must suspect people near to him. He acts like there are spies all around, and perhaps we should too."

"I'll be careful." Alden leaned forward, pulling Olea into his arms, kissing her.

"No, I mean it!" Olea struggled.

"I'll be careful, my love," Alden breathed, brushing his lips over Olea's. "Besides... you'll be by my side. Nothing bad can happen to me or Elyasin while you're here. I'm just going to start quietly asking a few questions. Maybe I'll start with the palace staff. *Someone* should have seen something that night. I'll send a raven to Vennet and have Vicoute Arlen den'Selthir tell us what he knows. We'll get to the bottom of this, you and I. And then my father can rest easy."

"*Carefully*," Olea admonished.

Alden brushed his lips over hers. "Carefully."

"ALDEN!" Olea snapped upright in her bed, her nightshirt soaked with sweat. Tears tracked down her face, making a puddle in the hollow of her throat – but Olea did not wipe them away as she paused, every sense prickling in the night. Honing her hearing, she listened. Something had woken her, but now all was quiet, only whispers of air moving through her open window. In the darkness, her eyes took in every corner of her room, one hand ready upon the longknife beneath her pillow. But there was no intruder – only these unsettled dreams from everything Vargen had told her the night before.

Suddenly, a soft sound came at her ironbound door, like the tap of a finger. Clad only in her silk undershirt and underwear with her longknife to hand, Olea paced to the door and threw it wide, her knife poised to skewer a throat.

And saw Dhenra Elyasin blink in surprise in the torchlight of the soldier's hall.

"Forgive me, Dhenra!" Olea hastily lowered her knife, stepping back. The Dhenra took a shaky breath, then just as hastily stepped inside Olea's rooms, glancing furtively around as she entered. Olea checked the corridor also, but the Dhenra had timed it perfectly, avoiding the night-patrols. Although she had slipped her guards again, and Olea made a mental note to put Aldris on the Dhenra's watch personally until the coronation and wedding were over.

Olea shut the door and striking a phosphor match, lit candles upon the mantle, then set her longknife beside them. Turning to her liege, she sank to one knee, but the Dhenra was distracted, pacing Olea's sparse quarters. Stopping in front of the only decoration in Olea's simple room, Elyasin eyed a five-foot gilt-framed wall mirror. A gaudy piece, Olea had asked the Castellan to have it removed a number of times, and a number of times he had agreed but it had never been done.

A gripping sensation hit Olea's gut suddenly, as she realized this mirror probably provided a way for someone to watch her rooms, just like Vargen had seen behind the walls of Roushenn. The Dhenra stared at the mirror now, watching her reflection – and Olea wondered if someone was watching back. If someone could hear and see their conversation from the mirror's spying oculus. She was suddenly very aware of keeping this conversation, whatever it was going to be about, clean of anything that might threaten the Dhenra's life.

"Dhenra, how can I serve at this late hour?" Olea prompted.

"Such starkness," Elyasin's gaze rested upon the mirror, seeing the entire room. "It is a wonder to me that you choose to live this way, Olea, with but a single ornament upon the wall. But I suppose it was how you were raised, wasn't it?"

"Kingsmen have no need for idle treasures." Olea murmured. She had just readied herself to ask Elyasin to walk outside where they could really talk, so she could disclose everything Vargen had told her, when Elyasin turned, pinning Olea with her regal gaze.

"Did he come here? Alden? Did my brother spend time with you here?"

Astonished, Olea's eyelids flickered, as if Elyasin had somehow read her dreams. At last, she sighed, knowing this was ancient news if anyone was listening. "Sometimes. He would slip his guards just like you do, and put out the rumor that he was whoring and drinking in the Queen's Quarter."

"I miss him." Elyasin sank down upon the bed as her hand passed over Olea's buckwheat-grain pillow. "I can't believe it's been two years since he died. Sometimes I feel like he's just around the corner. If I walk the right hall, or find the right suit of armor, Alden will be inside, waiting to surprise me."

"Alden was a troublemaker." Olea's mouth quirked despite the tears that choked her.

"He loved you."

Olea took one long, slow breath. When she had composure, she came to sit upon her bed next to the Dhenra. "Elyasin. What's this all about?"

"I miss him," the Dhenra flushed, her body tight with misery. "It should be him taking father's throne this summer with you by his side, making him strong like you always did. How am I supposed to do this? Who will stand with me, to help make me strong?"

And suddenly, Elyasin was shattering, falling into Olea's arms with renting sobs. The Dhenra was a proud woman and a fighter, so much so that Olea often forgot she was still young. Wrapping her arms around Elyasin just as she had upon receiving the news of Alden's death, tears threatened and Olea blinked them back as the young woman clung to her.

"I couldn't protect him," Olea whispered, her voice rasping. "I was supposed to protect him so he could be here for you. I'm so sorry, Elyasin..."

"It should be Alden ascending the throne. He was prepared to rule." Elyasin's words were choked as she snuggled close, her chin on Olea's shoulder. "I know he chafed at it. It was his duty not his desire, but he would have been right for it."

"He would have." Olea sighed, stroking Elyasin's golden locks.

"Tell me about the day you met, Olea." She murmured. "I know you've told me over and over but... the story gives me strength."

Olea sighed as the young woman pulled back, watching her now as Olea gathered her thoughts, then at last spoke. "Alden first saw me upon the practice grounds nine years ago on midwinter solstice. I was twenty-one, Inked, and placed in the Palace Guard from my ability with weapons."

"Alden said you were a better swordsman than Captain-General den'Norrin." Elyasin smiled at the remembrance as she brushed tears from her cheeks. "He said you beat den'Norrin in three bouts back to back the morning you and Alden met."

"I did." Olea chuckled with a soft smile, lacing her hands around one knee and leaning back on her bed. "I slapped my Captain-General on the butt with my sword after the third bout, just for spite. But before the captain could skin my hide, Alden stepped onto the field, bare-chested and ready with his own sword. He waved den'Norrin away and grinned at me, and said, *come on then, let's see what you've got.*"

"He got more than he bargained for." Elyasin smiled, a mischevious glitter in her green eyes now.

"I beat him five for five." Olea smiled, enjoying the remembrance. "Alden insisted upon continuing, even though he was getting weaker each time. I drove him to his knees on the last bout, got my blade to his throat. Den'Norrin was furious. He motioned ten men forward for raising a blade to my Dhenir, but Alden waved them off. He just knelt there, watching me. I couldn't move, couldn't take my blade from his throat. I wanted to kill him. I wanted to take from King Uhlas what he had taken from me. But I paused. Alden was just... too beautiful, too fierce. At last he spoke, and it was his words that broke me."

"What did he say?"

"He said, *do it, if you want to. I would understand*. I dropped my blade. I couldn't kill him, even though a part of me craved it for my people."

Reaching out, Elyasin stroked gentle fingers over Olea's Inkings, and Olea startled at the Dhenra's touch. "A yhulen-thorn, father used to call you, like the story of the Yhulen-Thorn and King Trevius' Sleep. My father never was very fond of you, was he?"

But Olea stared at the mirror, and suddenly, she knew she had to tell her Dhenra everything. Uhlas' secrets had run them all into blind corners. Alden had paid the price for it, and so had Olea, then finally the King himself. And now Elyasin was at risk. It was far past time, that she hear everything. As long as it didn't threaten her safety.

"Dhenra. You have to know something." Olea murmured. "I thought Alden was the one who changed my life that first year, promoting me,. But I found out later Uhlas had told him to do it. And Captain-General den'Norrin had secret orders directly from your father to tolerate Kingskinder, as did the other military Generals. We were not to be harmed in the ranks."

"*What?*" Elyasin's hand lowered from Olea's Inkings, one golden eyebrow arched. "I thought my father hated you! He was always so cold with you..."

"It was a ruse." Olea murmured. "Your father and I were actually very close, in our way. Though we could never meet openly, we developed... an understanding. Over time."

"What do you mean?" Elyasin murmured, her body tense.

Olea took a deep breath. And then she began her story, just as she'd once told it to Alden in this very same room. Of how Olea had first seen Uhlas in the palace Annals as she searched to prove his Summons unlawful and how Uhlas had approached her that midwinter's eve, speaking of his Summons. Of how Uhlas had engineered for Olea and Alden to meet the very next day and become close. And how Uhlas also knew of Elyasin learning Kingsmen arts from Olea, even as secret as they tried to be.

"A few months after that," Olea spoke at last as Elyasin listened gravely, "I found two slender tomes in the Annals. They'd been left in a pile of books I'd sequestered into my reading alcove. Uhlas was lingering nearby, watching when I discovered them. He never spoke a word, but he smiled – as if he'd planted them for me to find. Two volumes from his own personal collection..."

Olea's gaze fell upon the stack of books in one corner of her room. She had smuggled those two tomes out of the Annals and hidden them deep in the pile. Two slender cobalt leather volumes that spoke of the true Line of Kings, the original Alrashemni whose blood filled the Alrou-Mendera royal house. Uhlas's veins, Alden's – and Elyasin's.

All of them, Alrashemni by blood.

Uhlas had known it and had pointed Olea to the proof, those two tomes that chronicled house after house all the way back to the founding of the nation, when the Alrashemni immigrants finally made peace with the native Menderian tribes. A history that went all the way down the royal line, the Linea den'Alrahel. The Line of the Dawn. The Line of Kings.

Olea's own family line.

Olea needed to move those volumes. They weren't safe in her quarters, nor anyplace in Roushenn. But her gaze flicked to the gilt-edged mirror, knowing now that if she moved them, someone might see. The candles had burned low upon the hearth and the blush of dawn now lightened her solitary window, the trill of a fhrel-wren blossoming somewhere outside.

"We have to get you back, Dhenra. You have courtiers to meet in a few hours."

"But you've hardly begun telling me about my father! And what about these books he ensured you'd find?" Elyasin sat up, suddenly tempestuous.

"I can't say more now. It's not safe to talk here. Invite me out for a ride tomorrow."

"A *ride?*" Elyasin blinked. "I don't have time for a ride tomorrow! My schedule is packed solid with meeting suitors and discussing trade. You will tell me the rest now, Olea."

Olea's stomach clenched. If someone was watching, anything more she said could mean her Dhenra's death. And so Olea chose to abide her Dhenra's wrath, which she could feel coming like a thunderstorm as an angry formality settled about Elyasin. "Dhenra. With all due respect. I will continue my story upon the morrow. Invite me out for a ride."

"You are defying a direct order from your liege, Captain." Elyasin's eyes tightened, her lips set in a line. And Olea saw again how similar the two royal siblings had been; one a panther, the other a lioness. Elyasin was a born ruler despite her youth, and had taken over the realm as her father became senile and bedridden after Alden's death. Olea had suspicions about Uhlas' death, his King's Physician conveniently killed only a month before Uhlas' own demise.

And now, there was only one thing the tempestuous Elyasin would understand.

Sliding from the bed, Olea knelt, one palm to her Inkings. "Dhenra. Alden trusted me for a reason. Our hidden courtship had passion, but always I was his guard, even while we slept. I am your guard now. And I withhold information from you because I deem it unsafe to disclose at this time and place."

"If you are withholding information that is vital to my *realm*, Captain-General, I will have you tossed in the cells!" Elyasin spoke frostily. "My father kept secrets from me, and now I find Alden did, too. And you, whom I've always trusted, have kept secrets from me for *years*. Roushenn holds secrets from its liege – secrets as elusive as the Black Ghost of its halls! The Kingsmen Summons is an issue of national security. And finding out these secrets is *vital* to me holding my throne. You've raised my ire, Captain. Whatever you and Alden found out, you will tell me. Now."

It was a scathing tirade. But Elyasin had no idea the danger she would be in, should such information come out within Roushenn's walls.

"Alden was sent to Ghrec with the merchant fleet to keep him safe, far from Roushenn!" Olea growled, her own temper flaring now as she rose. "I was thrown in the cells because *someone* found out about us. And when Castellan Lhaurent revealed our affair before the Chancellate, Uhlas' hand was forced, to part Alden from his protection! In that gap, both son and father were killed, one undone by treachery and the other by what I believe was a slow poison. So I withhold information from you now because I deem it *unsafe*, Dhenra. Please. You have to trust me. And we have to get you back to your rooms before anyone knows you've been here!"

Seizing her shirt from a nearby chair, Olea yanked it on, followed by her breeches, boots, and cobalt jerkin. Her fingers raced up her shirt's laces, covering her Inkings as she buckled her jerkin, then slung on her baldric. Running her fingers through her blue-black curls viciously, Olea turned, regarding her almost-Queen. To see a thoughtful woman now before her, Elyasin's temper lessened as her gaze flicked to the window. It was going to be a hot summer day; Olea could smell it in the air.

"Take me back to my rooms, Captain. We will continue our conversation later."

"As my Queen commands."

But Elyasin's green eyes flicked back, razor-keen. "I'm not your Queen yet. But when I am, we will have some frank discussions, you and I. And you will tell me *everything* I ask. And you will tell me everything that I don't even know to ask. Are we quite clear, Captain?"

"Yes my liege." Olea nodded, letting out a single breath to bleed off the last of her own temper. She had come close to being thrown in the cells tonight. She could see it in the vibrating tension that rippled through the Dhenra as Elyasin's fine jaw set, hard.

Elyasin could be pissed that information was being withheld from her, but at least she would remain alive. Striding to the door, Olea hauled it open, glancing both ways. She heard no boots in the soldier's hall, and Elyasin whisked out quickly when she nodded. Closing her door, Olea offered her arm, but Elyasin raised her chin and strode forward, denying Olea the honor of escorting her. Suppressing a growl, Olea fell into step behind her liege.

She had never been allowed to walk next to Alden either, despite everything.

But once, monarchs and Kingsmen had walked side by side. And once, the kings of Alrou-Mendera had known they held Alrashemni blood. A secret that had pushed Uhlas into the shadows and made him paranoid after his Kingsmen had fallen to treachery in his very own palace. A secret that Uhlas had only trusted Olea with, knowing that perhaps she was the only one who could do something about it. Who could protect what was left of the Alrashemni royal line.

Elyasin. Herself. Elohl.

Striding down the torchlit hall behind her Dhenra, Olea's hand touched her sword as her gaze scanned the shadows for threats – just as a true Kingsman would for her blood-kin liege.

18

ELOHL

Elohl's eyes snapped open to a yell down below. His first thought was that he felt amazing, despite having slept all night atop the high bluestone column. As sunshine blessed his skin now, a sweet breeze of spring foxglove and linden wafting around the column, Elohl felt a deep ease. He felt good, such as he'd not felt in a long time.

But his attention sharpened suddenly, as another yell came from down below.

"*Hey!* Are you asleep up there?! Dammit, Elohl..."

Elohl's tension eased as he heard Eleshen's curses waft up on the warming air. If she'd been under attack, she'd not waste breath chastising him. As he listened, a scuffling came from the base of the Stone and Elohl peered over. Watching Eleshen's fruitless attempts at climbing, he was unable to stop himself from chuckling, enjoying her antics. She placed a bad foothold and went sprawling on her pretty ass, having ascended not even a foot above the ground. A natural, amused laugh rolled out from Elohl's throat as she gazed upwards, shading her eyes.

"Ha, ha! Very funny! Just sit up there and laugh at me bruising my ass all day! What *are* you doing up there? And how the hell did you get up this thing?" Testy, Eleshen slapped the stone with one hand.

"Hang on, I'm coming down." Elohl chuckled again, loving how fierce she was. Standing and rolling out his shoulders, he stretched, breathing deep. The morning was warm up on the ridge and Elohl blinked, trying to remember his dreams. But he found them fleeting today, just out of mind. All he recalled was a feeling of expansiveness so blissful that it lingered, as if his heart was wide as the sky and light as the dawn. He remembered waking in the night, the pulsing of the column, and feeling called to climb. But that was where the memory stopped – and Elohl supposed he had simply fallen asleep once he'd reached the lookout.

Shaking out his legs, he stretched his arms, pushing worry away. It was too beautiful a day. Backing down over the side of the column, he made it to the ground in moments. Eleshen's eyes were wide as he dusted his hands off at the bottom.

"Aeon's brows, Elohl, where did you learn to climb like that?"

"You learn to climb trees fast when your twin is always hunting you down." He grinned rakishly. He felt rakish this morning, and gazing at Eleshen now, he suddenly wanted to kiss the Halsos out of her until she squeaked and hit him for mercy. Reaching out, he netted her at the waist, pulling her close.

"Practice my ass." Eleshen grumped good-naturedly, grinning at his attention. Elohl knew she was coming with him now, even if it meant following ten paces behind the whole way to Lintesh, and strangely, he felt fine about it this morning. Pulling her in for a kiss, their lips were just about to meet when Eleshen's fingers suddenly flew to the neck of his shirt, pulling his laces open.

"What the...?"

Elohl chuckled with a masculine heat as he moved his fingers to her bodice-laces. "I suppose we have time—"

"No, Elohl! Your *skin!*" Her face was shocked as she slapped his hands away, her fussy fingers tugging his shirt out of his breeches. "And your wounds are *gone!*"

"What?" Confused, Elohl glanced down at his chest. There, where the gash from yesterday should have been, whorls and scripts in gold flowed out from his black Inkings and over his collarbones, disappearing beneath his shirt. As Elohl shucked his shirt quickly, he saw his body made anew. Like a spider's filaments, his chest was limned with tenuous filigree, sweeping arcs of gold radiating out from the Kingsmount and Stars and cascading across his chest, curling over his collarbones and cresting over his shoulders. Lines of gold dove downward, too, marking his abdomen like the blade of a longsword and diving below his belt. And where the lines went, they formed patterns, arcane sigils surrounded by a flowing script in a hand so minute it was barely recognizable.

And all of his slashes from yesterday were gone – as if they had never been.

"Aeon's hands!" Eleshen traced the golden markings with light fingers. Moving behind him, she traced from his shoulders all the way down his spine and up his nape to the base of his skull. Lingering in the center of his back, her fingers traced a circular shape up over his shoulder blades and around his spine. "It's beautiful! The front is uncanny, but you should see the back!"

"What is it?" He murmured, stunned as he gazed at the lines of script upon his front.

"A dragon! And a wolf." She murmured to the breeze.

Something in Elohl went cold, the bliss of the sunny day dimming.

"Describe it for me."

"Well, they're trying to kill one another! The wolf has the dragon's neck in its jaws, and the dragon is disemboweling the wolf with talons, but it seems perfectly balanced—"

"As if neither is actually winning," Elohl breathed. He could see it all, every part of it just the same as it had been upon the Deephouse doors of Roushenn long ago.

"Precisely! But there's more! They fight inside a ring of fire, like the blaze of the sun, with thirteen flaming spokes! Aeon, Elohl, what happened to you up there last night?"

Turning back towards the monolith, Elohl regarded the towering Alranstone. Standing behind it, he could see nothing of the eyes upon the other side. Moving like a sleepwalker, he circled around, already knowing what he would see, already feeling it vibrating in his body like a swarm of bees. An eye was open near the ground. He circled further, his breath catching as he saw all the eyes upon the massive Stone were wide in the morning sunlight. One had an iris of malachite, one an iris of flat jet. One was white moonstone, one a sunlight-flooded citrine. One was the red fire-opal that had gazed upon him at the top of the column, one was blue lapis. And the center eye upon the column carried every color within it, reflecting a radiance so bright it outshone diamonds.

"Well, they weren't like that yesterday." Standing next to him, Eleshen gaped at the Stone. Thrumming filled Elohl, building in his sinews. The Stone was aware of him now. Aware, and waiting. Reaching out a hand, Elohl placed it on the massive obelisk. And when his fingers contacted it, all seven eyes upon the column *blinked*.

Placing his other hand to the Stone, the column blinked again.

"Get your things," Elohl murmured to Eleshen, "I think it will let us travel now."

With a hasty nod, Eleshen moved off. Elohl heard her jangling her pack, stuffing away pots and bedrolls, but transfixed, he stood at the Stone with his eyes closed now as he leaned into his palms. Something almost came to him of the night before. A flash of a stern countenance. A feeling of purpose, like someone challenged him.

Rennkavi.

"Elohl? Are you all right?" Eleshen was back, one pack upon her shoulders, the other dragged across the overgrown flagstones.

"Fine." Elohl blinked, realizing he'd been deep in trance. "Are you ready? Prepare for pain, Eleshen. And shuck your pack. Just hold it between your knees."

"Women know all about pain." She waved a hand dismissively, handing his pack over then doing as he suggested with hers. "Let's do this."

Setting his hands to the Stone as Eleshen did also, Elohl closed his eyes, digging into that trance again, feeling the Stone's sight crawling all over him now, demanding. Demanding what, he didn't know – but firstly, that Elohl travel.

"All right. I'll do it, you bastard," Elohl breathed. "I'll take it."

He'd not known why he'd spoken those words rather than the words Alranstones supposedly responded to. But in a clap of thunder that split Elohl's ears, he was sucked in, twisted and writhing in screaming madness. Pain ripped him, and just when he thought death had come, it spat them out upon the other side, in a sprawling heap in the wooded grotto near Lintesh. They collapsed into the tall grass, and gasping, Elohl could do nothing for a few moments. Feather-blume was in season, the tall wispy fronds obscuring the rest of the forest. Keens of pain came from Eleshen beside him as his faculties returned. Rising to his feet, Elohl offered her a hand and with a grimace, she took it and rose.

"Let's *never* do that again...!" She growled, picking up her pack and slinging it on.

But though Elohl agreed about traveling through the Alranstones, something still felt lighter inside him today, more purposeful than ever before. Yesterday he'd been a gruff, tired soldier, but today, he felt changed – as if the Stone had done something to him overnight. Something inside him felt lighter, less lost, as if he had a plan for his life for the very first time. A flicker of dream pushed through; a man standing before him, decorated by red and white sigils.

But just as Elohl focused upon it, it slipped away.

Taking a spare Brigadier jerkin from his pack rather than wear his Kingsman Greys in the city, Elohl buckled his jerkin's crossover flap tight. Though a few tendrils of gold crept up the sides of his neck above his jerkin's high collar, most of his new golden marks were covered. The thin lines above his collar would raise eyebrows, but only because Inking was not common in Alrou-Mendera, though there were places on the borders where customs had come from other lands. Soldiers were often Inked in various ways if they had traveled. Stepping close, Eleshen adjusted his collar, covering up more of the new markings as she watched him.

"Well? What now? Your plan for contacting your sister better be a good one for all that misery we just endured!"

Hefting his pack from the ground, Elohl responded, "I'm a loyal Brigadier, honorably discharged. I'm instructed to pick up my discharge pension at the West Guardhouse, so we'll start there. Hopefully, we can find some Guardsmen to speak to, someone who might have known Olea."

"Good a plan as any." Eleshen quipped, as she motioned for him to take the lead.

Starting off through the woods, Elohl followed the stream as it coursed out of the grotto, down the forest's slope towards the city. He knew the way by heart from all those years ago, though the pain of those memories seemed distant today. As if the ice that lived within him had been sloughed away, he felt easy and calm as they moved through the woods, his long strides matched by Eleshen's short, quick ones.

They were soon through the Kingswood, the margins of the forest breaking to fields as they approached the Watercourse Gate of Lintesh. The gate was bustling with activity, people passing with carts and oxen, higher lords moving through upon horseback. The Elhambrian Valley was dry this far down the mountains, hot with the sweeping fugue of summertime. Crickets chirruped to their passing, cicadas whirring in the oaks that dappled the edge of the forest. Striding onto the blue-grey grit of the thoroughfare, Elohl and Eleshen joined the activity that kicked up dust beyond the massive gates with their fanged portcullis in the towering guard-wall of Lintesh's First Tier.

The whole thing looked like a wolf's maw to Elohl suddenly. Halting, he watched people moving in and out beneath those cruel iron fangs, engulfed and regorged by the beast. And though Elohl's attention drew into a spot behind his heart, humming and prickling, it was nothing that signified immediate danger. Squaring his shoulders, he adopted a pose of command and strode forwards, towards a knot of guards that kept foot traffic flowing. Fishing out his discharge notice from his leather belt-purse, he walked up to a likely guard with blond hair and a posture that spoke of rank. The man noted his approach, his eyes flicking over the small amount of gold that could be seen upon Elohl's neck, before noting Eleshen with obvious pleasure.

"Business in the King's City, soldier?"

Elohl nodded and handed over his notice. The man scanned it then looked up, his eyebrows raised with respect. "High Brigade, and a Lead Hand? Honorable discharge of *completed* service? We don't get many of these. Not many Lead Hands make it ten years. Seen some action?"

"Skirmishes the past few summers." Elohl nodded, though he found he was smiling. "But the Red Valor tend to not assault the border when the snows are more than ten feet deep in the low crags."

"And in the high crags?"

"High pass climbing is all snow, all the time." Elohl smiled at the man. "We pick our way up frozen gorges and waterfalls. Gotta watch out in summer, though. The waterfalls aren't as stout as they seem."

The man blinked. "You are one ballsy—" he glanced at Eleshen, "—gentleman."

"Whatever you say." Elohl laughed, then clapped the fellow on the back. "I'm just glad it's over. Where do I go to pick up my King's Pension?"

"The Captain-General should be in the West Guardhouse right about now." The Guardsman spoke briskly. "She's the one to see. Her secretary can't dispense funds without her present, so if she's not there, you'll have to wait. But there's plenty of shopping and amusement in the Central Plaza, good taverns, too. The White Wheat makes a great lamb mitlass, not to mention has a private contract with the Jenners for their best pale ale every season. Lots to do while you wait for Captain den'Alrahel."

"Captain den'Alrahel?" Elohl spoke, stunned, his heart hammering in his chest.

"Your captain is a woman?" Eleshen spoke up, beaming at the news.

"Most beautiful goddess of the sword you've ever met!" The guard grinned as he winked at Eleshen. "But don't tell Captain Olea I said that. She'd gut me, knives fast as she has and a temper thrice as quick! And a word of advice? No matter your feelings on the Kingsmen Treason, don't mention her Inkings. She got 'em, she flaunts 'em, and she'll not give you your pension if you get nasty."

Prattling on, the man gave directions to the Central Plaza of Lintesh, which Elohl barely heard. With a salute to Elohl and a bow over Eleshen's hand, he turned away, back to managing traffic as Elohl and Eleshen moved through the gates under the chill shadows of the First Tier wall.

Elohl's heart soared at the news about Olea as he and Eleshen wove through the midday traffic of the Tradesman Quarter, carts and people lingering at colorful awnings and market-stalls all along the main avenue. He barely saw the pennants with the cobalt crest of House den'Ildrian that fluttered in the hot breeze, lofted upon wrought-iron poles between buildings of solid bluestone carved from crags of the Kingsmount, houses of thatch-and-beam crammed in-between like an afterthought.

Staring around with brightness surging through his heart that Olea lived, Elohl saw such a different city today than he remembered from ten years ago, full of life. Lintesh's broad avenues were deeply worn from time, dust swirling into the air with the reek of a city; sweat and horse, shit and piss. Wash lines extended from every window, fluttering like festival flags as folk laughed, worn faces smiling as they drank ale, listening to a bard belting out a humorous song on a tavern porch. A troupe of Travelers performed at a fountain, tambourines chiming, drums pounding as a sextet of tumblers launched each other into the air.

It was so hot and bright that something warm glowed in Elohl's chest as he took it all in. Something purposeful and good, that made him smile as he saw a tiny girl enjoying the hell out of a ripe sour-melon. Bright green juice smeared her chubby little cheeks, being wiped at to no avail by her scolding mother. Something bubbled up inside him and he laughed, his heart soaring.

But they'd arrived at the center of the city, and Elohl's gaze was suddenly pinned to the main gates of Roushenn Palace, looming between two stone towers. Austere, the East and West Guardhouses were made of solid bluestone carven with arrow-slits and topped with niches for a whole host of archers to rain hell down upon invaders. The massive guard-wall above the gate was crowned with trebuchets, glinting well-oiled in the sunlight. But the palace, the gates, and the throng that dappled the broad market-plaza with its sprawling byrunstone fountain might as well have not been there.

Because standing at the steps to the West Guardhouse, was his life.

Olea.

Elohl's feet sped over the cobbles as sound died away, as thought died away. Taking a break in the sunshine, Olea curried her fingers though her blue-black curls, fanning that river of hair from her neck in the sweltering heat. In her cobalt Guardsman's jerkin, her Inking was brazenly displayed, her slender-muscled height beautiful as a sword. Closing the distance, Elohl saw the sea-grey of her eyes, so clear and luminous – like her very being had been spun of pure light. A smile Elohl hadn't felt in ages blossomed over his face as he shucked his pack to the dusty flagstones – and Olea gasped, her eyes wide as she saw him. But she had no more time to react as Elohl scooped his twin into his arms, pulling her close, feeling every part of her come back to him.

Joy flooded him. Peace. Crushing her close, he felt her, though her body was thinner than he remembered, corded with sinew. He could feel ribs beneath her jerkin, as if she wasn't eating well. As he pressed his lips to her wayward curls, a sense of completion overtook him. Elohl tasted salt – and realized he was crying.

"Elohl!" She breathed, her arms fierce around his neck. "You came!"

"Olea!" He murmured into her hair. "Aeon, where have you been?!"

"I've been here, the whole time!" She spoke as she squeezed him tight. "When you stopped writing, I thought... but your name never came off the lists, no one ever reported you dead or missing!"

Pulling back, Elohl gazed down into her lovely grey eyes, the storms in them roiling to match his own, but lighter, safer. His twin. A part of his being, a part of his very self and yet not. Emotion flooded him, drowning him, lifting him, cracking whatever remained of his ice sending it shuddering through his veins in a blissful tremor. He seized her face, kissing her brow, pressing their foreheads together.

"I never stopped writing, Olea! Every month, I wrote."

"What?" Olea pulled back, her eyes red-rimmed. "But I stopped getting letters eight years ago!"

"I stopped getting yours at the same time..." Trepidation rippled Elohl's gut as he realized what they were both saying.

Olea's grey eyes suddenly went hard as she realized it also, flicking around the wide plaza. "Not here. Inside. Hold your tongue until I say it's safe. Too many people may have seen us."

Stepping out of his arms, Olea was brusque suddenly as if nothing had happened. Turning, she leaped the guardhouse stairs and Elohl followed, perplexed, with Eleshen upon his heels. Once they were inside in the stifling gloom it was all business, Olea accepting Elohl's notice of discharge and filing it in one of the many racks of scrolls and tomes that ringed the first level. Producing a formal writ, she had it witnessed by herself and her young secretary, then stamped with a seal, her manner kind but distant. She left the room and Elohl heard the clanking of a lockbox. Returning, she handed over a King's Note for the majority of Elohl's pension and the rest in gold and smaller change in a leather pouch.

Coin changed hands. A formal thanks was given. Olea was escorting Elohl and Eleshen to the door, when she leaned in and said, "Follow the man at the fountain. I'll be along." Then she clasped Elohl's arm as if they were strangers and shut the guardhouse door.

"Some homecoming! What was that all about?" Eleshen huffed once they were back outside.

"Not now," Elohl murmured.

Scanning the throng in the plaza, Elohl wondered whom Olea had meant. But then, he felt a prickling through his sensate sphere. He was being watched. Turning, his gaze sharpened upon the fountain. There, lounging upon the rim sat a man who was clearly Alrashemni. Broad-shouldered like a mountain, he was all stone and strength, his black curls shining blue in the sun. The man at the fountain stood as Elohl noticed him, his gaze skating over Elohl, then Eleshen. Turning, he moved off through the crowd, dodging carts with an ease any other man his size could never have mastered.

His movement confirmed what Elohl had already known.

That he and Eleshen were in good hands.

Elohl let out a breath he hadn't known he was holding. Winding through quiet alleys, then dipping back into the throng under the portcullises, they moved back down through the Tiers. In the Tradesman Quarter, the man disappeared down an alley, and when Elohl turned in, he saw the double-doors of a workshop open at the end. With a glance at Eleshen, he strode forwards, feeling for any threat. But there was none as they gained the end of the alley and slipped in the doors, out of the muggy heat into a cool, well-drafted workshop that smelled of silver tang.

Inside, the mountainous man studied Elohl, leaning at a workbench with his arms crossed. The forge-fires were unlit in his shop, a soft gloom suffusing the space as light filtered down from panes of smoky glass along the shop's apex. At last, the man took a knee. Putting a hand to his side where a sword should have been, he set his fingers to a ruin of scars upon his chest.

"*Alrashemnesh ars veitriya rhovagnen,*" he recited formally, a common start to Alrashemni negotiations. "Alrashemni are welcomers of truth."

Shucking his pack, Elohl took a knee also, making the same motion with one hand to a longknife at his hip as his sword was currently strapped to his back. His other palm went to his leather jerkin, over his Inkings. "*Alrashemnesh ars veitriya rhovagnen.* I also welcome truth, and will speak whatever I can."

A kind smile lifted the man's scar-riven face as he rose from his bow. "You look just like your father, lad. Elohl, is it? Your sister said to expect you."

"You knew my father?" A strange peace filled Elohl as he gazed upon this man, feeling the truth about him, kind and gentle.

"Some." The Kingsman gave a small smile. "Urloel was a great man. I hadn't the occasion to meet him more than thrice when he visited Dhemman, but he was tremendously wise and patient, an accomplished negotiator. You should be proud, lad. He was a shining example of how we all should be."

Elohl's throat choked to hear such kindness. But there was no burn of anger in him today, no freeze of woe. His emotions came naturally today, in a ripple that moved out from his heart and made him murmur, "Thank you."

The big man nodded, stern but kind as his deep grey eyes bored into Elohl. "You'd be a Rakhan now if such things still existed. I can see the depth of leadership all over you, lad, and feel it in my heart. You're Urloel's son through and through. Hardship has only honed it. Like it did for all of us."

Tears pricked Elohl as Eleshen stood silent at his side. Her fingers stole out, clasping his as Elohl swallowed hard. Thoughts swirled of a time long gone, seeing how his life might have unfolded. It must have shown upon his face, because the big man took a massive breath, then sighed. "Forgive me. I didn't mean to—"

Just then, Olea strode in through the workshop's heavy halberd-wood doors. Elohl couldn't stop himself from smiling, his heart singing like harp strings. She came to him and Elohl wrapped his twin in his arms fiercely as she embraced him back.

"Elohl. Aeon be praised!" Olea breathed at his cheek, shuddering with emotion as she gripped him. "You don't know how hard it's been! Feeling you were alive but without any confirmation of it!"

"I told you I would find you." He murmured, kissing her temple. "That I would always come for you. No matter how far apart we are. When I find out who was waylaying our letters..." A fierce anger rose in Elohl, raging in his gut. Protective, he clutched Olea closer, never wanting to be separated from her again. In a moment of fierce love, he felt stillness wrap them both. Heaving a massive breath, Olea sighed. Elohl set his lips to her forehead as she closed her eyes, breathing quietly.

But rather than indulge emotions further, it was Olea who pulled back at last, setting her hands to his shoulders and regarding him with a frank intensity. Elohl saw his own hardship and maturation staring back at him in her opal-grey gaze, ten years honed in Halsos' Hell. Olea had weathered it, same as he. And come out fighting with the strength and righteous presence of a commander. Elohl had always had to fight his inner rage to be calm.

But Olea had steadiness in abundance, a true leader for war.

"We have information that must be shared, Elohl." Brisk and efficient, she gave him a shake at the shoulders as she spoke. "I'm afraid you've come home under a strange moon. The interference in us keeping contact is not the only atrocity that's been brewed against the Kingsmen all these years." As her hands fell from his shoulders, she turned, glancing at Vargen. "What did I miss?"

"We were just introducing ourselves," Vargen rumbled gently. "But I didn't get your name, milady?" He smiled at Eleshen, welcoming.

Eleshen flushed noticeably. If she'd taken a step out to shake Vargen's hand, Elohl was certain she'd have bumbled it. Even so, she flicked her long honey-blonde braid distractedly, managing to get it tangled in her pack-strap. Hauling it out, she ripped a number of strands of hair, all with her wide eyes pinned to the big Kingsman. "Eleshen." She cleared her throat. "Eleshen den'Fhenrir."

"Welcome, Eleshen." Vargen's lips lifted in a warm smile. "Welcome to a Council of the Kingsmen. Though you bear no Inking, I can see you are a friend. But be warned. Anything you see, hear, or do in our presence may put you at risk. It should be your choice, to stay for our council or no."

"Well." She cleared her throat again. "Forgive me, big man, but I've already been involved in two assassination attacks since meeting Elohl. I'm thinking I'm safer here with the three of you in this workshop than anywhere else in the nation! So. I'll stay put. Thank you very much."

"Assassination attacks?" Olea's grey eyes were livid. "What? *Who?*"

"I don't know who." Elohl murmured, reaching out grip her shoulder. "And I don't know why. But my life has been attempted a number of times these past years, Olea."

She blinked at him, perusing his face, his skin, and his forearms where he had his shirtsleeves rolled up from the heat. He saw her note the blade-scars on the backs of his forearms from fighting, though his other wrist-scars were hidden. Her gaze traveled up, noting how his jerkin was fully buckled even in the heat. And then her gaze lingered upon the sides of his neck, as she blinked.

"Did you have yourself Inked with gold-leaf? Where in Aeon's blazes did you have that done?"

"Those happened yesterday." Elohl felt himself smile. "Well, last night, actually."

Olea raised her eyebrows as Elohl filled her in on the seven-eye tower and of his golden Inkings, giving her a succinct briefing. He watched Olea become more and more astonished with every word, and when Elohl had finished, she reached out and touched the golden marks above his collar. Indulging her, he unbuckled the crossover flap of his leather jerkin, unlacing his shirt so she could see the pattern's tendrils where they commingled with his true Inkings.

"Holy gods above..." He heard Vargen utter softly.

"I always thought there was something special about you." Olea spoke as her calloused fingertips traced the sigils of gold, lingering over the lines of minute script. "Mother used to say it. *Protect Elohl, look out for him. He has a wyrrian way about him*."

"There's more on my back." Elohl murmured. "A sigil of a wolf and dragon, fighting inside a flaming sun."

"Like the emblem in Roushenn's throne hall! And upon the Deephouse doors." Olea's gaze flicked to his, stunned. Her grey eyes went distant, and Elohl saw thoughts burning through her like a wildfire as her brows knit. "Elohl. We need to speak privately. I have some... information I need to share with you."

"I believe this conversation requires dinner and ale." Vargen interrupted as he cleared his throat. "Allow me to go out to the tavern down the street. I will fetch whatever we need tonight. Eleshen, would you care to accompany me?"

"I'd be honored to," Eleshen stammered as she flushed to the roots of her hair, then glanced to Elohl.

"Go." Elohl murmured. "You'll be as safe with him as you'd be with me. Safer, maybe."

She nodded, a complex emotion sliding through her. But when Vargen offered his arm, she took it, the two of them issuing out through the double doors. Vargen glanced back to Olea and murmured, "Look for us within the hour. If we're not back, ask the weaver across the alley. She has a reliable network of street lads, they're good at finding people and gaining information."

"I will." Olea murmured.

Vargen nodded. He and Eleshen moved off, shutting the massive doors. Once they were gone, Olea turned back to Elohl. "Elohl. I have to tell you something right away. Information about our kin's disappearance will come out when Vargen returns, and you will hear everything that has so startled me these weeks since Vargen and I made acquaintance. Since the Dhenra bid me re-open the investigation I was once making into the Kingsmen treachery with the Dhenir right before it killed him. But I have something else I must say first."

Elohl blinked at the tirade of information spilling from his sister's lips. Startling information that made his heart jump. "What do you mean? What have you found?"

"Later." She spoke, her grey eyes shining with ferocity – and fear. "For now, you have to know… that you and I are of the *King's own line*. The surname den'Alrahel is ancient, and once they held the crown. Men and women of House den'Alrahel, *Linea den'Alrahel*, have actually sat the throne, Elohl, and House den'Ildrian is closely related. House den'Ildrian have Alrashemni blood – King Uhlas, Dhenir Alden, and Dhenra Elyasin. And ours is no less royal."

"Royal?" Elohl's lips fell open. His mind roiled, wanting to forget what he had just heard. But like a storm, it built within him, spinning, burning. A fierce knowing came with it, as a face surfaced in his mind, stern and wild with whorls of red and white Inkings. Elohl's legs turned to water as he sat upon a stool nearby. Like they'd been called, his golden Inkings began to itch and burn, searing upon his chest, shoulders, and all down his back.

"King Uhlas knew." Olea came to sit beside him. "He gave me two tomes of *Alrashemni* royal lineage, back to the founding of Alrou-Mendera."

"But House den'Ildrian hold the throne. We're sworn to them. The family who killed our people." Elohl's mind fought desperately for excuses, but his golden Inkings surged as his gaze flicked to Olea.

"So we are, Elohl." She nodded. "And I hold to it. I want no throne; I will never challenge Elyasin. She is our Queen-to-come, and I will fight for that with my very last breath. But this secret has been worth killing over. Someone knows. The Kingsmen Summons was not given by Uhlas. He was deceived, as we were. I've had my share of assassination attempts too, but they never get close enough, surrounded by Guardsmen as I am. But what Vargen will tell you when he returns is horrible, Elohl. Prepare yourself. Our kin did not leave Roushenn alive, of that I am now certain."

"They're gone." Elohl breathed softly. Some part of him had known. Some part of him had always known that it had been the Kingsmen's last day, that morning he had escaped Roushenn.

"They're all gone." Olea murmured, reaching out to clasp his hand, her gaze frank upon him. "But we're not. And the Dhenra's not. Though someone wishes we were."

* * *

ELOHL AND OLEA were speaking quietly of her life in the Guard as Vargen and Eleshen returned. Bottled ales were hefted to a worktable and they all sat, tucking in to roast boar with cucumber sauce and a fruit salad of fresh melon with summer strawberries. Stories were told late into the evening. Elohl heard Vargen's wretched tale about the Kingsmen killings, the demon, and the cursed back halls of Roushenn. He heard of Olea's investigation with the Dhenir and now the Dhenra, and how she feared for her liege's safety with the massive public event of Elyasin's coronation at midsummer.

The conversation turned to suppositions, of what King Uhlas might have known, and suspicions that the Chancellate or perhaps the Castellan knew of Roushenn's secret halls and the slaughter of the Kingsmen. But as conversation turned to Ghrenna's vision and the mystery of the clockwork puzzle, Elohl suddenly sat up, blinking away stupor and drink.

"You still have the clockwork?"

"I had a bad feeling before we returned to Alrashesh that morning." Olea nodded as Vargen moved to a side-bench and unlocked a drawer, pulling out a wooden cataloguing box and setting it upon the workbench. "So I hid your belt-purse in our log. The rotting one, in the forest hollow where we used to play pirates. Then I went back for it when I had some relief time from the Guard."

"So you've had it all these years?" An inebriated smile lifted Elohl's lips, impressed as he gazed at the pieces of the clockwork in the cataloguing-box before him. Vargen had separated each piece into cataloguing squares, and as the silver-smith brought out papers, Elohl saw each one corresponded to a numbered space in the box, sigils upon each wheel and fulcrum copied in painstaking fashion on the papers.

"See here," Vargen spread the papers upon the workbench, carefully pushing aside food and ale. "I've tested each piece. Each is wrought of either solid silver, gold, or platian, not alloyed. But there are thirteen pieces of rhoyanis. Rhoyanis is very rare, priceless, and comes from meteors that struck down in Ghrec and the deserts further south. You can only make something with it if you melt down ancient artifacts, as all the natural rhoyanis was used up long ago. What you have here is a very expensive, very old puzzle, whose origins may be near Ghrec. I've been to the First Abbey and scoured their language compendiums, even asked a few Jenner scholars if they could make anything of those markings. They couldn't. It's not any language they've heard of, so they can't say for sure the age of this script, or its origin. So, this is a *deep* mystery as well as a good puzzle."

"Can you put it back together?" Elohl interjected.

Vargen glanced up. "I was rather hoping you'd give me that information. When you first saw it, can you remember what shape it was before it fell apart?"

"I can sketch it for you." Elohl reached for a sheet of paper, his weathered fingers sketching in careful motions. "It was rectangular and fit in the palm of my hand. In the center was a dial with spokes like the Jenner sun. I think it was that rhoyanis piece there, I remember it shining even in the darkness of the cavern, like moonstone. Those long rods might be the spokes. The backing of the wheel was like a teardrop... maybe that piece there." He pushed his sketch back to Vargen.

"It's something to start with at least." The man rumbled. "May I ask what this object is?"

Olea and Elohl glanced at each other in unison, but it was Olea who answered. "We have no idea."

Elohl cleared his throat. "There was supposed to be something else in the box. Our comrade Ghrenna had a vision that there would be a ruby ring. And with the ring, we would be able to bring the Alrashemni justice. But there was no ring, just this. The box fell to pieces when I handled it. Whatever this is, it was in there for a god's age. And Ghrenna was wrong, though her visions were never wrong prior to this."

"So whatever your friend saw in the box was... what? A portent?" Vargen grunted.

"Or perhaps the clockwork is related to the ring." Eleshen's fingers were hovering near the pieces as if she might start picking them out of the cataloguing box. Vargen slid the box cautiously out of reach, and she pouted.

"What?" Elohl blinked at her.

"Well, the clockwork is clearly magic!" She huffed with a wry smile. "It fell apart when you touched it! But it's withstood all of time's other weathering? That just doesn't make sense. Unless the clockwork has magic, just like Alranstones that open all seven eyes to your touch, Elohl, and ink you in gold! Whatever it is, it's tied to *you*. You're the common link. Maybe your mother was right. Maybe you do have a *way* about you."

Elohl stared at her. He could feel his cheeks blushing, embarrassed by her suggestions as he rubbed his short beard with one hand. "But that still doesn't help us figure out why the clockwork was in the box and not the ring. Or what they do. Or how they are supposed to help us."

"Well. Shit." Eleshen's smug visage fell. She chewed her lower lip, frowning.

"She's got a point, Elohl." Vargen spoke, his gaze resting upon Elohl. "I can't say about the clockwork, but I've heard about this phenomenon with the Stone you came through, the opening of all seven eyes."

"What do you know of it?" Elohl asked, curious to know if Vargen had the answer to his strange night. He'd already told everyone how he'd received his golden Inkings and that he remembered little of the dream, only the man and the word *rennkavi.*

"Legends say seven-eye Stones were used for great teachings," Vargen continued, taking a pull of ale from his mug. "There are only three seven-eye Stones in Alrou-Mendera, and a few scattered around the other nations, but there is a legend about them in the Jenner cannon – the parable of the Heimkellen. *And the Uniter of the Tribes will open the eye of every septen Alranstone, from the mountain fasthold of Uhrkhennig to the Valley of the Ninth Seal. And all will come to him, refugees near and far. And the Lost Tribe will be found again. The heimkeller will celebrate at last, united.*"

"Where did you hear all that?" Elohl blinked.

"I looked into becoming a Jenner monk for a time." A wry smile graced Vargen's lips. "Back when I was still... unsettled after the Summons. But history says there used to be a religious sect among the Alrashemni called the *Jhennik Alremani*. They had strong opinions about god, and were unable to be impartial enough to act as moderators. So eight hundred years ago, they seceded from the Alrashemni. The Jhennik took over the Alrashemni's ancient fortress in Lintesh and created the First Abbey, started brewing ales and leading a life of monasticism. I had one of their books of prayer and prophecy."

"The Jenner monks." Elohl leaned forward, intrigued.

"Just so." Vargen nodded. "In any case, the Jenners consider themselves the *heimkeller*, the Ones Who Will Return Home. And that there will come a person who can open the eye of every Alranstone, the Uniter of the Tribes, to get them there. It's really more of a spiritual parable than something they actually *believe*. You know, the *heimkeller* are sinners who have forgotten Aeon, they will Return Home when one comes to teach them how to live in brotherly love, unity, and eternal bliss, that sort of thing. If you want to know more, you had better talk to the Jenners. But don't tell them you opened every eye on a seven-eye Stone, lad. It might break their minds to hear a parable come to life."

Elohl blinked. Something about Vargen's words resonated with him, yet he felt the information was right but also far from right. Suddenly, the image rose in his mind of the dark alehouse so long ago – and the wolf and dragon upon the ironwood doors, roiling and struggling as the torchlight guttered.

"Well. That's it then." Eleshen perked beside him. "We'll get some lodgings in the city, then go visit these drunk monks and see what they can tell us."

"Jenners don't drink." Elohl murmured absently.

"Well. That's just crap." Eleshen snarked as she swigged off the rest of her beer. "Brewing all those ales? I'm sure they get soused, they just like to pretend they're holy men. So. Time to unravel this knot of wool and find out who's hunting you."

Elohl glanced over. Eleshen was beautiful in a no-nonsense way, her determination showing in the stubborn set of her jaw and the lift of one golden eyebrow. Elohl couldn't help but smile as his fingers stole out upon the table, seeking hers. She gripped his hand and Elohl saw Olea's gaze flick to it – saw her blink in surprise before she smiled. Sitting back, she took it in – that Elohl had found someone other than Ghrenna after all these years.

Cerulean eyes surfaced in his vision.

Elohl pushed them away.

19

DHERRAN

The ready-tent was stifling as Dherran watched Khenria roll out her shoulders, the heat of the day baking through the thick canvas like a brick oven. He could practically feel her nervous tension flooding the space as calls went around outside, people betting and wagering, drunk with liquor and anticipation. Out in the rabble, Grump would be doing his usual, pushing men into wagering more with his capable wheedling. Khenria was fighting at the strike of noon, and the day was sweltering already. Dherran's fight wasn't until fourth bell, but sweat had begun to glisten them both in the humidity of the tent as skinny Khenria paced in her training halter and loose cotton pants.

Stepping over with a dipper of water, Dherran noted with a twinge how much her skin was about to get bloodied and bruised as he extended the dipper. "Have some water, Khen. Hold it in your mouth and let it soak in. If you get hit, you'll regret having a bellyful of fluid. Remember, no nasty tricks. If you do, you'll be disqualified. Fight fair, but fight for your life if you have to."

She nodded, doing as he said, though fear widened her eyes.

"Have another." Dherran instructed, continuing his last-moment speech, his capstone to their training all week in preparation for Khenria's First Seal test. "You'll have this tent again if you win, to rest before the next bout as the other contenders take the ring to determine your second opponent. Remember – first bout is easy, second bout is hard. Second bout is twenty minutes after the first, and your energy is sapped, you're heady from winning, and you're hungry and thirsty after your jitters have worn off. Second bout is where it counts, if you get there. One more sip."

Khenria took another sip, rinsing it around her mouth and letting the water soak in. But as she did, the bell sounded, calling the women to the field for the first match. Khenria looked ready to jump out of her skin, terrified, as she spat her mouthful of water into a nearby bucket.

"*Focus!*" Seizing her by the shoulders, Dherran gave her a little shake – enough to rattle her but not enough to hurt. "You've done this a hundred times! Let your opponent move first. Watch how she does it; even a footstep is enough to go by. Watch her balance." Seizing Khenria's chin, he shook it, making her bristle now instead of being fearful. "Find her weakness and rip her apart, Hawk-Talon."

That centered her. Hearing the name made Khenria's courage rise, ready to fight as the bell rang again for the fighters to take the field. Turning towards the tent-flap, Khenria held her head high now, though her body was still tense. Reaching out fast, Dherran slapped her on the ass as she departed, hard. With a yelp, she turned a fierce glower upon him.

"What the fuck, Dherran?!"

"You'll thank me later." He spoke as he shoved her towards the tent-flap. "Go sink your talons in."

"Fuck you."

Ferocious at last from his uncouth send-off, Khenria stood tall, stalking to the exit and ripping the tent flap back viciously. She was alert now and the tension had gone from her muscles as her fury at Dherran's treatment made her pace from the tent with a bristling energy. Dherran followed her out through another panel, trailing her along the black spears, knowing she could feel his support even though her concentration was fixed upon the ring. Shoving forward, Dherran pushed through men who cursed drunkenly until they saw his size and scowl.

Through the spears, he saw the two women face off, slight Khenria with a stocky older blonde opponent built like an anvil. The bell rang for the fight to begin, and Khenria waited as Dherran had instructed, watching the blonde. The woman took a step, and Dherran saw Khenria note it; heavy and sluggish. Khenria was as spry as they came, and knew what to do with a heavy, slow opponent. With one fast sweep of her leg, she took the blonde down, letting the woman's momentum and weight slam her to the ground. The blonde didn't know how to roll, and hit the hard-packed dirt of the fairway with a sickening thud. She scrabbled on the ground as Khenria followed her down to wrestle in the dirt, trying to use her weight and big muscles to her advantage. But though she was whip-skinny, Khenria was both fast and strong, and had the blonde trussed up into a choke-out in moments.

In thirty-eight seconds, the match was over.

Khenria crowed, releasing the blonde as she flashed to standing. The crowd cheered for the skinny young woman with fast moves, and she grinned as she wiped dirt from her face and paced back to the line of spears. She was all elation as she returned to the tent to wait as the second match was decided. As Dherran massaged her out and gave her water, they listened to the second women's fight happening in the ring. There was cheering, then booing, then cheering again from the drunken rabble beyond the tent – when suddenly, a painful scream rang out through the heat. Khenria startled, rattled, as silence swallowed the crowd. A few tense moments passed, and then the bell rang.

"What was that, Dherran?" She asked him, her grey eyes round.

"Probably a broken bone, or a popped tendon. Shit hurts like Halsos' Hells." He spoke quietly, listening for more, though they were too far away from the fight-ring to hear much.

"How often does that happen?" Khenria asked, still rattled.

"Not that often," Dherran murmured, still listening. "But it can happen when you've got a talented opponent who carries a lot of wrath and doesn't care if they break someone. Breathe, Khenria. Second bout is harder. Not just because of how you feel physically, but because you just got to listen to your next opponent out-match someone."

Khenria nodded, and just then the bell rang again, calling the next match to the field. She wasn't as steady as she exited this time, still unnerved by what had happened in the previous minutes, but her head was high as she went, proud. Just as Dherran had anticipated from that scream, Khenria's second bout was vicious, her opponent brutal. Khenria got hit four times right away, testing punches from a quick redhead with Elsthemi Highlander braids who was all muscle and no extra. The redhead was fierce, and Khenria was resting on her laurels from her previous bout. A black eye and a nasty punch to the right side of her jaw cured that, then another on her left ear that Dherran knew had rung her bell.

Khenria's eyes dazed. And then Dherran saw her rage rise, surfacing like a demon as it tore through her limbs, making them shiver and shake. She roared like an animal, making her opponent take a quick step back, though the redhead was still weighing her with a calm precision. And here it was. Khenria was about to make her worst mistake, about to step in close as her rage bested her.

And get the shit beat out of her.

"Khenria! Focus!" Dherran roared from beyond the black spears of the summer-ring. Others shrank back, cursing at his tremendous snarl that could thunder across a battlefield. But though it startled the drunken louts all around him, his roar had the intended effect on his fighter.

Khenria blinked, shivering like a horse in battle, then settled as the redhead stepped in to re-engage the fight. The redhead threw a punch towards Khenria's face, and like a hawk in mid-dive, Khenria feathered to the side, putting her weight behind a vicious uppercut that cracked the redhead's teeth, followed by an elbow to the head that snapped the redhead's neck. The redhead crumpled, her eyes rolling up in her head as she went down. Cheers rang through the crowd, and Khenria's face was all triumph as she thrust her hands high.

But Dherran was watching the woman on the ground. She was faking, taking a moment to rest and gather herself. Before Khenria knew it, the redhead was in action, sweeping Khenria from her feet just as Khenria had done in the earlier match and making her hit the ground hard. Khenria knew how to roll, and just managed it, when the redhead was on her, knocking her to her back and pinning her with a forearm to the throat, choking her out. Khenria panicked, beginning to kick. But then Dherran saw her get control, tangling her legs in the other woman's and twisting her hips, rolling the redhead off and getting the woman in a head-lock. The redhead struggled, panicked – and threw a fistful of dirt up into Khenria's eyes. Khenria shrieked like a falcon, but only locked her talons down harder for the kill.

The redhead choked out.

Khenria hardly waited to be named the victor as she strode from the ring, vicious and fuming as she wiped angrily at her eyes. Blinded and feeling her way out along the line of spears, Dherran met her at the tent flap, hastily leading her inside after listening a moment for the verdict from the judges. Guiding her to a bench, he picked up a ceramic wash-basin and set it next to her, guiding her hands to it.

"Easy, Khenria!" He soothed. "Here's the basin. Time to rinse out."

"My eyes feel like glass! Fuck that bitch!!" Khenria hissed as she started to rinse her eyes at the wash-basin, winced, then pouted at Dherran. Something about it was both adorable and fierce, and he couldn't help but chuckle as he guided her hands back to the basin again. "Keep going, Hawk-Talon. Rinse your eyes out. They'll be better by the time you do your next bout, though they're going to water and sting like venom. You almost lost your temper on that one. Lose your temper, lose your First Seal."

"Fuck her! She had all sorts of dirty tricks." Khenria fumed as she began washing her eyes out again, blinking rapidly to distribute the water beneath her eyelids.

"Some do." Dherran spoke soberly. "You have to fight them anyway, be the better woman. Not everyone is trained by a Kingsman. You're one of few people these days who's learned to fight with both efficient skill and precision. A lot of people don't have that. So they have to use dirty tricks."

"I never thought of it that way." Khenria looked up at that, thoughtful as she blinked her red eyes.

"She was disqualified for throwing sand." Dherran spoke, leaning in to lift her eyelids and inspect for grit. "You did well, choking her out after that grappling, but know that you can step away after a move like that, and the judges will call the match in your favor. Though in a real battle, it doesn't work that way."

Khenria's eyes were clean, and though they were viciously irritated, Dherran knew she'd be fine soon. As the bell for the next match rang and people started cheering drunkenly outside, Dherran touched Khenria's swelling jaw and cheek-bone, then her ear, producing a wince as his fingertips perused her skull on that side. "Open your mouth. Any clicking in the joint? Ok, you're whole. Nothing broken."

"Good. I would have torn that bitch limb from limb for her asshole moves if the match hadn't ended." Khenria growled as she rinsed her mouth with some of the water and spat again.

"Remember, Hawk-Talon." Dherran continued as he moved to her shoulders, massaging them out for her third match as the interim bout continued beyond the tent. "Fighting is only part of what we do as Kingsmen. Sometimes you have to negotiate. Study, learn, find your opponent's weaknesses and use them in battle. In a ring-fight, you can use the crowd to break them. Ready?"

The bell had rung, concluding the interim match and Khenria nodded as she took another sip of water and stood. They had no words for each other now, and Dherran sent her out of the tent with a nod. Following Khenria to the ring, Dherran saw her third bout would be well-matched. Khenria's third opponent was of average stature, muscled but not thick, with a calm demeanor and a tight bun to hold back her brown hair. From his place outside the spears, Dherran could see she was cool and calculating, almost dispassionate as she fought, and it actually brought out the best in Khenria. A number of test punches were thrown in both directions this time; some landing, some glancing, some missing. Their footwork was agile and challenging in the dust, both women breathing steadily to keep cool as the sun scorched down. But then, Khenria missed a punch, and the woman landed a stout hook on Khenria's already-damaged left ear. Wincing, Khenria dropped into a backwards roll to get some space as she shook out her head.

And the crowd booed.

Khenria's eyes snapped wide as she noticed the crowd for the first time. A rotten head of lettuce was thrown at her, then another. Dherran saw her hiss at the crowd's displeasure, then approach the brunette again. This time, Khenria let a punch land, a jab to the gut. Allowing her breath to flow as Dherran had taught her, she soon had the woman pummeled with a tight combination of punches, and the brunette staggered backwards out of reach, breathing hard to re-gain her equilibrium. The crowd booed the brunette now. Rotten pears were thrown, and Khenria wasted no time. Surging on the momentum of the crowd, she rushed into a strike, breaking the brunette with a tidy collection of fast punches.

With one last punch to her neck, it was over. Khenria did not celebrate as the crowd cheered, merely nodded to either side with her spine straight and head high, glorious like a fucking Queen. The crowd cheered harder, and she smirked at Dherran, then stalked off towards the ready-tent with a swagger that set Dherran's loins pulsing. But he saw the scoreman beckon, marking Dherran as Khenria's trainer. Dherran went over, had a few low words, and finally made for Khenria's tent.

Thrusting the tent-flap aside, he clapped, his heart expansive with pride. "That's it, Khen. You're done."

"What?!" She was livid as she surged up from the wooden bench. "I'm supposed to fight one more! That fight was clean – I didn't use a single dirty trick! I can't be disqualified!"

Dherran laughed. Khenria was gorgeous, all beaten up, sweat-streaked, and vicious as they came. And suddenly, Dherran didn't want to try so hard to resist her. She was a warrior, every bit as fierce as Suchinne had been, the kind of woman that made his heart swell. Surging forward, he gathered her up, kissing her hard despite all the bruises, dirt, and sweat. She gave a muffled squeak, then relaxed into it, kissing him back before she at last pulled away, flushed, and Dherran let her.

"I have to focus..." She breathed unsteadily. "Damn you... I've got one more fight...!"

Dherran kissed her again and she melted into him, kissing him back until they were both breathless. His heart pounded in his chest and his loins heated as they wound into each other in a sweaty, sexy mess. "You're done. Your final opponent resigned." Dherran finally managed to tell her between kisses. "She's got a broken foot. Finished her last bout, but she's out. You won."

"I won?" Khenria's eyebrows shot up as she pulled back, breaking their kiss at last. "Do I get my First Seal?"

"Congratulations, Khenria den'Bhaelen, Hawk-Talon of the Bhaelen Alrashemni," Dherran smoothed her sweaty curls back with a smile. "Your First Seal is complete."

With an enormous grin, it was Khenria who corralled him now, kissing him hard and deep. And Dherran didn't resist it, this relationship building between them as he kissed her back. It was tempestuous and sweet, it was confusing and hot, but it was something Dherran found he didn't want to stop as they wound into each other in the stifling humidity of the ready-tent. They were still kissing a minute later as Grump swooped into the tent, breaking up their afternoon delight by rattling purses full of coins – both from his wagering and Khenria's winnings.

Khenria was all elation as she got cleaned up and changed back into her regular menswear, and then they tromped back to the inn for the midday break. It was packed to the rafters for the festival, and a hearty cheer sounded as Khenria entered. Everyone recognized her now, and the beaming innkeeper's wife showed them to a table that was quickly cleared of other guests, the rotund, jowly innkeeper blustering and smiling as he fetched them a veritable feast. Their repast was on the house, and they ate like kings, roast guinea-fowl with a sauce of aged dark vinegar and summer strawberries, not to mention as many ales as they could drink.

Khenria wolfed it all down like the skinny young woman she was, as a parade of townsmen and women came by to congratulate her. Surrounded by ogling men, Khenria soaked up the attention, grinning and flirting ferociously as she regaled everyone with her version of the fights. Normally, it wouldn't have bothered Dherran, but he found that in the wake of everything that had passed between them in the ready-tent, all the male attention focused on her suddenly irritated him tremendously. Though he tried to tell himself her admirers were nothing, he found himself scowling at them as Khenria laughed and flirted, a hot jealousy simmering in his chest.

But as Khenria enjoyed the attention, Grump, drunk as bats, suddenly lurched up out of his seat. "Got to see to the horses, Dherran! Back in a trice!"

Dherran blinked at the man's sudden departure, as Grump stumbled quickly to the rear door of the inn and out towards the stables. But he'd barely turned the corner when a clarion baritone voice called out through the crowded dining-room, "The dark beauty of the day!"

Clipped with the precise, elegant tones of the aristocracy, the voice matched a sword-thin older man with iron-blond hair that suddenly interrupted Khenria's circle of admirers. Other men stepped back quickly, removing hats from their heads as they noted him. Dressed in a rich russet leather jerkin with gold embroidery and a fine silk shirt, the lord was solicitous, bowing over Khenria's hand and kissing it with perfect manners. Handsome in the extreme, he was still in his prime, his husky-blue gaze sliding over Khenria in precisely the way that made women wilt rather than fume – his perfect manners and poise only accentuating his exquisite handsomeness.

"Khenria den'Bhaelen, was it?" The lord murmured as he arched one ash-blond eyebrow, his lips holding a slight smile. "You had your opponents on the run this afternoon. Well-fought, milady."

"Thank you." Khenria breathed, impressed.

As then man lingered over her hand, Khenria swooned into his fine manners. Dherran didn't like it one bit, certain that this calculating fellow had a reputation with women. Leaning back at the table, Dherran crossed his arms menacingly over his broad chest, staring the fellow down. The lord's pale blue eyes flicked over, a battle-hard glint in his gaze as it roved Dherran's hair and face, then landing at the center of his chest where Dherran's Inkings were hidden by his mostly-buckled jerkin. As the man's gaze perused him, Dherran had the creeping sensation that his measure was being taken – almost as if the man wished to fight him.

"Are you her trainer?" The lord murmured at last.

"I am." Dherran was not solicitous, his tone blunt. "I didn't get your name. *Sir.*"

"I am the Vicoute Arlen den'Selthir." Though the lord inclined his head, his pale gaze never left Dherran's, challenging and almost angry. "The lands in and around Vennet are mine to caretake. But I offer my congratulations to you, sirrah. The lady is a very fine fighter. I recall seeing moves like that in the Khessian Hills when the Kingsmen came to settle a dispute among the border lords. It was settled by individual combat, as the leader of the Khessian Rebels was a haughty man. He didn't last long. But that is all ancient history, as they say."

Leaning down, the lord lifted Khenria's hand to his lips again, his eyes pinning her as she flushed, easy prey to the man's perfect manners. "Milady. Congratulations again. If you are lingering in Vennet for the festival, you must come stay at my manor. You and your trainer, and your servingman whom I noticed leave to tend your beasts. My title is Vicoute, but you may simply call me Arlen."

"My trainer fights at fourth bell this afternoon, Vicoute Arlen." Khenria spoke flirtatiously as she lifted an eyebrow. "If you stay for the men's fights, you may see the impetus of my genius."

"Does he?" The lord's cool blue eyes roved Dherran again – once more displaying anger as if Dherran had personally wronged him. "I will attend. I must see the origin of this maelstrom. Until then." Bowing regally, he turned away, men of lower birth parting before him like water as he departed the inn with his two brawny retainers in tow.

And though the lord was gone, the heat inside Dherran wasn't. Fuming viciously at their interaction, he turned to Khenria. "What in Halsos was that?"

"What?" She pouted fiercely, crossing her arms as she scowled at him, echoing his dark mood now.

"You did everything but flash your breasts at him!" Dherran snarled, knowing his words were sour but suddenly unable to stop them. His hot jealousy was roaring from the afternoon, his stomach churning with gall. Even though Dherran chastised himself from going so quickly from elation of Khenria's wins, to love for her passion, and now to rage at the attention she was getting, he couldn't stop it. Wrapped around her littlest talon, he felt hooked now that he'd decided to open his heart – caught in love once again.

And oh, how it burned.

"Gods, Dherran!" Khenria threw up her hands, scoffing in exasperation as her mood soured to his. "We were only talking! It's what people do, talk. And so what if a lord was interested in my fights? He seemed very nice."

"You'll have all the lords scraping and bowing to your simpering, Khenria." Dherran spoke sourly as he took a large swig of ale, then banged the tankard on the table.

"Fuck you, Dherran!" She hissed at him as she set her own tankard aside, leaning in and piercing him with her stormy grey eyes. "I don't need your rampant jealousy today. You and I haven't even fucked! You've got no right to treat me this way."

"You're right, I don't!" Dherran barked back, livid as he pushed up from the table with red tingeing the edges of his vision now. "So if you're just going to tease me my entire life and keep stringing me along, why don't you just go fuck him?"

Dherran saw her face crumble to his horrible words. He saw how he'd hurt her as her eyebrows shot up, astonished, as she shrank back from how much of a callous brute he was being. But red poured through Dherran now, and there was no stopping it. Like it or not, her talons had sunk into him deep, and now they both had to deal with everything it provoked. There was a reason Dherran didn't let himself love anyone. There was a reason he was cold to the whores he bedded. Because once his love began to rise, terrible things rose with it.

Staggering back, Dherran breathed hard, fighting for control over his emotions. Turning, he made for the stairs out the back of the inn, ignoring Khenria as she called out behind him at the table.

20

THEROUN

Beside the gilded desk, Chancellor Theroun stood with his arms crossed, like he always had during a conference of war. He really didn't see suitor's negotiations any differently, his customary scowl firmly in place as he watched Dhenra Elyasin glide into the Mirror Hall. Sitting behind the ample desk topped by the papers from Theroun's rooms, his secretary Thaddeus sorted everything into stacks as Elyasin entered with her retinue of Chancellors and Guards, stirring the potted palms that flanked the hall's gilded mirrors. And though everything was just as it had been for the Dhenra to welcome her other suitors these past weeks, for Theroun, today was distinctly different.

Today he had a role to play – for the Khehemni Lothren.

It was an informal meeting in this small drawing-room with its white granite columns and walls full of gilded mirrors flanked by potted palms, to begin broaching issues of trade with the Elsthemi Highlands should a union take place. Elyasin was resplendent as she moved to the center of the hall, clad in a pale yellow silk gown that clung to her every movement. Her hair was done in Elsthemi fashion, with ornately carved bone pins long enough to stab a man corralling up her bright waves. Midnight-grey hahled-opals dripped from her ears and neck, their veins of red fire catching the afternoon light that streamed in through the hall's vaulted windows. It was fetching, the hahled-opals native to Elsthemen and a nod to Elyasin's suitor today as her silk slippers whispered over the polished bluestone floor inlaid with pearlvein.

Elyasin was going to slaughter King Therel Alramir today, but her beauty was not what made pain lance in Theroun's side as the Dhenra proffered her hand to him. Bending into a bow over her hand to cover his agony, Theroun noted the Dhenra was quiet as she acknowledged him.

"Chancellor Theroun." She spoke as he straightened. "I have read your treatise on the Elsthemi Highlands. My thanks to you and your apprentice for assembling it."

"Your highness." Theroun nodded curtly.

Dismissing him, Elyasin glanced at Lhaurent lingering with a small army of servers near a table full of delicacies and wine. The Castellan slid forward, his soft grey boots whispering over the floor as he bent over the Dhenra's hand. "Dhenra. How may I serve?"

"Please show the Elsthemi delegation in from the Crown Room. I am ready to receive them."

Bowing deeply, Lhaurent slid away as the Dhenra motioned her guards back into alcoves around the hall, leaving only Captain den'Alrahel close to her person. The Captain-General of the Guard was a mess, her dark curls windblown and her cobalt jerkin half-undone, brazenly baring her Inkings. Theroun felt like keshar-cats stalked his grave as her grey gaze pinned him, but Olea's attention flicked past, scouring the room as the Dhenra stood before a broad circle of chairs in the center of the hall to receive her guests.

The double-doors to the Mirror Hall opened with a boom, stirring the potted palms that flanked the doors. As Lhaurent stepped aside, King Therel Alramir of Elsthemen strode in, followed by a cluster of men and women all wearing buckled leathers and furs in the Elsthemi Highlands fashion. Tall and graceful, King Therel strode across the pearlvein floor as his light blue eyes scoured the room with a wolf-like attentiveness, setting one hand to a plain, functional sword at his hip. Handsome, the young King was in his middle twenties, his military-short ash-blond hair and stubble displaying a seductive yet sharp personality, though he was resplendent in a light grey cloak with a grey wolf pelt around his shoulders. Wearing a black leather jerkin with black boots and grey breeches, only his etched silver buckles showed his station, his boots all function and no pomp, buckled up the side with knives.

But upon seeing the Dhenra stand to receive him, he startled suddenly. Halting, he looked at her, *really* looked at her in a way her other suitors had not, though the Dhenra had been just as lovely upon those days. Uncanny, King Therel's regard sharpened upon Elyasin so keenly that had he been a lance, he would have pierced right through her breast as a moment passed in the hall. Confused, Therel's retainers halted at his back, glancing at the Dhenra, then back to their liege.

But as quickly as her radiance had stopped him, King Therel recovered. A smile of eager pleasure curled his lips, his pale blue eyes rapt with attention as he strode forward once more. Giving a swirl of his cloak, he showed a crimson lining as he gained the circle of chairs, and reaching out, he took Elyasin's hand, bowing over it with a snap of his boots. It was a showy gesture, but well-reasoned. He didn't have to bow. She was a Queen-heir, but he was a full King already, his father having died three years prior. Regardless, King Therel Alramir played a smart entrance, coming to their first meeting with no circlet upon his brow, nor much wealth of note. A long pendant upon a silver chain dangled when he bowed, though as he rose it slipped back inside his shirt. But Theroun had glimpsed it long enough to know it was a keshar-claw inscribed with silver runes that hung over the Elsthemi King's heart.

The Highlanders were wildmen – as wild as the cats they rode to battle.

"King Therel Alramir of Elsthemen." The Dhenra spoke pleasantly. "Be welcome. Are your suites to your liking?"

"Dhenra Elyasin." King Therel's speech held the rolling accent of the north like a cat's purr as he lifted her hand to his lips, his pale blue eyes riveted to hers. "We are richly accommodated. Your palace is a wealth of gracious hospitality, and I give my humblest thanks."

Brushing his lips over her fingers, his kiss lingered, and it flared poor Elyasin. Theroun stifled a growl as he watched his Dhenra fidget, rubbing her knuckles at her side as King Therel took his liberty, her green eyes wide, her breath high and lips parted. When the King removed Elyasin's fingers from his lips, he held her hand close to his mouth so she could feel the heat of his breath as he inclined his head. Theroun saw the Dhenra succumb even more to the young wolf-king, her breath quick and her cheeks flushed as she reclaimed her hand.

Something in Theroun growled at Lhaurent, watching in his best servile manner with his hands clasped nearby. That damn man had known King Therel of Elsthemen would be the first to make such an impression upon the Dhenra, her prior suitors old hounds or young bucks without lands and monies worth the Dhenra's alliance. But this suitor was a bright young wolf, and a wealthy one – and his impression had been smoothly made.

"Please, my King." Elyasin spoke as she gestured to the chairs. "Sit. I invite your retainers to retire to the Rotunda Room to discuss trade benefits for the clans over wine and games with Chancellor Evshein, whom you have already had the pleasure of meeting. My Castellan will show them through."

"You are most kind, Dhenra."

King Therel nodded and a generous portion of his entourage peeled away, along with all the Dhenra's Chancellors besides Theroun, following Lhaurent through a side door. Along with Therel's most richly dressed retainers, a small cadre of guards remained, scattering through room as the landholders sat. Two guards remained by their liege, including one older Highlander with white hair. Upright and proud, his dark eyes were flinty, the man wearing an unembellished sword at his hip and a snowbear pelt around his shoulders.

A man whom Theroun recognized as Devresh Khir, the First Sword of Elsthemen.

But Elsthemen's First Sword was peaceable as King Therel unclasped his cloak and handed it to a thick-muscled bear of a man, though he left the grey wolf-pelt over his jerkin, giving him a wild, roguish look as he settled upon a high-backed seat near the Dhenra. Folding his arms with his customary glower, Theroun eyed the Elsthemi, the First Sword eying Theroun back with mild hostility as he settled into a comfortable stance behind his liege.

Returning to wait upon the company, Castellan Lhaurent rolled a silver trestle laden with beverages and delicacies to the King's side. At the Dhenra's nod, Lhaurent cut the wax on a sealed bottle of wine with a flourish and poured a gilt-rimmed goblet. All watched as Lhaurent tasted it solemnly, then handed it to the Elsthemi King with a deep bow. Pouring one for Elyasin also and tasting it, he at last stepped back, folding his hands and blending seamlessly into the mirrored hall.

King Therel swirled his wine, admiring it for color and clarity. After a sip, he nodded and smiled, breaking the yawning silence with well-versed courtly manners. "Very lovely. Your grapes bloom full and sweet, the mellow base complementing a high heady fragrance. It intoxicates me, Dhenra." Sipping again, he leaned leisurely upon one arm of his gilded chair – his ice-blue eyes never leaving Elyasin's.

Her cheeks colored, but Theroun noted she did not duck her head at his scrutiny. Instead, Elyasin had a very regal sip of her own wine, regarding Therel with shrewd appraisal. "You appreciate our southern grapes? We do not import grapes from any other nation, though the wines of Praough sweeten the palate as well as any."

Praough has an heir near marrying age, is what she means.

At a wave of her hand, Lhaurent's army were suddenly in motion, serving everyone else around the circle with goblets of wine and trays of delicacies as the talks formally began. But King Therel only chuckled as he continued to eye the Dhenra, swirling his wine like a rapacious young wolf.

"Far southern climes are too hot for proper grapes," he spoke again as he sipped. "In Alrou-Mendera, grapes are chilled by ocean mists and snowmelt streams, while heated by fine summer suns, making your strains the perfect combination of tenacity and delicacy. Dhenra."

"And yet the far southern grapes are hardy indeed. Do you think our grapes wan, easily taken by frost or drought?" She countered archly, lifting an eyebrow at him.

"Wan? No, not hardly so." King Therel's smile was all seduction as he lifted an eyebrow back. "The beauty of Menderian grapes is that they persevere in the face of much hardship. Erosion of soil from snows and a touch of frost or blight only intensify the flavor of such heady grapes. A flavor which I long to taste, to swirl in its chalice as I take my leisure by the light of roaring fires in the dead of night. For what man wants a wan or hard grape? A man wants a supple grape, one that is ripe with beauty and bursting with juices upon the tongue. One that is only made more luscious by hardship, by scorching, a touch of mist, and the deep wells of snow from between crevasses. Only such a grape does a man wish to take at the height of summer, to punish beneath his bared skin into the sweetest of mellowed wines."

Even Theroun was nearly gaping at the end of this onslaught. Papers shuffled beside him, and Theroun held a hand out, forestalling Thaddeus' fidgeting. The Dhenra's eyes were riveted to King Therel, her breath fast, her face and chest blooming crimson. She was silent a long moment, then gestured regally, albeit somewhat shakily, for her Castellan.

"Please... Another cup of wine for our honored guest."

Lhaurent slid forward, refilling the King's goblet. As he backed away, Therel saluted Elyasin. "To Menderian wines, the finest in all the land."

"To gracious guests," the Dhenra spoke archly, though she flushed again, "who know quality when they see it."

"Who know quality when they *taste* it." Therel added, his lips curling into a rapacious smile.

Theroun thought the Dhenra was going to drop her wine, so violently did she tremble. She managed to not spill any, though Theroun noted her gaze did not leave King Therel as it came time for petty conversation, her fingers rubbing her knuckles violently as they began the suitor's negotiations. And so it went – him with innuendo though ostensibly speaking of trade, her trying desperately to counter, growing more and more fidgety. It was agonizing, and after twenty minutes, even Thaddeus was shuffling so furiously Theroun had to press his hand down upon the stack of papers to get the lad to quit. Thad blushed, nodding at the scene unfurling before them.

Theroun shook his head, letting Thad know any interruption would be a severe breach of station.

The Dhenra had to maneuver the raw sexuality of Therel Alramir all by herself. This wasn't harder than managing a war, which Elyasin had done in a vastly capable way for nigh-on two years. Crossing his arms, Theroun watched the pair duel it out as the Dhenra's power slipped and slid, nearly obliterated by King Therel's salacious talk as innuendo dripped from the King's lips like honey.

But when light banter gave way to more precise talk of trade and tariffs, Elyasin came into her element at last. Standing with the briskness of a battle commander, she stepped to the desk, asking for a few lists. Hastily, Thad handed them over and Elyasin spread them out, leaning upon the desk in a decidedly unladylike way as she looked them over, nearly ignoring the Elsthemi King.

In that moment, King Therel morphed into a man of business. Innuendo was quite suddenly shelved as he came to the Dhenra's side, examining the lists. Now, as they came together pouring through numbers and figures, they seemed almost a team. Commenting side-by-side on various matters, they pointed out pieces of trade each would like to maintain, and other areas for negotiation.

Theroun watched it with growing pleasure as Elyasin showed her prowess now, thumping the Elsthemi brigand of a King with her wits as she performed complicated sums on the fly in her head, raising the King's blond eyebrows. And just like this, they continued as the hours flew by, deep in conversation as if the rest of the room had utterly disappeared. Theroun found himself suppressing a smile as he took in Uhlas' daughter. She wasn't some wealthy, idle waif just waiting for a man to show her the way to the bedchamber.

And the Highlander King had it coming if he presumed otherwise.

But King Therel did presume at one point, as the sun was finally dying beyond the high-gabled windows, lighting the gilded mirrors in flaming oranges and reds. As they leaned over a map together, heads close while discussing the mining of silver in the Eleskis, Therel quite suddenly laid a few fingers upon Elyasin's elbow. It was a small gesture, almost a passing touch like one might do with a friend – but the Dhenra nearly jumped out of her skin. Snapping upright, she shuddered so badly that King Therel actually blanched, concern suffusing his visage as they stared at each other, Elyasin breathing hard. Standing near the desk, Guard-Captain den'Alrahel had her hand on her sword as a long moment stretched in the mirrored hall – the vast silence bouncing off the marbled granite gables as the light whispered gold and red.

"Forgive me." King Therel murmured, heartfelt as he paused as if searching for the right words. For the first time all afternoon, he seemed vulnerable, as if something deep inside him might break should Elyasin reject him.

Theroun's gaze sharpened upon the man, watching this sudden, strange weakness.

"I can see our conversation has many benefits, Dhenra," the King recovered at last, his speech smooth but surprisingly free of innuendo. "Perhaps we should adjourn for the evening and take this up again upon the morrow? My clansmen are quite tired from the journey. And though they would never say so, I think an ale and a good leg of roast meat would do them well, rather than sweets and wine."

Theroun blinked. Tact was not something he'd have expected out of the Highlander King as Elyasin recovered also, giving a kind smile – though something in her green gaze seemed disappointed. "Of course. We forget our duties. A banquet has been set in the Small Hall, milord, for you and your men. A welcome for your journey, with feasting and music. I will attend anon. Though my schedule has been quite busy, you must understand, and I shall need to retire early."

"Of course." King Therel dipped his chin in a nod, though his eyes never left hers. "But I would request, milady... the pleasure of a dance at the banquet. Before you retire for the night."

A beat passed between them and Theroun watched it intently. He saw how Elyasin's eyes shone to hear the King's bold request. He saw King Therel waiting, strung out now that he'd made such a plain move. And Elyasin saw it too as her gaze lingered upon him, a clever smile lifting her lips.

"There will be dancing, I am sure, milord." She spoke smoothly. "And you will see me at the banquet. Until then, my Castellan will show you and your men back to your rooms so you may make ready. I look forward to taking a cup of wine with you at the festivities."

With a gracious nod, Elyasin let her gaze fall from the King's, demure and frustrating as hell. Sidling by, she was close enough that her sleek silk brushed the King, making him linger upon her scent. Theroun watched the man break, the young wolf-King of the Highlands watching Elyasin go with agony in his eyes – desperation far more than any man should have when watching a beautiful woman tease him. Without turning, Elyasin clapped her hands smartly and the assembled Highlanders and Chancellors rose, Therel and his men ushering from the hall while Elyasin stood proudly by her gilded chair with her Guard-Captain at her side.

Just at the last moment, Elyasin raised her voice. "King Therel!"

"Yes, my Dhenra?" Breathless, he spun, his pale blue eyes simmering to have been called by her.

"Save a dance for me."

As Elyasin gave a roguish grin, King Therel's retainers broke into the raucousness for which they were famed. Hollering and pounding their fists to the walls and door, they clapped Therel upon his shoulders, jostling him in a familiar way no King would have ever allowed from his men. But Highlanders were different. Theroun saw how they were family, how the King cared for his men and they for him, looking out for each other through haunting winter nights full of burying snows.

Breaking into the most pleased, most sexually dark smile Theroun had ever seen, King Therel said, "My Dhenra," with such a rolling thrum that Theroun thought it might just drop the Dhenra where she stood.

It didn't. She stood tall, regal and challenging with one golden eyebrow arched and a slight smile upon her lips. Placing a palm to his chest and one hand to his sword, King Therel sank down upon one knee, holding his bow for a count of ten before he rose. It was an Alrashemni bow – and it wasn't wasted upon Elyasin. She startled, and Captain den'Alrahel beside her, as Theroun suddenly realized why the Khehemni Lothren wanted a war with Elsthemen. They didn't just want to frame this young, roguish King for Elyasin's assassination and provoke a war to kill off Alrashemni in the ranks.

They wanted to kill him – Alrashemni by blood, right smack in the middle of the Elsthemen royal line.

His bow had shaken the Dhenra. She turned, giving the Highland King one last ornately tortured glance as she moved off towards the doors back to her suites, her Guard-Captain on her heels. King Therel watched her go. And then roused his clansmen, gesturing them after Castellan Laurent.

"Thad!" Theroun snapped his fingers with a growl at Thaddeus, who was still frozen, gaping at the scene. "Pick up those lists and follow me. The Dhenra will need to study them tonight in her quarters. Things are progressing here, and she needs to be prepared for the morrow."

With a blink, Thad gaped at Theroun.

And then nodded hastily, gathering everything up with hurried hands.

* * *

INSPECTING his raw knuckles in the morning, Theroun flexed his hand to make certain everything still worked, before slinging on a hunter green leather jerkin and affixing his Chancellor's pin to the high collar. Though it hurt like Halsos' Hells this morning, his bruised hand wasn't from the raucous Highlander banquet the night before – though Theroun had stood by with Thaddeus beneath the gilded chandeliers, watching the Highlanders make merry and down their ale like there'd be no more, ever.

Theroun thought back on the party as he pulled on his boots at his desk, knowing Elyasin's summons this morning was far more important than her usual requests for a briefing from him at breakfast-time. The Highlanders had been lively the night before, just the kind of liveliness Elyasin enjoyed as they'd spontaneously taken over the festivities, interrupting the musicians and taking their instruments, forming their own band and thundering the hall with the stamping of feet for their boisterous dances.

As the fires in the hearths had burned high, King Therel had gotten his dance with Elyasin, a folk-reel known in Alrou-Mendera and the Highlands. She'd been spun from partner to partner, women of her coterie and female Highlands warriors filling in the line as men came to dance, seeing the Dhenra upon the floor. But none came so avidly as Therel Alramir, a dark pleasure illuminating his visage every time they came together for a promenade or a bow, a spin or a daring lift.

Setting his jaw this morning as he stood and straightened his jerkin, Theroun thought back over the young King and the Dhenra's interactions. He'd seen how Therel had let Elyasin slide down his body in her thin silks from every lift, how she'd melted into his touch every time they partnered. Heat blistered between them; sex. And when it was over, Therel had bowed over her hand, pressing it with a hard, daring kiss and watching her flush as he breathed fast from the dance.

Elyasin had left the hall after that, leaving the Highlanders to dine on. Theroun had too, leaving Thad to enjoy the revelry, pacing back to his suite with bitterness choking his throat. He'd slept with nightmares, tossing and turning, and woken at dawn in a fierce temper, flowing through his sword forms with more violence than usual.

And when the Dhenra's summons had come, Theroun had slammed his fist into his desk so hard it bled.

Wrapping it in clean linen now, he strode out his doors in a bitter anger. It was still early as he knocked upon the Dhenra's gilded double-doors between two flanking guards. The doors boomed open, placid First-Lieutenant Fenton den'Kharel admitting Theroun with a nod and a genial smile. Theroun nodded back; Fenton was a decent sort, the kind of warrior he respected. And though the Dhenra should have been primping with her maids, readying for her morning with the only other proper King on the docket, Arthe den'Tourmalin of the Tourmaline Isles, Theroun gazed into the vaulted chambers to see that the Dhenra was hardly dressed.

Sunlight flooded in through the high bank of windows as Theroun entered the Dhenra's sitting-parlor, potted greenery growing in a riot among the cobalt velvet chaises. The Dhenra was curled up on a chaise in the sunshine, clad in a robin's egg dressing-gown edged with dripping lace, sipping coffee from a piece of midnight-blue Jadounian porcelain. The gold rim winked in the sun as she brought it to her lips, and eyeing him above her coffee, the Dhenra did not stand for Theroun's arrival and Theroun did not sit. It had been the same with Uhlas, and Elyasin drew the lace of her dressing gown securely closed as she shifted to a more proper posture upon the chaise.

"Theroun," she spoke without preamble, regarding him with Uhlas' level stare as she tapped the rim of her cup with one buffed fingernail. "What do you think of King Therel Alramir?"

And here it was. Theroun knew his time had finally come for the Khehemni Lothren, to open his mouth and dance upon their puppet strings. Giving his customary glower, neither more nor less than usual, Theroun barked casually, "Therel is very full of himself, Dhenra."

"I can always depend on you for an honest opinion, can't I?" A smile quirked Elyasin's lips as she sipped her coffee again.

"I give frank opinions as I once did upon the battlefield for your father, Dhenra. When Generals hold things back studying the fields of engagement, good men die."

"Men always die in war, Theroun," she said smoothly, turning and setting her coffee aside on a gilded table. "I am asking you how much of a risk Therel is."

"To the nation? Not much." Theroun did not break his scowl, though his insides churned and his old wound in his side gripped like fire. "An alliance with House Alramir has benefited our country for more decades than I can count. They are strong supporters of your House, though they did not approve of the war with Valenghia. It almost cost us our trade."

"The Elsthemi Highlands provide most of our wool and ghennie-fleece," the Dhenra's gaze drifted to the windows as she spoke. "Not to mention nearly a million bales of pevel yearly, plus precious ores, gems, and dyes. Therel has been most gracious in preparatory trade discussions. He has offered the pevel at half its usual price and the wool at two-thirds, in addition to other sundries of note."

"Very generous, Dhenra." Theroun had heard it all at the desk the afternoon before.

"Generous indeed." Elyasin took up her porcelain cup again, sipping from the gold rim. "What are his ulterior motives, Chancellor?"

"Ulterior motives?" Theroun barked, almost laughing at her. "You're young, beautiful, wealthy, the only heir to the throne from the direct line of den'Ildrian. What King in his right mind wouldn't want to take that to bed?"

"Chancellor!" Coughing in the middle of her next sip, she set down her cup upon its saucer with a vicious clink. "When I require opinions in matters of the bedchamber, I will ask for them!"

"Forgive me, Dhenra, but my opinion stands," Theroun returned. "The young Elsthemi King is clever, daring, and motivated – and you are his ultimate conquest. His flagrant behavior yesterday, both at the negotiations and at the banquet, have made that inescapably plain."

"And once he has me?" The heat in her green eyes withered.

Theroun cursed himself, covering his next lie with his usual scowl. "Once men capture the golden idol, they never cease to luxuriate in its presence. Dhenra."

Elyasin brightened, foolish already for the Highlander King. Theroun could see it in the way the pulse in her neck sped, the way she breathed faster, and how she began to flush just thinking of the young wolf. "And once the idol is captured, do men like Therel smash the temple from whence it came? Would he?"

Rubbing his jaw with one hand, Theroun held back a bitter sigh. This was too easy. Dhenra Elyasin and King Therel were practically wedding themselves – right into the Lothren's plans for their destruction. "I believe King Therel to be a man of his word, Dhenra. Indeed, you may enjoy more freedom with him than with most men. Elsthemen has had split kingdoms before and Elsthemi tradition is to invite any outlander Queen to spend half the year with her King, while she spends the other half-year in residence at her own kingdom. Decisions are generally agreed upon jointly, and women enjoy freedoms more broad in Elsthemen than anywhere else upon the continent. They have an entire regiment of women keshar-cavalry, women can own property same as here, and when there is not a King upon the throne, there is a Queen. You would not usurp his power, and he would not usurp yours. From what I've seen of Therel so far, he has his father's demeanor. Flagrant, compelling, naturally magnetic and unabashedly innuendous, but with a keen mind for ruling. And he has... a camaraderie with his retainers that leads me to believe he is of good temper overall."

"I heard he stuffed some poor woman in a trunk after dismembering her." Elyasin arched a regal eyebrow, and Theroun scowled harder.

"Rumors can be petty and misleading."

"I see." Elyasin took a small sip of her coffee. "What time am I meeting with King Arthe den'Tourmalin of the Isles?"

"Ninth bell, Dhenra. Just after his delegation has enjoyed a morning repast. Castellan Lhaurent has planned a brief sitting in the Mirror Room, then a walk of the Greenhouse. Apparently, King Arthe likes to walk while he discusses business."

"You should know, Theroun," she eyed him candidly. "I am considering King Arthe den'Tourmalin rather seriously. The Tourmaline Isles command an impressive spice trade."

"Indeed?" Theroun could have laughed at how she was trying to deceive herself. He knew the Dhenra's heart would not lead her to the King of the Isles. But since she'd brought it up, he had to address it. "May I be frank?"

"Of course." She blinked. "From you, I expect it, really."

"I think you'll find King Arthe to be a bit much like your father, Dhenra." Theroun commented. "He's older, stern, and a man of few words. He's been married, and though his previous Queen died, he has four healthy heirs and needs no more. Technically, he is King, but the Isles are run by the Septhan, comprised of a representative from each of the seven Tourmaline Islands. The Tourmalines are more a federation than a monarchy, banded together under egalitarian values from their ancient history as pirates. Their King is merely their tiebreaker for voting, and their foreign diplomat. For the Isles, you would be a figurehead only. Your power to affect change would be limited, as Arthe's is, though his populace love him tremendously."

Theroun saw his words strike Elyasin deep as her green eyes shrouded over. If nothing else, Elyasin was an idealist, and maintaining her power and wielding it with surety, grace, and a strong hand were of vital importance to her, just as it had been with Uhlas. Theroun watched her consider his words, and when her eyes cleared, he knew she'd chosen.

Aeon help them all.

"Very well. We will discuss King Arthe den'Tourmalin after he and I have met. When is my next meeting with King Therel Alramir?"

"This afternoon." Theroun spoke curtly. "First bell again. Your schedule has been cleared of all other matters until the banquet for the Islemen in the evening."

"Very good, Chancellor. You may go. And I thank you for your candor this morning."

As Elyasin gave him a nod to go, calm with clarity, Theroun gave his curt military bow. Turning, he startled to realize First-Lieutenant Fenton den'Kharel had been standing behind him the entire time, slouching in a casual but ready way at the door. Theroun nodded and den'Kharel nodded back. Hauling open the door to the Dhenra's suites, Theroun strode out, his old battle-wound in his side twingeing viciously from what he'd just done.

And his heart gripping him even worse.

21

ELOHL

In the dusty thoroughfare outside the Jenner compound, Elohl pulled the bell-chain near the massive main gates of red cendarie wood, then pulled it twice more. Shading his eyes from the mid-morning sun, he gazed up the fifty-foot byrunstone wall to turrets with guard lookouts. The First Abbey of the Jenner Penitents was a city within the city, the fortress-wall that ringed it speaking of ancient martial history. Arrow-slits dominated the upper reaches, an edifice from more disastrous times – but though Elohl narrowed his eyes, searching the battlements for life, he saw none.

No sentries, and no one watching the doors in the noontime heat.

It was the seventh time he had rung. For the past five days, it had been like this. The routine was wearing upon him and Eleshen, as all five days they had spoken with a curt, angry brother who had insisted, *it is a bad day for visitors, would you please come back when the deliveries of ale for the Queen's Coronation are concluded?* Today, the heat was thick, dust high in the air, and yet again they were being ignored as sweat dripped inside Elohl's collar, his well-buckled jerkin stifling. He had half a mind to just visit by night in his Alrashemni gear and case the place, but their mission was to actually speak with a Jenner Brother, and that they could not do by subterfuge.

Elohl was about to ring again when Eleshen strode forward, rattling the ornate iron grille before the small welcome-door next to the main gates with a huff. "Well, where are they?"

"Maybe they're praying. Or still readying the Queen's ale deliveries." Elohl sighed, rifling a hand through his short black hair, fanning out the sweat.

"Ha, ha. Very funny." Eleshen eyeballed him, all piss and vinegar today. "They're lazy, that's what they're doing. A fat lot of nothing! Open up! *Answer your goddamn door!*"

Rattling the grate again, Eleshen kicked it – and suddenly, the small door beside the main gates opened. A tall man stood there, a different fellow than the past few days. Of later of years, he had a drooping face with a gray beard and stooped shoulders. Wearing black Jenner robes, his cowl was up despite the heat, its draping sleeves hiding his hands. The long robe had a belt of black cordage, and as he shuffled forward to unlock the wrought-iron grille, gnarled toes peeked from beneath his robe, his bare feet filthy. Dropping into a moderate bow with one foot behind the other, the man placed two fingers to his lips with far more respect than they had been given the previous days.

"Milord. Milady. Blessings be upon you." The old Jenner's smile was of gentle temperament as he straightened. "Do you have business in the First Abbey?"

"Penitent." Elohl inclined his head, of a mind to be civil to this fellow, relieved they weren't being summarily dismissed today. "We have no pre-arranged business, but I do have questions about the Penitent faith."

"Come in then, come in!" The man's face opened into a smile of delight as he motioned them forward with one gnarled old hand. "Please forgive my lateness in opening the door. You have come on a busy day, a busy few weeks. We ready libations for the Queen's coronation seven days hence, and there is yet much to do. But we always have time for those who wish to ask about the Faith. Perhaps we can find a Brother in the history office to answer your questions."

Elohl nodded and stepped in through the iron gate, Eleshen on his heels. But as she passed through, the old man stepped to the side, gathering a long white shawl from a basket in a niche carven into the inside of the wall.

"Please, milady, if you don't mind?" His eyebrows raised expectantly as he extended the shawl.

Eleshen's brows furrowed, not understanding, but Elohl answered quickly, "Of course."

"What?" Eleshen glanced from one man to the other.

"Cover up a little." Elohl motioned to her hair, her bare collarbones, and chest.

"Our Sisters," the old Penitent coughed, "go about the Abbey with modesty. As do all the Brothers. Though we move together about our duties, there are some who could be... distracted."

"Oh!" Eleshen's face opened in understanding as she accepted the shawl. "Because you're celibate, you mean?"

"Most are, by choice." The Penitent mimed her winding it up over her hair and covering her upper torso and shoulders. "Some are not. *Relations* are not prohibited among us, simply frowned upon as a distraction from true bliss." Eleshen had finished winding her shawl and now waited expectantly, but the man frowned. "The, ah... finer trimmings of feminine beauty, ah... please."

"What finer trimmings?" Eleshen quipped, oblivious.

Glancing over, Elohl saw Eleshen's cleavage was still clearly visible below the shawl, above her buckled lambswool corset and shirt. Elohl held back a chuckle, which turned into a cleared throat. "Your breasts."

"Oh!" As she glanced down, Eleshen missed the old Penitent going red as a beet as he also looked. Tugging the shawl over them, Eleshen grinned at the Jenner, completely amused by the man's squeamishness. "Better?"

"My name is Brother Sheldran." The old Jenner was still shamefaced. "Shall we proceed to the Abbey?"

"Lead the way." Elohl nodded with a smile.

Proceeding in, Brother Sheldran led them through manicured gardens, along a path that led away from the main thoroughfare through the gates. Similar to Alrashesh, the compound of the First Abbey brought Elohl right back to his childhood with its well-organized layout, each building made of byrunstone blocks with cap-fitted rhivenstone shingles upon peaked roofs. Pearled glass windows created triptychs and single-pane stories from the Penitent holy texts. The gables were high enough to shed snow at the foot of the Kingsmount, even barns for livestock ornate as cathedrals.

Unlike Lintesh, every building in the First Abbey was exquisitely carved. Flowering vines of byrunstone writhed up every corner, gargoyles and fanciful beasts graced every roofline, their wide mouths spouts for water-collection into rain barrels. They passed a granary entirely carven to look like fields of wheat and oats, and as Elohl peered closer, he saw foxes, rabbit, and small dragons creeping through the stalks. A storehouse was carven with panels telling the story of hops from planting to beer. A section of wall they passed under served as an aqueduct from one part of the compound to lavish gardens, the arched stone portal flowing with the rising Jenner Sun over a land of well-tilled fields.

Absorbed in it all, Elohl hadn't noticed he'd been silent until Eleshen spoke beside him. "It's beautiful! All the stone carving! Brother Sheldran, how long does such a thing take?"

Gazing around with a fatherly smile as they walked through a quadrangle with a fountain at its center, he responded indulgently, "We have carved these stones for as long as Lintesh has been a city, young lady. Stories tell of the Abbey being founded just a single year after the palace was hewn from the mountain. A panel like that one there," he pointed to a five-foot piece depicting incredibly lifelike deer in a forest, "takes ten carvers a year. And one master can take five or ten years on such a piece, depending on how complex it is."

"Don't they get bored?" Eleshen quipped, astounded.

"Not really." The Jenner's chuckle was indulgent. "The carving is an act of Penitence. The careful consideration of what is to be carved, the feel of the stone, the dedication to do it day in and day out. Many take vows of celibacy and silence while they work on a piece, to absorb themselves in the task. The Doing is the Way, the humbling loss of self into a greater Knowing. This is the Lost Way, which we must remember. Ah, here we are; our First Dwelling. The first cathedral built upon our beloved grounds."

Gesturing up a set of byrunstone steps, Brother Sheldran indicated a building more ornately carven than the rest, clearly ancient from the amount of weathering it had taken. Though a newer and far larger cathedral stood next to it with high arches, domes, and gargoyled turrets, this space had a simple elegance to it, as if those who had built it had done so in haste, only afterwards honing it to beauty. Hauling on a massive iron ring to open one of the tall cendarie double-doors, Brother Sheldran ushered them inside. "Please enter. Speech is currently permitted as prayers are not in session, but please keep your voices respectful."

Nodding, Elohl and Eleshen stepped inside. Vaulted, the cathedral's interior was lit by thirty-foot panels of opalescent glass at the far end, a musky incense curling through the air from bronze censers near the doors. Rows of cendarie benches with meditation pillows proceeded to the central domed nave, the colored-glass windows depicting the Jenner Sun with its thirteen golden spokes.

Dark halls flashed back to Elohl as he blinked, recognizing the same image burned into his mind from the torch-lit doors of Roushenn's Deephouse long ago. Inside the Jenner Sun, a dragon and wolf fought each other, tumbling in their vicious glory. Staring up at the tableau, nausea hit Elohl as the tension of that night flooded through him. Done here in sparkling ruby glass for the dragon, with opalescent greys and whites for the wolf, living flame wreathed the beasts, the gold of the Jenner Sun trapping their fight in the center.

But as Elohl looked, he saw this image was different. In Roushenn, the wolf and dragon had been equally opposed, but here, the wolf was triumphant, the dragon's neck in its bloody jaws as it stood over the great serpent coiling upon its back. But still, the red eyes of the dragon blazed, furious as it yet lived – hateful of the wolf.

"The Battle of Wolf and Dragon. A fight to the death." Brother Sheldran murmured as he gazed at the glass rotunda also. "Do you like it?"

"It's ferocious." Elohl murmured as he blinked, the spell of the tableau broken. "What does it signify?"

But the Brother merely shrugged. "Only the most learned have read deeply into the symbolism of the Wolf and Dragon. You should query Brother Temlin, who I am taking you to meet. He has made some study of it with the Abbess Lenuria, who is an expert on arcane symbology."

Leading them to the right, Brother Sheldran took them towards stone arches that opened into reading-rooms packed with shelves of books and scrolls. As he led them to a cramped study-room cluttered with tomes and odd items, Elohl saw a wire-framed older man with white streaking his red waves sitting behind a stout cendarie desk. His nose firmly planted in his tome, he blinked up through reading half-spectacles, then lowered his chin and gazed over them, his green eyes sharp as eagle talons. Elohl liked the look of the man immediately – fierce like an old war-general past his prime, now engaged in a war of the mind in his advancing years.

"Brother Temlin?" Their guide knocked at the open door. "The young man has a few questions about our faith. Are you occupied?"

Smoothing his trim russet beard, the man let his leather-bound tome thud to the table irreverently. Raking a hand through his yet-thick hair, he stood with the energy of a fox but the stiffness of a turtle, as if his joints hurt and he didn't expect them to. Gesturing them in, he barked, "Come! I was just finishing a treatise on

House del'Ilio of Cennetia. Conniving, money-grubbing bastards the lot of them, with a quick hand to the poisons whenever it suited them! Come in, come in!"

"Please excuse Brother Temlin." Brother Sheldran coughed, his face red. "He is... opinionated."

"Leave them here, Shel. Have Brother Berian bring ale for our guests, with bread and butter. They look thirsty. Shoo! Well now!" Removing his spectacles and tapping them on the desk, Brother Temlin's keen gaze took in Elohl and Eleshen after he'd shooed Brother Sheldran out of the cramped study. "Have a seat! Never mind the scrolls. Useless, the lot of them. Sit upon them if you like." He gestured amiably to an overstuffed couch on the far side of the desk and Elohl gingerly shoved over a few ragged scrolls to make room for himself and Eleshen. When they sat, the sofa revealed a puff of fine dust.

"Now. I am Brother Temlin, Second Historian of the Abbey. Are you wanting to convert, lad, or does something else about the Faith pique your interest?" The Brother reclaimed his seat, though humor in his green eyes said he already knew Elohl had no intention of joining the monks.

"I am not interested in conversion, Brother Temlin." A smile flitted across Elohl's face as he shook his head. "I have questions about your history and cannon."

"Well." Brother Temlin leaned his chair back on two legs as he stroked his trim beard. "That would take all year. Is there something specific about the cannon you want to know?"

A nervous-looking young man suddenly appeared at the door with a wide trencher of hot-buttered bread and two pewter flagons. Brother Temlin motioned him in and the lad placed it all on the desk, nearly slopping ale in his haste. Temlin eyed him sharply and the lad paled, practically racing out the door as Brother Temlin leaned over the flagons and inhaled.

"Ah. Our famous honey-red with the baelin-malt." Straightening, Brother Temlin gestured to the food and drink. "Sup, friends. You repay our efforts with detailed commentary on the brew. Once you're soused."

He winked.

Reaching for a mug with a smile, enjoying the man's directness, Elohl passed it to Eleshen, then nudged the bread towards her. She set to as Elohl took a mug, sipping a lovely summer ale with a crisp floral taste from the honey and malt, an expansive bouquet with very little bitter. He nodded appreciatively as he had another sip, then answered Brother Temlin's question. "I'm looking for information on the Alranstones. In particular, what the number of eyes signify. I've heard the Penitents have an origin story surrounding them."

"Better to have asked the Alrashemni, lad, they knew about the Alranstones. Are you a scholar?" Stroking his white-streaked beard, Brother Temlin's face softened into wistfulness as his gaze passed over Elohl – lingering upon the golden marks just visible above his jerkin's high collar.

Elohl's gaze flicked to the open cendarie door, wondering if he should close it. Having noticed Elohl's glance, Brother Temlin pulled a piece of parchment from a drawer and wrote a short sentence with a charcoal nib, passing it to Elohl, as Eleshen leaned over his shoulder to read along. *Tongues wag less around here if doors remain open. Anything you wish not spoken, please write. You may take it with you and burn it in the cathedral braziers at the end of our session today. Many come here to write meditations and burn them, releasing them to the Way. It will not be notable.*

Elohl nodded, though he still took a moment to spread his sensate sphere, monitoring for anyone lurking in the hall. There was no one. Undoing a few jerkin buckles, he unlaced his shirt, pulling it down so the Brother caught a glimpse of both his gold and black Inkings, before buckling everything back up. Though the Jenner betrayed surprise, Elohl saw a deep understanding move through the man's gaze before it was banished. Elohl's pulse quickened, knowing he'd find answers here at last. But before he could speak, the Brother held up one gnarled hand, forestalling Elohl.

"I must tell you, lad. We Penitents do not involve ourselves in political movements. Ours is a peaceful order, and if this is about vendetta, you may leave now."

"Though I war with my own demons, my query is not about vendetta, Brother." Elohl shook his head. Setting the nib to paper, he wrote, *I need information about the Alranstones because these gold Inkings were given to me by a seven-eye Stone,* and slid it back.

Brother Temlin read it, blanched, and read it again as his lips fell open. Looking up, his green eyes tightened. "Do you jest with me, lad?"

"No." Elohl shook his head. "What you've just seen was given me by no hand of man."

Brother Temlin went very still, his gaze roving Elohl's neck where the gold was visible. Elohl felt a moment of concern, that the man could be part of the cabal sending assassins after him. But locking eyes with the old Jenner, Elohl had an impression of intolerance, as if the man abhorred secrets. It eased Elohl, and when Brother Temlin gestured for Elohl's mug, he slid it over. Brother Temlin took a very long swig, then slid it back. Settling into his chair with his arms crossed, he displayed the firm chest and shoulders of a man who had once used a sword.

"I think I would like to feed the ducks." The Brother quipped suddenly. "How about you? Would the two of you like the take a walk out to the ponds?"

Elohl nodded, understanding the need for privacy. Draining his ale, he stood, Eleshen close upon his heels. Exiting the study, the Jenner Brother led them through the cathedral's annex and out a back door that opened into a sprawling herb garden. Crunching along gravel paths towards the glimmer of water, they reached the duck-ponds. Pleasant and cool, the area had artfully sculpted paths for walking and byrunstone benches beneath cascading willows. Prattling on about the Penitent canon, stalling, Brother Temlin led them to a secluded area near the outer wall. Elohl's view over the ponds was uninterrupted; they would see anyone coming thirty yards away. Having a seat on the bench Brother Temlin indicated beneath a bower of lhumen-vine, their full yellow blossoms smelling of honey and reminiscent of squash, Brother Temlin followed his gaze up the wall.

"Don't worry, lad, we can speak privately here. This section of the wall plays tricks on sound. We'll hear anyone coming before they hear us. Only us old-timers know it, though." He winked conspiratorially. "So. Your golden marks were Inked by a seven-eye Stone."

"I was hoping someone here would know about it." Elohl nodded. "A friend told me the Jenners have a history with the Alrashemni and Alranstones. Something called me to climb the Stone, to sit atop it at midnight. A pulse, like a heartbeat. I know I dreamed, but the only thing I can remember is the word *rennkavi* and a vague impression of a man with red and white Inkings. When I woke in the morning, every eye on the Stone was open. And when I placed my hands upon it... they blinked."

"And you swear this is all truth, lad?" Brother Temlin's eyebrows had climbed his face.

"I saw it." Eleshen piped up. "One day he just had his Kingsmount and Stars, and the damn Stone wouldn't even open a single eye. The next morning, he had all that gold and *every damn eye* was open, and when he set his hands to the Stone, they blinked. Then we traveled through."

"The Stone let *you* go through?" Brother Temlin blinked at her. "Correct me if I'm wrong, but you're not Alrashemni."

"I'm not." Eleshen shook her head.

Brother Temlin sat back, stroking his white beard. "Tell me, lad, what color were the eyes on the seven-eye Stone?"

"The lowest eye was jet, then lapis, then malachite. The one in the center shone every color like a diamond. The fifth was moonstone, then citrine, and at the top was Elsthemi fire opal, a hahled-stone."

"By the Light of the Way," Brother Temlin murmured, sitting back on the bench. "And you swear to me you've never read any Jenner cannon?"

"Never." Elohl shook his head. "Like I said, my friend told me about it."

"Then he told you the Heimkellen. The prophecy of the Lost Tribe, and the Uniter."

"I don't claim to be this man in your prophecy, Brother," Elohl nodded. "I just need to find out what all this means."

"Tell me, lad, do you know what the word *rennkavi* means in ancient Alrashemni?" Brother Temlin asked, still stroking his beard. Elohl shook his head, but leaned in, ready to listen.

"*Rennkavi* is often is translated as *binding*," Brother Temlin continued. "But to the ancient Alrashemni, it carries many interpretations. This word can sometimes mean *to bind* or *make bound*, as in binding a wound or tying things together. Or it can mean, *one who binds* or *he who remembers*. Some interpret it as indicating a wise man, like a sage or a scholar. But I believe the word has yet another meaning. The suffix *-kavi* was traditionally used to mean *unity*, like the unbroken circle of the sun. The prefix *renn* means *to bring*. But in High Alrakhan, such a combination was often used as a noun. So the word actually means *unifier* or *unity bringer*. The person who embodied the *rennkavi* was a person to bring others together. A leader."

"So why do I remember that and nothing else?" Elohl asked, rapt.

"You should rather ask," Brother Temlin eyed him, "how in the Great Way did you open all the eyes upon an Alranstone and get those golden marks Inked upon you. I've made a study of Alranstones from historical accounts; you described the iris colors perfectly. But you must know, most of that knowledge was kept by the Alrashemni. When the Jenners were kicked out of the Alrashemni, the Rakhan at the time would not allow us access to the old annals. He feared we would retaliate against him, and sent the annals to a mountain stronghold somewhere. So we do not have those records."

"Has there been nothing written about the Stones since?" Eleshen voiced Elohl's question.

"There are a series of tomes about thirty years old that apply," Brother Temlin continued. "The journals of Sister Mollia den'Lhorissian, who joined the Jenners in her teens against the wishes of her family, a long line of palace healers. She was training to be an Alran-keeper, a post that has not been observed in hundreds of years, due to the lack of anyone with the suitable gifts for it. But Mollia took up the ancient trainings, writing down what she learned about Alranstones from her experimentations with them, and those journals are in our keeping."

"What did Sister Mollia's writings say?" Eleshen quipped eagerly.

"Much, and little." Brother Temlin shrugged with a sigh. "Her language is cryptic, some of the text in High Alrakhan, which can have many meanings. Some of it was written in a cipher so complex it still has not been unwound, entire pages filled with unidentifiable sigils. Many thought Sister Mollia went mad from interacting with the Stones. Apparently, Alran-keepers often did go mad. It was one of the reasons the Alrashemni decided to no longer train young minds in such mystics, as it involved frequent usage of very potent mind-altering plants. Mollia became quite addicted, and quite addled, even by age twenty-five."

"You speak as if you knew her." Eleshen's voice was somber, her comment perceptive.

"I did." The old Jenner glanced over, sharp. "Yes, I did. A very sad tale."

Elohl paused, then unbuckled the upper part of his jerkin to bare his golden Inkings. "Do any of these sigils look familiar?"

Leaning close, Brother Temlin donned his spectacles, squinting. "Could be. But it's been a long while since I read Sister Mollia's works. I'd have to get permission from the First Historian to get into the Rare Tomes Room to view them."

"Could you ask him?" Elohl spoke as he buckled his jerkin back up.

"Not right now." Brother Temlin shook his head. "He's away in Rhaventia, in conference with our sect there. He'll be gone a month or more."

"I can't wait that long." Elohl sighed, feeling they had reached a dead-end.

Pulling off his spectacles, Brother Temlin began to polish them as he gazed at Elohl. "You look like a man of *capability*, Kingsman. The Rare Tomes Room is near the Fifth Spoke, the guard-tower near the Annex where we began our conversation today. It's an underground vault accessed by a crypt behind the Statue of Sage Lherrick, he's the one with the birds on his shoulders. The vault is cleaned weekly on Dornast, but none have permission to visit while the First Historian is away, other than the Abbott and Abbess. There is a key in the Annex office, clearly labeled. The office watch changes at midnight and again at noon. If you are interested in such things."

A smile spread across Elohl's face, understanding the man's meaning. "Many thanks for answering my questions about the Jenner Faith, Brother."

"Glad I could be of assistance." Brother Temlin winked. "Anything else?"

"Actually..." Unease moved through Elohl as one more question surfaced that he wanted answered. "Can you tell me about the emblem in the First Dwelling – the Wolf and Dragon?"

"An ancient symbol." Brother Temlin smiled knowingly. "It signifies conflict, so the oldest sources say. Unceasing conflict, the kind that tears a man's soul apart. Have you seen it before?"

"Once." Elohl nodded. "But it was different. Balanced, with neither animal winning."

"You've been inside Roushenn, then. You've seen it in the Throne Room or on the doors of the Deephouse." Brother Temlin crossed his arms over his chest as a knowing look flickered over his features. "It's the same in all the Great Palaces. Eight of them, all through our vast continent. Where those palaces were built, a strong center of commerce took root where none existed before. A symbol of blessing? Perhaps. Ringed in fire, the classic tableau depicts the two ever-battling, neither vanquished. The symbol goes far back, to the Alrashemni's foreign origins."

"Yet here in your Abbey, it shows the wolf victorious, and rather than a ring of fire we see the Jenner Sun encircling it all."

"Observant." Brother Temlin's green eyes were searching. "Does it bother you, lad? That tableau?"

Elohl shifted, feeling that this man was far cleverer than he'd supposed.

"It disturbs many." Brother Temlin smirked, feeling Elohl's unrest. "Conflict is ever thus. But I'll tell you something. I've heard it described as a blessing, the balance the wolf and dragon have in the classic tableau. And though the wolf is victorious here in the Abbey, which some suppose is the triumph of righteousness over deceit, I've heard a different tale. That the Jenner Sun imprisons the conflict, lending power to the wolf, where otherwise there would have been none. Ancient symbolism, of a war waged long ago. A war your Alrashemni ancestors had something to do with."

"My mother used to tell such tales. That we fled our ancient home because of that war." Elohl murmured. "So are the Alrashemni depicted by the wolf, in the tableau?"

"Or are they the dragon? Or does the tableau signify something else entirely?" Rising stiffly to his feet, Brother Temlin smiled. "Please. You both must stay in the Abbey tonight. We have quarters for guests, and I can have rooms made up in a trice, with a hot meal and a bath. I'm sure our Abbott and Abbess would be interested in meeting you and asking about your experiences with the Alranstone. My Abbess Lenuria den'Brae may be able to answer your questions further, as she is far more learned than I on the ancient mysteries. Not to mention it would give you better... access. To precious information." Brother Temlin's green eyes glittered in the afternoon sun, intelligent and foxlike.

It was generous offer, but suddenly Elohl felt his golden Inkings tingle in a burning sensation across his shoulders and back. Something in Brother Temlin's last words had triggered it, and unease rose in Elohl, feeling this sensation was somehow similar to his premonitions of danger from his *wyrric* gift. "Thank you, but not tonight," Elohl found himself politely declining. "We've rooms in the city and they're paid for. Besides, I've not got any of my gear upon me, Brother. Though I would like to return and speak with you again in a few days, after I've had some... reading time."

"I suppose it's not convenient at the moment. Very well." The older man chuckled as he clasped Elohl's arm, little infirmity in that old swordsman's grip, though his green eyes were hard as stone and twice as sharp as he regarded Elohl. "But here, lad. Know that the Jenners didn't secede from the Alrashemni because of a lack of passion, merely a belief in a more sustainable Way. And we haven't forgotten our Brothers and Sisters of the Kingsmount. My offer to stay here in the Abbey stands if you want it. Protected."

Elohl paused as he regarded the Jenner in a moment of gripping intensity, Brother Temlin so vicious in his support of the Alrashemni that it made Elohl question suddenly whether the tingle in his Inkings had been a warning or something else.

Elohl paused, then spoke. "I'll consider it."

“As you like, lad.” Brother Temlin spoke solemnly, though his green eyes still flashed fire. “As you like. Just know we’re here should you need any further advice. Shall we?”

As Brother Temlin gestured back towards the Abbey with one gnarled hand, Elohl nodded, silent as they began the trek back towards the cathedrals in the high noon sunshine.

22

OLEA

Olea stood at attention in the Throne Hall, her hands folded over the pommel of her sheathed sword as she kept watch up on the white marble dais, a step behind the throne and to the left. Below the dais, suitors and their entourages packed the hall for the opening reception of Coronation Week, along with lords from Alrou-Mendera. Dwarfed by the vaulted recesses of the enormous space, richly-dressed men and women lingered by the massive bluestone columns, others standing in the center of the checkered black and white marble floor near the red carpet that split the hall to the steps of the dais. Liveried servants moved around with ewers of iced lemon-water crushed with mint, and honeyed mead freshened with lavender to ease parched throats in the sweltering heat of the day.

But the Dhenra stood regal upon the dais before her byrunstone throne, clad in sky-blue silk with a high collar of starched lace, with lace dripping from her sleeves nearly to the floor. Sapphires and diamonds were woven into her hair, again done with ornate Elsthemi bone needles. Olea had insisted upon the hair needles this week, as Elyasin needed a weapon, and her poured-on formal silks didn't allow for a blade. Positioning her Guardsmen all along the main floor, Olea's men stood stern in their cobalt jerkins at the columns, ready for any disruption. And Olea had personally set Fenton and Aldris at the foot of the dais – watchful of those approaching the Dhenra.

The proceedings had taken six hours so far, and Olea shifted, feeling another trickle of sweat roll down between her shoulder-blades. Her gaze drifting up, Olea noted the Dhenra's cobalt banners with the lion of den'Ildrian hanging from the vaulted stone ribs of the ceiling, their crossed scepter and olive branch crowned by the Mountain and Stars lending credence to Elyasin's authority as ruler of the nation. Not a breath of air stirred them today, though every door and window in the hall had been thrown wide to catch a breeze. All along the upper galleries, fans were aflutter in the hands of watching commoners, their gazes rapt upon the proceedings below. Crowding the balconies, they leaned in to catch the Dhenra's conversations with her suitors as each approached, one by one.

Olea's garb was new today, except her sword and longknives, and her knees and ankles throbbed from standing in her new boots. Elyasin had insisted upon her Guard-Captain being presentable this week, but the stiffness of the new leather was agonizing, and Olea's silk undershirt was entirely soaked with sweat beneath her new jerkin in the punishing heat. A movement caught her eye and her gaze flicked, noting a servant entering from a side door with an ewer of chilled wine.

Behind the throne, the massive carving of the Wolf and Dragon covered the wall fifty feet high, some long-ago architect having inscribed this symbol in the throne hall of every palace he'd built like a signature. Olea admired it now, having seen the gold Inkings upon Elohl's back, wondering what it meant. But this image was different from Elohl's markings, as Alrou-Mendera's carving showed the beasts fighting around a scepter, while Olea had heard the one in Valenghia showed them doing so around a vine.

As a minor lordling of Alrou-Mendera approached the dais, Olea dismissed the carving. Judging the suitor a non-threat, her gaze roved the hall, seeing Castellan Lhaurent to the left of the dais, silently directing servants. Olea's gaze raked the silvered mirrors along the sides of the hall behind the bluestone columns, wondering if Lhaurent had an army of spies watching today. Though Elyasin had been chilly towards Olea since their night talking, her mood volatile from stress, she had still insisted her Guard-Captain stand as her personal protector in the throne hall today. Olea would also be stationed to guard the Dhenra during the most important events of the week, concerned as they both were about threats to Elyasin's person before she came into her power with the coronation.

And though Olea had cased her rooms, running her fingers over the grit upon the frame of the gaudy mirror, she hadn't found evidence of disturbance. But just because Lhaurent hadn't moved that mirror recently didn't mean he wasn't standing behind it in the dark. Olea had still not come up with a good way to remove the two tomes chronicling Alrashemni royalty from her room.

And so they were still there, hidden – dangerous like an avalanche about to break loose.

Another bead of sweat seeped down and Olea shifted, rolling her shoulders as she watched House den'Tourmalin of the Isles approach the dais. King Arthe den'Tourmalin was a tall, brooding fellow with a stern jaw, salt-spray black hair, and sea-grey eyes. But for all his taciturn brusqueness, Olea liked the Isleman King. He had spoken plainly in trade negotiations, and was not pressuring the Dhenra to wed. Even today, he made no attempt to sway her as his herald presented his gift, a lovely ironwood sea-chest full of spices and pearls. An honorable man from a very old house, King Arthe deliberately glanced to Olea, spreading his hands to signify a lack of armament as he stepped up the dais. Only when Olea nodded did he step forward, clasping Elyasin's hand with gravitas.

"Dhenra." King Arthe's murmur was private, reaching only Elyasin and Olea's ears. "I received a courier this morning from the Isles, and you should know of it. These past years, the Isles have had unmarked ships sneaking through our Straits at night – fleet, painted black with black sails, and running passably silent. The missive I received said we were finally able to catch one. It was crewed by Perthians and Thurumen, and had a belly full of Jadounian slaves. The crew would not speak, but some of the captives talked freely. It seems they had been coerced into sailing by threats against their families. They were given the choice of indentured servitude, fighting in the war upon the Menderian-Valenghian border, or else see their womenfolk raped and the youngest of their children slain. They chose to sail."

Olea's breath had ceased in astonishment at this news, while the Dhenra was very pale, though she held her composure. "And were the slaves to fight for Alrou-Mendera at the border?"

"Yes and no." Arthe den'Tourmalin continued. "Some believed they were to serve Valenghia in the war. Some thought they had been conscripted for Alrou-Mendera. Some thought they were destined for the emerald mines along Alrou-Mendera's southeastern coast."

"Conscripted by whom?" Elyasin's green eyes went hard.

"The slaves didn't know." King Arthe spoke soberly. "But we did find a writ of payment to the ship's captain signed by one Helios den'Garnesh. My people know Helios; he is Harbormaster of Ligenia, on your southeastern coast. I would recommend that you send someone *quietly* to investigate this situation, Dhenra."

"Arthe." Elyasin spoke as she clasped his hands. "You are a true friend to Alrou-Mendera. If I can repay you this kindness..."

Reaching up, he set his palm to her face in a fatherly gesture, his sea-scoured visage kind. "Your father would be proud of who you've become, Elyasin. I know I am not the one for you, and I do not believe we need to unify our houses with a marriage, as our trade is already strong and fair. Take this gift of information freely. And if you ever have need to arrange your own personal network of... quiet observers, send word. I will sail straightaway, and give any and all counsel you need."

"Thank you." Elyasin murmured. King Arthe was a good man, and Olea could see a mutual understanding between the two monarchs. It was unfortunate he was so much older than Elyasin.

Leaning forward, Arthe mimed kissing Elyasin upon the cheek, but instead spoke, "Trust no one. Confirm everything, even from those close to you. That is the first law of ruling." Bowing over Elyasin's hand, he brushed it with a formal kiss then moved on, summoning his retainers to stride from the hall.

Elyasin watched King Arthe go, her face unreadable though Olea saw her tap her finger upon her gown, a nervous tic that meant Elyasin was rattled by what she'd just heard. But as Olea gazed down the long hall, she realized her Dhenra was also rattled by this next suitor. King Therel Alramir of Elsthemen loped down the red carpet with six of his fur-clad swordsmen, once again wearing the plain garb and wolf pelt Olea had seen him in all week, though he'd added a circlet of gold today upon his ash-blond hair. Presenting his gifts with a flourish at the foot of the dais – a trunk full of keshar pelts and silver bars – he stepped up the dais. Olea's gaze roved Therel's retainers, including the First Sword with the white hair, but his men idled placidly at the foot of the dais with Fenton and Aldris.

As the Highlander King drew near, the Dhenra began to rub viciously at one knuckle as she flushed to the roots of her golden hair. King Therel had been intimately alluring with the Dhenra all week, though sometimes he'd shown an almost tender side – and Elyasin returned that attention. But as he bent to kiss her hand, Therel Alramir's pale blue eyes roiled with lust and precision, as if he was certain he had already won the prize so formally fought-over today. Though he was the picture of courtly grace, he had the air of a wild wolf, howling victorious in the darkness.

Olea recalled the rumors about him, that he was ruthless when necessary, and wondered if she might find Elyasin diced up in trophy jars after their nuptials. Olea gave the man her best glower, and she thought she saw a hint of smile at his lips as his pale eyes roved her – before moving back to the Dhenra.

"Elyasin." Clasping the Dhenra's hand, King Therel was far too familiar, and Elyasin trembled at his touch as he stepped close, reaching up to stroke her face with his knuckles. "You're shivering. On such a hot day, in such fine silks, one would think the sweetgrapes would be sweating upon the vine, dripping with moisture..."

"King Therel." The Dhenra's voice was breathy, though she held her strong posture. "We look forward to mutually beneficial trade with your noble nation."

"As do I." Therel Alramir's chuckle was sexual. "Trade with you would be most sweet, Dhenra. I would lick your wine from my fingers, and plunge my tongue into the moist chalice from whence it came."

Executing a perfect bow over her hand, he did not take his gaze from Elyasin as heat simmered between them like the thickness of air before lightning. As King Therel straightened, he rubbed his thumb over her fingers and Elyasin shuddered with a small sound – as Olea's fingers tightened on her sword. Olea saw Therel note her subtle change; he was no fool. With a rapacious smile, he was gone, striding back down to his retainers and moving off. Making a mental note to double her guard around the Elsthemi suites, Olea resolved to have Therel Alramir tailed until the end of the week.

King or no, men like that caused trouble wherever they went.

At last, the list of suitors had come to an end. Raising her voice, Elyasin gave a pretty speech about prosperity for all lands, and the lords and ladies in the long hall clapped politely as a raucous cheering came from the balconies above. Lifting her gaze, Elyasin nodded to her commoners, which made them cheer more. She had made this concession for them the entire week, that the balconies be available to the general populace, though many of her Chancellors had advised against it. It had raised her popularity overnight, and people had thronged the Central Plaza all night just to be here today, a trend likely to continue for the duration of the week.

Near the dais, clarion hunting-horns called an end to the proceedings and Elyasin turned, sweeping from the hall. Falling into step just behind her, Olea canvassed the gables as they recessed through an alcove, Chancellors of Elyasin's cabinet and the Castellan following also as Elyasin retired to the Sun Lounge. Late afternoon sunlight slanted through the south-facing windows, which curved up and over in a latticework, giving the impression of an arched waterfall of glass over a forest. Built like a greenhouse, the Sun Lounge was a nightmare of places for an assassin to hide, and Olea's gaze swept the densely-vegetated space, wilting today in the humidity.

"I must rest before the banquet tonight. All of you, leave me." Elyasin dismissed her Chancellors curtly. All left with murmurs and bows, except Castellan Lhaurent in his grey silks, who hovered expectantly. "You, too, Lhaurent. I need to be alone."

"My Dhenra. May I send in a tray and beverages to refresh you? And some of your ladies to attend?" Dripping with false demurity, Lhaurent didn't even spare Olea a glance, and it was all she could do to not draw her sword and strike his head from his shoulders. But she had no proof he was connected with the Kingsmen killings, and setting her jaw, Olea gave Lhaurent a glower – which he consummately ignored.

"Give me an hour before you do." Elyasin spoke over one shoulder. "I wish to be undisturbed a while."

"As my Dhenra commands." Castellan Lhaurent frowned. But he knew his place in public, bowing and turning to leave. Glancing over, the Dhenra regarded her Guard-Captain and Olea dropped to one knee. Elyasin's fingers passed over her hair, which had been coaxed into something honorable earlier by one of the Dhenra's ladies.

"Your hair is longer than I thought." Elyasin spoke as her mouth quirked, her fingers falling away. "I'm afraid one might almost call you respectable, Captain."

"I thank you for your kind gifts, Dhenra." Olea spoke as she stood with a small smile. "But the boots will be scuffed terribly by the end of the day."

"Alden could never keep new boots nice, either." Elyasin's face softened into wistfulness, then deepened into a frown. "Olea. I must have your opinion on what King Arthe—"

"Which is something that takes the fresh air of the Rose Courtyard to help us review. Shall we?" Olea cut her off quickly before she could say anything dangerous inside Roushenn, offering her arm.

The Dhenra's green eyes narrowed, but then she sighed. "Yes, I suppose it is stifling in here. And the Rose Courtyard should be quiet from any celebrations."

Elyasin took her arm, and together they made their way through the Sun Lounge, Olea scanning for threats, Elyasin clearly exhausted from standing for the past hours in the scathing heat. Selecting a staircase that wound down through the Sixth and Fifth Tiers and opened out into the gardens, Olea led them through a set of tall hedges into a small courtyard of fountains and topiary. Native roses wound up trellises in hardy abundance, while brightly-glazed pots held rare varietals from over the southern seas. Guards lingered at the entrance and Olea flicked her fingers, sending them in to sweep the stone arches before she and the Dhenra strolled. Olea saw Aldris step into the courtyard, saluting as he leaned upon a centaur statue, just out of earshot. Stopping to smell the roses in their early-summer riot, Elyasin and Olea enjoyed the drowning scent as an afternoon breeze finally cooled their sweat.

"Why the garden, Olea," Elyasin spoke as they walked, "to discuss what King Arthe just said to me? What aren't you telling me that you began to the other night?"

They'd come to it at last. Olea would have preferred a less stressful moment to speak to her Dhenra about Roushenn, but the young woman had not made time in the past week. This news had to be told – and like King Arthe den'Tourmalin's news, now might be Olea's only opportunity. Taking a breath, she spoke. "The palace isn't safe, Dhenra. Not for such discussion. And not for you."

"Not safe? Your men and women patrol it, Captain," Elyasin snorted, waving a tired hand. "You've sealed off the Unterhaft as a precaution for my coronation, correct?"

"As you commanded, yes, and the halls my men patrol are safe as they can be." Olea spoke low so her voice didn't carry. "But the palace isn't safe because there is a palace *behind* the palace! That's what I wanted to tell you the other night. An entire labyrinth of rooms and corridors exists behind the walls, where people can spy and listen – all of it accessed by secret means..."

Halting, Elyasin blinked in surprise, her hand falling from Olea's arm as she fidgeted with her knuckles. Olea knew the Dhenra had gotten too much distressing news today – and when Elyasin became upset, she became angry. Olea saw her Dhenra become a storm about to break, visible in every line of the young woman's body as fury heated her cheeks. "What do you mean, a palace *behind* the palace?"

"The walls of the palace move," Olea breathed, though she knew how it would sound. "I don't know how, but they do. There are passages behind the walls, and it's part of how the Alrashemni were killed the night they came to Roushenn. They were shown to rooms and while they slept, the *walls moved on them*. Changing, confusing them. Some kind of poison was released into the air to disorient them and make it impossible to fight back. They were slaughtered to a man, quietly. Because *Roushenn is a weapon for whomever controls those walls!* I still don't know why the Kingsmen were killed, but I know partly how it was done. And if the palace wasn't safe then, it's certainly not safe now. Security for your coronation is already compromised, Dhenra. There's no possible way I can keep you safe if any wall could move at any time. We need to postpone the coronation until we know more. Or move it to the Winter Palace in Fhouria. And get you out of here. Tonight."

"Are you *jesting* with me, Captain?!" Elyasin gaped at Olea, furious now. "Do you think to dissuade me from my coronation, from *ruling* by making me feel unsafe in my own palace? Have you seen this yourself?"

Olea shook her head, her heart sinking that Elyasin was suddenly taking the advice King Arthe had given. "No, but I met an Alrashemni Kingsman who escaped that night, and I trust his word. And Dhenra, I have seen things myself. A piece of furniture replaced here. A twist to the hall that I don't remember there."

"But have you seen this *behind-the-palace*? Have you verified any of this?" The Dhenra spoke scathingly, the situation going from bad to worse.

"No, Dhenra, I have not seen it, but I assure you it's true." Olea spoke as her mind raced frantically for any information that could convince Elyasin of the truth. "Those tomes I told you about, the ones Uhlas led me to find, they chronicle the history of the royal house. Your lineage is Alrashemni, right back to the founding of this nation. House den'Ildrian is directly related to House den'Alrahel, the original founders of Alrou-Mendera—"

"Den'Alrahel." Elyasin went very still. "Are you saying you believe your *own house* to be royal?"

"So it said in the tomes Uhlas gave me, but you're missing the point, Dhenra. Your lineage is Alrashemni and whoever is killing Kingsmen—"

"*Silence*!" Elyasin was livid now, reacting and not thinking as Olea's dire warnings became badly misinterpreted. The Dhenra's temper roared, her green eyes searing wrath as she shouted, her voice ringing around the courtyard. "I asked you to uncover the fate of the Kingsmen, and you give me fae-yarns – today of all days! You know what this week means to me! Are you trying to derail this coronation? My marriage? My rule? *Are you trying to set yourself up as Queen by asserting a blood-relation to the throne?!*"

Olea knelt quickly to the gravel path, one hand going to her Inkings without even thinking, desperate. "Dhenra, no! I swear to you, I would never—"

"Silence! Guards!" Five of Olea's guards came running from behind a set of potted rose-trees, confusion spreading over their features to see their Captain-General on her knees before their livid soon-to-be-Queen. "Take her!"

Two of Olea's best hustled in, still confused but unable to shy from a direct order. Seizing Olea, they hauled her up, relieving her of weapons with apology in their eyes. Someone coughed by a rosebush and Olea glanced over to see Aldris, his green eyes flicking nervously between Olea and the Dhenra.

"Pardon, Dhenra." Aldris spoke, his clarion tenor cutting through the commotion. "Where are we to take Captain-General den'Alrahel?"

"Somewhere... anywhere!" Elyasin was rubbing her knuckles viciously, flushed with fury. "Out of my sight! You are *dismissed* from duty, Captain, until my nuptials and coronation are over! Your First-Lieutenant Fenton den'Kharel will be my bodyguard for the duration. And you will spend the week in the Upper Cells thinking about why it is *unwise* to spin fae-yarns and falsehoods to me!"

The Dhenra nodded to the guards and Olea did not resist. Her eyes locked upon Aldris as she was hustled away, and he gave her a very discreet, very worried nod.

TORCHES FLICKERED in brackets all along the stone wall as Aldris den'Farahan offered a flagon of klippas-ale through the bars of Olea's cell. The Upper Cells smelled damp with rot and rat droppings, but at least they were warm as a potato cellar rather than a glacier. Olea's cell had a cot with a pallet of fresh straw plus a thick wool blanket, a ceramic basin with a pitcher of water, and a chamber-pot with an actual lid. It was generous compared to the cesspit starkness of the Lower

Cells, but though Aldris seemed amused as he leaned up against Olea's bars, she could see his vast worry.

"Pissed off the Queen. Nice move, Captain."

"She's not Queen yet, not for another six days." Olea spoke as she took a swig from the flagon, anger ripping her gut. "Dammit! She needs me up there to protect her, Aldris, not rotting away down here all week!"

"Seems she doesn't think so." Aldris shrugged as he received the flagon back and took a swig. "Thinks she can protect herself, apparently. Maybe she'll wind up stuffed in a trunk on her wedding day..."

"That isn't funny." Olea leaned on the bars with her arms crossed, giving Aldris a scowl.

"She gussies you up, then shits in your stew?" He grinned as he handed the flagon back. "You must have pissed her off good. Everyone knows she allows you liberties she doesn't give anyone. The men call you the Dhenra's Champion, did you know that?"

"Some champion." Olea scowled. "I can't do anything for her from down here."

"What got her lace in a bunch?"

"Don't ask me about it." Olea shook her head.

"The same *don't ask me* that gets me and Fenton covering your shifts while you sneak off around the city?" Aldris smiled knowingly, aware that she was hiding something. "Where have you been going, Olea? I was going to tail you, but Fenton said you'd hear me and chuck me down here in the cells." Aldris laughed, then took a swig from the flask.

"Fenton was right," Olea glowered at Aldris. "You two stay out of it. It's the Dhenra's business."

"Boys who took you in told me they overheard you and the Dhenra shouting before I got close." Aldris shrugged as he gave her the flagon. "Something about investigating the Kingsman disappearance."

Olea's stomach gripped to know Elyasin had been overheard. Their secret missive was out now, and Olea knew it would be all over the barracks by sundown. It was a short eavesdropping before the veritable army of palace maids, cooks, and porters knew – and Lhaurent. Olea tried to shake off the feeling of being watched as she glanced to the shadows of the torch-lit hallway, paranoid as Uhlas had been at the end. Rousing herself, she gave Aldris a forbidding glare. "I said it's the Dhenra's business. Leave it. And shut up any fool mouths you hear passing that information around."

Aldris nodded, but his green eyes were narrowed now, watchful. As Olea handed the flagon back through the bars, Aldris shook his head. "Keep the drink. I gotta get back up to the banquet. Fenton is getting lonely guarding the Dhenra's pretty ass. Anything you need, Captain? I've arranged for a bit of banquet left-overs to be brought down later for you."

Olea shook her head, then thought better of it, reaching through the bars and grabbing Aldris by the jerkin, pulling him close.

"Last kiss?" Aldris raised his eyebrows, grinning.

"Shut up and listen." Olea snapped, and Aldris' smirk was wiped clean, replaced by that cool calculation Olea had promoted him for. "I believe Elyasin is in very serious danger, and this week is the most serious. I have reason to believe Dhenir Alden and King Uhlas were both murdered because they had a personal connection to the Alrashemni. And Elyasin is next."

"Personal? How personal?" Aldris murmured, his eyebrows lifting in surprise.

"Blood-kin personal." Olea breathed. "If I'm right, whoever killed the Kingsmen will try to strike Elyasin before her Queen's Writ is signed, before she's technically able to rule without the Chancellate. Triple her guard. From now on, either you or Fenton plus one of my six best are there like flies on pigs, whether she's awake or sleeping. Trust nothing and *no one*."

"Damn. I mean, shit." Aldris' eyebrows rose.

With a growl, Olea yanked Aldris closer. "Roushenn holds its secrets, Aldris, more than any of us ever suspected. There are passages *behind* every passage, that we know nothing of and can't control. The walls of Roushenn move. They fucking move and I don't know who or what controls it! Only that it secured the end of the Kingsmen – all of them in a single night. They never escaped this palace, Aldris. The fucking *Kingsmen*, the most talented fighters on the entire continent, couldn't escape Roushenn. They died here. And I think Castellan Lhaurent knows about it. I think he knows what the walls can do... or maybe has access to it. And assassins where we can't find them."

As she let Aldris go, he gaped at her like she had gone mad. "Are you fucking *serious*?"

"Do I look serious?" Olea narrowed her eyes.

"Yeah." Aldris nodded with a deep grimness. "You look really fucking deadly, actually, like you mean every word you just said."

Yanking her shirt open, Olea bared her Inking beneath her unbuckled jerkin. "Then hear me. I am an Alrashemni Kingsman to the death, and Elyasin is *my King*. So swear me to Aeon, if anything happens to her, I will begin a bloodbath until my blade runs through every last throat involved. Are we clear, Guardsman?"

"Clear as diamond, Captain." Aldris nodded, his green eyes holding no laughter.

With a nod, Olea released her shirt, and Aldris turned, moving swiftly down the flickering hall to fulfill her orders. Sinking back against the bars with a growl, Olea felt caged as worry gnawed at her. Pacing her small cell, she mussed her hair violently, ripping at the strands in a way she'd not done since she was a child. A tingling feeling skittered over her like roaches and Olea halted; breathing, listening. But other than the first-year Guardsman currently on duty trimming his fingernails with his knife, there was no one.

The sensation of being watched dogged her as she began to pace again. Olea tried to breathe past her paranoia, past her rage at being in here, and her terrible fear that something was about to happen. As she paced her cell for the umpteenth time, her tray finally came down from the banquet. Trim and wiry, Fenton den'Kharel approached with her dinner like lightning over ice. Sliding her tray into her cell via the pass-through, he hunkered, interlacing his calloused fingers, his dark brows brooding. Olea hunkered also, eating from the tray with her hands. Smeared with peach chutney, the roast goose was still warm, a fennel salad with roasted honey-nuts disappearing into her mouth as fast as the goose. It had been a long time since breakfast, and Olea found herself eating quickly, reliving memories of starving in the Lower Cells nearly two years ago.

Fenton watched her in silence, and when Olea finally wiped her mouth, his eyebrows rose expectantly.

"Is Aldris guarding the Dhenra?" Olea asked at last.

"She's asleep." Fenton nodded, his gold-brown eyes thoughtful by the torchlight. "Aldris and den'Thanut will take watch until noon tomorrow. I convinced the Dhenra that security was needed inside her rooms and attending her person for the duration of the week. I placed a guard of four on each entry to her suites, and we've got three men on the walls watching her windows. They'll rotate every six hours."

"It's not enough." Olea leaned back against the bars with a sigh. "We have to get her out of the palace entirely. Dammit!"

Tracing a pattern in the dirt on the stones with one calloused finger, Fenton spoke quietly, "What's this about, Olea?"

"You'd think I'm insane if I told you," Olea grimaced.

"I've seen a lot of things in my time, Captain." He continued tracing, but his quiet gold-brown eyes were sharp upon her, his face chiseled with intensity though still smooth. "I'm older than I look, and younger than I feel sometimes. But I'm wise enough to know insanity and den'Alrahel don't connect. You've always been steady and loyal. Everyone knows you'd be the first to die for the Dhenra, as you were for the Dhenir." His fingers traced on, and Olea noticed the pattern stabilize into a Kingsmount and Stars in the dust. "What I mean to say, Captain, is that I know what you've been up to."

"*Everyone* knows now, dammit." Olea scowled.

"What the Dhenra said today confirmed it," he nodded. "But I knew before then. Aldris wanted to tail you, but he's too sloppy. I know it wasn't wise, but sometimes I'm not known for being wise."

"You've been following me." Olea blinked, stunned. She'd not heard a damn thing.

Fenton nodded, still tracing, his gold-brown eyes knowing as he looked up. "I've seen the silversmith, seen his scars. I've seen your brother and his pretty woman, and followed them to the Jenner compound. I've followed you quite a few times over the years. And the Dhenir, back when he would *wander* at night. And I follow Elyasin, sometimes..."

Fear ripped through Olea, quickly followed by a vicious anger. She snarled through the bars, gripping them hard as a heat like fighting animals roared through her. "Whom do you serve, cur?! To whom do you give all this information?!"

"I am First-Lieutenant Guardsman," Fenton spoke as he rose to standing, dusting off his hands. "I report to my Captain-General. But there's also this."

Confused, Olea paused in the tirade she'd been about to unleash as Fenton put one hand to his heart, his gaze holding Olea's as he moved close to the bars. He began undoing his jerkin buckles, and Olea realized he was close enough that if anyone was watching from the hall, they couldn't see. At last, she saw what Fenton wanted her to, the Kingsmount and Stars plain upon his chest – though strangely done in red ink, a bloody nick in the center like someone had scored him with a blade. But Fenton had never had a Kingsmount and Stars. Olea had seen him without his shirt countless times, and she fought to keep her face neutral, despite her immense surprise.

Fenton was Alrashemni.

Some kind of secret, underground Alrashemni.

"I am one of you yet I'm not," Fenton murmured, confirming her thoughts. "We were close to the throne once and we are still, but not as close. Not in the way that matters. But you are, with Elyasin as you were with Alden."

"Who are you? How many of you are out there?" Olea could barely breathe.

"Enough. But I can't speak of it here. Not now." Fenton's visage was fierce.

"Aldris, is he also?"

Fenton nodded, and Olea's world spun like a badly-made top. Shadows flickered all around, as that sensation of being watched crept back, itching between her shoulder-blades and raising the small hairs at the back of her neck. Suddenly, Olea knew they were at war. Whatever this was, whatever was happening here, if it had driven Fenton to expose such a secret, then all her fears were founded.

"Find my brother, Fenton." Olea's voice cracked with a sudden urgency. "Find Elohl. Tell him what has happened and that the Dhenra needs protection. Now. He's the fastest swordsman I know. He needs to be close to her. Especially at the coronation."

Fenton nodded, his fingers racing back up his lacings and buckles as he leaned close to the bars, his next words barely a whisper. "Olea. I have to tell you. What you found out about the walls..."

"You *knew?!*" Shock hit Olea like a staff to the knees.

"I did." Woe suffused Fenton's gaze as he finished his buckles. "I had to keep that secret, for reasons I cannot give. But you must understand, your assumptions are correct. Lhaurent keeps an army behind the walls, in the Hinterhaft. I've seen it. But you cannot flush him out of that labyrinth, Olea. He has ways of keeping himself safe if he retreats there. Which he can do at a moment's notice. Be wary of him. Be very, very wary."

Fenton's gold-brown eyes were drowning with some emotion Olea didn't understand as he reached through the bars, cupping her face. "I fear for you, trapped in here, though I can't get you out, not right now. But I swear to you, that someone is watching you... someone who will get you out, if any threat comes. He would die for you. Just like I would."

"Fenton..." Something cold dove into Olea's gut. "What are you talking about?"

"I can't say more." He shook his head, his touch falling away. "But please trust me. I will go to your brother, get him into the Guard for the coronation. We'll keep Elyasin safe. I promise."

Setting his jaw, Fenton's demeanor was ferocious, deadly with his promise. With an intensity like lightning flashing in the deeps, he turned, and was gone up the shadowed stairs before Olea could blink.

23

DHERRAN

Dherran was sweeping the men's finals in Vennet. His first four fights had gone decently this afternoon, yielding only a fat lip, a bruised cheekbone, and a few purpling areas over his ribs and torso. For the first time this summer, he strode bare-chested to the ring of spears with cheering in his ears, people eager to see him fight once more. The populace of Vennet didn't seem to care that Dherran was a Kingsman, and their energy fed him like a raging flood.

But beneath it all, Dherran was simmering. Khenria had been vicious with him all afternoon, ever since their argument at the inn, and the sweltering late afternoon heat only made Dherran's frustrations with her today deepen. As he faced his last opponent now, Arvale den'Whestin, the reigning free-hand champion in this region, Dherran felt himself boiling inside as red tried to swamp his vision yet again. He'd managed to control his passionate rage enough to win his earlier fights, but now Dherran was tired, his body hurting and his vision blurred from so many matches against talented opponents back-to-back.

Taking the measure of his final opponent as they squared off before the bell, Dherran saw the man was a featherweight, wiry but made like well-tempered steel. Shifting from foot to foot upon the dry earth, the man's feet and ankles were wrapped better than his hands, and Dherran realized as they took each other's measure that the man was a kick-fighter in the old Praoughian style. It was a style that was rarely seen in Alrou-Mendera, though as an Alrashemni, Dherran had once learned it as a child before it was clear he was a bull in the ring, rather than a bantam.

Gazing at this man now, Dherran saw his thighs were corded muscle, his calves the same. The bell sounded for the fight to begin and Dherran paced slowly with his guard up, trying to think only of his opponent and not let his rage with Khenria swamp him. Allowing his back heel to square to the dirt rather than his usual agile stance, Dherran faked a heavier posture than normal, needing this man to think he was thick, slow, and his footwork too heavy.

He heard the crowd settle into a hush as the match began. The lean rooster bounced, getting his feet beneath him, then tried an experimental set of punches at Dherran's face. Flowing out of the way with tiny movements, Dherran didn't move his feet, and then the man tried a set of kicks. Dherran swiveled his hips, keeping his frame aligned and allowing each kick to pass him by, again not moving his feet. The bantam rooster scowled, bouncing from foot to foot. But now that the man had gotten Dherran's measure, he came at Dherran for real, and they began to engage.

Keeping to a small space, Dherran used his alignment to dodge kicks and strikes while throwing falsely heavy punches, still not really moving his feet. He shuffled through the dirt as high kicks came, barely getting out of the way each time as he crouched, dodged, and slipped past. The rooster was getting angry now, his face red and his scowl deep as he batted at his heavier, immutable opponent. Both he and Dherran knew he could take down a big, stout lug of a man if he got the right kick to Dherran's head – but though Dherran was faking slow, he was just quick enough that it was pissing the rooster off.

Finally, the punch came that Dherran was waiting for. The rooster faked and Dherran slipped sideways so the punch actually came at his face, as he had intended. He pretended being caught off-guard, throwing his right hand up to defend and leaving his right flank unprotected. The rooster crowed, whirling into a kick with the full force of his steel-lithe body, meaning to give Dherran a nasty blow to the kidneys that would make him crumble from pain, followed by a kick to his head to finish the match.

But the kick to Dherran's flank came straight to Dherran's inner elbow now. Using his arm to absorb the kick, he folded it in to his torso and took the man's foot with it. It was a slick, fast maneuver the kick-fighter hadn't expected, and spiraling his right arm up and in, Dherran twisted his hips with agile speed, and had the man's leg pinned. As he turned, it sent the man into a flying twist, meant to either dislocate his hip or spin him horizontal to the ground and smash him into the dust, a blow to end the match.

It fact, it did neither.

With a vicious crack that rent the air, the man's femur broke in a spiral, his leg turning into the twist, but his body not following through. He hit the ground like a sack of rocks, screaming, his leg riven and twisted unnaturally. Dherran released the man, shock flooding Dherran as dizziness took him, surprised by what had just happened. He had been distracted and had twisted too efficiently, too true to the killing nature of his Kingsman training, training meant to break a man upon the battlefield.

He had been thinking of Khenria, letting his fury get the best of him – and this was the outcome.

Screams filled Dherran's ears, the shrieks of a mauled animal as the man reached for his leg, his hands hovering, not daring to touch it. The scorekeeper rushed to the ring and the fight-medic stepped between the two opponents, motioning Dherran away. Still breathing hard in shock at what had just happened, Dherran stepped back, unable to hear, unable to see anything but that mangled flesh. The medic reached out to touch the man's leg as he screamed, then snarled at Dherran with murderous hate.

"Fucking whoresbane! You've ruined me!"

The kick-fighter gasped sobs as the medic tried to assess the extent of the break. Silence filled the square beyond the spears, the faces of the crowd shocked. Though Dherran had done well today in the men's final rounds, Arvale den'Whestin had been favored to win, from his excellent record these past ten years in Vennet. He wasn't a traveling fighter, just an outstanding local one; but now as Dherran watched that twisted, mangled flesh he realized the man would probably never fight again. Maybe never even walk again. The scorekeeper was muttering low to den'Whestin, but as the medic touched his leg, he screamed again.

Finally, Arvale gave a curt nod and the scorekeeper stood, facing the crowd with his hands high. "Dherran den'Lhust, for the win!"

But the moment was rent by the man cursing on the hard-packed dirt. "Halsos' Bane! How can you call yourself a Kingsman?! You're nothing but a brute! All that training, all that knowledge, and this is what you do? *Break men* in a clean fight? You'll pay for this, you... you *boar!*"

Gathering saliva, he spat into the dirt.

And that was all it took. Dherran's rage gathered, an unstoppable torrent. It had been bad today because of Khenria, but now it was like a demon unleashed as red swamped his vision and buzzing filled his ears. Logic and reason fled as Dherran strode to the man on the ground like a mountain in swift avalanche, seizing him by his hair and shaking his head roughly.

"What did you think was going to happen, kick-fighting against someone with my training?!" He bellowed, furious. "You see these Inkings?! Look at them! Do you remember the Battle of Gheirn? A hundred Kingsmen held back three thousand Valenghian Longriders, protecting this valley for *two days* until the King's army could get here! *Two days!* Without sleep, without food... protecting Vennet! That was only thirteen years ago. Most of you were alive then! My father and mother both fought for Vennet! How dare you forget them!"

Thrusting the man's head to the dirt with a growl, Dherran made Arvale yelp, but Dherran didn't care anymore. He was winding up, his vision bleeding into a dark red haze. He could barely see the shocked faces around him as his hot rage was turned on the crowd. People shrank back from the ring of spears as mouths muttered, but only a buzzing like seething hornets filled Dherran's ears. A light hand fell on his arm suddenly – and Suchinne's beatific face rose in his mind, interrupting the red.

But when he turned he saw it was Khenria, her face frightened as she stood strong, confronting him within the ring of spears.

"Come away, Dherran. You've won. These people aren't your enemy."

Dherran shook his head, trying to process what she was saying, but his head was stuffed with burning steel wool. Her words didn't make sense; nothing made sense in the burning, seething maelstrom that filled him. Everything inside him roared for battle, for retribution, for death – but somehow his fingers wound up in her hand. Somehow, he was walking towards the ready-tent as an angry susurration devoured the plaza behind him. Somehow, he was moving away from the battle he'd been about to unleash, as he shook his head again and stumbled into the tent.

"Dherran!" Khenria's grey eyes were worried as she seized his face in both hands. "Dherran! Can you hear me?"

Dherran shook his head, trying to understand, but everything was red, everything was burning. Taking up a pitcher of water, Khenria doused him with it and the cold water shocked his senses, awareness beginning to return at last. The red rolled back; suddenly he could hear again through the buzz that devoured his ears. Shaking his head to clear it and taking a few quick drinks to cool the burning inside his body, Dherran listened to the crowd outside. He finally noticed Grump was absent from the tent, and Khenria had Dherran's winnings purse set aside upon the wooden bench.

"Khenria... what?" Dherran spoke, confused as his faculties began to return.

"You broke their champion," she spoke quickly, her grey eyes still enormous at what had taken Dherran, still fearful of him as she stood with the water pitcher – near but not too near. "They're pissed, Dherran. And you... I don't know what happened to you just then, but I think you would have killed Arvale if I hadn't stepped in."

"Where's Grump?" Dherran gasped a few deep breaths to calm himself as he curried cold water through his hair, splashing his face and behind his neck to push the burning back further.

"I saw him doing his rounds before the match for the betting, but not since." She shook her head, still watching Dherran like he was a raging animal about to attack.

"We gotta go. I broke their champion... we gotta leave town." Unwrapping his hands quickly, Dherran took up his shirt and leather jerkin from the nearby bench and pulled them on. "Get the horses, we'll check the inn for Grump—"

"You both are two of a kind. Reckless."

An iron-hard voice behind him made Dherran snarl as he turned fast – to find himself facing a tall, lean man in a handsome red leather jerkin, cold fury in his husky-blue eyes. There was nothing idle about the Vicoute Arlen den'Selthir as he stared Dherran down. His sword-honed frame might have been swathed in riches, but Dherran would have bet his right nut the man had expert training in the arts of war. As the Vicoute eased forward into the tent, Dherran saw him move like liquid on fire – like the most dangerous predator in the darkness.

"What are you doing here?!" Dherran snarled, feeling his red rage pour back like lava, ready to hit the man as he turned the fire of his gaze on Khenria. "What the fuck is he doing here?"

"Your protégé has nothing to do with this." The Vicoute's pale blue eyes were flat with anger as he stared Dherran down, a sensation of knives bristling from his person. "This is between you and me, *Kingsman*. If that's what you actually believe you are."

"You and I have nothing to say to each other," Dherran growled as he hefted his saddlebags up onto one shoulder from the rough wooden bench. "You don't know anything about me."

"But I do, Kingsman. I know quite a lot, actually." The Vicoute spoke, pinning Dherran with those icy eyes, though he didn't make any motion to stop Dherran from departing. "I know you're going to have a mob in about five minutes, and you need somewhere to go. I know every inn for ten miles is full-up from of the festival. And I know that you are going to accept my invitation to sup for dinner, and to stay the week at my manor."

"And why's that?" Dherran snarled rudely, surging up to the man now and getting in his face.

"Because the lady hasn't ever slept in a manor before, and she's never dined with a Vicoute." Den'Selthir gave a hard, emotionless smirk, not taking Dherran's bait to fight, though Dherran was right up in his face now. Staring Dherran down like a cool meltwater flood to his blistering lava, the Vicoute's gaze flicked to Dherran's Inkings at the cleft of his shirt as his lips lifted in a small snarl. "And because you, Kingsman, owe me a fighter. That was my man you ruined. He was sworn to my service. And I demand restitution."

The roar of the mob surged outside the tent. Dherran paused, listening. It would take five full minutes to ready the horses, and by then the mob would be all over them. Facing off with this lord before him again, Dherran felt the man had steel and wrath in his veins, but what Dherran didn't know was what would happen if he went with the Vicoute – though he had the distinct impression he would soon find out. It was a risk either way. Dherran could put himself and Khenria the mercy of the mob, or at the mercy of a pissed Vicoute who had not yet lifted a hand to harm them.

"I have three saddled horses waiting outside." The Vicoute raised an ash-blond eyebrow. "Bring your winnings. Stuff your gear under the benches behind that hay bale and I will send my men back for it later. I'll have someone wait here for your servingman, also."

Dherran glanced at Khenria, and he saw her lift her black brows in a silent plea. It was that look that broke him, that finally sluiced away all his rage and left him feeling ashamed at everything that had just happened. A dark fear devoured him suddenly, that he had put her in danger. Not just from a mob again, but from his own wrath, unleashed in a way it hadn't been since before he had met her and Grump. Pausing, Dherran digested it all, how bad it could have turned.

And then realized Khenria had calmed him, just like Suchinne had once been able to do, when he'd been about to rage mad.

"Fine." With a hard out-breath, Dherran stuffed his saddlebags behind the hay bale, snatched up the winnings purse, and then the party was out the back tent-flap fast. Hot afternoon dust choked them as they stepped out into the stifling late afternoon. But the Vicoute was good as his word, and Dherran immediately saw a small knot of retainers on horseback with their swords out, facing off with the seething crowd at the rear of the tent. Three horses waited inside the ring of mounted men. Racing to a white gelding, Khenria was up in a flash. Dherran vaulted up to a sturdy roan, while the Vicoute mounted up on a richly-appointed black charger that was clearly his own.

Wheeling his charger to the front of the mob, the Vicoute roared out, "Populace of Vennet!"

It was a slicing bellow, the snarling roar of a commander that would not have been out of place upon a battlefield. Dherran blinked, having not heard the man speak with such a furious sound in his tone yet, and all around the knot of horsemen, people quieted in a slow wave. As the Vicoute wheeled his horse in a circle, men backing away to a respectable distance now as they looked shame-faced, pulling hats from their heads and calming, Dherran realized how much clout the Vicoute had here in town.

And how much of a blessing it was that the fellow had come to their rescue.

"You have seen a brutal fight today!" The Vicoute roared, riding tall on his impressive black charger as he faced the mob. "My champion has been mangled, and I have demanded restitution from the fighter who broke him. Rest assured that until the debt is paid, he will answer to me! But now is not the time for violence. We have seen too much already today. Go to your inns. Sup, drink. Your first ale of the night comes from my coffers from this disappointing spectacle today, for which I take full responsibility. Drink and let your evening be merriment rather than pain! And I will take care of the pain-giving."

A vicious cheer went up from the crowd, pleased with the Vicoute's words. Dherran felt himself simmer in anger at the things the man had said, but Khenria's glance as she heeled her horse close forestalled him. It was better this way, leaving with protection. Though they had no inkling as to what would come next, there was no more time to think about it.

Kicking his charger hard, the Vicoute broke a path through the crowd, his riders flanking him. Dherran and Khenria had no choice but to follow, riding hard in a canter out from the dusty square, heeling through the market to the outskirts of the city. Following a dusty lane flanked by fig orchards and grape arbors, they kept pace for a number of miles, riding hard through the sweltering day. And only when they'd turned down a wide dirt lane past a long row of cypress trees did they slow to a walk.

Coming up over a rise, Dherran saw fields and orchards spreading to every horizon. And there at the end of the lane towered an enormous manor-house of white granite with marble pillars. Four stories high, the massive house was more than grand, imposing and keen in its lofty elegance. As they neared, a number of retainers paused in their duties near an impressive stable large enough for forty horses.

But though the Vicoute nodded at his household, he did not stop. The column rode straight to the steps of the main house, the Vicoute slinging down from his charger and handing its reins off to a stable boy, who took them with a bow. The other swordsmen in his retinue followed suit, handing their horses off to grooms, and Dherran and Khenria dismounted, doing the same. Without turning or saying anything to Dherran and Khenria, the Vicoute marched up his marble manor-steps, stopping in brief conversation with a liveried butler just inside the doors of an airy white marble entrance hall. The butler nodded, and the Vicoute strode on through the hall without looking back.

But when Dherran made to follow, the cheeky butler suddenly stepped in his path.

"Sirrah. I am to show you and the lady to your suites. The Vicoute has invited you to dine with him tonight, but until then, you may rest and refresh yourself. If you would come with me?"

Dherran glanced at Khenria, and she shrugged. Apparently, neither of them had any clue what was happening here.

"We would love to refresh." Khenria stepped in, managing the situation. "Thank you for your Vicoute's gracious hospitality."

The butler nodded, and with a sweep of one hand and a bow, invited them in.

24

GHRENNA

Ambling arm-in-arm down a main avenue in the Abbey Quarter, Luc and Ghrenna took in the city of Lintesh; gaudy and garish, bright and full of life. For the first time, sunshine was not a bane to Ghrenna, and she was able to admire the fountain plaza teeming with folk enjoying Coronation Week as the sun scorched down. They had been in the city two days after the week-long journey up from Fhouria. Luc had been treating Ghrenna with his miraculous hands the entire way, and today her headache was merely a subtle irritation deep inside her temples, her visions and seizures nonexistent.

Lintesh soared with good humor this week as the Dhenra's cobalt banners rippled in a sweltering breeze. Since their guild had arrived, it had become evident they weren't going to get anywhere near the palace to find Olea, not until the week's revelry was concluded. The Dhenra had apparently opened her galleries to commoners for the week, and the Third Tier had become a madhouse of people waiting for their chance to see inside the palace.

And to see the young soon-to-be-Queen.

Passing the time, Ghrenna and Luc moved along a tree-lined promenade today, searching for scores. Shara and Gherris were canvassing the Craftsman Quarter, every inch of the main thoroughfares occupied by hawkers and gawkers, merchants and menagerie all throughout the city. Tumblers in bright red silk climbed each other's shoulders, balancing in contorted poses as a man near the fountain ate fire, juggling it on lit batons and blowing flames from his mouth. Guards in cobalt were present at every intersection, watching the populace with their hands folded over the pommels of their swords. Coronation memorabilia was being sold everywhere, from silver rings etched with Dhenra Elyasin's profile to full-sized portraits on black velvet. They passed one stand, the portrait-hawker swearing he had done a real sitting for the Dhenra, from which he'd captured her likeness.

"Elyasin looks nothing like that." Luc scoffed as they passed, lifting an eyebrow at the paintings.

"You've met the Dhenra?" Ghrenna smiled easily, still wondering that it didn't hurt. She hadn't even touched her pipe today. But it was in her belt-pouch over her flax dress and summer lambswool corset, just in case.

"I used to live in the palace; Elyasin was just a girl then." Luc shrugged as they ambled on. "But Uhlas was a straight-nosed man with heavy brows. Elyasin is pretty, but she has her father's stern features when she's not smiling. This woman in the portrait is all plump curves and a button nose. She looks like a dumpling."

Ghrenna laughed, amused at Luc's commentary and Luc smiled, glancing over. "It's good to hear you laugh, Ghren."

"It's good to be able to." Ghrenna nodded. "I can't remember the last time laughing didn't hurt."

Stopping their promenade, Luc reached a hand up to smooth back her loose waves of white-blonde hair, nudging his fingers in to touch her scalp. Ghrenna felt a cool wave pass through her head, and what little pain there was rolled back further.

"You didn't need to do that." She murmured, smiling. "My head hardly hurts at all today."

"I know," Luc muttered, standing close. "But I like the way you succumb when I do it." But where Luc might have once tried for a kiss like a rogue, he merely held her now, with a tenderness that was far more honest since they'd shared secrets over a week ago. Luc had become more solicitous, and they'd come to each other's beds every night since then, for quiet lovemaking by the campfire while on the road. Now something complicated slid through his gaze as he watched her, before his hands eased from her scalp.

"Better?" He murmured, his fingers lingering at her neck, massaging beneath her hair.

"It wasn't bad to begin with." Ghrenna closed her eyes, absorbing his touch as the noise of the street faded. She felt him draw near; felt his breath on her lips. As his lips touched hers, she lingered in it, letting him draw her in as she let herself enjoy it.

As the moment stretched between them, Luc finally drew away and Ghrenna opened her eyes to see him smiling. His green eyes were entirely light as he smiled at her, as if something good had blossomed out of this handsome rogue, beaming through his every sinew. It made Ghrenna feel terrible suddenly and she pulled away, something clenching deep inside her, resisting that light. Breaking eye contact, she pulled back and he let her go. As they stood silent and awkward now in the raucousness all around, Luc gave a chuckle. But it was harsh and Ghrenna flushed, moving her gaze to the houses around them, scouting the broad bluestone mansions so she could forget that kiss, for now.

"Are you seeing what I'm seeing?" Luc spoke at last, in a briskly professional tone. Ghrenna glanced at him, but he was gazing at the buildings now just as she was, and she couldn't see his face.

"Good pickings." She spoke in the same professional tone, surveying the lay of the rooflines and the way the mansions were packed just a bit too tightly in the cramped space of the Quarter. Most had wrought-iron fences to keep out gutter trash and petty burglars, and in front of some Ghrenna saw dogs or house guards, with ornate iron grilles protecting doors and first-story windows. But gazing down a long alley, she saw the neighborhood was backed by a towering bluestone wall, raised ten feet or more above the mansions.

"Over there." Ghrenna spoke as she nudged Luc. "We could get on the roofs from that wall, have our pick."

"The First Abbey of the Jenners." Luc squinted in the hot afternoon sunlight, professional as he always was on a case, as if their kiss hadn't happened. "They run a watch on that wall at night, or they used to. Remnant of tougher times, you know? I wonder if they still do..."

"Only one way to find out." Ghrenna spoke as she nodded her chin towards the alley and the wall.

"The Jenners brew all the beer for Lintesh and the surrounding countryside." Luc grinned, his roguish humor returned now that their awkwardness over that kiss had diminished. "If you pretend to be interested in the Faith, they give you free samples."

Cocking her head, Ghrenna considered it. Thanks to Luc's regular treatments, for the first time in her life she could enjoy an afternoon of drinking without throwing her guts up in the morning. It made her feel grateful for him, and their day of canvassing would be well-complimented by a mid-afternoon ale. But something still clenched Ghrenna, something that needed easing.

Which an ale would help, also.

"Then let's go get some religion."

Luc laughed; a full, bright sound. Offering his arm again, they angled down the alley away from the bustle of the main thoroughfare and towards the distant wall. Both were quiet as they took in the details of the buildings flanking the Abbey. It was their usual scouting, and would come in handy later when they conferred, each having noted different aspects of the architecture, security measures, and rooflines.

At last, they reached the wall and headed to a side-door covered by a wrought-iron grille. Posing as a married couple visiting from Fhouria for the coronation and curious about the Jenner faith, they gained entrance without difficulty. The Jenners were solicitous, and provided them with ample brew as they gained a tour of the Coronation Week sights from the five-story wall, their flagons refreshed by two young Brothers who blushed and stammered to see Ghrenna.

More lighthearted than she'd been in years, Ghrenna had laughed when Luc mimed pinching the ass of one young Brother as he leaned over to collect more brew from a tray he'd placed on the stones. But laughter had never felt so good, and at last the Brothers had left them alone to admire the view. They gave the giggling Luc and Ghrenna strange looks as they departed – and she and Luc burst into laughter so badly she had to lean over the wall to catch her breath, fanning her white-blonde hair.

Though Ghrenna had not a single twinge of headache, and she took a tremendous breath, feeling alive at last.

"Aeon, Ghren!" Luc was still in a fit of chortling, wiping at his eyes. "I never knew you could be so much fun! Always so calculating – and all this time I thought you were just a sour apple. But you're not! Quiet, mysterious, but not really sour at all...!"

"I never knew I *could* be fun, Luc." Ghrenna spoke as she took another swig from her pewter flagon. Their fifth round of beer was hearty, a good stout with a caramel head of foam. Leaning on the battlement as she gazed out over the city,

Ghrenna twirled a lock of hair, a tic she hadn't had since her youth. "Having pain, it just... saps you. Everything you have, everything you could ever be, until you only focus on surviving one moment to the next. I never realized I could actually *live*."

"Any visions since I started treating you?" Luc stepped up next to her, close enough that their forearms touched as he gazed at her.

"No. Thank all that's holy." Ghrenna took another swig of her ale.

"You don't miss them? You don't want them back?" He frowned.

"No." Turning, Ghrenna studied the golden-blond thief before her. "It's a burden, Luc. It's something I can't control. I never know when the visions will strike or how terrifying they'll be."

"You never saw anything nice? Like winning at cards?" Luc leaned his tall frame over the battlement, his flagon cupped in his long fingers as he gazed at her with a mixture of thoughtfulness and concern. It was a good look, a look Ghrenna wanted in her life. Suddenly, her heart swelled for the golden-handsome bastard before her. Luc had risked everything coming here, and Ghrenna sobered as a twinge of guilt gripped her – a feeling like she was deceiving him. Something about it made her feel empty, as she turned back to the view with a wry smile.

"It doesn't work that way, Luc. I see what my *wyrria* wants me to see."

An old woe seemed to haunt Luc as he reached out, stroking her neck drunkenly, playing with a lock of her hair. "Those lake-blue eyes of yours... they make me wonder what you see. Fates of men? Have you seen my death?"

Shock flooded Ghrenna, and it took her a moment to realize Luc meant it to be teasing. But a strange emotion had contorted his face, and gazing once more over the rooftops, his attention fixed upon the palace. As Ghrenna watched, his jaw flexed in anger. It made Ghrenna worry for him; Luc had been morose on and off since they had entered Lintesh, and this was more of what haunted him.

"Do you think you're going to die because you're here in Lintesh?" Ghrenna asked quietly.

Luc chuckled ominously, his gaze never breaking from the palace, lit gold now in the late-afternoon sun. A shiver passed through him, his gaze was still fixed upon it as he spoke. "I may seem like a flippant fool sometimes, or a callow lout, but whatever I am, I tell you this. A curse runs through my family, walking those halls. My mother died there, and I had an aunt Mollia who died there before she even made it to age seventeen. I never met her. And now my brother and father have died there. *Every* Lhorissian dies there – too young. If I go serve the Dhenra... I'm going to meet a tragic end."

Ghrenna shifted, pulling away. Luc's words pricked her, as if stirring memories that went too deep, things better left dead and buried. "You could die anytime, Luc. We all could. You could fall and break your neck tomorrow trying to raid one of those mansions."

"Then my death would be a story, not a curse." He chuckled again, resting his flagon upon the stone wall. "I tell you, Ghrenna, death walks the halls of Roushenn. Untimely, secret death. My mother—" But he stopped abruptly, shutting his mouth as he stared out over the rooftops.

"Your mother?"

"Enough." Luc snapped suddenly. "Focus, Ghrenna. We're supposed to be scouting mansions. That's what this whole trip up here was all about today."

"As you say, Luc." Ghrenna blinked, feeling like he had just slapped her in the face.

But it was unsettling, the thoughts Luc had provoked today. As Ghrenna tried to blink away her ale-fugue, gazing out over the roof tiles of Lintesh, she found her thoughts wandering into images of death and battle, of starving out in deep snows, and being cut to ribbons by blades. Death after death plagued her, sourced from too many of her past visions. A late afternoon breeze caught the ramparts, stirring her white locks, cooling her sweat. Looking up, Ghrenna gazed at the pinnacle of the glacier-capped Kingsmount, wishing the breeze could take her away from her own mind.

A NORTHERN MOUNTAIN wind snaked through the city tonight, cool and fresh as Ghrenna shivered in her Kingsman Greys, feeling chill for the first time since they'd arrived in Lintesh. Peeper-frogs chorused in the darkness as she waited for the signal from Gherris, who had climbed an ancient darkoak across the street, watching the First Abbey's wall for the Jenner patrol. Crouched in the shadows of a hedge, Ghrenna waited. Once the patrol passed, she would have twenty minutes to climb, set a grapple, then get everyone up and hidden in one of the turrets to wait for a second guard to pass before stringing lines across the avenue to the nearest rooftop.

Their target tonight was a mid-sized mansion across from the Jenner compound. Luc and Ghrenna had timed the Jenner patrols, while Shara and Gherris had earned a tour of a similar mansion available for purchase to identify roof accesses. Tonight's mansion in the Abbey Quarter was a test for getting up on the Jenner wall, the house empty since the lord in question had moved his family into rooms at the palace for the Queen's coronation.

Waiting behind the hedge, Ghrenna eyed the wall again. "You sure you can get up there, Luc?"

"With your rope? Absolutely." Luc crouched in the darkness by her side in his thieves' blacks, breathing softly in the night.

"Light a fire under your ass." Ghrenna eyeballed him. "That's a fifty-foot climb."

"I'm not that bad a climber, Ghren." Luc gave her a cheeky smile, though it was strained tonight. The call of a nighthawk sheared the darkness from the oak across the avenue – their signal. Lifting the rope-and-grapple up over Ghrenna's head, Luc settled the grapple on her back. "Time to go. No falling this time. You got your pipe?"

"Just in case." Ghrenna patted her leather belt-pouch over her Kingsman Greys.

"Up you go, sweetheart."

Luc slapped her ass, though not hard enough to make any sound as Ghrenna set her hands to the wall, found purchase, and began her ascent. The top of the wall was silent beneath a halo of stars in a new-moon night. As she finally swung over the edge of the battlement, breathing hard, Ghrenna froze in her customary crouch – willing herself to be unseen.

Holding immaculately still, she used all her faculties to feel for any disturbance. But they'd timed it perfectly; no one was atop the wall between the guard-towers. Setting to with the grapple, she secured it in a block of byrunstone. Ghrenna was about to toss the rope over the side when the crunch of a footstep caught her ears. She froze, her face turned in the direction of the sound. A shadow was climbing the turret next to her, nearly as high as the parapet Ghrenna was on.

Someone else was working the rooftops of Lintesh tonight.

Stilling her body, Ghrenna willed herself to be unnoticed as her heart hammered. Fear slid through her gut and she felt her *wyrria* moving out, ready to turn any eyes that scanned the wall in her direction. Ghrenna's guild hadn't yet made contact with the Lintesh Thieves' Consortium, and if they were caught working tonight, they could be blacklisted or worse.

Much worse.

Ghrenna held motionless, hardly breathing as she watched the man upon the turret – an agile climber far better than she. Lean and tall, he moved like the night breeze, lifting easily between holds as he let his momentum do the work. Glancing to the top of the turret, he changed his mind, angling for the parapet upon which Ghrenna stood. Within moments, he was swinging lithely over the byrunstone battlement, landing upon soundless feet in the darkness.

Close now. He was so close; barely ten paces in front of her, and he still had not noticed her in the darkness. Ghrenna spread her tendrils out, willing him to see nothing but the night. But as she gazed at him, then squinted at his garb, she found it was familiar.

Because she was wearing the same thing.

It was a Kingsman in his Greys who stood before her in the night. She could see the tooling of the Kingsmount and Stars upon his belt and sword-harness in the starlight, his deep hood, and the quadrant-split panels of his long jerkin. The leather was soft like it had been used hard over the years, though the man stood before her with effortless strength, lean and honed like a blade.

A nighthawk cry sounded down below; Gherris' signal asking what the holdup was. Ghrenna couldn't answer. But the call startled the man upon the wall and he crouched, frozen a few moments. Leaning out at last, he scoured the darkness below, looking intently at the darkoak across the avenue. As he scrutinized the wall, the gardens, and the street, lingering in the places where Luc and Shara were hidden, Ghrenna caught a glimpse of a well-boned, handsome face in his deep hood. Turning his attention back to the parapet, he looked directly at her now. Ghrenna suppressed her fear, holding perfectly still. Spreading her will out, she pressed it towards his mind like pressing putty into a stone block. Breathing softly, she honed it, shaped it, slid it into his body and mind – to not see her.

His dark eyes swept her by.

Ghrenna let a silent breath pass, easing her focus. But then his gaze flicked back. His eyes narrowed and he stepped forward a pace, then another. Slipping towards her like a heron, all lithe patience and sinuous muscle, he stood only four paces from her when his gaze suddenly sharpened. He blinked, then straightened, closing the distance. As he did, his face became clear in the thin starlight. Ghrenna breathed out, her heart thundering, her stillness shattered. Her focus broke as the night seemed to expand all around them and contract at the same time – swaddling them in stillness like a dream.

Her dream. Her vision.

"Elohl." Ghrenna could hardly whisper his name, her tongue dry in her mouth, her heart beating fast. A void yawned inside her, a keening emptiness that had only grown more engulfing for ten long years – watching him from afar, seeing him but unable to touch. His grey eyes shone in the darkness, and the force of their hold drew her forward, and him also. Inches away, he was so close he could have caught her in his arms as he stared down at her, transfixed – Ghrenna's heart lifting up through her throat.

"You're here." Elohl's breath was a whisper in the night, his storm-grey eyes fixed upon her, his gaze dark and bright all at once. Rough and weathered, Ghrenna could smell his warm musk on the night air, basalm-fir and lemonbalm, his short beard hinting at nights buried in snow without warmth. Need roiled through his gaze; terrible and anguished as his hand reached up, hesitating as if not believing she was real. Fierce and wild, a flood of desire found Ghrenna, ripping her downstream with the force of a snowmelt avalanche – at the same time feeling as if this was only a mirage, ready to evaporate at the merest caress.

As Ghrenna's breath ceased, wanting but afraid, Elohl's gaze softened. And there it was, all the love they'd missed, all the days of pleasure and nights of bliss wrapped in each other's embrace. All the living that had stalled, that had been ripped away by a bitter Summons and a failed quest. And now they faced the truth of those lost years, gazing into each other's eyes in the depths of the night.

Soft as gossamer, Elohl touched her face, his rough fingers tracing gently along her jaw. Bliss sighed through Ghrenna, ecstasy as she heard his breath catch; a soft parting of lips as he had done when they kissed by the balewick trees near Alrashesh. She felt his love, even stronger than before – as if his very essence had reached out with that touch, embracing her into its diamond serenity. For a moment, everything filled with light. For a moment, Ghrenna saw a white spire in the darkness, felt it twine them together, lancing up from their bodies and spearing the sky.

For a moment, everything disappeared but this light, this bliss.

But his touch was obliterated as Ghrenna's head gave a vicious surge. Lights ricocheted across her vision, too fast. Suddenly, a riot of light chased darkness chased light, spinning with every color, twisting and tearing. Ghrenna shrieked, clutching her head as the pain blossomed into a nightmare – and her spasm came like a falling star.

Seizing ripped through Ghrenna's body. Her jaw locked, she tasted blood, and her world went black. It was only moments later that she came to, trussed by her hands around the neck of a man who was all sinewed muscle. Slung upon his back, she was still seizing, torn with pain, and she keened out. But Elohl's movement never faltered, sure and swift as he scurried them down to the ground, then ran them across the dark avenue. She could feel his alarm in every corded muscle and smell it in the way his musk had changed, acrid.

Elohl was terrified for her.

Ghrenna was terrified also.

Some part of her recognized her seizures should have ceased by now. Some part of her felt pierced by something that had lanced into her body, causing mayhem. It was deep and old, something that had dark and horrible memories – and while it had begun when Elohl touched her, it wasn't going to end there. Another fit took her, whipping her body and almost toppling them, but Elohl was sure-footed, strong like braided mast-line from his time in the mountains.

"Hold on, Ghrenna, hold on..."

As Elohl gave the call of a nighthawk beneath the darkoak tree by the hedge, sharp and urgent, three hooded figures emerged from behind it, armed and ready to strike. Gherris did strike, a knife whizzing past Elohl's ear as he ducked, the blade barely missing Ghrenna's cheek as another fit of rigors took her, clenching her teeth.

"Don't throw knives at me, you fuckstone!" Elohl's growl was deeper than Ghrenna remembered it – the furious voice of a Rakhan, a seasoned commander just like his father.

"Who the hell are you?" Gherris' challenge was rabid, all silence in the night forgotten.

"Put her down, shadow." Luc's voice was smoother but strained as it reached Ghrenna's ears.

"Ghrenna's having convulsions! Do any of you have threllis?" Elohl was lifting her from his shoulders to set her in the grass beneath the towering oak, untying her hands as he felt her forehead and pulses. But though Ghrenna yearned for his touch, where his hands went, her seizing was triggered like poison. Keening weakly in the darkness, it was the only sound she could make as another spasm ripped through every muscle.

"Get away from her! You're hurting her!" Luc shoved Elohl aside, and Ghrenna felt the cool balm of his hands, his sweet nectar flowing through her skull. Her keening dwindled to whimpers, and finally, she was able to catch a breath as her heart thundered in her chest. Her breaths were small sips, rapid and uneven as the sensation of cool water poured from Luc's hands, surging into her head and down into her locked body. "Easy, sweetheart, easy..."

"Do you have someplace we can take her?" Elohl's low baritone was all concern beside her.

"How do you know her name?" Shara interjected nearby. "How do you know she needs threllis?"

"We grew up together."

"Fuck Aeon!" Shara breathed. "You're Elohl – from her dreams! From her visions!"

Ghrenna was barely able to open her eyes, just enough to see Elohl blink at Shara in surprise – but then she was suddenly hoisted into Luc's strong arms. "Come on, sweetheart. We gotta get you to the inn. You! Elohl, shadow, whatever your name is. You'd better follow and explain all this, or so help me Karthor, I'm going to let Gherris disembowel you! He hasn't murdered anyone since we got to Lintesh, and I'm sure he's hungry for a first."

Sliding down into a pool of darkness as pain consumed her, Ghrenna didn't hear the rest.

25

ELOHL

They hadn't dared bring Ghrenna in the front of the guesthouse with everyone dressed in thieves' garb, so Elohl climbed her up the side of the inn through the window. Ghrenna keened in pain, thrashing atop Elohl's back and it was pandemonium as he rushed her to the bed, her screaming whenever they touched skin to skin. Stepping back in tortured frustration, Elohl made way for the lanky man in thieves' blacks as he ripped off his gloves and threw them at the bureau with a murderous glance at Elohl. Sliding to the bed in haste, the golden-maned thief laid his hands to Ghrenna's temples just as he had in the shadows of the hedge.

She was deathly pale, and still thrashing violently as Elohl's heart twisted while he watched, helpless. Something inside him gaped raw and open, in agony every time she thrashed. Here she was at last, and he couldn't touch her, couldn't soothe her, couldn't even cup her face in his hands and stare into those mesmerizing blue eyes.

Because every time he did, she seized.

The other two had made it in the window and were now lighting the lamps as Elohl knelt on the bare floorboards by Ghrenna's bedside. Clearly, whatever the thief was doing was having a positive effect; Ghrenna's jerking was quieting and her color was returning. As the tall man worked, her eyelids started to flutter.

And finally opened.

Ghrenna's gaze fixed upon Elohl, penetrating and ancient. Her irises were a darker blue than he remembered, twin pools of midnight, and his mouth ran dry. They were eyes that knew too much, had seen too much, and they bored into Elohl's soul. Tingling spreading over his chest and shoulders, down his spine, collecting in the center of his back. From the moment their eyes had first connected tonight, this sensation had risen inside Elohl, flaring his skin and searing through his muscles. His goldenmarks were alive with fire, surging whenever he looked at her, blistering whenever they touched – running like lightning through his limbs now as they stared at each other in the flickering lamplight.

Unearthly in her intensity, Ghrenna drew him, yet also made him want to be anywhere but in her presence. Looking at her now, Elohl could feel them both shivering with the connection like they stood upon the topmost peak of the Eleskis during a thunderstorm. Her beauty was terrible and luminous, a tundra-pale allure like a full-moon night over snowfields, something that didn't belong upon this earth. Twin spots of color brushed her cheeks like the first rise of dawn over ice as her full lips breathed with a wraithlike warmth, seductive and destroying.

And her eyes. It was as if they *knew* things, things Ghrenna herself didn't even know, drawing a future into place that was only just set in motion. And now they pinned Elohl, laid him bare as if to accuse him that he was supposed to be doing more.

Doing something – starting something.

"Aeon! I thought I lost you, woman!"

For a moment Elohl was confused, having thought the words came from his own lips. But then he saw Ghrenna's attention shift, taking in the golden-maned thief who still had his hands wound in her white-blonde waves.

"I'm alright, Luc. The pain's down. You can stop." A wisp of smile lifted Ghrenna's lips for the rogue and Elohl's gut clenched in a sudden fury.

"You're *not* all right." The thief Luc glared over his shoulder at Elohl. "If my hands weren't busy right now I'd be throttling you, Kingsman. What the fuck did you do to her?!"

Elohl had no words and merely shook his head as Ghrenna responded. "He didn't do anything, Luc. I was just triggered again."

"Bullshit! He touches you and you start thrashing like your head is being split by spears."

"That never used to happen."

"Never used to…?" Luc glanced at Elohl then back to Ghrenna, his green eyes incredulous and pissed. "You two used to be *lovers?!*"

"It was a long time ago." Elohl murmured.

Ghrenna looked at him again with her unfathomable gaze and Elohl's golden Inkings roared like liquid flame through his flesh. Ten years hadn't been long enough to forget those eyes; eyes that ruined his heart. All Elohl wanted was to touch her, to drink her in and surrender himself to those fathomless pools. Whenever he was alone he felt them, and there was no place he could go to outrun them. They haunted him when the wind howled, when blizzards raged five days long. They reflected in the ice of a waterfall when his hands were numb and his iceaxe dull and every movement was agony. They blinked him awake into a nightmare when an assassin's knife was at his throat.

And now they were here – watching him.

"It was a long time ago." Ghrenna finally echoed, showing Elohl all the howling in her soul before she wrapped it up into stillness. Closing her eyes, she sighed as if their connection was too much, and Elohl felt her relief, his Inkings quieting also.

Ghrenna pushed up to sitting, the thieves Luc and Shara helping her. As she got settled, propped up against the headboard, Shara fetched water then hustled downstairs to fetch everyone a late supper. The young cur who had thrown a knife at Elohl was pacing by the window. But though Elohl sensed the young man had a short fuse, he was strangely respectful, keeping his distance. But the thief Luc still shot Elohl vicious glowers. Even when Luc's hands fell from Ghrenna's head at her insistence she was better, Elohl saw his fingers strayed to her neck, possessive. At last, Ghrenna took a deep breath, her midnight-eyes seeking Elohl again.

"Elohl, the last time I saw you, you were on a road in the mountains."

"You've been having visions of me?" Elohl wanted to take her hand but held still, knowing what would happen if he gave in to temptation. Luc glowered, his fingers straying to Ghrenna's neck again, and Elohl heard a cough from the young dark-haired man near the window.

"I saw you almost die in an avalanche, once." Ghrenna spoke, her gaze fixed upon Elohl. "Ice-climbs, an assassin who tried to slit your throat. I saw you on the road. And then on top of that Stone."

"You saw me on the Alranstone?" Something trembled Elohl, a fae wind in his goldenmarks.

"You seemed asleep, but there was a man with you." Ghrenna eyed Elohl's Greys, done up tight and not showing his golden Inkings except at the neck. But her gaze traced his chest and shoulders as if seeing them anyways. "He had the Kingsmount on him, but it was different. And Inkings of red and white like Elsthemi fire-opals all over his shoulders, chest, and spine. He was speaking to you."

"Could you hear what he was saying?" Elohl asked, wondering if Ghrenna could illuminate what had happened atop that Stone.

But Ghrenna merely shook her head. "I only glimpsed the scene."

Disappointment hollowed Elohl's gut. Here again was a dead end as far as what had been done to him. And now it was worse, his golden Inkings triggering a dire reaction between himself and Ghrenna, something neither of them understood.

Something that split them apart.

"Did you come here looking for me?" Elohl murmured, needing the answer.

"No." Ghrenna blushed as she spoke, her blue eyes pinning him with truth. "We were looking for Olea. I didn't know you were in Lintesh. I never knew where to find you, Elohl. If I had, I would have come. But all I ever saw were ice-climbs, mountain vistas, hovels of snow..."

Ghrenna's gaze was wretched and Elohl's heart surged for her even though some part of him chilled, knowing she hadn't been looking for him. Conflict filled him at her words, a seeping darkness like cold water flooding against the burning of his golden Inkings. Ghrenna hadn't meant to be hurtful; his lonliness wasn't her fault. Elohl knew she couldn't control her visions and that she'd been just as helpless as he, feeling their connection all these years yet unable to find each other.

"I forgive you." He spoke at last, meaning it even though conflict stilled warred inside him.

Ghrenna's breath hitched and her eyes tightened though she held her emotions just as she always had. "Have you found Olea, here in the city?"

"I have." A smile wisped over Elohl's lips at last, a golden sensation filling him as he thought about his twin. "She's Captain-General of the Guard, actually. We've been meeting when she has moments free over the past few days."

"I'm so glad." Ghrenna's answering smile was relieved. But then it faded. "Elohl, you should know... Suchinne is dead."

"How did it happen?" Elohl spoke quietly in shock as he raised his palm to his chest. Though he had always hoped he would see everyone again, he supposed it had been too much to believe they would all survive ten years.

"She died in battle at the Valenghian border. But at least Dherran is hot-tempered as ever." A smile flickered over Ghrenna's face, though it was still sad. "He's a prizefighter; went renegade from his regiment like I did. After he tracked down and killed Suchinne's... murderers."

Elohl nodded and the silence stretched as he ran a hand through his black hair. There was so much Ghrenna wasn't saying, so much he wasn't saying – but around the others, he didn't trust himself to say more, and knew she didn't either. "Olea's done well as Captain-General. She's close to the Dhenra."

"I know." Ghrenna spoke with a small smile. "She had a private relationship with the Dhenir, also."

"Forgive me for interrupting," Luc piped up, showing sudden interest, "but your sister was fucking Dhenir Alden? And now she's close to Elyasin? How in blazes did she manage that? I thought every Kingsman left would be in prison, if not hung."

"What do you care?" Elohl kept his voice measured, trying to hold back a rising ire with the healer.

"That's *my* business, Kingsshit," Luc scowled under his golden brows. "And I don't think your presence here is doing anyone any favors! Just because you're a Kingsman and have a sister close to the throne doesn't mean you're better than everyone else. And what *were* you doing skulking around the Jenner compound tonight anyway? Not so noble now, are you?"

Elohl didn't say anything, just kept the man firmly in his gaze. Authority rolled from him in cool waves until at last, Luc flinched. "I was up on the wall tonight trying to find out information from the Jenners. If you have a problem with me, thief, I invite you to challenge me in single combat."

"You're on, whoresshit!" Luc's face flushed as he began to rise from Ghrenna's bedside. "I'll fight you anytime, anywh—"

"You don't want to fight Elohl." Luc got no further as Ghrenna's hand alighted on his arm. Her gaze flicked to Elohl and there was a plea in them that choked his heart. Ghrenna and the thief were lovers; it was obvious in the furious set of Luc's shoulders and the way Ghrenna held Elohl's gaze, willing him to see how alone she had been all these years – lonely just like him.

"Well why the fuck not?" Luc simmered. "He's a good inch shorter than me, and no more than eighty stone soaking wet!"

"Because he'll kill you." Ghrenna murmured, her attention still upon Elohl.

"Him?" Luc eyed Elohl with consideration. "Bullshit. I can take him."

"Don't fight him, Luc. Please." The young dark-haired man spoke suddenly as he stepped forward from the window.

"Never heard you say *that* before." Luc seemed to settle at the young man's plea, eyeing him.

"I've never said it before. But I'll say it again. *Please*, don't take his challenge. If he kills you, we lose our livelihood. If you kill him..." The young man looked stricken, a mixture of hope and woe in his gaze as he glanced at Elohl. "If you kill him, I'll never have anyone to call Rakhan."

Elohl blinked in surprise as silence passed through the room. And then he put his palm to his chest. "*Alrashemnesh aere veitriya Rennkavi rhavesin. Sin Rakhan. Siere tut me lhin.*"

"You're not a Rakhan?" The young man looked crestfallen. "You seemed so—"

"My father was Rakhan of Alrashesh." Elohl spoke, his palm still over his Inkings. "I gained a certain... way... from him. But I was never inducted as Rakhan."

"What? You *should* be Rakhan! Why have you turned from your father's path?" The young man was shaking now, shivering with a deep inner battle Elohl knew nothing of.

"What's your name, Kingskinder?" Elohl spoke quietly.

"Gherris. Gherris den'Mal." The young man snarled.

And at last, Elohl understood the young man's wrath. "My father often met with Rakhan Ghennys den'Mal, from the Second Court of Valdhera. Are you from Valdhera?"

"Yes." The young man snarled, his dark eyes flashing bitter anger.

A soft inhalation came from Shara, who had returned during their conversation with a basket of food. Standing beside Gherris as if she wanted to reach out to comfort him, she had better sense, instead hovering just out of reach. Elohl's gaze roved the young man, judging him to be no more than twenty-five. He'd lost his family at fifteen when the Summons came – and had been fighting the ghost of his father ever since.

"I'm sorry for your loss." Elohl murmured.

"You know nothing of it!" The young cur snarled.

"You're right, I don't. I only know the desperate lengths I went to, to protect my own family, and a depression so deep after they disappeared that I tried to kill myself no less than thirteen times." Unbuckling his charcoal Kingsman jerkin and pulling open the laces of his shirt, Elohl knew it was time to bare it all; to admit to himself just how dark his years had been. And strangely, he felt it was right tonight, calm suffusing him as he began to roll up his shirt sleeves.

"Three failed attempts to slit my wrists," Elohl spoke, showing the scars on his wrists. "One failed attempt to slit my own throat. Two thwarted attempts to leap from a waterfall. Six tries to drink myself to death. I started a riot in a bar once, to see who could best me to the grave. None of us Kingskinder escaped; all of us are damaged, Gherris. It's just that some scars show more than others. But no scar," he pulled his shirt down, baring his Kingsmount and Stars, "is more important than this. This binds us as family. And I intend to see that family reunited someday. With your help, and Ghrenna's, and anyone else here," his gaze touched on Luc and Shara, "we just might have that again someday. Unity. And justice."

"Justice." Gherris licked his lips like a hungry dog.

"Justice is found in a court of law. Not by vigilantism." Elohl admonished sternly.

Gherris blinked, startled that Elohl had read him. "Tell me of law and I will find it."

"Not me, Gherris. We need my sister Olea for that. Politics and negotiation are her strengths. For now, do you know the Alrashemni code? Do you know what each star of our Inkings means?"

The young man licked his lips again as his tortured grey eyes found Elohl's Inkings. "Strength. Flexibility. Wisdom. Knowledge. Patience."

"Patience." Elohl repeated, touching the leftmost star on his chest. "Patience, Kingskinder."

Though his gaze was alight with a fever Elohl knew all too well, Gherris nodded, mollified for now. With a scalding sensation through his golden Inkings, Ghrenna's pull caught Elohl once more and he glanced to her, watching her eyes. Spearing his heart, they sank into him like a curl of blue fire on the coldest winter's night. Yet again, Elohl felt that they demanded he do something, start something.

Something far more than he knew how to.

* * *

It was the deep quiet of near-dawn when Ghrenna padded to Elohl's blankets upon the bare floorboards. Luc was fast asleep on the bed, snoring softly, the other two in the adjacent suite with the door closed. Elohl felt Ghrenna's gaze in the semi-dark, licking over his skin like slow fire as he motioned her over. Still in her Kingsman Greys from the night, she stretched out upon her side on the floorboards with him, watching him with her head propped on her hand. Her fathomless eyes seemed to shine in the early light, mysterious as her shroud of white-blonde hair. Ghrenna's pale northern beauty caught Elohl like it always had, and he lifted his blanket so she could slide under. But he was careful not to touch her, as if they were First Seals once more.

"Did I wake you?" Her voice was a whisper in the dawn.

"I was already awake." Elohl nodded at the bed and the snoring. "Does his healing really stop your headaches and seizures?"

"It does. Luc's a natural-born healer. My visions are unpredictable, but I haven't had one since he first helped me." Ghrenna's smile was shy as she stretched out her fingers, toying with one of Elohl's shirt-laces. It was a smile Elohl used to see when he would undress her by moonlight at the edge of Fherrow's Pond, and he caught his breath. Using all his discipline, he held still so they wouldn't touch.

"I used to dream you would find me, Elohl," she murmured again. "That you would climb us both up a white spire so high that we entered the clouds – a palace of solace and mist. We would lay there in the clouds, just... touching. Until they cleared and we could see the world, lit by diamond brilliance."

Reaching out as if to touch his bare chest and the golden Ink in the grey light, her fingers hovered as a subtle tremor rippled her. "I still dream of it. Before Luc began healing me, the only time I knew a world without pain was when you and I were there. But now you've been marked by something... powerful. And I don't know why. Nor why it keeps us apart when we should be one."

Her whisper held a dire portent that made Elohl shiver and ache. He could feel the heat in her fingertips, so close yet unendingly far. Her eyes were twin pools of sorrow, and Elohl's heart twisted as her fingers hovered over his chest. Drawn in, he moved forward, their faces close as his lips breathed over hers. He could taste her sweet scent upon his tongue like wintermint and pine as she breathed hard now, and Elohl couldn't stop himself matching her pull. He couldn't stop wanting her until the world burned. Aeon suffer him, he'd never been able to stop. Risking touch, Ghrenna brushed her fingertips over his bare skin, along a line of gold ink – as Elohl lifted his lips. For a moment, Elohl burned as they kissed.

And then Ghrenna was seizing again.

As Elohl came to his knees in his blankets, trying to hold her steady, Luc launched from the bed in the wan light. "Dammit, Kingsman! Let her go! You're making it worse!" Elbowing him out of the way, Luc got a firm grip on Ghrenna's head, staying clear of her thrashing. In a moment, he had the violence down to a shiver though her eyelids still fluttered madly.

"What did you do?!" Luc snarled, murderous as his green eyes flashed in the dawn.

"I kissed her." Anguish twisted Elohl's heart as he watched Ghrenna, knowing he had just jeopardized her life. Again.

"Fucking hells!" But Luc's sigh was more irritated than angry now. "You know this strains me, Kingsman. Each time I work on her, I get sapped. I'm not the fountain of bloody youth! Ghrenna? Ghren sweetheart, come on back..."

Luc was tender with her, and as Elohl regarded the man, he saw the sweet love the thief held for Ghrenna from everything they had shared over the years. Ice crept into Elohl's chest and he spiraled into a bitter despair, his newfound peace sliding away as Ghrenna's twitching subsided. Even so, Luc still moved his hands slowly, cradling her head. Reaching out, Elohl's fingers whispered over a lock of Ghrenna's white-blonde hair where it spilled across the floorboards.

"I envy you, Luc." Elohl spoke, his eyes burning as he gave a soft laugh of despair. "You can touch her, love her, be with her. I've waited ten years hoping she lived... All I ever wanted was to be with her. All I ever hoped for was that she and I would have a chance once my service was finished. Once I could have my own life back again. But now I'll never have it – any of it. Aeon, curse me for a fool!"

Standing abruptly, Elohl pulled the lacings of his shirt closed, shrugging into his jerkin and weapons harness as he glanced out the grimy window at a bitter dawn. Tears falling thick and fast, he sat in a chair, pulling on his boots. Rising, he headed for the door and had his hand on the bolt when Luc's voice called out behind him.

"Hey! Kingsman! Where can she find you?"

"Do you really want to know?" Elohl turned, not bothering to scrub his tears away.

"I don't. I could give two shits. But she will. And Ghrenna leads our guild, not me."

Elohl considered the tall man upon the floorboards, still with his hands beneath Ghrenna's head. The thief was a decent fellow, the sort of man Ghrenna deserved. A man who could be kind to her, who could give her laughter and warm nights rather than pain and bitter memories. But jealousy seared a cold path into Elohl's heart, and some part of him rose suddenly in promise.

He would find a way to touch her again – or die trying.

"I'm at the King's Cross in the Tradesman Quarter," Elohl spoke at last. "Ask for Elohl den'Alrahel, Veteran High Brigade."

"Veteran High Brigade?" Luc's attention flicked over Elohl as if seeing something new suddenly. "High Brigade is a death sentence."

"So they told me when I was conscripted." Elohl gazed over Ghrenna's luminous beauty one last time, steeling himself in his promise as he paused with his hand on the door.

"She loves you, you know." Luc growled, bitter but honest. "The way she speaks of you. You'd be a daft bastard to leave her like this."

Lingering, some part of Elohl died deep inside to know that Ghrenna still loved him. "Tell her I'm at the King's Cross?"

The thief was silent a moment, but at last nodded. Opening the door, Elohl stepped out into the dim lamplight of the hall without looking back.

26

TEMLIN

Brother Temlin den'Ildrian massaged his beard as he stared down at the Ghenje board, contemplating his dark and light stones. Abbott Lhem den'Ulio had backed him into a corner. The fat old walrus was grinning now, his dark grey eyes still sharp though he was ten years Temlin's elder. The lamps were bright in the Abbott's high-gabled apartments on the third story of the Annex, the scent of burning lamp-oil drafting out the open windows and into the frog-chorused night. Both geezers needed the lamps bright so they could squint at the pine gaming board, contemplating their moves – two mugs of honey-brown ale sitting on the Abbott's supper table adding to their fun.

"Get on, then, Temlin! What're you gonna do now, huh?" Lifting his mug to his generous white mustachios with a drunken wink, Abbott Lhem's cheeks were ruddy with ale. His bark was that of a military General, still hale and deep – though the First Abbot of the Jenners was infamous for his political maneuvering, and it showed in his Ghenje. Temlin wondered again how such a man had ever sought the monastic life. But he kept a tight ship at the First Abbey, and his agile mind was always something to behold.

Temlin stroked his beard again, pondering his move.

"Keep messing with that beard and you're gonna lose what's left of your hair." Abbott Lhem growled.

"Keep swigging that honey-brown, and the younger Brothers are going to know their Abbot is drunk as a badger." Temlin returned smartly.

"Ah! Fuck the little men. I can drink if I want to." Lhem swigged again, defiant.

"*The Way is the Life, and the Life is full of mellow wealth.*" Temlin chuckled, still considering the board. "*Seek you to calm your passions, neither drink to pass your lips, nor the riots of flesh to grace your skin, and ye shall find the Way of Inner Release.*"

"Don't quote catechism at me, old man!" Lhem leveled a thick finger at Temlin. "I could quote you around the Wall and back."

"So you could." Temlin chuckled peaceably. They had enjoyed such a battle before, and it had gone on for an entire week before one of the younger Brothers pleaded for a truce between them. "But sometimes I wonder how much the Way really sinks in for you..."

"For fuck's sake, Temlin! Get a move on!"

"In time, my friend. One must not rush the Bliss of the Way..." But Temlin flicked his eyes up over his half-spectacles to Abbot Lhem, grinning. Lhem leveled his meaty finger at Temlin, bouncing it like he was going to explode into a tirade. But then he began to chuckle, to belly laugh, and then finally dissolved his laughs into his beer.

"You old possum. Devious as the Ghost of Roushenn! Make your move, then."

Temlin finally did, sliding his polished white stone into an unoccupied space in the lower left corner of the board, trying to secure his left flank. He was losing already – he knew it and Lhem knew it. They were just playing to see how close it would be as the evening deepened. Their games were often within three points of each other, and playing to the bitter end pleased them both long into the night.

Finally permitting himself a sip of ale, Temlin swished it around his mouth while sitting back into his overstuffed chair. Some might have called their Ghenje nights sacrilege, but Temlin chose to consider them enjoyment; the Jenner Way had no tenets against enjoyment, just distractions and addictions. Though Temlin only allowed himself a beer when he and the Abbott gamed. His love of alcohol was an addiction, ancient and strong, which was why he allowed himself only one – and only under the direct supervision of Lhem's stern mustachios on Ghenje night.

But there was something else Temlin needed to address tonight, and now that the Abbott was relaxed from the day and winning their game, the time was right to bring it up.

"I had an interesting visit today," Temlin began conversationally as Abbot Lhem stroked his ample mustaches, considering the board. "A young man, perhaps thirty. He was a Kingsman. Inked."

"Inked?" Surprise flitted over Lhem's ruddy features as his grey eyes flicked up, sharp as flaying-knives. Straightening, he sipped from his flagon as he sat his plethoric bulk back into his plush chair, his sharp eyes never leaving Temlin's. "Continue."

"Inked as a Kingsman, but also marked in another way," Temlin spoke as he took a sip of beer, enjoying drawing out the suspense for his Abbott. "He was Inked by a seven-eye Alranstone, just a few days ago. Inked in gold – all over his chest, shoulders, and back."

"He was Goldenmarked? And you're just telling me this now?!" Abbot Lhem slammed his flagon down so hard upon the table that ale slopped from the rim. "Dammit, Temlin! Are you certain about this? Does anyone else know?!"

"So he said, and so I believe." Temlin spoke as he sipped his beer. "I took him to the Far Ponds, to the bench. No one overheard us as we spoke. His woman knew about the Goldenmarks, and she could corroborate the event. One night, he wakes up, climbs a seven-eye Stone, and in the morning he's Inked in gold and can't remember a damn thing except the word *rennkavi*. And when he climbs down, *every eye* upon the Stone is open, and they blink at his touch. He described the Alranstone's irises perfectly, Lhem. And when he traveled through it to get here to Lintesh, it took the woman through, too."

"Sweet Nectar of the Way." Lhem took an enormous swig of beer, his attention riveted upon Temlin as he wiped his mouth with his black sleeve. "And you let the lad *leave?!*"

"He was a stubborn young man, he wouldn't stay here at the Abbey," Temlin chuckled. "Got squirrelly for some reason and I had to let him go. But he'll be back. He wanted information on Alranstones, trying to find out what had happened to him. I may have told him how to get into the Rare Tomes Room to review Mollia's journals. Unofficially."

"You old goat." A smile spread across Abbot Lhem's face, lifting his mustachios at the corners.

"Kingsmen have impressive talents." Temlin swirled his beer in his mug. "I expect him sometime tonight after midnight bell, once evening's gloaming is completely gone from the sky. After our game, you and I and Abbess Lenuria could be doing some late-night research in the Rare Tomes Room... and oops! Catch him in the act of stealing rare journals and have a chat with him."

Lhem gave a devious chuckle. But suddenly all mirth dropped from his mustachios as he settled back into his high-backed chair with a scowl. Reaching up, he scratched at one ruddy ear. It was one of the Abbott's few tells, and it communicated to Temlin that Lhem was acutely worried about this news. Taking a swig of ale, Temlin watched his longtime friend in the Shemout Alrashemni as Lhem sat in silence a long moment, contemplating Temlin's information.

As a Jenner, Lhem knew the common version of the Uniter of the Tribes, just like Temlin. Most thought the Prophecy was simply a redemption parable about finding unity within oneself; finding peace and acceptance in life. The problem was, the true Prophecy of the Uniter had been laid down by a Seer some thousand years ago. That a seven-eye Stone would open for the Uniter was part of the official parable – but that the Uniter would be Inked by an Alranstone was not.

That was a very deep secret. A secret still passed on among the Shemout Alrashemni, part of an ancient oral lore they had to memorize to earn their hidden Bloodmark. Which Temlin and Lhem both wore – though no one would ever see it on their ancient old chests unless they were pricked by a blade.

But the exact tenets of the Prophecy had been fractured so badly over the centuries that no one really knew the entirety of it. Part myth, part hedge-legend, the original Prophecy of the Uniter was such a mess no one had ever really bothered to track it. But two of those who knew a few hidden secrets of that conundrum were staring at each other now, sipping beer. And now there was a flesh-and-blood man who wore the prophesied Goldenmarks of the Uniter asking questions around Lintesh. As Temlin rubbed his hidden Inkings beneath his black Jenner-robes, he noticed Lhem doing the same, staring off into space.

At last, the Abbott looked back and they locked eyes. "Have you heard from Arlen den'Selthir lately? Or has Abbess Lenuria?"

"No," Temlin shook his head. "The channels have been quiet, and we've had no hawks. Den'Selthir is keeping a very low profile since Uhlas' death. I don't blame him."

"So is Sister Mollia." Lhem murmured. "She hasn't come through the Abbeystone for two years now. If she's not dead up in that secluded valley of hers, that is."

"Molli's always been strange." Temlin countered as his heart gripped him, feeling an old sadness lance his chest. He'd not thought about Mollia for so long, but whenever she came up, there it was, agonizing as ever. Love was truly bitter fruit, even for a man past his prime. "Perhaps she's in seclusion. Uhlas kept her a secret from the world for a reason."

"Your brother was wise, Temlin. It's not everyday a King falls in love with a mad Seer."

"Molli's not mad." Temlin bit tersely, feeling himself go hard as flint as the rage of a far younger man surfaced beneath his hard-won Jenner patience. "She saw this day, Lhem. She saw the *Man with Goldenmarks* coming right to the First Abbey. And she saw we couldn't turn him away. You know as well as I what happens if we don't give him our help."

"Annihilation of the Alrashemni, right to our very bones." Lhem sighed heavily, drumming his thick fingers upon the table. "Perhaps the *Man with Goldenmarks* coming to us means the Khehemni will finally gut us once and for all."

"They've had their turn." Temlin spoke angrily as he drained the last of his beer, then slammed it to the table. "They did a fine job gutting us with that fucking Summons ten years ago. Speaking of the Khehemni – what are you going to do about the Chancellate and Castellan Lhaurent?"

"Fuck them." Lhem scowled like a raging bear. "Evshein and Lhaurent have tried to blackmail the First Abbey into their sick operations one too many times. But we need to wait. They've yet to show a strong play against us."

"I say the time for waiting is finished, Lhem," Temlin growled in his throat. "It's long past time for the Jhennik Alremani to join the war – for us to wake the sleeping giant that is the Abbey and support the Crown! It was time when my nephew Alden died; it was time when my brother Uhlas succumbed!"

"Temlin. Don't let your family's downfall affect your judgment." Abbot Lhem spoke as he gave Temlin a very stern eyeball. "We can't move against the Khehemni Lothren yet; we still have no idea how they are coordinating much of their dealings. And you're not technically House den'Ildrian anymore, though you keep the name. Don't forget your father had you *removed* from the King's line, and your brother Uhlas was just unbendable enough that he never once invited you to the palace to meet his children, simply because your father decreed you anathema!"

"Don't tell me I can't protect my niece!" Temlin snarled, his old ferociousness raging as he lurched to standing, pressing his fingers to the tabletop. "The rest of her family is gone; she's all alone! I'm Shemout Alrashemni, dammit, so sworn since I was fifteen years old – and I'm still Elyasin's uncle!"

"*You* are a Brother of the Abbey." Lhem barked sternly as he leveled a meaty finger at Temlin, his plethoric face flushed as he rose to his feet also, his bear-thick bulk thrice Temlin's. "That is what you are these past thirty years! We can't simply rope the First Abbey behind you, Temlin, nor can we support Elyasin! The First Abbey is an *independent* organization. A few of us Shemout Alrashemni hide in the Jenner ranks, but only because of the *access* it grants us! The rest are regular men and women of the Faith. They believe in peace and calm. Meditation, my friend. Something you would do well to learn."

"I meditate just fine." Temlin grumbled, crossing his arms over his chest.

"You cogitate and read, you old goat," Lhem countered sternly, "to pass time while your insides stew. You've a temper as much as you've always had, Temlin. You need those quiet ponds and soothing platitudes far more than anyone I've ever met."

"Beer will do."

"Speaking of." Lhem lifted a bushy white eyebrow. "How many have you had tonight?"

"Just one, dammit! Just this one here."

"Good. Once a drunk, always a drunk, Temlin."

"Fuck Aeon, I know!" Temlin growled sourly. "You don't need to remind me of my past, nor of how I wound up here. That was a long time ago."

"In any case." Lhem eyeballed him, his thick mustachios set in a frown. "We can't simply rally the First Abbey for Elyasin, nor expose ourselves as Shemout Alrashemni. Such things must be done *cautiously*. Most Jenner Brothers and Sisters don't know anything about the Alrashemni's real history. They think the Uniter is a redemption parable. But if this young man is who we think he is, we need to find him. We need to get him to Molli and have her read his mind; see if he would be useful to us."

"If Molli will ever make contact." Temlin couldn't stop a sinking feeling in his heart. Despite their tortured history, he still missed Mollia – a woman he'd loved but who had never really been his. But Abbot Lhem didn't notice, his gaze faraway with machinations, his thick fingers drumming upon the table. Heading to a silk bell-pull on the wall, Lhem gave it a yank, summoning one of the runner-lads from their bunks next door. Presently, a sleep-tousled youth knocked upon the door, sticking his head around the frame and blinking at the bright lamps.

"Yes, Abbott?" He yawned.

"Get to the Abbess, lad," Abbott Lhem grumped sternly, a hard frown upon his ample white mustachios. "Wake her if she's sleeping. Tell Lenuria to meet us in the Rare Tomes Room with all haste, and that it's *vitally* important. Someone's going to try breaking in tonight. Go. Now."

The lad blinked, then nodded hastily and disappeared, the heavy door latching shut behind him.

"Come on." Abbott Lhem spoke, lifting his flagon to his lips and draining it. "Let's get a move on with these old joints."

"Speak for yourself." Reaching to the pitcher of ale, Temlin refilled his flagon then tipped it back, swallowing ale down without a single breath like a practiced drunk. Dark thoughts swirled; rage about his niece's predicament. Filling his flagon again, he drained it once more just for good measure.

When he turned, Lhem was giving him a disastrously severe eyeball.

"Ale won't help you restore your youth, Temlin," he murmured. "It won't bring Mollia back, and it won't help your niece any. All it does is make you wind up facedown in horse shit."

"Fuckitall, I know." Wiping a hand over his lips, Temlin scrubbed his beard, realizing his chin was already numb. He hated it and loved it all at once. But his joints screamed less after a few pints, and he'd be able to walk faster in Lhem's prodigious wake. "Let's go."

The big man eyed him again, then turned to the door. In a trice, Lhem had the heavy ironbound door open and they marched into the hall. The First Abbey was quiet, no one about in the Annex as they trod a circular stairwell down to the ground floor and out the doors into the night. Temlin felt himself closing in from the ale, brooding as his stride became brisk, the chronic pain in his knees and back dulled. His gaze sharpened as he scanned the darkness; old habits of battle from a youth long gone. Circling around the Annex to the arched vault that marked the entrance to the catacombs below, they took up oil-lamps from pegs upon the wall, kindling them by fire sticks in a brazier.

Temlin's heart hammered, realizing a figure stood right by the brazier. He'd not seen her in the night, yet Abbess Lenuria den'Brae was already there to meet them, her dark grey eyes glittering in her black hood with her hands folded into the sleeves of her robe. Drawing up to her full five-foot-nothing, their tiny Abbess with her striking silver-black braid gave them her most formidable eye, as if the two old farts had kept her waiting hours. Both men instinctively cringed from Lenuria's set jaw and straight-browed scowl. Her gaze was like an eagle, missing nothing about their shoddy appearance, and Temlin almost pitied the Sisters of the First Abbey. Lhem could be bought with beer if one did something amiss.

Lenuria couldn't be bought for all the jade in Perthe.

"You two are drunk." Lenuria's words held a cutting edge, slicing through the night. "Brother Temlin, how many times must one cite catechisms against addictive imbibing to you?"

"My dear Abbess. My deepest apologies. I am nothing but an old skunk." Sinking to both knees upon the stone foyer before the catacomb's entrance, Temlin was dramatic. He was in a mood and didn't care who knew it.

"Temlin old man, don't make it worse." Abbott Lhem swept a low bow for their Abbess, who was technically his superior both at the Abbey and in the Shemout Alrashemni – the Jenners having been founded by a woman originally.

"Oh, for Aeon's sake! Get up! I could hardly punish you more than you punish yourself, Temlin." Abbess Lenuria gave Temlin her sternest eyeball as she ignored Lhem – though not for long. As Temlin rose with audible pops in his knees and back, Lenuria rounded on Lhem, her teensy frame formidable as she faced his walrus-like bulk. "And you! Encouraging him! Be an example for your Brothers, Abbott, or I will remove you from your station! Let me remind you that being Abbott is not necessarily a lifetime appointment. It is *earned*."

Lhem gave the proper downcast visage and mutterings of apology, though Temlin could tell the old musk-ox was smiling beneath his ample white mustachios.

"Now." Lenuria smoothed a hand over her silver-streaked braid. "What's this all about? You have news someone is breaking into the Rare Tomes Room tonight and we are supposed to just *sit here* and wait for him? Why shouldn't I simply summon guards?"

"Well, Leni, if Temlin is right, we're going to have a very interesting visitor tonight. Inked in gold."

If Temlin had thought Lhem's reaction to his news was interesting, Lenuria's was positively astounding as her eyes flew wide, her mouth dropping open. Though she covered her astonishment with one hand, Temlin saw that hand was trembling violently. Lenuria never trembled. Solid as marble, she'd been a fighter long before she came to the Abbey, and was neither doddering nor infirm. The small braids running through her silver-streaked larger braid proved she'd adopted Highlands fighting fashions long ago, of their women keshari regiments who rode to war upon battle-cats. But she was trembling now, so violently that Temlin had a sudden concern for her, and reached out to steady her by the shoulder.

Lenuria's gaze swung up, and in her grey eyes shone more fear than Temlin had ever seen from her. But also a light, like the deepest hope. "Is it true? Did you see a man with golden Inkings all over his shoulders, back, and chest?"

"So I did, Lenuria." Temlin murmured, sober now after the reaction of his stalwart Abbess to his news. "And his story was stranger still. He said they had been inked all in one night after an Alranstone called him to climb it. He slept atop it, dreaming. And woke with the word *rennkavi* upon his lips, and the Goldenmarks upon his skin."

"The Alranstone inked him in gold and and named him Rennkavi. The Uniter." Lenuria was pale as porcelain by the brazier's glow as her attention flicked to Lhem, then back to Temlin. "Come. Let us go inside. And I will tell you what I know about the Prophecy of the Uniter while we wait."

Shrugging off Temlin's hand, she turned, reaching out to unlock the iron grate that barred the door down to the Tomes Room. Giving it to Temlin to haul back, she unlocked the heavy inner sanctum door and they proceeded into thick darkness, lifting their lanterns as they descended the corkscrewing stone stairwell. Down three turns, the stairs ended in a comfortable sitting-area with a broad cendarie desk, ornate rugs, and a number of reading chairs. Beyond the main reading area were the byrunstone stacks of the Tomes Room – rows upon rows of arcane writings and scrolls all carefully catalogued and preserved in the vaulted crypts beneath the First Dwelling.

Other religious sects kept dead sages entombed below their cathedrals, but not the Jenners. Their dead were burned upon pyres, released back to the Way, their ashes scattered upon the gardens so fruitfulness could come from their passing. Temlin admired the ancient bluestone architecture of the massive underground crypt as they lit lanterns in every arch to push back the darkness.

Brightening the sprawling catacombs to a warm glow and banishing shadows, the cathedral-like underground chamber was soon visible down every aisle and up into every dome.

When at last they selected places upon a pair of red velvet reading couches next to a group of magnifying-lanterns, Abbess Lenuria finally spoke. "I don't know much about the Prophecy of the Uniter beyond the standard catechisms we learned in our Shemout Alrashemni training, but I've heard extensive tales about the Uniter of the Tribes from my travels when I was young – word-of-mouth tales from the nomads of Ghrec all the way to the tundra above Elsthemen."

"I didn't know you had traveled so extensively in your youth," Lhem boomed, before lowering his voice in the echoing space.

"What you don't know about me could fill volumes, Abbott." Lenuria shot him a look. "I lived a long and complicated life before I came here to the Abbey, seeking solace. But suffice it to say that I heard tales. And wherever I traveled, on campaign or not, I asked about the Uniter, what tales different peoples knew."

"And what did you learn?" Temlin leaned forward upon the edge of his couch, rapt.

"There is a tribe of caravan people who call themselves the Berounhim," Lenuria spoke, "who live in Cennetia down through Ghrec and into the southern deserts. They're similar to the Travelers here in Alrou-Mendera, but they worship the Uniter, the *Rennkavi*. They believe the man we describe in our *heimkeller* parable is a real person yet to come – a savior who will be able to right a most horrible wrong that happened in the distant past. Apparently, there was once an actual King of the Khehemni, over a thousand years ago. He was vastly wronged by the Alrashemni and sought retribution. So he waged a great war, laying waste to his own nation and all the other nearby nations to kill the Alrashemni off. He was at last brought low, but the ruin was done. A great migration of people on both sides left their decimated land to seek better fortunes. The Berounhim remember there was a Prophecy at that time. That someday a person would come, Goldenmarked by one of their Great Teachers, who could repair the damage done so long ago. Who could Unite both sides of the ancient war."

"An origin story explaining the reason for Khehemni and Alrashemni conflict these past thousand years," Lhem spoke as he chewed his mustachios, his thick fingers tapping the velvet couch. "Well, that's not one I've heard before. So this man, this *Rennkavi* is supposed to bring peace to us? How?"

"No one knows what is actually supposed to happen when the Uniter comes," Lenuria shrugged. "Great peace – or tremendous war? The Berounhim couldn't say. Only that in the end, all would be United. But would that end be bloody? Apparently some Berounhim believe it will be a destructive end, where all are United in death. Whereas others disagree, believing the Unity will actually be the ushering in of a Great High Age. In any case, our Shemout Alrashemni story and the resultant Jenner parable are a fluffy, simplistic version of the original tale, passed down through word of mouth for a thousand years and changing considerably the entire way." Lenuria heaved a sigh as she came to silence.

"So." Lhem chewed his mustachios, scowling. "What do we do if this young man comes tonight?"

"You've already met the Rennkavi," Lenuria glanced at Temlin. "Did you feel anything... *unusual* about him?"

"Other than being a very righteous sort of young Kingsman, and well-hardened by war in the highpasses... he seemed rather ordinary." Temlin sighed as he thought back through his beer-fogged mind. "Tall, striking in that traditional Alrashemni way, certainly – but ordinary."

"I suppose we'd best hope he comes tonight, then." Abbess Lenuria gave a sad smile.

"I suppose we'd best," Temlin responded.

Settling into silence, the three old Shemout Alrashemni watched the night as the oil-lamps spluttered and hissed in the great stacks of tomes.

27

ELOHL

Elohl had slipped back to his apartments at the King's Cross just as the true light of dawn spilled over the Eleskis. Shutting the door, he glanced at the bed where Eleshen was sprawled in sleep. Naked and lovely by the light coming in through the open window, her honeyed hair was spread over the pillows, one leg slung up over the covers. An energetic sleeper, she was always tangled in the blankets, and Elohl would have smiled except his heart was twisted in knots. Emotions long buried had swamped him tonight, and nothing was simple anymore; it never had been. He'd been lying to himself that he could have a life with Eleshen when Ghrenna was still out there, her lake-blue eyes still pulling at him.

And now he knew exactly where Ghrenna was – and that she still loved him.

Looking at Eleshen's golden beauty in the rising light, Elohl's gut twisted, his heart cavernous. He felt like a cur, but whether he was betraying Eleshen or Ghrenna, he only knew he was a bastard either way – and that soon he'd have to make a choice. With a soft sigh, Elohl turned to the pegs on the wall, unbuckling his climbing harness and hanging it up by his longsword. A knock suddenly came on the ironwood door, startling Elohl. Fast as instinct, he had a longknife to hand from its sheath on his climbing harness and spreading his sensate sphere, felt for a threat on the other side of the door.

The knock came again. Whoever it was, was trying to be civil and Elohl lowered his knife, suspecting that Luc had decided to follow him and give him an earful. Hauling open the door, he intended to tell the man to go back to Ghrenna – but instead found himself face to face with a cobalt-jerkined Palace Guardsman.

"Elohl den'Alrahel?" Lean and of average stature, the Guardsman was wiry as a mountain-cat, something about his lithe, alert presence reminding Elohl of a keshar as he spoke. The man's baritone voice held a soothing ripple like a well-practiced bard, his eyes a curious shade of brown ringed with gold that caught the lamplight of the hall as his gaze flicked to Elohl's longknife. His russet-brown waves were carefully curried back from his forehead, and something about the set of his jaw commanded instant respect.

A deep calm suffused him, utterly at ease under Elohl's scrutiny.

"Who are you?" Elohl's growl was low, not wanting to wake Eleshen but purposefully putting menace in against a man he knew nothing about. He didn't brandish his knife at the Guardsman, but he didn't put it away, either. Elohl still had his Kingsman Greys on, and he used their notoriety now, lowering his chin as he gave an air of stern authority.

"Your sister Olea, my Captain-General, sent me to find you." The Guardsman's gold-brown gaze glimmered with a sudden wry humor. "Don't even try denying who you are, you look just like her. But taller; more masculine. Obviously. And your Kingsman Greys rather give you away. In any case, Olea's been imprisoned by the Dhenra and needs your help."

"Fucking hells." Elohl hadn't realized he'd spoken until it was out of his mouth. Reaching out to collect his longsword and climbing harness from the peg, his gear was buckled on swiftly. He hadn't even realized how fast he'd moved at the man's information until he was already reaching up, adjusting the longsword's grip in its scabbard over his shoulder. But the Guardsman stood there with a placid readiness, and Elohl felt truthfulness in the man's steady gaze. The glint of a silver First-Lieutenant's pin caught the light at his high collar – the same rank Elohl had once held in the High Brigade.

"Where is Olea? Is she in danger?" Elohl frowned as he finished checking his longknives in their sheaths.

"Olea's fine, for the moment." The Lieutenant spoke, though his brown eyes betrayed a subtle worry. "She just had a very unfortunate argument with the Dhenra and she's been put in the Upper Cells of Roushenn for the week. They're harmless; cells for nobility. But I warn you if you pull heroics and break her out, she will be untrustworthy of the Crown. She *must* remain where she is. But she sends you a plea: she wants you to protect the Dhenra. Elyasin is in danger, or so Olea believes. And I am tempted to confirm it with some of the things I suspect."

"And who are you?" Elohl eyed the man, taking in the Guardsman's lean frame and sinewed, calloused hands.

"Fenton den'Kharel, First-Lieutenant of the Palace Guard. Your sister's right hand officer."

Elohl's brows raised as shock filled him. The name Fenton den'Kharel was legend among the High Brigade. Like Elohl, the man had never set a bad route, but unlike Elohl, he'd managed to keep his entire team alive his full ten years of service, then served another five for no reason at all. Ihbram den'Sennia had regaled Elohl with tales of Lead Hand den'Kharel, of daring ascents and skirmishes won, whom Ihbram had had the pleasure of serving under for five years. But the infamous Lead Hand had left for warmer climes just prior to the Summons and war breaking out upon the Valenghian border – and Elohl had never met the legend Ihbram had often spoken of.

"Fenton den'Kharel? Veteran High Brigade?" Elohl raised an eyebrow. "I heard you served fifteen years and never once lost a man on your team."

"You heard right." Fenton's gold-dark eyes glimmered as a small smile lifted his lips, though serenity still flowed through his every sinew. "Olea said her twin was a Brigadier. It's nice to meet another one come home."

"Likewise." Impressed, Elohl gave a lazy Brigadier salute. The Lieutenant returned it just as lazily, and as Elohl grinned the grin was returned. Setting his hands casually to his hips, Fenton cocked his head, scuffing one boot on the floorboards of the hallway.

"Who did you hear from about me, may I ask?"

"Ihbram den'Sennia."

"Ihbram." And to Elohl's surprise, the man before him gave a good-natured chuckle, shaking his head with a grin. "We'd better get going. Olea's expecting us. Shall we?"

Elohl found he was at ease now that he knew whom Olea had for her good right hand. He checked his gear, then looked to Eleshen, still sleeping in the early morning hours. But he couldn't just leave her wondering where he'd gone, so he turned back to Fenton. "Give me a minute?"

Fenton's gaze strayed within, then acutely away. "Of course. I'll wait here in the hall."

With a nod, Elohl shut the door. Eleshen was awake upon the bed, watching him as he turned back. Her face was sad as she sat up, tucking the covers up over her breasts. "Only a few days into Lintesh, and you're already in the serpent's maw."

"Were you awake?"

"I was. Eavesdropping. I heard the whole thing. I'm so sorry, Elohl... I didn't know you'd be thrust right back into danger coming here." As she brushed her long honey-blonde hair over one shoulder, the gesture tore at Elohl's heart, reminding him of Ghrenna. Sliding onto the bed, he wrapped an arm around Eleshen and she snuggled close, laying her head upon his shoulder. He felt guilty holding her when his mind kept straying to Ghrenna. His gut twisted, demanding that he tell her everything, but Elohl pushed it away. Let it wait a day, or a few. Holding Eleshen close, breathing in her lavender and spice scent, he pressed his lips to her temple.

"No place is safe for me, Eleshen." Elohl breathed. "I didn't imagine Lintesh was going to be any different. But as a Kingsman, my sworn liege needs me now. And Olea needs me. I have to go."

Eleshen nodded, taking it all in stride. "Did you get into the Abbey tonight?"

"I ran into a complication." Elohl shook his head.

"Complication?"

"A group of thieves." Elohl decided to tell the truth, as much of it as he could stand right now. "One was a Kingsman. She was scouting the wall and we had a run-in. She got hurt before I recognized her. She's one of those I told you about, from my past. Ghrenna."

"The one with visions?" Eleshen blinked wide.

"Eleshen..." Elohl murmured as his gut twisted again, telling him he was a bastard. "I have to go to the palace, but can you take a message to Ghrenna, today? She's staying at the Proud Marlin in the Abbey Quarter."

"Of course!" Eleshen spoke, eager to be helpful – and blissfully unaware of Elohl and Ghrenna's history, or what had happened tonight.

"Tell Ghrenna the Dhenra needs her to earn her Inkings, if she's well enough. Tell her to come to the West Guardhouse and ask for Fenton den'Kharel, First-Lieutenant Guardsman, and to not leave until she speaks with him. And tell her... I will find a way to get in touch after all these years."

Elohl died inside, saying all this to Eleshen for her to relay. It was horrible – he was worse than a lout, but the message had to be sent by someone he trusted. Elohl couldn't give her a proper embrace as he departed, with so many wrenching emotions boiling inside him. All he could do was snug her close around the shoulders and press another kiss to her temple. "Be safe. I'll be back soon, I promise. If you need anything while I'm gone today, go to Vargen's."

"How long will you be gone?" She murmured, twisting and looking up at him so he had to face those lovely green eyes.

"Hopefully not long."

Eleshen nodded, taking it in stride. Lifting up, she pressed her lips to his in a tender kiss, her warm goodness and dedication flooding him. It was more than he deserved. Elohl pressed his forehead to hers, feeling her love for a moment; letting it soothe him. And then he rose, leaving her behind and heading for the door.

Elohl didn't look back as he left; it was too painful. Shutting the door with a sinking feeling in his chest, he turned down the hallway with Fenton den'Kharel. Together, they tromped down the wooden stairs and through the common room, the inn waking with sounds of banging pots as the innkeeper and his wife prepared for the day in the kitchen. The fireplaces had been lit and already the common area smelled of baking bread, cinnamon, and rosemary – all the good smells of hearth and home that were Eleshen's.

Elohl pushed the thought away as he and Fenton tromped out the inn's weathered door. Today he had been called to duty, his reprieve of dreaming about a simple life ended. Pulled by Ghrenna's gaze into an inescapable reminder of what he was, he'd been tossed into the mystery of his golden Inkings, and now had been roped right back into service to royalty.

But it was a service Elohl wouldn't run from. He was a Kingsman. Even though he told himself he did it for Olea, because it was her request for him to help protect the young Dhenra, Elohl knew better. He'd never earned his Inkings; never stood strong for any King. And now, a young soon-to-be-Queen whose House his people had sworn allegiance to for generations was in trouble, and Elohl was in a position to do something about it. Dhenra Elyasin wasn't her father.

And if the things Olea had said were true – she was family.

As they moved up the cobbled avenue at a good clip, golden sunlight started to slant through the buildings, a cool morning breeze lifting the dust on the cobbles. Glancing over, Fenton must have picked up on Elohl's dire mood because he frowned, before opening his mouth to speak.

"So. Ihbram was blabbing about me?" Fenton gave Elohl a sidelong glance as he moved up the avenue, one hand on the hilt of his longsword. "I suppose that redheaded half-Elsthemi miscreant is still alive?"

"He was when I left." Distracted, Elohl looked over, his spirits beginning to lift with Fenton's easy camaraderie and the early bustle of the streets. "He was headed to Valenghia. Served fifteen years, just like you."

"Did he?" Something like pride shone from Fenton. "Good lad."

"Lad?" Elohl blinked, taking in Fenton's appearance. "He's got more grey in his hair than you do."

"I was his superior officer." Fenton shrugged easily. "They will always be my lads. Ihbram was under my care, same as the rest of my team. And so I gather, under yours?"

"I was a Lead Hand almost from the first," Elohl nodded. "Nine years. Once Captain Arlus den'Pell saw me climb and fight – he made sure of it."

"Kingsmen do know how to fight." Fenton glanced over with an almost approving smile on his lips, though Elohl saw questions in his gold-brown eyes. "How did you manage to keep your Greys all these years? Olea hasn't got hers."

"I was arrested in them, and they were confiscated." Elohl spoke quietly. "I managed to slip into the armory at night to liberate them, then hide them in a root-hollow before they got burned. I was whipped for it, but eventually Arlus just let me wear the damn things whenever we engaged. Found out they instilled fear when we skirmished with the Red Valor, especially during night raids. But most of the time he still made me wear military-issue browns. When I finished my service, I had both."

"Well," Fenton chuckled good-naturedly. "You'll get a change of gear when we get to the palace. You're going on the Dhenra's guard, so we have to get you a set of the blue, though I will put your Greys someplace safe for the duration. You're lucky, keeping your Alrashemni gear. Olea had to burn hers the first week she was in the guard, at the King's insistence. I can't imagine what that must have felt like."

Fenton's mention of Olea brought Elohl back to the moment as they chose a shortcut through a narrow alley, Fenton moving with lithe grace around barrels of rain and garbage. "So what do we do about Olea?"

"Unless you want to be a fool, nothing." The Guardsman's eyes went hard as he ducked a waterspout on a low roofline. "I've got a man watching her cell, discreetly. He'll keep her safe. But the Dhenra is another matter. They're only two men I trust on her guard besides Olea, and one is myself. Do you know any other Kingsmen in the city? How many can we summon to aid the Dhenra?"

The question caused Elohl to blink, unused to having someone trust him because of his Inkings. "Only two, other than myself and Olea. There's a Kingsman hiding as a silversmith in the lower city."

"Vargen den'Khalderian." Fenton's speech was prompt. "I just met him. Olea sent me to him also. He's already at the palace getting outfitted to act as a new guard. Who's the third Kingsman in the city?"

"Her name's Ghrenna," Elohl continued. "But she's not well; she may be out for this. Do you know any Kingsmen? You talk like there are more here in the city."

Fenton glanced around, making sure they were the only people in their stretch of narrow street before responding. "I know five Alrashemni hiding in Lintesh, including myself. But only myself and one other can assist us with the Dhenra. The others have duties elsewhere."

"*What?*" Elohl stopped dead in the middle of the street, his eyes flicking to Fenton's immaculately buckled cobalt jerkin. Moving close, he murmured low so no one could hear. "You're a Kingsman? But wouldn't Olea have told me?"

"She didn't know." Fenton's chuckle was wry as he motioned them to continue up the narrow avenue as if nothing had happened. Striding on, Fenton walked close, speaking low. "I told Olea last night, just as I'm telling you now – nor was she aware of my associate's identity until last night. She still doesn't know any of the others, and it will remain thus. It's not my place to disclose the Shemout Alrashemni who are not part of the Palace Guard. But I have a feeling all of us who are left will be coming out of the woodwork soon. We need solidarity, if we suspect an attack on the Dhenra's life."

"The Shemout... what? But hasn't Olea seen your Inkings?" Elohl countered, confused.

"I don't have the traditional Inkings, Elohl." Fenton spoke as he sidled close. "I'm of an Alrashemni sect that is not supposed to exist, the Shemout Alrashemni. We're a special sect of Alrashemni political spies who have operated discreetly for generations. We're not out in the open, so we didn't attend the

Summons. Thus, we survived when it happened. I couldn't tell Olea what I was. But things are changing. She, you, and our Dhenra need me to make myself known. So I'm breaking my ancient oaths of secrecy to keep our liege safe. But this knowledge goes no further than you and I. Do you understand?"

Something in that direct admission of Fenton's held the power of decades, and Elohl spoke soberly in response. "I understand."

But reaching out suddenly, Fenton stopped Elohl with a hand to the jerkin. Eyeing Elohl, a number of complex emotions moved through the man's gaze as they paused in the avenue. Elohl thought he saw Fenton's eyes flash red for a moment, but it was just a trick of the morning light reflecting from the water of a nearby fountain as the First-Lieutenant Guardsman regarded him.

"I must know..." Fenton spoke suddenly. "Are you still a Kingsman, Elohl, through and through? Despite all that's happened these past ten years?"

Elohl knew what he was really asking – if he would be loyal to a Dhenra whose father had had his people slain, supposedly.

"My father told me once," Elohl answered quietly, "that the primary Alrashemni law to remember when mediating and passing judgment is that the transgressions of the father shall not be passed to his children. Elyasin is not her father. And her father may not have been the traitor I thought he was... these past ten years."

"Wise words. Words to live by." Some old sadness lingered in Fenton's gold-tinged eyes, his eyebrows knit, his gaze faraway before he blinked, his reverie disappearing. "In any case, the Dhenra will get as much protection as we can muster for her, and I'm glad to hear your position on the matter."

"Olea is a Kingsman, sworn to the Crown. I am no less." Elohl agreed quietly. "A sword through my chest before the Dhenra is harmed. I swear it."

"Very well." Fenton nodded as if satisfied, something conflicted seeming to clear within him. "Pick up your steps, Brigadier. This may be a very long few days until the coronation."

"If it means clearing Olea's name and protecting my liege, I'll do anything I have to." Elohl nodded.

Cocking his head again, a small smile lingered about Fenton's lips. "Let's hope those words aren't tested." Moving on up the avenue at a brisk pace, his lithe yet somehow furiously energized boot-falls reminded Elohl of a keshar-cat's roaring grace.

28

GHRENNA

Ghrenna's head had finally ceased throbbing after breakfast. Luc had insisted she eat, so she had taken a bit of oat porridge with honey from a tray the inn's goodwife had brought up. The goodwife had been all bustle, trying to shove more pillows behind Ghrenna so she could eat sitting up. Ghrenna hated the attention, but her body felt weak as a three-day-old kitten. Luc had pushed the goodwife from the room, and now the porridge bowl was empty upon the tray across Ghrenna's legs. As she tried to lift the heavy tray by its iron handles to set it aside, she found her arms shaking from the strain.

Luc was there quickly, whisking it away without a single teasing comment. In fact, he hadn't said much this morning, only really opened his mouth to tell Shara and Gherris to get out scouting manses. But now he sat at the edge of the bed, reaching up to stroke the nape of Ghrenna's neck, and though it was tender, she noted the possessiveness in it since her encounter with Elohl last night.

A jealousy both men had shared.

"How is your head?" Luc's green eyes were all concern as his fingers stroked her neck. Ghrenna could feel traces of his gift soothing her, but it was sluggish. And though Luc was attentive this morning, his eyelids were drooping.

"Better," Ghrenna admitted. "You were right, food helped. But you should rest, Luc."

"No." He shook his head, blinking hard as if to clear his fatigue. "You're not healed yet."

"Luc, you're exhausted." Ghrenna protested quietly. "Healing me is taking it out of you. If you continue, it'll put both of us out of commission. The team can't have that."

"You shouldn't have kissed him." Luc's glower was sullen suddenly, and Ghrenna felt a flush spread across her cheeks. Here it was, despite all the years she had tried to avoid this very conversation. Now Luc knew the truth – and had seen perhaps more than a man could bear.

Looking down, Ghrenna stared at her hands. "I know."

He was silent a long while, his golden brows knit before he spoke again. "Did you see anything? When you spasmed?"

"Yes and no." Ghrenna spoke, trying to recall the visions she'd had when she and Elohl kissed. Most of it was muddled, but there were flashes that almost made sense. "I saw byrunstone halls lined with torches. There were armed men rushing through the halls; some wore the blue of the Palace Guard so I assume it was Roushenn, though I can't be sure. I saw a high-gabled room filled with nobles in silk and gems; a ceremony of some sort. A regally-dressed woman with red-gold hair grabbed her stomach, and then there was chaos. People panicking, fleeing..."

"It could have been the Dhenra at her coronation." Luc's face was grim as he digested the news.

"She had the right color hair, and I thought of the Dhenra as well. But the ceremony? The hall was hardly large enough to be her coronation." Ghrenna leaned back against the headboard, tired. She hadn't even risen today, except one shaky trip to the privy that Shara had helped with. And though her vision was muddled and vague, every part of this seeing had been seared with the blood-iron taste of truth to it – the taste of death.

"There was more," Ghrenna continued softly, recalling the images. "I saw a woman with all-white eyes standing by an Alranstone with a half-lidded, bloody eye. She gestured to me. And I saw two tall wildmen, Inked in different colors, so tall they seemed like Alranstones..."

"Alranstones?" Luc blinked, then frowned at her.

"Anyway, we don't even know who I saw in my visions. Or what event." Ghrenna shook her head, returning to the moment.

"So will you run off now, to go be a Kingsman and save the day?" Luc set his jaw, his tone scathing.

"I don't know, Luc." Exhausted, Ghrenna closed her eyes, knowing what he really meant and not able to face it yet. "Once I was a young woman with a righteous fire, burning for the Kingsmen who saved me. I had training to ease my anger and help me process the pain and fear of my visions. But when it all was ripped away, when my mind was broken and I was hauled off to the Fleetrunners for ten years... I don't know. I don't feel any honor for the Crown anymore. I just try to get by."

"Do I help you get by?" The vulnerability in Luc's voice was heartbreaking.

"Of course." Ghrenna opened her eyes to look at him. "You and Shara and Gherris."

"Am I no better to you than Shara and Gherris?" His half-smile was bitter.

"You know that's not true. I might be dead right now if it wasn't for you."

He shrugged, debonair and mocking and vulnerable all at once as his fingers stroked her neck, his healing touch gone. "Do you love him?"

Ghrenna's gaze snapped up at the question. It was unlike Luc to get right to the point. He used to mope dramatically over women, moaning about this beautiful lady who had spurned him, and that creature of darkness that had denied him. But Ghrenna had never seen him like this. He was bold and angry now, direct, and there was a suffering in his gaze that for all the women he'd bedded and lost, none had caused him dismay like this. Because of all those women, he'd loved none of them. Except Ghrenna could see his love now, plain in the weariness that devoured him, in the defiant angle of his chin, and the utter vulnerability of those hard, cynical green eyes.

"I do love him," Ghrenna whispered. "I've always loved him."

It was a blade through Luc's heart. Ghrenna saw it thrust in, saw it twist – saw him flinch as his fingers spasmed at her neck. A veil dropped over his eyes. One moment he was Luc and the next a dramatic hauteur settled in to cover his pain. A wry twist graced his mouth, and just like that, the real Luc was gone, replaced by a sham. Rising with a dramatic sigh, he went to the window, throwing it wide and letting in the late morning heat.

"The lovely lady of the twin lakes takes my heart," he jested, "and wears it upon a chain around her neck."

"Luc, please..." Ghrenna pleaded. He didn't turn to look at her. Slouching by the window, he crossed his arms, staring out over the street.

Staring out towards the bluestone palace in the distance.

A knock came at the door suddenly. Luc noted it with a glance, but didn't turn from the window. With a sigh, Ghrenna struggled to swing her legs out of bed. There was nothing she could do for Luc, but at least she could get the door. She had just managed getting to the edge of the bed, when Luc scoffed and strode to the door, a knife tucked up behind his forearm. Swinging the door wide, he revealed a pretty petite woman with a long honey-blonde braid, who startled at Luc's quick motion.

She caught her breath, gazing up at him with big green eyes.

Adopting a lazy slouch against the doorframe, Luc grinned at the pretty creature before him. He posed in just such a way that it showed off his fit abdomen beneath his leathers, and Ghrenna saw the woman's eyelashes flicker as she noted everything there was to note about the handsome rogue. Sweeping into the courtly bow that made ladies at wealthy parties faint, Luc was absolutely lecherous, catching up one of the woman's slender hands and pressing it with a lingering kiss.

"My, my! A pretty maid comes to my door with sorrow in her eyes! How can I banish that sorrow for you, good lady?"

The blonde was overcome for a moment, before she snatched away her hand – though a pleased little smile curled her lips at the attention. "That will be *quite* enough of that! I'm looking for a woman named Ghrenna? The goodwife of the inn said she could be found in this room. I bear an urgent message from Elohl den'Alrahel."

Stepping back from the doorway, Luc gestured her in. He was on the hunt now to ease his pain, every movement honed to perfection. Proceeding in, the pretty blonde sidled around him, her attention fixed upon Ghrenna while Luc shut the door, slipping his knife out of sight in a quick gesture the woman completely missed. The blonde's jade eyes flickered over Ghrenna, taking her in before she turned, looking at Luc – who was still slouching against the door with his arms crossed sexily over his chest. He gave his most smoldering smile before the woman faced Ghrenna once more.

"You're Ghrenna?" The blonde spoke briskly. "Elohl said you weren't well, and I can see why. You look terrible!"

"You have a message from Elohl?" Sitting up on the edge of the bed, Ghrenna tried to adopt a more commanding pose, though it took effort. Still clad only in her silk undershirt and breeches of her Greys from the night before, her limbs trembled as she tried to appear businesslike.

"May we speak privately?" The woman countered as she fiddled with her long braid, her gaze flicking to Luc.

"Whatever you have to say may be said in front of my associate."

"Well, in that case." The woman fiddled with her long honey-blonde braid again. "Elohl says to tell you the Dhenra needs you to earn your Inkings, if you're well enough. You must go to the West Guardhouse and ask for Fenton den'Kharel, First-Lieutenant Guardsman, and to not take no for an answer. And he also says..." The woman balked as a flicker of jealousy flared through her, along with a fierce temper. "He says he will find a way to get in touch after all these years."

"Get in *touch*." Ghrenna heard Luc's snort from the doorway. "Brilliant. Subtle."

"And who are you?" Ghrenna asked the woman, as she tried to not let her fatigue show with Luc's ire.

"My name is Eleshen den'Fhenrir." The blonde quipped smartly. "I'm Elohl's traveling companion."

"Traveling companion?" Luc rose from his slouch at the door, stepping into the conversation with heat for the lady Eleshen. "If you traveled with me, I'd treat you better. I'd call you my Queen of dreams and take your burdens both day and night."

His courting backfired on Eleshen, who rounded upon him with vinegar on her tongue. "And I would slap that language from you until you couldn't stand straight! I know a rogue when I see one!"

"Slap me, lovely," Luc murmured as he slid forward a pace, seductive, using his height and golden good looks to his advantage. "Slap me until I can't stand, and I will kneel at your feet. My blood pounds in your hands..."

"Oh, for Aeon's sake," Ghrenna bit as Eleshen gaped at Luc, blushing and flustered. "Luc! Leave off!"

"*You* can't tell me what to do." Rounding on Ghrenna with a hard snarl to his voice, Luc stared Ghrenna down. He was trying to make her jealous, flaunting everything they'd shared right in her face. And though she'd done the same thing to him last night, it didn't make it any better. Her gut twisted, as tension lanced her temples, agonizing. Eleshen moved back a pace as she glanced quickly from one to the other, feeling the tension in the room.

"I can see I've come at a bad time. Do you have a return message for Elohl?"

"Wait." Ghrenna raised a hand, forestalling her departure. "What does he need me to do? Who is this Fenton den'Kharel?"

Eleshen seemed on the edge of bundling herself up and leaving, but something like pity settled in her eyes. "I overheard a conversation Elohl had with this Fenton fellow early this morning. The Dhenra is in danger, or so Elohl's sister Olea says. Olea's been imprisoned, and asked her First-Lieutenant Fenton den'Kharel to protect the Dhenra in her stead. They're arranging Elohl to be smuggled into the palace as a guard, to protect the Dhenra. I think Elohl needs your help."

Ghrenna started to stand as an unconscious impulse to go to Elohl flooded her. She got halfway up from the bed, then felt blood wash from her head as her vision tunneled. Tipping, she sprawled onto the bedside table and Luc was there instantly – scooping her up and settling her back to the bed. Taking slow, deep breaths, Ghrenna willed her consciousness back from the brink as her vision gradually returned. But her body was even more shaky than before, and she felt suddenly like she might be sick as pounding intensified in her temples.

"You're *really* not well." Eleshen spoke as she moved forward, a worried expression on her face.

"I'm fine. I've got to get to the palace, and tell Elohl about my vision. If it's the Dhenra I saw..." Ghrenna gasped though her pain, feeling the pounding spreading around the sides of her head. Soon it would form a band, and once it did, her head would be trapped in a vise-grip of suffering.

"No, you're not fine." Eleshen spoke sadly, her gaze sympathetic now. "I've seen killing-fevers less severe than this."

"You can't even stand, Ghren. There's no way you're going to the palace, much less fighting like this." Luc's voice was sad at her side, echoing Eleshen's as he smoothed Ghrenna's blonde waves out of her face. As she leaned forward, the room spinning drastically, he held her hair back. "Do you need a basin?"

Ghrenna nodded quickly. Vomit was rising no matter how she choked it down.

"I'll get it." Eleshen hustled away, nearly tripping over her own feet. The basin appeared between Ghrenna's feet not a moment too soon. Luc held her steady as she retched, keeping her hair back as Eleshen dipped a washcloth into a water pitcher, sliding it behind Ghrenna's neck. Ghrenna vomited again and then a third time, the world tilting, her vision fading. Finally, there was no more porridge to bring back up and she spit, her head a dance of misery, whirling and pounding. Clearing her nose, she wiped it with the cloth.

Which came away red with blood – a lot of blood.

"Oh, dear." Eleshen's voice was all motherly concern. "Here now, let me hold that. It should stop in a moment. Probably just the pressure from vomiting."

Ghrenna was reeling. She didn't even know she had keened until she felt Luc's arms wind around her, cradling her like a child. "Shh, Ghren... here, lean back on me."

She did, her head a maddening fury now, one of her worst. Luc absorbed her weight as he wound his hands through her hair. Where he touched, an ocean of sweet release seeped in. But those kind fingers were daggers to Ghrenna's heart, as her chest became cavernous with sorrow. Suddenly, she broke into sobs, wracking and awful – that it wasn't Elohl who was holding her now, that she was so terribly weak.

That Luc was being so kind.

Steady and gentle, Luc worked his fingers across her skull as exhaustion swept Ghrenna. Her sobs finished, her eyelids settled closed as a few snippets of conversation came to her before she fell asleep.

"Aeon... what's wrong with her?" Eleshen murmured quietly.

"She loves a man she cannot touch." Luc's voice was sad now, all trace of flirtation gone. "And doesn't want the man she can."

* * *

Ghrenna came awake listening to muted conversation in the adjacent room. Tucked back in bed, she saw the now-washed basin and a pitcher of water upon the bedside table. It wasn't much later, the sun high beyond the window and the room muggy, though Ghrenna shivered with a chill. Conversation in the next room rose from a murmur to a sharp lash, as Luc's voice became hot in anger. Another voice took charge, low and growling but young – Gherris.

At last, the door was flung open and Gherris stormed through, sliding knives into his leather harness. "I don't care what we're up against, Luc! If Elohl needs help, we're going. Protecting the Dhenra was supposed to be my birthright, and I will stand by that if he is at our lead! You're the one who hates that I kill – let me use it for once. If Elohl is a good enough climber to surprise Ghrenna on the wall, he's good enough to take lead for us."

"I'm not going to the palace!" Luc growled, severe. "There are guards all over that place."

"We'll *be* the guards, if I'm not mistaken." Gherris give Luc a withering stare.

"That seems to be what this Fenton fellow has planned." Eleshen was fast on Luc's heels as she followed from the other room.

"I'll be singled out if I show up at the palace as a fighter," Shara followed, her eyebrows knit. "There can't be that many Guardswomen at Roushenn. Do you think this Fenton fellow could get me disguised as a noble instead?"

"I really don't know *what* he can do," Eleshen shrugged. "But Elohl seemed to trust him right off, which is something."

"That's it. I'm in." Gherris threw his knife point-down into the floorboards. "Shara?"

"In." She nodded, pulling a knife and throwing it down also. "Luc?"

"I'm going to regret this." Luc huffed grandiosely, as he threw his knife down also. "If *anyone* at the palace recognizes me, I swear I will cut my way out."

"Done." Gherris collected his knife. "Browns and tans everyone, blacks underneath. We're going to scout the guardhouse and ask around for this Fenton fellow."

"I need to go with you..." Ghrenna spoke weakly as she tried to struggle up to a seat. Her headache was a dull throb, but the weakness was crushing as she barely managed to pull herself to sitting. When she looked up, everyone was watching her.

"You stay put." Luc's command was non-negotiable. "I'll tell Elohl what you saw in your vision."

"I'll stay with her." Eleshen crossed her arms with determination as she stared Ghrenna down. "I've got no business at Roushenn. You all know what Elohl looks like?"

"We do." Shara intoned as the thieves all nodded, moving about the room and gathering their scouting clothes in dun colors to put on over their blacks. As Shara wriggled into a tan and blue dress, rolling up the sleeves of her blacks and unlacing the shirt to tuck beneath the bodice, she asked, "But what does this Vargen fellow and Fenton look like?"

"Vargen you can't possibly miss," Eleshen fired like a weapons drill-master as her lips quirked in a smile. "Just look for the biggest man you've ever seen, blacksmith's build, with hair like Elohl's. He'll probably also be the most soft-spoken person in the room, but with a voice like boulders crashing downhill. Fenton is wiry, taller than me but shorter than Elohl. Brown hair and fairly lovely gold-brown eyes, with a resonant voice like a harper. You'd think him plain at first glance, but he's... stunning, somehow. I can't explain it."

"Got it." Shara threw a cloak on over her dress, hiding the lumps of her garb. "You boys ready?"

Luc and Gherris had tan flax clothing on that made them look like farmers, soft but homespun. Both outfits hid their gear nicely, and Gherris added a straw hat to hide his scowl. Both Luc and Gherris added knives beneath their wrist bracers and down into their black leather boots. Black boots didn't fit either man's outfit, but most people never looked at your feet.

"Ready." Gherris spoke, his dark grey eyes flashing beneath his hat.

"As I'll ever be, I suppose." Luc was dramatically put-upon as he glanced at Ghrenna, weighing her. "How's the head?"

"I'll manage. I had threllis long before you came around."

"Right, then." Luc flinched as if she had struck him. "We'll try to check in by nightfall."

"Just go." Ghrenna nodded, wishing she had said something kinder. "Find Elohl."

"We'll make the Kingsmen proud, Ghren." Gherris spoke, fierce as they moved out the door into the hall. Luc lingered, his hand on the door as the other two stalked off. Eleshen had bustled to the other room, and it left Luc and Ghrenna alone a moment.

"I'm sorry, Luc," Ghrenna murmured. It left so much unsaid between them, but it was honest, and it was all she had.

"Not as much as I am, Ghren." Luc's demeanor was bitter as he watched her. "But if this is what it takes to prove to you what kind of man I am, I'll do it. What does Elohl have that I don't? History? You can start rewriting your history anytime, Ghrenna. I did."

"I can't run from this, Luc." She spoke softly. "This connection with Elohl, these visions... they'll either kill me or I'll figure out what they're for. Either way, I need Elohl's help."

"But you need me, too." Luc's eyes were fervent now, determined.

"I never said I didn't." Ghrenna murmured, feeling split inside.

He paused at that, his golden eyebrows knitting. "But you'll never admit that you do."

Luc was out the door like smoke, shutting it soundly behind him. Ghrenna sat back against the pillows, feeling hollow. Unable to stop staring at the door, she wondered if Luc would come back, or Elohl. Perhaps they would both leave and she would be alone again; alone and unloved. Maybe they would tear each other apart because of her, leaving them all to die out in the snow. An image filled Ghrenna suddenly; a waking vision of two men upon their knees before her, stripped to the waist and bloody from fighting. In a cavern of ice, they knelt before her upon sigils that glowed with blue-white fire, then flamed orange and red.

And with her bared knife, Ghrenna felt herself slay them both.

Ghrenna jolted as her headache flared in agony. Eleshen had returned from the adjacent room and was peering at her concernedly, Ghrenna pale and sweating cold despite the stifling heat in their rooms. As Eleshen offered another washcloth, Ghrenna took it gratefully, laying it over her forehead. Resting back on the pillows, she tried to forget what she had just seen – the raw brutality of it.

"Are you all right?"

"I've had worse."

"Does this always happen when you have a vision?" Eleshen eyed her.

"I'm usually weak, and there's a headache," Ghrenna nodded, "but sometimes I seize. The nosebleed was new, though." She could still taste the iron tang of it in her mouth.

"The others say Elohl triggered your seizing, last night."

This time, it was Ghrenna who eyed Eleshen. "You're his woman, aren't you?"

"I'm not his *woman*." She sniffed in irritation. "I'm not a cow. We're simply traveling together."

"Could have fooled me." Ghrenna lifted an eyebrow, got a spike of pain, then relaxed back against the headboard. "You were taking my measure the moment Luc opened the door. And his charms usually work on women."

"I'm not the type to be charmed by rogues!" Eleshen spat, all hot vinegar and quicksilver now, her arms crossed. "Anyway, that Luc has eyes for only one woman, and you're a damn fool if you don't see it! He's wrapped around your little toe, Seer, and you're squashing his love like a cockroach!"

"You're feisty." Ghrenna blinked, moving the cold washcloth to the back of her neck. "You would have made a good Kingsman. You've the gall for it. And a sharp mind."

"What? I..." Eleshen's lips dropped open and she looked flustered a moment, fiddling with her long blonde braid. Her cheeks flushed, lovely in an innocent kind of way Ghrenna would never have. "I wanted to be a Kingsman when I was younger. Elohl's father saved me, you know, from a burning building. I would have died were it not for him. Ever since then, I used to dream about it. Heroic fancies and all that."

"Where are you from?"

"Quelsis. My father Eiric den'Fhenrir was Dhepan of Quelsis. He always called the Kingsmen in when there was trouble. Our family was declared treasonous for trying to put pressure on the Crown after the Summons. I've been keeping an inn in the mountains ever since. I never got to live those childish dreams."

"Neither did I." Ghrenna murmured, feeling lost as a deep silence stretched between them.

"I owe you an apology." Eleshen spoke suddenly, blushing. "I was... possessive of Elohl. I never thought how all your lives must have been after that horrible Summons. Something rides him, Ghrenna. Something hard and brutal. He's been lighter since the seven-eye Stone, but – sometimes I still feel that darkness in him."

"Elohl wasn't always troubled." Ghrenna swallowed at the woman's kindness, stilling tears. "He always demanded much of himself, but he used to be lighthearted. It's good that he has you now. He needs someone... bright. Happy."

"Isn't there anything I can do for you?" Eleshen was all kindness now as she reached out to take Ghrenna's hand.

"There's a tin in my pack, there on the nightstand," Ghrenna nodded. "Will you bring it? And a glass pipe in the leather pouch on my harness, on the chair. Light it please, set it here by bed."

Eleshen did, and as Ghrenna settled back down into the covers, she quipped with a hopeful smile, "Was your vision something happy, at least, to compensate for all this pain?"

"You have so much hope." Ghrenna smiled a little, the threllis wafting through the air swaddling her in a blanket of fog now and taking the edge off her pain. "No. My visions are mostly dire tidings. I used to think that was why I get so much pain when I have them. Because the visions are nothing I want to see. And I fight them..."

"That's awful." Eleshen had taken Ghrenna's hand like a sister, her eyes full of sorrow. "What did you see this time?"

"Nothing I can ever unsee." Ghrenna's gaze went long, staring past Eleshen towards the door. "Nothing I can ever unburden myself from."

"Sometimes talking about these things helps," Eleshen murmured.

Ghrenna glanced at her. Eleshen's pretty heart-shaped face was tight with concern, and Ghrenna saw again why Elohl kept her close. The little woman was filled with an empathy that Ghrenna could practically feel, as if her heart was as wide as the sky. Drawing a deep breath of threllis-smoke, Ghrenna sighed, relaxing as she stared up at the ceiling now. "My visions are often indistinct, but sometimes I feel them, like I'm the one being hurt. This time I saw a woman, experienced it, *felt* her pain as she was stabbed..."

Ghrenna found herself opening up to Elohl's bright-eyed confidante, telling everything of the event she had witnessed, and of the white-eyed woman beckoning from the Alranstone with the bloody half-lidded oculus. It felt good to unburden herself for once, telling all the pain of the vision, every horrible agony. Telling someone how Ghrenna had felt herself dying as the woman had been stabbed in the ceremony felt her own body screaming from the wound. That she'd been witness in the vision, and also *inside* the woman's body, all at the same time.

Eleshen listened to it all, taking in every awful detail. And when Ghrenna was done, she lifted a hand, smoothing Ghrenna's sweat-streaked waves from her forehead with the kindness of a mother. "I'm glad you told me. No one should have to bear such things alone."

Something about her simple kindness broke Ghrenna, and tingling pricked her eyes.

"I think I need to sleep a while," Ghrenna murmured.

"I'll leave the pitcher of water." Eleshen eyed Ghrenna, her brows pinched in concern. Then she seemed to change her mind, wrinkling her nose at the threllis. "Do you mind if I take a walk, actually?"

"Sure." Ghrenna nodded. "The pipe will be out in half an hour, and I should be asleep by then. I usually sleep three to four hours. Do what you need to."

"Perfect. I'll inform the goodwife to check in on you if I'm not back soon."

Rising to her feet regally, Eleshen nearly spoiled it by tripping over herself as she turned for the door. Ghrenna nodded, but her mind was already clouding into sleep as she heard the latch click.

29

DHERRAN

The Vicoute Arlen den'Selthir's butler escorted Dherran and Khenria up a grand staircase of white marble, then down a long hall on the second floor of the manor. Decorated with suits of ancient armor, hunting horns, lances, and steel shields, the hall was a wonder of military treasures, a fine cobalt silk carpet with gilded runners whispering beneath Dherran's boots. There were more than thirty doors along the hall, and finally stopping at one of the last ones, the butler opened it, gesturing them in. The suite Dherran entered was opulent, and he couldn't help but stare. Richly carved white oak furniture was everywhere, cobalt silk carpets with the crest of a lance and bitter-holly sprigs swathed the well-polished floorboards. Wandering through the massive apartment with her mouth agog, Khenria opened a side-door to find they had separate but adjoining bedrooms.

As the butler bowed his way out, closing the white oak door behind himself, Dherran turned to Khenria, so completely befuddled at their welcome that he had forgotten his rage. "What the hell is going on?"

"I guess we're supposed to get cleaned up." Khenria had moved to an elegant copper tub in one corner of the room, gliding her fingers over its well-polished gloss. Fiddling with some brass knobs on the wall, she suddenly had the tub sluiced with steaming water from a spout and Dherran moved over, marveling at it.

"Look Dherran!" Khenria gasped. "Hot and cold water brought directly to the tub!"

"I've heard such piping existed in lord's homes and in Roushenn Palace, but I've never experienced it." Dherran murmured, touching the knobs, fascinated.

"Well, I'm taking advantage of it." Already disrobing, Khenria was naked in a trice, her round ass and narrow hips enticing as she climbed in. Dherran tried to ignore her; tried to remind himself he was pissed at her today. But she was magnificently distracting as she washed. How she moved, how she cocked her head curious as a raven as she smelled the soaps upon the silver tray near the bath, trying them all upon her skin. Brushing with a boar-bristle scrubber on a long wooden handle, Khenria's movements were completely distracting, and Dherran's eyes strayed to her shoulders above the rim of the tub, lean but hard with muscle. She still had bruises from her fights earlier, and sitting upon the bed, Dherran found himself staring at those reminders of her ferocity; wanting every curve and angle of her. He was about to stride to the bath and haul her out, when she spoke suddenly.

"Are you worried about Grump, Dherran?"

It took him aback, cooling his ardor somewhat. And suddenly, he realized he was worried about what had happened to Grump – why he'd not been in the tent after the fight. "Yeah. I am. Are you?"

"Not really." She murmured, brushing with the scrubber.

"Why not?" Waiting while Khenria lounged in the bath was driving him insane, but he tried to focus upon the conversation, distracting himself by wandering around the suite and examining the finer details of the decor and carved furniture.

"He's disappeared like this before." Khenria sighed, sluicing clean with water now. "Once for a whole week. Another time, he hid me in a cave for five days, without telling me what he was doing. He generally leaves after he gets quiet for a few days. Although, I thought he was just quiet this time because of what I said at the inn today. I did apologize."

"Did he take it well?" Dherran frowned, glancing at her from where he idled by the unlit fireplace.

"He seemed to." With that, she rose from the bath, water cascading from every luscious curve. Reaching out to claim a thick cotton towel from a gilded stand and tuck it about her, Khenria looked back over her shoulder, meeting his gaze. She was aware of what she was doing to him and the fires in Dherran surged as he moved over to her, catching her in his arms.

"I want you." Dherran murmured, hot with passion.

"You're filthy. I'm clean." Khenria flushed as she touched his chest over his open shirt collar, her desire flaring also. "Wash first."

With a frustrated growl, Dherran stepped back. Stripping fast, he was in the tub lathering soap into his hands and scrubbing everything with haste. In two minutes he was back out, the costly oils in the water having soothed his lust not at all.

Striding to Khenria without toweling off, he wrangled her in his arms and they fell to the bed. As she landed upon the cobalt silk coverlet, her grey eyes challenging him, her towel gaped, baring a long swath of hip and making the last of Dherran's resistance break. He wanted her, now. She was such a bitch, and she was so beautiful, and he loved the way she'd strung him along, and he wanted to punish her for it. He wanted to rip that towel away and take those firm curves in his hands and suckle her little breasts until she cried out like a falcon for him.

Barely containing his lust, Dherran stroked his fingers down her hip, enjoying her shudder. "You are such a cruel mistress. Teasing me, holding a knife to my throat to try and get me to take you. You don't give me much choice about what I'm going to do to you."

"And what do you think you can do to me?" Her grey eyes were veiled now, hot with feral anticipation as Dherran growled in his throat. Grasping her wrists, he pinned her arms above her head, the towel coming undone as he leaned down, kissing her neck and pressing his hips to hers. Wrapping her long legs up around him, Khenria moaned as he slid himself, hard and ready, between her legs but not inside yet. Dipping his head, he took one nipple in his mouth, beginning to suck it slowly as Khenria writhed beneath him, so ready for this game.

"Aeon, Dherran!" She gasped, arching beneath him. "Gods don't stop...!"

She was so hot, so wet where he rubbed between her legs. But this wasn't about consummation, this was about punishment as Dherran suckled her breast harder and she mewled for him, bucking. He moved to the other breast, making her writhe, making her need him as he moved his hips just so, to slide over her but not slip in – not yet.

Suddenly, a knock rapped upon the door, as if a servant had been out in the hall waiting for just the right moment to cause violent frustration. Snapping like a bowstring, Dherran soured as he yelled, "*What, dammit?!*" at the door.

"Dinner in fifteen minutes, sirrah!" The servant called through the door. Footsteps moved off down the hall, and growling in frustration, Dherran repositioned himself over Khenria, taking her nipple back into his mouth.

"Dherran!" She squeaked, laughing now instead of writhing.

"What?" His growl was peeved as he moved to her ribs, still kissing her, determined.

"We've got to go to dinner!" Khenria laughed, squirreling out from underneath him and jumping off the bed, her lean hips and little breasts frustratingly gorgeous. "We've been summoned by a *lord*. You don't just keep a lord waiting while you fuck in his guest suites!"

"I can. And I will." Dherran made a swipe for her, his need aching like Halsos' hells now. Khenria laughed as she dodged his swipe, then darted in to fondle him.

"Keep it warm for me, Dherran."

"You bitch!" Dherran growled as he flopped back to the coverlet, gasping for breath. Breathing hard, he tried to push back the swamping tide of his arousal, but it wasn't working; she'd gotten him good. She laughed and Dherran glared though he smiled also, then lurched from the bed to where his clothes lay by the bathtub. Reaching for his trousers with an incredulous smile, he yanked them on so hard the fabric strained at his still-needful crotch.

"Don't you want to wear something nicer?" Khenria suddenly spoke from the gilded white oak wardrobe near the tub, where she pawed through fancy clothes bare-ass naked. "There are fresh shirts in here, and trousers, with a jerkin or two that might fit you. Their weave is so very fine..."

"I don't think so." Dherran started buckling his belt, not about to please the Vicoute by dressing in fancy garb for the evening.

"You can't go to supper at a Vicoute's manor dressed like you slept under the trees, Dherran!" She scowled back at him, her straight brows set in a stubborn line now.

"My own clothes will do, Khenria." Dherran insisted as he glanced at her, getting irritated now. "Leave it."

"Fine." She narrowed her eyes at him. "Be a filthy lout. But I'm getting dressed properly for dinner with a fine lord." Striding from the room naked, Khenria slammed the door between their rooms with a swift backhand. Dherran heard a bell pulled from her room, then the voices of two women, then laughter, then a buzz of chatter. Fully dressed now in his own clothes, he paced his room waiting, when another knock came at his door. Striding to it, Dherran threw it open – a dark-haired, fit servingman in an elegant leather jerkin recoiling as Dherran snarled in his face.

"*What?!*"

"If you please, sirrah." The servingman spoke, his face a cultured mask. Not the butler, this man had good-shouldered brawn and a trim waist like he spent most of his time upon the practice yards rather than in the house. His dark brown eyes showed disdain as he eyed Dherran's clothes like Dherran was a filthy urchin. "The lady has asked for dressing-maids. Would you appreciate some assistance with your wardrobe for dinner?"

"No. Get out." Dherran tried to shut the door in the man's face, but the servingman cheekily put his boot in the door as he stared Dherran down with an edge of iron in his demeanor now.

"You know, if I had the opportunity to dine at a Vicoute's table," the fellow spoke softly, "I would make full use of it. I hear Kingsmen are experts at negotiation. One does not negotiate an evening with a Vicoute dressed like a bandit. *Sirrah.*"

And despite his temper, Dherran knew the man was right. With a growl, he opened the door wide, gesturing angrily to the wardrobe. "What do you suggest?"

With only a slight smirk of victory, the man stepped inside, shutting the door. Pacing to the wardrobe, he threw it wide, then paused. Glancing at Dherran's frame, his eyes narrowed. And then he pulled out breeches, a shirt and jerkin, leather boots, and a belt, thrusting them all into Dherran's hands. "Wear these. At least you'll not look like a pauper."

Dherran was about to cuss him, but the disdain in the man's face suddenly made him feel ashamed. Dherran was uncultured and he knew it; a far cry from how he'd been raised. Something in him resolved to try harder as he buried his growling, shucking his clothes and stepping into the new ones without protest. The cream silk shirt was the softest thing he'd ever worn; the breeches nearly as soft, a tight fit in dark green lambswool that showed off his muscled thighs. The dark leather boots were creamy smooth, the belt tooled with a rushing river. His jerkin was doe-leather, dyed dark green like the trousers with a high collar. It was a crossover military cut, and suited his athletic frame like a second skin.

Dherran waved away a tray of men's jewelry, and the servingman backed off with an amused nod. Running a hand through his blond hair, Dherran glanced in the full-length mirror by the wardrobe – and didn't recognize himself. The man who stared back at him looked every inch the lord, tall and well-built, with hard green eyes and lines of temperance in the face of his youth.

Dherran looked like his father, he realized. With a hard sigh, he turned from the gilded mirror, gesturing to the door. The servingman led, and pacing down the long hall of armor and oddities, Dherran stewed, silent and brooding. Moving down the marble stairs, he was led through a parquet-floor ballroom, then a sitting parlor crowded with potted ferns. At last, they came through a set of gilded white oak doors into a massive dining hall flooded with light from an entire wall of windows. Early evening sun caught crystals in the chandeliers, throwing rainbows about the room.

Surging up from a chair at the white marble table, Khenria's face lit to see Dherran in his fine lord's garb. The silk of her gown shone a rich emerald in the evening light, pouring like water over her curves as white lace delved to her plunging décolletage. Lace fell from her sleeves, cascading towards the floor, and when she moved, a lace-covered slit parted in her gown, slashed scandalously high over one hip. An emerald pendant the size of Dherran's thumb nestled between her breasts, emeralds dripping from her earlobes also. Her lips rouged and eyelids lined, Khenria's short black curls had been expertly arranged, and she smoldered for him as talons sank deep into Dherran's heart – gaping at her like a fool.

"She looks just as beautiful within the fighting ring as without, does she not?" Vicoute Arlen den'Selthir had stood from his own seat at the table, motioning Dherran forward. Large enough for forty people, the banquet table was set for only three at one end, tall tapers lit against the oncoming night. "Come, join us! Your lovely student has just been telling me of your most unusual training tactics."

Wearing a jerkin of crimson silk with gilded embroidery, charcoal riding breeches, and well-fitted leather boots, the Vicoute was dressed in finer clothes than what he'd had on earlier in town. His iron-shot blond waves were oiled back artfully, his person smelling of sandalwood incense. Rings graced his fingers, costly with rubies and sapphires, and a sapphire set in gold pierced one ear. Like a royal rogue, Arlen den'Selthir had a hard yet sophisticated edge of a man who took what he wanted.

As his approving gaze flicked to Khenria, Dherran felt himself sear with jealousy.

"Has she?" Dherran sneered.

"Indeed." Den'Selthir motioned again for Dherran to take a seat. As he did, his host also sat. "Challenges of surprise combat, even while the other is fast asleep. Interesting."

Dherran growled as a servingman stepped forward to fill his wine goblet. Primping at the table, Khenria leaned forward, batting her dark eyelashes at the Vicoute, who was now engaging her in banter that Dherran couldn't hear through the jealousy that hummed his veins. They laughed and Dherran glowered, taking a generous swig of his wine and missing the conversation entirely.

"Dherran?" Khenria was looking at him oddly.

"What?" He blinked.

"The Vicoute just asked if you would show him a few fighting moves after supper."

"I have an indoor training arena beneath the manor." The Vicoute supplied as he swirled his wine, watching Dherran. "I would be honored to have you show me a few famous Kingsmen moves later, if you're up for it."

"If you want to get hit, sure." Dherran swigged his wine, his tongue acerbic.

"You are a man of very little tact, Kingsman." The Vicoute leaned forward, swirling his goblet, his pale blue eyes suddenly sharp as a cold fire moved in him. He did not even glance down as an opulent plate of ghennie-fowl in a cranberry sauce was placed before him. "Tell me, how did one such as you escape a lynching all these years? Flaunting your Blackmarks at every bout, inciting riots. I'm sure today has not been the first occasion your hide was almost skinned, nor may it be your last."

"I can be persuasive when I need to be." Dherran swigged his wine, to show his lack of care about tact.

"With fists, perhaps." Den'Selthir chuckled, swirling his wine, though his arctic blue gaze still pierced Dherran like a lance. "But is it enough? How many times have you had to run for your life?"

Dherran was about to answer with an epithet, but Khenria answered for him. "Eight times in two years."

"Eight times? You are a survivor, it seems." Den'Selthir's eyebrows lifted, his gaze acutely disapproving. "With the harvest-time Kingsman Burnings, I'm surprised you've survived this long."

"They don't actually burn Kingsmen at harvest fest," Dherran dismissed.

"But how long before they get the idea to have an *actual* Kingsman Burning?" Den'Selthir leaned forward, his eyes hard now, intense. "How many times do you have to piss off a public before it's *your* body they truss to the burning-pole and not a stuffy-guy? When it's not a burlap sack of straw dressed all in black, but a living flesh-and-blood man they want to watch burn? Or a woman?"

His gaze flicked to Khenria, and that was all Dherran needed. This Vicoute was no friend to them, no matter his fine ways and opulent suites. Lurching up out of his chair, Dherran left his food untouched on its gilded china plate. "That's it. Khenria, we've leaving."

"But you've hardly arrived." Den'Selthir's tone was hard as iron as he lingered in his posture of repose, swirling his wine with his eyes locked on Dherran, cold fury in their ice-blue depths. "You do owe me, after all, for breaking my liege-man. For saving your life. For teaching you manners like a *real* Kingsman – hardly worthy of those markings you flaunt."

Something inside Dherran snapped. Like a demon, his rage rose, surging towards the man who goaded it. Part of Dherran's mind knew den'Selthir was unarmed; had roved the Vicoute's fine clothes when he had risen from the table in greeting. Part of him knew the servingmen were similarly unarmed in their fine jerkins for table-waiting.

The rest of him didn't care, as Dherran lunged for the Vicoute. But suddenly, den'Selthir had launched from his chair, sending it flying backwards. He pivoted so Dherran's attack found nothing but air as he seized Dherran by the throat. And in one move, the Vicoute lifted Dherran from his feet, tipping him back and slamming him into the marble floor-tiles so hard that a tile cracked beneath Dherran's broad back. All breath was driven from him as his head rang, lights pulsing in his eyes from his head hitting the marble. Gasping beneath the Vicoute's iron grip, Dherran was vaguely aware of Khenria surging up from her chair to attack the man who still had Dherran pinned by the throat.

"Stay back, girl!" The Vicoute snarled viciously, all pretense of lordly manners gone as his icy eyes flashed fury. "This is between your *incomplete* mentor and myself. Touch me and I will break your arm to teach you a lesson in mis-timed courage! And *you*," he snarled coldly at Dherran. "Your parents should have named you Dherrennic, the Gutting Boar! For you will surely secure this fate for us all if you continue on as you are! Kharlos! Seal the doors. No one comes in or out tonight, unless Whelan comes with the Khehemnas in custody. If he does, have him sleep in the cells, guarding the man."

A servingman rushed to comply, his fine clothes, Dherran suddenly realized, a costume for a far more dangerous man beneath – just like the entire persona the Vicoute had showed until this very moment. Dherran stopped struggling and was at last able to gasp a ragged breath as the Vicoute's strength pinned him.

"Khehemnas?" Dherran coughed. "What...?"

"You travel with the enemy, *boy*." The Vicoute was cold steel as he regarded Dherran.

"And who the fuck are you?" Dherran growled through his damaged throat.

"I am the Vicoute Arlen den'Selthir," the Vicoute's grip tightened warningly upon Dherran's throat, "and I have a people to protect. *Alrashemnari aenta trethan lheroun!* And you are *fucking it all up*."

At last, the Vicoute released him. Massaging his throat, feeling it swelling where the Vicoute had manhandled him like a fool, Dherran sat up, then managed to get up into a chair at the table. As he sat stunned, both from his sudden besting and also from the Vicoute's High Alrakhan, Khenria sat silent also, sipping her wine with her eyes agog.

Moving close, a servingman set a mug of something before Dherran, murmuring, "For the pain, sirrah."

Dherran was suddenly aware of pain lancing through his head, neck, and back – a distinct tender area near his spine where he'd probably bruised a rib. Taking the mug, he sipped a bitter herb tea and his headache began to roll back as he chanced a look at the Vicoute. Seated, the lord had lapsed into a dangerous, simmering silence. He'd allowed Dherran to rejoin civilization at the table, but Dherran had a feeling anything he might say would only provoke another beating at the moment.

Looking at the Vicoute now, seeing his sword-honed sinew and dangerous demeanor, Dherran wondered just what kind of person he was dealing with. Dherran's gaze flicked to the man's well-covered chest, wondering if he wore Inkings, when at last, the Vicoute heaved an irritated sigh. Taking a sip of wine, he swirled it as his cultured masque of a lord fell into place once more. But it was a masque and it wasn't. Dherran had the feeling this man had actually been a Vicoute all his life, in addition to being a Kingsman, somehow.

"Listen, boy, and listen well to what I am about to say." Arlen den'Selthir spoke at last in a flat, imperious tone. "After tonight, you may not speak of it, you may not ask me of it, and you may not mention *anything* of what or who I am to anyone outside this room. Do you understand?"

Dherran nodded as he cleared his throat. "I understand."

Den'Selthir's icy gaze fell upon Khenria.

"I understand," she spoke quickly.

The Vicoute nodded regally, pinning Dherran again with his gaze. "Every person on this entire estate is either a Kingsman or Kingskinder in hiding. The man you broke today was the same. The Kingsmen living here were on political missions away from Lintesh and the Three Courts when the Summons was sent down ten years ago. We were not able to make it in time to renew our vows. But when we heard of how everyone else had disappeared, naturally we all went underground. Fortunately for me, my position has always *been* underground. After the Summons, the King met with me on his travels back from failed negotiations in Valenghia. He told me to spread word among the gentry and the military that the Kingskinder were to be protected *at any cost* once they had been put into positions of trades-craft or soldiering throughout the nation. Now, why do you think the King would send a Summons calling the Kingsmen traitors and make them disappear at Roushenn *while he was away on a political mission to Valenghia,* then cruelly capture our children, then turn right back around and *protect* our children immediately afterwards?"

Dherran's entire world shattered as disbelief filled him from the Vicoute's words. Glancing down, he saw his hands were shaking in his lap, but not from fury this time – from fear. The same feeling he ran from, that he fought, that he burned to forget. The terror of having to run home the day of the Summons, hoping his family weren't dead. The horror of facing off with soldiers in Alrashesh and the man in herringbone leathers who'd captured them. The agony of Suchinne's death, and escaping imprisonment for his actions afterwards. Fleeing from every town, from their slurs and hate of what he was.

The terror – that there was something darker at work beneath all of it.

"The Summons didn't come from the King..." Dherran whispered in the flooding silence.

"There are brains in there after all." The Vicoute was acerbic as he stared Dherran down. "Yes. The King was *not even at* Roushenn the day of the Summons. He was in Valenghia, secretly trying to salvage trade relations before it could turn into a war. Which obviously failed."

"So the King comes here on his way back, and hears what has happened to the Kingsmen for the first time." Khenria jumped in, her eyes wide.

"Precisely." Den'Selthir nodded coldly. "And finds he has been betrayed, but by whom? Suddenly, he realizes his palace is dangerous, which even our own agents inside Roushenn knew nothing of. How do you suddenly *lose* two thousand people? In any case, the King issues a secret edict to protect the surviving Kingskinder, which goes out only through *our* channels – Kingsman channels. Agents were assigned to keep each and every one of you ungrateful miscreants alive. Ever have a friend who saved your hide, perhaps more than once?"

Dherran swallowed hard, his mouth dry. He remembered the day his mentor Ottavio in the Stone Valley Guard took a blade for him, helping him escape prison in Quelsis. As Dherran glanced over at Khenria, he saw she was pale. He didn't know much about her past before Grump, but Dherran could see the terror in her of something awful that she had somehow escaped, maybe with help.

"Hear me now, and hear me well." Arlen den'Selthir sighed suddenly, world-weary as he watched them. "There is a dark power behind the throne of Alrou-Mendera – a throne the Alrashemni once held, which has now been usurped. For centuries, a secret group called the Khehemni have been a thorn in our side; a blade without mercy both here and abroad. Myself and other Alrashemni in hiding believe the Khehemni were behind the Summons, as well as the deaths of Dhenir Alden and King Uhlas den'Ildrian. But we have no proof. Meanwhile, popular opinion of the Kingsmen dwindles to little more than pure hate, augmented by false whispers and traditions like the Kingsman Burnings. And *you*," he glared at Dherran, "are making it all worse. I hereby *forbid* either of you to fight in public spectacle from here on out. Do I make myself clear?"

"Very." Khenria whispered fearfully.

"And who are you to give such an edict?" Dherran murmured, subdued now but needing to know.

"I am your Elder, boy." Den'Selthir eyed him coldly. "And if you want to *earn* those markings you had so foolishly had Inked before you were ready to fulfill them, you will do as I say. *Alrashemnesh aere veitriya Rakhan rhavesin.*"

"You're a Rakhan?" Dherran swallowed hard in his bruised throat.

Den'Selthir did not blink. "I am Rakhan of a Court you've never heard of, and a name I will never again repeat. I am Rakhan of the Shemout Alrashemni."

"Shemout. *The Hidden People.*" Dherran murmured, remembering his High Alrakhan.

"Just so." The Vicoute nodded. "We are the Kingsmen behind the Kingsmen. We are born in secret, we live in secret, and we die in secret. And we comprise almost all of the Alrashemni who are left."

As he spoke, Arlen den'Selthir began unbuckling his red silk jerkin, pulling his fine white shirt open. Without pause, he took up the steak knife by his plate and drew it across his chest, biting into the skin and drawing blood. As Dherran watched, curls of crimson began to lance out from the wound, swirling through the Vicoute's skin like ink through water as they moved outwards – stabilizing into a Mountain with five crowning Stars like fresh-spilled blood.

"To the world, I was born a Vicoute, and I will die a Vicoute," Arlen den'Selthir spoke, his blue eyes ice-cold as they rested upon Dherran. "But to the Kingsmen, I am the best weapon we have now. And you are no less."

30

TEMLIN

Blinking back fatigue, sweat slid down Brother Temlin's neck as he perused a tome in his reading-chamber. The cramped study was stifling this afternoon despite the thickness of the Abbey's stone, and dust motes tracked lazily through a shaft of pearled-glass light, weaving from blue, to yellow, to green. Realizing he had been lost for minutes staring at them, Temlin sighed and leaned his wooden chair back on two legs, tossing his spectacles to the desk.

The Kingsman hadn't come last night. All night they'd waited in the Rare Tomes Room, until they'd lost track of the hour in the underground catacomb and walked out to another ferociously sunny day. Abbess Lenuria had locked the doors with a curt dismissal and an eyeball of reprimand for Temlin. And now it was past mid-afternoon, and Temlin writhed in the muggy heat – still feeling the vast displeasure of his Abbott and Abbess, that he had let such an important person out of the Shemout's grip.

Without so much as getting his name or the location of his lodgings.

Rubbing the bridge of his nose, Temlin suddenly needed a drink with a roaring fever. But after last night, he needed to earn his superior's trust back. An old twist of responsibility filled him, and fast on its heels was unrest. Once, he'd been the King's son and younger brother to the heir, leading armies on the battlefield. Now he was an old spy, rotting away in this abbey and expected to be both celibate and sober – not to mention obedient, which had never been his strongest attribute.

Currying his greying red hair with his hands and massaging his tired eyes, Temlin took up his spectacles from the desk. Donning them, he peered once more at Mollia den'Lhorissian's journal, wishing for the hundredth time that he could make sense of it. This was her final volume before she had blocked up the Abbey-stone two years ago after Uhlas' death, never to be seen again – and the most unintelligible. Complicated sigils dominated entire pages, while others were squeezed in with a tiny hand. Words wound through the sigils; some in High Alrakhan, some Lhemvian, others Menderian but with strange diacritical marks. There were still languages and sigils no one had ever been able to identify, and Temlin growled in frustration as he noted a word in High Alrakhan that summed up his mood nicely.

Blutengen. Blood's teeth.

That was what Temlin got for trying to decipher a mad blind woman's journal. Yet just as he thought of Mollia, his wretched heart twisted again, still loving her after all these years. They had been so young when he and Uhlas had both fallen for her at the palace. She had been unspoiled then, without her madness, still with beautiful cobalt eyes Temlin could have drowned in forever. And yet, Temlin had been cursed, always in the shadow of his brother. Uhlas had won Molli – won her hand, won her bed, won her completely.

And then had to hide his young love in the Abbey as she grew more and more insane – raving with madness though she was only eighteen at the time.

Uhlas never could have married her, but still he kept her in the Abbey as she'd succumbed to raving by her mid-twenties. Temlin had been disowned from the line of succession by then, chucked in here to rot also, mad with drink and rage. But unlike Temlin, Mollia's madness was something an abstinence from drink couldn't cure. She'd broken Uhlas' heart, and when it became clear she'd never be normal, he'd wedded Sorilea den'Ihlent, second-daughter of the King of Praough.

Temlin's heart gave a vicious twist, thinking about his ancient rivalry with Uhlas over Molli. But now no one had heard from her in two years, and Temlin didn't even know if she lived. Slamming the tome shut with a growl and tossing his spectacles to the desk again, he was about to shuffle himself off to the brewery, damn his promise, when a tow-headed young brother popped his head around the door.

"Brother Temlin?" He spoke breathlessly.

"I'm busy! You are not a beer!" Temlin snarled as the lad blinked in surprise.

"Sorry for the interruption, Brother, but there's a *woman* to see you!"

Rising from his chair, Temlin found himself curious at the lad's eagerness. There had been a time when Molli had stirred lust in Temlin's loins like that, and a beast in his heart. But as he saw the lovely creature with the honey-blonde braid trip amusingly over her own feet as she entered his study, Temlin suddenly broke into a smile, his worries vanished. This woman was welcome, and not just because she was lovely.

But because she was the companion of the Goldenmarked Kingsman.

"Away with you lad, quit gawking at her pretty breasts!" Temlin snapped at the young brother lingering in the doorway. "Fetch a mug of ale for our guest and some bread. Fuck it all, it's hot! Fetch two mugs!"

The young brother flushed to the roots of his hair as he stammered something unintelligible, gazing at the woman's cleavage below her shawl. He tried to stop gazing, couldn't, tripped himself around the doorframe, nearly fell on his ass, then rushed away. Temlin burst into laughter as the young woman sat upon his couch.

"Ah! He'll be drowning himself in ale for weeks at the sight of you, young lady, I'll give you that!"

The pretty blonde flushed, appreciative that someone had noticed her beauty, then spoke with sincerity. "Brother Temlin, my apologies for the interruption again today, but I was wondering if you could assist me with something?"

"Anything a Brother of the Way can do, he will." Temlin spoke genially as he resumed his seat behind his desk. "And how is your handsome friend from yesterday? I rather expected him to be back visiting us by now..."

"Elohl has... business in the city." She spoke with hesitation.

"Ah." Setting his elbows to his armrests and steepling his fingers, Temlin gazed at the young woman. She was going to play coy with him today – that was fine. He'd still get the information he needed out of her, and had already gotten a first name. "And how may I help you... what is your name?"

"Eleshen." She quipped brightly. "Eleshen den'Fhenrir."

"Den'Fhenrir? Interesting. It means *wolf's child* in High Alrakhan. What is it I may do for you, Eleshen?"

"I'm seeking a physician." She spoke quickly, as she fiddled with her long braid. "I need a rather special kind of physician, one who could help a friend with severe headaches and seizures. She's a... a dreamer."

"Dreamer?" Temlin frowned. "Is your friend having nightmares?"

"No." Eleshen shook her head. "She has visions, actually. Visions that come true."

"I see." Temlin sat back in his chair, astounded by this information and unable to keep his astonishment hidden. The young woman traveled with notable and interestingly gifted companions. Companions he needed more information about – especially if one had true visions and the other was Goldenmarked. Lacing his bony old fingers, Temlin leaned forward with his elbows on the desk. "Not a *dreamer* then, but in the language of the north, a *Dremor* or a *True Seer*. And why do you think I can help such a person?"

"Because..." Eleshen chewed her lip, then beckoned to a sheaf of papers on the side of Temlin's desk. He fetched one with a nib of charcoal, passing them over. She wrote, then passed it back.

Because you're a Kingsman.

Temlin's brows shot to the ceiling as he gave her a hard look, knowing his glower was still formidable. She fidgeted with her braid again, though her gaze remained bold upon him. "And what makes you think this?"

"You have a... *way* about you." She shrugged. "I could be wrong, but I bet a mug of ale I'm not."

Brother Temlin felt a slow smile spread over his face. It had been a long time since he had met a woman with such wit and instincts. No matter that she couldn't keep her feet underneath her legs.

Not everyone was born for war.

"Walk with me, Eleshen. Let's stop by the brewery on our way to the ponds."

Rising, Temlin beckoned out the door, ignoring the stiffness in his old joints. Eleshen smiled as she rose from the couch and stepped to his side, and together they walked out from the Annex into the sweltering sunshine. Temlin engaged her in petty conversation about herbs for headaches as they walked to the taproom and secured a pair of ales – though stern Brother Sebasos gave Temlin the eyeball beneath his commanding black brows, his blacksmith's square jaw set with disapproval. Temlin gave Sebasos a cheeky salute with his mug, then drank right in front of him, knowing Sebasos would probably report it to Lenuria. Temlin didn't give two shits. Ale was already furthering his conversation with Eleshen, as they meandered down the gravel path that led to Temlin's favorite bench.

Gesturing for Eleshen to sit as he also did, Temlin broke into the topic of interest at last. "So you knew I was Alrashemni. How? And don't give me that *way about you* horseshit."

Eleshen lifted an eyebrow at his language, though she smiled as she sipped her beer. "You wear your robe laced all the way to your neck, though you wear the cowl down. Most Brothers have it the other way around, unlacing the collar in this heat but keeping their head covered. You're sweating – clearly you could do with more breeze, but you're hiding something, perhaps Inkings like Elohl and the other two men I've met recently in the city. And you walk like you've trained with weapons. Though you're rheumatic, you pace on the balls of your feet like a cat when you step, just like Elohl."

Lifting an eyebrow with a sly smile, Temlin took a drink. She was impressively shrewd and he liked it, but he needed to dig for just how shrewd. "And if I took you 'round the Brothers, could you identify any more who are Kingsmen?"

"Possibly."

"And these men you've met in the city, they are Kingsmen also?"

"I'm not here to talk about them." Eleshen suddenly stonewalled him, cagey and stubborn. "I'm here to discuss my friend, to see if you can help her."

"You're quite careful, aren't you?" Temlin's mouth quirked in amusement, though he was even more impressed now.

"My friends are in danger," she shot back testily, "and I don't know that I can trust you."

"But you came because you think I can help. And you trust Kingsmen," Temlin countered.

She paused, her lips open as if she would retort, then sighed. "Honestly, I don't know whom to trust. But you seem decent enough."

Temlin barked a laugh and she shot him a very stern eyeball. Still chuckling, he took a swig of his ale. "Tell me about your ailing friend. Why do you think she's a True Seer? Does your friend vomit in the morning or after eating? Has she started bleeding or bruising yet?"

Eleshen blinked, going pale. "She had a nosebleed just this morning. How did you know?"

"I've known a True Seer. Her health was very bad until she learned how to master her gift." Temlin spoke solemnly. "And your friend's visions? How do they manifest?"

"She says she... experiences them," Eleshen continued. "She's inside the bodies of the people she sees in her visions and feels their pain, as well as being outside the vision, watching it."

The girl's description was exactly like Molli's visions when she'd been young and Temlin sobered quickly, narrowing his eyes. "Your friend. She's in a dire way right now. Very ill, isn't she? So ill you're worried she might die any day?"

Eleshen paled, and Temlin saw fear slide through her eyes as she nodded. "Ghrenna seems... worse than fevered. She's very weak and having horrible seizures, plus her headaches. Even though this last vision was indistinct, it was terrible. A regal woman in a packed hall, signing documents. Dressed in cobalt and sky-blue silk, with sun-gold hair. She was gutted by a sword during the ceremony. And then Ghrenna saw a petite woman with all-white eyes beckoning to her from an Alranstone with a half-lidded, blood-red eye..."

"She saw Molli." Temlin's blood ran cold. His gaze snapped to Eleshen, ferociousness rising in his old body along with a horrible fear. "She saw Molli here at the Abbeystone, and she saw Elyasin getting assassinated at her Writ Signings!" As Temlin launched to his feet, abandoning his ale on the bench, a long stream of cursing exited his mouth. "I need to get word to Fenton! Dammit, dammit, dammit!!"

"Fenton den'Kharel?" The young woman startled. "But he brought news to Elohl just this morning that the Guard-Captain Olea's been imprisoned by the Dhenra! She's in Roushenn's cells, apparently—"

"*Imprisoned?!*" Temlin coughed, the world suddenly dropping out from underneath him as he seized Eleshen by the arm, hauling her up. "Come girl! You're in it, now. Up, up, walk fast!"

As Temlin marched from the ponds, Eleshen followed quickly. His joints still hurt, but urgency leant him speed he hadn't felt in decades as her information spiraled in his mind. Ancient fears rose, the same fears that had swamped Temlin when he'd found out about his nephew Alden's death, and then his brother Uhlas. There had been too much tragedy around the throne; Temlin had seen it all over the years, and news like this had a pattern to it.

Temlin's niece had made a terrible mistake with that temper of hers. A mistake that was about to be capitalized upon by the Khehemni Lothren, and get her killed. It was time to see Lhem, to push him to act. Temlin spiraled so viciously into his determination that he didn't realize he'd already led Eleshen inside and up the staircase, straight to the Abbott's apartments. As his blood boiled, Temlin didn't just knock upon the Abbott's door, he pounded with all his might, the muscles of a swordsman still present in his iron-wrought frame.

As his rage seethed – his vision bleeding red like it had done all those years ago.

"Enter!" Abbott Lhem's bark was that of an old veteran. Pressing the latch, Temlin hauled on the ironbound door, whisking inside and pulling Eleshen along. But the Abbott was not alone in his suite, two young scribes attending him as they bent over documents upon the massive desk. All looked up, startled by Temlin's entrance. The young men blushed to see a woman, but Temlin growled impatiently as he slammed the heavy door behind Eleshen, thinking of a ruse that would get the youngsters out and communicate everything Lhem needed to know – fast.

"Brother Temlin!" Lhem was blinking at him. "What's this?"

"Abbott." Temlin spoke briskly. "I must formally request a hearing to atone for my sins. I have slept with this married woman. Please, hear our confession regarding the Foundations of the Abbey."

Abbott Lhem rose to his feet, his ruddy face a thundercloud of incredulity, though it was a sham. He'd understood Temlin's meaning, that Temlin wanted a private meeting at the Abbeystone with Eleshen present. "Such a rash deed, Brother Temlin! I must hear your confession at once. Brothers, you are dismissed. We will address the final lists of ale for the Dhenra's coronation later this evening."

Like frightened hares, the two young men bowed their way out. Once the door was securely bolted, Lhem motioned to one side of his ample quarters, pressing a catch beneath his desk. A section of wall groaned and then stones slid back – a façade controlled by intricate mechanisms on a track.

"Confession of intimate relations!" Lhem chortled as he beckoned into the darkness beyond. "Good one, Temlin!"

As the Abbott set the pace with his brisk bulk, Temlin shooed the startled Eleshen on before him. The short, dark passage took a few turns, running through the walls of the Annex, then descended in spiral stairs to a sub-basement. Neither Temlin nor Lhem needed any light, knowing the way by heart, until at last the tunnel opened into a natural cavern of byrunstone beneath the Abbey grounds, the center of which was dominated by a single edifice.

The Abbeystone.

A secret known only to those of the highest echelon at the First Abbey, and to the Shemout Alrashemni, the towering Abbeystone dwarfed the circular chamber, ascending high into the darkness. Its seven eyes were all closed except the lowest – that one half-lidded, the red iris of garnet barely visible but throwing a bloody light around the cavern. The Stone didn't work anymore. Temlin, Lhem, and Lenuria had all tried traveling by it, but it would let no-one through these past two years, the half-lidded eye never changing. Mollia had done something to it when Uhlas had died two years ago, so no one could contact her in her isolated valley beyond the Stone now.

And she had not once come back through.

As they arrived in the blood-red chamber, Eleshen rounded on Temlin. "What is going on? What is this place?"

"Peace, girl." Lhem rumbled, turning to Temlin also. "Temlin. What's this all about?"

"Lhem, this young woman just told me Olea den'Alrahel's been imprisoned by the Dhenra! Elyasin has removed her sole obvious Alrashemni protection, and more than that, Eleshen knows a True Seer, suffering from the exact same maladies Molli had. The seer had a vision of Elyasin at her Writ Signings, getting gutted by a swordsman! The Khehemni Lothren are moving, Lhem. They're plotting a strike against Elyasin that would solidify their position in the Chancellate. The coronation's only three days away! We need to get Olea back on the Dhenra's guard. Now."

"Aeon's balls." Lhem cursed darkly, his ample mustachios turning down as he fixed Eleshen in his gaze. "You. Tell me about this vision and the news you heard. Everything."

Eleshen began to fidget with her braid. Temlin had expected her to launch into a diatribe in her usual manner, but instead she shut her mouth uncertainly and looked to him. With a blink, Temlin suddenly realized she was wary of Lhem.

"You can trust our Abbott," Temlin assured her gently. "If you wish to help Alrashemni Kingsmen, well you're standing in a closed room with two of them. Two old farts of Kingsmen who haven't fought in years, but Kingsmen all the same."

Eleshen's wariness seemed to ease at his words. She paused, then repeated everything she'd said to Temlin at the bench. Lhem scowled through it all, chewing his mustachios, his face acquiring the plethoric rage of a thundercloud. As Eleshen finished, Lhem suddenly released a furious growl.

"Aeon fuckitall. We can't interfere, Temlin. We have to leave Olea be."

"*What?!*" Temlin roared, incensed.

"We can't risk exposing our network during such a crucial time," Lhem nodded decisively. "If the Dhenra threw her Guard-Captain in the cells, they're most likely having a spat. Let Fenton smooth things over; he's got a slick tongue, he should be able to talk the Dhenra out of whatever's got her incensed. If not, well, Fenton's as capable as Olea. He'll make sure the Dhenra's well-protected at the Coronation and Writ Signing. Unless we can confirm proof of any plot and the persons involved, we have to wait until the Khehemni Lothren make a blatant move."

"*Blatant move?!*" Temlin roared, setting his hands to his hips and wishing for a sword right now to go protect his niece. "We can't just sit here, we need to do something!"

"You will do as the Shemout says, Temlin!" Lhem barked back. "I am still your superior, and Olea will stay put. Lenuria and I will send word to Fenton to make certain the Dhenra is safe for her coronation events! That's the best we can do for now, my friend."

"Lhem." Temlin pleaded, desperate. "Eleshen is also the traveling partner of the young man with the Goldenmarks."

Lhem's beady eyes swung to Eleshen, his presence, deadly. "Tell me, girl, where is your companion with the golden Ink?"

"Olea's brother has gone to guard the Dhenra." Eleshen quipped, crossing her arms irately.

"Olea's brother? Are you telling us this Elohl you travel with is Olea's twin brother Elohl den'Alrahel?" Temlin gaped at Eleshen, shocked. He'd known the den'Alrahel family of old, and now Temlin knew why the Kingsman had seemed so familiar to him. The young man looked just like Rakhan Urloel den'Alrahel in his prime, and Temlin reeled, realizing his grievous mistake in not keeping Elohl at the Abbey when he had a chance.

"Fool, Temlin!" Abbott Lhem voiced his mistake for him as he cursed brusquely. "You had the Rakhan of Alrashesh's son in your office, Goldenmarked, and you let him go! All for want of asking his name! Dammit! So they've all gone to the palace, you say?"

“They’re going to masquerade as Guardsmen during the coronation, to protect the Dhenra. Olea asked Fenton to put it together and involve Elohl,” Eleshen nodded alertly.

“The Dhenra will have extra protection, then. Good.” Lhem nodded.

“Lhem, we need to send word to our remaining Shemout Alrashemni cells about the situation.” Temlin prodded, feeling a deep urgency to do more. “We can put pressure on any Khehemni who might take advantage at the coronation, but we have to be united in coming forward. We must assume the Dhenra is being pushed to marry a Khehemni-allied noble. If she lives long enough to wed, we will discover alliances quickly. But if she dies, we learn nothing.”

Lhem chewed his mustachios as he turned, pacing his ample bulk before the blood-tinged Abbeystone. “Ravens and hawks will never get to our agents outside Lintesh fast enough. Besides, if we try to place more agents in Elyasin’s Guard, she will question too many new faces. If the Abbey withholds deliveries of ale to delay the celebrations, it will spark riots, which will only destabilize Elyasin’s hold over her subjects. If we come forward openly as Alrashemni, we might be slaughtered. No, none of that will do. We’ll have to rely upon Olea’s plan to halt an assassination attempt. Elohl will have Fenton and Aldris at his side in the Small Hall. They’ll fight for Elyasin to the death.”

“I still don’t like it,” Temlin scrubbed a hand over his beard, fuming still. “But we have more problems than just the coronation, Lhem. Eleshen’s True Seer friend could be of use to us, if she saw something as important as an assassination attempt. But she has the headaches, seizures, and bleeding, just like Molli did when she was young. And you know how Molli almost died before she got her gifts under control.”

“Is Ghrenna going to die?” Eleshen’s whisper was very soft.

“Not if we can help it.” Temlin reached out, taking her hand. “But True Seers are more than rare. We need to bring her here. If anything can help her, it’s the Abbeystone. Physicians can do nothing.”

“She has a friend with pain-easing abilities – it helps when he puts his hands to her head.”

“Pain-easing abilities in his hands?” Lhem frowned, lifting a white eyebrow. “I’ll bet that’s young Luc den’Lhorissian. He disappeared from the palace before he could be confirmed in his position after his gifts surfaced. But with the deaths of his brother and father, it seems the last of the King’s Physicians has returned to

Lintesh." Lhem's attention returned to Eleshen. "A Lhorissian may be able to keep your friend alive for a little while. But a True Seer will continue to wither unless trained properly by an Alranstone."

"We shall send a few Brothers to collect your ailing True Seer." Temlin spoke with fire in his veins, as he gripped Eleshen's hand. "She *must* be brought here so we can protect her. Such a treasure is nearly as important to the Kingsmen as protecting our future Queen. We will send a litter for her immediately, with an escort of our trusted agents."

"You mean Kingsmen agents?" Eleshen spoke hopefully.

"Technically, we're *Brothers*. Got it?" Temlin smiled at her wryly, though he still felt Lhem's response to his news had been less than adequate. "And I think I don't need to tell you how very secret all of this information you just heard must remain, if you want to keep your friends safe."

31

OLEA

Tracing sigils in the dust of her cell by torchlight, Olea tried to ignore a tingling sensation that lifted the hairs on her neck as her fingertips circled again. A creeping feeling of being watched, it had come often in the past few hours, though she had seen no one. Even if she was being watched by spies from behind the walls of her cell, there wasn't a damn thing she could do about it. And rising to alertness every time she felt that tingle was making her as paranoid as Uhlas had been at the end.

Moving in a light meditation, Olea traced sigils remembered from the clockwork in her white pouch, perused night after night for years. A sound caught her attention suddenly, a whisper in the darkness and Olea sharpened her hearing, waiting. After a moment it came again; a scrape like a soft leather boot over grit-covered stone. Just out of the torch's light, she felt a shadow by the bars of her cell, his breathing soft and fluid. Olea could just hear the beat of blood in his veins, steady and slow, and in the darkness, his skin smelled of pine musk and oiled leather.

A familiar scent – Elohl.

Olea smiled, relieved he'd come. Elohl's stealth had improved over the years, and glancing through her bars at the Guardsman by the stairs, Khenner den'Ihs, Olea saw he was bored. Staring straight ahead, he lounged at the wall with his arms crossed, a vague scowl upon his face. He hadn't noticed a thing, and though normally Olea would have berated her Guardsman for his lack of attention, tonight it was a boon.

"Elohl. Thank the gods." Olea's whisper was soft; she knew Elohl could hear her.

"Olea, I'm here." His answer came just as soft, hardly a breath in the darkness. "What can I do to get you out of here?"

"I'm fine. I need you to protect the Dhenra."

"She's being watched." Elohl breathed back. "Fenton, Vargen, and your man Aldris are on her detail. Olea, did you know Fenton was Alrashemni?"

"Not until last night." Olea breathed, surprised that Fenton had also outed his Shemout Alrashemni status to Elohl. "Believe me, I was as surprised as you probably were."

"How many more of these Shemout Alrashemni are there in hiding, do you think?" Elohl asked quietly, and even without looking at him, Olea could feel the wheels in her twin's mind churning.

"I don't think they're hiding, Elohl," Olea paused, considering questions she'd been stewing over for the past day. "I think they operate outside the Kingsman Oath to the Crown, a secret sect of Alrashemni with no liege."

"Then why help the Dhenra, if they don't serve the Crown?" He countered quietly. "Is it because of House den'Ildrian's Alrashemni history?"

"Elohl... I think there's a dangerous game being played here." Olea chewed her lip. "It's bigger than the Crown, and I think Alrashemni are the pawns. We always have been. The Summons was a deliberate move by someone to eradicate us. And it wasn't King Uhlas."

"Maybe Ghrenna will be able to see something to illuminate the situation." Elohl spoke softly.

"Ghrenna?!" Olea startled to hear the name, and it was all she could do to not turn and stare at her twin in the darkness. "You've seen Ghrenna? Where? When?!"

"She's alive, here in the city." But Elohl paused, and Olea knew something was vastly wrong.

"Just alive?" Olea breathed, frowning. Elohl's words had an ominous ring, and if Olea knew her brother, he was leaving quite a lot out.

"She's bad, Olea. Really bad." Elohl's next words were strained, and in them, Olea could hear her twin's terrible heartbreak. "I can't even touch her. She spasms if I so much as touch her hand, and the headaches devour her, worse than ever."

"Elohl..." Telling him she was sorry wouldn't help. It never did, with Elohl. He would grieve and grieve until it consumed him, and not utter one more breath about his love, nor how it tore him to shreds. He had always suffered that way, with the silence of a glacier.

"In any case," Elohl continued, mastering himself, "Fenton's set me up as a Guardsman now. How do I approach the Dhenra to tell her what's happening?"

"You don't, not unless you want to be stuck in the cells here with me," Olea sighed, wanting to discuss so much more with Elohl but knowing now wasn't the time. "Elyasin's got a temper, and she had reason to use it upon me, not to mention on some nobody she's never met. Don't try to approach her or speak with her. Just stay on her ass like a leech and spread your senses wide. Don't let *anything* slip through unnoticed. Fenton and Aldris are sharp swordsmen, but they don't have what you have."

"I'll do my best." She saw the shadow nod. "I love you, Lea."

And with a faint swish of air where he'd been, Elohl slipped away.

"I love you too, Elohl." Olea breathed, but she knew he'd already gone.

Moving back from the bars, Olea settled upon her pallet bed. Leaning back against the stone wall, she ignored her paranoia as her mind drifted through too many thoughts. Images became sharp, her memories turning to her last time alone with Alden. Nearly two years ago, her memory was of the palace practice-yards. Dust swirled in the hot summer sun, and Olea heard Alden's throaty laugh as she got a knife-jab into his ribs. Oaks and cendarie beyond the palace whispered of summer, cicadas whirring as Alden strode in again with his sword ready – never to be undone by the number of times Olea had mock-killed him in the ring.

"Olea. You should know I've had two letters sent by hawk, recently." Alden began a conversation as he breathed hard, slipping Olea's deft strikes. No one was around to hear their discussion, the palace practice yards empty as everyone was out on rounds in the hot mid-afternoon.

"From Arlen den'Selthir?" Olea spoke as she struck again, and Alden lithely slipped away.

"No." He chuckled as he parried her next strikes. "It's been so long since we sent that hawk, I think it might have gotten shot and eaten. No, I've had two letters from Amlenport. The first was from the Amlenport Harbormaster, Lugol den'Fhillian, regarding the raid on the *Dauntless* and their shipment of emeralds we were looking into. He told me about a corrupt dock-keeper's trial that pointed to a deal with Thurumanian pirates to accomplish the raid. And though the man confessed to piracy, the trial was apparently a very odd affair."

"Odd, how?" Olea spoke as she blocked a cut from Alden's sword, sliding out with ease.

"Well, the dock-keeper was put to the question by some of our Guardsmen, Fenton den'Kharel and Aldris den'Farahan." Alden huffed between parries. "I don't know how those two were chosen to question a corrupt dock-keeper so far from Lintesh, but they were. The man broke quickly – too quickly, giving up the name of a Thuruman pirating vessel that made spoils off the raid. I asked Fenton about the trial while we were drinking together last night. He said the same thing – that the man had broken too easily, babbling on and on almost incoherently about pirates and planning the raid at Amlenport's Alranstone."

"Why was the man incoherent?" Olea stepped back, ceasing their duel.

"Fenton didn't know. But when it came time to execute the dock-keeper for piracy, the man started shrieking, *I don't know these thoughts!* And shrieking about his mind being broken by *the man in grey and the woman of slow sighs* so he would spew lies about the raid."

"Like what that man in black herringbone armor did the day us Kingskinder were captured." Olea held up a hand, passing it over her eyes. "He broke into our minds – gave us all so much pain that none of us could fight back."

"Yes, except the dock-keeper was screaming that he was supposed to tell lies about the raid. That it wasn't pirates who had stolen those emeralds, but someone else."

"So who did steal the emeralds from the *Dauntless*?" Olea lifted an eyebrow.

"Unfortunately, the dock-keeper was put to death before that information came out." Alden sighed. "The local judiciary of Amlenport were supposed to wait to hang him until Fenton was present as King's Witness. But Fenton and Aldris were still getting dressed to attend the hanging when they heard the gallows drop in the square."

"Someone was trying to cover up the real emerald thieves and their agenda," Olea mused. "The descriptions of the people who swayed the dock-keeper are vague, but maybe it's a place to start. What did the second letter say?"

"It was a follow-up letter from Amlenport, from Vicoute den'Jhenn." Alden put a hand to his sweaty black hair, tousling it in a frustrated way. "Apparently, Harbormaster Lugol den'Fhillian has been murdered. Just two days after sending his letter to me. Knife in the night."

"Alden." Olea blinked, sliding her sword away. "Harbormaster Lugol den'Fhillian was Kingsman-trained. House den'Fhillian are an old family that followed the tradition of sending their sons to train with the Kingsmen until age twenty-one. Lugol wouldn't have been easy to kill."

"So someone with equal or better training killed him." Alden planted his sword tip in the dirt with an exasperated huff, something young Elyasin was already copying him at. "You know Olea, the more we look into this ball of yarn, the more it feels like we're dealing with a massive network. To make so many Kingsmen disappear in a single night, and all these strange dealings revolving around emeralds these past ten years – you'd have to involve thousands of people! Did you talk to Fenton about his task?"

"Yes." Olea nodded. "Fenton said he found no Guardsmen declared missing from palace duties the day of the Summons, or the day the Kingskinder were collected. But what he did find was a shipment of three hundred cobalt jerkins reported stolen two weeks prior to the Summons."

"So the Guardsmen involved in the capture of the Kingskinder could have been hired mercenaries. Impostors." Alden scowled now, furious. "They had carts and horses, right? I'm seeing Lhaurent in a few minutes to plan supplies for the merchant fleet venture to Ghrec. I'll ask him if anything was reported missing from the palace stables prior to the Kingsmen disappearance. And then we'll know if anyone from Roushenn was involved."

"Careful, Alden. We don't know whom to trust." Olea warned.

"We took a chance with Fenton and Aldris," he countered. "They've been alright. And Lhaurent has been an institution at this palace since my father was born. Don't worry, Olea. It's just a few questions about supplies. I'll say I'm just doing a retrospective inventory on the stables."

"*Careful.*"

"I'll be careful, Olea!" Alden strode forward, seizing Olea around the waist and pressing her with a hard kiss right out in the open where anyone could have seen. Fortunately, the practice yards were empty, and Olea's hasty glance showed no one at the windows overlooking the yards. But all the same, she glowered at Alden's indiscretion as he pulled away, chuckling. Striding out of the sand ring with a haughty jaunt in his step, he slid his practice sword back into the rack by the infirmary doors.

"Oh, and by the way, Olea!" Alden spoke as he turned back. "You're coming as my bodyguard on the trading-run to Ghrec when the merchant fleet leaves in two days. Get your things packed. We'll have all the time in the world to trade blows while we sample spices in hot climes a few days hence!" Alden gave her a cheeky wink. "See you in the Chancellate Hall for the meeting at sixth bell."

Turning his back, Alden strode away through the dust.

The memory broke suddenly as Olea heard another pair of feet coming to her cell. This time, it was a swish of soft boots descending the stone staircase, and as Olea peered out, she saw the Guardsman salute. The tall figure of Lhaurent den'Karthus approached, his regular pearl-grey outfit switched tonight for a fine doublet and breeches of silver-embroidered dark blue silk. His chains of office hung shining at his collar, and he clasped his hands behind his back as he came to stand before her bars. Rising from her pallet, Olea scuffed her boots through the clockwork sigils she had been tracing earlier, discreetly obliterating them.

"Captain-General." Lhaurent spoke coldly, eyeing her with his regular disdain.

"Castellan." Olea matched his frigid tone, and did him one better.

"You might be a little politer, Captain. I am here on your behalf." He spoke with a slight smirk.

"Oh?" Olea was saccharine as she smiled. "Did the Dhenra send you to return me to my duties?"

"No, I'm afraid." His smirk was benignly apologetic. "I'm merely to inquire about your health."

"As well as can be expected for the Captain-General of the Guard who is caged up and prevented from protecting her liege in a den of butchers who hide behind sliding walls and see-through mirrors." Olea growled, her hackles rising.

"Ah, I see..." Lhaurent spoke as he clasped his oily hands before him now, raising a well-groomed eyebrow. "And do you think Roushenn so unfit a place for Elyasin?"

It was practically an admission that Lhaurent knew or was somehow involved in the palace's hidden secrets, and Olea gaped at him, before she surged at the bars of her cells, gripping them with a fierce growl. "You bastard! I knew it! How did you kill the Kingsmen when they came here after the Summons, Lhaurent? How did you make the palace walls move? What are you after? The throne, the kingdom?"

"My, my! What a vivid imagination you have, dear Captain!" Lhaurent chuckled smoothly. But his grey gaze went cold as he stared her down, glittering in the darkness as a smile played about his smooth lips. "Thrones and crowns... such paltry treasures to be heaped upon these unwilling shoulders. No. When I look in the mirror, I see... possibility. A world *behind* the world. A world that can be what we make of it, through subtle grace like sunlight underwater. What do you see when you look in the mirror, Captain? Power, influence? A position to the right of the throne?"

"I see *your face*, you bastard, *watching* me!" Olea seethed at the bars, rabid.

"Do you think me so callous, Captain?" Lhaurent's eyebrows rose with mock affront as his odious lips gave an oily smirk. "To observe whom a woman does or does not take to bed at night? I do not peek through keyholes. But I do watch from behind your bars. For the palace is a prison to you. Whereas to me, it is freedom. Ultimate freedom."

"It was you all along, wasn't it?" Olea seethed, her breath hot, her face inches from the bars, her knuckles white where she gripped cold iron. If she could have, she would have ripped his smirking mouth off his face with her teeth. "When you exposed Alden and I's affair that day before the Chancellate, I thought it was a maid who had seen us kiss in the practice yards! I thought we had been careless, but it was *you!* You were watching behind the walls of my *bedchamber*, you disgusting piece of filth! From behind that fucking gilded mirror you never removed from my quarters!!"

"Temper, Captain." Lhaurent stared her down, not bothering to conceal his cold smirk. "You should be more careful whom you accuse. It might not go well for you. As it did not go so well for Alden. Or even Uhlas, for that matter."

"You killed Alden, didn't you?" Olea snarled, grief like a knife striking her heart. "You bribed someone to put out the lighthouse at Amlenport because you knew Uhlas would put me right back at Alden's side once he returned from Ghrec, and you couldn't get to him while I was around."

"Rumor and conjecture, my dear." Lhaurent examined his buffed fingernails, his odious smile still upon his smooth lips. "Amlenport is a very busy city of trade. There are a thousand thieves who would bribe a lighthouse-keeper to make a beacon go dark there. Besides, Alden was rash. He was bound to get killed sooner or later."

"All so that he and I would never get a chance to expose the threads we were following – threads that led right to you, I'm sure!"

Lhaurent's eyes went hard as he stared her down, all pretense of coyness falling away to reveal his true, dark nature. "Follow the tail of the hydra, my dear, and you'll find more than you bargained for."

"There may be more heads, but you're the true snake in the grass," Olea growled. "Now I know that Uhlas was on to you."

"Ahh, Uhlas. So paranoid at the end. Almost as if someone were *watching* him day and night, don't you think?" Lhaurent's lips lifted at the corners. "Uhlas suspected much, but unfortunately, knew nothing. Uhlas knew what I told him to know, and what I told him was to drink his medicine so his health would recover. Which he did. And for a few hours after every vial he felt tremendously improved."

"Before he felt even worse and had to have another. You poisoned him, you bastard!" Olea snarled.

"I urged an ailing, paranoid liege to take his medicine for the good of his kingdom, and for his daughter. His only remaining heir."

"What are you plotting against Elyasin?!" Olea surged at the bars.

"Elyasin will enjoy being Queen. For as long as she may." With a lift of one well-combed eyebrow, Lhaurent turned to go, his gossamer step sliding away over the stones.

"I *will* expose you for the crimes you've committed!" Olea screamed out behind him. "I will find the missing link and figure out how you orchestrated so many deaths! And I *will* expose this palace for what it is, Lhaurent!"

"And who is going to believe you, Captain?" Turning back, Lhaurent den'Karthus' grey eyes were feverish with disdain. "What would happen if the tired, superstitious masses knew the secrets kings keep? What riots would they incite, what tumult would they create? Foolish people do foolish things with precious information. The Alrashemni knew it. But they have kept far too many secrets for far too long. And secrets have a way of strangling those who wield them."

"I'm going to strangle you with yours, Lhaurent." Olea growled through her bars.

"Not if I strangle you with yours first." His glittering grey gaze was feral now as a sneer curled his lips. "I seem to recall you have two interesting tomes in your quarters, which you peruse at very late hours. *Treason* interesting, some might say, to assert that the soon-to-be-Queen comes from the same lineage as the traitorous Alrashemni Kingsmen – or that *you* come from a bloodline more royal than she! That might give the populace a nice reason to flay you. I wonder... would the people of Lintesh enjoy having a Kingswoman traitor who is *also* a witch to burn upon their pyre for harvest-fest?"

"I'm no witch!" Olea recoiled, horrified at the things Lhaurent was saying.

"With hearing like you have?" He smirked. "It seems a witch-talent that you can even come *close* to hearing me when I enter a room. But I'm afraid I must depart now. I have a coronation to prepare for in a few days. The spectacle of which I am very much looking forward to. Goodnight, Captain."

Swishing away over the stones, Lhaurent was soon out of sight beyond the torchlight. With a growl, Olea threw her weight upon the bars, desperate in her imprisonment. Her heart hammered, her mind frozen into a loop of terror at everything Lhaurent had wrought – and at everything was going to.

Olea's knees buckled and she sat down hard upon her pallet. Staring at the wall, her mind churned, desperate and utterly trapped behind her cell bars in the flickering darkness. Drawing her knees in to her chest, the creeping sensation of being watched filled her again, lifting the hairs at the nape of her neck and locking her body tight with an animal panic.

32

THEROUN

The Dhenra had officially decided on a wedding to House Alramir of Elsthemen. Her coronation was to be tomorrow, with the wedding celebrations immediately afterward. Theroun stood in his apartments this afternoon, gazing down at documents drawn up in a fine, flowing hand upon his stout desk. The King's Calligrapher had done a magnificent job with the Writ of Betrothal, and now it bore signatures of both the Dhenra and King Therel Alramir. Witnessed by Theroun and the other six members of the Dhenra's Chancellate, as well as a number of high-ranking members of King Therel's cabinet, the betrothal was official.

The Writ of Marriage sat beside it upon Theroun's desk, ready to be signed tomorrow.

Though his quarters were blistering in the late heat, Theroun wanted to light the hearth and cast both documents into the fire – then stuff Lhaurent's mouth with the ashes before he ran the man through. Swirling wine in a silver goblet as he stood by the desk, Theroun felt ghosts crowding him despite the brightness of the afternoon. As he looked at those documents, he saw the bleached earth of Thelkomen's Crossing, the first village he had slaughtered in his madness upon the Aphellian Way.

As he sipped his wine, he tasted blood – the blood of innocents being shed.

Thelkomen's Crossing hadn't deserved what he'd done to them. A Menderian village on the Aphellian Way near Valenghia, Theroun had commanded the villagers be killed in his madness – Uhlas' own people. Children had been run through by spearmen. Goodwives had burned in their homes when dry thatch was torched and doors barricaded. Farmers had been slashed across their guts so they would die in their own shit and piss.

All because everyone in the village bore the Alrashemni Blackmark – to the last man, woman, and child.

Sighing, Theroun swirled his wine. Maddened by grief and fever from the murder of his family and his assassin-wounds, and hopped up on fennewith for the pain, he didn't even recall half his orders as he'd marched his army into Valenghia. Ruthless, he'd hung Menderian and Valenghian Alrashemni to every monolith of the Way, torsos bare to display the treasonous Mountain and Stars. Caught in a devil of madness, he'd strung up dead and alive alike, and it had continued to the next village, then the next. Theroun's madness had spread like a curse to his men, making them brutal, but he hadn't cared in his vengeful fever.

Dead Alrashemni had lined the Aphellian Way for thirty leagues into Valenghia before King Uhlas had gotten word of it and sent General Ghuryen to stop Theroun.

It should have been Theroun's death, carted back to Roushenn in manacles to face the furious Uhlas. But the Khehemni Lothren had been quick to conscript Theroun after witnessing what he was capable of. It had been Lothren agents, Castellan Lhaurent and Chancellor Evshein, who had convinced the King to send his physician rather than chuck Theroun in the cells; to give Theroun a second chance. Tales of horror had been suppressed, Theroun's armies disbanded into other regiments.

War-crimes were committed in every nation, and Theroun's formidable ability to manage armies had value.

It was then the Khehemni Lothren had made themselves known to Theroun. Their purpose had been aligned with Theroun's at the time, and he'd agreed to be positioned as a Chancellor, to be close to the crown and help secure the annihilation of Alrashemni in every nation. Regret had not come until later. But he did feel remorse now, looking at Elyasin's signed death-note. He hadn't joined the Khehemni to end the King's line. He hadn't joined them to slaughter Uhlas' daughter and start a war that would kill thousands of innocents and loyal subjects.

"The Black Viper of the Aphellian Way." Theroun's gaze fixed upon the Writs on his desk as he spoke. Lifting his goblet, he drained it, tasting blood with every swallow. Setting it carefully aside so no wine was near the white parchment, he took up the two documents, opened a drawer of his desk, slid them in, and locked it. Rifling a hand through his hair, Theroun felt a thunderstorm pushing this heat over the mountains, though it still hadn't broken. A walk was what he needed to clear his mind. Leaving his apartments and locking them, he strode down the hall, turning down a spiral staircase and egressing into the Rose Courtyard.

Walking slowly as his old wound stitched from inner conflict, Theroun took the air, stopping to smell the blooms upon their spreading trellises. A military man with a military father, Theroun had grown up hard and been denied the finer things in life. But his mother had always kept a small rose garden, and it had been his vice. Roses and Generals didn't mix, but as a Chancellor now, no one thought it odd for him to stroll and think, to bend and inhale a flower.

And mourn the death of innocents.

Theroun's scowl was more morose than usual as he bent to smell yet another flower. Its scent was pure as dreams, but to him its heady fragrance was the sweetness of rotting corpses. Pacing to the next bloom, he found he could not remove the taste of char and bile from his tongue. Inside, Theroun twisted, though on the outside he remained stoic. It wasn't every day a woman he thought of like a daughter would go to her death. King Therel Alramir was going to be arrested for the actions of his First Sword, and then he would be hung.

And then they would have a war.

Another one.

Idling near a white-thorn bush, Theroun admired its snow-pale blossoms as he thought about Devresh Khir, the Elsthemi First Sword with his all-white hair and cold blue eyes. The man had served the throne of Elsthemen for nearly thirty years and was still sharp, immeasurably talented, and utterly deadly. Born Khehemni, he was willing to die for his beliefs, and Theroun's right side spasmed around his old wounds, that Uhlas' treasured daughter was going to get stuck like a pig tomorrow. Hearing a soft crunch upon the gravel – a lean figure with a light tread coming up behind him – Theroun turned with his jaw set, expecting to see the Eel of Roushenn.

But instead found himself facing Thaddeus.

"Looked for you at your quarters, sir, but you weren't there." Thad smiled apologetically at his intrusion, a leather folio under one arm and a basket upon the other, stuffed with food. “Guessed you’d be out here where it’s more pleasant. I thought you might want a spot of late lunch, sir. And a quick review of how accepting trade agreements with Elsthemen will change our negotiating positions with other nations.”

“Very thoughtful, Thaddeus.” Theroun was in fact grateful for Thad’s thoughtfulness, always bringing foodstuffs and drink to make sure Theroun didn’t starve working through meals. Turning, Theroun motioned him through the greenery towards a stone bench and table they often shared near a three-tier fountain. The fountain masked their conversation, and Theroun sat at his usual place, his view pleasantly long in all directions so he could see anyone who idled near enough to listen. Laying the folio atop the table, Thad began to spread out a cloth, cheese and jams, bread and butter, and cured meats.

“Thaddeus,” Theroun began as he opened the folio and perused it, though he had other ideas he needed to flesh out this evening. And Thaddeus was the perfect agent with which to explore those thoughts. “Let us resume our conversation about the Kingsmen from the other night.”

Thaddeus had been doling out meat and slathering herbed butter on the crusty loaf of bread when he froze like a mouse in an open field. Setting the knife down, he stared at Theroun from behind his wire-rimmed spectacles. “Why?”

“Because you have a keen mind, lad, and I want to see what’s to be done with it.” Theroun barked gently enough so no one nearby could hear. “Go ahead and eat. Pretend we are having our usual discussions about nations and trade.”

Thad blinked, then eyed the folio. Theroun saw him note that though Theroun had opened it, he’d not removed any papers. Reaching for the buttered bread, Thad piled it with cheese and meat, taking a bite though his eyes remained on Theroun. Theroun took food also, keeping up the ruse for anyone watching.

“Now,” Theroun spoke with his mouth full. “Ask me questions, lad. And I will answer what I may.”

Thaddeus blinked, but his hesitation was brief before he dove in. “Is Alrou-Mendera in a situation like Cennetia was once? Where a force behind our throne is manipulating the nation? And if so, do you know what or whom is behind it?”

“Yes and yes.”

Thad paled, but continued. “Are you one of them, sir?”

“Marginally. Yes.”

“Why?” Thad blinked, shock taking his face as he set his bread down.

"Because I hate Alrashemni for killing my family," Theroun answered quietly. "Or once I did."

"Who is more central in this endeavor?" Thad was leaning forward now, rapt, his food forgotten. "And if you can't give me names, can I guess them?"

"No. To do so would secure your death." Theroun growled. "Be smart, lad."

Thad swallowed, but had courage and plowed on. "Are there others like you in the palace, close to the Dhenra, maybe even swaying her choices?"

"Yes."

"Do you sway her into continuing war with Valenghia, sir?"

"Yes. I have been ordered to by my superiors."

"Can you tell me by whom?" Thad whispered, though as Theroun gave him a chiding glower, he nodded hastily. "My death, of course. Forgive me. What do you know of the Kingsmen Summons, sir?"

This was an unexpected turn, and Theroun cocked his head. "Little. I know only that Uhlas did not give it."

"He didn't?" Thad's eyes widened. "Who did?"

"I don't know." Theroun set his jaw. "I was readying armies at the time, Thad, not yet a part of this scheme, just a General in the field. Uhlas was in Valenghia, trying to forestall imminent war with every negotiation skill he had."

"One of your people sent a false Summons from the King…" Thaddeus was quick, putting all the pieces together with ease. "What happened to the Kingsmen after they entered the palace?"

"I have no information on that account." Theroun shook his head. "I know only that the Unterhaft and all the halls were thoroughly searched after they disappeared. They simply vanished; no trace of them was left."

"That's impossible. People don't just vanish." Thaddeus narrowed his eyes. "Someone knows what happened. All traces of the Alrashemni Kingsmen history have been removed from the library and armor-halls also, as if there was a cover-up."

"Smart lad. Go on." Theroun took a bite of bread and meat, knowing he was encouraging the lad down his own line of suppositions. But it was imperative he watch someone else put it together, that he make certain his assumptions were sound through another mind quite possibly as brilliant as his own, though still young. "And who has access to all details of housekeeping inside Roushenn?"

"Castellan Lhaurent." Thad blinked. "Castellan Lhaurent knows about the

Kingsmen disappearance. He knows what happened. He covered it up, then removed all the evidence."

"I wouldn't say that name with such suppositions if I were you, lad." Theroun leaned forward. "They might get you killed. Badly."

"I'm right, aren't I?" Thaddeus went deathly pale.

"I cannot confirm any of it." Theroun took a drink of the wine Thad had brought.

"And if you could? Don't you hate Kingsmen? Weren't you happy to hear they disappeared?"

"Not at the time. I supported the Kingsmen before I became the Black Viper of the Aphellian Way. They were a formidable military asset."

"And now?"

"Now I am caught between stone and stone, Thad." Theroun gave his secretary a hard look. "I am not in a position to have regrets; I cannot reverse my choices. All I can do is make more agile choices from here on out."

"Is Lhaurent threatening you, sir?" Thad leaned forward. "Pressing you into doing... something?"

"Lhaurent does not know whom he threatens, Thaddeus." Theroun glowered.

"What is he pressing you into? What's going to happen?" Thaddeus swallowed, suddenly looking very scared, and very young.

"I will not risk your life so rashly as to tell you." Theroun set a hand to the lad's slender shoulder. "But what I want you to do is *dig*, Thaddeus. You have a keen mind. Dig, and come back to me with questions. I will answer what I can."

"Why?" Thaddeus whispered. "Why expose yourself, sir? I could go to the Guard, have you accused of High Treason for everything you've just admitted to me."

Theroun gave him a level look. He almost wished the lad would do it, if it meant exposing Lhaurent. But no, the game had to be subtler than that. Theroun had to figure out a better way to strike the head from the eel, a better way to prevent a war that would cost thousands of lives and probably the security of the entire nation.

And Elyasin's life.

"We're done here, Thad. I have documents to prepare." Rising from his seat at the stone bench, Theroun turned to go. But the lad was pale and very still, a kind of stillness that let Theroun know he had one more question.

"You didn't answer me, sir." Thad breathed.

"Yes, I did. Use your wits." Theroun scolded softly. "Would I be telling *anyone* this if I was secure in my position?"

"No." Thad swallowed. "You're afraid of what Lhaurent and the people behind him are about to do. You're regretting your decision to be one of them. Whatever is coming is not what you joined them for."

"Smart lad." Theroun nodded. "And if the Black Viper is afraid for our nation, Thaddeus... then you should be afraid. Very afraid. And very quiet. For now."

"Would you kill me, sir... to keep me quiet?" Frank terror was behind the lad's eyes, but also courage as he sat very still. He wasn't going to run from his death if it came today. Theroun took a deep breath, considering the lad's question.

"If I wanted you dead, you would be cold by now."

Thad was parchment-white, but he did not fidget.

"I have to go." Theroun murmured at last, satisfied with their discourse and knowing now that all his prior reasoning had been sound. "Stay quiet, and think over everything we've discussed. Study the broader implications of what you've learned, and why I've confessed these things to you. All Generals have to take into account every supply line, every watering hole, the amount a man sweats when fighting in full armor under the scorching summer sun, and how long he can do it without water. Think, Thad. Consider all the repercussions. Dig. We will speak again later."

Turning, Theroun crunched down the gravel path, wondering if he had just made a vast mistake beginning this discourse with Thaddeus.

Or if he'd set a pebble rolling that would soon cause an avalanche.

* * *

IT WAS VERY LATE when a knock came at Theroun's ironbound door. Theroun was sitting before the fireplace in his armchair, swirling wine in his goblet as he stared into the flames. Making sure his customary glower was in place, he barked, "Come!" at the door – but it wasn't the Castellan who whisked in. It was First-Lieutenant Fenton den'Kharel, lithe and brisk, a man any General would have been proud to have as one of his top commanders. Den'Kharel had a stunning record of service, and his demeanor was entirely steady as he stood at military ease once the door closed, calm and ready.

"Lieutenant den'Kharel," Theroun glowered as he rose from his chair to face the man, setting down his wine. "This is a very late visit."

"I know, Chancellor." The man nodded briskly. "But I would like to discuss security around the Dhenra and King Therel tomorrow for the coronation and wedding."

Theroun didn't reproach the Guardsman for his request; it was natural for the First-Lieutenant to want extra security at such an important event, especially since the Captain-General was still in the cells and den'Kharel had no one to consult other than the Dhenra. Rising, Theroun faced the man, ignoring a vicious twinge in his side.

"Let's hear it, den'Kharel. What do you suggest?"

"I want a retinue of a hundred Guardsmen on the floor of the Throne Hall for the coronation," the Lieutenant spoke promptly, "and another hundred in the balconies. Twenty close to the Dhenra on the dais. Four right next to the throne, tagged to her person the entire time, even for the procession, including myself. I also want fifty of those present at the Writ signing in the Small Hall."

This time, Theroun did sigh; it was too late to hide his weariness from the deluge of self-loathing that had worn him down all day. "That's a veritable *army*, Lieutenant."

"Yes, sir." Den'Kharel nodded, with a shrewd determination in his steady gold-brown eyes. "But I think the numbers prudent and sufficient, sir."

"Therel's not going to cut Elyasin up and stuff her in a trunk while they're signing their vows." Theroun barked sourly, crossing his arms over his chest as he stared the Guardsman down. But then, the First-Lieutenant slid forward a small step. It was a careful movement, and Theroun held himself in check as the man's presence suddenly *intensified* for no apparent reason. That one small movement had put Theroun on edge with his old fighter's instincts – as if Fenton might go for a blade to strike him.

But Fenton den'Kharel merely reached into the inner pocket of his blue jerkin, drawing out a folded piece of paper and handing it over. "Your pardon, Chancellor, but Captain den'Alrahel believes the Dhenra is in danger, and I quite agree. Read this to yourself, please."

Frowning, Theroun took the piece of paper and opened it. Skimming it quickly, his head snapped up as fury raged through his veins, genuinely shocked as he had not been in ages. A shiver of rage laced with terror surged through his body, twisting his damaged side with unimaginable pain.

"Is this some kind of *joke*, Lieutenant?!" Theroun seethed.

"No, sir." The First-Lieutenant shook his head, his gaze hard and ready. "Hence the tight security around the Dhenra tomorrow. And, I suggest, for the indefinite future."

Theroun crumpled the paper into his fist, livid at what was written upon it. The short paragraph of text had spoken of the walls of Roushenn as mobile, each and every hall in the palace hiding a second palace behind the palace – secret passages full of spies watching from every mirror and listening behind every hall. With a growl of battle-rage, Theroun turned, hurling the wad of paper into the fire where it caught and blazed at once. Rounding upon the First-Lieutenant with blistering fury, Theroun snarled, "Who else knows about this?!"

"I'm not sure, sir." The man spoke low, still calm even in the face of Theroun's rage. "Maybe everyone; maybe no-one. I don't know how deep the secret goes, or for how long. Generations, perhaps. I have an eyewitness, a Kingsman who was present for the Summons. He saw the walls move. And he saw the Kingsmen slaughtered that night because of it. We've been trying to get his testimony before the Dhenra but she won't make time."

A scowl thundered across Theroun's face as rage replaced every emotion within him, making him tremble, making the old wound in his side grip and sear. Of course there were passages behind the walls. How else could an entire army of people disappear in a single night? Rage seethed through him at the Lothren, who had never trusted him enough to tell him how the disappearance of the Kingsmen had happened – or that Roushenn had a palace behind the palace.

And then Theroun realized something else – that a Kingsman in hiding had come to den'Kharel, had trusted den'Kharel. As Theroun narrowed his eyes upon the Guardsman he saw Fenton den'Kharel was tidy, the row of buckles on his cobalt jerkin done up to the shoulder. Fit like a keshar, he was muscle and sinew and nothing else, his gold-brown eyes utterly steady. Theroun had thought the man was sinewed and calm because he had been High Brigade, but now he knew better. Fenton den'Kharel was fine-honed Alrashemni Kingsmen steel, the finest blades ever wrought. And a Kingsman had come to him, trusted him, because they were the same.

Fenton hadn't changed his posture, but his persona intensified again as he waited under Theroun's blistering scrutiny – the unmistakable feel of Kingsman protectiveness.

But den'Kharel and his secret wasn't the issue at hand. Lhaurent was. As Theroun ground his teeth together so hard they ached, certain to the depths of his gut that Lhaurent was behind it all, he pictured how lovely the eel's head would look on a pike, displayed for the crows to pick. The Castellan had control of the palace somehow – that's why the bastard always looked so smug and certain of himself. How many times had Theroun been watched in his quarters? How much had Lhaurent studied him, listened to his conversations? Theroun had always suspected the Castellan had spies among the servants, listening at niches or peep-holes in the walls, but this was insanity.

And if Roushenn's regular servants knew nothing of those secret passages, then who did Lhaurent have within the walls? And how many?

Enough to kill two thousand Kingsmen in a single night.

"Halsos in chains..." Theroun breathed. Standing a moment, he ground his jaw, his teeth close to cracking. The game was up – his hands were tied. If he refused the First-Lieutenant his extra Guardsmen, Fenton would be suspicious of Theroun when the Dhenra's assassination came. But permit it, and Theroun was risking Lhaurent knowing that Theroun had betrayed the Khehemni Lothren's assassination by allowing too many guards in the hall. Now was the moment to decide, just like decisions came upon the battlefield. Attack, defend, change course, regroup.

Let the pieces fall where they may.

General Theroun den'Vekir took command. Moving to his desk, he wrote a quick sentence on a scrap of paper in a hand small enough to be very to read from the vantage of any wall. *Disregard everything I say and follow what I write here,* he wrote. *You have your men. Protect the Dhenra at all costs. I never gave you these orders – Captain-General den'Alrahel did.* Folding the note, Theroun stepped to Fenton and handed it over.

Placing his faith in a Kingsman.

"This is for your Captain-General." Theroun spoke brusquely, as if dismissing the man. "You may read it and give it to her in the cells. I do *not* permit any additional Guardsmen at the coronation or the Writ signing. Fifty will do in the Throne Hall, and the regular thirty in the Small Hall. That is all."

Seething anger burned in Fenton den'Kharel's commonly placid brown eyes, though he did not tremble as he took the note. At the end of Theroun's speech, he snapped his well-polished boots smartly and inclined his head, though Theroun could tell the man was itching to pull a blade and run it right through Theroun's throat for denying the extra security. Without a word, the Kingsman spun on his heels, yanking Theroun's door open and slamming it behind him, trembling the iron fittings and the lock from the power in his wiry frame. Theroun took a deep breath, then let it out.

Hopefully, den'Kharel would read the note in the next few minutes.

"I may not be much of a man now, Uhlas," once-General Theroun den'Vekir spoke softly as he went to the table, taking a very long drink of wine. "But I will protect the innocent. Fuck Lhaurent, and fuck the Khehemni Lothren. Let there be war between us, though it blister my bones and crow-pick me clean."

33

JHERRICK

Jherrick stood in the fey darkness of the Hinterhaft, watching as an argument ensued between Castellan Lhaurent and the Elsthemi First Sword. He wasn't supposed to have overheard it. He'd only come to report on Guard-Captain Olea's activities prior to having gotten herself chucked in a cell by the Dhenra, and about her investigating the Kingsmen disappearance. But though it was the usual hour when the Castellan expected him in the octagonal hall, he'd come at a bad time, and now was party to an argument as he stepped back, deep into the shadows of the grand vaulted arch.

Listening to the tense conversation echo as blue orbs floated around the center of the room.

"You've been Khehemnas all your life, Devresh," Lhaurent was arguing in his smooth, impeccably cultured voice. A tension in his vocal chords was the only thing that indicated he was furious. "I don't see why this one more task for the Lothren would be any different."

The Elsthemi First Sword had his hands planted on his lean hips in the vague blue light, his stubborn swordsman's stance outlined by a single lantern lit upon the octagonal table. "I practically raised that boy, Lhaurent." He growled in a thick Northern accent. "I won't kill his bride the day they wed. It's disgusting."

"Disgusting or not, it needs doing. And you promised to do it. At your last visit here, don't you recall? Just a few weeks ago." Lhaurent was firm, his hands folded neatly before him, his body deceptively quiet in his impeccable silk attire.

"I've changed my mind." The man growled back, setting a hand to the pommel of his sword. "I don't know why I ever agreed to that. You don't know Therel – he's *besotted* with Elyasin, in a way I've never seen before. Let them have a few weeks together at least."

"Giving them a few weeks together would give them time to plan together, time to strengthen their alliance." Lhaurent spoke calmly, though with an edge of steel to his voice now. "It must not happen. We need riots in Lintesh to create instability here, my friend, and it cannot happen without Elyasin's demise. We need to give the Chancellate power to move things forward against Elsthemen so all our mutual aims can be met."

"Find someone else to be patsy to the Lothren's crimes!" The Elsthemi First Sword growled like a bear, echoing up to the cavernous blue vaults. "I'm done. When this plan was first laid, I agreed to spy for the Lothren in Elsthemen and cause a disruption at the coronation by mistakenly skewering one of the Menderian Chancellate going for a blade against Therel – not by killing Therel's bride, goddammit! To that original agreement, I hold now. Not to the one you somehow forced me to agree to a few weeks ago, you leech."

Jherrick went immaculately still in the shadows of the arch; his heart hammered and he was almost certain they could hear it. Dusky blue swamped his vision as his head reeled, his body deciding whether it would panic at this sudden news. But he kept himself in check, breathing steadily and silently as he digested the information he'd just heard.

The Khehemni Lothren were planning to kill the Dhenra. It would send the nation into turmoil. It would send Lintesh into turmoil, and Roushenn – everything in Jherrick's life. Suddenly, he saw the grand scheme. How the Lothren would take command of Alrou-Mendera once the dust had settled from this event. How rule of the country would fall to the Chancellate, to Chancellor Evshein and other key players at the head of the nation that Jherrick wasn't high up enough to know about.

How rule of Roushenn would fall to Lhaurent with the King's line dead.

Watching closely, Jherrick buried his emotions under stillness, straining his hearing to catch more. But the conversation had paused now, as Lhaurent narrowed his eyes upon the Elsthemi First Sword, a sign of severe displeasure at the slur the First Sword had just leveled at him. The First Sword was standoffish, still bristling with his hand upon his blade, though from his posture, it didn't look like he was going to draw steel.

But then Lhaurent gave a liquid, placating smile and a regal gesture with one hand. "Walk with me, Devresh. On behalf of the Lothren in Alrou-Mendera, I am willing to hear your argument for an alternative scenario, but I find myself in need of exercise and a bite of refreshment. If you will accompany me, I'm certain we can solve this dilemma appropriately for all parties concerned. Please."

Lhaurent gestured again down the length of the vaulted chamber, amiably. The Elsthemi First Sword growled in his throat, scowled, then ripped a hand through his thick white mane of hair. "Fine. Lead the way. But make it quick, Lhaurent. Therel expects me back within the hour."

"Oh, this shall take no time at all. This way, my friend." Lhaurent turned graciously, and the First Sword followed, towards a far arch that led toward a vast room Jherrick was not permitted in. It was a room no one was permitted inside, actually, part of an entire section of the Hinterhaft that was off-limits. Jherrick narrowed his eyes, watching their forms become swallowed in blue shadows as they walked off towards the forbidden halls, wondering why Lhaurent would take the First Sword to such a private area.

He didn't know what occurred back in that private section, and Jherrick's other contact in the Lothren, Chancellor Evshein den'Lhamann, only ever met Lhaurent in his quarters. They never met in the Hinterhaft where Lhaurent did his dirty work, and never in that secret section, a massive chamber right at the very heart of the Hinterhaft that was off-limits to all on pain of torture.

Jherrick breathed softly where he stood, his mind and emotions in tumult as he wondered if he should stay. If he should move or if he would be discovered by some other agent of Lhaurent's if he chanced returning to Roushenn proper. As he debated, the hairs on the back of his neck suddenly raised. He stiffened with a hand on the hilt of one longknife, his heart hammering as he cast his glance about in the fey blue light of the octagonal hall, feeling another of Lhaurent's agents close by but seeing no one. Just as Jherrick was about to draw steel and raise a challenge to the unseen intruder, a hand pressed atop his from the shadows right beside him – trapping his fingers to his blade-hilt.

"Draw no steel, boy." A man's voice murmured to his left. "I am no adversary to you."

Jherrick hissed in surprise, almost drawing his blade from sheer terror that someone could get so close to him in the shadows without having been seen. Jherrick's back was to the stone, and tucked into the archway, he should have been impossible to sneak up on, but somehow this fellow had managed it. Not only that, the man had gotten close enough to lay a hand on Jherrick without betraying a single sound in the darkness. Jherrick's gut dropped through the floor as he breathed hard in surprise, his entire body shivering with battle-energy, though he had to suppress it.

"Are you Lothren?" He growled to the intruder.

"No, boy," the shadow breathed back, low and calm. "I serve only the Castellan. I know he is anticipating your report. Stay put. He shall return shortly."

"Who are you?" Jherrick turned his head, searching for the man in the shadows. He could barely make the fellow out, lean and trim but tall, swathed entirely in black the same flat charcoal color as the shadows. His head was covered by a black hood, his lower face wrapped with soft black cloth so only two pairs of dark grey eyes watched Jherrick from the shadows. Wearing trousers and a long shirt woven of flat charcoal silk, his garb was strangely bound by black cordage to keep it tight over his thighs and arms. Even the buckles on his supple leather jerkin and boots had been blackened, or perhaps crafted that way, so he seemed to disappear into the stone beside Jherrick as he stood in the shadows. Weapons of a masterful variety bristled about his person upon an ornate leather harness, all of their steel and leather crafted black to be unnotable in the darkness.

A lot of weapons.

"I'm no-one, boy," the shadow breathed, his eyes calm and strangely empty of emotion. "I'm no one to note, and no one to trifle with. Your master will return shortly. Wait for him."

With that, the fellow melted right back into the wall.

Jherrick's breath stopped. His heart nearly stopped. The man had walked backwards, *right into the wall.* And now he was gone. Jherrick's heart restarted, furiously fast from what he'd just seen, wondering if he'd been addled somehow. But other than terrified, his veins racing with energy and shock, he felt unaltered. And he had no more time to think about it as a moment later, the Castellan and Elsthemi First Sword reappeared down the long hallway, emerging back into the vaulted octagonal chamber. To Jherrick's surprise, the Elsthemi First Sword was talking genially with Lhaurent now, almost smiling as they returned to the hall, which looked odd on his battle-lined face.

As he turned to take his leave, he offered his arm to the Castellan. "Lhaurent. If we don't speak again, good fortune to you."

"Devresh." The Castellan clasped arms with a pleasant smile. "You will be lauded in history, my friend. The Lothren appreciate your sacrifice, and will remember your deeds. A brave end to a brave life."

"I am honored to do the Lothren such service." With a deep bow to Lhaurent, the First Sword turned and strode away, up the nearest set of stairs that would take him to one of the few Hinterhaft access-points and back to Roushenn proper.

Jherrick knew his lips had fallen open; he couldn't shut them. Questions whirled in Jherrick's mind that the Elsthemi First Sword had had such a change of heart in such a short span of time. The only conclusion he came to was that the First Sword had been drugged by the Castellan in that private off-limits chamber. But he hadn't looked drugged when he strode away. He'd not stumbled, not swayed. Not even so much as moved slowly to indicate they'd shared a goblet of wine.

But before he could mull on it further, the Castellan was suddenly upon him. "Ah. Jherrick." Lhaurent's voice was intimately pleasant as he moved gracefully towards Jherrick at the side of the arch, a smile curling his lips. "How much of that did you see just now?"

Jherrick's veins ran cold suddenly, knowing what Lhaurent would do to him if he lied or tried to play the man false. "Just a minute or so before you walked down the corridor, my Lothren. And this bit as you returned. Forgive me. I merely came to give my usual report, I didn't expect—"

"You did right to wait for me." Lhaurent smiled benignly, though there was something deeply cold within that smile. "And do you have any opposition to anything you just saw or heard?"

Jherrick could see death in the Castellan's cold grey eyes, luminous beneath the fae blue globes that lit the chamber. He could feel that he was disposable; that his life meant nothing to the Castellan, and only information mattered. The privacy of that information was everything, and if Jherrick couldn't keep that privacy – then he was already dead.

As dead as Dhenra Elyasin would be at her coronation tomorrow.

"I serve the Lothren, my liege," Jherrick murmured, stilling his body and face to betray nothing. "I am Khehemni."

"You may serve the Lothren, but do you *oppose* anything you just witnessed, boy?" Lhaurent slid forward a step, his grey eyes taken with a vicious shine now that chilled Jherrick to his very core.

Jherrick stilled himself beyond flesh. He was stone; he was granite. He would betray nothing of his feelings – not now or ever. "No, my Lothren."

Lhaurent did not smile right away, his opal-grey gaze boring into Jherrick's marrow as if trying to read his holy soul. And when the Castellan did finally smile, it was cold, cold, cold. "Up to the cells, then Jherrick. I believe you are on duty for the coronation, are you not? Guarding Captain den'Alrahel?"

"Yes, my Lothren."

"Good. Report to me again in three days' time."

"Yes, my Lothren."

With that, Lhaurent turned and slid silently away, back in the direction of the forbidden halls. Jherrick departed also, something clenched deep inside him, though he was utterly relieved to still have his hide on his bones after that interaction with Lhaurent. Moving back through the Hinterhaft the way he'd come today, Jherrick's mind churned furiously, battle-tension still gripping every muscle. He realized he'd not told Lhaurent about the black-clad man – though from the way Lhaurent had looked at him just now, he'd been glad to keep their interaction as brief as possible.

Passing shadowy figures as he egressed, other agents of the Lothren who gave only a silent nod as they slipped about their business, Jherrick realized everyone was moving behind the walls today. The Hinterhaft was strangely abustle compared to its usual cavernous silence. Lhaurent kept a veritable army behind the walls, people who served the Lothren through him. Though his regular Roushenn spies consisted of cooks, maids, and porters, those permitted behind the walls were quiet mercenaries, spies, and thieves. A foreigner passed at a turn of the corridor, dark-skinned with the swarthy build of a pirate, probably from Jadoun. He was followed by a Perthian raider with rows of ear piercings, and a Ghreccan with black curls and geometric tattoos upon his neck. Everyone passed in silence, hardly sparing Jherrick a glance. Unsavory men all, Lhaurent's go-to men were a strong network for the Khehemni Lothren, but Jherrick found himself wondering suddenly just how much the Lothren knew about Lhaurent.

Especially if the man kept a black-clad assassin that could melt through solid stone somehow.

At last, Jherrick came to one of the access-junctures, sliding out through a pivoting section of stone into a dark niche behind a statue of antique armor in the West Armory. Making his way up to Roushenn's regular halls, he stepped lithely around a bustle of maids, porters, and visitors all crowding Roushenn for the impending coronation and wedding. But Jherrick hardly noted the swirl of people around him as he strode onward. Inside, he stewed, wondering about Lhaurent – and about what he'd done to the Elsthemi First Sword.

Suddenly, he knew where his feet were leading him. There was only one person he could report such suspicions to, and Jherrick glanced both ways down the hall, making sure none saw as he rapped smartly upon the door to Chancellor Evshein's personal quarters. There were no mirrors in this hall by which Lhaurent or any of his house-spies could see, though there still might be hearing-niches behind the corridor. But Jherrick had to take the risk, and he pounded again, harder, his heart racing.

Suddenly, the door was thrown back by a scowling guard, one of Evshein's personal attendants.

"Corporal den'Tharn!" The brawny Guardsman blinked. "Do you need something?"

Jherrick couldn't help that he'd been recognized. He did work in the office where the entire Guard came to collect their week's pay, after all. "Lieutenant den'Bhliss. I have an urgent matter for the Chancellor."

"Just a moment." The guard turned and shut the door in Jherrick's face. It was another moment of gut-wrenching waiting before he returned. "You have five minutes, den'Tharn. The Chancellor is very busy today with the Dhenra's coronation tomorrow. So make it quick."

"Absolutely." Jherrick sidled in, casting his eyes about the sumptuous apartments until he spied the elderly white-haired Chancellor Evshein den'Lhamann sitting at his desk in the adjacent room. He wasted no time, striding through the sitting-room, straight to the Chancellor. Evshein blinked rapidly behind his gold-rimmed spectacles to see Jherrick, his hooked nose and eagle-eyed scowl formidable as he cast his spectacles to the desk and rose, this thin frame stiff in his voluminous black state robes with gold embroidery. Beckoning Jherrick to the open-air balcony adjacent to his office, Evshein dismissed his guard.

"Chancellor," Jherrick murmured as they stepped out to the balcony, Evshein closing the balcony doors behind them. "I require a private word, sir—"

"Jherrick! You are forbidden to contact me—" The elderly Chancellor growled, irate.

"Forgive me, Chancellor. But I have news of import that you must hear right away."

"Go on." The Chancellor crossed his skinny sun-spotted hands into the voluminous sleeves of his gilt-edged robe.

"Sir," Jherrick cast his eyes about, making sure no others were out upon nearby balconies as he kept his voice low in the hot, sunny morning. "Do you know what the Elsthemi First Sword is planning tomorrow? Tasked to him by Castellan Lhaurent?"

The Chancellor blinked, then scowled. Glancing around also, he gripped Jherrick's arm in a claw of steel as he hissed, "Fool, boy! I should slit your throat for bringing this to me in such an obvious manner today! But since we are quite alone, I will put your mind at rest. Trust the Lothren. The First Sword serves our plans, and our Castellan does but ensure those plans."

"But I heard them arguing, sir! The First Sword doesn't want to do it!" Jherrick hissed.

"He swore he would." Evshein blinked. "Ever since Lhaurent brought him here for the Elsthemi preparatory conferences, he was amenable to his task."

"I swear to you he's not," Jherrick argued. "Just now, I heard them arguing in the Hinterhaft, and Lhaurent took him away to a chamber he never lets anyone enter. And then they returned, and the First Sword was ... joyous. To give up his life."

"Many are joyous to serve the Broken Circle." Evshein admonished severely.

"But I swear to you, his attitude was entirely different before and after he entered that room. Like he'd been drugged."

"Lhaurent is a master of persuasion, lad. Let it go."

"This was beyond persuasion! I've seen Lhaurent's tactics of persuasion, and all of them involve threats and blood. This was something else." Fervent, Jherrick wasn't about to let it drop. Something about Lhaurent was off, and someone who could do something about it needed to know.

Evshein was scowling now as he lifted one gnarled old hand to brush his bushy white eyebrows. "A room in the Hinterhaft he never lets anyone else see, you say?"

"A vast room." Jherrick nodded. "I've walked all around it. It's larger than the Throne Hall, sir."

"And you think he keeps a poison apothecary in there to make others do his bidding?"

"I don't know." Jherrick shook his head. "But I worry that he serves himself, not the Lothren."

And here, Evshein gave him a very stern eyeball. "You will tell no-one what you suppose, Jherrick den'Tharn. Let me deal with it. Lhaurent has served the Lothren long, but always he has built his network in secret, and we allow it because he is excessively efficient and effective. Attend to your regular duties, den'Tharn. And if you breathe a word of this—"

"I know, Chancellor."

Chancellor Evshein den'Lhamann gave him one last pointed look, then motioned Jherrick out. Jherrick knew his position, and went with the curt bow that any Guardsman would give a superior. His walk was brisk as he left, his nod to his fellow Guardsman without passion or emotion as he departed.

But inside, his gut churned to know what was about to happen tomorrow, his palms broken into a cold sweat.

34

KHOUREN

Stepping briskly through the fey blue passages behind Roushenn's walls, Khouren Alodwine tried not to think about the price of blood that would be paid tomorrow at the coronation – only about the glory of the Unification, come at last. Into the Hinterhaft he plunged, then back to wan midnight torchlight. Through closed cendarie doors, through ironbound locks and stout frames, through walls of solid byrunstone and halls of polished marble, no barrier restricted him. For the walls of Roushenn were of no import to Khouren – walls being of no import the entirety of his four hundred year span. Flowing through everything he touched as if barriers turned to thick water, his body created an ease of passage like stepping through a waterfall – with only a sensation of pressure and a popping in his ears.

Clad in the darkest storm-grey, he wore the ancient garb of the caravanserai, the *Berounhim* who had led his clan out of a brutal desert war nearly a thousand years ago. It had been long before Khouren was born, but his garb recalled theirs, silken and bound tight at the hips and arms so he moved silently in the dark. A silk *shouf* covered his lower face beneath the leather hood of his jerkin, leaving only his grey eyes to pierce the night. Beneath his buckled leather jerkin and weapons harness was a shirt of the softest charcoal silk, supple gloves covering his hands. Twin longknives of an ancient, sickled variety rode his back rather than a sword, more knives of various kinds secured upon his weapons harness.

Khouren had never mastered the sword. Knives were better for close, confined spaces like Roushenn's halls.

But though part of him scanned for enemies in the dark like always, Khouren maintained a part of his mind upon his feet as he traversed the palace. He had to maintain a sliver of attention in his feet when he walked upon anything but solid earth. The House of Alodwine, the original Scions of Khehem, had always possessed the most peculiar gifts, their *wyrria* of *Werus et Khehem* yielding formidable abilities. Khouren had somehow acquired his oddity, along with House Alodwine's longevity, but with it came a tendency to fall through man-made structures. He'd broken his share of bones over the years – though fortunately, his long life also included mending quickly.

The blessing of his ancient clan was this firmness of body and mind – for more years than perhaps they should have lingered.

Taking a shortcut to his destination, Khouren emerged in a catacombed larder, snatching up a hunk of bread and a small round of cheese as he went. A scullery-maid was sorting potatoes in the corner of the larder by lantern light and shrieked as she saw him materialize from the wall, clapping her hands to her mouth, her brown eyes enormous. Shuddering in terror, she was frozen to the spot, unable to move or even breathe as he strode through.

"The Black Ghost of Roushenn!" She whispered with a squeak as he neared.

The Black Ghost of Roushenn. What a laugh.

Khouren didn't mind the nickname; in fact, he found it appropriate to his nature. He played his part, staring her down with a commanding, terrifying presence as he moved past, then melted through the wall past a crate of pears. He heard a sigh of her fainting before he moved through the wall, but then with a rush like water and a chill like mist, he was through, back to the darkness of the Hinterhaft upon the other side. Taking a bite of bread and cheese, a vague smile lifted Khouren's lips in the darkness; in these halls, he was through anything in moments, silent as a ghost and often surprising servants and guards as if he was one.

From which the most amazing tales of Roushenn's hauntings had sprouted.

But he was alone in his strange gift; to his knowledge no one else in his family line had been born with such an oddity. There weren't many of them now, the Alodwine lineage having a particular *wyrria* that made bearing children difficult. But their supreme longevity had always made them suspicious, and so the House of Alodwine had always lived in the shadows. Some had sided with the Khehemni over the years, their original bloodline. Some had sided with the Alrashemni, opposing atrocities now committed by a people who had forgotten their past.

But most had simply declined to engage the ancient war.

Because the lineage of Alodwine kept the true tales of the Thirteen Tribes, the Prophecy of the Goldenmarks and the Rennkavi, and the great Unity to come. They alone carried hope through all these bitter years of war, waiting for the one who would unite them at last, who would undo the vast wrongs done long ago in Khehem. And forty years ago, when a palace page had accidentally stumbled into Khouren's domain, the *wyrria* within the lad strong enough to open the walls to the Hinterhaft, Khouren had seen the Goldenmarks upon the boy's flesh. He had stepped from the shadows and knelt before his true Rennkavi.

The one who would Unite them all in glory.

Now, his feet hummed to be doing the his Rennkavi's will. Tomorrow was to be a day of glory even as much as it would be a day of bloodshed and mourning for the nation. Khouren felt the cold burn of conflict within him as he stepped through muted halls lit by blue orbs weaving like drunken moths high above. Tomorrow was the day his Rennkavi would take command of his rightful place leading the country, though he would let the Khehemni Lothren believe they were still in charge, for now. Tomorrow all worlds would tilt, all perceptions shift, all foundations be shaken.

And his Rennkavi would step into that dearth of leadership like a phoenix of glory – Uniting all the peoples at last.

Stepping quickly through Roushenn's dark halls, Khouren slipped through another wall and into his destination at last – his Rennkavi's private rooms in the palace. Though many plots were in play for tomorrow, most of them known to the Khehemni Lothren, there was one task which was Khouren's alone, just as it had been ten years ago when the Alrashemni Kingsmen had come to Roushenn.

Stepping quickly over the plush silk carpets to his Rennkavi's ornately carved desk, the fire's low flicker was the only light in the sumptuous apartments as he saw the item he'd been promised. The same as ten years ago, the small glass vial shone in the firelight, nestled in an open box of ironwood upon the desk with a black velvet lining. Capped in pure gold, the contents of the vial were clear, and as Khouren lifted the vial to examine it, he mused that anyone else might have thought it contained water, or a tincture of distilled white wine with medicinal herbs.

But this tincture wasn't for healing – only death.

Unbottling it, Khouren wafted it beneath his nose. The faint smell of rotten citrus made his stomach churn, and he stoppered it tightly before slipping it into his leather belt pouch. Turning to the low-lit fireplace, he found the second item he needed for tomorrow's events. A large bronze censer hung upon a chain over the fireplace, an unnotable item such as the Jenner priesthood often used for burning healing incense when one was ill. Retrieving it from its iron hook, he hunkered at the yet-glowing coals, brushing back ashes to make them burn hotter. Twisting the censer open, Khouren raked in a few coals then assembled it, holding it by a short length of chain so it wouldn't swing.

Turning, he stepped to the nearest wall and melted into it – back the way he'd come.

With his items collected, Khouren moved through dark halls and light, cool halls and warm. Descending stair after stair though Roushenn's sub-basements and deep in the bowels of the Hinterhaft, he at last came to the place where he knew his items would be safe until he could come back for them tomorrow. Melting through the wall, the ancient crypt below the palace soared around him with silence and utter darkness. There were no sounds in the deep as Khouren moved through the space by instinct and touch – placing the bronze censer and glass vial on a flat bier of stone to be safe until the morrow.

Blowing on the coals gently through the censer's fine filigree, he heated them to an eerie light, casting the bier in strange red shadows. Like blood over water, it seemed to Khouren, as he watched the curling light move eerily over the cold bier of blue byrunstone. He knew the censer would stay lit down here until he needed it tomorrow; this crypt had a strange way of preserving the life of all things – even things that consumed or had already perished.

Turning away, he strode back through the bloody light – vanishing again into darkness.

Retracing his steps up to the sub-basements, his next stop tonight was an errand for his grandfather. It wasn't precisely an errand for his Rennkavi, but it had been on numerous occasions, and Khouren was content to believe that even now under the current circumstances, his charge should continue – a charge he distinctly enjoyed. In a dark section of Hinterhaft at the level of the Upper Cells, Khouren slid into a wall, only his nose and eyes emerging from the wall into the fresher shadows of a small, barred cell. Well out of the torch's reach at the guard station by the stairs, no light found him as he came to stillness within the wall, breathing slowly and maintaining focus so he didn't move right through.

Khouren's eyes were adjusted to the dark, and his charge tonight was crowned by the halo of torch-light in their brackets behind her. Reclining on her pallet bed near the bars, her long black curls shone blue in the unsteady light, her face angelic yet hard like queens of old. With her striking cheekbones and sharp jaw, her soft, kissable mouth, and skin that somehow remained white despite all the time she spent out upon the Tiers, she was a rare beauty.

And a rare joy to behold, like always.

She slept upon her pallet bed. Khouren loved watching her sleep. Ever since his Rennkavi had bid him keep an eye upon her ten years ago when she arrived at the palace, he'd enjoyed his duty. Sometimes she would twist in her sheets and cry out, sweating with nightmares, and at those times Khouren felt his heart riven for how she suffered. Sometimes she would surge, flushed and scraping away her blankets in the dead of night as she took her Dhenir in dreams. Khouren loved to watch those moments, to see how she rode her beloved even two long years past his death. Sometimes he would place himself within the wall just like this with only his eyes to watch her, touching himself as she spasmed and cried out in bliss.

Sometimes he'd done that when she'd actually been with her callous princeling – jealous and seething to watch her fucking another man.

She wasn't his, but she was. Khouren knew no one could appreciate her like he could. No one knew the pureness of her lineage like he did, the vastness of *wyrria* that still lived inside her bloodlines. This creature before him was his true Queen, unlike the pretty sun-haired woman who would never make it to see Queenship upon the morrow. But now as he watched her sleep, her straight brows became knit in a frown, a troubled look he'd seen her make many a night.

Khouren had the urge, as he always did, to soothe her.

Sliding from the wall in the darkness as he removed his gloves, Khouren kept to the deepest shadows, making no sound in the night. Moving closer with an impeccable silence practiced over hundreds of years, he paused his breath and slowed his heart to his will, giving nothing away to her formidable *wyrric* hearing. In her deepest cycle of sleep now, she breathed steady and slow, a pattern he had mapped over the years. She would not wake; not unless something startled her. But the guard was drowsing at his station and the palace was silent in the deepest dark before Coronation Day dawned.

Now was his time – and hers – to be together.

Khouren's grandfather had bid him keep her safe while she was incarcerated, and it was not precisely against his Rennkavi's orders, so safe was how Khouren would keep her. At last, he gained her side, next to her pallet bed. She hadn't stirred, and reaching out as he had done a thousand times before, he brushed his bare fingers gently over those beautiful curls. She sighed in the night; her little frown eased to feel his gentle caress. A rapturous peace stole over her face, lifting the corners of her lips in a beautiful smile.

Oh, how she smiled for him. It filled Khouren with light, his heart bright as a thousand suns to feel that smile, that benevolence turned upon him. She had never been Goldenmarked, it was not her who was called to be his Rennkavi, but if it had been, Khouren would have followed her beyond the grave to do her bidding. Of royal blood from two ancient lines, Khehemni through her mother and Alrashemni through her father, she was the same as his Rennkavi – precisely the the same.

Except he'd been Goldenmarked and she had not.

A vast mistake, so Khouren thought as he smiled in the darkness, still brushing his fingers tenderly over her curls. As he caressed her with the barest touch, she sighed for him again, curling deeper into her thin blanket. Turning her face up, she sensed him close, though she still dreamed. Her smile was bliss for him, radiant in the night. Every time he'd touched her like this, she'd shone like sunlight upon water like that.

All for him.

As he touched her, her lips fell open and she made a subtle movement; a movement of wanting. Without a sound, Khouren leaned down until his lips hovered over hers. She turned her face up more, a sigh of breath issuing from her lips as Khouren slowly stroked his hand over her jaw, touching his fingertips to her skin in the sweetest caress. She sighed again in her dreams, feeling him. And like the night wind, Khouren whispered his lips over hers – touching his lips to hers a peaceful kiss in the undisturbed silence of the cells. When it was finished, she sighed for him, her lips curling into a sweet smile as Khouren's lingered.

"I love you." He whispered to the night.

"Alden..." She sighed, snuggling down into her thin blanket, smiling.

Lifting his chin, Khouren nuzzled her nose softly, just like the Dhenir had once done. "Always."

And then he rose, melting back into the wall to watch over her until dawn.

35

ELOHL

Coronation Day dawned hot, the sky heavy with humidity, which quickly began gathering into burgeoning towers of cumulus over the mountains. Sweat trickled down Elohl's neck beneath the high collar of his cobalt jerkin as he stood at attention in the Small Hall. Fifty Guardsmen stood stock-still through the moderately-sized hall with their hands resting on the pommels of their swords, all waiting just like Elohl. They'd spent all morning securing routes from the Dhenra and King Therel's apartments, clearing them of personnel. The noontime hour had been spent sweeping the Throne Hall, the Small Hall, and all adjacent rooms for the revelry that would take place after the ceremonies.

But no nobles were here yet, the hall still empty except for Guardsmen. Gazing at the tall blonde thief Luc, now in cobalt gear directly across from him in the niche on the far wall, Elohl also saw the sullen young thief Gherris further down the row. Luc held Elohl's gaze, haughty and angry, and the two hadn't exchanged three words today, except when Luc had told Elohl that Ghrenna had had a vision of the Dhenra getting hurt – possibly this afternoon.

Suddenly, the double-doors at the end of the hall boomed open, admitting a draft in the sweltering mid-afternoon heat. A procession of Chancellors in black and gold doublets with long open robes strolled across the inlaid white marble floor, talking amongst themselves. A small army of servers hustled about the room after them, directed by a tall, lean man dressed in impeccable grey silks that Elohl recognized as the King's Castellan. The Castellan directed the servers with firm smoothness, making sure everything was in last-minute order. As porters wheeled in trestle-tables with small bites and pitchers of lemon water to place along the richly plastered and gilded walls, the Castellan's gaze took in all the Guardsmen stationed around the room with a flicker of distaste.

Elohl was parched, salivating at the thought of water freshened with lemon. But this hardship was little compared to what he had faced in the highmountains as another drip of sweat rolled down his neck, itching in his short beard. He didn't scratch or move. But he found himself thinking about the feel of ice beneath his bare hands, the sensation of cold wind across his neck from a glacier to make the heat tolerable.

It helped. Barely.

After the servers, lords and ladies began filing in. Only those of highest station were permitted to the Writ Signings, small as this hall was. Those of lesser station would be permitted in the Throne Hall for the pomp of the Coronation Ceremony and Royal Wedding directly after all the official documents had been signed here. This short event was where all the most important individuals of both Elsthemen and Alrou-Mendera needed to be to witness the official coronation and wedding, privately. Elohl narrowed his eyes upon the retinue of leather- and fur-clad men and women from Elsthemen, noting a plethora of weapons about them.

But all seemed in a gay mood, chatting amongst themselves in their rolling native Elsthemi. His gaze still roving the hall, Elohl picked out the thief Shara, blending in with a retinue from the Tourmaline Isles. Masquerading as a noble, her turquoise silk dress in the flowing Isleman fashion was scandalous, though Elohl knew there were knives hidden beneath. All smiles and flirtation, she was expert at intrigue, drawing a crowd of men. Expectation sang high in the hall, the temperature of the nobles merry. Virtually no one scowled today except for a stern, warlike man dressed in a rich hunter-green jerkin who had been identified by Fenton as Chancellor Theroun den'Vekir – speaking low with his secretary by a gilded desk set with lit candelabra and pots of flowering cobalt lilac at the front of the room.

At last, a clarion call sounded. The ringing fanfare of hunting horns split the humid air, signifying the Dhenra and King's approach. It was Elohl's signal. As nobles stirred to look and conversation died, Elohl and the other Guardsmen worked their way forward, positioning themselves in a spread double-line on either side of the long red carpet, from the hall's entrance to the gilded desk. Hands on swords, they pressed the crowd back with their presence and hard eyes, corralling nobles away from the carpet.

Elohl watched the Dhenra and King approach from the corner of his eye, holding the line though nobles pressed forward to get a look at the royal pair. They were resplendent. Dhenra Elyasin den'Ildrian wore a clinging gown of snow-blue silk with cobalt trimmings, Alrou-Mendera's colors, the long train whispering behind her and her person dripping with jewelry of sapphires and diamonds. Her golden tresses were wound up through a diamond and sapphire circlet set in gold, the white ermine Stole of the Queen about her shoulders.

King Therel Alramir had dressed per his nations colors also, in crimson and black for the keshar-banner of Elsthemen. Richly brocaded black breeches rode his thighs, chased with gold thread, a long crimson cloak cascading from his shoulders that was embroidered the same. Though a plain circlet of gold sat upon his brow and ash-blond hair, he'd maintained the wilder look of the Highlands, a shaggy grey wolf-pelt over his cloak and a black leather jerkin with silver buckles on beneath. His tall black boots were functional, buckled with twin bootknives, and a nondescript sword rode his hip. Almost predatory, his pale blue eyes swept the hall as he moved down the velvet carpet with his soon-to-be-Queen on his arm.

As King Therel and Dhenra Elyasin stepped to the desk at the front of the hall, their retinue of four Guardsmen parted. Fenton was among them, and Olea's Second-Lieutenant Aldris den'Farahan. Elohl stood close to the desk at the head of the red carpet, Luc across from him. As the Dhenra and King stood before the desk, a few of Therel's Highswords near the Dhenra's guards, a skinny old man with a hound-wrinkled face stepped behind the desk and raised his arms. One of the Dhenra's Chancellors, gold medallions of office winked across his shoulders and over the front of his rich black velvet robes with their gold embroidery. Another blast rang from the horns, and Chancellor Evshein den'Lhamann, the master of these proceedings, raised his thin, reedy voice in welcome.

Elohl's gaze raked the attendants of the Dhenra and King Therel, and the nobility nearby as the Chancellor droned on. A thin Elsthemi lord with bushy white eyebrows sniffed and itched his nose. An Islewoman in green silk reached to her cleavage, but it was only for a handkerchief to mop her face. King Therel's white-haired First Sword shifted his stance, both hands settled easily upon the pommel of his sword. A dark-haired man from Alrou-Mendera grumbled and reached into his doublet, but it was only for a set of gold-rimmed spectacles to blink more closely at the event in progress. The King's Castellan hovered by the paneled wall, immaculately still in his grey silks, his hands clasped servilely as he watched the proceedings.

Elohl kept sweeping the room, one hand on his sword and the other ready at his longknife upon his belt. The Chancellor had at last concluded and the Dhenra was now saying a few words. Heads nodded; faces smiled. Handkerchiefs and lace fans were stilled so all could hear in the stifling hall. But a boom of thunder sounded suddenly, ringing through the vaults, and a number of people jumped as the Dhenra paused. As its rolling wave died, the Dhenra continued, calm and practiced. Elohl's gaze fell upon Fenton, seeing him tight with tension, his gaze rapt upon Elyasin as she finished, King Therel Alramir saying a few words next. More people mopped faces and fanned themselves, the heat in the space thick now as another boom of thunder rippled the hall. A few nobles were moving to the walls, enjoying a chalice of lemon-water and a bite to eat as the proceedings dragged on.

At last, it was time for the signing. Elohl had been informed there were two signings, the first a Pledge of Queenship for Elyasin alone to sign, conferring to her authority as ruling monarch of Alrou-Mendera. The second was the Writ of Marriage, securing the alignment of a Queen-proper to a King. Dhenra Elyasin said a few words and then her Chancellor did, handing her a gilded fountain pen with a fluffy tourli-feather from the desk, then a small, ornate scepter. Dipping her pen in a gilded inkwell, Elyasin affixed her signature to the Pledge of Queenship while holding the scepter. The Chancellor raised his hands, conferred her in as Queen, and the hall erupted into applause.

It went on a long while. Elohl's eyes roved the hall, watching as the clapping died down. Elyasin handed the scepter back to the Chancellor, who set it in its velvet-lined box. The pen she handed to King Therel Alramir, who dipped it in the gilded inkwell. After reciting a short pledge, he bent and affixed his name to the Writ of Marriage, then handed the fountain-pen to the Dhenra. Elyasin dipped the pen, recited her pledge and bent, scrawling her name.

The Writ of Marriage was signed.

But that's when Elohl felt it suddenly. Like a nudge from beside the desk, he felt an intent movement from King Therel's First Sword. Elohl's gaze snapped to the white-haired man, seeing in an instant how his stance had changed, just a shift of his hips and feet. But that simple movement suddenly put the Dhenra within reach of that long, plain steel sword at the man's hip – and Elohl was in motion before he knew it. Sensate sphere tingling, his golden Inkings burning, his sword whistled from its scabbard. Frightened shouts rang in the hall; other Guardsmen began to turn, too slow. Fenton was like liquid lightning beside him, but Elohl was faster. His sword was already slashing the white-haired First Sword across the neck, a deep cut that nearly took the man's head off – a moment before Fenton's sword pierced the man's heart.

But the damage was done.

As the First Sword of Elsthemen gurgled and went down, his eyes rolling up in his head, the Dhenra clutched her side. Her other hand still held the gilded pen, her jade eyes wide as crimson bloomed beneath her fingers in a broad flush over her flank, soaking the rent blue silk of her gown. As the Elsthemi First Sword bled out upon the white marble floor and Elohl kicked his sword away, Elyasin staggered, gasping. Elohl rushed in to catch the Dhenra as she sank sideways, but her King and now-husband Therel Alramir was there first, scooping Elyasin up.

Elohl spun, his back to the King and Queen and his sword out, ready for other attackers as battle-fever roared through his veins in a vicious heat. Red tinged his vision, his sensate sphere roaring wide, feeling for other threats. Searing like lightning, his golden Inkings felt alive beneath his jerkin as his gaze frisked the terror of the hall. But though everything was in confusion now, everyone moving, Elohl felt no other imminent threats.

Though he found one man who was not in confusion – not at all. Cold grey eyes held Elohl's, hands clasped demurely in his grey silks as the King's Castellan stared Elohl down. And Elohl felt a darkness and deep wrath in the man – that Elohl had thwarted something the Castellan had intended. A sea of people moved between Elohl and the Castellan suddenly, obscuring Elohl's vision. When they moved, the Castellan was gone and Elohl cursed, furious. He had no choice but to follow King Therel, now briskly carrying the injured Elyasin from the hall, kicking a side door open with one powerful boot. Elohl was fast on his heels, Fenton and Aldris a step behind, a few of Therel's burly Highswords with them. Lords and ladies were screaming, fleeing like frightened cows from the hall as Luc rushed in a moment before King Therel's men barricaded the door.

Cradling her head carefully, his eyes a wreak of concern, King Therel was laying Elyasin down upon the thick cobalt carpet in the empty room. Screams still issued from the hall, shouts, a clash ringing out of sword on sword. Blood was pooling beneath the Queen, soaking into the carpet in a grisly spread as Elyasin gasped in short bursts that kept her belly as still as possible, pain tearing her eyes.

"Let me through!" Luc's snarl sliced through Elohl's battle-fugue as the thief pushed roughly past, dropping to his knees by Elyasin. King Therel tried to shove him away, but Luc threw a smart punch, knocking the King square on the jaw, and Therel blinked. Elohl saw him go for a dagger, but Elohl reached out fast, gripping the Elsthemi King's wrist.

"He's a healer!" Elohl spoke quickly.

"I'm a fucking King's Physician!" Luc snarled as he pressed his hands to Elyasin's wound. "She's my charge, dammitall! Hold on, Elyasin, hold on, girl..."

"Luc?" She murmured, blinking to see the golden-blond thief leaning over her. "How...?"

"Yeah, it's me... fuckitall..." He growled, though a deep tenderness was in his eyes as he curled his hands over her wound. "Lay still girl, you're hurt pretty bad. We can't move you yet. Give me a minute."

"Like when I fell from the orange tree... cracked my head..." Elyasin murmured, barely audible now, her eyes fluttering closed.

And Elohl saw something he thought he'd never see from the thief. Tears pooled in Luc's eyes as his face fell into a hard woe, hopeless. "Yeah, yeah... Like the time at the orange tree. Gods fuckitall to hell..."

"In the name of the Highlands, open up!" Pounding began on one barricaded door suddenly. "Or we'll break our way in!"

"My Highswords." King Therel raised his voice, calling out to them. "Not now!"

"My liege!" A big voice boomed on the other side of the door. "The

Menderian Chancellate are calling for your head! We need to get you out! A third of our retinue have already been arrested!"

Therel blinked, his handsome visage twisting into bleak anger. "Control the hall, Yhurgen! We need a route cleared to the West Stables. Send men ahead to our grooms and protect our horses! And fuck it, they'd better be ready to ride by the time I get there!"

"Yes, my King!" The Elsthemi voice growled quickly.

But then another voice growled from outside the door, like boulders crushing trees. "Elohl! Fenton! We can't hold! The Chancellate have taken over the Palace Guard, they're issuing orders for the Elsthemi King's death! The thieves Gherris and Shara rallied with clans Visk and Brackthorn, enough so we could get to you, but the Guard have them pinned! They'll break through any moment now! You have to go!"

"Vargen!" Elohl shouted back. "We're going with the King! Hold them off and meet us at the West Stables!" King Therel lifted his eyebrows, and Elohl caught his look. "Your Queen is going with you. And so am I."

"Elohl!" Vargen shouted again, "I've got to get Olea out of the cells!"

"I'll go with Vargen." Aldris spoke quickly as he shoved furniture away from the door. "I know a fast route to the cells. We'll meet you at the stables. *Alrashemnari aere alranesh vhekhan!* Long live the Alrashemni!" He shoved his way out as Elsthemi retainers flooded in with hooded eyes and weapons bared. Elohl heard a sigh beside him and glanced over to see Luc, white with fatigue, wipe his sweaty brow with one arm.

"We can move her now. She's still bleeding internally, but I can do the rest later."

"Come on, my sweetgrape, don't let them crush you yet..." King Therel was careful as he scooped Elyasin up from the soaked carpet, her blood-slicked silk clinging. She keened as he hefted her into his arms and then her head dangled, passed out from the pain. Therel roared then, his handsome visage rippling in a cruel, cold snarl like a wolf baring fangs. "Whoever set this up is going to *pay! Alrashemnari aenta trethan lheroun, ahle fhis brethii!*"

Alrashemni keep their promises, to the bitter end.

Elohl pressed one palm to his heart, his other hand upon his sword. King Therel paused, regarding his gesture deeply, then gave curt nod. Fenton had stepped to the wall and stood by an open servant's door that had been well-concealed in the wainscoting. Therel turned with Elyasin in his arms, making for the door. Elohl glanced at Fenton as thunder rolled through the room, a hard patter of rain beginning upon the byrunstone roof tiles of Roushenn. Fenton was livid, trembling with a hard rage, his gold-brown eyes so hot with wrath they seemed to burn in the dim light as heavy green storm clouds swallowed the day beyond the high windows.

He shared Elohl's glance for a moment – a lash of intensity between them making Elohl's golden Inkings surge with fire.

But as quickly as the sensation had come, it left as Fenton looked away, falling into step ahead of King Therel and leading them out by the servant's passage. Through twists and turns of long corridors, dodging and weaving in tight spaces, they startled footmen and maids as they took back ways through the servant's halls. Twice they met with a knot of Guardsmen and engaged arms in the cramped halls, protecting King Therel with the Queen still unconscious in his arms. Elohl was a blur of speed, fighting with both sword and longknife in the close confines, his cobalt jerkin spattered with the blood of other men as Fenton proved a strong and vastly capable fighter at his side. Though King Therel lost two of his Highswords, the Guardsmen were slaughtered to a man, slow from their confusion facing some of their own and seeing the dying Queen in King Therel's arms.

Taking a turn, they angled down a long empty hall, jogging quickly.

"Two more passages, and we're out." Fenton spoke with easy breath, as if the fighting had affected him not at all, and Elohl nodded, moving forward swiftly.

When suddenly, the walls of Roushenn *shifted.*

One moment, they were running a straight course, but the next, the long hall began to split from the middle – walls starting to rotate, mirrors flashing into view where nothing but byrunstone had been before. Doorways slid into place between the mirrors, then slid more, creating impossible corners and angles.

"*To me!*" King Therel roared, as the hall suddenly became a vast confusion all around them.

Elohl skidded to a halt, his heart thundering in his ears as he backed close to the Elsthemi King next to Fenton, weapons out as they created a tight knot around the King and Queen. The hallway roiled and buckled in all directions; impossible, terrifying. What had been a hallway was now a maze, multiple branches and halls opening outward from their position, sliding and shifting and sliding again with grinding sounds of stone on stone. Mirrors reflected each other, creating an infinity of halls – an infinity of men gathered in a tight knot. Only Fenton seemed unphased, standing grim beside Elohl with a hard readiness, his courage steady.

Suddenly, Elohl's world tilted and he staggered as his vision warped. The maze before him seemed to stretch, a scent in the air of sweetness and stench like lemons gone to rot in a honey-crock. Reeling from the fragrance permeating the air, Elohl sank hard to one knee. His head was full of the lemon-sick odor; his stomach churned with it, bile rising. Disoriented, his eyes wouldn't focus, his muscles couldn't keep him steady.

Everything was reeling – poison flowing thick as death through the air.

"Fenton!" He yelled, coughing. "Poison! We need to move!"

Just then, a roar like some tremendous beast split the moving hall – a shattering, shrieking roar like a hawk's whistle given the power of a lion in battle. Mirrors burst on the walls, showering glass over the company, and a flash of a black leathery body caught Elohl's eye in the mirror-shards. Fear rushed through Elohl, a vast, obliterating terror that chilled his every vein as a scream sounded behind him, then another. From the corner of his eye, he saw two Highswords go down in the rear of their company, fast movements like an animal spearing his blurring vision – a leather-skinned creature like alligators but whip-lean and standing upright, twice the height of a man.

Pressure flashed at Elohl, and he whipped his head back as talons big as butcher-knives raked past his neck, red-tipped with gore and stinking of entrails. Screams sounded nearby, then King Therel's roars as Elohl felt someone else stagger behind him. The creature shrieked, its piercing tone slicing Elohl's eardrums as its knife-like talons reflected in the churning mirrors. He saw its massive head, with corkscrewing horns like a ram and jaws like a lean, ravaged wolf. Thick with muscle, lean and fast, it dove in, slashing and leaping as Elohl threw himself sideways, shoving Therel and Elyasin out of the way. Jaws wide and fangs massive, its mouth was full of blood and slicker things as the creature turned – scrabbling for purchase as its massive claws punched solid bluestone to turn back for another attack.

Suddenly, Elohl saw the flash of a man in cobalt rolling in under those swiping knives of death. Lunging upward in a powerful move, he drove a longsword right into the beast's bony chest and the creature shrieked, enraged, looking down at its wound as it staggered backwards. It was Fenton den'Kharel who had pinned the beast, surging upwards now and driving his sword to the hilt into the creature, the blade ringing as it was wedged between blocks of stone in a non-moving wall. Twice his size, towering over him with its long, powerful limbs, the beast snarled at Fenton, gnashing teeth as it swiped with razored claws, enraged that it was pinned to the wall. So fast he blurred in Elohl's reeling vision, Fenton rolled backwards, springing up with both hands beneath Elohl's armpits, hauling him to standing.

"Get them up and run, Undoer be damned! *RUN!*" Fenton roared in Elohl's face, his brown-gold eyes flashing red in the light of the shifting halls. "The Kets al'Roch is nothing you can best!"

Elohl staggered, disoriented, watching the spinning walls. The pinned beast whirled in his drugged vision as it struggled at the wall, but Fenton grasped Elohl by the shoulders, slapping him hard across the face to sober him. Elohl's golden Inkings surged at the contact, a fire of pain shocking his mind to clarity.

"You're the only one who can get them out!" Fenton roared at him. "Use your gifts, dammit! Close your eyes and use your gifts to get them out!"

Quickly, Elohl sheathed his sword and dagger. Taking a breath, he found the space of calm that lived below his waking mind – the space of his instinct that knew direction and danger without being told. His vision was warping, his head reeling, but through it all he saw Fenton hauling up King Therel and depositing Elyasin back in his arms, then hauling up the healer Luc and the few Highswords left to their decimated company, roaring at the King to follow Elohl.

Elohl shut his eyes, feeling out with his sensate sphere. A massive sensation like wings spread in his mind; touching the spinning walls, feeling the position and density of the beast, still occupied trying to claw the sword from its chest. But here in his gift he was steady, needing no eyesight to keep his course. And far off to the right he felt it, where dense walls of stone gave way to air at last.

The way out.

"King Therel! Follow me! Stay close!" Elohl bellowed.

Sliding forward, lithe and fast like a heron in a stream being shot full of arrows, Elohl dodged his way through the ever-shifting halls by the touch of his gift alone. By his *wyrria* he could feel the solid, lean bulk of King Therel following, the Dhenra in his arms and the others close in a tight knot as they flowed like water through the twisting, churning maze of Roushenn.

But the last thing he felt as he dashed on was a man standing alone. Facing off with the beast, Fenton den'Kharel stood defiant with two longknives drawn in the passage behind them. As the company left him behind, a pressure built around Fenton that surged in Elohl's ears – pummeling through the sphere of his gift like a gathering thunderstorm.

36

KHOUREN

Khouren was motionless in the churning hallway, his eyes wide as he took in the spectacle. Of all the things his Rennkavi had planned for this day, it hadn't included his grandfather facing off with the Kets al'Roch, freed from its ancient oubliette for the first time in ten years. Of the House of Alodwine, only Khouren had ever seen this creature of his great-great-grandfather's malevolent planning – seen its ruthless glory and felt its slashing knives as it parted bone from flesh ten years ago. The first time it had ever been freed in living memory, slipping silently from room to room as it prowled the Hinterhaft, it had wound its deadly way through sliding walls in the middle of the night, slashing talons like knives across the necks of Alrashemni Kingsmen. All the Kingsmen. One after another until thousands of corpses had decorated the Hinterhaft's blue halls, dragged there by mercenaries hired to clean up after the creature.

Unaffected by the aerial poison he'd unleashed from the glass vial and doused upon the censer – a poison which both decimated the senses and attracted the beast – Khouren watched the chaos now with horrible clarity. He'd taken the antidote long ago just as his grandfather had once done, and Khouren and his grandfather were both unaffected by the lemon-rot stench as the demon of legend screeched unholy hell in the face of Khouren's defiant grandfather. It was angry that it had been pierced by a weapon and was now pinned to the wall. With a tremendous wrench, it finally broke the sword, freeing itself and hauling the blade from its own chest – hurling it aside with a deafening roar.

But Khouren's grandfather roared back, furious, his gold-brown eyes flashing red fire in the light of the still-shifting halls. Standing strong in his cobalt Guardsman's jerkin, Fentleith Alodwine raised one longknife, pointing at the beast. Khouren's grandfather did not cower, he did not shrink from the demon. He stood tall, imposing as the ancient Kings of Khehem and snarled in its face – matching its livid rage.

"Back, spawn of the Undoer! Or I will do worse than pin you!"

It swiped at him. With a snarling roar like a lupine dragon, Fentleith slashed back. His blade found finger joints, parting talons from the beast. It roared; he roared back. Thunder concussed in the yet-moving halls of Roushenn as pressure built in Khouren's ears; the pressure of a thousand summer storms, his grandfather's masterpiece. The creature swiped again with fast strikes, lunging.

And with a clap of thunder that shook the walls, Fentleith Alodwine engaged.

Spinning in, he was ruthless, fast. Khouren had never in all his years seen such speed as his grandfather in battle. All he could do was watch from a motionless spot in the yet-spinning walls as his grandfather and the creature battled, dodging rotating walls as they fought. A flash of lightning split the dim hall as his grandfather unleashed his unholy *wyrric* gifts. A shriek lanced Khouren's ears as the creature was struck by that bolt and thunder broke whatever mirrors were left, glass skittering past. Longknives flashed in the moving torchlight. But then a sickening, ripping sound came as the creature snarled out of sight beyond a wall – the sound of blades tearing leather and flesh.

And a man's scream.

Khouren's gut dropped; his heart wrenched. He saw his grandfather stagger around the side of a sliding column, blood seeping from his middle, ducking as the creature swiped again. He pierced for its eyes with one longknife and the knife hit home, but Fentleith Alodwine paid the price. The creature sank fangs into his shoulder, ripping at the joint and he bellowed, stabbing its long bony muzzle with his free blade. Lightning ripped the corridor, lancing the beast in the neck. It screamed, spasming, its flesh charring red and smoldering with smoke.

Fentleith's dire mark.

But Khouren's grandfather staggered back as he was released, dropping to his knees. Khouren could see the mortal wound he'd taken. Not the savaged shoulder, but a deep, livid gash across the belly, spilling his guts a rich red through his cobalt jerkin. Khouren could stand by no longer. Rushing forward, he careened through the spinning walls to his grandfather's side.

But there was the beast, wickedly fast, is razor-talons coming for Khouren's neck. He began to spin, knives up to parry, but it was too late. The creature's talon was deflected by his knife, but the other massive hand of talons slapped Khouren down hard, pinning him beneath the creature's weight as it tried to crush him into the stones. Khouren was no hero. He was a blade in the night; he was a ghost behind the walls. He'd not been born a fighter – and the creature had him.

Its massive jaws descended, open in a bite meant to take his head.

"Khouren!"

His grandfather's scream of dismay was heartbreaking, and with a jolt of terror, Khouren did the only thing he could think of – he dropped through the floor. Just at the last moment, he threw his arms around the beast's talons, drawing it with him as he went. Falling, he landed hard on his back in a dark cellar-passage below, but he'd made his mark. The creature was screaming in the hall above, shrieking, trapped by its own mistake – its taloned hand scrabbling, trapped in the ceiling above Khouren's head.

An explosion came from the hall above, a blaze of lightning powerful enough to flare light through cracks in the stone above Khouren's head.

And then everything went silent.

Khouren launched to the nearest wall. Hauling himself up it and through the floor above, he emerged back in the passage. It was ruined. Walls had been blown off their hinges; metal gears and the clockworks that moved them were jammed, broken. The Kets al'Roch had been blasted backward, severed from its trapped appendage, shattering the wall behind it. And now it lay in a tangled lump of hide and protruding bones, its pool of black, tarry blood spreading out over the stones of the floor.

Khouren's grandfather lay slumped against a broken wall, one hand clutching his middle. His breath was a rasp in a way Khouren had never heard it as Khouren approached, trembling. Close now, he could see by the light of a shattered torch the way slick ropes of intestine protruded from between Fentleith's fingers – a spreading pool of tacky blood beneath his grandfather's torn form.

"Grandfather?" Khouren's voice was low, careful. Even now, a stray flash of Fentleith's rageful lightning could kill him, even when his grandfather lay dying.

"Khouren?" Fentleith looked up, his brows knit in pain, his gold-brown eyes flashing no red. He grit his teeth, sucking air slowly through them. But even so, a low keen of pain issued from him. Khouren hastened to his grandfather's side, dropping to his knees as his hand flashed out to feel his grandfather's abdomen.

"We need a pressure bandage." Whipping back his hood, Khouren unwound his charcoal silk *shouf* – a gift, originally, from Fentleith.

"No." His grandfather stilled Khouren's motion with a light, faltering touch. "The beast cut too deep. Just one claw, but it's enough. You can't staunch this... I can't..." Suddenly, his grandfather's eyes rolled up. Eyelids closing, his eyelashes flickering, his entire body twitched in the spasm that comes before death as his head lolled back over Khouren's arm.

"No!" Desperation raced through Khouren. His grandfather was dying. After all these years, after all they had been through, Fentleith Alodwine, the last Scion of Khehem, was going to die. This wasn't the way; this wasn't what they'd held fast for all these years.

Not to have him die and leave them untethered.

Khouren couldn't lose him. Without thinking, he wrapped his *shouf* tight around Fentleith's middle, trapping in the torn bowels. Taking a knee, he hauled his slighter grandfather up over his shoulders, the weight feeling as nothing. Khouren could have carried a bear had he needed to, especially with all the fire and determination flooding his veins right now.

But as he stood, his gaze caught on a man watching through one of the broken hallways of the Hinterhaft. Standing very still in his impeccable grey silk robes, imperious, his cold grey eyes were flat with rage upon Khouren. Khouren shivered, feeling the chill judgment of his Rennkavi. But before the Rennkavi could say anything, before he could arrest Khouren's intent with any command, Khouren turned – stepping through the nearest wall with his grandfather slung across his shoulders.

It was a fair distance to the heart of Roushenn. Sliding through walls, trotting briskly through larders, jogging fast through long expanses of fey blue Hinterhaft, Khouren needed no compass to navigate the bowels of the ancient fortress. A fortress that was his by lineage, or so the House of Alodwine had discovered when they'd traveled out from Khehem a thousand years ago. So many years of

Khouren's four-hundred span had been spent wandering these halls, discovering its secrets, realizing the extent of his great-great-grandfather's madness. Or genius. Only a mad mind, a brilliantly corrupted mind teeming with thoughts of betrayal could have made a palace such as this.

A stronghold of moving walls, maze-like passages, and hidden horrors – like the oubliette chamber of the Kets al'Roch.

Khouren set his jaw, determined, feeling the weary beats of his grandfather's heart slowing as blood poured down over Khouren's shoulder and spine, soaking his garb. But here was the larder next to the six-foot-thick stone at the center of Roushenn. Here was the Clockwork Room, the massive central chamber at the heart of the palace with its plethora of gears larger than a man, all humming and churning in their deafening clatter and precise timing. Though it was a sight to behold, Khouren raced straight through the all the chugging gears and humming machinery, his grandfather across his shoulders just as permeable as Khouren as long as their skin touched.

And there it was at last, the center of the madness. Here, in the very center of the clockworks, at the heart of all of Roushenn, was a secret spot with hardly room to stand. No doors led here; no passages would take a person through the deadly gears. It was a secret Khouren knew because he alone had found it, wandering one night through all the chugging, clanking machinery.

A secret he'd only ever told his grandfather about.

Standing in the very heart of Roushenn surrounded by clanking clockworks, he eyed the small pyramid of filigreed white stone atop its waist-high byrunstone plinth. No larger than an apple, its surface was luminous in the dim space, cut with a pattern of scepters signifying the right to rule – the conflict of authority and leadership. Suspended in the air inside the pyramid was a flat, plain river stone, marked crudely upon the surface as if etched by a knife blade. A wolf and dragon circled each other in the stone's etching, fighting in perfect balance and surrounded by a wreath of flame.

The *Werus et Khehem*. The eternal conflict of the Wolf and Dragon, symbol of Khouren's House.

Symbol of the ancient Kings of Khehem.

"Leith Alodwine, hear my prayer." Khouren whispered, staring at the talisman. "Whatever magic you gave this place, help us now. Fentleith, your grandson, he needs you. If anything of you yet lives in this palace you built... let it restore my own grandfather now."

Kneeling, Khouren lifted his grandfather's bloody hand.

And set it to the filigreed stone.

Fentleith came awake with a gasp, spasming atop Khouren's shoulders the moment his palm touched the pyramid. Heat blazed through Fentleith in a wave as a crackle of energy flooded from him through Khouren, making Khouren shudder with pain and exhilaration. But though the energy had revived his grandfather, a scream ripped from Fentleith's throat, an agonizing sound of beasts tearing each other's flesh yet fighting on to the death. Machinery slowed as energy poured through Fentleith, the clockworks lurching around them to a low hum – then surged once more, buffering Fentleith's scream.

There was no time for whatever additional help the stone could give; not if the Rennkavi had heard that scream. Taking his grandfather's hand from the talisman and thanking whatever gods there were, Khouren turned quickly, hefting his grandfather and fleeing back through the chugging machinery. Fentleith spasmed atop his shoulders, curling and uncurling, screaming with blood-wracked pain through clenched teeth. Bronze cogs flashed by as Khouren ran, silver wheels and steel pistons as he fled through the ancient clockworks with his heart in his throat. Slipping through walls until he was safely away from the center of Roushenn, he finally stopped in a blind oubliette filled with crumbling books and ancient scrolls.

Breathing hard, Khouren struck a spark from his flint into an ancient torch in a bracket upon the wall. It caught with a crackling blaze, casting the tiny octagonal room in shifting shadows. Sinking to the dust-choked floor, Khouren slid his grandfather gently from his shoulders. Fentleith was breathing hard, sweat-streaked and pale, his hands clutching spastically at his middle over the blood-soaked *shouf*.

But he was alive.

"Let me see, let me see..." Khouren crooned, pulling Fentleith's hands away and lifting the edge of the fabric. There, even as he watched, he saw flesh knitting – bowels working themselves back inside as muscles slipped and sealed closed.

"Shaper and Undoer!" Khouren breathed out as relief flooded him.

"This never would have happened if you'd heeded me."

Khouren's gaze snapped to his grandfather's face – only to see Fentleith's dark brows set in a hard line in the flickering torchlight, his gold-brown eyes furious. Ever-young, he looked just as Khouren first knew him as a child even after four hundred years, with just a touch of lines at his eyes and mouth.

But tonight, those eyes and mouth were set hard, livid.

"I did what I had to, grandfather," Khouren murmured quietly. "You know I did."

"Bullshit." Fentleith snarled, more enraged than Khouren had seen him in a god's age. "You gave that man what he wanted. Again. You led the Kets al'Roch right to us, Khouren! It doesn't live in that part of the palace, you and I both know that. You acted as the bait just like ten years ago, leading that thing through Lhaurent's gauntlet of walls like running a bull through a chute! Until it finds something to slaughter, as you *poisoned* the air to make men fodder for it! Yet again, Lhaurent has his bloodshed, all in the name of *peace.* But this time, the blood shed was mine."

"I never meant to risk your life!" Khouren pleaded, desperate as a dark conflict churned within him. "You weren't supposed to go with them! The Kets al'Roch was only a failsafe, only to be used if the Dhenra made it out of the coronation hall alive!"

"I am sworn to protect her life." His grandfather's eyes flashed red, dangerous.

"You are sworn to the Rennkavi! The Uniter!" Khouren hissed back. "By your own words, by your own hand!! You are sworn to the one who wears the Golden-marks lest fire take you, just as I am! And that man is here in these very halls! Our Rennkavi is the Castellan, grandfather, though you accept it not."

"I will *never* accept him." Fentleith spat at Khouren, a scathing fury in his eyes. "A man who annihilates *thousands* is no Uniter of mine! And *you are responsible for all those deaths!* The blood of the Alrashemni is upon *your* hands, Khouren! For the part you played in unleashing the beast, in giving Lhaurent the tools to plan it all on behalf of the Khehemni Lothren. Your hands."

Slowly, Khouren sat back, a cold emptiness devouring his heart at his grandfather's words. "And does a King do any less upon the battlefield, to secure a better future for his nation?"

Fentleith Alodwine struggled up to his elbows then to his bloody hands, a terrible fury in his gaze. And though he flinched from pain and one hand yet clutched his abdomen, his eyes burned red into Khouren's very soul. "You're no King. Take me back to the stables, Khouren. I will follow the ones I serve, and you will follow yours. I disown you – right here, right now. I disown you and any scions you may ever have. You are no grandson of mine, following that beast of a man Lhaurent. And though you saved my life today, I owe you no debt, because it was *you* who put the Ghenje pieces into play. Giving Lhaurent my grandfather's ring to resonate the palace walls. Showing him the Clockworks. Allowing him to summon the Puzzle from its resting place and start the machine that controls the walls. Causing unholy hell today. And now this—!"

Fentleith hitched a hard breath, his brows knit in pain and a deep, unfathomable sorrow as he closed his eyes.

"This?" A curl of fear took Khouren, not understanding his grandfather's words.

"I feel him." Fentleith's sigh was a breath in the flickering dark as his hand lifted to rub his chest. "I feel Leith! A part of him is now in me – his magic, his *wyrria*. His conflict. Undoer, Khouren! What were you thinking, setting my hand to my grandfather's talisman and letting it drink my blood?!"

"I didn't know!" Khouren's eyes were wide, his breath racing as fear drove deep into his heart. He hadn't considered that when he'd set his grandfather's palm to the filigreed stone in desperation. He hadn't understood that his beloved, mild-tempered grandfather had now absorbed the *wyrria* of a madman – a mad conqueror – by letting the stone take his blood.

Leith Alodwine. The Last King of Khehem.

"I feel him stirring within me..." Fentleith murmured, his eyes still closed as a stricken look etched his face. "I feel him hot like forge-sparks and chill like dragon's breath. And I feel the palace stirring too, far beneath the earth, deep under Lintesh. It's awake. It's all awake."

"All awake?" Khouren asked. "What do you mean?"

Fentleith's eyes snapped open, burning like coals as they sharpened upon Khouren. "Only a part of Roushenn woke to Lhaurent slipping on Leith's ring thirty years ago. Now the entirety of the mechanism beneath the city wakes to me, Khouren! To *my* blood, stronger than any Khehemni lineage Lhaurent possesses. It wakes to me. But Lhaurent has the ring – he has my grandfather's ring. He controls it all! Don't you understand what you've done?!"

"I've given him the city at last." Khouren sat back on his heels, his breath stilling as he understood the full import of what had just happened. "All of Lintesh is awake... for my Rennkavi to command."

But Fentleith's eyes were sad upon him, sad and dead of love for his grandson. "You've given a tyrant a fortress none can ever breach. And now you will live to see what he does with it. Let me out of here, Khouren. I go to the West Stables."

Khouren blanched, feeling the dismissal of his grandfather's dire words. That was it, then; they were through. He had been disowned and there was no going back. Tonight, they parted ways forever, at odds now with one another in a way they had never truly been before.

And someday, one of them would pay the price for it.

"I love you, grandfather." Khouren murmured.

"Take me to the stables, Khouren."

Fentleith Alodwine staggered to his feet, stumbled and caught the wall, not looking at his grandson. Slowly, Khouren stood also, stepping to his grandfather's side and feeling the cool, empty space between them. Lightly, he took his grandfather's bare fingers. But there was no love there, not anymore. Not like there had been when he was a boy, his mother dead and entombed in the bowels of Roushenn, a child of only seven sobbing over her stone effigy. His grandfather Fentleith had taken him by the hand then, wrapping him close in a bittersweet, loving embrace.

But there would be no embrace now – perhaps never again.

Khouren swallowed hard. He'd made his choice. Following the Rennkavi was more important than a grandfather's love. Stepping forward through the wall, he led a man he no longer knew through the wall behind him.

LHAURENT FOUND him quite a while later as Khouren sat in their regular meeting-place, a rectangular hall in the Hinterhaft with a long table for war-conferences. He had lit all the torches in the room, pushing back the dark, but they could not push back the heaviness in his heart. Now as he sat upon the table, his fingers leafed idly through an ancient tome bound in goat-hide, but he was not looking at the beautiful illuminations of medicinal plants within. He heard the scrape of the wall as it swung inward over ancient dust, then the soft, nearly soundless step of Lhaurent as he slipped in. After the closing scrape of the wall, a scent of perfume wafted through the room, heady like ripening plums.

"Khouren." Lhaurent den'Karthus' tone dripped icy scorn. "You have gravely disappointed me, interrupting my plans."

Khouren did not look up from his tome. "Injuring someone dear to me was not supposed to happen today."

Khouren heard Lhaurent pause, thinking about this information, still behind him near the wall. "Who was that man who wielded lightning, who killed the Kets al'Roch? What did you do with him, Khouren? He would be a great asset to our cause..."

"My grandfather will never come to you." Khouren sighed, as Lhaurent den'Karthus stepped around the table into view, one long-fingered hand wisping over the dust upon the table. On Lhaurent's index finger was the ruby ring of Khouren's great-great-grandfather. The ring of Leith Alodwine with its wolf and dragon fighting around a ruby, ringed by white fire of a metal come from the heavens themselves. The ring that controlled the walls, for the right man with the talent.

The ring that controlled Roushenn – and now controlled an entire city.

"Your grandfather?" Lhaurent's voice was soft, intrigued. "But the man I saw battling the creature... looked like First-Lieutenant Fenton den'Kharel."

"Just so." Khouren heaved a deep sigh then looked up, meeting Lhaurent's curious grey eyes. "Don't ask me to go after him. He'll never come to your cause. He believes in the Dhenra. Nothing I've ever said has convinced him that you're the one, the Rennkavi. The Uniter of the Tribes."

Lhaurent was silent another long moment. But rather than angry as Khouren expected, he seemed eager, as a soft wonder suffused his face. "Khouren. Something's – happened. I feel a change in the pull coming from the ring; from the entire palace. It feels stretched, wider, deeper. As if leagues and leagues of walls and floors and ceilings have suddenly wakened, hearkening to the *wyrria* in the ring. They're... humming... all around me. Far into the city..."

Khouren gave a deep, tired sigh. With a slow grace he rose, then sank to one knee. "Rennkavi, the city of my great-great-grandfather Leith has awakened. It is yours to command."

Lhaurent startled visibly, a twitch taking him from head to heels. "What are you saying?"

Khouren looked up, feeling sick, feeling elated – feeling vast conflict deep in his very bones. "The entire city of Lintesh lives by the *wyrria* of Khehem, the same as the walls of Roushenn do. My great-great-grandfather's city has awakened, yoked now to the magic in the Clockworks. All those walls, the streets of Lintesh, they will move for you now. I awakened it today by the blood of my line. And it will hearken to you – to the power in your ring, the ring of Khehem's ancient royalty. Keep it well, my Rennkavi. For now you control far more than a mere palace. You control a city. Right beneath the very boots of any who might oppose you."

Lhaurent den'Karthus had taken a deep breath. Slowly, he sighed it out, his grey eyes shining with a vast fever. "Khouren. Your opposition of me today is excused."

Something deep inside Khouren shifted then, restless as he watched the man before him. Goldenmarks were upon Lhaurent, Inked there so many years ago by a seven-eye Alranstone just like the Prophecy had said. And yet. As Khouren watched those shining grey eyes, that serpentine pleasure in his lord and master's gaze, he wondered for the first time if his grandfather had been right.

Right to not follow this Rennkavi.

Right to wait, hoping against hope that another one would come.

37

ELOHL

Elohl opened his eyes as they burst through a side-door to the palace, rushing across a courtyard that was quickly churning into slick mud from the thundering downpour. Lightning forked across the burgeoning sky as wind lashed the pines and cendarie upon the mountainside. They were out, but it had cost them. Three more of King Therel's men had been swallowed in the ever-shifting halls. Only Elohl, Luc, King Therel with Queen Elyasin, and four of his Highswords were left. A grim company, they rushed to the stables in a tight knot, throwing themselves through the stable doors. Dead Guardsmen in cobalt littered the stables, blood soaking the straw upon the flag-stones. Twenty of Therel's Highswords held the stable, roaring in triumph at their King's arrival – but Olea, Vargen, and Aldris were not there.

Nor were Ghrenna's thieves.

"Ride!" King Therel roared above the crash of thunder. All around him, Highswords mounted up in haste, as Elohl helped the King lift his Queen up before him upon his tall black charger. As Elohl helped bind her unconscious form to King Therel with a belt so Therel had his hands free to manage his horse, a clarion horn sounded. A second wave of cobalt-jerkined Guardsmen rushed around the side of the stables, bristling with weapons in the downpour.

"Yah!" King Therel wheeled his horse, whipping it into a rear and charging the open stable-doors. Guardsmen stumbled back, shouting as Therel's retinue thundered through their break, churning muck and splattering the Guardsmen as they passed. Elohl slung up fast to the only horse left, a heat-eyed grey who pranced sideways and tried to bite as he mounted. As he reigned the beast, he said a quick prayer for Olea's safety, hoping Vargen and Aldris were as good as their devotion to her.

His heart sundered to leave her behind when they had just been reunited, but there was no time. He'd be cut to bits if he lingered, and wheeling his horse, Elohl charged after King Therel's line, galloping through Guardsmen trying to block his way. Guardsmen readied swords to slice his legs and Elohl drew his longsword, protecting himself and his horse as he galloped past, clashing blades in sparks that lit the dark afternoon. He glanced back as he charged out – looking to the palace side-door, hoping against hope to see Olea come bursting through it.

But there was no one – not even Fenton, who had remained behind to save them all.

Burying his emotions, Elohl dug his heels in, charging his horse after the Highswords fast as thunder in the driving summer rain. Sleet slashed his face, driven by the wind and Elohl leaned down tight to his horse's withers, kicking it hard past the gate to the Fourth Tier. Decimated by Therel's fierce clansmen, cobalt-jerkined Guards lay motionless in the puddles, blood spreading from them like ink stains. Sawing his mount up onto the narrow palace hunting-trail, Elohl followed the churned-up hoof prints of King Therel's retinue.

Elohl's grey stallion was full of piss, heaving over boulders to take the trail up into the forest cover of evergreens, hot with speed in the driving rain. Elohl kicked it harder, needing to catch up to the main retinue and it snorted, bucking beneath him though it gave more speed, racing up the switchbacks as the trail climbed the mountainside. Gaining King Therel's line at last, Elohl found their party grim, Highswords glancing back with hooded eyes to check for pursuit as they struggled up the mountain quickly, horses slipping on the wet rocks and muck of the narrow trail.

Rain drenched Elohl, sliding down his collar and soaking his undershirt. Flicking it out of his eyes and currying rain out of his hair, he followed at a brisk gallop as the trail leveled, following the curve of the Kingsmount's southwestern slope up and further up. Branches scratched, catching at his leathers. Lightning split the heavy green sky, eerie in the false darkness of the day.

Elohl pressed his beast hard, trying not to think about everything he was leaving. Trying not to think of Olea, Eleshen – and Ghrenna. Olea fell further behind with every heave of his horse's flanks. Ghrenna fell further behind with every roar of thunder. Gazing up at the terrible sky, Elohl roiled with fury, his golden Inkings burning through him with every flash of lightning.

Gritting his teeth, his throat clenched tight, Elohl struggled against the agony that was rising inside him like a demon. Bubbling up his throat, his fury and woe came out suddenly as a scream, drowned in a vicious flash of lightning and a roll of thunder from the heavy grey sky. His head falling back, rain pelted his face as he hauled in a great lungful of air and screamed again, making his horse whicker in alarm and toss its head. Highswords looked behind from their own mounts, their eyebrows raised.

But Elohl's roars came like the thunder, rolling from him like the rain. Until he had nothing left; until he was empty inside. Until every emotion that had frozen him and burned him for so many years was utterly still.

At last, he heard nothing but the patter of the rain and the hard breathing of his horse as he rode. The heat of his own breath curled away in the chill air and Elohl opened his eyes, seeing the vastness of the forest, dark and expansive in the dim afternoon. Stillness slipped into him from every swaying bough; dripping into him with every patter of rain upon the leaves. Stillness rocked him with the rhythm of his horse's muscles and with the tide of his own breath like some vast, susurrating ocean.

Stillness came to his golden Inkings – a deep quiet that opened Elohl's heart.

Suddenly, he could feel – everything. His heart breathed in that moment, opening, expanding through the storm until it touched Therel's Highswords riding before him, then the empty trail behind. He felt it like some enormous spread of wings, expanding until their gossamer touch brushed the city of Lintesh now far behind. Out it reached, out and further still, until it whispered softly through those he cherished, finding each and every one of them in the grey afternoon and whispering of his love.

He could feel them. If he breathed softly enough, he could feel them. Moving his horse into a better line, Elohl came to quiet at last. His focus shifting, he listened to the forest, touching out with his sensate sphere to the back-trail and feeling for pursuit. Focusing on the now, on surviving today, he let the past go; everything. All the pain, all the passion. All the certainty of how his life was supposed to go. All the rage at how it had been arrested and taken from him by twist after cruel twist of fate.

Letting it all go, Elohl listened to the rain, breathing deeply in the soft silence of the forest, and riding hard up the endless trail.

* * *

THEY RODE out to the northwest in the towering midsummer storm until nightfall. Circling the base of the Kingsmount on a craggy hunting-track upon the western slopes, they pushed the horses hard through the driving rain. Climbing towards the high-country along the rough, little-used track, they avoided the valley. Scouts had been sent ahead and lingered behind, but no news came of pursuit. Rain churned the steep trail to muck, and though they galloped where they could, even the resolute warhorses were hard-pressed to maintain a continuous trot, sliding and shying from mud over slippery rocks.

Suddenly, the column pulled up at a broad spot in the trail. Reining in, Elohl paced up alongside one broad-shouldered beast of a Highsword with long red braids and a braided red beard, a man he recognized from their flight in the halls.

"What's going on?" Elohl asked the big Highsword fellow.

"The Physician's treating the Queen." The man was brief as he spoke in a deep, rolling Northern accent, nodding towards King Therel's black charger. Elohl could see that Luc had pulled alongside King Therel's horse and was reaching over, his hands moving slowly over Queen Elyasin's abdomen. Therel had wrapped her in his crimson cloak, keeping her warm, but even so, Elohl could see how pale she was. Deathly pale. And as Luc moved his hands, Elohl saw how much blood had soaked her silk gown.

"We need to stop for the night," Elohl heard Luc murmur through the driving of the rain, his face grim. "Get her off the road. I can't get the wound to close if it's constantly shifting and pulling."

Glancing at the light above the trail, the sky now heavy with impending nightfall, King Therel narrowed his eyes on the horses. And Elohl saw what the King saw, that all the chargers were heaving and blowing hard from their fast climb up the mountain, their stamina nearly gone. They were well-trained mounts, and none of them were complaining or slowing in their determined ascent, but still, they were nearly done for.

And if they blew out their horses now, they'd have to take to their feet, trekking across the highmountain wilderness.

"Off the road!" Therel barked at last. "We'll camp in the trees."

Sawing his horse to the side, he walked it off the trail to the north into the thick vegetation, the trees dripping with moss, the ground cover thick with ferns. But just as the retinue led their horses from the road, the sound of hooves came up the trail behind them, hitting the muck hard in an earth-churning gallop. Elohl heard King Therel curse his rear scouts, and steel rang in the damp air as Therel drew his sword in a rush even with his Queen slumped over his pommel. Wheeling his horse hard, he faced the oncoming enemy with his Highswords bristling at his sides.

But as the dark bay neared, lathered in sweat and rain, Elohl picked out a familiar face wearing the cobalt jerkin of the Palace Guard, and he raised his hand, fast. "Hold! He was with us in the halls! It's Fenton den'Kharel, one of my sister Olea's best lieutenants!"

"Aeon dammitall!" King Therel cursed a blue streak in his native Elsthemi, then thrust his sword away. "Tell him to not sneak up, for fuck's sake!"

Wheeling his horse in a vile temper, King Therel stalked it off further into the trees, Highswords at his hocks. Elohl held his temperamental stallion in place with a determined rein, waiting for Fenton. The man slowed his lathered beast to a trot, then to a walk thirty paces down the weathered path, and Elohl saw the relief upon Fenton's face as he neared – and the pain. Disbelief moved through Elohl as his gaze flicked over Fenton's garb, seeing the massive rent in his leather jerkin, and his torn shoulder like the beast had gotten fangs into him and savaged him.

Blood soaked everything – just everything. Breathing hard and deeply ashen, Fenton was exhausted and drenched in addition to all the mess. He had tied himself to his horse as he rode; lashed himself to the saddle with a length of leather rein. Men didn't do that unless they had to stay mounted with a deadly wound, and Elohl's gaze flicked over Fenton's blood-soaked leathers again, noting how much blood there was – nearly as much as had coated Queen Elyasin. Elohl's eyes went wide as Fenton reigned in, stopping his blowing mount.

"Aeon fuck me...!" Elohl breathed as he took in the Guardsman's ruined state. "Fenton! Are you sure you can ride?"

"I wouldn't exactly call it riding, more like getting fucked on horseback." Fenton's mouth was a hard line of pain as he spoke, but still, it quirked up at one corner with soldier's humor. "I feel like shit and I know I must look it, but I'll make it a bit further. Lead the way."

Elohl couldn't fathom how bad Fenton's injuries must have been under all that mess, and he couldn't comprehend how Fenton had faced down that creature in the hall. But like a true veteran soldier, Fenton was already focused on the next problem, and that didn't include tending his wounds or wasting time discussing a finished battle. So Elohl just nodded, clucking his tongue and kicking his heels lightly into his horse's flanks to make it walk on. Leading it down into the gully beside the trail and off into the forest, he followed the muddy hoof prints of Therel's company through the ferns.

They rode in silence for a while. As soon as it became obvious that King Therel meant to lead them far off through the wilderland until dusk, Elohl chanced a look over. Fenton was reeling in the saddle, lurching a bit too much with his horse's every hoof-fall, not able to keep himself upright. He'd taken a deep injury from the beast in the halls, something dire, and his eyes fluttered shut a moment. Elohl heard the Guardsman hiss softly through his teeth as one of Fenton's hands strayed to his middle where the bloody rent in his jerkin was.

"Bad?" Elohl murmured, watching him.

"Bad enough." Fenton glanced over, his face drawn with pain. "But I'll live. We don't need to stop and tend it."

"How did you best that thing?" Elohl spoke, curiosity overcoming him at last. "The creature in the hall?"

"I didn't." Fenton glanced over again, a wry twist upon his lips as he breathed shallow from pain. "I dodged a few turning walls and the damn thing followed me, got itself squished. Not before tearing me up a bit, though. Took me a while to get out. Then I had to hide until the stables weren't watched, to steal a horse and follow you."

Elohl knew it was a lie, right as the man spoke it. The speed of Fenton's movements while fighting the creature had not escaped him; and his strength, to skewer the beast with a sword right through the bones of its massive chest was something no regular man could accomplish. Fenton also hadn't seemed affected by the aroma of poison in the corridor, and in the heat of battle, Elohl had almost sworn the man's eyes had flashed red as he roared for them to get out. But it was clear Fenton didn't want to talk about how he'd killed the creature, and Elohl set that line of inquiry aside – for a later time.

"How did you know about my gift? That I could lead the others out?" Elohl asked, wanting to know something else from the heat of battle that had not escaped him.

"Your gift?" Fenton glanced up, still holding a hand to his middle. "Olea told me."

"You two were close?" Elohl frowned, wondering how much about him Olea had shared with the Guardsman. And then wondering if she'd told Fenton anything at all, or if the man had figured out Elohl's *wyrric* gift himself.

"We weren't close like that." Fenton smiled more, understanding Elohl's meaning. "Olea and I were just good friends."

Elohl nodded, changing the subject, as the topic of Olea was too hard yet to bear and it was clear Fenton wasn't going to be straight with him right now about the battle in the halls. "We're losing the light. We should pick up the pace. Catch up to the main host."

"Lead on, den'Alrahel. I'll follow."

Kicking his horse, Elohl picked up a trot to follow the Highlander's pulped hoof prints through the thickening vegetation. Conversation ended as he and Fenton moved faster through the trees, until at last the main party was in sight. King Therel and his men were stopped now, dismounting in a small clearing ringed by tall cendarie evergreens that would serve as camp for the night. But as Elohl sawed his bad-tempered grey to a halt within the copse, Fenton suddenly slumped over his pommel in a dead faint.

Quickly, Elohl leaped from his horse, rushing to catch Fenton as the wiry man slid sideways out of his saddle. Hauling him over beneath a broad cendarie, Elohl laid him out upon the dry needles. Luc was there in a trice, his hands already at Fenton's abdomen, lifting away a dark grey silk wrap soaked in blood and peering beneath. But strangely enough, the gash in Fenton's abdomen, though it was wide and ragged, wasn't terribly deep. It didn't even go down through the muscle, and seemed hardly a scratch for a fighter as fierce as the First-Lieutenant Guardsman. Likewise, Fenton's savaged shoulder seemed to be far less damage than the pulped leather and blood on his jerkin suggested, and after peering at the shoulder, Luc left it be and went back to Fenton's middle.

Luc tended Fenton's wound, though he was drained and it showed. The healer's breathing was a harsh rasp, his hands trembling as he attended to the Guardsman. After a few minutes, he took his hands away, rubbing sweat and rain from his brow. "He'll live. He's got some deep wounds worse than we can see, but I've fixed what I could. I've got to tend Elyasin."

Rising, Luc stepped away with haste – and without a single bad-tempered scowl for Elohl.

With nothing more he could do for the unconscious Fenton, Elohl left the Guardsman for the moment beneath the dry cendarie tree. Returning to the horses and fetching their leads, he tied them to a tree out of the rain in a spot where there was plenty of grass. Therel's Highswords were already establishing a rough camp of lean-tos beneath the evergreens, from supplies they had pilfered from the stables. Oilcloaks made coverings, lashed between the trees with rope. Lanterns began to flicker in the damp nightfall, strung up to some of the lean-tos. A fairly ample oiled canvas stretched over a patch of moss between two towering cendaries, oilcloaks covering the ground. It was there that King Therel took Elyasin – a shabby palace of exile for them to share their first night together.

But as Elohl finished with the horses and approached the King's tent, he saw there would be no wedding night for the royal couple. Hunkering next to the unconscious Elyasin, her pale hand pressed between his, King Therel was a picture of disheveled distraction and wretched exhaustion as Luc came to his knees beside the wounded Queen. Highswords idled nearby, ostensibly going about the duties of making camp, though Elohl could tell most were watching the dire situation inside the royal tent.

"Save my sweetgrape, physician..." Therel Alramir's voice was raw with anger and a plea as he spoke to Luc, his pale blue eyes hard and miserable. Luc merely nodded, setting his hands to Elyasin's wounds, and as Elohl hunkered nearby, the healer dipped his chin and closed his eyes.

Time ceased beneath the lean-to, the moment trapped in a cast of sorrow as Luc began his healing yet again.

"My Liege." The big Highsword Elohl recognized from the road, clad in a hulking bearskin and ragtag buckled leathers, stepped up to the shabby tent. Hunkering next to King Therel, he combed a hand back through his long, wet red braids, then shucked water from his braided red beard with his fingertips. "We'd go faster on the main road, down in the valley."

King Therel's lupine blue eyes were still pinned to Elyasin as Luc worked, and he shook his head. "I'll not take her through the Valley of Doors, Lhesher. It's too exposed. The walls of the canyon are too steep. Any pursuit could flush us out faster than we should ride with her injured."

"We could have an escort of keshari. We have scouts watching the border. Transfer her to a cat and ride hard for Lhen Fhekran." The big man spoke again.

Therel paused this time. But again, Elohl watched him shake his head with a growl. "We can't assume our scouts are still alive, Lhesher. This betrayal was organized. And if there are no cats waiting for us at the border, we'll be caught in the valley. I won't risk it. We ride on, up over the western side of the Kingsmount. We'll go slow, give Luc time to heal her, pace the streams to throw off any dogs in pursuit. I will make it back to Lhen Fhekran with my Queen alive. By all the gods, I swear it."

The big man, Lhesher, nodded solemnly, then clapped a sturdy hand upon King Therel's shoulder. Therel nodded back, his eyes never leaving Elyasin. Elohl watched the proceedings for a while, but seeing no more he could do, he finally rose and returned to Fenton beneath the evergreens. To find that the big northerner Lhesher had erected a lean-to over Fenton and was now adjusting it so it cast off the majority of the rain and made a generous dry spot beneath the cendarie tree.

Elohl nodded to the big redheaded Highsword and the man nodded back, taking a seat on some cendarie boughs he'd cut down with his belt-hatchet, and beckoning as he made room for Elohl to sit. Together, they stared out over the camp, watching Elsthemi swordsmen tend horses and weapons in the dripping dusk, settling in to make what they could of the wet camp beneath the trees. Elohl sighed, leaning back against the cendarie's trunk, soaked to his bones and wishing for his Kingsmen Greys, or even his High Brigade gear.

But all of that was gone now – left behind in Lintesh like the rest of his life.

"Lhesher Khoum." The big Highsword next to Elohl extended a massive paw of a hand suddenly.

"Elohl den'Alrahel." Turning, Elohl clasped the big man's wrist. "Thanks for the lean-to."

"My pleasure. Fuck-all of a day, huh?" Pulling out a pipe from his leather belt-pouch, Lhesher stuffed it with some leaves Elohl didn't recognize, then lit it with a dry phosphor match. Taking a few draws, he held it out to Elohl, who accepted it and took a deep pull. The smoke was mellow and smooth with a slight flavor of cherries. Puffing a few more times in silent gratefulness as darkness finally swaddled their camp, Elohl watched the lamps flicker among the lean-tos like fireflies in oblivion.

His heart reached out, searching in the night for Olea, for Eleshen – and for Ghrenna.

Cerulean eyes surfaced in his vision, a lake of blue seeking him. Calling.

Handing the pipe over with a nod, Elohl dropped his head back against the tree trunk behind him, exhausted to his bones. "Yeah. Fuck-all of a day."

38

JHERRICK

Keeping watch at the guard station of the Upper Cells, Jherrick stood with his hands clasped upon the pommel of his sword. In the flickering torchlight, Olea den'Alrahel was like a tigress as she paced the bars of her cell. Even with days of sweat-rumpled dirt upon her, she shone like freshly-sharpened throwing knives as she ripped a hand through her black curls, displaying a heightening unrest – one Jherrick resonated with. A tight knot of worry had grown in him over the past hours, because up in the highest Tiers of Roushenn the coronation was proceeding, the Dhenra signing her Writs about now.

And the Elsthemi First Sword would be making his lunge to kill her.

Suddenly, the palace erupted in noise, and Jherrick and Olea both froze to hear the clanking rush of heavily-armed Guardsmen sprinting through the hall at the top of the stairs. The Upper Cells lay close to the formal halls, and shouts were being raised in the level above. Jherrick's ears strained, hearing battle-roars and a crash of swords on shields – then screams.

The screams that happen when men are pierced and dying.

Fear rose in Jherrick's gut, tightening his throat and raising his pulse as his mind sluiced furiously through all the information he had heard from Lhaurent's meetings in the Hinterhaft. No one had ever spoken of Roushenn under attack, or mentioned an army sweeping in on Coronation Day. An assassination was one thing, but there shouldn't have been this much fighting unless something had gone wrong with the Lothren's plan. Jherrick's eyes met Olea's across the stone corridor as her hands gripped the bars hard, her knuckles white and grey eyes fierce.

"Jherrick. Something's wrong. Get me out of here!"

"What's going on, Captain?" Jherrick fingered the key ring at his belt as he took a step forward with wide eyes, playing the terrified innocent.

"If fighting is happening inside Roushenn, then an attempt has been made on the Dhenra's life, just as I feared!" Olea snarled like a furious animal. "Get me out, Jherrick! I'm needed up there!"

Jherrick took another step forward, debating his options as a true fear gripped him. If he released his Captain, his life would be forfeit to Lhaurent. Jherrick had seen in exquisite detail what Lhaurent could do to someone who betrayed him – he'd be tortured, maimed, and most likely made to suffer like an animal. But battle was chaos, and in chaos there was opportunity – even to break free of Lhaurent's horrid games, perhaps.

Opportunity to truly serve the Khehemni Lothren and find out what Lhaurent was really up to.

"Dammit, Jherrick, release me!"

Olea's roar was a strangled, desperate thing, and something about it caused Jherrick to make his decision, finally moving forward with the keys. Mild-mannered, lack-limbed Jherrick den'Tharn, Corporal in the Palace Guard and bookkeeper of lists would assist his Captain-General in a time like this. Wherever it led him, whatever it meant next, he would keep his ears open and his mind sharp – and make his decisions as he went.

Sliding the keys into the lock, Jherrick threw the bar back and Olea den'Alrahel sprang from her cage like a lioness. Jherrick was with her, darting to the weapons rack at the Guard station and unlocking it in haste, throwing open the bracing. As Olea claimed her baldric and blades, Jherrick unlocked an armor-hutch to equip them both for whatever was happening above.

"Stay out the fighting," Olea spoke hastily as she buckled on lightweight leather gauntlets and greaves, then threw a full set of leather armor at Jherrick, which he fumbled like Jherrick would. He buckled on only what he needed as she spoke, equipping her baldric and checking her weapons fast. "I don't want you coming with me up to the Throne Hall. What I need you to do is find Aldris and

Fenton and send them to me. If you see fighting, choose a different hall. Stay alive, dammit! And get my best up to me to help control whatever the fuck is going on."

"Do you think the Dhenra's been killed?" Jherrick's breath was fast, his voice appropriately scared as he checked his baldric and weapons. It wasn't entirely an act. He'd never been in a melee before, and his heart was betraying him, thundering his blood through his veins.

"If she has, then everyone involved will eat my blade before the day is out." Olea's grey eyes had the furious sheen of retribution in the torchlight, and Jherrick's world closed in suddenly at her pronouncement. A tremor passed through him as he saw what a killer she was. Lhaurent would dismember Jherrick for betrayal, but Olea would skewer him in wrath if she ever found out the game he'd been playing. Jherrick had a vision of himself at the end of her sword, dying in the torchlight – a shining moment of truth in his dark life of duplicity. Something must have showed in his eyes because Olea clapped a hand to his shoulder, her grey gaze hard but kind.

"Breathe, Jherrick. We'll worry about all that later. Just find Aldris and Fenton for me."

But just as she was turning to go, a familiar voice shouted. "*OLEA!*"

Second-Lieutenant Aldris den'Farahan's clarion tenor was unmistakable as he came barreling down the stone stairs and into the torchlight, breathing hard. Fresh blood smeared his cheek and bright blond hair as he reached them, his green eyes hard with fury, as a giant mountain of a man in Guardsman cobalt stormed into the torchlight behind him. "Olea! Thank Aeon's fuck you're safe!"

"Aldris!" Olea gripped his forearm hard. "What's happened?!"

"No time! We have to run!" Aldris was all snarl as he seized Olea's arm, turning her down the long black passage away from the sounds of fighting. "Corporal den'Tharn, get that grate at the end of the hall open *now*, or so help me I will gut the living shit out of you! Move!"

"Lieutenant den'Farahan?" Jherrick played the dumb desk-lad as he backed up a pace.

"*NOW!*" Aldris roared. "Let's go!"

Jherrick roused himself, his wide eyes startled as his mousey alter ego, then did as he was told. Sheathing his sword, he darted towards an unused iron grate at the far end of the cells, jangling keys off his belt and nearly dropping them in haste. Unlocking the grate, he swung it open as the others seized torches from brackets and extra gear from the weapons rack. The grate led deep into the palace bowels, a part of the Unterhaft that never saw daylight. Aldris paced forward with his head cocked, listening to the fighting above as Olea and the huge man equipped, then all three dashed for the grate. Olea nodded her thanks to Jherrick as they moved through quickly.

"Lock it." Aldris growled. "We can't be followed."

Jherrick did as he was told, but as they turned, he saw the big man press a small white silk pouch to Olea's hand. "I didn't want to leave them in the workshop."

Olea nodded, slipping the pouch quickly into her leather belt purse. In a trice, they were running down the dust-slick stones into a deepening silence, without looking back.

"Aldris. Tell me what's going on." Olea spoke once they were a decent distance from the cells, her breath unruffled as they ran.

"The Queen signed her writs," Aldris growled, his face drawn in the torch-light, measuring his breath as they jogged. "But she's been attacked; run through by the Elsthemi First Sword. Elohl and Fenton got to him fast, making the First Sword miss his mark, but the Queen's wound is deep, possibly lethal. King Therel Alramir seems to have no knowledge of the plot, but the Chancellors are calling for his head. Chancellor Evshein took over the Guard and ordered the Guard after King Therel and the Elsthemi. Ordered them to kill. Guardsmen are fighting Elsthemi retainers in the halls, and a number of Elsthemi have already fought to their deaths. King Therel, Fenton, and your brother have Elyasin, with a healer named Luc. They're going to make a run for it. Whatever this was, whoever provoked it wanted this chaos, Olea. No one loyal to Elyasin is safe right now."

"My brother and Fenton will get the Queen and King Therel out." Olea's face was grim, determined as they darted down another dark Unterhaft hall by the flicker of their torches. "Fenton knows this palace better than any of us, and Elohl is a better fighter than I am. We just have to get ourselves out now."

"Easier said than done with all the madness in the halls right now." Suddenly, Aldris turned towards a narrow staircase Jherrick hadn't known was there and issued them up. They came out in a niche behind a bookcase, through a grate that was already unlocked. Back in the main halls of Roushenn, they ran in a terse silence, listening to the echoing sounds of fighting somewhere behind them. A raging thunderstorm played counterpart to vague screams and clanks of metal, rattling windows in their high gables with every slash of lightning.

But Aldris was keen, listening for battle and not the storm. When a clank of metal sounded in the halls ahead, Aldris dodged down a side corridor. When the corridor echoed with footsteps and shouts, he ducked through a panel and down a corkscrewing servant's stair. When the stairway was blocked by a gate, he picked it smoothly, leading into unlit tunnels. Jherrick found himself impressed with the Second-Lieutenant, a man Jherrick had generally dismissed as a ribald nuisance and a womanizing drunk. Deep beneath the palace now, there were no more sounds of fighting, echoes of thunder muted through earth and stone as they ran on.

"Aldris! Here. This one."

Olea stopped suddenly at a small wrought-iron gate, and beyond, Jherrick could see a black corridor that caught the torchlight and threw it back slick with wet. The stone corridor was treacherous with slime and seeping water, but though Aldris lifted his eyebrows, he said nothing, picking it with ease and re-locking it behind them.

Sliding on mold-slick stones, they tromped through ankle-deep water as the passage angled down, the seepage soon up to their knees. Rounding a corner, they slogged on, the water flowing now with a current as Jherrick heard a roaring up ahead. Hefting herself up to a lip of stone high as Jherrick's chest, Olea beckoned the others up just as the current around their knees began to drag. Creeping along the narrow lip, the party kept their heads low to avoid hitting the ceiling of the shaft – when suddenly, the vaults above their heads opened up into an enormous underground grotto.

Water cascaded from the passage, joining the thundering rush of a waterfall next to them. Barely seen beyond the torchlight, a river flowed through the underground, black and fast, the air chill as glaciers as it rushed through the space with a fell wind. The lip of stone they were on transitioned into a high retaining berm carved from the grotto wall, and traversing the berm, they came to slime-slick stairs cut into the stone that wound sharply upwards. Jherrick soon had a sheen of sweat from climbing, as they ascended what felt like hundreds of feet through the underground river-way. At last, the stairs dug into the mountain, in a tunnel away from the underground river. It was a short way to another gate, ornate and crumbling with the rust of time. But it was already unlocked, and as Aldris pushed it open, they stepped out onto the roof of the world.

Storm winds whipped this far up the mountainside as rain lashed Jherrick's face, cold and fat. Shivering in his blue jerkin, he wished for a hood even as his breath was stolen by the mist-wreathed view. Far below, the rooftops of Roushenn were lit as a fork of summer lightning slit the black-bellied clouds. A thousand feet up the Kingsmount, everyone was breathing hard from their climb. Only Olea had poise as she stared out over the city with her grey eyes steely as the storm's underbelly, her hands resting upon a stone retaining wall. At last she turned, a terrible anguish in her eyes as the wet slicked her curls and dripped off her nose.

"My thanks for my freedom, gentlemen. I am in all of your debt."

"Clever, Olea, taking the Weeping Tunnel." Aldris spoke as he stepped to her, his hands tucked under his armpits for warmth. "Even if the Chancellate use dogs, they won't be able to track us."

"If Elyasin dies, it won't matter!" Olea growled, seething with fury as she ripped a hand through her obsidian-blue curls, combing their wet lengths back from her face as tears began welling in her eyes. "We've *failed*, Aldris! *I've* failed. I couldn't protect Alden. I couldn't protect Uhlas, and now Elyasin! Gods of darkness smite me down...!"

Stepping close, Aldris laid a hand upon Olea's shoulder as hot, furious tears spilled down Olea's cheeks. Jherrick felt an irrational twinge of jealousy that the Second-Lieutenant was so blatantly familiar with Olea, as a lone sunbeam sliced through the clouds, cutting through that black silk and falling upon her. He resisted the urge to draw his blade and cut off Aldris' presumptive hand as Olea's grey irises shone, luminous under the darkened sky. Her black curls glowed in that fey light and Jherrick's body thrummed with her pull. Watching his Captain-General break was a beautiful, terrible thing – full of pain, and misery, and honor. The honor that binds a faithful heart to her most sacred duty.

The honor of a good woman trying to do what was right in the world.

"Elohl and Fenton will keep Elyasin safe, " Aldris murmured gently. "Trust in that. Trust in the Kingsmen now."

As the rain slackened, mist curling around their boots, it was all Jherrick could do to not go to Olea. To soothe her and run his hands through those wet curls as he held her, kissing away each and every tear. Shame flooded Jherrick like some vast, bitter sea as he suddenly thought of a dead boy's glassy eyes – of everything he'd been party to under Lhaurent's cold sways. Instead of Jherrick, the big mountain of a man stepped forward, wrapping Olea in his massive arms as Jherrick's gaze strayed out over Lintesh, now curling with mist from the breaking storm.

The entire Elhambrian Valley shone emerald with the midsummer rain, the mountains capped in glaciers and wreathed in clouds. From the corner of his vision, Jherrick saw Olea push both men off, then lean on the stone wall with her fists pressed down hard, her shoulders shaking and head hanging. At length, wrenching sobs tore through her and Jherrick's gut twisted. This was what Lhaurent had wrought. A good woman broken, a good Queen murdered, and a nation sundered. Rage twisted into a cold, hard knot in Jherrick's gut as his tears dried. He fell into a deadly silence as he watched the big man wrap his arms around Olea, bringing a scream from her.

She turned in his arms, burying her face in his broad chest as she wept.

"I couldn't protect them, Vargen!" She sobbed, her words vague upon the brisk summer wind. "My parents! Alrashesh! Elohl! And *Uhlas' entire line!*"

"I couldn't keep my wife safe, either," the big man sighed as he kissed Olea's curls. "Or my son Khergen, or my court. Kingsmen do what we must. We *must* let people die, Olea. We *must* let battle take them. We *must* keep our patience and hold our spines straight for another day. Cry yourself dry, then put away your tears and come with me. I am not going to stop, not like I did before. I am done giving up. I am a man reborn, because you need me to remind you who we are, and that Kingsmen never quit. We will find Elohl, Fenton, and the Queen. And when we do, the men behind this will already be corpses. To the Fifth Price and beyond."

THE STORM HAD BLOWN itself out as the sun descended over the Kingsmount, a brisk wind scudding clouds into high wisps above. The temperature was falling fast this high up the mountain, and Jherrick shivered in his soaked jerkin as he rubbed his chest to keep warm. Huddling in a small circle behind the stone wall to break the wind, he kept silent as their party decided what course of action to pursue next. Seemingly loyal and devoted to his Captain-General, he hung upon Olea's every word, voicing no doubts at breaking from the Palace Guard to follow a band of Kingsmen outlaws.

"Fenton and I have a network in the city." Aldris spoke beside Jherrick as they dug into a discussion of their options. "We should make contact with them."

"It's too risky to go back to Lintesh." Olea shook her head, calm and in command once more. "The Chancellate will have the Guard looking for us. Every Guardsman knows me, and you, Aldris. No. Where else?"

"The only other contact I have is in Vennet," Aldris growled with hard sigh. "But that's a good two weeks from here. We'd need horses, and supplies. Without going to Lintesh, we'd be hard-pressed to trade for what we need. Every hamlet for leagues is emptied, everyone flooding to the city for the coronation."

Olea tousled her damp curls and Jherrick absorbed that motion with his eyes. He would take a sword in the gut to hold her, just to touch those curls even once. Gazing over at two sets of steps that led away from their lookout, one up the Kingsmount, one down, Olea nodded suddenly. "Aldris, how far have you taken the upper path here?"

"Only a few leagues." Aldris shook his head, his golden brows knitting. "There are some fortress ruins about four leagues up, probably an escape for the royal family at one time. The stairs go further, but Fenton says they dead-end at an unclimbable wall of sheer volcanic glass. No way around, no way up."

"Well, that won't get us supplies," Olea murmured.

"What about going back into the underground?" The big Kingsman Vargen spoke. "That river must be the one that lets out beyond the First Tier."

"Unless you are expert at surviving getting drowned, I don't suggest it." Olea gave him a tired smile. "There are no places to walk beside that torrent, though it does flow right underneath the entire city."

"There's no way to float that beast." Aldris grunted in confirmation. "But we could backtrack to the Weeping Tunnel and take the Unterhaft."

"The palace will be crawling with dogs by now." Olea shook her head. "If we backtrack, they'll catch our scent."

"Where does the lower path go?" Jherrick chimed in, playing his part of young ignoramus as he nodded at the path leading down the mountainside.

"That goes down just behind Roushenn." Aldris' mouth quirked. "There's a gate behind the barracks that we keep Guards on at all times. No one ever uses it, except huntsmen for game and kitchen girls for herb-gathering up the mountainside."

"Serpent's maw or serpent's maw," the big Kingsman rumbled. "Any way we go leads straight back into Roushenn."

"We could take the path most of the way down," Olea spoke up suddenly, a thoughtful look upon her face, "then split through the woods and track around Lintesh on the mountainside. That would put us near the Alranstone grotto in the Kingswood, at the foot of the mountain to the east."

"Is there an Alranstone near Vennet?" The big Kingsman Vargen asked with a thoughtful scowl. "We might be able to travel through the Stone here to Aldris' contacts."

"Not that I know of." Aldris murmured with the same thoughtful look in his eyes now. "But there's a Stone near Quelsis. Perhaps we could take the Alranstone out of the Kingswood here and make it to the eastern reaches. No one would know we were outlaws. We could trade for supplies and get down to Vennet quickly."

Jherrick didn't miss the fact that Aldris spoke like he could wrest passage through an Alranstone like a Kingsman. More and more today, Jherrick was realizing Second-Lieutenant Aldris den'Farahan was truly something other than he seemed, his jaunty demeanor tempered into cold, ruthless steel at their current predicament. But Jherrick had seen Aldris shirtless in the practice yards, and the man wasn't Inked.

But then again, technically, neither was Jherrick.

"Quelsis is nearly a hundred leagues northeast of Vennet." Olea pursed her lips, thoughtful. "We could cover the distance quickly if we stole a few horses. But only if that Stone lets us pass through."

"The question is... is our need great?" Vargen ventured in his rumbling basso.

"Our need is great." Olea met the big Kingsman's eyes, determination in her every sinew. "For who am I without a King or Queen to guard? Who are all of us, Vargen, if we're not Kingsmen anymore?"

"Down the mountain, then," Vargen rumbled with a sober nod. "We split from the trail and head east to find the Stone-grotto in the Kingswood. Let's get going before this wind whips us off the ledge."

The Kingsman Vargen stood in a decisive motion, and just like that, their council was ended. As the party made for the wet-slicked stairs, Jherrick rose to follow. Tromping down steps carven out of byrunstone bedrock, they went briskly but carefully, the stairs running with water, which often gave way to washed out gullies. As violet evening tinged the storm-clouds rose and gold, they at last left the rocky scree and entered the hardy evergreens of the Kingswood, the path turning into a muddy track beneath their feet. Twice Jherrick pretended to trip and fall into the steadying arm of Vargen, displaying ineptitude that sharply contrasted with the three trained veterans.

He wasn't a Kingsman, and he made sure it showed.

Dim shadows had taken the forest by the time they split from the path and headed deeper into the woods. The sun was long set behind the Kingsmount, and Jherrick increased his stumbling accordingly, damp moss making the mud treacherous underfoot. Every tree began to look like all the rest, when suddenly Jherrick felt the spongy moss flatten out. He knew a moment of fear as they passed the clearing where he'd dumped bodies for the wolves and a hungry howl went up. Jherrick wondered if they could scent their regular purveyor of meat, but the prickling of his neck gradually subsided as they crossed the wolves' hunting grounds and into a thick stand of silveroak.

At last, they heard the bubbling of the Stone-grotto's spring. Only a thin band of starlight held court around the Alranstone, the night breeze warm down near the city as it rippled tall grasses in the clearing. The Stone was silent as the four approached it, though Jherrick felt that strange ripple over his skin as he passed a certain boundary, as if the Stone was watching him. He'd never liked being near Alranstones; he felt accused, judged for what he was, what he had agreed to. Olea, Aldris, and Vargen shivered also as they crossed the Stone's boundary, and as everyone put their hands to its smooth surface, Jherrick felt a thrumming in the air and through his palms as if it were singing.

Reciting Kingsman words Jherrick had never heard, Olea implored the Alranstone for passage. The Stone's vibration surged for a moment, then dimmed, but otherwise it did nothing. With a frown, Vargen recited the words next, and the Stone surged again but still did not permit them passage. Clearing his throat, Aldris then recited the words, confirming Jherrick's suspicions about him – but still the Alranstone did not permit them to travel.

"Well, I suppose that's it then." Vargen heaved a heavy sigh, his hands falling from the Stone as an aura of defeat settled over the party.

But just as Jherrick was about to remove his hands from the Stone's surface, he felt the thrumming suddenly increase in his chest, humming through his body like a whir of owl wings. His heart thundered, his breath gripping as a vast touch brushed through him – and Jherrick felt himself *compelled*. Shuddering from a fear that had no name, he leaned into his sweat-cold palms where they touched the Stone. Something deep and ancient slid into his mind, whispering, and Jherrick shuddered in terror as he felt himself entered by that watchful, powerful presence. The thrumming of the Stone increased to a fever pitch and Jherrick barely heard Vargen's astonished intake of breath.

"Something's happening! Everyone put your hands on the Stone and recite together!"

As everyone else recited their Kingsman words once more, the Alranstone's shuddering gripped into Jherrick's core, the whispering solidifying in his mind. *Traitor. Their need is great but yours is more. I taste blood on your hands, death in your soul, and fury in your mind. But there is only one thing that can make your heart truly weep, child. And only those tears will redeem you.*

Suddenly, the lowest eye upon the three-eye Stone blinked wide – a vicious, bloody red. There was a thunderclap and a violent tearing of space, and Jherrick screamed as he was threaded though to a vast nowhere. Turned inside-out, his ears were stuffed into his entrails as he was viciously pulled through the Stone and spat out upon the other side. Sprawling, retching, he fell into hot white sand beneath a high-noon sun as blistering heat accosted him like a scalding forge. White blinded his vision, sand searing his hands. Stumbling quickly to his feet, he saw the others doing the same, brushing off white sand beneath a cloudless azure sky.

Suddenly, a clarion call rang through the desert, the deafening tone issuing from the Alranstone that had spat them out upon the baking sand. To its ear-splitting call, a tirade of armed warriors flooded from the shade behind tumbled columns that ringed the Stone, and Jherrick found himself surrounded by dark-haired, grey-eyed men and women. Clad in desert leathers with loose white head-wraps, they bristled with razor-tipped spears – all those spears aimed directly at the party's throats.

"*Taile arabine ghenya shefan!*"

Spears still leveled, the warriors parted to let a tall man stride forward, his silver-worked helmet with a mane of red bristles showing his leadership. Well-muscled though slender, he set the butt of a spear taller than he in the sand with a graceful, authoritative motion, and Jherrick heard it clink upon stone beneath the drifts. A sheer wrap of white fabric with a silver and red-edged border draped his shoulders to keep off the sun, a harness and breastplate of leather beneath that, woven with red bristles. Leather gauntlets graced his wrists and a leather-paneled skirt came to mid-thigh. Light leather boots laced to his knees, with silver shin guards like his helmet.

"*Taile arabine ghenya shefan!*" The warrior-captain's grey eyes were hard as stone as he made an unknown demand of them yet again.

"Anyone have any idea what he's saying?" Aldris murmured with a wry tension. "I'd like to not get my throat slit today."

"I think it's a form of Ghrec! Aeon, we must be somewhere on their trade routes." Olea murmured, frowning, then stepped forward slightly to respond. "*Talim enenya khoum vhris.*"

The warrior-captain blinked as he studied her a moment.

"You are Menderian dogs!" He spoke at last, the words twisting his tongue as he leveled his spear at them with a snarl. Turning his head, he spat into the white sand with disdain. "Did you come to bribe us again with your worthless emeralds? You stink like the eel you serve! Go back to your slippery master and I will spare your worthless hides!"

Jherrick's insides twisted; there was only one man to whom such a phrase could refer. Carefully but with obvious authority, Olea stepped forward, positioning herself between the spear-captain and their group. The man with the crested helmet shifted his spear's point right to her throat.

But Olea never flinched, her grey eyes steely.

"We do not know of what you speak, fellow," she murmured in a calming tone. "My name is Olea den'Alrahel. I'm a Kingsman, Alrashemni. These are my comrades. Was there someone else you were expecting to come through that Stone?"

The man startled at Olea's words as a ripple of astonishment went through the surrounding spearmen. Suddenly, he lifted his spear decisively from her throat. Striding forward with his spear still in hand, he stepped close to Olea. Jherrick could see the tension of her stillness as she resisted going for a weapon. But the spearman didn't move to harm her, only reached out, tracing her face with his fingertips – running his fingers through her blue-black mane and holding her chin to peer at her storm-grey eyes.

And it hit Jherrick suddenly, how similar they looked.

"*Alrashemnari... Alrahel?*" The spear-captain murmured.

"Yes." Olea held his gaze calmly. "Olea den'Alrahel. Alrashemni. Kingsman."

"*Olea dihm Alrahel?*" The spear-captain's fingers traced her face again as wonder spilled over his features suddenly. His face amazed, he sank to one knee, laying his spear reverently upon the white sand. Slowly, he lifted his crested helmet off with both hands, baring a brush-cut mane of blue-black curls just like Olea's, then unbuckled his leather breastplate with its red weavings, setting those aside also.

And beneath his breastplate, Jherrick's eyes widened to see the most beautifully Inked Mountain and Stars. But his Inking was done in twelve different colors with twelve stars rather than five, tendrils twining and weaving through the rest, interspersed with intricate sigils and script spilling over the warrior's chest and collarbones.

Placing his palm flat upon his multihued Inkings, the spear-captain bowed his head.

"*Sei Olea brethan khoum tantha Alrahel.*" He murmured, reverently.

Like sighing sand, the rest of the spearmen and women sank to one knee also, laying their spears aside and pressing palms to their chests. As they did, Jherrick resisted the urge to run. The Alranstone had put him through – right into a nest of Alrashemni vipers.

"What just happened? What did he just say?" Aldris murmured.

"*She is the Olive Tree that brings peace with the Dawn.*" Olea spoke quietly – her eyes open wide in astonishment at the men and women kneeling all around her in the white desert sand.

EPILOGUE

DHERRAN

In the vaulted stone basement that was the Vicoute Arlen den'Selthir's training arena, Dherran moved jerkily now after five hours of bouting, everything sore and screaming. A puddle of sweat, his breath was shallow from all the bruises upon his body, but Arlen's blue eyes were still cold as glaciers where he stood across from Dherran in the sand pit. The Vicoute's shirt and breeches still had no stains of sweat, his posture impeccable, not a bruise or a scratch showing upon him in the lamplight that illuminated the space. Nearby, other men and women sparred, weapons ringing in pits of sand like the one in which Dherran stood – Kingsmen practicing their formidable arts.

"Again!" The Vicoute barked, readying his quarterstaff.

"No." Dherran had taken enough beatings today, and letting his temper best him at last, he threw his staff to the sand. Though as soon as it left his fingers, den'Selthir swept in, ruthlessly flipping Dherran's feet out from underneath him. Landing on his back with a grunt, Dherran heard sniggers echo around the vaulted cellar as Arlen leveled his staff at Dherran's throat.

"Up, Dherran!"

"I said no." Crossing his aching arms over his chest, Dherran tried to make his voice firm despite lying upon his back with a staff threatening his throat. Gazing past the Vicoute, his eyes lit upon the massive tableau set into the far stone wall worked in silver. A wolf and dragon fought each other, perfectly balanced within a ring of golden flame. It was captivating, and had distracted Dherran ample times over the past weeks – getting him hit in the process. But he had time to stare at it now, because he wasn't getting up. "We've been at this for hours. And you had me running sprints half the night, then carrying water to the animals all morning. I'm done."

A swift rap caught him on his abdomen and Dherran huffed, trying to not hold the tension of the blow. Bracing for blows only made things hurt more around Arlen den'Selthir.

"You are lazy, fat, and arrogant," den'Selthir lectured as he had for weeks now, "and have no respect for the marks you wear. I could skewer you, Dherran, yet you wear Inkings that are important to me. Get up!" Another sharp rap came to his abdomen.

"I respect these marks no matter what you say, because in my own way, I believe in them and strive to be worthy of them everyday. Not that it matters to you." Still on his back, Dherran focused on keeping his breathing easy. Expecting another hit with the staff for his impertinence, he ground his jaw tighter, though he didn't budge, willing himself to stay calm. Horrible things happened when one lost their cool around the Vicoute, as he had learned their first day together. Arlen was fast as a viper and five times stronger than he looked. A lifelong Kingsman, he hadn't ever stopped training.

Not a single day.

Silence came from the Vicoute and Dherran tried not to tense, waiting for another swift rap with the staff. But then a proffered hand came instead. Frozen in surprise, Dherran blinked – Arlen had not offered him a hand up from the sand in all their long hours training yet. But now it was offered so Dherran took it, the Vicoute hauling him to his feet.

"You've got tenacity, I'll give you that." Arlen gazed at Dherran appraisingly as he handed his quarterstaff off to his waiting armsman Philo. "Nine out of ten fighters break under my treatment on just the third day. Indeed, you *have* something you believe in, or you would not have lasted these past three weeks under my tutelage. You're a decent fighter, Dherran. But Kingsmen don't rub their assholes in people's faces and swing their cocks about to give the world a great big fucking. Breaking the beloved icons of a community will only get our name detested, and that's what you do when you fight popular opponents and *ruin* them."

"I've apologized for breaking Arvale," Dherran spoke stubbornly. "Countless times."

"I know. And he is healing. This is bigger than that. Come."

Stepping from the sand ring, Arlen flicked his fingers regally for his armsman, who stepped in with fresh towels. Taking one, Dherran rubbed sand out of his hair and off his sweat-streaked torso, not to mention some dry blood. Arlen only used his towel to wipe a sheen of sweat from his neck and face. It was a routine they had undergone every evening, though every other practice had ended with Dherran too weary to stand or even see straight. Den'Selthir had pitted Dherran against two Kingsmen, then three, then four, and finally up to six before he had manhandled Dherran himself the first week.

And had been beating him to a pulp ever since.

Usually after practice, den'Selthir nodded a curt goodnight, and Dherran went back to his rooms to soak out his aches in the copper tub. But tonight Arlen beckoned, and curious, Dherran followed. Walking a short way down the vaulted underground catacomb, they pushed through a heavy cendarie door into a small chamber, the Vicoute's saunas. Dherran had been down a few times with Khenria, as the saunas were open to all, though never with Arlen. Pegs hung on the wall, some already laden with clothes, some with fresh robes and towels, boots lining the wall by the door.

Disrobing and shucking his boots, Arlen hung his garments on a peg, and Dherran realized it was the first time he had seen the man shirtless, as the Vicoute always fought with his shirt on. Disrobing also, Dherran glanced over to see Arlen had no Inkings upon his chest, and Dherran frowned in confusion, as Arlen made much of *respecting the Inkings* at every turn. But the Vicoute simply slung his towel over one shoulder and headed for another door, passing through with the grace of a lynx.

Dherran followed, soon swallowed by the thick steam of the saunas. Steam billowed through vents in the walls, a few Kingsmen and women sitting upon cendarie benches in the hot mist. Some had the traditional black Inkings, some had a plethora of battle-scars. Some were younger and unmarked, Kingskinder still earning their Seals upon the Vicoute's estate. While some like Arlen had no Inkings whatsoever. Yet again, it raised Dherran's curiosity, and as they entered, a number of heads nodded, the Vicoute clasping arms in greeting.

"Arlen." A grey-maned boar of a man growled, clasping the Vicoute's forearm.

"Ghevran." Arlen acknowledged him.

"Arlen." A wire-framed mid-aged retainer clasped arms with the Vicoute.

"Ihlen." Arlen spoke genially. Out upon the estate, the Vicoute treated his men like retainers, civil but brusque like a lord. But down here in the training-pits and saunas, all were Kingsmen and all equal, Arlen greeting his kin accordingly. As the Vicoute pushed open another cendarie door, they came to a second steam room where few men lounged. Upon seeing the Vicoute, these stood with a nod, gathering their towels and stepping out, leaving Dherran and Arlen alone.

Taking a seat upon a bench with a sigh, Arlen scrubbed away perspiration on his face with his towel. Hanging it around his shoulders, he leaned back on the cendarie-paneled wall, closing his eyes. Still not knowing what he was doing here, Dherran sat a respectful distance away. The Vicoute was not a man to get cozy with, no matter that they had known each other three weeks now. The steam was rich with a loamy smell, something that mellowed the mind, easing tension from screaming muscles. After a few breaths, Dherran had closed his eyes, leaning back against the wall.

But after a moment, he opened his eyes, gazing at the Vicoute's bare chest. "Vicoute."

Taking a long, deep breath of steam, Arlen spoke. "Down here, you may call me Arlen, Dherran."

"Why is that?"

"Because at the end of a day when a man has done everything he needs to do," Arlen sighed, his eyes yet closed, "when he has upheld his integrity and lived a day worthy of his Inkings, then he may enjoy solace just as a man. Just as we all are, in our bones and flesh. Equal."

"Why do you not have Inkings?"

"I have them." One of Arlen's eyes cracked open. "They are just not seen until you pierce me with a blade. One day soon you will best me, Dherran. And when you do, you may have the honor of striking a mark upon my chest until Ink burns in my blood. But you must best me first." A low chuckle came from the Vicoute, haughty and amused.

"I will best you." Dherran spoke stubbornly.

"I know." Den'Selthir chuckled again. "Your skill impresses me, for having gone so long without a proper teacher. But know this: I am not here to teach you the sword. I am here to teach you that which you lack most. In order to lead men in battle, one must be clever, patient, and thoughtful. One must play to the strengths of those around you and win their hearts, so their loyalty to you never wavers even for a moment. Why do you think the people of Vennet love me, Dherran?"

"Because you're their lord." Dherran frowned.

"No." Arlen chuckled again, though he did not open his eyes now. "They love me because I send men and women for charity duties in town. I hold a school for children to learn their letters. I invest in community works like bridges, water piping, and roads. I sponsor events for the town to enliven their spirits. And all is done with the name *Vicoute* Arlen den'Selthir. That is how they know me. And should the day ever come that I must bare my Inkings upon my chest and rally this town – this entire valley behind the Kingsmen – I could see it done. But for the spear you lanced right in my well-greased wheel. You have the courage and stamina of a great leader, but up to three weeks ago, you've been dumb as a stump and making enemies the entire way."

"Why do you care?" Dherran couldn't resist crossing his arms over his chest, anger rising at the sting in the Vicoute's words. "If I'm such a lost cause, just dump me and be done with it. Khenria and I can make our own way, even with Grump gone."

"Your *Grump*, as you call him, will be found, sneaky fox that he is. And when he is, he will be put to justice." Arlen gave an irritated sigh, scratching both hands through his brush-cut blond hair now. As Dherran made a sound to retort, Arlen held up a hand, forestalling any argument. "I know he aided you and Khenria, her especially, and I am grateful to the man for preserving our Kingskinder. But it does not excuse what he *is*, Dherran. He is a Khehemni agent. And he will die like one."

"I don't see why he has to die," Dherran scowled, the familiar argument one he and Arlen had discussed at length already.

"Where there is one Khehemnas, there are ten." Arlen spoke patiently, though with an edge of iron in his voice now. "And where there are ten, there are a hundred. Breaking even one, Dherran, may lead us to the hundred. I will not repeat myself on this matter again."

"You can't just keep leaving me in the dark." Dherran growled now. "You've explained less than nothing about Grump, or what Khenria and I are really doing here. We've waited long enough, training with your retainers day after day. I think we're due some answers."

"You've waited ten years for answers, and you can't wait one more day?" A curl of a smile graced Arlen's lips, but he still did not open his eyes.

"I could slit your throat down here, and your retainers wouldn't hear it."

"Go ahead and try, Dherran." Arlen's smile turned into an amused smirk, both of them knowing Dherran's threat was useless. Scrubbing a hand through his iron-streaked blond hair again and wiping away sweat, Arlen continued, "In any case, I've brought you here to give you answers – you've earned them today. You controlled your temper and made a decision about what was best for your army, which today was simply your body, but that's where one begins. Armies can't fight day in and day out. Men get injured and sore, horses wear out, supply lines run thin. No one gets any sleep and people are up at odd hours doing tasks that weary them, like watering the animals. Commanders have even less time to rest, and must take it when the moment is non-critical. So ask your questions. I will give you only five answers tonight. Choose wisely what you ask."

Dherran clenched his jaw, part of him irate yet part of him impressed. He finally saw now what the previous weeks had meant, and found he was mulling it over. He'd not realized Arlen had been surreptitiously training him in how to be a commander rather than just a fighter. But thinking back on all the bizarre lessons Arlen had impressed upon him these past weeks, he realized every lesson had a deeper kernel in it concerning commanding armies and what a man had to learn in order to do so. It was something Dherran had never really thought himself capable of, commanding regiments – but now that Arlen had opened his mind to it, he found himself deeply considering the idea.

But there were other questions to ask the Vicoute first.

"How did you know Grump was Khehemni?" Dherran began, calm taking him now as he regarded the Vicoute.

"I first met *Grump* in the Khessian Hills," Den'Selthir sighed at length. "He was in the rebel camp we routed. I chained him up myself, to be brought to trial for war crimes. But he escaped. In the morning, we found a number of our Kingsmen dead. He'd been spying on us and knew which of us carried black

Inkings, and he targeted them. I don't know if he planned his capture so he could get close to our ranks, or if it was accident, but he stands accused of the deaths of thirteen Kingsmen. He will pay the Fifth Price, once we catch him. What else would you ask?"

Dherran thought a moment, wondering if this information about Grump was actually the truth, though his next question was already clear. "Who are the Khehemni? And why do they plague Alrashemni?"

"We know and we know not." Arlen gave a wry smile, his eyes still closed. "They have been a force opposing us in secret for nigh-on a thousand years, yet the *why* of it is not exactly known. They are passionate about tearing down things Alrashemni create, and do so in utter secrecy. Khehemni often come through a family line, though some are conscripted. We know their governing council is called the Lothren, though we have only suspicions about certain individuals involved. Khehemni are notorious for being able to withstand torture and rarely give names, though they have been found in Cennetia, Praough, Valenghia, Elsthemen, and here. They wear a Bloodmark upon the left shoulder that appears when the skin is cut, the same kind of Ink I have for my Shemout mark, though their Inking shows a dragon fighting a wolf inside a broken circle."

"Like the tableau upon your basement wall?" Dherran blinked.

"Like it yet different." The Vicoute nodded. "My wall depicts the classic emblem of the warrior's way, the Marriage of Conflict in perfect balance. The Khehemni blood-inking has the dragon and wolf, though fighting inside a circle broken into pieces. We don't know the significance of the difference."

Dherran paused, taking in this information, then pushed forward with a topic of interest to him. "How does a Kingsman become Shemout Alrashemni?"

"*You* don't!" The Vicoute barked a laugh. "You've flaunted your Inkings over half the Realm! To become Shemout, one must keep a low profile. Or a very high one, so no one would ever suspect you of being what you are. Some Shemout are born into it, as I was. Others are conscripted, but never with a history as brazen as yours."

"Who leads the Shemout Alrashemni?" Dherran leaned forward now with interest.

"Telling you that would secure your obedience here." Opening his eyes, Arlen eyed Dherran deeply now. "I won't let you leave this estate, not if you have that knowledge, Dherran. You or Khenria."

"It's you, isn't it?" Dherran sobered, watching the way Arlen sat perfectly, intensely still. "You're the leader of the entire Shemout, not just their Rakhan, their battle-commander. How many of your men and women here know what you are?"

"Only the ones who sport no Blackmark." Arlen's icy eyes were riveting as he stared Dherran down. "If you loose your tongue about this, Dherran, even to men and women here on the estate, I will have it silenced."

"But who becomes leader of the Shemout if you die?" Dherran did not back down, digging for answers.

"You have earned the right to be answered tonight," the Vicoute spoke coldly. "But after tonight, I will answer no more questions about the Shemout, and you are to repeat nothing of what you've heard. My Second if I die, is a Jenner – the Abbess of the First Abbey in Lintesh. Her name is Lenuria den'Brae. If I die, you are to ride out with the Bloodmarked from my retinue, and pass word *immediately* to Abbess Lenuria. Can you do that, Dherran?"

"Why are you asking me to do this?" Dherran murmured, perplexed.

"Because if someone kills me, it will either be you," Arlen eyed Dherran almost appreciatively, "or it will be a *very* skilled opponent. And if she kills me, I want you to run like hell, and protect as many as you can along the way. Abbess Lenuria can help you do that. Promise me that if I fall, you'll pass word to Lenuria."

"She?" Dherran blinked at him. "You already know who it is that could kill you?"

"Yes." A wry, bitter smile curled Arlen's lips of memories long gone. "She spared my life once, barely. That is all I will say about it."

Dherran held the man's gaze a long moment as the curling steam passed between them. He didn't know why Arlen was asking him to take up this particular task if Arlen was ever struck down, but he realized suddenly that the Vicoute was placing a deep trust in him. It impressed Dherran, and he felt all his previous anger with the man sigh away, cooled by a deep understanding.

Arlen had seen something in Dherran. Something he was willing to gamble on – if Dherran was willing to gamble on it himself.

Recalling the way he'd looked in the mirror the first time he'd dressed in lordly attire in the Vicoute's manor, Dherran took a deep breath. "If I leave here, I may never find out what happened to my family. So you have my vow, Arlen. I will stay here on the estate and learn what you have to teach. And if you ever die... I will pass word to the Abbess. I swear it."

"*Alrashemnari aenta trethan lheroun.*" Arlen den'Selthir's nod was grave with respect as his gaze rested upon Dherran – for the first time since they'd known each other.

"*Alrashemnari aenta trethan lheroun.*" Dherran nodded back, feeling respect for the Vicoute for the first time also.

* * *

THE NEXT MORNING, a servingman came early with a brisk rap at Dherran's door. Dherran opened his eyes to a trickle of light passing over the eastern mountains, the sky brightening slowly out his open window. It wasn't quite morning and he groaned as he sat up, Khenria peeping irritably beneath the covers beside him. Though he had slept deeply, all the effects of the Vicoute's steam-room upon Dherran's battered muscles were gone this morning. Everything screamed with miserable fury as he swung his legs out of bed, and hauling a blanket off the bed to cover his nakedness, he stumbled to the door and threw it wide.

"What?! Aeon and all the gods..." Dherran slurred with less than his usual vinegar, still half-asleep. A Blackmarked Kingsman named Fhennic stood in the hall, the servingman who had dressed Dherran his first night here. The two had become friendly over the past weeks, and Fhennic did not sneer now at Dherran's disheveled state as he spoke soberly.

"The Vicoute has called a meeting, Dherran. Everyone. Rouse Khenria and bring her down at once."

"What? Does he do this often?" Dherran's eyebrows shot up as he blinked, rubbing his face to clear the sleep.

"Never." The man's eyes hardened. "Just throw something on and come down to the dining hall. Excuse me, I have others to wake." Stepping quickly past, Fhennic jogged off down the hall. Dherran watched him go, noticing that he sported a full brace of knives on a baldric today with a longsword across his back. Something in Dherran's gut tightened, uneasy. Fhennic never wore weapons in the house. Closing the door, Dherran strode quickly to the bed, shaking Khenria by the shoulder.

"Khenria, love, get up. We need to dress."

"What? Hmm?" Her sleepy tousled head was irresistible, her puffy face imprinted with the blankets. Khenria had become a heavy sleeper since coming to the Vicoute's manse, training with the women fighters nearly as hard as Dherran did with the Vicoute.

"Up. Clothes. Let's go." Dherran threw her the first thing to hand, a flimsy silk underdress. Pulling it on over her lithe nakedness, she put it on backwards at first and had to haul it off again. Dherran paused, caught in the beauty of her pert little breasts and lean curves. They'd been intimate numerous times now since arriving at the Vicoute's manse, but Dherran still found himself caught in her beauty every night when they fell into bed exhausted from training, and every morning when they woke.

But Fhennic had been wearing weapons, and it didn't bode well. Stuffing down his lust, Dherran hauled on his trousers and a loose shirt, then his boots. At last, Khenria was out of bed, the thin shift clinging to her slender frame like mist. Dherran wanted nothing more than to rip it off her and trundle her back to the bed, but he stuffed his ardor down.

"Whaddre we doing? Running 'way?" Khenria yawned as she donned a pair of silk house slippers.

"Meeting with the Vicoute, Hawk Talon." Wrapping her in his arms, Dherran kissed her gently on the lips. "Splash some water on your face and let's go."

Moving to the basin, she splashed her face, combing down her wild mane as she blinked awake. When she turned back, a ready woman faced him. "Weapons?"

"Maybe." Dherran nodded, reaching out to buckle on his sword belt. Khenria slung on a leather longknife harness the Vicoute had given her, which was strangely perfect with her slinky underdress. She nodded, and Dherran heard her light steps follow as he moved to the door and hauled it open. They strode into the hall, a few of their Kingsmen comrades already jogging towards the stairs and disappearing down them. Picking up his feet, Dherran jogged also, Khenria on his heels. The feeling of foreboding in his gut grew as they stepped quickly through the formal halls to the massive dining room, lit only by the blush of dawn through the arched windows.

Fhennic had not exaggerated when he'd said everyone was called to the meeting. Over a hundred people crowded the dining hall – the entire estate. Kingsmen and women in various stages of dress, all were armed as they stood or sat around the long table, steely-eyed. Dherran and Khenria were among the last to arrive just as the Vicoute entered from a side door, two of his best men tailing him – all three fully armed. Standing at the head of the table, Arlen placed his fingertips upon its polished top and a hush settled over the long dining hall.

"I have had a rider just this morning," den'Selthir began, his eyes even more icy than usual, "from Lintesh. Two weeks ago, there was an assassination attempt at the Queen's coronation. The Queen is missing and presumed dead. Her assassin was the Elsthemi First Sword, and the Chancellate have called for justice from King Therel Alramir of Elsthemen, who abducted her and fled. The Chancellate have made a public show of executing Elsthemi retainers they captured during the fighting, and declared an emergency power of state. They are preparing for all-out war with Elsthemen."

Murmurs rose around the table, growled expletives from the Kingsmen. Dherran's eyes went around, taking in the hard set of every jaw, the cold readiness in their eyes at this terrible news. He was surprised to feel how well it fit him; the bristle of anger around the hall intoxicating, surging with a current of fury barely kept in check.

That much rage in a hall of Kingsmen could have brought down an army. But alone among them, Arlen den'Selthir stood calm and collected – all trace of the haughty lord gone, replaced by a battle-hardened commander.

"My contacts in Lintesh have reason to believe the Elsthemi King is not at fault," he continued, his iron-hard voice echoing to the highest gables. "Two Kingsmen were seen leaving with King Therel Alramir as he escaped, Kingsmen who had been posing as palace Guards, and King Therel was carrying the Queen, who may have still been alive. Other Kingsmen are missing from the palace, and we believe this to be a Khehemni-induced plot. I have told you all about the Khehemni's supposed link to the Summons and Purge. Know this: they are at work again here, and we cannot abide a war with Elsthemen, where Alrashemni are numerous. I need three volunteers to go as ambassadors to the Elsthemi King and tell him we stand ready to support him. Who will go?"

Hands went up around the hall. The Vicoute nodded at three – two men and one woman. "Den'Bherlus, den'Khan, den'Buir. Good. Make ready anything you need and be upon the road in two hours. My thanks to you gentlemen, and lady. Please be excused, the rest does not concern you."

As Arlen placed a solemn palm to his chest, the three bowed back in Alrashemni fashion, striding from the hall as den'Selthir continued. "The rest of you, listen closely. We are beginning a campaign. From now on, each of you will leave this manse once a day and travel somewhere new. A map will be kept of all locations in the training room. We begin a war of slander against the Chancellors and this rash Elsthemi invasion."

The Vicoute paused, swinging his icy gaze around to take in everyone in the hall. "Take coin from den'Thurgard, spend it on your travels. You will drink in taverns, gossip in the markets, visit a brothel and a smithy. You will spread word of what is happening in Lintesh, using language such as, *plot against our Queen, unnecessary, two-front war, reaching too far, stretching too thin, outnumbered* and the like. The populace *must* be made to agree that this war is a terrible idea. In two weeks' time, we will re-visit the marked areas and begin to rabble-rouse."

"But what if the Queen's dead, Arlen?" One of Arlen's retainers broke in, a brawny man named Dhuth, his dark-browed face frowning.

The Vicoute drew a long, slow breath, the single breath of his training, before answering. "Hopefully by then, we will have confirmation of the Queen's safety, Dhuth. But even if she's not alive, we must avoid a war at all costs. I will hear suggestions in my study all day today, and will consider all thoughts. Get some breakfast, think of your destinations. Only the most minimal chores are to be observed upon the estate – cooking, feeding the animals, groomsmen duties, and the smithy. If you have one of these, please plan your visit somewhere local. Telsen, engage an inventory of all weapons. Arthur, recruit as many hands at the smithy as you need to anticipate an engagement. Dismissed."

Palms went to hearts all around the room, and hands to blades. More than a hundred Kingsmen-in-hiding pledged their duty, their eyes flashing with readiness to finally be able to retaliate after all these years. Though it was a small ripple den'Selthir had started, Dherran felt the power it created like lightning in his limbs.

He felt his own heart hungry for retribution now – feral like a wild boar about to charge.

"Dherran, Khenria." Den'Selthir's eyes pinned them. "With me. You will observe all proceedings for the next few days and keep my notes. Get dressed properly, then bring breakfast to my study. Go."

"Vicoute." Already bowing, Khenria set one palm to Inkings that were not even there yet, her grey eyes shining for war.

Dherran nodded also, feeling battle bristle in his soul.

* * *

The adventure continues in *Bloodmark: The Kingsmen Chronicles #2*

Love this series? Help Jean write more by leaving a review!

THE ADVENTURE CONTINUES

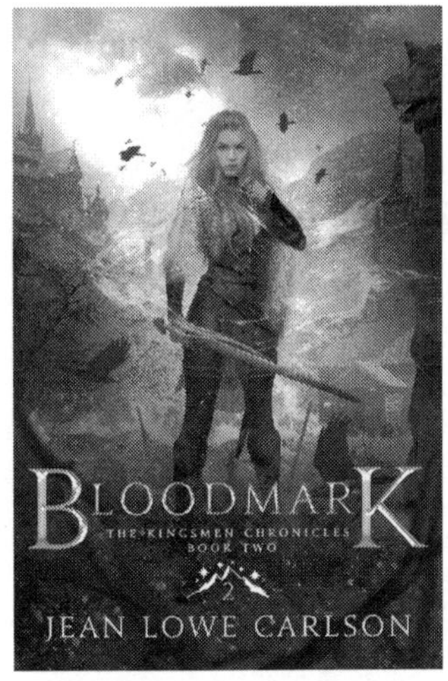

The epic adventure continues in *Bloodmark: The Kingsmen Chronicles #2*. Learn more at **www.JeanLoweCarlson.com** or visit:

APPENDIX 1: PRONUNCIATION GUIDE

WORD BEGINNINGS:

Dh/Jh/Kh/Lh – Hard consonant, "h" is silent (Ex. Dherran [Dair-ren] like "dare", Jherrick [Jair-rick] like "jester", Khouren [Koor-en] like "kick", Lhaurent [Lao-rahnt] like "laugh")

Gh/G – Hard "g" sound (Ex. Ghrenna [Gren-na], Gherris [Gair-ris] like "good")

Ih – Long "ee" sound (Ex. Ihbram [Ee-brum] like "helium")

Th – Soft "th" combination (Ex. Theroun [Thair-oon] like "thespian")

Uh/U – Long "oo" sound (Ex. Uhlas [Oo-las] like "tulips")

O – Proper "oh" sound if begins a word (Ex. Olea [Oh-lay-a] like "ocean")

El – Open "eh" sound (Ex. Elohl [Eh-loll] like "elephant")

Il – Soft "ihl" sound (Ex. Ildrian [Ihl-drēe-an] like "ill")

MIDDLE OF WORDS:

-i- If in the middle of a word, long "ee" sound (Ex. Elyasin [Ehl-ya-seen] like "do re mi")
Exception: Aldris [Al-dris, not Al-drees]

-ch- Soft "sh" sound (Ex. Suchinne [Soo-sheen])

-ou- Long "oo" sound (Ex. Roushenn [Roo-shen] like "frou-frou")

PHRASES IN ALRASHEMNI (HIGH ALRAKHAN):

Alrashemnesh aere phelo Areseitya rhavesin.
In the Alrashemni, I am of the order of True Seers righteous.

Alrashemnari aenta trethan lheroun!
Alrashemni keep promises theirs! (Alrashemni keep their promises.)

Alrashemnesh aere veitriya Rakhan rhavesin.
In the Alrashemni, I am truthfully the Battle Commander righteous.

Alrashemnesh aere veitriya Rennkavi rhavesin.
In the Alrashemni, I am truthfully the Binder righteous.

Sin Rakhan. Siere tut me lhin.
Not the Battle Commander. These are all of my sorrows. (I'm sorry.)

Alrashemnari aere alranesh vhekhan.
Alrashemni I am my life entire. (Long live the Alrashemni!)

Alrashemnari aenta trethan lheroun, ahle fhis brethii!
Alrashemni keep promises theirs, to the end bitter!
(Alrashemni keep their promises to the bitter end!)

PHRASES IN KHOUREK (Oasis Ghellen):

Taile arabine ghenya shefan!
You uncloak all your cowls! (Declare yourselves!)

Alrashemnari... Alrahel?
Alrashemni...dawn?

Olea dihm Alrahel?
Olive tree of the Dawn?

Sei Olea brethan khoum tantha Alrahel!
She is the olive tree that brings peace with the dawn!

PHRASES IN GHREC:

Talim enenya khoum vhris.
We mean you harm none. (We mean you no harm.)

APPENDIX 2: CHARACTERS

ALRASHEMNI KINGSMEN:

Elohl den'Alrahel – First-Lieutenant of the High Brigade, twin to Olea
Olea den'Alrahel – Captain-General of the Palace Guard, twin to Elohl, Fourth Captain of the Realm
Ghrenna den'Tanuk – Kingswoman, a thief
Dherran den'Lhust – Kingsman, a prize-fighter
Suchinne den'Thaon – Kingswoman (deceased)
Vargen den'Khalderian – A silversmith, Kingsman-in-hiding

ROUSHENN PALACE:

Elyasin den'Ildrian – Dhenra and heir to the throne of Alrou-Mendera
Uhlas den'Ildrian – King of Alrou-Mendera (deceased)
Alden den'Ildrian – Dhenir of Alrou-Mendera (deceased)
Lhaurent den'Karthus – King's Castellan
Jherrick den'Tharn – Corporal in the Guard
Aldris den'Farahan – Second-Lieutenant of the Guard
Fenton den'Kharel – First-Lieutenant of the Guard

Theroun den'Vekir – King's Chancellor, ex-General, Black Viper of the Aphellian Way
Thaddeus den'Lhor – Secretary to Chancellor Theroun
Evshein den'Lhamann – Head Chancellor
Rudaric den'Ghen – King's Chancellor
Arthe den'Tourmalin – King of the Tourmaline Isles
Khouren Alodwine – The Ghost of Roushenn

FIRST ABBEY OF LINTESH:

Brother Temlin den'Ildrian – Second Historian of the Jenners
Abbot Lhem den'Ulio – Abbot of the Jenners
Abbess Lenuria den'Brae – Abbess of the Jenners
Mollia den'Lhorissian – A Seer of the Jenners

HIGH BRIGADE:

Ihbram den'Sennia – Second-Hand to Elohl
Wereth den'Bhariye – A troublemaker
Eleshen den'Fenrir – An innkeeper
Arlus den'Pell – Captain of the High Brigade

VENNET:

Grump – Friend to Dherran
Khenria den'Bhaelen – Friend to Dherran
Muk – A horse
Merrow – A horse
Vicoute Arlen den'Selthir – Vicoute of Vennet

FHOURIA:

Luc den'Orrisian – A thief of the Fhouria Thieves' Consortium
Gherris den'Mal – A thief of the Fhouria Thieves' Consortium, once Kingskinder

Shara den'Lhoruhan – A thief of the Fhouria Thieves' Consortium, defector from the Fleetrunners

ELSTHEMEN:

Therel Alramir – King of the Highlands
Lhesher Khoum – Highsword to King Therel
Devresh Khir – First Sword of Elsthemen
Hahled Ferrian – One of the Brother Kings of Elsthemen

VALENGHIA:

The Vhinesse – Queen of Valenghia

APPENDIX 3: PLACES AND THINGS

PLACES:

ALROU-MENDERA:

Lintesh (The King's City) – City at the base of the Kingsmount
Watercourse Gate – Gate of Lintesh that leads to the Elhambria Forest
Elhambria Forest – Aka the Kingswood - by Lintesh, contains an Alran-stone in a grotto with a spring
Elhambrian Valley – Valley at the edge of Lintesh
Elhambrian River (The Kingsriver) – River on the border of Alrou-Mendera and Elsthemen
Elesk (The Kingsmount) – By Lintesh
The Eleskis (The Kingsmountains) – Border of Valenghia and Elsthemen
Elsee – Lake in the Eleskis
Alrashesh – First Court of the Alrashemni (Kingsmen), a city
Valdhera – Second Court of the Alrashemni in Alrou-Mendera, a city
Dhemman – Third Court of the Alrashemni in Alrou-Mendera, a city
Kepsburg-on-the-Rhine – Ruins, a safe-house for the Alrashemni
High Camp – High Brigade base camp, on the Elsee

Arden – A city on the coast of Alrou-Mendera
Vennet – A city on the eastern bogs, home of Vicoute Arlen den'Selthir
Rhaventia – A city in central Alrou-Mendera
Quelsis – A city in the foothills of Alrou-Mendera
Fhouria – A city in southwestern Alrou-Mendera, home of Ghrenna's Consortium
Thalanout Plain – Where most of the fighting is against Valenghia
Aphellian Way – Site of the Black Viper's slaughter
Lheshen Valley – In the mountains near Quelsis, has seen vicious fighting, now well-protected
Gerrov-Tel (Mount Gerrov) – Ruins in the Kingsmountains, site of Haled's Stone
Gerthoun – City on the border of Elsthemen and Alrou-Mendera
Lhennian – City on the plains of Alrou-Mendera

ROUSHENN PALACE:

The Deephouse – A natural cavern, now a tavern in the bowels of Roushenn
Small Hall – A meeting-room in the palace for dignitaries and small events
Viewing Gallery – A portrait gallery in the palace
West Guardhouse – The Captain's guardhouse
West Armory – Antiquities hall under Roushenn
Great Hall – Aka the Throne Hall, site of large events
Royal Galleries – A portrait gallery of the royal line
Greenhouse – Indoor palace gardens
Dawn Room – Private area for the King's family
Receiving Hall – Main reception hall at Roushenn's entrance
Dressing Gallery – Dressing for royal events
Central Plaza – Main fountain and trade plaza in the city

ELSTHEMEN:

Lhen Fhekran – Capitol city of Elsthemen
Fhekran Palace – Therel Alramir's palace at Lhen Fhekran
Kherven Valley (Valley of Doors) – Leads from Alrou-Mendera to Lhen Fhekran, has ancient ruins

VALENGHIA:

Velkennish – Capitol city of Valenghia
Palace of the Vhinesse – The White Palace in Velkennish

TOURMALINE ISLES:

Straits of Luthor – Straits through the Isles
Isle of Luthor – Capitol island of the seven Tourmaline Isles

OTHER NATIONS:

Cennetia, Praough – Nations annexed by Valenghia
Thuruman (Cape of Lost Hope) – Far eastern nation
Ghrec (Sea of Ghrec, Ghreccan Desert) – Far eastern nation
Lhemvian Isles – Islands in the Archipelago of Crasos
Crasos – Island to the west of Cennetia
Jadoun, Perthe – Southwest countries to Alrou-Mendera
Unaligned Lands – To the northeast, nomadic lands

THINGS:

Aeon – God of the Air, like Zeus
Aeon's sack – A curse
Alrashemni Kingsmen – Elite fighters and peacekeepers sworn to the King of Alrou-Mendera
Arawein – A grain, like amaranth
Bales – How straw and raw goods are measured
Barreloak – A stout timber tree of Alrou-Mendera
Blackmark – A derogatory slur used for Kingsmen, refers to the mountain and stars Inking
Byrunstone (Bluestone) – Common bluegrey stone in Alrou-Mendera
Carrow-deer – A small deer in Alrou-Mendera, like a gazelle
Cendarie – Like a cedar tree
Centime – Unit of money, like a penny

Chandria – Yellow mushrooms, edible, grow in woods
Chirus Alrashemni (Alrashemni Inking) – "Dedicated of the Land" received after Eighth Seal
Claw-feet – Like crampons for climbing
Consortium – An operating group of thieves in each major city
Courhe den'Byrune – "Heart of Bluestone", Ghrenna's nickname from her team
Dragon-snaps – Like a snap-pea, but wild, edible
Eldunne – Like an elder tree
Eloi – A fast-climbing lizard, like a gecko
Essenac – A pain-dampening herb
Fennewith – A drug that is smoked, like opium, seeds can also be chewed, like fennel
First through Eighth Seal – Rites of passage for the Alrashemni, start at age 14, end at 21
Ghennie – A slur, refers to idle lordlings
Halsos – Lord of the Underworld, like Hades
Hecane – A measurement of mass, like a ton
High Alrakhan – The ancient Alrashemni language
Highsummer – Summer solstice
Holy Penitence – A curse
Hopt-ale – Like beer
Hopt-blume – Like hops
Jenner's Penitent – An order of monks in Lintesh at the First Abbey
Karthor – A vengeful god of war, like Aries
Keshar – A large battle-cat/saber-tooth cat, like a cougar but huge
Khehemni – A shadowy faction in opposition to the Alrashemni
Kingskinder – Children of the Alrashemni, not yet 21
Kipper-flisk – A river fish, like trout
League – Mile (measurement)
Leavonswood, bairn, ironwood – Different kinds of trees
Lhoru-butter – Like yak butter
Mellon-blume wine – A sweet wine
Mitlass – A type of wild-game stew
Oaths of Reinstatement – Oaths Alrashemni take before the King upon their Eight Seal at age 21

Oilcloak – Used to keep the rain off in the mountains
Pay the Fifth Price – An Alrashemni Kingsman threat, killing five people for a transgression
Rou – Currency of Alrou-Mendera, like the dollar
Seeproot, vheldan, morris-blossom – More herbs for medicine, from the southwest
Shouf – A trade grain from Alrou-Mendera
Summons of the Kingsmen – Historical event ten years prior
The Lothren – High council of the Khehemni
The Red Valor – The high brigade regiment of Valenghia
Threllis – A drug that is smoked, like marijuana with cocaine
Travelers – Like gypsies, put on plays and stories
Vellas-wine – A wine from Praough
Wesl-root, thranac-leaf, bitterbark – Herbs for medicine, from the Isles
Yegovian cider – A strong pear cider, like brandy
Yhulen-thorn – Like a holly bush, but more prickly

RANKS OF LORDS (Least to Greatest):

Dhepan – Mayor of a town/city
Vicoute/Vicenne – A lower Viscount, manages a moderate area around cities/townships
Couthis/Couthenna – A higher Count, manages large areas including multiple cities
Duchev/Duchevy – A Duke/Duchess, manages major sections of the nation
Chancellor (King's Chancellor) – Advisers to the king
Dhenir/Dhenra – Prince/Princess of Alrou-Mendera
King/Queen – Monarch of Alrou-Mendera

ALROU-MENDERA WAR BRIGADES:

High Brigade – Operate in the highest mountains in the Valenghian border
Longvalley Brigade – Operate in a well-protected valley on the Valenghian border
Fleetrunners – Messengers at the Valenghian border

Stone Valley Brigade – Special tactical unit, fierce fighters, called in where necessary

ACKNOWLEDGMENTS

To everyone who made this labor of love come true, you rock! Special thanks to Ben Rayack for helping craft languages and their grammar, to Anders Reis von Crooks for his dedicated proofreading and marketing ideas, and to Susanne Lakin for her wonderful critiquing on characters and flow. Many thanks to Carrie Petersen and Michelle Graden for their early-draft critiques, vast encouragement, and great suggestions. Love to my family Wendy, Steph, and Dave for their continued support, as well as my grandparents. Thanks to my friends Josh and Lela, Sam and Ben, and Anders and Nadine for letting me talk their ear off about fantasy books! Love to Amber, for letting me know that creativity is absolutely worth it.

But most of all, thanks to my incredible husband Matt Carlson. I honestly could not have done this without all your plot twists, fight scene suggestions, mapmaking abilities, heaps of encouragement, and so much more! You make my life worth it in every way, baby!

Made in the USA
Las Vegas, NV
30 August 2022